The Best of Fiction on the Web

1996-2017

*Rock on
Patrick!*

Fish.

Edited by Charlie Fish

The Best of Fiction on the Web is published by Charlie Fish, 121 Leigham Vale, London SW2 3JH, United Kingdom.

Cover design and typesetting by Raffaele Teo.
Printed with Amazon CreateSpace.

ISBN 978-0992693916

Website: www.fictionontheweb.co.uk

The Best of Fiction on the Web is typeset in Georgia.

Table of Contents

||||||||||||||||||||||||||||||||||||||||||||||||||||||||||||||||||||||||||||||||||||||||||||||||||||||||||||||||||||

Preface

The fifty-four stories collected here represent the diversity of the stories I publish at Fiction on the Web. The first story, "Above Candles", was the fifth I ever published, way back in 1996; over two decades later, when choosing the stories for this volume, I still vividly remembered the opening paragraphs in which a priest gives a penance to a young orphan for killing two hundred and twenty-seven men. (Three Hail Marys does the trick.)

Nine other stories made the cut from the olden days of Fiction on the Web, before I gave the site a major facelift. The rest are from the last five years. These stories lingered in my brain because they made me laugh out loud ("CLAM$", "Smart Car"), or openly sob in the middle of the staff canteen ("One Oh for Tillie", "What the Creek Carries Away"). Some evoked a sense of wonder ("The Bird on Silver Strand", "The Rooming House"), and some a visceral fear ("East", "War Baby").

These stories have transported me all over America – Alaska to Maine; Baltimore to Los Angeles – and the UK – Belfast to Scarborough; Glenlivet to London. Further afield as well: Canada, France, Nigeria, the Philippines, New Zealand. (The one set in the Philippines, "Gladiator", is about jungle children betting on spider battles.)

Let's not forget the crisply realised fantasy worlds, full of hardship and redemption ("Across the Oar", "The Place of Endurance"). And the magical tales that take place in a world that's *almost* ours, but with longer necks ("The Neck"), less solid walls ("The Wall"), or revenant relatives ("Relativity").

The themes of the stories cover huge swathes of the human experience. Love and betrayal ("Hearts and Darts", "The Kindness of Strangers"); justice and redemption ("One on One", "The Right of Wrong"); life and death ("Lost in Glass Slippers", "The Bridge"); sex with space aliens ("Purr", "Spurs that Jingle Jangle Jingle").

The stories are categorised according to the six genres I use at Fiction on the Web:

Funny stories – for when you need a laugh
Creepy stories – to make your hair stand on end
Fantastic stories – orcs, swords, magic and fantasy
Futuristic stories – many worlds of science fiction
Criminal stories – crooks and detectives
Real life stories – everyday life and relationships

But even within each category, several genres are explored. The "criminal" stories here include a heist, a noir, a caper, a courtroom drama, a corporate conspiracy, and a sweeping condemnation of corruption in the upper echelons of the Catholic Church. (The latter is "Vatican Bag Man".)

Some of my favourite authors are here: "The Debacle" by Beryl Ensor-Smith is one of twenty-five delightful comedies of hers I've published, about gossiping wives in small-town South Africa. I can't get enough of Hanja Kochansky's wonderful autobiographical anecdotes, as in "Goodbye Butterfly". And some authors have gone on to great things after featuring in Fiction on the Web: Rob Boffard has published a series of breathtaking science fiction novels. Rotimi Babatunde won the Caine Prize for African Writing, and has written plays staged in several theatres including London's Young Vic.

There is one story of mine in this collection. In 2013 I was asked to contribute a story for a horror anthology called *Bleed*, published to raise money for The National Children's Cancer Society. Bleed turned out to be brilliant, the highest standard of writing of any anthology I've been published in, but at first I thought it was a terrible idea: Can you imagine anything more depressing than reading a whole book of stories monstrously personifying cancer? I only wanted to contribute a story if I could come up with an angle that no one else would be exploring. So I wrote "Remission". It's a science fiction space tale, but also a metaphor for the less obvious side effects of dealing with a serious illness: loneliness, loss, fear, isolation, stress on family and friends. My baby daughter was very ill when I wrote it, and the story is infused with some of the trauma and desperate hopefulness I was feeling.

My daughter owes her life to the staff of St Thomas' Hospital and Evelina London Children's Hospital. So I'm proud to be able to say that all proceeds from the sale of this book – every penny – will go to Guy's and St Thomas' NHS Foundation Trust.

That is only possible because my patrons, those loyal few who donate monthly to Fiction on the Web, have paid for the editing, design and typesetting of this book. So I owe a huge debt of gratitude to John F. Furth, Ceinwen Haydon, Jeff Alphin, Jeff Weddle, Theresa Amarilio, Orion D. Hegre, David Valenzia, Andrew Smith, James Mulhern, J. H. Otterstrom, Kelly Shackelford, Charles H. Wise, Brooke Fieldhouse, Irena Pasvinter, Doug Hawley, Martin Green, Rob Boffard, Giovanni Valentino, William Belle, Shayne McClendon, Artie Knapp, Deborah Smith, Minkette, Gerald Warfield, Bruce Costello, Elizabeth Archer, Adi Bracken, Nancy McGuire, Julie Carpenter, Ted Morrissey, David Perlmutter, Laura T. Weddle, L. S. Sharrow, Alex Artukovich, Paul von Hippel, Steven Lucas, Melissa Davis, Tom Harrington, Tom Minder, Leo X. Robertson, Arun Dawani, Courteny L., Andrew Miller, Michael King, Paul Beckman, Monica Nelson, Pineapple Pineapple, David Haight, Mike Florian, Greg Szulgit, Gene J. Parola, Sharon Frame Gay, Patricia Crandall, John Mullen, Don Herald, Jerry W. Crews, Jim Bartlett, Seren Roberts, Katherine Parker, Anthony Billinghurst and Adrian Kalil.

Thank you to all the authors and especially the commenters who support Fiction on the Web. And thanks to Dave Aldhouse for the incredible animation on my Patreon page, Raffaele Teo for the elegant design and typesetting of this book, Julia Bell for contributing the foreword, Sue Tyley for her meticulous copy-editing, my Nomads for their continuing moral support, and above all Emma, for everything.

Charlie Fish
London, December 2017

Foreword: Real Artists Ship
JULIA BELL

eal artists ship. Steve Jobs is credited with this phrase, spoken at a boot camp in the early 80s where he was trying to encourage his team to produce better, more creative tech. What he meant was that real artists put their stuff out there – they don't dream up useless prototypes of things that will never work, they invent things that go on to be seen and used. They move on and through their work.

Since the rise of the internet it's never been easier for real artists to ship – to put their work out there for everyone to see, through social media, blogs and personal websites. Increasingly writers are making their reputations as artists from sharing work on the internet: Rebecca Solnit's essay "Men Explain Things to Me", about the phenomenon that came to be called "mansplaining", was first published and widely shared on the internet, turning a well-regarded poet-essayist into an international public intellectual. There's the poet Hera Lindsay Bird with her viral poem "Monica" – or just recently Kristen Roupenian with her story "Cat Person", published in full on *The New Yorker* online, which also went viral, creating a massive and surprising audience for the short story.

We're only beginning to understand the power of the internet to disrupt traditional publishing. Kindles are evidently not going to replace physical books, and bookshops are – just – withstanding the distribution monolith of Amazon. But in the short term and in the UK, at least, it's made publishers somewhat risk averse – there has been a glut of psychological thrillers and, before that, dystopian YA. Now I think publishing is increasingly taking its cues from the net. We might doubt the quality of the work by Rupi Kaur, but her audience, mostly teenage girls, has found something relatable in her Instagram poetry and her first book of poems has been a big bestseller. A viral phenomenon which a publisher could neither spot nor manufacture – though they are quick to publish a slew of copyists.

Shipping your stuff through the traditional publishing route used to be the best and only way to get noticed. Now it's perfectly possible to publish yourself and find a huge audience for it without relying on the heavy machinery of a publishing company and its marketing and sales departments and dependence on the shrinking power of traditional media.

This shift is only going to accelerate and it will be interesting to see what other writers like Hera Lindsay Bird or Kristen Roupenian do, now that they can share their work directly with their growing numbers of fans. With their work, the relationship between print and internet becomes even closer. Their success also seems to me to prove the motto quoted to me once by a publishing executive at a dinner party: *If you want to be a successful writer you need to be first, best or different.* And even inside the churn of the internet it's possible to be so new or so best or so different that the work finds – sometimes in the space of a few hours – an audience it would never have reached through the bookshop.

This anthology comes from that impulse to make curated work available on the net for free, and the success of the site is leading to a print publication. This, I think, will be the model of the future of print publication. The book will follow the net, and not the other way around. Teaching writing, I can see how more and more of the students – especially those who grew up with tech – see it as a part of their writing practice. Each one of them is the curator of their own media, some of them worrying over Twitter updates as if they were poems.

But to go back to the idea of shipping – that first step of putting your stuff out there. Shipping as Jobs meant it is an Americanism – in British English we are more likely to say deliver – but I like the double meaning. The idea of seafaring, of stories launched like messages in a bottle, something that might float on the sea of data until one day it beaches itself on the screen of a reader. To launch it and throw it out there is a mark of artistic seriousness. You want people to read your stuff, even if it's still – always – work in progress. The artists in this book are real and they know there is only one way to test their work, out in the world where there are readers.

Above Candles
D. K. SMITH

||||||||||||||||||||||||||||||||||||||||||||||||||||||||||||||||||||||||||||||||||||||||||||||||||||||||||||||||||||||||||||||||||||||

A wayward orphan girl seeks solace in the church, and the beleaguered priest feels conflicted about helping her.

"Oh. Um… is there anything I can do?" "Can you bring five children back to life?"

"**B**less me Father, for I have sinned."

Father Moriarty inspected the black metal bars which separated him from the familiar voice. For the tenth time that Sunday he heard confession. The sessions had been emotionally trying.

"How so, my daughter?"

Her tone was tense. "Father, I killed two hundred and twenty-seven men."

Moriarty's face melted into a smile despite himself. "Three Hail Marys."

"What!"

"The penance must meet the sin, my child."

He heard the sounds of quick movement, and with a gust his booth's curtain flew open. In the sudden light appeared a girl. Her hair was short, curly and black. Her velvet dress was black too, a dark shadow surrounding her flushed skin.

"I can't even get absolution in this crummy church!" she raged. He lost restraint and burst into laughter. "Oh sure, laugh, laugh!" Her voice had an edge of panic. "Just laugh at me!"

1

With an effort and a clutch of his stomach, he stopped laughing and rose. "Peace, my daughter." He took a deep breath. "Mary," he said calmly, "you must come to realise that killing people in games and killing people in real life is . . ." He put his hands together. ". . . different in the eyes of the Lord. Now I'm sure you feel very deeply about this –"

"Blood was everywhere!"

"Ah, yes, but people have been playing computer games, or arcade games, all sorts of electronic games for half a century now. All children and teenagers play them. And I assure you there's nothing wrong with blasting away digital opponents for a little fun. It's not real, child. Just the other day in the news I heard that scientific studies strongly suggest that this release of stress is beneficial."

"You just don't understand!" Mary spun and stalked past the dirty pews, her rush tugging at the candle flames before the Cross. "I've been having these nightmares about Hell!"

"Nightmares?"

Stopping and raising her hands, she said, "There was this red river flowing into the base of a mountain, and everything was skewed, like there wasn't a straight line anywhere, it was all wavy and bloody. All around were these giant statues of heads, like the heads of gods, just staring. They had no expressions, they just kept watching me, watching watching watching. They were relentlessly and unchangeably there, watching, staring, staring –"

Again, her voice held that edge of panic. "It was just a dream, my child," Father Moriarty said soothingly.

"And I was all alone – totally and completely alone!" Mary burst into tears.

Father Moriarty moved quickly to comfort the girl, who sagged against him. He was shocked by the lightness of her body. "My goodness, child, when was the last time you ate?"

"Yesterday," she sniffed. "I didn't have another chance. I had to spend the day fighting the Hordes in cyberspace." As she spoke he seated her on a pew. "I could use a cracker or something," she admitted. "How about those crunchy things you're always giving out on Sundays?"

"I don't think so," he said mildly. "Ah . . . I'll be right back." Quietly he walked to a room at the back of the church, and he shut the door behind him.

Then he crossed himself. What was he to do with this strange girl? A week ago she had started coming to confession every single day, always declaring these utterly peculiar "sins" of cyberspace. How she had blown up this building, or cast an evil spell, or some such nonsense. Her parents – if she even had any – obviously had not taught her the difference between reality and fantasy, and now, for whatever reason, she wouldn't stop pestering him.

He had long ago determined that she wasn't Catholic, that she didn't come here from any real belief in God. As far as he could tell this was just another place of fantasy for her, a peculiar extension of the hours and hours she spent playing electronic games. Apparently she had seen some movie about a priest a couple of weeks ago and now she thought his church was her private toy. If only she'd leave him alone –

"No," he said to himself. He was a priest, here to serve the Lord Christ. All who came to him would receive his help. But he had absolutely no idea what to do with that girl, and now was the worst of times for her to be here.

Taking his hand from his brow, he turned to the church's small kitchen. Quickly riffling through the pantry, he returned to the church proper with a tray. She remained where he'd left her. From a distance her thin body looked pale and small, and her black, voluminous dress – very odd attire, perhaps another quirk of her warped imagination – swelled hugely around her figure. Her bright brown eyes were locked on the Cross.

She studied the Christ as if mapping His every feature, as if trying to discover His every secret. He approached her quickly, horrified that anyone would dare so blatantly scrutinise Jesus, like she were trying to render Him naked and peer into the very soul of Him Himself. "Here." He interposed himself in her view and thrust the tray into her hands. She caught it with surprise. "I'm afraid," he said brusquely, "that I'm going to have to ask you to leave. You see, I have a very important sermon to give today. But if you truly wish, you can come back and have another confession tomorrow."

He forced himself not to frown. She was just a girl, after all, not even a Catholic. But when he thought of all the people who came in here with real problems and real sorrows he couldn't help but add, "If you feel you can stand the guilt for that long."

She stared at him, and again, that look of panic came to her eyes, as if . . . as if – Gentling his voice, he asked, "My daughter, why were you studying the Cross?"

Lowering the tray to her knees, Mary selected from its contents without looking. She chewed carefully while her eyes studied his. Only the steady crunching of her teeth came between them. Finally she said,

"Well, I'd never really looked at one in real life before. I've seen them in a movie and some TV shows, and in the pics all these people clustered around them, and they all seemed . . . well, like that Cross really mattered to them. You know?"

Crunch, crunch, crunch. Her eyes never left his.

"I'd think it would matter to them," he said. "It is Christ their Lord."

"Can Christ be my Lord, too?" she asked.

"Christ is everyone's Lord, my daughter."

"Really?" She brightened considerably. "Then that means someone loves me?"

"Christ loves everyone, my child."

"Oh, goody!" She leaped to her feet, spilling the tray onto the floor. "That means I'll never be alone again! I'll have someone to talk to, someone to play with, someone to help me sleep, someone to help me defeat the Hordes! It'll be just like in that Humphrey Bogart movie I saw!" She thrust past him and beamed up at the Cross. "Hi, Jesus, I'm Mary!"

"No, no, no!" Father Moriarty struggled to contain himself. He bent and started putting the fallen food back on the tray.

"Oh, don't worry about that," said Mary, stooping to help him. "I dropped it, I'll take care of it – in fact, think of how much I'll be able to help you, now that I'll be staying here!"

"What!"

"Well, if Christ loves me here, then I'll –"

"No! Christ loves you everywhere and anywhere! Now please, would you mind going home?"

"Why?"

"I –" He crossed himself again. "Mary, I have a very important guest coming this evening. The . . ." his voice hushed to a whisper, ". . . the Bishop is coming to my church."

"Who and what's the Bishop?" she asked.

He fought down his irritation. "My boss!"

"The Bishop's your boss? Humphrey Bogart said something like his boss being –"

"He's my immediate boss! And he's coming to my church! You couldn't understand, you obviously know nothing about the Church –"

"Try me!" she exclaimed indignantly. "Billy Jobeson said I wouldn't know how to operate a flight simulator after all those X-Wing sims. I showed him! Go on – try me!"

"My church is in one of the filthiest slums in the city. Homeless people sleep on the pews during my services. Criminals conduct their crimes inside these walls. I used to think I could help them – I used to think I could help them all – but now I've learned to ignore them, now I don't even blink an eye. And today the Bishop's coming, part of his campaign to make the dying Church more popular with the people – like people even really care –"

He stopped. Her eyes were wide, and she was listening intently, and for a moment he thought she was really trying to understand. He cursed himself, cursed himself for flying into an almost blasphemous tirade before a girl who couldn't understand . . .

"Don't you have any family?" he asked finally, his voice calm, soothing.

"They died in a drive-by shooting," she said, "when I was three."

Oh, God.

He turned from her, crossed himself.

"I live in the orphanage on Sixth Street. It's no big deal. I just usually don't tell people because then they have to give all this pity and it makes me uncomfortable."

"Wasn't there a shooting," he said, his voice sounding strange to him, "about a week ago, in the orphanage on Sixth Street?"

"Oh, no," she said. He turned slowly to face her. Her eyes were wide and distracted. "There was no shooting. It was just a day like every other. I played on the computer with Billy Jobeson. He was beating me as usual. He was the only one who ever could."

"That's the second time you've mentioned Billy. Are you close to him?"

"Huh? Oh, no, Billy had to go away for a while."

"Really?"

"Ms Garleson said he had to last week. She said he wouldn't ever come back, that he was going to a better place. She took us all out to see a movie with Sister Edna – she hardly ever does that. I usually don't like movies, ya know? You just sit there and you don't have any control over anything. There's nothing to shoot, nothing to do at all but just sit there and watch a flat screen. It's so boring. But this time it was different. There was this man I've never seen before – Humphrey Bogart was what Ms Garleson said his name was – and he was a priest like you, and he was kind and loving and brave and he didn't think shooting people was always a good thing. I'd never seen anything like it before, not ever. He's all I've been able to think about since Billy had to go."

She turned, and pointed at the Cross without any reverence at all, and said, "But I don't have to worry about that any more. Does he have a nickname? Billy had a nickname – 'Shooter'. Mine's 'Muerte'."

He approached her slowly, and put his hand on her shoulder. "No, he . . . he's just called 'Our Lord'."

"Just like what Humphrey Bogart called him!"

"Yes, um . . . have you ever read something called 'The Bible'?"

"Every now and then Sister Edna comes to the orphanage and tries to get us to read it. Ms Garleson doesn't like it, because the Federal Government says it's wrong to do that in a federally funded institution, but I don't really care. I mean, books are even more boring than movies."

"I see."

"Please don't make me leave! I'll clean up the mess! I just want to stay!"

Father Moriarty sighed. What could he do?

"You may stay, my daughter, but please, be quiet."

"Great! I'll clean up the mess right away! Do you have a broom and stuff in that back room? I'll go get it!" She rushed off like a sprite.

Alone, Father Moriarty looked with supplication at the Cross. "Why did You send her to me? Can't You see there's nothing I can do to help her? There's nothing I can do to help any of the people You've sent me. Nothing I can do for the homeless, nothing I can do for the criminals, nothing I can do for the adulterers and the young pregnant women, nothing at all. The times are changing so fast, and now I have a child who doesn't even know what's real. What do You expect me to do? What do You expect me to –"

A giant crash rang from the back room. "Damn!" Hesitantly, the door opened. "I wasn't supposed to say that, was I?" she asked meekly. "Sister Edna's very particular about saying things like shit and piss – oops, I wasn't supposed to say those either!" She giggled. "I don't know why – everyone uses those words, anyway, when she's not listening." She slid through the door, and one by one revealed a mop and a dustpan. "Sister Edna's really a drag, actually, but Ms Garleson lets her come because she helps around the orphanage."

"Mary, um . . . look, child, maybe you should go back to the orphanage. It's getting to be dinner time, and the Bishop's going to be here soon."

"You mean your boss? Gee, if your boss is coming, shouldn't you clean the place up? After all, most people want to impress their bosses, just like Ms Garleson does –"

"On the other hand, why don't you remain right here," Father

Moriarty said, tiredly. "No, I didn't clean the place up. Serve the Bishop right to walk into a . . . dirty place like this. He spends all his time in the lovely affluent section of the city, where they don't have muggers in the pews. Now if you'll excuse me, I think I need a moment . . ."

He passed her to enter the church's back room. He paused by the door to ask, "Haven't you been to school? Surely you would have heard about Christ in school."

"Sometimes I saw the name 'Christ' written in graffiti in the classrooms. But I try not to go to school, and Ms Garleson doesn't really make me. You know what they say – going to school in the projects is a good way to get killed." She winked.

He nodded slowly and began to shut the door, but she stopped him. "Will Christ really love me? Anywhere I go?"

"Yes," he said, though not with the vigour he might have hoped.

"Really? I mean . . ." and for the first time, her voice lowered, and a hint of seriousness touched her tone, ". . . I mean, like, Christ is something like God, right? And God takes care of things. I mean, Ms Garleson said Billy had gone with God, so if I know God, I can be with Billy, right? 'Cause I'd really like to be with Billy. And if God's here, then that means that sooner or later, Billy will be too, right? And God will keep us safe, that's what Sister Edna keeps telling us. So I can't leave here, you see, I gotta wait for Billy to come, so we can play the games again. But maybe we won't play the killing games any more because they've been giving me such nightmares . . . Please, can I stay, Mister Moriarty? Can I stay?"

"You . . . can stay, I already said so."

"Until Billy comes?"

He swallowed, hard.

"Because Billy will come, right?"

"Billy . . . 'left' around the time of the shooting at your orphanage, ri–" He stopped in mid-word, as without warning that almost palpable sense of PANIC came to her eyes and he reached and touched her arm. "You can stay, Mary, you can stay until Billy comes."

A barely perceptible sigh came from her lips, and the panic faded, and then he'd never even know it had been there. "I'll be right with the cleaning," she said eagerly. "I'll clean the whole place up, don't you worry, it'll look great when I'm through – you go do whatever you need to for your boss. Don't you worry – don't you worry!"

He nodded, and started to shut the door once more. She stopped him again and threw her arms around him, and squeezed him with the strength only the desperate could muster. Then she ran off into the pews, swinging the mop through the air like she was a ballerina, making strange karate noises. "I'm the Cleaning Ninja! Just like on TV!"

He shut the door.

"Now I've lied for You," he said, looking to the Cross above the nearby desk. "What was I supposed to say to her? What, that Billy's never coming? Maybe that would have been better. Maybe that's what I should have said. Told her to go back to the orphanage, that she can't stay here, that's she's completely out of touch with the world, that she's doggone nuts. I should have tossed her out of Your House, is that what I should have done? Tossed her weeping onto the streets?

"But no, how could I do that? How could I do that when I'm supposed to be kind and wise? I'm not wise. I'm a fool." He clenched his hand. "A doggoned fool."

He walked to the desk, and opened a phone book. It took only a few minutes to find the number for the orphanage.

"Hello?" answered a tired voice on the other end of the line.

"Hello. May I speak to Ms Garleson, please?"

"Speaking."

"Hello, I'm Father Moriarty. Listen, I think I have one of your wards, her name's Mary?"

"Which Mary? I've got three of them."

"Um . . . I don't know . . . are they all missing?"

"Never mind. Does she have black hair and brown eyes? Is she wearing a widow's gown?"

"A widow's gown – Ms Garleson, wasn't there a shooting –"

"Yes."

The voice was heavy and cold.

"Oh. Um . . . is there anything I can do?"

"Can you bring five children back to life?"

He was silent.

"I'll send Sister Edna over. She's here telling everyone that God has five new angels in Heaven, the damned bitch. Oh gosh, what did I just say . . . Sorry Father, um . . . it's been really tough over here." The woman sounded like she was fighting back tears. "I'll send Sister Edna over, she really does care. Maybe she'll take them to another movie. I can't believe she dragged me to the last one. Mary – the one with you – she's really quite taken with Humphrey Bogart. It's something I guess, better than those cheap games she always plays."

"I'll be waiting for her."

"Thank you, Father . . . Goodbye."

He turned from the phone. "It's amazing all the suffering You managed to cram into the world," he said to the air. "Do You feel proud of Yourself sometimes?" But how could he say that? Had God shot up the orphanage? Who was he supposed to blame, the gunman or the Lord?

He walked to the door. Just as he was about to open it, it was thrown open from the opposite side, and he was confronted with Mary's flushed face. "Hurry, Mister Moriarty, your boss is here!"

She tugged him out of the room, and he stood amazed. Half of the pews were shiny and clean, scrubbed with soap. The floor was a bit less grimy, the littered debris on the pews was gone. "My God!" he said.

"I know, I know – I didn't get a chance to clean everything. I tried – Look, is that your boss?"

Indeed it was. The Bishop entered wearing his regal white robes and tall mitre. He was a handsome man, dark in colouring and known for his charisma, and he seemed totally unflustered by the two men with tiny mini-cams hovering around him. One cameraman was in front, another at his back, and they circled him like monkeys scrambling for a view. Behind them came several of the Bishop's assistants. They had their clipboards and notes –

"No!" one of the assistants cried. "This place looks like a festering dump!"

"Stop the camera, stop the camera!" another assistant cried. "This is not the image we want to present!"

The Bishop stopped and turned, as if seeing the church for the first time. His mouth fell open, and Father Moriarty suspected he wasn't pleased. "It's . . . dirty," he said, like he couldn't believe it.

"Someone at least started to clean the front pews," said a third assistant. "Where's the priest who runs this trash heap?"

Father Moriarty broke from Mary's grasp and walked forward with as much dignity as he could muster. "Welcome –" he started to say.

"Couldn't you at least have cleaned up the place?" the Bishop asked. "How am I supposed to better our public image? How am I supposed to convince people we're helping the poor and needy when the church looks like a pigsty? I thought this place had stained-glass windows – all I see is cardboard."

"Stained-glass windows show the glory of God," Father Moriarty said, "but they're fearfully fragile when it comes to bullets."

"But we chose this church because it's in one of the poorest areas of the city! We're featuring you on national television! Couldn't you at least have made an effort to make the place look even a little better? It looks like . . . like . . ."

"Like we're in a slum?"

"Exactly!" the Bishop shouted, steadily losing his composure. "How are we supposed to convince people we're helping them when the place looks like it's part of the problem? This is supposed to be God's House, it's supposed to at least be clean . . ."

"I petitioned your office for someone to help me maintain the church. My petition was refused."

"The Church is poor, man, the Church is broke! We don't have the money to fund your laziness with maids and butlers, now do we?"

"Unlike the maid and butler the Bishop is reputed to have in his own church?" The Bishop's mouth closed with a snap and he turned beet red. "A simple nun would have done, Your Excellency. Please, I mean no disrespect, simply I have petitioned the Church many times, sometimes for only a modicum of assistance, and always my requests were refused."

"Perhaps what this church really needs is a new priest," the Bishop said darkly.

"Perhaps," Father Moriarty said.

The Bishop scowled. "The front pews are the cleanest. Let's film it there." He started forward, and the assistants and the cameramen scurried after him. "Maybe you're right, Father," the Bishop called over his shoulder as he stopped by one of the pews and daintily brushed away a scrap of dirt. "Having the place look a bit run-down gives it a touch of realism I hadn't foreseen. If handled right, maybe we could tug at a few hearts, touch a few chequebooks. Yes." The Bishop turned his attention to his cameramen. "Get a shot of that window only – it's still got some glass. And who's this girl here? Father, I thought you said you hadn't got a nun."

"She's not a nun, Your Excellency."

"Of course not, she wears no habit. What's your name, girl?"

"Muerte," Mary answered eagerly.

"What?"

"Her name's Mary," Father Moriarty said.

"Oh, you mean my real name," Mary said, "not my nickname! Yes, Mary it is."

"Why would anyone have the nickname of Muerte?" the Bishop asked.

"It's Spanish for Death," Mary volunteered. "That's what they call me in cyberspace."

"A gamer, huh? It's good to see that even gamers take an interest in the Church. Perhaps we're not in such dire straits after all. See, Father, with all your complaints and your filthy church, even right here is a bastion of hope for our cause. Sit right here beside me . . . Mary? Oh, what a beautiful name. Named right after the Virgin herself."

"Hey, don't call me a virgin!" Mary exclaimed. "It's bad enough that everyone teases me about it anyway! If Billy hadn't left, I might have –"

Mary turned away. Though her back was to him, Father Moriarty could almost imagine that expression in her eyes again. Mary looked at the Cross for a long moment.

When she turned around, her face was bright and smiling. "But don't worry! Jesus will make sure it's OK!"

"That's the way!" the Bishop boomed. "Come, have a seat by me! Ah, that grim Father Moriarty! Ignore him! Always talking about the poor and the suffering – sure there's suffering! Anyone who's not Catholic's going to suffer! What do they expect?"

"Well . . ." Mary looked puzzled. "Well sure, you're going to suffer if you don't have friends. Jesus is my friend. Right, Mister Moriarty?"

"Father Moriarty," he immediately corrected. "You have to forgive her, Bishop, she's –"

"Well, a Catholic in the slums can't be perfect. Come, Mary, sit by me! Of course you have a friend. You have a whole world of friends. Everyone does, if they believe in Him." He took Mary's hand as the two sat together in the front pew. "You got those cameras ready?" he asked one of his assistants.

"Just a moment or so, Your Excellency."

"Mmm, well hurry it up, will you? I have a dinner engagement." Turning to Father Moriarty, the Bishop said, "I purposely selected the smallest cameras possible, but they're a bit of a pain to set up, so I'll have to take up just a wee bit more of your time. Small cameras are great for shots taken in public – they're concealed and they don't make people nervous."

Father Moriarty walked to the Bishop's side and said in a low voice, "Your Excellency, may I have a word with you?"

The Bishop scowled again, then studied Father Moriarty through squinted eyes. "Hold on here, little Mary," he said, patting her hand. It was obvious that Mary didn't like being called little, but she let it pass.

They took a few steps from the pews and the Bishop said, "What?"

"I was wondering if perhaps you could think of a place for that girl over there," Father Moriarty said. "I know it's hard to tell by the look of her, but she's . . . well, she's been traumatised."

"Nonsense!" exclaimed the Bishop.

"A week ago, the orphanage where she lives was shot up by a gunman. Five kids, including her closest friend, died."

"Dear Lord." The Bishop crossed himself. "How even the young must pay in this world. Just what do you expect me to do, Father?"

"I . . . was hoping you might have a place for her. I know you live in the affluent section of the city, and I was hoping that maybe you could use your influence to find her a situation somewhere in that section of town. Your Excellency, she's really a bright girl, even a cheerful girl, but . . . she's dimming down here, Your Excellency. It's like she's fading away. I know it's not really obvious, but I've seen her, I've seen those like her, and if we or someone or God can't get her out of here, I daren't imagine what will become of her. Your Excellency, I can't even bear to imagine what will become of her. She's got no education, no family – she's not even living in this world. Is there nothing you can do, Your Excellency, nothing at all?"

The Bishop's face was sombre. "How long have you known her?" he asked.

"A week."

"A week? You'd think you had known her for years the way you were carrying on!"

Father Moriarty felt his face grow red. "Sometimes the Lord grants insight, Your Excellency. Sometimes living in Hell can give you a sort of warped understanding not found in the high-rise condos downtown."

"Seems to me like you've been down here too long," the Bishop said. "But I'll let your accursed impudence pass again. I'll help her, Father Moriarty, I'll help her just like you ask, provided you can answer one question."

"Yes, Your Excellency?"

"Has she been baptised?"

"Ah . . . no."

"Is she Catholic?"

". . . no."

Instantly Father Moriarty wished he had lied.

"No, hmm? Well then, explain to me why I should take the time to rescue one – just one, mind you – little gutter girl from the slums, when there are surely a thousand more just like her. I save this one, and then there's the next, and the next, and the next. I can't find placements for every child here. No, Father, no, it wouldn't even be right. It's not the solution, you must see that. The solution is to eradicate the slums, eradicate the poverty, but not, my dear friend, to just save one child."

The Bishop clapped Father Moriarty's arm. "But obviously you're a kind chap –"

"What difference does it make, whether she's Catholic or not?" Father Moriarty asked bitterly.

"Don't you know, Father?" the Bishop asked. "According to our beliefs, everyone who's not a Catholic, who's not been baptised, is going to the Flame. If she had been baptised, maybe it would have been worth my time. But she's doomed anyway, and there are a thousand more like her."

"You're just sorry you can't save a Catholic girl," Father Moriarty almost shouted. "Why did I even bother to speak to you? Your entire life is but a damned public relations scam and hoax!"

"Oh, are we cursing now, Father? Perhaps you should meet me in confession later." The Bishop smiled blandly and turned away.

Father Moriarty raised his fist, he aimed at the back of the Bishop's head and –

"Hey, Mister Moriarty!" The Bishop's and Father Moriarty's attention was called to the Cross. Mary stood there, her face flushed before the flickering candles. "Look what I found!"

She raised her arms. Both the Father and the Bishop gasped. "Good Lord!" said the Bishop.

Draped upon Mary's either arm were easily a dozen crosses, all dangling from their gold and silver and bronze chains from her uplifted arms and hands, all throwing flashing reflections of light which danced through the dark church and upon her black dress and glowing face. The crosses floated above candles. She was a disembodied angel with bright brown eyes and crucifix wings . . .

"Put those down now!" the Bishop cried. "You have no right to be . . . playing with what's holy!"

"But they're so cool!" she exclaimed, slowly swaying her arms so that the crosses clinked against each other.

"Put them down!" the Bishop shouted, and Mary's smile faltered.

Father Moriarty walked towards Mary and took her hand, leading her away from the candles and the Cross. "Give them to me," he said quietly.

"I was just trying to look pretty," she whispered back. "It's like jewellery. I've never really worn much jewellery. I just wanted to show the Bishop that I wasn't a little girl, like he said. And I always wanted to look pretty for Billy . . ."

"I know, I know . . ." He wasn't prepared for when she softly put her head against his chest and hugged him again, crosses and all. "I miss him," she whispered, "I really, really miss him . . . When's he coming back? I miss him . . ."

"It's all right, my daughter," he said. He kissed her curly black hair. "You'll find him again some day, we'll all find our Billy some day . . ."

She sobbed into his chest, delicate and frail and small. He held her and the candles before the Cross flickered and wavered . . .

"The cameras are ready, Your Excellency."

"Give those crosses to Father Moriarty, child," said the Bishop, his tone softer but not quite kind. Mary wiped the tears from her eyes, then began clumsily doing as the Bishop said. The Bishop smiled and turned to his anxious assistants who were crowding around him.

"Mary," said Father Moriarty, putting his hands on her shoulders. "You must understand – the Catholic Church is so much more than you see here. Some of the most glorious art in the world is inside Catholic churches, like the Sistine Chapel."

"The sixteen what?"

"The Bishop there – he's not your typical bishop. Every religion has its faults, just like every man or woman has their faults. The Bishop is just very concerned about the image of the Church, that is all. Other bishops, other priests and nuns would give you their heart on a silver platter. It's just that this world is falling apart, dear Mary. Don't let these little injustices make you think –"

"Like you?" she asked.

"Think like me? What . . . what do you mean?" he faltered. "No, not like me."

"No, no," she said. She handed him the crosses, their chains all tangled together. "I think . . . I think what I'm saying is that you're everything I'd ever hoped a priest would be, Mister Moriarty."

"Father Moriarty. You call a priest 'Father'."

"Oh. That's why they kept doing that in the movie. Just like 'Sister Edna'. What I mean is, you've been just as nice to me as Ms Garleson or Billy. I sort of feel like . . ."

"It's all right, Mary. You don't have to talk."

"No! I never had a chance to tell Billy how I really felt, so now I'm always going to say what I really feel, no matter what. You've given me your heart on a silver platter too, Father Moriarty, by letting me stay here. I haven't found a lot of people who'd even give me the time of day, and . . . well, thank you," she finished, her voice nearly a whisper. She smiled, blinking wet eyes.

He swallowed. "Bless you, my daughter."

"Father!" the Bishop called. "We're all ready here! Come and take your place. That black girl can sit in the pews at the back."

Father Moriarty's jaw tensed in rage.

"At the back!" Mary exclaimed. "But I didn't even clean those!"

"Can't she sit just a couple of pews back, Your Excellency?" Father Moriarty asked, his voice small and tight.

"Fine. Just as long as she's not in the camera shot. Who knows what she might do?"

"Go on, my child."

"Sit at the back. Who does he think he is? If we were in cyberspace I'd . . ."

The church door opened, and the first of Father Moriarty's regulars entered, a wrinkled black lady so old she made the sun look young. Father Moriarty welcomed her with open arms. "Welcome, Ms Jeffreys. Did you have a good weekend?"

"Yes, yes," she wheezed. "No bullets came through my door, it was a good weekend. Thanks for asking, Father." She took her seat.

She was followed by a crowd of others. After the few devout had entered, the many scum came in, and Father Moriarty greeted them, too. After all, everyone was welcome in God's House.

There was Blade, who always wore a mix of cheap jewellery and leather. His face was scarred, his eyes were cold, and his wide shoulders barely fitted through the doorway. Father Moriarty nodded to him, and was ignored, as usual. The big man's eyes scrutinised the Bishop and his contingent, who seemed obviously out of place. Yet the Bishop's regal robes had no real significance to him, and after his examination the big punk sneered. "Rich fuck," he muttered.

Blade was the biggest and baddest of them all. A couple of his crew followed him, two oily bad-ass toughs who wore baggy rapper clothes and sported the darkest sunglasses imaginable. Most of the others were winos and addicts, some pushers, a few others homeless who smiled at Moriarty's greeting. Not that many came here, only the ones who thought they could get away with crimes where the police would never think of looking.

From the corner of his eye, Father Moriarty watched the Bishop slowly pale with each new arrival. The Bishop had probably not even dreamed a church could hold such people. It served the Bishop right. It satisfied Father Moriarty very deeply to know that at least for an hour the Bishop would glimpse life as it could be . . .

Before taking the pulpit Father Moriarty stopped by Mary's seat. She seemed nervous and restless, and he laid a soothing hand on her shoulder.

"What's with all those bad people?" she asked. "Some of those guys look like the enemies I blasted away in that old game Rumble."

"Don't worry. Just don't stare at them, or even look at them."

She watched him walk away, to take his place at the pulpit. He felt his sleeves slide upon his arms as he set his hands on the paper where he had scrawled the notes for his sermon. The pews of the dirty church faced him back, like a question he had never been quite able to answer. Would anyone hear his words today? Did anyone ever hear them? Surely the drug dealers and the addicts near the back didn't care, nor the people who regularly walked in and out of the church to surreptitiously score from Blade. How had the Holy Church come to this? Why did he even bother?

If only he had the strength or passion to move these people. If only he'd ever had the courage to throw this trash out of God's House. Often he told himself that the church had to be open to everyone, but even he doubted he believed that completely.

He took a deep breath.

"There have been times when people have asked me about the practicality of faith. Isn't the concept of Eternal Damnation a bit cruel in these modern times? How can someone realistically practise and uphold in today's world the black-and-white ethics that faith demands? Our world has become increasingly hard, more and more backbiting as everyone fights for an edge, and not just for capital gain, or greed, but sometimes simply for survival. Can you blame the starving thief? Can you curse the uneducated gangster?

"Our world is a mad world, where half suffer and half feast. Is there no way to catch the ear of the wealthy? Is there no way to widen the eyes of the oppressed? Are we only animals under God? Is there not some way to convince people that their cause is not the only one –"

Shouts rose abruptly from the back of the church. Father Moriarty's hands clenched spasmodically – it was hard to see, but in the back of the church, was that a gun?

It was.

The flash lit the grey walls and the sound made everyone duck. The flash repeated itself three more times. Father Moriarty glimpsed the agony on the face of a falling man. Blade was grinning like an animal, livid joy in his eyes.

Silence, a moment's silence, mock silence.

The Bishop stood, his mouth hanging open. The damned fool didn't even have the wits to stay down. He rose to his full measure, and with rage pointed at Blade, and shouted, "The Lord will punish you –"

Blade casually aimed at the Bishop's chest. His Excellency's words faltered and fear coloured his face. A sudden scurrying filled the air as the homeless and winos made a break for the exit. Ms Jeffreys was clutching her chest, her nostrils flaring with each hard-won breath. And his hands were trembling. He was frozen motionless at the pulpit, the only movement his shaking hands . . .

Mary rose from her seat.

"No," he whispered, eyes fastened on her. "No, get down –"

Mary raised her hands. In them was a black 9 millimetre.

Blade never saw it coming. Perhaps it was because the church was dark, or maybe it was because Mary was wearing a dark dress, or perhaps because she was so small. Her face was cool and her eyes were serene. She squeezed the trigger like it was nothing but the press of a joystick button.

Red exploded from Blade's chest, like pulp. It splattered across the pews and suddenly all the joy was gone from his face. He spun crazily toward the direction of the shot and Mary let him have it in the face.

Teeth flew through the air.

One of Blade's two lackeys went for his piece, a quick move to his vest. He never finished the motion. The second already had his out. Mary ducked and the shots went wild. She ran crouched along the pews, like some easy cyberwarrior, came up from a different position and now there were four dead people on the ground.

Slowly, Mary rose to her full height. Most everyone else had left by now. The Bishop had fallen sobbing onto the floor, begging God to have mercy on him. Father Moriarty wasn't sure, but he might have wet himself. In the front pews Ms Jeffreys composed herself, then crossed herself. She kicked at the huddled white mass of the Bishop. "Get up you old fool, it's over. Think you'd never been in the projects before," she wheezed.

Somehow Father Moriarty forced himself from the pulpit. He took a few steps towards Mary, then stopped, unable to go any further.

"It's just like the games," Mary said, a tone of wonder in her voice. "I . . . always thought it'd be different in real life." The gun fell from her hands, smacked the pew with a sharp clatter. "The gun, though . . . I had no idea it was so heavy, so loud . . ." She raised her hands to her ears, then lowered them. "There's all this . . . powder on my fingers . . ."

"Mary," Father Moriarty said, his voice hoarse and foreign to him, "where'd you get the gun?"

Mary looked at him, without really seeing him. "Well, that's funny," she said. "I'd never have expected to have gotten it from her."

"Who?"

"Ms Garleson. She gave it to me. Said I should never let what happened to Billy happen to me, so I . . . I took the gun . . ." Mary clutched her head. "I . . . I won't start having the nightmares again, will I? I was only trying to do what was right. I don't want to have the nightmares again. I . . . Father?" She looked at him, her eyes suddenly frightened and wet, so different from just a moment ago. "Father?" she said, like he was really her father, like – "Father, did I do right?"

"You . . . killed in God's House . . ." he heard himself say, but no, that wasn't the thing to say. He wasn't anyone's Father, no. Not when he was glad that Blade was dead, not when he was glad at the Bishop's cowering –

The Bishop was in the arms of his assistants. One was calling the police on his cell phone.

"It's just like the games, the movies . . . Just like Billy said, there's no difference." Mary smiled. "If I could just have done that for Billy."

Again, Father Moriarty forced himself to move. He was nearly beside Mary when without warning he started to cry. "Why couldn't I have been there for Billy?" she kept saying, as Father Moriarty took her into his arms. "Why couldn't I have been there for him . . . ?"

"It's OK, it's OK," he sobbed. In the distance he could hear the wail of sirens.

"Sister Edna said we needed to take it all back. She said God and Jesus said we had to kill and fight now, just like them. She said God was going to punish the person who shot Billy in Hell and that the shooter deserved to die." Father Moriarty held her tighter. Mary looked up at him. "Did I do my part for Billy, Father? Did I do my part for God? Will God love me now?"

Father Moriarty couldn't answer.

"I had to defend Billy's church, that's what you were saying, right, I had to defend Billy's church . . ."

A creaking sound distracted them. Above candles the Cross tilted, then fell forward. Father Moriarty glimpsed two bullet holes in the wood before it fell upon the candle flames, extinguishing the light and engulfing the church in a terrible gloom.

Across the Oar
GREG SZULGIT

||||||||||||||||||||||||||||||||||||||||||||||||||||||||||||||||||||||||||||||||||||||||||||||||||||||||||||||||||||||||||||||||||||||||

A pilgrim stops to hear a warrior's troubling confession in this thoughtful short fantasy. First published in GenrePub.

"I can't get this old Jowl out of my head, Pilgrim."

> I had planted the oar at the crossroads . . .
> . . . And they were all I loved.
> – John Ciardi, "Ulysses"

The pilgrim was aware of the man who had been following him for some time. He did not, however, feel endangered or concerned, as it was common for people to stalk him in a way, gathering their courage to approach him for confession. Often, the idea of a telling had not been planned on the teller's part; the need welling up in them only after a confessor crossed their path unexpectedly. If a friend had asked what was bothering them of late, why they drank more heavily, or hit their children, or handled their affairs with impatience, they might reply honestly, albeit naively, that there was nothing wrong. The sight of a pilgrim's oar blade bobbing along above the heads of a crowd could, however, cause a man to look into himself and, like Aldam and his wives in the Orchard, feel a sudden shame at his nakedness. And so it was on this day, when the hard-browed man had been on his way to collect his order of nails from the blacksmith, that he found himself drawn to the bearded pilgrim in the red robes who chanced to be passing through his town.

"Pilgrim, will you know me?"

The man had approached before the oar had been customarily planted in the ground at a crossroads; an action that spoke either to his lack of etiquette or to his desperation. The pilgrim nodded to the man to let him know that he had been heard and would be tended, and then began setting up the sarjatar, the prayer station. He did not rush, as the time that it took him to prepare was usually helpful to those who approached him. It allowed the troubles within them to roil to the surface and, often, they would open the telling by simply sobbing with a rush of emotions never before confronted. There were even times when this was all that was needed, and the teller would leave without a word.

When the oar was set flat on the ground, and the life-bowl was placed in the centre of its blade, the pilgrim knelt and poured a handful of sand into the bowl, saying, "There is nothing new in this world." He then struck it hard and waited for the ringing to subside, following the ever-fading tone until the distinctions between it, and silence, and the world were incomprehensible. And he waited for the man across from him to speak.

"I can't get this old Jowl out of my head, Pilgrim."

The pilgrim raised his eyebrows but did not speak.

"I was flank-guarding a small caravan to Kaad, through the hinters, last fall. During our lunch stop, two of us bars went to collect mistletoe in the hills – we usually get enough to cover our gift-giving for Woses' Day. Anyroad, we were far from the caravan, walking fast but quiet, thinking that we might spook up a stewing rabbit if we were lucky, and we saw these two Jowl kids hunting. They didn't see us, but they must have heard us because they looked around real concerned and then started heading away, deeper into the hills. We knew if we followed them we might be late on roll-call but Lucas, our High Bar, would understand when we told him that we spotted Jowls. So, we followed them and they led us back to a small group of tents. We figured it for just a minute or so – it was a day camp for hunting and there was just the one family there."

The pilgrim readied himself for what he knew would follow. His mentor had taught that a pilgrim should remove himself from the telling; that any reaction to the confession was certain to alter its purity or, in a worst case, alter it entire. If the teller felt judged, then the confessor had cheated them egregiously, and in their most important moment, their assenting. Still, the pilgrim was no master and he had to make a conscious effort to suppress judgement at times. Having lost his own children to war, this was sure to be one of those circumstances.

"There was thick brush on one side of the camp and a rock wall on the other. Perfect for the 'river net' they teach in first-weeks. We never tried it in the field, so we were excited for the chance to make good on our training. We got up a good run and, when we reached the camp, my partner charged straight to the other side to block any retreat. He passed one of the kids, who was tending the fire, but didn't break form and swing at him because he needed to 'set the net'. He's a good soldier. I was hoping to get to the kid before he had much of a chance to yell out, but I was too slow and he called out for his great-dad before I could split him. An old man come hot out of the main tent, along with the other kid who we tracked before, but neither one had anything more dangerous than a skinning knife or the pot they was eating from."

The pilgrim tried not to visualise the scene and told himself that this was in the past; that the victims were at rest now and that it was only the living who mourned the outcomes of such encounters.

"So I went straight for the great-dad, knowing that my partner would be ready for the kid when he tried to break off. The old man tried to block my Brelling with his cooking tin, but I cut him at the wrist and then back-bladed him at the eyes. He fell on the ground and yelled something, probably his great-son's name, before I stuck him in the ribs. The kid was already down and Mathew was finishing him before I even could help. It all happened so quick."

If the pilgrim had let himself be affected by the story, the teller didn't seem to notice, going on with a fervency born of confessional release.

"We weighed bearings and decided that all enemies were tended. And then, as if he's back from the dead, I see the old Jowl on the ground raising up his head and trying to gasp out something. He's lying there, like a fish out of water, trying to get some air into him, and he gets enough to mouth some word, but I can't hear what it is. I couldn't even believe he was still alive. So Mathew stands on the old Jowl's hands while I lock his head between my ankles. I tell him, 'What are you mumblin at, old man?' But you know these fuckin Jowls. He probably don't even speak Wendish. He gurgles something, some m-word that probably means 'you pig-fuckers!' He's obviously not about to answer me with the respect owed a bar, so I cut the guy's pants free while Mathew steadies his head. I ask him one more time, but he's still doing the fish-gasping thing. So I punch my sword up his ass. That woke him up!"

The pilgrim had dropped his eyes at this point, which was against the teachings, but he feared that to not do so would betray his revulsion; his memories. He found himself back at that moment, eight years ago, that still defined his present more than he would admit. It was the end of the planting season and he had gone quarrying, expecting it to take all day, but the rock was well-fractured from the hard winter and he finished gathering a wagon of shards by high noon. He considered going directly home, but the spring air was sweet, and he was in no rush to resume the routines of his life. Instead, he indulged himself with a trip to town, where he spent more than he should have on a hair pin for his wife and smash-taffies for his two littles and his teens, being sure to include some ferments for the latter. So it was in high spirits that he returned to his stead to find that the expectations for his life had been fractured and scattered, left for him to reassemble into a new, ugly mosaic of guilt, anger, and loss.

As he approached the cabin, he didn't hear the pigs, nor the chickens, nor the dog. Then he saw the door, splintered and hanging on one hinge, and broke into a run. The shambles of the interior were lost to him as he searched the room for his family. He found his wife under the overturned table, her lifeless hands still clutching the youngest, dead child. He found the eldest in the well, his mouth stuffed with straw, pig faeces, and two of his own fingers. His daughter, Cynthia, was never found, though a few fistfuls of scalp-torn golden hair were left behind.

He had been a fool, and he knew it now. The People's Protectorate had spread the word, months earlier, that they expected taboda to be planted for their use, and that all farmers were advised to aid in The Protection by doing do. He had done as they asked, but had planted too much too quickly, suggesting to the group that he had a substantial amount of cash at hand, as taboda sprouts were not cheap. He had tried his best to appease them, but his thoughtlessness had cost everything.

"So the guy kicks his head back and howls out the same curse as earlier, squirming around and kickin the dirt like a wee one having a tantrum. I gave the pommel one good, hard kick, and drove the blade in about as far as it'd go. I must have hit an upper chakra because he stopped moving after a few more jerks, but not before he spit out that word again: 'munda'. Gotta give him credit, he was a feisty old fuck.

"Anyroad, Mathew and I requisitioned their portables and got ourselves back to the caravan to report to Lucas. He was right pleased with our work and even rode alongside of us, chatting to us about the incident and Jowls in general. He knew them good and said he even spoke some Jowlese, so I asked him what 'munda' meant. I thought it was gonna be something awful. I figured the old man was cursing me, or God, or the whole fucking world. Well, do you know what Lucas tells me?"

The pilgrim sat.

"He says that 'munda' means 'why'. Can you imagine, I'm sticking a sword up this guy's ass and his great-children are hacked apart, and all he can say to me is, Why?"

Several moments passed in silence. A gusty breeze whistled over the top of the life-bowl, causing a few grains of the sand within to dance slightly, and the man with the hard brow began to wince with long-overdue tears in his eyes. The Jowl's question was the reason that the man had stopped the pilgrim; it was the thing that had been eating him from the inside.

The pilgrim brought his hands together to call an end to the session. It seemed that this man, if one could grace him with such a term, had come away from the caravan experience a better person, even if it took the lives of an untold number in his past to get him there.

"And now that you have learned the value of all persons, may you be more at peace," declared the pilgrim. It was contrary to the stricter interpretations of the teachings to add his own commentary to a telling, and he knew this, but he did it as much for himself as for the man with the tears in his eyes. He needed to quiet the ghosts that had been awakened by the soldier's story, banishing them to the space that he had surrendered to his past, along with his name.

A change came over the man's face, slowly at first, but with an increasing intensity that pulled his lips taut and hardened his stare more than when the two had first sat down. "Value?" the man shouted, spittle careening off his words. "Value? Those fuckers! Who's gonna pay them back, Pilgrim? Who's gonna pay them for Wessad Mountain? I was there, and it's all true! Who's gonna pay them for Meisser Pass? Do you think I'm sorry for what I did? I'm not! Little Jowls grow up! They grow to be big Jowls; fucking pig-people! All men know this."

The pilgrim sat aghast, horrified by what he had done. All of the shame that he had previously felt for the soldier, he now turned on himself. How could he have been so arrogant? Now, due to his pride, his weakness, he had robbed the universe of an assenting, and probably doomed more innocent people to death at the hands of the angry man on the other side of the oar.

After a long pause, the man took a deep breath and steadied himself. He closed his eyes and concentrated on his words. "It doesn't bother me to ask why the Jowls are shit, or why they have to be hunted to the last. I know what's right. But since that day, I can't get the question out of my head: Why? Why does it have to be this way? Why can't we live another way?"

The two sat for a few minutes, both stirring the telling in their heads. Each knew that there would not be a cathartic ending, but they also knew that change and peace do not always come easily – that sometimes stories cannot be finished in one sitting. And so, the pilgrim brought his hands together and pointed them towards the bowl, inviting the teller to strike it with the oar pin that lay beside it. As the single, clear tone rang out, the pilgrim looked the soldier in the eyes and felt a hope return that he had abandoned only minutes earlier. Neither smiled, but a tension had cleared, and he sensed a sort of kinship with the man. The feeling surprised him, and then sickened him a little, and then was gone.

When the man was done following the tone, he took the bowl in his hands, stood, and poured the sand out onto the ground, watching as much of it was carried away in the crosswind. As he finished doing so, the pilgrim recited, "Today is not tomorrow; be at peace." With that, a faint smile crept over the soldier's face and he nodded to the pilgrim, turned his collar up against the wind, and walked towards the blacksmith's shop with steps that became ever stronger and more even.

After the Bombardment
BROOKE FIELDHOUSE

Mefta, an Asian man expelled from Uganda, battles his self-centred landlord to try and make ends meet as a pensioner in Scarborough.

"How could mankind expect to comprehend eternity when he was no more than a temporal being?"

Mefta dreaded the Scarborough foghorn. It wasn't so much the dismal adenoidal hum which it made every few seconds; it was the silence that followed each dead note. It seemed that during the intervals between its grim dirges, everything else in the world ceased to exist.

On a clear day, he would have had a view of the harbour with its white lighthouse, would have enjoyed watching gulls soaring over fishing boats. Today he couldn't even see across the Valley.

There had been heavy rain during the night, and he stared gloomily at the six inches of khaki-coloured water outside his window. It should have drained away by now, but there was nowhere for it to go. The gullies were blocked, gutters full of holes, the roof leaked, and most of the window frames were rotten.

The local Civic Society boasted that Sitwell View had the "finest carved Victorian bargeboards in the town". But that was no good if every time Mefta went out, he found fragments of them – the texture of nicely soaked Weetabix – lying in the front garden. Something had to be done.

Sitwell View rose to the height of six storeys. Such was the phenomenon of houses built on the side of the Valley. Folk who didn't know – or who hadn't visited before – would approach from the top road and see what appeared to be a conventional Victorian villa of two or three storeys. Then they would peer over the railings and get a surprise. Mefta certainly had done, when he came to view the flat twenty-six years ago. He was glad that he had the ground floor. There was no lift, and now he was eighty.

Mefta had three neighbours. Laura, an elderly librarian from the Local History department, was on the first floor; Jim, a retired insurance underwriter, lived on the second; while Atticus Strata, a geologist turned novelist – and at seventy, the youngest of the four – lived on the third floor. The rain-soaked attic and musty basement were used as stores.

At last, Mefta began to see sunlight through the fog, and he found himself contemplating that it was indeed a strange journey that he had made through life.

He had once been the owner of a thriving sugar company in Uganda, but then one night in 1972 came a hammering on the door, and the barking of a policeman. "You've got twelve hours to leave the country, or you and your family will be interned." He couldn't even get his money out of his bank before having to flee.

The family settled in Leicester, and with the help of sympathetic landlords they began to find their feet. While his brother struggled to set up a secondhand-furniture business, Mefta began to buy and sell porcelain and brassware. The move to Scarborough came with the opportunity to rent a small shop on Valley Bridge Parade, and he found sufficient interest in what locals referred to as bric-a-brac and knick-knacks to make a modest living. His three children – now all married with kids of their own – welcomed a trip to the seaside, so he was still able to see his family.

Nobody in Sitwell View was well off. Atticus never had two pennies to rub together; Laura lived frugally. Jim had a generous pension, but had unselfishly volunteered his entire lump sum to finance a kidney operation in America for his granddaughter. Money was a worry, and never far away was the problem of repairs to the house.

* * *

In a small village twelve miles away Dick Braggingham filled the doorway between the dining room and conservatory of his bungalow. Opposite stood his architect.

Dick had boasted that this was "his architect", but nothing was settled yet. Why did architects always talk about "fee proposals"? Why couldn't they just give you a bloody estimate like normal people?

"I'm an ex-miner so I'm a down-to-earth bloke," Dick warned the younger, anorak-clad man standing in front of him. "Aryer a Yorkshireman?" he continued – rather matily he thought. "Know how copper wire was invented, do yer? It was a Scotsman and a Yorkshireman fighting over a penny!" The architect smiled weakly and exhaled. Dick always knew when he had won somebody over.

Last year Dick and Sireen had "done" the PVCu conservatory. Two years ago it had been double-glazed windows, this year it was going to be a new car . . . and at last that loft extension. The trouble was, Dick couldn't help thinking about Sitwell View. It was like a dark Victorian Gothic cloud hanging over him, all those bloody repairs to do. He knew he'd never do them. He wanted to sell the freehold and have done with it, but Sireen wouldn't let him.

"Dundrearie is merely our village bungalow," Sireen liked to tell folk. "We also own a large property in town." "It lets people know how well you've done in life," she insisted to Dick. "What's more, it tells those toffee-nosed tossers who live there that ordinary working-class people like us can be landlords."

They were fuddy-duddies, thought Dick. He recalled his last visit to the house five years ago – to discuss . . . something or other with that coffee-coloured fella.

"Gedda life!" he'd shouted, as the door closed behind him and he leapt into the street punching the air.

Dick had inherited Sitwell View from his grandmother, who had been "in service" there. She unexpectedly got the lot after the owner died, and his son buggered off to South Africa. Penny-pinching? She was as bad as Dick – patched it up after the First World War, kept the freehold, but sold leases on four of the floors. Ninety-nine years each. That was another reason Sireen was right to hang on to it – there were only five years to run on the leases.

It was a good job there was going to be better income from Sitwell View. All this spending was putting pressure on Dick's pension. He also worried about the constant flow into the house of creams, lotions, nourishers, serums, energisers, and salon-quality shampoos.

Sireen hadn't worked since the modelling jobs dried up – apart from a recent feature for *Total Tattoo*. She had one on each shoulder, and a Celtic emblem on her bum. Dick had said that it "didn't look like the Celtic strip" to him, and anyway, if push had come to shove, he would have supported Rangers.

Mum and Dad had wanted her to become a nurse, but in 1965, at the age of seventeen, she won the Miss Grimethorpe beauty contest. Dick had some of the magazine originals framed in the hall. Black and white of course; hot pants. Stunning or what!

* * *

"We can force Braggingham to sell the freehold." Jim's suggestion made Mefta tremble, as he sat chairing the residents meeting. Meetings always took place in Laura's flat on the first floor, so that nobody had to do too much climbing of stairs.

House policy had always been to keep the buildings insurance and external repairs the responsibility of Braggingham, but things clearly weren't going to improve. Even a council enforcement order failed to do the trick.

Now the clock was ticking, the leases would soon expire and . . . goodness knows what would happen then.

It appeared that Jim had already done some work on the subject.

"Brightwell's suggest we offer a figure of £60,000. That's ten per floor."

Mefta swallowed hard. Fifteen each was half his total savings.

"Look," reasoned Jim, "if it's ours, then we can at least sell the whole house, repairs done or not. At the moment, with the leases practically expired, we've nothing to offer."

Mefta tried to rally himself with one of his father's sayings: "The worst hazard in the world is to not take a risk."

* * *

It was early morning. Dick was dressed – too nervous to go back to bed, so he sat, fidgeted, and gazed at his sleeping wife.

Her hair, still brunette after sixty-five years – she never dyed it – was worn in a close crop. Folk in the village had nicknamed her "the bulldog". True, her nose might be just a little flat, her jaw a trifle square, and her thighs solidly built, but by 'eck, she still looked cracking in a pair of hot pants. She could knock spots off that Felicity Prerequisite who ran the flower-arranging classes.

Dick could feel a sickening anxiety creeping over him. He knew he had something to discuss with Sireen, but it could wait. He wasn't going to wake her, not just yet.

His eye wandered over the encampment of bottles, tubes, and

dispensers on the nightstand. He'd always been at a loss to know the difference between "visible effects nourishment", "firming nourishment", and "hydro nourishment". As far as he was concerned, nourishment was a full English, and at least a couple of pints.

Dick had never learned to read or write. There was no point, Sireen always covered for him. He could read a bit, and as he leaned closer to the nightstand, his finger traced the words on two of the jars: *Duwop Plumperazzi*, and *Balmbini Palette*. "Christ!" he muttered.

He felt his shaved head suddenly grow hot as he recalled the time when Sireen had sent him to Boots to pick up an order.

"Is Mrs Braggingham exfoliating at the moment?" asked the soft-spoken male assistant. Dick told him that his wife's periods were none of his business.

Dick and Sireen had no children. He'd been keen, but not her. She was always on about "elasticity", and something that went by the rather nauseating name of "body butter". He sometimes felt that all these pots and tubes were the enemy of their love life. Sireen couldn't wake up without rubbing some stuff or other over her arms and legs, and even as he had brought her an early cup of tea, a hand had stretched out and grabbed the Dr Feelgood Complexion Balm.

It hadn't prevented their early-morning session though. It had been short, but it had taken the edge off the nervous craving which he could feel eating away at him. Sireen was always quiet as a mouse, but Dick liked to bellow loudly as he reached his climax. It was one of the benefits of owning a detached property.

Sireen never actually talked about sex. She would boast about something called Nude Beige she was keen on. She liked the sound of Bare Minimals Ready Bronzer, and the phrase Naked Strangers was always on the tip of her tongue. A lip gloss, she said it was.

Dick reckoned that she liked his bald head – something he had sported after his blond curls began to desert him. "From Harpo Marx to Yul Brynner – overnight," he had bragged at the pub. "Who do you prefer?"

She opened her eyes, began to stretch, and Dick felt his stomach turn over as he looked down at the letter he was holding.

"They want to buy the freehold," he blurted.

"Well they can't," she pouted, taking hold of a stick of Duwop Lip Venom.

Dick could feel drops of perspiration running into his eyebrows.

"Brightwell's seem to think they can. It's the law apparently."

"Stuff that!" The lipstick had been replaced by a cigarette paper containing half a thimble of Golden Virginia. She fidgeted it into a microscopic white tube and let it dangle from her pale-pink lips as she repeatedly snapped at the gas lighter.

"Get Sodwell's on the phone and we'll see."

Even the mention of the name plunged Dick further into despair. Sodwell, Handslip and Trolley had been his solicitors ever since he'd been down the mines. Victor Sodwell was a rogue, grotesquely disguised as hail-fellow-well-met.

Oh Lord! That incident five years ago, shortly after their arrival in the village! He and Sireen had been drinking at the Cormorant and Shag. It was late autumn, when Sireen – as was her wont – adopted a facial hue of something approaching bitter chocolate. A group of students from Hull University had been gathered in the snug, when Sireen thought she overheard one of them refer to her as looking "rather simian". Dick didn't know what it meant.

"It means that I look like a bloody monkey, so what are you going to do about it?"

Dick pictured the ghastly scene as he escorted the reluctant undergraduate to the beer garden. Even before he'd decked the youth, he caught sight of Felicity Prerequisite, who just happened to be walking past.

The charge against Sireen, of disturbing the peace by repeatedly chanting, "Let him have it, Dick," was dropped, but in spite of Sodwell's mitigation, Dick got four months.

"If you don't speak to Victor, then I will." Sireen stared at Dick, and then with the artificial smile of a stand-up comic, "Victor and I were very intimate once."

As far as Dick was concerned, Sodwell was as queer as they come. This was a bizarre revelation, no doubt intended to goad him.

* * *

"The Bragginghams have declined our offer." Jim's news came as some reassurance to Mefta. Of course he knew that surveyors would have to be appointed on both sides to arrive at a "fair" value.

Jim's advice was to commission a detailed "invasive" survey.

"The surveys for valuation are superficial," he insisted. "We need to find out exactly what we're in for, in terms of a scope of works for repairs."

"It will be fair to both parties," conceded Mefta.

Solicitor Simon Brightwell suggested that they ask Braggingham to contribute to the cost of the specialist survey.

"After all, it's in his interest."

Mefta decided that rather than sending a letter, or telephoning, he would go and see Mr Braggingham himself. He had been there once before, and it wasn't a pleasant memory, but perhaps this was the last time he would need to go.

The Bragginghams' bungalow was at Plumpton, a small clifftop village twelve miles south of Scarborough. Mr Mefta no longer owned a car, but his daughter Azmena was coming to see him, and was keen to visit the bird sanctuary. They would mix business with pleasure.

"'E's out picking up the new Mercedes-Benz!" A disembodied female voice came through the bathroom window. Mefta was sure that Mr Braggingham had said two o'clock, and he was surprised to see the bungalow covered in scaffolding.

"Just look at the length of those camera lenses!" exclaimed Mefta, as father and daughter spent an exhilarating hour in the hot sun, watching gulls and kittiwakes swooping in the warm air currents, three hundred feet above the sea. "I've never seen so many birdwatchers."

Back at the bungalow Mefta once again pressed the cuckoo-chime doorbell. There was still no sign of Mr Braggingham. Then he heard Mrs Braggingham's voice, this time coming from the back garden. "It's one of your tenants, Dick – that coffee-coloured one."

As Mefta stepped back, he caught sight of Mr Braggingham on the scaffolding directly above him.

"Come and have a look at the building works," boomed Braggingham. "Three weeks done and three to go," he specified, as if he was describing a prison sentence.

Surely Mr B didn't expect him to go up there? He glanced across to where Azmena was sitting in the car, just out of sight. Mr B clearly wasn't coming down so up went Mefta.

"Hot, isn't it?" bellowed Braggingham as Mefta climbed gingerly. "You'll be used to it though."

"Hey!" whispered Braggingham conspiratorially. Mefta could feel the other man's elbow in his ribs as he was struggling to right himself on the timber planks after his climb. "Englishman says to an Indian, 'We buggered up your country for two hundred years.' The Indian says, 'Yes, but we buggered up your language for ever!' No offence, mate," he added with a nervous chuckle.

It *was* offensive, and as Mefta glanced across towards where the car was parked he was glad Azmena could not see them. All hell would have been let loose. Mr Braggingham said that he would think about the survey, and discuss it with Mrs Braggingham.

As Mefta turned to go, he could feel Braggingham's hands inexplicably marauding his shoulders. It was a strange touch, as if they were working sponge – almost sexual.

There was a lot of activity on the scaffolding, and workmen were moving to and fro, some of them singing tunelessly along to a radio. One of them was decent enough to offer Mefta a hand.

As Mefta carefully descended, his eye wandered through and beyond the rungs of the ladder. Not more than six feet away from the base of the scaffolding, and in full view of the entire workforce, stood a tangerine-coloured lounger on which lay Mrs Braggingham. Her eyes were shaded, her body bikinied; her skin was the hue of charred walnut, and the texture of a well-basted goose.

* * *

It was a shock – no doubt to all concerned, and certainly to Mefta – when the valuations for the freehold came in lower than expected. Brightwell's man had valued at £15,000, while Sodwell's surveyor had said that, "Under the circumstances he was unable to supply a figure higher than £70,000." The resulting agreed sum of £42,500 came as a relief to Mefta.

"Serve Braggingham right," commented Atticus. "He should have accepted our first offer!"

The specialist survey – which Braggingham had refused to contribute to – took two days. Test bores were dug to examine the foundations; small sections of wall were removed. There had been great excitement about the discovery of substantial shards of metal in the walls and floor cavities, particularly in Jim's flat.

A week later Mr Mefta read an email from the surveyor:

> . . . We expect the full report to be completed next week, but I thought you would be interested to know that the fragments of metal, taken from the superstructure of your property at 1st- and 2nd-floor levels, came from a shell fired from a German warship on 16th December 1914 . . .

Mefta had heard of "the German raid on Scarborough", but knew nothing further. Atticus, it appeared, was an expert on the subject.

"There were three of them – battlecruisers: *Derfflinger, Von der*

Tann, and *Kolberg*," he announced. "Two of them did the shelling, while *Kolberg* went to lay mines near Flamborough Head. It began just after 0800 hours and lasted an hour and a half. Then they sailed up the coast attacking Whitby, followed by Hartlepool. Over eighty-seven were killed at Hartlepool, seventeen at Scarborough, plus the injured. There was panic – people were convinced they were going to land."

"Why?" Mefta looked nonplussed at Atticus.

"The target was a wireless station which they never actually hit. Also it was strategy – trying to split the British fleet prior to the Battle of Jutland. Basically, though, it was to put the fear of God into folk – and because they could."

That evening, in the warmth of the approaching dusk, Mefta felt an urge to walk down to the sea. The wind, in summer or winter, was capable of howling up or down the Valley, but this late-June evening was one of those rare moments when time seemed to stand still.

As he walked under Cliff Bridge onto Foreshore Road, Mefta could smell the air, ozone-laden after the earthiness of the Valley. He could hear the soft incoming tide; the gentle sounds were almost like those of suckling. Was sand suckling salt water, or was water feeding off sand?

He stopped in front of the Futurist Theatre – as far as he dared go without his stick – and gazed out to sea. There were no waves. For a moment he shut his eyes, and as he listened, he felt as if he was in the presence of some large benign farm animal, quietly inhaling and exhaling.

Mefta's eyes suddenly sprang open, as he imagined he could see two towering mountains of steel, floating no more than five hundred yards from the harbour mouth, and spitting fire into the winter dawn mist. He turned and pictured the smoke and dust coming from the hits on the buildings behind him, from the several hundred shells which came walloping into the town that morning long ago. He visualised the panic as people crowded into the railway station – some carrying Christmas cake hastily crammed into tins – only to be told that there were no trains, and that they would have to flee as best they could. They were convinced that they would be bayoneted by the invading Germans.

He recollected his own fear, as his family prepared to leave Uganda that night forty-two years ago, his panic at the sight of the policeman at the door of his house.

"Don't worry," the man had reassured him, "Amin has promised us land and property, I'm not going to shoot you. Always remember, a dog with a bone in its mouth can't bite you!"

Mefta thought about Mr Braggingham's absurd behaviour on the roof of his bungalow, his inappropriate humour – yet he too, as a miner, must have known fear. The man had looked so beseechingly at him; childless, friendless, and possibly even loveless.

Mefta stared towards the indefinable boundary between sea and sky, and there were tears running down his cheeks. Whether these were of joy or sorrow did not matter, for as a student of reality he knew that there *were* no boundaries. Here could become there; now would sooner or later turn into then. Inside was out, outside was in, there was no beginning, there was no end. How could mankind expect to comprehend eternity when he was no more than a temporal being?

The long warm evenings of June and July gave way once again to the fogs of November. Completion had been achieved, the freehold was now theirs, and Jim was masterminding an insurance claim for the repairs.

"Repairs" was – as Mefta wistfully observed – a euphemism for a rebuild. The original foundations had always been inadequate, and the damage done by the German shell was insidious. The engineer's report said "no immediate danger", but recommended reconstruction within a year.

Sitting alone in his apartment Mefta was struggling to cope with the magnitude of it all when there came an urgent thumping on his door. It was Atticus and Jim in a high state of excitement.

"I'll let Jim do the talking," volunteered Atticus. "He's done most of the work on this."

"It would appear that we are eligible to claim compensation for war damage."

"But it happened a hundred years ago." Mefta smiled in spite of himself.

"It doesn't matter," said Jim. "We've taken the liberty of talking to the Ministry of Defence, and discovered an extraordinary blip in the system. The statute talks about 'reasonable defence measures in the face of attack by a foreign power'."

Mefta was beginning to feel like taking one of his walks, or even better, a "lie down". Jim rambled on.

"If our property was in Hartlepool and we had discovered similar damage, then we wouldn't be able to claim. That's because Hartlepool was defended on the day of the attack by three six-inch guns. But Scarborough was defenceless, and it seems that no one ever put a time limit on claims."

"What does this all mean?" Mefta's legs felt like jelly.

Jim sat back for a moment, so Atticus could have his turn.

"The Ministry of Defence have told us that in principle they'll support our claim, but you can bet your bottom dollar that if we're successful, then Parliament will change the statute pronto."

"Brightwell thinks our claim could be a first," interrupted Jim.

"And the bombshell," added Atticus, laughing at the irony of the phrase, "is that the claim could be backdated. The cost of rebuild, plus internal refits at today's prices, including VAT – that's £800,000, plus compound interest since 1914. That's well over a million!"

"Brightwell did use the phrase 'a shot in the dark'!" added Jim.

Mefta closed his eyes. A shot in the dark? All he could see were the bursts of flame coming from the guns of *Derfflinger* and *Von der Tann*, the pistol in the holster of the Ugandan policeman, and Mr Braggingham raising the Union Jack for the topping-out ceremony at his bungalow.

Several months later, Mefta had just nicely come to after his afternoon nap, when the phone rang. It was Simon Brightwell, and he sounded ecstatic.

"You've done it! Customs and Excise have asked me to set up an account on your behalf, ready for a transfer by twelve noon tomorrow. And by the way, your colleague Jim got his sums wrong – he forgot all those years we had of soaring interest rates. The payment to the four of you is a smidgen under £5 million – less my fee of course, ha ha ha . . ." The phone went dead.

All Mefta could think about was Azmena, his two sons, and their children. Never again would they have to wake up in the morning and wonder, "Can we manage till Christmas?"

* * *

Spring is here, and Dick is feeling very springlike indeed. He's spent most of the day with Gary the garage mechanic. There's been a lot of, "You owe me, yeh, you owe me!"

Perhaps unwisely, Gary challenged Dick during a darts match at the Cormorant and Shag. As far as Dick can recall, it went something like:

"Triple top to finish, mate, and I'll give your Merc a free MOT!"

Dick got the triple top, so apart from taking a lot of finger-poking into his ribs, there wasn't much Gary could do other than put his money where his mouth was.

What a day! Fifty quid in; wait till he tells Sireen. Scampi and chips in a basket all round, eh!

Dick swings the Merc into the drive. Funny, seven o'clock on a March evening and the bungalow's in darkness. Power cut? Kitchen door's open.

"Fifty quid in on Gary, eh!" he chants. "Not bad?"

Silence.

Dick enters the dining room.

Sireen's there after all, sitting at the table, staring out of the window into the evening murk. In front of her is a copy of the *Scarborough Evening News*, but still she does not speak.

Dick leans forward, and in the gloom, he slowly traces with his finger the headline, *Scarborough Pensioners in War-Damage Property Compensation Windfall*. It means nothing to him.

An Unfinished Husband
ADRIAN KALIL

||||||||||||||||||||||||||||||||||||||||||||||||||||||||||||||||||||||||||||||||||||||||||||||||||||||||||||||||||||||||||||||||||||||||||||

A family man feels there is something missing from his life, and finds it is not what he expected.

"Larry wondered if they would ever forgive him for what he was thinking."

"I 'm not really sure I understand what it is you need," said Kate.

Larry looked out over the vast blue ocean that lay before him and smiled. "A new car," he said quietly.

He squinted to see beyond the spread of brown beach that lay between him and the water. The sun glared; its heat was relentless and oppressive. Larry was tired and longed for the respite of some shade and a large, cold beer. He coveted gulping it indiscreetly and enjoying a satisfying belch, but he'd given up drinking a few months back and, deferring to the moment, thought better of it. Moreover he had, of all things, begun jogging again, though usually quite slowly, along the familiar beach where its firm sand met the water. Alone like this, his uninhibited mind would travel through foreign and forbidden ground.

Kate had said nothing about these ascetic changes but Larry knew it pleased her, if only in passing. For her husband to surrender something gave the woman a strange aura of stifling superiority that dispelled all remaining myth, all hope, that he was any longer the head of their household.

He didn't really care, as his passion to lead had faltered, as had his unquenching desire to be with her most every night. It gave Kate great, unwavering satisfaction to get her way, no matter what the cost, and Larry wondered if that, too, had been a part of her plan. Over the years she had exerted more and more subtle influence over the decisions he was accustomed to making and had become more manipulative, more precise in her methods and intent.

"What on earth do you want with a new car?" she pushed. "We already *have* one." Her accusing eyes were upon him and he did not look back.

"It's yours, really," he said, "the one we have is yours." With that he turned away and thought, too, that he had been the one to pay for it. Their last vehicle was merely a fresh example of most everything, including the children, that was once theirs and that she had somehow endeavoured to make hers. Miles separated their reclining beach chairs.

The children were playing in the water a few dozen yards away and were unaware their father was watching them so closely, so lovingly. They were growing up so quickly, he could not grasp how long he would know them or how many years they would wish to know him and share their unconditional affection. As he sat there next to their pale, colourless mother, Larry wondered if they would ever forgive him for what he was thinking. They were so young and beautiful, so trusting at this age.

It's a shame, he thought, that adolescence sometimes arrives abruptly, blossoming at the door, at the cost of such sweet innocence.

He wondered, too, if Kate could read his mind. She paused and blinked, then slowly returned a bemused gaze to her book as she slid her sunglasses back on her nose with a single, slender finger. He felt her panting and sweating behind her eyes, crouching like a hungry lioness in the summer heat. She swallowed and he sensed she tasted blood.

He didn't hate his wife, but had lost respect for her a long time ago. From the things she had said, the distance she kept, he knew there was no more fire, no more of the passion they had once enjoyed. Lately, when she was asleep and he lay next to her, confused and torn, he would watch her breathe, watch her breasts rhythmically rise and fall. He would look deep into his heart, his anticipation and passion unrequited, and think of being somewhere else.

Long ago he had held onto some remote delusion of becoming the perfect husband, and soon found himself on the generous and selfless, yet quickly unsatisfying end of a disparate equation. It was clear she'd become accustomed to his constant desire to please and to keep her comfortable and secure, wanting nothing. She began, then, to expect more than he could muster, and her need for attention and satiety soon outgrew his spousal abilities. Her appetite swiftly turned into rejection.

Their early courtship was captivating and seductive, but had blinded him cold to the reality of such barren and desolate love. Once she knew she had the security their association held, she stopped giving. Even after the arrival of their children, events that should have pulled them together, she turned away.

He had been exquisite in his passions to no avail, for she grew unmoved by his attempts to please her. For a while he thought he had succeeded, but she had a way of turning her displeasure into wanton void, and in her wake festered a cloud of guilt that hovered low over black, frigid water. To subject one's soul to unceasing self-scrutiny, more critical than anyone else could ever imagine, defied definition, and Larry became shackled into looking hard at both sides of his dark mirror.

Kate's dispassionate submissions stemmed only from obligation and, after a while, she grew weary and bored. They still slept in the same bed and he was rewarded with occasional lusty satisfactions, but he knew her bitter heart heard a voice that was not his. His love became a discarded beach shell; a music unheard, a melody he could no longer sing. He did not like what he saw, nor what they had become.

Where do I begin? he thought. He wanted to want something in his life, and longed to know what it felt like to care about something passionately again. He wanted someone to want him in the way he had once known, but found the thought of himself revealed, his raw soul, the fragile vulnerabilities and the exposed flaws, profoundly frightening. Sitting next to her, he shivered hard in the afternoon heat.

Every weekday morning he would leave the house at the same time and drive the same comfortable road to the familiar grey parking lot behind his office. More often than not his wife would be sleeping as he prepared for the day and would arise as the front door closed. If Kate happened to be up with the children, she maintained a glacial wall of silence as she manoeuvred through her morning tasks, efficient and unanimated in her routine. At these times, the bleak chasm between them was deafening and the sound would shake his soul.

Despite the omniscient darkness that arose from such occasions, Larry preferred it to her frequent critical diatribes, however difficult it may have become. He closed the door behind him and, in silent concession, breathed a new day. He paused for a moment on the porch.

It's not as if I'm running from anything, he thought. More that he felt the need to run to something fresh, yet undefined. Only the unconditional love of his children drew him back to their home.

A few months ago, faced with malignant boredom and a manifest desire unfulfilled, Larry began to notice things he had otherwise ignored. To break the day's routine, he made a point of slowly driving past showrooms, their floors glistening with shiny new vehicles. He would often park his old car and peer into the window, his reflection an apparition of longing and dissatisfaction, his eyes watching the caged, painted beauties. They seemed so far beyond him and so far from what he felt he deserved, but he could not look away.

One dealership was close to the office and he took to walking by on his lunch break, mesmerised by the sights and smells of raw, new power, of an unbridled sensuality waiting for his touch. He felt stronger and more independent when he looked at these magnificent, unattainable creatures and dreamed that somehow they could be his.

One day while taking in the charm of a late model, he noticed something in the background and a bit out of his focus move, rise, and then move again. He looked up from the polished, refined temptations to see a handsome young man standing tall in a sea of human mediocrity. The gentleman acknowledged his interest with a kind and dignified nod, his eyes on Larry for what seemed a colourful and luxuriant moment.

As others in the showroom remained occupied with their deals and clever distractions, the young man's face was a welcome sight. Ignoring everything else, as at the time it all seemed quite unimportant, Larry walked over. The cool, soft room was a pleasant respite from the sun's incessant glare and the hot, melting sidewalk outside. The exquisite aroma of untouched cars filled his nostrils and lay rich within his senses. However steady and sure he felt upon entering, he flushed with caution as he approached. The young man's hand then extended and, with it, a smile quite unlike the historical artifice of others.

"Hello. I'm Dash."

Larry looked at his nametag. It read "Dashiell". *Fascinating*, he thought.

"Hi, I'm Laurence," he said, caught a bit off guard. "Larry, please. It's Larry."

Dash's hand gripped his in a solid and knowing way. It was strong and certain. For a brief moment, Larry was unsure what to do or say next, yet, somehow, he felt taller facing this man, as if he had unexpectedly found new ground.

"Please, take your time and look around. Anything in particular I may show you?"

A new life, he thought, but just smiled to himself and thanked Dash as he walked around the room, feigning interest in the white sidewalls and shiny chrome. Dash walked alongside him, confident and slow, as if he could anticipate his next steps. Larry became aware of Dash's cologne and was reminded of distant summer nights and rugged health. His company was an attractive, unobtrusive presence, and he regarded Dash carefully.

"Tell me about this one, the red one," he asked. Larry twisted his wedding band as he felt sweat forming under his shirt. It dripped slowly down his side as his clothing clung uncomfortably to his skin.

"A fine model. Aggressive, solid. Smooth ride and handles well under the most unforgiving conditions. Low maintenance."

Good God, he thought, *could everyone read me?* Although a little flustered, Larry found this guy unexpectedly pleasant and openly welcomed the attention.

"Well, I am undecided right now," said Larry, as he laughed at the irony of the obvious. "But, I would like to look more, just not today."

"Feel free to come in any time, and ask for me." He handed Larry his card and, again, his warm hand. This time Larry noticed the man wore no rings.

"Anything I can do for you," said Dash, "let me know. Anything." His words lingered like a fragrance, long overdue, and Larry drank it in.

He walked out and back to his office, holding the card tightly in his damp hand before slipping it into his pocket. He did not look back, but felt Dash watching him as he turned the corner. Larry thought of his children and the questions they asked during those tender and trusting hours they were together, when they would often astound him with their precocious insight. He thought of Kate and all the things he would never reveal to her and vowed to not go back to the showroom, to not ask for Dash, but he knew he was kidding himself. It was, he sensed, just a matter of time.

Dash represented more than a benevolent salesman. To Larry he seemed a step into the light; his words and self-respect a taste of new wine and Larry's soul was thirsty. Larry was certain he wanted to see him, to talk with him, but was unsure how to pursue it. This budding attraction was new and didn't make much sense, but the thought of spending even a little time with someone so kind and civil was powerfully seductive to his aching and hungry self. Within the context of his marriage, he had endured abuse for too many years and felt the time spent with his wife was taking him down to an eternal abyss from which he saw no respite, no return. Beyond family, he had never dared to tread any uncertain ground before, but now yearned for the covenant of fresh direction.

A few days later he walked by the showroom early when he thought Dash might be working and, as he approached the corner, he saw him. Larry watched him cross the street and walk towards the dealership, head held high, eyes bright and forward. Dash was lean and tall and wore his clothes well, at once projecting youth and maturity. For a moment Larry wondered what he drove, how much money he made, what his life was like away from the cars and deals. He seemed to stand out from the crowd, and appeared more sincere than most other people Larry had met. He imagined him successful in his work or, for that matter, most anything. Dash was athletic-looking and carried himself well, as would a man reaching for a goal. Larry found himself watching intently from the sidewalk, as if on a hovering cloud, when Dash looked up and saw him. He stopped and waved, then crossed to where Larry was standing.

"Hello! I thought you might return," he said.

"Uh, I was hoping to talk with you about −"

Dash interrupted. "Hey, it's not busy right now and I could get away. Breakfast?"

"Uh, yes. That would be nice, thanks." He glanced at his watch. "I have the time." *Such eyes*, he thought.

They walked around the corner but quickly decided against the noisy café too familiar with its mundane occupants. Dash suggested they walk a little further to a place neither had tried, but that looked tempting and interesting. They entered and found a rather private corner and a table with some fresh flowers. Their blossoms were young and fragile, perched alone, white and lavender, wanting company. The waitress arrived and greeted them; Dash acknowledged her warmly. Larry found it difficult to find his voice and fidgeted with the vase until Dash spoke his name.

"Look, Larry, I'm not trying to make a sale. I just hoped you might stop back so we could visit."

As he spoke, Dash looked directly into his eyes and, as Larry's gaze met his, they both stopped. Neither said a word. Larry was aware that something unique was about to happen, something unimaginable before now, and the moment seemed to herald a turning point in his thoughts, his concepts and all the familiar notions of what men are to one another. He felt the fire's embers, a gateway into the realm of the imagination. He swiftly became far more at ease with this man than he could ever have believed. He smiled and breathed a faint sigh of relief as they opened their menus.

"I was not sure," he began. "I had no intention of anything other than to look at the cars, but I think meeting you has opened up a door."

"How's that?" asked Dash. He again looked up.

"I'm not sure. Listen, if I am not making any sense, or if I am looking up the wrong road, I will –"

"No, that's OK. I understand. Let's just eat and you can tell me something about yourself."

Over the next hour, as if time stood still, Larry opened up to Dash in a way he had not imagined possible and with an ease he had long forgotten. Something from within surfaced through the years of suppressed emotion, and the layers of armour and doubt slowly, gradually fell aside. The infant seed that had been growing, gaining independence, emerged from the soil in search of new light. He was hungry and wanting. Dash listened without agenda or judgement and heard his words, their depth and the pain behind them. For a brief and gratifying moment, Larry thought of his children and their undying devotion in a soft and kind way. He soon forgot about his troubles with Kate, her relentless disappointment, and the misery their marriage had become. He now was certain he needed some new ground on which to anchor this evolving foundation. It caught him like a swift current, pulling him along towards the deep, enveloping sea.

When he was done, he took a sip of his coffee and sat back.

"And that's really it," he said. "You may have seen something coming, but I didn't. I feel as if I am entering through the back door, long overdue, while everything else has been tried and has failed."

"You're a good father, aren't you?"

"Yes," replied Larry, "and an imperfect husband."

Dash smiled. "I think you need a friend. Meet me here tomorrow, same time. We'll talk more."

That evening after work while Kate was out, Larry held his children in his lap, read them each a story, and rocked them until they were asleep. They did not once ask about their mother. As he closed the door to their room he smiled. A great burden had been lifted and the future looked bright.

The two men met several more times before work and, over the next several weeks, a few evenings for dinner. Dash would offer occasional fragments of insight into his private, young life, but usually passed their time listening. As Larry talked, he slowly filled his void with the freedom of new conversation and the joy of opening one's heart without expectation. At home, Kate didn't question his odd schedule or his occasional absence when she thought he should be around. The change in routine was good for Larry and helped lift him from the cruel certainties around which his life had come to exist.

Each time they met they grew more familiar in thought and word. Larry was not alarmed when Dash's hand would sometimes rest on his shoulder, or reach out across the table and hold his in a gesture of warmth and comfort. He would sometimes find their knees touching under the table, or when they sat side by side after a walk. At first Larry was hesitant, but Dash possessed such a broad and evident confidence that Larry found himself more comfortable with each new touch and increasingly open to Dash's gestures of affection. He found that, should space and opportunity allow, he would sit a little closer to Dash, exploring his profile, the way he held his eyes, the way he spoke as words emerged from his golden voice. He grew eager for the chance to be in his company and began to find new meaning in his life as this extraordinary situation continued to unfold.

As profound as their conversations had become, more enjoyable were the increasing moments where there was fertile silence. They would walk for hours or sometimes run slowly along the shore and paths Larry knew. Stride for stride, in steady tempo with their strong heartbeat and uniform breath, little was spoken, but they quickly realised a common understanding more powerful than words could convey. They knew just how fast to go, just how far to take it. Neither led, neither followed as they enjoyed their wordless, cadent rhythm.

A few weeks later, and after a long and difficult run, having covered more distance than they had been accustomed to, Larry fell exhausted on the ground, his eyes closed, panting for air. Dash stood by him for a moment, then also dropped to the ground and, propped up on one elbow, leaned close to where Larry lay. He reached over, stroked his hair, and gently kissed him.

Larry looked up to see Dash's intense eyes, full of strength and passion.

"No, no . . . I . . ." he mumbled, still catching his breath as he began to pull away.

"Shhh, shhh. Stay," Dash said, and gently touched his face.

"Is it you?" he asked.

"Yes, Larry, I'm here."

Larry reached up, brushed Dash's cheek and, looking directly into his beautiful eyes, cautiously kissed him in return.

"Night is falling," he said.

"I know."

"I must be going . . ."

"No, come with me."

"But, the kids . . ."

"They will still love you tomorrow."

"I . . ."

"No one will know, Larry. No one."

That night, in the soft colours of dusk and dreams, they faced each other and slowly removed their damp clothing. They explored each other with the freshness and innocence of adolescence. Dash was patient and allowed Larry to venture uninhibited as he delighted in their inevitable consummation. Their passion was without limit as the two men found a place in which both their lives became complete.

"If I didn't come to see you tomorrow," Larry asked, "what would you do?"

"I would learn to not expect you."

As their tongues explored salty skin there formed a bridge of masculine solitude from which grew a deep and personal, brilliant understanding. Here was left something fresh and believable, far removed from the oppressive and critical love Larry had known.

No one had ever touched him that gently, passionately, and powerfully. The simmering, volcanic feelings he had known for so long finally surfaced, bursting into a new light, a new way to see his life. Dash's grip was strong and tender as he held Larry's wide, trembling shoulders in his hands. Their exploration knew no bounds and, amidst thunder and life itself, their unbridled rhythm began to build, escalating to fullness.

Several hours passed and they lay exhausted. Larry felt he had never belonged as he did now, nestled in this man's arms; his head resting on Dash's chest, his mouth breathing the same air.

Larry slowly sat up and watched the man as he slept. He then quietly dressed and closed the apartment door behind him. It was late and the deep-blue evening was cool. As he anticipated the imminent discovery of what they had shared he felt no shame. Larry slowly walked home.

How can one explain, he thought, *if one has never been there? We are, after all, only visitors. You make your own hell; you make your own heaven. When all is gone, when all else has perished, I will continue to be.*

A Planned Retirement
BILL MONKS

A fascinating tale of a lovable rogue's plan to escape to a lifetime of wealth and happiness.

"My conscience was fairly clear considering the magnitude of the crime."

I sat on the sand watching the breakers beat upon the beach. I found it hard to believe that I had been on Maura for five years. The early-morning surf fishing finished, I gathered up my gear and ambled up to my villa on the hill. By my appearance, I could be taken for a native islander. The part of my body that was not covered by my sarong was brown as a coffee bean. My long, white hair, partially covered by a red bandanna, was tied in a knot.

On deciding to become a permanent resident on the island I had purchased a large tract of beach property and had a villa erected on the hill overlooking a lagoon on one side and the endless Pacific on the other. I had brought the blueprints of my new home with me, all part of my retirement plan. I imported the workers and material from Kyushu for its construction.

It cost a fortune, but as my father always said, "If you got it, spend it," and I did have it. The villa had all the comforts one would want and yet was not ostentatious. I made sure it wasn't the Hearst Castle of Maura.

I had only been seated on my veranda for a moment when my

beautiful native companion Gabriela approached with my morning libation, rye and vermouth. A drink named after another island that would never again feel my footfall.

We silently held hands for a moment as we shared the sea breeze. Gabriela was tall and graceful, with long black hair draped over her shapely mahogany form. I had never seen such perfect teeth; their whiteness brought out the stark black of her eyes. I never tired of admiring her beauty. She was my true treasure, my money only a tool.

Without speaking, she departed back into the villa. I sipped on my drink looking out at, and yet not seeing, my Pacific bulwark. I thought how marvellous it was that we should have met. Gabriela had become, as they say, the very beat of my heart. Her villa and mine were the only two on the hill.

What started out as being good neighbours grew into a powerful love relationship. Our strange encounter came about one evening while I stood on my veranda gazing at the moon reflecting off the ocean. I was suddenly captivated by the sound of a haunting violin drifting through the night air. It was Mendelssohn's Allegro molto appassionato, which had always held me spellbound. The music was emanating from the home of my only neighbour on the hill. I knew a woman occupied the villa, but I had never seen her. I followed the sound of the music as if in a daze. I found myself standing in her garden, entranced by her virtuosity.

After hearing the last note, I could not resist going to her door and introducing myself. The occupant appeared with the instrument still in hand. Her beauty was excelled only by her music. I thanked her for the most ecstatic rendition of the Appassionato that I had ever heard. She smiled, graciously accepting my compliments, saying that she thought it time we met. Had she been calling me?

It was the beginning of a relationship that I could only compare to the gift of Eve to Adam. The highlight of our time together was when this gorgeous woman joined me on my veranda each evening to play for me. With the eerie sound of a beguine filling the night air, the palms swaying beneath the moon, I would be caught up in a reverie of years long past.

The trinket about her neck sparkled in the bright moonlight – the Gates necklace, shown at its best when worn by a beautiful woman, not to be hidden away in a vault. I had presented it to Gabriela with the understanding that she would never wear it off the hill. I told her I still hadn't had it insured and a thing of such beauty would only cause envy and jealousy among our beloved friends. She had no idea of its history or value.

Gabriela was a descendent of Captain Nathaniel Savory, a whaler from New Bedford, who had settled on Maura in 1830. She was educated in Japan and studied music in Australia; while there she became an accomplished violinist. During a musical tour in Australia, she met and married a physician and bore him two children. Her husband was killed during the war while serving in New Guinea. Never recovering from this loss, after raising her children, she returned to Maura alone. Though she was in great demand to tour the continent, she preferred seclusion on the island, a tragic loss to the music world.

We were extremely close, but I never revealed to Gabriela my background or true identity. Bill Kias had ceased to exist. I had mailed my son a letter on the last day on the job, telling him I would always treasure our past relationship and would never forget him. I knew my boy was involved with his own family and would stand the pain.

There was no doubt in my mind that the careful effort and length of time I had expended to be here had been a small price to pay for the rapture I now enjoyed.

* * *

"Mr Shaw, sir. This is Jim Bates. I'm down in the vault. I'm the new vault manager."

"Yes, Jim, how can I help you?"

"Well sir, my very first customer, a Mrs Ziner, tells me the box that I removed from her safe is not hers. She is mad as hell! Could you come down here? What do I do? I've got four customers waiting!"

Shaw thought that old guy Kias must have taken care of two customers at the same time, which is a no-no. He returned the two boxes to the vault in one trip, placing them in the wrong safes. It was the only possible way he could mix them up.

"Stay cool, Jim, I'm on my way. Take care of the other customers. Place Mrs Ziner in one of your conference rooms."

As Shaw headed downstairs to the vault, he thought old Kias, who had retired Friday, should have gotten out much earlier. You can't spend twenty years in a vault without losing it.

He hadn't met Jim yet. He knew he was fresh out of Yale and had just started the bank's Officers Training Programme. He was going to work as a vault manager for a two-month stint – part of the course – and then move to back office and up the line.

Shaw found it hard to believe what Jim had reported about the switch. It just couldn't happen. Kias had written the Safe Deposit

Manual. He taught classes at the training centre covering every aspect of the security required for an efficient safe deposit facility.

It was an extremely controlled environment that called for a thorough yearly audit. Every facet of gaining access to and locking a safe deposit box had been written in cement for at least a hundred years. In today's crime-ridden society the safe deposit facility was the last bastion for the protection of an individual's valuables.

The bank, assuming the responsibility for the customer's wealth, takes every possible measure to safeguard it. The customer, when renting the box, is informed that he is receiving the only two keys to his safe. These keys are presented to him in a sealed envelope that has a serial number and a safe number. The customer signs the envelope, verifying that it was given to him sealed. The metal seal could not be broken. The only way to open the envelope was to cut it open with scissors.

When a safe is surrendered, the keys are immediately placed in the slot of a safe to which the vault manager does not have access. The Lock Change Co., upon removing these keys from the safe, randomly switches the locks from the surrendered safes. The keys are then placed in the sealed envelopes and the safes re-rented.

The safe contains a tin box into which the customer places his valuables. At each access he is directed to a small room where he can open his tin in private. He is told to always keep the tin in full view while it is being removed, carried and placed back in his safe.

Shaw laughed to himself. The kid certainly sounded shaken. I'll just call up the other customer and soft-soap him into coming in with his key. That should do it. His name must be in the tin box. I just hope he isn't a bastard. Shaw felt beat; it was always a pain in the neck to come in after a three-day holiday.

As Shaw approached the vault gate, he saw a young man standing behind a desk, surrounded by four extremely irate customers. The guy behind the desk, with his mouth open, white as a sheet, had to be the new man.

As Jim approached the gate to let Shaw in, he whispered, "God help us! I gave access to three more customers. They all maintain I have given them the wrong tin. What the hell happened? What am I supposed to say? What do I do with the tins? Mr Shaw, are we permitted to give out addresses? A Mr Ortez wants to know Mr Kias's home address."

God, not Mr Ortez, thought Shaw. He was jokingly known as Mr Coffee in the branch. He was supposed to have a large "plantation" outside of Cali in Colombia. One tough hombre.

Kias, that son of a bitch – had that bastard switched all the boxes? How the hell did he do it?

Shaw, ignoring the now berserk customers, walked past the desk into the conference room, where he found Mrs Ziner sitting at a table with someone else's coffer. There was only one way to play it: absolute calm, without a sign of panic.

"We have a little problem here. Let me just see who owns this box. I'll have him hop over here and you will soon have the right one."

Opening it, he quickly managed to identify the owner, a John Cody. Thank God, Shaw knew him.

"John, this is Jack Shaw at the bank. How are you doing? Great. Listen, could you come over to the branch for a moment? Come down to the vault. We just want to correct a slight error – and remember to bring your key. Yes, as quickly as possible. Thanks, John."

They waited quietly. Shaw didn't dare go out to Jim's desk where there seemed to be a crowd gathering. He overheard the word "kill" being repeated.

Cody finally showed. He was quite amenable and could understand how Kias, as an old timer in a hurry, could make that error. Cody was an all-right guy, thank God. But even at midnight it can get darker. Opening Cody's box it was discovered that a third hand was being dealt. The tin in Cody's safe did not belong to Mrs Ziner, but to the LOL Abortion Clinic. Mrs Ziner's box was still missing.

It suddenly hit Shaw. That bastard not only switched the boxes but he did it randomly. How the hell did he do it, right in front of their eyes? Kias is the only person who knows where the boxes are. He must have been in every box. What the hell is Head Office going to think of this? One thing for sure, my butt is going to be nailed to the vault door. Before this is over that door is going to be covered with butt. What did Kias know that we didn't? God help us. What will the newspapers do with this? Our credibility will be destroyed. We signed contracts with our customers guaranteeing them the safety and confidentiality of the contents of their safes. There won't be an unemployed lawyer for the next ten years.

It was a common belief in the branch that there was more cash in the customers' safe deposit boxes than it had in its own safes. It was the largest branch in Gotham City. The customers, many of them on the Forbes 500 list, were spread all over the globe. The total value of the contents of the safes could only be guessed. It was sure to run into a multi-million figure.

Shaw thought of a horrible scenario. Harry the Tout opens Von Camp's tin in the private room and finds it stuffed with gold krugerrands. Harry gives the empty box back to Jim, signs the surrender and disappears a winner. A day later Von Camp opens what he thinks is his tin only to find a priceless collection of snuff bottles. All these boxes will have to be sealed and then inventoried. Here was a catastrophic dilemma. They could only be opened with the permission of the lessee. How could a customer authorise the opening of a box that did not contain his tin? How would the absent customers feel about their boxes being in the bank's possession without their permission? How many boxes belonged to Pandora?

Shaw's mind boggled. Kias must have been planning this for years. There was only one question answered.

"Why do you keep turning down promotion?"

How much did he take? How did he get it out? Why did he randomly switch the boxes? Where in the world was Kias?

* * *

I was on Maura, in the Central Pacific, with twenty million in cash, the culmination of my retirement plan.

You say how could he steal that amount?

Planning, my boy, planning. Once the plan was conceived it was a piece of strawberry shortcake.

The Gotham Safe Deposit Co., whose vaults were situated beneath the branches of the Gotham Bank, had always been a separate company, in order to limit the bank's liability. The Gotham Bank changed its policy shortly after I was employed. They dissolved the Gotham Safe Deposit Co., making each branch responsible for its own safe deposit facility.

I waited in vain for a new safe deposit administration to take form in order to oversee our vaults. It never happened. The bank had not shot itself in the foot, it had cut its own throat. They say every man has his price but this was going to be one heck of an overpayment.

My retirement plan first occurred to me when I realised that there was no longer anyone watching the store. The store being the largest safe deposit vault in Gotham City. The millions in the vault were up for grabs. All that was needed was patience and the conception of a foolproof take-and-keep plan. I knew that Diogenes would be the only person not looking for me.

I first became aware of this strange situation when by attrition and experience I found myself to be known throughout the bank as the safe deposit authority. My odd situation occurred to me after receiving numerous telephone calls on questions concerning safe deposit policy, procedure and accounting practices. When I was stumped for an answer I realised there was nobody for me to call. I had become God by default.

We were a ship without a rudder sailing on the Sea of Limbo. When it came to procedure to be followed, there was no wrong way. The situation was incredible. Our very tight auditing department had ceased to be. The safe deposit manager, being the only person in the branch who knew how to audit the department's keys and locks, became the safe deposit auditor, a very unbankish state of affairs. What hath the bank wrought?

My spouse had recently passed away. My boy Bill, an FBI agent, had recently married and had settled on the coast. There was nothing stopping me from going for the gold ring. All the chess pieces were in place. There would be an opening, middle and an end game. Possibly I had spent too much time in the vault, but I could not turn down the challenge. I was finally answering that haunting call to return to Maura.

I was originally introduced to Maura at the close of the war while serving with a small Marine detachment in 1945. Its beauty and isolation immediately struck me. There was no island comparable to it in the Pacific. It had the entire splendour and solitude of the mythical Bali Ha'i. While serving there, I disappeared from my outfit for a week, spending the time as Adam wandering through the Garden of Eden. I had seen enough of hell to know that this was where man was meant to live. My hiatus cost me five days in the brig on piss and punk; well worth it. For twenty years after leaving the island, I never gave up my dream of returning to Paradise.

I would feel no guilt. I had always thought of the bank as a heartless machine, not a person. The sleeping giant had no idea the game was afoot. The thing had malfunctioned; it could no longer protect its hoard. I would look at it as only a financial coup. The system would be held responsible. Jack Shaw was not chargeable for the system. He would escape with his hair.

My opening gambit was to gain control of the surrendered safe deposit keys. The fact that the lock-change mechanics switched the locks on surrendered safes and resealed the keys was not a problem. I could duplicate the surrendered key and place a matching mark on the back of the lock before I placed the key out of my control. This was basically a simple operation. It would take time, but each key could be worth a fortune.

It was easy enough to purchase a key-making machine and a supply of key blanks. I was in no hurry. I had all the time in the world. Each night, at home, I duplicated the keys that were surrendered that day. I then placed the new keys on a concealed pegboard in my basement. The following day, returning to the job, I placed the customers' keys in the slotted safe belonging to the lock-change mechanics.

I glanced at my mark on the back of the lock when opening a box as a new rental. I noted the box number in my journal next to the corresponding key. In a fashion I was slowly moving the largest safe deposit vault in Gotham City into my home.

As the years passed I managed to hang a key on every peg. While the keys were accumulating I carefully planned my getaway to Maura. During my leisure time I perused each box, keeping a record of the blocks of stored cash. Oh, the jewellery that people have, but I was only in search of cash. I must admit that my knees buckled when I gazed upon the famous Gates necklace. Forty of the most perfect diamonds in the world were on one strand. I had read it had been appraised at fifteen million. Should I? I had no intention of taking anything but cash. I would take it, but of course I would never sell it.

I must say I did come across other interesting items such as narcotics, guns and an occasional bottle of whisky that would add zest to the customer's lunch hour and help him finish his day. In one box I found an axe, covered with dried blood, along with a newspaper clipping mentioning a decapitated Mafia don. I switched this box with that of a police lieutenant.

I was quite sure the millions in cash that I had carefully selected from the safes were other people's ill-gotten gains. There was no reason for this large amount of cash being kept in the vault, not drawing interest. You might say I was going to separate the wheat from the chaff. I had always followed the bank's policy of explaining to the customers, when they rented a box, that the bank was not responsible for cash. Of course I knew that a lot of bad guys, along with Mr Coffee's minions, would never stop searching for me. It was obvious Mr Coffee had a laundry problem. The contents of both his boxes were well over two million.

The Mayor's chauffeur, apparently his bagman, was the keeper of a stash of at least a million. He would be no problem. I doubted the chauffeur would ever honk his horn. That was going to be our little secret; I had become a confidant of the Mayor.

My conscience was fairly clear considering the magnitude of the crime; I had no doubt caused a great deal of confusion, but no lasting damage to any innocent parties. The random switching of the boxes was only a temporary insurance ploy, to be used as a trade-off if my plan had failed and I was forced to barter for a light sentence.

I left a letter in my desk stating that, if I had successfully eluded my pursuers, in a month's time, I would provide the bank with my journal designating the true location of each tin. Everything going as planned, I lived up to my letter without revealing my whereabouts.

As far as the States were concerned, there was no evidence that Bill Kias had left the country. Bill Montesque's name and all his necessary papers, including his passport, had been provided by the FBI. My son had used the same documents years before while working undercover for the Bureau. Before the documents were returned, I had managed to duplicate the complete dossier on "the man who never was". I had breathed life into the FBI myth. It would never occur to them that Montesque was alive and a very rich man.

According to the FBI background cover, Montesque had been a design engineer for Lockheed, residing in CA. I moved his mailing address to a post office box in Gotham City. Subscribing to several aerospace journals, using his post office box, Montesque was continually receiving invitations to attend all sorts of aerospace roundtables and lectures in Washington. It seemed that the Bureau had made him a respected associate in his field. It is easier to kill a man than to get him off a mailing list. In fact, up to the time I retired, Montesque appeared to be growing in stature. His silence must have been his strong point. According to Montesque's last change of address, he was now retired and residing on the island of Maura in the Central Pacific. I had managed to hoist the Bureau on their own lie.

I spent my vacations on Maura, during my last years at the bank, posing as Bill Montesque. They were expensive trips but a necessary investment. During my brief stays I made it a point to establish my identity as a person who loved the island and intended to retire there.

I was accepted as a man who had suffered a horrible tragedy back in the States. I never spoke about it. But rumour had it that my whole family had been killed in the crash of my private plane. I had managed to be the source of the rumour. One night, while pretending to be drunk and in a deep depression, I gave a friendly native woman a brief capsule of the accident, without mentioning facts that could be verified. My cover story, which was swallowed by all, went something like this: After leaving Lockheed, where I had worked as a design engineer, I had developed a hydrogen pump that I sold to the French government for a very large sum, which left me a wealthy man.

The island was so small that it did not appear on most maps, an ideal abode for Montesque. After five years I formed close friendships with the small group of families that were the residents of the island. Their blood was a mixture of American, Australian and Japanese. Oceanographers were attracted to the island each spring for a brief period, when the offshore waters became a whale playground. The rest of the year we were left happily alone.

There was much more cash than I expected. I actually felt a little agita when a customer went to one of my boxes that contained cash. On my completion of the journal of safe contents, and having a key for every safe, I announced that I would take an early retirement in two months.

While the keys were accumulating I had carefully laid out each step of my departure. The end game looked very promising. If everything went well, Bill Kias would no longer exist. Bill Montesque rested in his coffin, awaiting the rising of the moon. When it was time, Montesque would come forth, being replaced by Kias in the nether world.

I knew I could still cancel the operation and avoid the possibility of spending twenty or thirty years in a very uncomfortable retirement home, but the roar of the surf on Maura was constantly ringing in my ears, drowning out any doubt of my success.

Naturally, I would have to walk out of the bank with bags of cash over my shoulder. This had to be done without anyone casting a suspicious eye.

You say preposterous. Planning, my boy, planning. Study the board. I decided that four of those extra-extra-large heavy-duty bags the branch used to contain their garbage would suffice as my coffers. On Friday, my last day, I quietly locked myself in the vault by closing the grille gate after the bank had been closed to the public. I could count on at least two undisturbed hours. Following my journal, I quickly removed the cash, stuffing it into the bags. I also moved tins randomly from one safe to another, keeping a record of each switch.

I had a brief interruption when a co-worker who could not make my retirement dinner, which was being held that evening, came to the main gate to say goodbye.

There were some boxes I did not move. I had become aware, over the years, that some of my customers had serious financial problems. I wasn't all bad. Like the *Gotham Times* I had also compiled a "Neediest Cases" list. Customers who were down on their luck and needed a boost. I only wished I could see their faces when they opened their boxes and found them stuffed with Mr Coffee's green beans.

I then moved the cash bags to the garbage storage area, known as the rat room, located a few feet from the vault. Garbage was not due to be removed from the branch till Tuesday. As planned, my last day fell on the Friday prior to a three-day holiday. The vault was closed on Saturday, but I would have no problem gaining access to the bank itself on the weekend. It was quite common that personnel occasionally entered the branch premises during that time to catch up on paperwork. Its time locks and Burns Electric Protection safely sealed the vault till nine o'clock Tuesday morning. The key to the door in the lobby would not be a problem. I had been given that key several years ago.

I proceeded Friday evening to my retirement dinner, to bid a fond adieu to my co-workers. I was the guest of honour at a bizarre farewell party for a "bank robber". Considering the effort and success of my past endeavour, I did think a celebration was in order. It did add a certain panache to the end game.

Remembering the busy day I faced on the morrow, I apologised for my early departure. My farewell speech was brief and a bit cryptic. "Who said you can't take it with you?" They knew, of course, I meant their love and affection. I was tempted to "amen" branch manager Jack Shaw's parting remark, "Bill, we will never forget you." They had given me a darn nice watch.

Saturday morning at nine o'clock I parked my van just around the corner of the branch. I wore a Gotham Bank sweatshirt for the occasion, plus a Gotham Bank baseball hat. As usual, there were people in the lobby using our cash machines. I opened the door, entering the branch proper. I brought up two bags of garbage from the rat room, to alleviate any suspicion. I opened them slightly to provide the proper aroma, and put them in plain view by the door leading out of the branch. The next four bags I placed directly into my van, which was out of sight of the cash machines. One of the customers was kind enough to hold the door open for me. I then returned to place the genuine garbage in front of the building.

I immediately drove to the garage that I had been renting for the past three months in my own name. Once in the garage, I placed the money in three crates addressed to Bill Montesque, Villa Montesque, Maura Jima, Bonin Islands, via Tokyo. The crates were labelled as books. I dropped them off at the shipping agency using a second van, rented in the name of Montesque. Returning the van, the now disguised Montesque proceeded to Kennedy, where he commenced a series of hedge-hopping flights to the West Coast. After spending a week in San

Francisco, Montesque caught a flight to Tokyo; here he boarded the Ogasawa Maru, the bi-monthly supply ship for Maura.

My last trip to Maura was the summer prior to my retirement. While there I made the arrangements for the arrival and storage of the crates.

It was a beautiful morning when I made my final and joyous landfall. My friends greeted me at dockside and that night we had one hell of a party celebrating Montesque putting down his roots. I couldn't contain my exhilaration. Gad, the plan had worked without a hitch.

Pacing myself carefully I used my wealth as a tool to maintain our paradise. I, of course, had to be careful that generosity shown to my neighbours did not draw attention to our island.

I contributed a sizeable amount to the building fund for our new church and medical facilities without flaunting my fortune. My beneficence caused a movement among the small populous that I be appointed the administrator. I quickly quashed this idea by feigning poor health. Any picture of me appearing anywhere would only bring tears to my eyes and Mr Coffee to my beach.

I have never actually counted my booty; it was just too much. I think I overdid it. It was huge and always growing. Occasionally I would leave the island for a trip to Tokyo; from there I would fly to my bank in Hong Kong, where large cash transactions were not questioned. Still, my financial adviser was always shocked when I would show up with large amounts of cash. He would often suggest that I make use of their safe deposit accommodations. I, of course, like all scallywags, trusted no one. I kept my main stash buried in an old cave, high up in the mountains.

My exhilaration was replaced by a strange let down. A flame deep inside of me was being quenched. I realised my great adventure was over. Kias had run with the tiger and now he was no more. It would take a while before Montesque adjusted to this new lifestyle. Surprisingly, he had no problem. Eden is Eden.

I always felt a twinge of guilt whenever Gabriela played for me. Surely, the whole world deserved to share in the pleasure of listening to an artist of such rare talent. How could one justify keeping the *Mona Lisa* in a closet? She had been constantly deluged with requests to tour North America. She finally permitted me to convince her to accept an invitation to participate in the celebration of the one-hundredth anniversary of the Metropolitan, in Gotham City.

From the moment her ship disappeared over the horizon I was in a depressed state. I did not realise how much of me I had given her. I now knew the pain of love. I lived for the moment I could witness her performance via television. I had a satellite dish installed on the roof of the villa for just that occasion.

The grand moment finally arrived. The announcer said that over five hundred million people would be able to view the concert. The stage darkened, a dim spotlight focused only on the outline of a woman playing a violin. The sound of Mendelssohn's *Concerto in E Minor* for violin penetrated the blackness of the stage. Slowly, as she played, the spotlight grew in intensity; the ravishing figure of Gabriela, dressed in a stunning black-lace gown, appeared, with her violin pressed to her chin. The three-movement work was being played with barely a pause between them. It was without doubt her finest performance. She never looked more exquisite, a feast for both the ear and the eye.

The audience, at the close of her performance, rose as one to give a crashing ovation. The cries of "Bravissima" rang throughout the house. The stage was covered with bouquets. Violin in one hand and bow in the other, she bowed gracefully, exposing the Gates necklace to five hundred million viewers. I had stolen my own noose.

"LIGHTS OUT LIGHTS OUT IN THERE!"

I can still hear the loud surf on Maura beating in my ears.

Bill Kias #P0897698 San Quentin Prison, CA.

Checkmate.

Auto-Da-Fé
ROTIMI BABATUNDE

|||||||||||||||||||||||||||||||||||||||||||||||||||||||||||||||||||||||||||||||||||||||||||||||||||||||||||||||||||||||||||||||||||||||

A group of African children want to test the mettle of the village boy in their class, but end up being tested themselves.

"We are going to burn the owlets. Let the god save them now if it can."

All day long the talk had only been of the film to be viewed that afternoon and already a small crowd of uniforms was clustering around the door of the screening hall but far away and lost to all the frenzy, the boy with eyes half closed stands rooted to the concrete expanse of the hostel rooftop, solitary on that giddy plane bare but for the cup crusted green in the corner and the sunbleached book gradually weathering to dust (beside the closed metal hatch door flat with the surface of the roof), his shirt billowing in the high winds gusting strong and steady.

Calmly he tilts his face into the coolness of the wind and taking in a deep breath his chest heaves, the sharpness of the rainclean air bringing a smile to his lips because now the same wind would be blowing tipped with the smell of ripe mangoes on his father's plantation. If not for school he would have been up on a mango tree hidden in its thick foliage, his teeth sunk in the fleshy sweetness of its foetus-shaped fruit freshly plucked while in the distance the women putting fruits into brown bags would be as small as dolls and in the other direction would be the stream – a long silver thread flowing without haste through the lush green.

His father always says the biggest catfish are to be found at the bends and every Saturday they would be seated on a promising bank, their hooks lost in the water. He hears the lazy purling of the stream on which skating insects enact strange dances and the rustling of bank leaves in the breeze, sharp, the boy gulping in lungfuls of freshness like a silent mantra fervently repeated, his eyes half closed.

They are startled wide open by a shout from below, a shout muffled by the concrete. A slight frown creases the boy's face and his body stiffens, keenly listening. Someone shouts again. There is a babble of excited voices, those of his fellow students, but he can identify none and only barely catches the phrases, the obscure babble.

They are hereby – Have you seen it? – It is gone – What did – Come again – Many of them I've found them! – What did he say? – Small ones – Says he's got them – Many? – Yeah! – Should I bring them?

Suddenly, all the voices shout together. Then silence. Again the mass shout comes and comes, alternating with brief silence, five shouts before someone breaks into a victory song. Other voices join in, welling it up to choral richness, and footsteps stamp down the staircase, running down with the victory chorus punctuated by whoops and the yells quickly getting fainter, then they are silent.

The boy's furrowed brow smooths out. A bird's hoarse shriek sounds, shattering the silence. He turns to peer in its direction, the courtyard of concrete and stone below. It is bounded on one side by the building atop which the boy stands and on the other by a building exactly similar. At the far end of the courtyard a water reservoir squats its mammoth haunches while the other end is open but smack in the centre of the courtyard stands a baobab tree. On it a hawk perches, flapping briefly now and then into the air, shrieking with a piercing larynx on the tree now completely bare of leaves.

The boy remembers a few weeks ago. The housemaster with a group of students hacked a groove around the tree's girth, deep like a purple noose. Into this he spilled several chemicals saying the tree's roots were wrecking the concrete. Then the mighty baobab was still crowned with leaves and in the boy's fancy the courtyard was the tree's, the surrounding architecture only there to showcase its gnarled splendour – maybe because it always brought to mind the even bigger baobab rooted on the outskirts of his father's plantation.

His father once told him the enormous tree was the ugliest thing he had ever seen, but also the most awesome. Coalblack scarification of lightning adorns it all over, like knifescars on the face of a veteran thug.

Thousands and thousands of ants with bite as painful as wasp-sting march ceaselessly on its boughs, the vast universe of branches. And the housekeeper said that in the old days childless women came from as far off as villages beyond the distant hills to dance naked round it under the full moon and some months after they were sure to have their bellies bulging as if it was the big moon itself they had swallowed.

But wasting away at the height of the verdant season the baobab between the school buildings was only a mere intimation of that forbidding grandness – a skeleton desolate of foliage, its fallen leaves on the courtyard swirling brown in the wind.

Nightly from its crown there was the regular hooting of an owl but for days now in the dead darkness the listening boy has heard nothing and he wonders why. Down below in the afternoon brightness there was just the hawk shrieking with savage power, flapping around the baobab and perching now and then on its branches the housemaster compared to the wicked fingers of a witch, the naked branches stretching upwards towards the rooftop where something startles the standing boy – a call from below that sounds like his name.

"Jide!" His name sounds once more, this time much nearer, and he knows the voice. Zuka's. His fingers bunch into fists, and as the steps get louder he knows they are from two pairs of feet. Zuka is coming with someone. The boy's gaze swings furiously, a wind vane in raging turbulence, swings in all directions across the expanse of the rooftop as if looking for a sanctuary, but the concrete on which he stands is bare, and with the footfalls memories of the day before rush again like the wind into his head.

The bell had shortly been rung calling the students in from the afternoon break. On Jide's entering the class Amoa and Zuka and the gang started shouting "Village Boy! Village Boy!" The boy walked on to his desk, his face blank of expression as if deaf. Someone pulled out his seat from under his buttocks as he sat. Then he was on the hard floor and the whole class was laughing, including the girls, shouting the painful chorus, "Village Boy! Village Boy!"

The footsteps stop, halting the echoing chorus. An irritant sound of grating as the rusty hatch flat with the rooftop is pulled ajar. Out of its mouth opening down a stairway a peeping head juts, then another, breaking the solitude of the rooftop; and seeing Jide the bodies of the two heads, two boys clamber onto the concrete.

"Jide, come here!" the taller boy shouts. "So this is where you hide."

"Leave me alone, Zuka."

"Village Boy! So you think you can run away from us." Zuka turns to his companion, a boy short and fat. "How did you even find him out? No one would have thought of this place."

"I saw the jerk when he was sneaking up here."

"We should even have locked the hatch from below. So that he can remain alone high up here till Judgement Day."

The two boys burst into laughter.

"What do you want from me? You had better leave me alone. Go away," Jide says.

Zuka begins walking towards him. "You are threatening me. Do you think you can beat me?" His voice rises. "You! An ordinary village boy!"

"If you touch me I'll grab you and push you down. I swear I'll grab you and push you down."

Zuka abruptly stops. He and Jide stare icily across the short distance straight into each other's eyes, with chests heaving, their fists bunched. Zuka licks his lips, and his fingers unclench. "I am not here to fight you. Who will waste his time fighting a local pig like you? We want you to check something for us."

"What?"

"We found some little birds in a nest in the toilet ceiling. The new toilet. One of the twins said you might know what sort of bird they are."

Jide's face instantly transfigures. His eager eyes shine as if lit from within. "Birds? Little birds. Where are they? How many? Let's go!" he gushes out, voice throbbing with excitement.

"Downstairs."

"What colour are they? Let's go quickly and see them." He takes only two steps before stopping and his face hardens. "This is just one of your dirty tricks. You think I won't know? Leave me alone."

"We are serious," says the fat boy. "Five of them. With very big eyes. Let's go, Zuka, if he doesn't want to come."

"Wait!" Jide shouts, despite himself.

And the three boys walk across the rooftop, to the hatch. One after the other their heads disappear as they descend through the hatchway. Grating harshly the hatch is closed above them, slicing the sunshaft dark. And they race through the dimness, down the flights of stairs, the rust-coated banisters swiftly running past, and in the onrush Jide sees nothing but images, magical, of little birds.

Those baby partridges one often sees hidden in thickets on the plantation (their mothers when startled towering skywards with the suddenness of gunshots) and the purple chicks of the water ducks running on shanks hardly thicker than broom strands – running behind their mothers along the banks together winding away with the stream. Then there were the nests plucked down by savage storms, like the one with the three warblers he tried being a wet nurse to, but watched helpless with watery eyes as they died within two days, his droplets of water and carefully prepared meals shunned like a defiled sacrifice. And more in the whirling kaleidoscope of trees and nests and chirping birds as the three boys race down the flights of stairs taking the steps in twos and threes, panting all excited down in the dimness.

Downstairs, they burst through the entranceway into the sunlight bathing the courtyard where two boys now stand. One clutching a lantern looks exactly like the fat boy that came to the rooftop, looks like his twin, must be his identical twin. The other is bespectacled. At his feet on the concrete lies a clump of pink flesh, a group of nestlings with feathers still limp as if freshly stuck and the gum not dried. The bespectacled boy repeatedly prods the awkward birds with his smart boots, his brows puzzled over with wrinkles, and looking up to stare at the new arrivals halted before him the round lenses of his spectacles glitter in the sunlight, two staring pools of swimming light.

"We found him," Zuka says, his breath coming fast and sharp.

"Where?" asks the boy in spectacles.

"Hiding on the rooftop."

Squatting, Jide observes the little birds closely. He looks up – at the bespectacled boy. "Amoa, you shouldn't have placed them like this on the concrete. Can't you feel it's hot? It is hurting them."

"No, it is not yet hot." Amoa looks down at the brood. "We are going to burn them. Then it *will* be hot."

"These little birds?"

"Yes."

"No, you can't. You will have to –"

Amoa cuts him short. "What sort of bird are they?"

"They are owls," Jide replies.

"Are you sure?"

"I'm dead sure. Owlets. See their eyes, and their moonround faces."

"What are owls?" Zuka asks.

"They are those birds that hang upside down in caves," says one twin.

Jide shakes his head. "Not at all. Those are bats but these are owls. The old women that work on our farm say owls are very wise. They fly and hunt at night. Sometimes at night you must have heard one hooting on this baobab. Some people say they are sacred to the god Esu."

"Fuck the god," says Amoa.

"We are going to burn the owlets. Let the god save them now if it can," Zuka adds, with a scowl.

There is silence. The five boys stand alert in the courtyard, glancing occasionally at each other, their breathing coming deep. At their feet under the hot sun the owlets squirm.

Amoa turns to the twin holding the lantern. "Are you with the matches?"

"Yes." The twin removes a matchbox from his shirt pocket. Smiling he shakes out of the lantern the splashing sound of liquid. "It is filled with kerosene."

"So you are really going to burn these owlets!" Jide exclaims, his face distorted by shock. "You must be crazy."

Amoa glances at him, his eyes stern. "Why on earth shouldn't we?"

"For one, they are living things . . ." Jide begins.

"Village Boy!" shout the twins.

Zuka looks down, and grins. "Wouldn't it be nice to see how they look when they are burning?"

"Of course, I'm dying for it," Amoa says.

"It will be horrible. You mustn't. Don't you –"

"Village Boy!" the boys shout. "Village Boy!"

"Listen to me." Jide is now nearly screaming. "The poor things are alive for Christ's sake. They feel pain. You can't just –"

"Village Boy! Village Boy!"

The four boys begin laughing. They speak quickly after each other.

"These birds came from the bush."

"From the jungle. From the darkness."

"Can he tell us what they are doing here, the local boy."

"My dad says the bush is backward."

"And our pastor also. He said it is our duty to spread the gospel into the bush areas."

"That must be because they still worship devils there."

"Like Esu."

"The bush boy said now that owls belong to Esu."

"They are heathens, these village people. Worshippers of –"

"Satan and all these black gods will burn for ever in hell fire."

"We're wasting time. Let's burn the birds."

"Yes, now!"

There is a pause. Jide's body jerks forward, his voice pleading earnestly, "Wait. Why don't you give them to the agric mistress instead?

She'll be delighted and may even give you marks."

"The agric mistress can go to blazes," says Zuka.

"Sure." Amoa takes a few steps forward bringing his face very close to Jide's. His voice is low. "In your heart you know that we should burn these owls. But you're simply scared. You are just being a chicken."

"No. I am not scared."

"Liar. You are just being a sissy."

"Stop it. I am no sissy."

"You are scared."

"I swear. I am not."

Amoa collects the lantern and matchbox from the twin. He presents them to Jide. "If not then strike the flame on them."

Jide's jaw drops, hanging his pink mouth wide open like his startled eyes. They starkly see the sootblack ruins of his father's poultry house destroyed overnight by fire last harmattan. And the holocaust of trapped birds burnt in the cages, bones stripped clean and dull ash, their charred flesh stuck to the metal bars still warm. He catches the faint whiff of acrid flesh. "I won't!" he shouts suddenly.

Amoa is smiling. "Didn't I say it? He's scared."

Zuka nods. "We will tell the whole school that you're not only a local boy but also a scaredy chicken. Scared of ordinary birds. Little birds!"

"I say I am not . . ."

Jide's voice ceases as he hears the laughter of students shouting – Local Chicken! – shouting at him in the desk-lined classroom, on the football field – Village Chicken! Scaredy Chicken! – laughing at him in the dining hall, their laughter following him all over the school like a dreaded shadow.

"I am not a chicken," he says again, but now weakly, his voice little more than whisper.

"Let's burn them without him," one of the twins says.

"Yes, we'll need some dry stuff to make the fire hotter," says the other.

"Those are dry leaves over there."

Chattering excitedly, the twins run off to bring fallen leaves from the foot of the baobab, leaving Zuka and Amoa standing together.

"He thinks he can be stubborn, Amoa. We'll show him we are city boys."

"He hasn't even been to the city before. Spent all his bloody life on his father's plantation. And the punk seems pretty proud of it."

"No flyovers. No traffic lights. No skyscrapers."

Amoa looks at Jide who is staring blankly at the floor, his head drooped. "You should cry for yourself. And if you don't strike the fire you'll see what we'll do to you. You'll see."

Jide looks up with a start, his eyes now bright with a strange new eagerness. "If I light the owlets will you tell them that I am not scared? That I am not a Village Boy?"

"Sure."

"Since you would have proved you are tough"

"Tough. Like real city boys. To be certain . . ."

"Be a good boy. We will even allow you to run around with us."

Jide collects the lantern and matchbox. "Then I will," he says. "I will burn them."

Looking down at the owlets pink on the concrete, something sharp catches like pain in his throat. Their wide soft faces remind him of his kittens at home. He sees them by the platter lapping up milk with their little pink tongues, the toys of utmost beauty. He winces as fire falls on them twisting their delicate bodies black. In a sudden gust of wind his shirt billows, and he shudders.

Zuka and Amoa are whooping with delight. Around the captured birds they circle a victory dance. Zuka hurting with eagerness implores the twins to hurry up. And arriving with their hands heaped with the baobab leaves they make a tinder ring around the owlets forever squirming on the floor, the ring like a nest of thorns. Then the four boys rise, their fingers twitching with suspense and expectant eyes fixed on Jide who sees instead a gallery of faces, the shocked faces of his father and the housekeeper and the farmhands and the picking women, their confronting masks of disappointment, but only briefly before the laughter comes again like the cries of the circling hawk and he knows what he should do.

"We are waiting for you," Amoa says.

Jide's shaking fingers tilt the fuel case of the lantern. The smell of kerosene fills the air, the colourless liquid spilling downwards. It splatters on the owlets animating them with life of surprising vigour like an instant storm in a teacup, the weak limbs raising a pink storm that takes them nowhere beyond their stasis under the spattering kerosene. It soaks into the dry leaves cradling the nestlings and further on around the cocoon, the volatile halo of fuel spreading quickly on the concrete.

The boy strikes several matches clumsily, breaking them on the box one after the other. Finally, he strikes one alight. He tilts his face gently skywards, his eyes closed as the matchstick slowly burns upwards. The silence is heavy as the creeping flame brings the searing heat right up to his nails before his fingers drop the burning stick, the four boys watching as the little flame falls landing right on the nest of owlets and raising from it a sudden blaze from which all the boys spring back.

The fire engulfs the birds in its yellow viciousness. Thick smoke belches skywards, and someone coughs. The fire intensifies as the dry leaves of the baobab catch, charring the feathers of the owlets and stretching them out into rigid stiffness, the heat exciting popping noises from their hissing flesh. The biting odour of roasting flesh thickens in the air. And before the watching eyes the birds transform with startling swiftness. The clump of burning flesh sizzles, the birds contracting in the only hell they'll ever know, getting smaller and smaller in the fire busy chewing blunt beaks and eyes hollow and without respite the tiny claws.

The boys stand still, saying nothing, their eyes avoiding contact in the silence shattered intermittently by the harsh cries coming from the baobab branches. With amazing haste the fire burns on, its intensity diminishing until it peters and only acrid smoke rises from the pyre.

In the hot ash there would be left only five little lumps of black flesh, featureless and anonymous on the concrete.

After a while, Zuka speaks. "I think . . . I guess we shouldn't have burnt those birds."

"I also," says a twin. "The smell was horrible."

"And the sight, the way they were twitching," Amoa adds.

"A time came when I started feeling bad in the stomach."

"No wonder Jide didn't want them burnt," says the other twin.

Zuka nods.

Jide is still staring at the burnt owlets, his eyes partially shut as if at painful light. He tears his eyes away from them. Raised, his face relaxes and meeting four complimenting faces a small smile sparkles rapture in his eyes. "It was nothing," he says.

"It was great of you," says Amoa. "He is now with us. What about that?"

"Yeah."

"Sure."

"This smell is terrible!"

The silence again. Smoke rises in wisps from the ashes on the floor, rising up in the silence which Zuka breaks. "Let's do something. We can't just continue standing here, in the midst of this evil odour. Let's go somewhere."

The boys glance inquisitively at each other.

"Hey! We nearly forgot the film," one twin exclaims. "The film will soon start."

"That's true!"

"We mustn't miss it." Amoa looks at Jide. "Will you go with us?"

"Of course."

"Then let's go."

Zuka doesn't move. He licks his lips. "I don't think I want to go," he slowly says.

"Why?"

"Is the film dull? I learnt it's a big hit."

"No." Zuka begins fidgeting. "It is not that it's dull . . ."

"Then what?" Amoa asks.

"I have seen the preview. It is only about someone going round burning babies."

"Why does he burn the babies?"

"Don't know. He's just burning the babies."

"Since there is a police chase then it is sure to be interesting," the other twin says. "But why don't you want to go?"

Zuka's darting eyes look worried. "I don't want to see any more bodies being burnt. The babies, they were burning . . ." He was almost choking on the words. "Those owlets were horrible!"

Jide takes a step towards Zuka. "Are you telling us you are scared?"

"How can I?" He pauses. His eyes roll in their sockets. "It's just that we don't want to see the film now."

Jide laughs. "We? Why not? That film is a big hit. We shouldn't miss it for anything." He whirls suddenly to face Amoa, startling him. "Are you also scared of the film?"

"I? Surely not. I ain't scared."

"Good. You see?" Jide turns to the first twin. "What about you?"

"No!"

"And you?"

"No," the other twin replies.

Jide swings back to face Zuka. He stares sternly at him. "So you are alone. When even the girls will flock down to watch the film."

There is a pause.

"If anyone asks of you we will have to say you didn't come because you were scared. Of only a film that even the girls will be around to watch. The whole school will know you are a sissy."

"Wait! Can't you understand? I saw the babies burning in the fire. They were screaming. I saw their little hands burning in the –"

Jide cuts in. "We want no sissy among us." He pauses, and looks questioningly at Amoa.

Amoa nods. "We want no chicken among us." Amoa's eyes stare hard at Zuka. His voice is flat. "Are you going to see the film? Yes or no?"

Zuka's face is now strained with anxiety. Looking round, each pair of eyes he meets is hard, like the concrete on which the boys stand. In the silence he licks his lips over and over again, then he sighs and his eyes fall. "I will. If all of you are going I don't . . ." The words stop, then he continues, "Yes I will. I will."

"Very good," Amoa says. He turns to gaze at a building in the distance, his palm a sunscreen over his squinting eyes. "Let's go. We mustn't be late."

The boys step into motion. They walk across the courtyard, each lost in his thoughts, Amoa and Jide in the lead and the twins immediately behind and Zuka taking the rear, dragging their feet across the concrete vastness. They walk past the baobab on whose large trunk a garish poster advertising the film is stuck, the tree's fallen leaves crunching like broken glass beneath their feet. And in silence the five boys move on towards the hall in the distance. By its door the small figures of their fellow students can be seen clustered. Behind them the hawk flaps again and again around the naked branches of the dying baobab, its cries sounding hoarse and harsh in the sunlight.

Belfast Girl
FREEDOM AHN

During Northern Ireland's Troubles, a teenage girl's life suddenly changes.

"Irish. Catholic.
Protestant. Politics.
Religion. It was all
just blood when you
had to bury it."

1978

November hung damp and heavy about her shoulders, as Kathleen pulled her collar up. The double-knit muffler she wore, her mother's Christmas gift to her last year, provided futile defence against the wind's frost-tipped claws. She had just turned the corner when sleet began to slap down around her. It would be a solid sheet of ice by morning. She could see the warm amber light in the front window, still a good fifteen-minute walk away. She'd be soaked through to the bone, by the time she got there. *The worst thing about working at the pub*, she mused, *they were all too drunk to give a ride home.* Not that it stopped them from offering most nights.

She felt the thin crust of ice shatter as she stepped in the puddle. The biting water crested her ankle-high boots, drowning her foot in a frigid slush.

Shite.

This was fast becoming the perfect end to a horrible day. Bad tips. Piss-poor weather. And the frigging soup she'd spilled on her new blouse. *Of course.*

Kathleen paused a moment on the front step, under the porch, and watched the icy snow pelt around her with increased intensity. She'd made it home, just in time. *Finally, my night is beginning to turn around.*

It was nearing nine o'clock when Mary heard the heavy knock on the door.

"On such a rainy night, Lord bless us all," she muttered as she went to answer it. She dried her work-worn hands on her apron before pulling the wooden door open. Eamonn and Padraig, her neighbours one lot over, faces stained by blood and fatigue, met her questioning eyes. Eamonn could only hold Mary's stare for a moment, before he slumped against the door frame, and shook his head softly.

"Kathleen, get your brother and sister. Go upstairs," Mary ordered. "Now!"

Kathleen thought for a moment of arguing her right to stay and help with whatever new trouble there was, but the brisk tone of Mary's voice eliminated any opportunity for refusal. Kathleen grabbed her brother Rauri by the hand, and went to gather Wellynd from the table. "Ma says to come upstairs now."

"But I'm making cookies," Wellynd defended.

"Not now you're not. Come on," Kathleen said. Taking the defiant Wellynd by one wrist, and with Rauri still securely held in her other hand, she tugged and dragged them upstairs under Mary's distant gaze. Eamonn and Padraig had come inside, just, and the door was closed behind them. Eamonn's eyes met Kathleen's and he dropped his head deeper. He ran his hand, swollen and broken, through his wet, dark hair. Kathleen was unsure whether the door frame was holding Eamonn up or the other way around. Nothing seemed solid at the moment. She reached the first landing, blocked from the view of the doorway, and tossed loose her grip on the small wrists of her prisoners. She approached her room, the last at the top of the hall, and ushered them in.

"You can play in here, if you're quiet," Kathleen offered. Never allowed to enter her room, it was an easy sell to the twins who were already beginning to sneak peeks into her laundry hamper and cosmetics drawer.

"I mean it, now, not a peep. If Ma hears you we'll all be done for. Do you hear me, Wellynd?" Although identical in appearance to her slightly older twin, Wellynd was the more responsible, mature one of the duo. She seemed to be able to grasp the reality of the grown-up world much too easily; an adult before she was ever a child. *Such were the lives of*

Mary O'Riordan's daughters, Kathleen mulled.

Wellynd looked up at her big sister with focus and determination and nodded her assent, pressing a chubby finger against her lips for emphasis. Kathleen smiled. Wellynd went to Rauri and soon the two were lost to the sparkling bangles and cheap fashion jewellery on the dresser.

Kathleen was careful to close the door gently. She made her way back to the landing. She was careful to avoid the plank outside the door that squeaked whenever she tried, without success, to sneak past her parents' room when even just a few minutes past curfew. She bent down to hear better, the banisters cool against the skin of her arms.

"Eoghan's gone, Mary. They tried. They all tried. They even had an ambulance bring him in, but . . . but . . ." Eamonn ran out of words.

Padraig could do nothing but pull Mary to him, his shirt soaked to the skin in a bath of rainwater and Eoghan's blood.

At first Mary struggled to free herself, failing to understand what they meant. *Gone?* Where had he gone? He couldn't *go* anywhere. That was ridiculous. They had no money to spare on *going*. What was Eamonn talking about? He'd been drinking, no doubt. You could smell it on him. And in this weather, too. And Padraig should know better than to be acting like this. Him holding on to her so tight. What if Eoghan were to come in? He could be jealous sometimes. And he'd have been to drinking, too. But no, they said Eoghan was gone. *Gone.*

"Gone?" Mary finally questioned, her voice faintly rising above Padraig's embrace.

Padraig held her tighter. She could feel the floor give way beneath her, her legs no longer able or willing to support her; her body incapable of being on its own.

Kathleen watched in horror as her mother fell to the floor, broken into pieces she knew would never quite fit back together again.

Kathleen slowly gathered herself and returned to the twins who had tired themselves with her jewellery and had started to doze on top of one another on the floor. She put them on her bed and pulled the bedspread over and around them. Mindlessly she sang to them, as Eoghan had sung her to sleep for years.

> *My Belfast Girl, so fair and so pretty*
> *With ivory skin, with crimson hair and moss-green eyes,*
> *I'll be with you, my child, through all your journeys,*
> *So hush, now, Belfast Girl, don't you cry*
> *I'll love you, Belfast Girl, until I die.*

Kathleen ran her finger along the window ledge, tracing the edge of ice that was creeping into her room. Eoghan had promised to teach her how to replace the seal this weekend. She reached into her laundry hamper and pulled out the first thing she came upon, her soiled blouse from the pub, and pushed it tight against the window, ruining the sheer fabric. She leaned in hard, against the ledge, supporting herself as her head came to rest against the cold glass. Da was gone.

In the distance Kathleen could see neighbours approaching. The sleet had stopped, but the belligerent wind threatened a second coming. She could hear the crunch of ice breaking beneath a parade of boots on their way, in a sign of sympathy and solidarity.

Eoghan's funeral was three days later, from St Anne's Cathedral. It was strange to see the church where she had so often gone with her parents, for Sunday Mass, for christenings and baptisms, for confirmations and first communions, for weddings and feast days, suddenly so solemnly decked out. To see so many of the townspeople's faces twisted, in grief and pity; and relief. Relief, that it was not them that had to bury their own.

Rauri and Wellynd, barely tall as the oak pews themselves, were dressed in their best clothes in the very first row. Wellynd held Rauri's hand and sat quietly watching, reminding her brother to be quiet in *God's House*. After the Monsignor finished his prayers for Eoghan's soul finding everlasting peace and happiness with his Lord and Saviour, one by one they filed out of the church, their clothes smelling of incense and candles. They each stopped to dip one finger into the holy water basin and then touch their forehead lightly in benediction, before beginning the soggy walk to the cemetery behind the hill. High heels sank deeply into the thawing muck, thanks to an uncommonly warm day, as their owners clung to their neighbours for balance; for comfort. Kathleen and the children were the last to leave, behind Mary, who walked alongside with Eoghan's coffin. She was last to arrive at the hole in the ground that would see them often; a place now to visit on holy days, on birthdays, on anniversaries, on any day really that you'd rather be anywhere but a damp soggy bog that held the rotting bones of your father.

Padraig came to Kathleen's side, after they lowered Eoghan into the ground. Nearby, two tired-looking men with soiled overalls and dirty fingernails smoked cigarettes as they stood waiting beside a truck that held their shovels and gravestones. They would wait until everyone left before beginning to lob the mounds of wet earth upon the coffin.

"You'll not be alone. I'll look out for you, you know that, right?"

Padraig smiled, and Kathleen nodded in diffuse agreement.

"I should get back to the house. Ma'll be needing help with the twins."

"I'll walk with you," he said, as he fell into step with her.

He held out his arm for her to steady herself, when they reached a particularly muddy part of the path. But Kathleen didn't reach for him. Padraig noticed that she was wearing Eoghan's old wellingtons on her feet, as she trudged deliberately towards the house.

A light mist was beginning to gather around the edges of the cemetery and the chill made Kathleen shiver. She stuffed her hands deeper into her pockets and fingered the hole in the left one she'd forgotten to fix. Padraig had fallen behind a little, to light a cigarette, and ran to catch up with her. They made their way to the porch of her house in silence. The screen door was closed, but inside the wake was just beginning to come into full swing. Soon, the sorrow would be replaced by stories from her father's misguided but well-intentioned youth, war stories, memories and a few lamenting ballads; each edged and eased into existence by another glass of Tullamore Dew or Clontarf.

Padraig stood between her and the screen door, holding it closed.

"Kathleen, I need to tell you something."

Kathleen didn't want to hear anything Padraig had to say. As far as she was concerned, if it wasn't for his nonsense her father would still be here with them. Eoghan's death was as much Padraig's doing as it was his own, and anything Padraig was going to offer wouldn't help.

"Ma'll need help with the twins," she said again, as she reached over his shoulder for the door handle.

Padraig took her hand from the door, in both of his. "I meant what I said earlier, Kathleen. I'll be here for you. I'll take care of you."

"Well . . . thanks," Kathleen said, as she tried to free her hand.

"What I mean is . . ." He stumbled on. "Kathleen, I'm not good with words, you know that. I just, well, without Eoghan, and well, you know what I mean."

She knew exactly what he meant, and her stomach sank with the knowledge.

"No, not really, Padraig," she fumbled, "but it's OK. Like I said, I really need to be going. Ma and all." She made a second attempt, this time with success, to free herself from Padraig's grip. She had just put her hand upon the latch, when Padraig stepped in front of her, pushing her backwards and blocking her entry to the house.

"Oh to hell with it," he spewed. "Listen, Kathleen, I'll marry ya."

He exhaled with relief. "There, I said it. It's the way Eoghan would have wanted it." Padraig turned to face the door. "We could tell them now. Some good news would do them well."

"No." Kathleen's tone was soft but undeniable.

Padraig turned to face her.

"Give me one good reason not to tell them tonight."

"No," she repeated.

"But it'll do them well to hear it."

"No." She took a step back from him. "I mean I don't want to marry you, Padraig. You're a good man, and I do like you, but . . ." She was fighting to be kind, for Mary's sake, for the twins' sake, who would still need help from the town. ". . . but I don't want to marry you. I don't want to marry anyone. Right now, at least." To Kathleen's surprise, Padraig didn't seem too put off or offended by her rejection, and she wondered if he had actually heard her.

"You need to marry someone who loves you, Padraig. And that's not me."

Padraig put his hand to the side of her face and let his fingers slide down the turn of her neck, caressing her collarbone. He looked into her defiant green eyes, and began to tighten his hold upon her shoulder. "I said I'd marry you, Kathleen."

The unexpected force of the hand upon her shoulder moved her easily and she found herself facing the gathering of unaware guests just inside the screen door.

"And we should tell them tonight, they'll do good for the good news," Padraig said through whiskey-steeped breath and clenched teeth.

"Let's go in, then," she offered. She felt Padraig's anger dissolve. *I'll be out of here by week's end*, she thought to herself. *The twins will be OK*, she reassured herself, *they're young*.

"Guess what!" Padraig's voice boomed above the crowd. "I'm to marry Kathleen."

The sorrow of loss was replaced by shouts of congratulations and good wishes in the easy embrace of family and friends. Mary made her way over to her daughter and held her in a tight embrace, saying nothing. *I'm sorry, Ma, but if I don't get out now I never will. I love you, but I will not become you.*

The night passed with laughter through tears and by daybreak much of their emotion had been spilled on the kitchen floor. Kathleen rose early and started a large pot of coffee for those that had spent the night.

She thought of Padraig, and of her parents, Mary and Eoghan, who had been together since they were fourteen; just three years younger than she was today. Sure, there were bad spots, but didn't everyone have those? But most of all, they were together. They *stayed* together. They faced the world *together*. The world didn't exist with just one of them. It needed them both to balance and keep it spinning on its axis. In one excruciating moment, the clarity of the new world had been forced upon her. Her father was gone. And what for? For God? What God? Irish. Catholic. Protestant. Politics. Religion. It was all just blood when you had to bury it.

"I'm happy for you," Mary said, as she passed through the room. Kathleen smiled in response.

"Do you love him?" her mother asked.

"No," Kathleen replied.

"No matter," Mary assured her. "He's a good man. He'll be a good provider. He'll be there for you," she said, fingering her wedding ring.

"Yes, Ma," Kathleen replied, turning away.

She looked in on the twins, asleep in her bed. They didn't stir. They were exhausted. She watched them and bent to brush the hair from Wellynd's face. She would miss them most of all, she thought, as she bent in to kiss them.

She pulled the velvet pouch from under her mattress and carefully counted her life's savings. £528. It would get her to London, and a few nights' lodging – so long as she wasn't proud where she slept. She packed only as much clothing as she could carry in her bag and headed downstairs, avoiding the third step for the last time.

She piled on Eoghan's sweater under her warm pea coat, boots, hat, muffler and mittens. She left a single manila envelope with her mother's name clearly written on it, along with the Claddagh ring from Padraig.

> Ma,
>
> I'm sorry to say goodbye this way, but I know if I waited to do it in person, you'd talk me out of it, and I couldn't let that happen. I would never be happy. I want to be happy, Ma, and I know you want that for me too.
>
> You know I don't love Padraig, and I can't marry someone I don't love. It does matter, to me. Please see that he gets his ring back.
>
> I don't know if I'll be back, or even in touch. I think a clean break might be best for us all.
>
> I talked with Father Quinn and he assured me he'd keep an eye out for you and the twins. Let him.

I have to go now, Ma. I'm sorry. I do love you.
All my love,
Kathleen

Mary read the note twice before tossing it into the fire. She watched the edges slowly crisp brown, then twist into a scorched curl. She slipped the silver ring into the top pocket of her apron for when she saw Padraig later that day.

"Damn fool, wanting to be happy," she muttered. "She gets that from you, Eoghan."

Boots
DC DIAMONDOPOLOUS

An Iraq war veteran struggling to get by sees an old comrade down on his luck on the streets of Los Angeles. First published in Our Day's Encounter.

"She unscrewed the top of the Bacardi, poured herself a shot and knocked it back. Liquid guilt."

The same sun scorched downtown Los Angeles that had seared the Iraq desert. Army Private First Class Samantha Cummings stood at attention holding a stack of boxes, her unwashed black hair slicked back in a ponytail and knotted military-style. She stared out from Roberts Shoe Store onto Broadway, transfixed by a homeless man with hair and scraggly beard the colour of ripe tomatoes. She'd only seen that hair colour once before, on Staff Sergeant Daniel O'Conner.

The man pushed his life in a shopping cart crammed with rags and stuffed trash bags. He glanced at Sam through the storefront window, his bloated face layered with dirt. His eyes had the meander of drink in them.

Sam hoped hers didn't. Since her return from Baghdad a year ago, her craving for alcohol sneaked up on her like an insurgent. Bathing took effort. She ate to exist. Friends disappeared. Her life started to look like the crusted bottom of her shot glass.

The morning hangover began its retreat to the back of her head.

The homeless man vanished down Broadway. She carried the boxes to the storeroom.

In 2012, Sam passed as an everywoman: white, black, brown, Asian. She was a coffee-coloured Frappuccino. Frap. That's what the soldiers nicknamed her. Her mother conceived her while on ecstasy during the days of big hair and shoulder pads. On Sam's eighteenth birthday, she enlisted in the army. She wanted a job and an education. But most of all she wanted to be part of a family.

"Let me help you," Hector said, coming up beside her.

"It's OK. I got it." Sam flipped the string of beads aside. Rows of shoe boxes lined both walls with ladders every ten feet. She crammed the boxes into their cubbyholes.

"Can I take you to lunch?" Hector asked, standing inside the curtain.

"I told you before. I'm not interested."

"We could be friends." He shrugged. "You could tell me about Iraq."

Sam thrust the last box into its space. The beads jangled. Hector left.

She glanced at the clock. Fifteen minutes until her lunch break. The slow workday gave her too much time to think. She needed a drink. It would keep away the flashbacks.

"C'mon, Sam," Hector said, outside the curtain.

"No."

Hector knew she was a vet. He didn't need to know any more about her.

On her way to the front of the store, Sam passed the imported Spanish sandals. Mr Goldberg carried high-quality shoes. He showcased them on polished wood displays. She loved the smell of new leather, and how Mr Goldberg played soft rock music in the background, with track lighting, and thick-padded chairs for the customers.

The best part of being a salesperson was taking off the customer's old shoes and putting on the new. The physical contact was honest. And she liked to watch people consider the new shoes – the trial walk, the mirror assessment – and if they made the purchase, everyone was happy.

Sam headed towards the door. Maria and Bob stood at the counter looking at the computer screen.

"Wait up," Maria said. The heavy Mexican woman hurried over. "You're leaving early again."

"No one's here," Sam said, towering over her. "I'll make it up, stay later. Or something."

"You better."

"Totally."

"Or you'll end up like that homeless man you were staring at."

"You think you're funny?"

"No, Sam. That's the point."

"He reminded me of someone."

"In Iraq?"

Sam turned away.

"Try the VA."

Sam looked back at Maria. "I have."

"Try again. You need to talk to someone. My cousin –"

"The VA doesn't do jack shit."

"Rafael sees a counsellor. It helps."

"Lucky him."

"So do the meds."

"I don't take pills."

"Oh, Sam."

"I'm OK." She liked Maria and especially Mr Goldberg, a Vietnam vet who not only hired her but rented her a room above the shoe store. "It's just a few minutes early."

Maria glared at her. "Mr Goldberg has a soft spot for you, but this is a business. Doesn't mean you won't get fired."

"I'll make it up." Sam shoved the door open into a blast of heat.

"Another thing," Maria said. "Change your top. It has stains on it."

Oh fuck, Sam thought. But it gave her a good reason to go upstairs.

She walked next door, up the narrow stairway and into her studio, the size of an iPhone. Curry reeked through the hundred-year-old walls from the Indian neighbours.

Sam took off her blouse and unstuck the dog tags between her breasts. The army had no use for her. *Take your meds, get counselling, then you can re-enlist.* But she wasn't going to end up like her drug-addicted mother.

The unmade Murphy bed screeched and dipped as she sat down in her bra and pants, the tousled sheets still damp from her night sweats.

The Bacardi bottle sat on the kitchenette counter. She glanced sideways at it and looked away.

The United States flag tacked over the peeling wallpaper dominated the room, but it was the image of herself and Marley on the wobbly dresser she carried with her.

Sam had taken the seventeen-year-old private under her wing. She'd been driving the Humvee in Tikrit with Marley beside her when an IED exploded, killing him while she escaped with a gash in her leg. Thoughts of mortar attacks, roadside bombs, and Marley looped over and over again. Her mind became a greater terrorist weapon than anything the enemy had.

Her combat boots sat next to the door, the tongues reversed, laces loose, prepared to slip into, ready for action. Sometimes she slept in them, would wear them to work if she could. Of all her souvenirs, the boots reminded her most of being a soldier. She never cleaned them, wanted to keep the Iraqi sand caked in the wedge between the midsoles and shanks.

The springs shrieked as Sam dug her fists into the mattress and stood. She walked to the counter, unscrewed the top of the Bacardi, poured herself a shot and knocked it back. Liquid guilt ran down her throat.

Sam picked up a blouse off the chair, smelled it and looked for stains. It would do. She dressed, grabbed a Snickers bar, took three strides and dashed out her room.

Heading south on Broadway, Sam longed to be part of the city. Paved sidewalks, gutters, frying tortillas, old movie palaces, jewellery stores, flower stands, square patches of green where trees grew – all of it wondrous – not like the fucking sandbox of Iraq.

The rum kicked in, made her thirsty as she continued down the historic centre of town. The sun's heat radiated from her soles to her scalp. A canopy of light siphoned the city of colour.

She watched a tourist slowly fold her map and use it as a fan. Businessmen slouched along, looking clammy in shirtsleeves. Women, their dresses moist with sweat, form-fitted to their skin. Even the cars seemed to droop.

Waves of heat shimmered off the pavement. They ambushed Sam, planting her back in Tikrit.

She heard the rat-a-tat-tat of a Tabuk sniper rifle. Ducked. Dodged bullets. Scrambled behind a trash bin. Searched around for casualties. She looked at the top of buildings wondering where in the hell the insurgents fired from.

"Hey, honey, whatsa matter?" An elderly black woman stooped over her.

"Get down, ma'am!"

"What for?"

Sam grabbed at the woman, but she moved away. "Get down, ma'am! You'll get killed!"

"Honey, it's just street drillin'. Those men over there, they're makin' holes in the cement."

Covered in sweat, Sam swerved to her left. A Buick and Chevrolet stopped at a red light. She saw the 4th Street sign below the one-way arrow. Her legs felt numb as she held on to the trash bin and lifted herself up.

"You a soldier?"

"Yes, ma'am," Sam said, looking into the face of the concerned woman.

"I can tell. You fellas always say 'ma'am' and 'sir', so polite-like. Take it easy, child, you're home now." The woman limped away.

Sam reeled, felt for the flask in her back pocket but it wasn't there. Construction workers whistled and made wolf calls at her. "Douche bags," she moaned. Alcohol had always numbed the flashbacks. Her counsellor in Baghdad told her they would fade. Why can't I get better, she asked herself? Shaking, she blinked several times, forcing her eyes to focus as she continued south past McDonald's.

At 6th, she saw the man with tomato-colour hair on the other side of the street, jostling his shopping cart. "It's Los Angeles, not Los Angelees!" he shouted. His voice rasped like the sick, but Sam heard something familiar in the tone. He pushed his cart around the corner.

The light turned green. Sam sprinted in front of the waiting cars to the other side of the road. She had grown up across the 6th Street Bridge that linked Boyle Heights to downtown. From the bedroom window of the apartment she shared with her mother, unless her mother had a boyfriend, Sam would gaze at the Los Angeles skyline.

She followed the man into skid row.

The smell hit her like a body slam. The stink of piss and shit, odours that mashed together like something died, made her eyes water. A block away, it was another world.

She trailed the man with hair colour people had an opinion about. The Towering Inferno. That's what they called Staff Sergeant Daniel O'Conner, but not to his face. He knew, though, and took the jibe well. After all, he had a sense of humour, was confident, tall and powerfully built, the last man to end up broken, not the hunched and defeated man she was following. No, Sam thought. It couldn't be him. It couldn't be her hero.

He shoved his gear into the guts of the city with Sam behind him. The last time she'd been to skid row was as a teenager, driving through with friends who taunted the homeless. The smell was one thing, but what she saw rocked her. City blocks of homeless lived under layers of tarp held up by shopping carts. Young and old, most black, and male, gathered on corners, sat on sidewalks, slouched against buildings, drug exchanges going down. Women too stoned or sick to worry about their bodies slumped over, their breasts falling out of their tops. It was hard for Sam to look into their faces, to see their despair. The whole damn place reeked of hopelessness. Refugees in the Middle East and Africa at least had tents and medicine.

Sam put on her ass-kicking face, the one that said, "Leave me the fuck alone, or I'll mess you up." She walked as if she had on her combat boots, spine straight, eyes in the back of her head.

Skid row mushroomed down side streets. Men staggered north towards 5th and the Mission. She stayed close behind the red-headed man. He turned left at San Pedro. And so did Sam.

It was worse than 6th Street. Not even in Iraq had she seen deprivation like this: cardboard tents, overflowing trash bins used as crude borders, men sleeping on the ground. She watched a man pull up his pant leg and stick a needle in his ankle. Another man, his face distorted by alcohol, drank freely from a bottle. The men looked older than on 6th. Some had cardboard signs. One read, *Veteran, please help me.* Several wore fatigues. One, dressed in a field jacket, was missing his lower leg. Most, Sam thought, were Vietnam or Desert Storm vets. She felt her throat tighten, the familiar invasion of anger afraid to express itself. She'd been told by the army never to show emotion in a war zone. But Sam brought the war home with her. So did the men slumped against the wall like human garbage.

The red-headed man passed a large metal dumpster heaped with trash bags. It stank of rotten fruit. He disappeared behind the metal container with his cart.

Sam looked at the angle of the sun. She had about ten minutes before thirteen hundred hours.

There was a doorway across the street. She went over and stood in it.

He sat against the brick wall emptying his bag of liquor bottles and beer cans. He shook one after another dry into his mouth. She understood his thirst, one that never reached an end until he passed out. He took a sack off the cart and emptied it: leftover Fritos bags, Oreo cookies, pretzels. He tore the bags apart and ran his tongue over the insides. He ate apple cores, chewed the strings off banana peels.

"What are you –" he growled. "You. Lookin' at?" His eyes roamed Sam's face.

Shards of sadness struck her heart. It was like seeing Marley's strewn body all over again. Staff Sergeant O'Conner's voice, even when drunk, was deep and rich. It identified him, like his hair. How could the man who saved her from being raped by two fellow soldiers and who refused to join in the witch-hunts of Don't Ask Don't Tell, a leader, who had a future of promotions and medals, end up on skid row?

"You remind me of someone," she said.

How could a once strapping man who led with courage and integrity eat scraps like a dog next to a dumpster? What happened that the army would leave behind one of their own? Like a militia, disillusionment and bitterness trampled over Sam's love of country.

She woke up to another hot morning. Her head throbbed from the shots of Bacardi she tossed back until midnight as she surfed the internet, including the VA, for a Daniel O'Conner. She found nothing.

For breakfast, she ate a doughnut and washed it down with rum. She pulled on a soiled khaki T-shirt and a pair of old jeans and slipped into her combat boots, the dog tags tucked between her breasts.

Sam knotted her ponytail, grabbed a canvas bag, stuffed it into her backpack and left. She had to be at work at twelve hundred hours.

If O'Conner slept off the booze, he might be lucid and recognise her.

At the liquor store, she filled the canvas bag with candy bars, cookies, trail mix, wrapped sandwiches and soda pop then headed down Broadway.

The morning sun streaked the sky orange and pink. Yellow rays sliced skyscrapers and turned windows into furnaces. Sam hurried south.

When she crossed Broadway at 6th, the same sun exposed skid row into a stunning morning of neglect. Lines of men pissed against walls, women squatted. She heard weeping.

Sweat ran down her armpits, her head pounded. Sam felt shaky, chewed sand, and looked around. Where was Marley? She stumbled backwards into a gate.

"Baby, whatchu doin'? You one fine piece of ass." The man reached over and yanked at her backpack.

"No!" Sam yelled. She didn't want to collect Marley's severed arms and legs to send home to his parents. "No," she whimpered, grabbing the sides of her head with her hands. "I can't do it," she said, sliding to the ground.

"Shit, you crazy. This is my spot, bitch. Outa here!" he said and kicked her.

Sam moaned and gripped her side. She saw a plastic water bottle lying on the sidewalk, crawled over and drank from it. A sign with arrows pointing to Little Tokyo and the Fashion District cut through the vapour of her flashback. Iraqi women wore abayas, not shorts and tank tops. Sitting in the middle of the sidewalk, Sam hit her fist against her forehead until it hurt.

She saw the American flag hoisted on a pulley from a cherry picker over the 6th Street Bridge, heard the click clack of a shopping cart, and the music of Lil Wayne. The sounds pulled her away from the memory, away from a place that had no walls to hang on to.

Sam held the bottle as she crawled to the edge of the sidewalk. She took deep breaths, focused and glanced around. What the fuck was she doing sitting on a kerb in skid row with a dirty water bottle? *You'll end up like that homeless man you were staring at.* "Oh Jesus." Sam dropped the bottle in the gutter and trudged towards San Pedro Street.

She had thought that when she came home, she'd get better, but living with her mother almost destroyed her. It began slowly, little agitations about housework, arguments that escalated into slammed doors. Then, one day, her mother called George Bush and Dick Cheney monsters who should be in prison. She accused Sam of murder for killing people who did nothing to the United States. Sam lunged at her, when she stumbled over a chair and fell.

Her mother ran screaming into the bathroom and locked the door. "Get outa my house and don't ever come back!"

"Don't worry! You're a piece of shit for a mother, anyway!"

She left and stayed with her friend Jenny until she told her to stop drinking and get her act together.

In her combat boots, Sam scuffled along, hoping to catch O'Conner awake and coherent.

She turned left. The shopping cart poked out from the trash bin. Sam walked to the dumpster and peered around it. O'Conner wasn't there, but his bags and blankets were. She stepped into his corner and was using the toe of her boot to kick away mouse droppings when someone grabbed her hair and yanked back her head, forcing her to her knees. Terrified, she caught a glimpse of orange.

"Private First Class Samantha Cummings, United States Army, Infantry Unit 23. Sergeant!" She raised her arms. Sweat streamed down her face.

His grip remained firm.

"Staff Sergeant O'Conner, I've brought provisions. They're in my backpack. Sandwiches, candy bars, pretzels!"

He let go of her hair. The ponytail fell between her shoulders.

"I'm going to take off my backpack, stand, and face you, Sergeant." Her fingers trembled, searched for the Velcro strap and ripped it aside. The bag slid to the ground. She rose with her back to him and turned around.

She saw the war in his eyes. "It's me. Frap." His skin, filthy and sunburnt, couldn't hide the yellow hue of infection. He smelled of faeces and urine. His jaw was slack, his gaze unsteady. "You want something to eat? I got all kinds of stuff," Sam said. Her emotions, buried in sand, began to tunnel, pushing aside lies and deceit.

O'Conner tore open the backpack and emptied out the canvas bag. "Booze."

She knelt beside him and unwrapped a ham and cheese sandwich. "No booze. Here, have this," she said, handing him the food. "Go on." Her arm touched his as she encouraged him to eat.

O'Conner sat back on his heels. "It's all . . ."

Sam leaned forward. "Go on."

"It's all . . . stuck!"

"What's stuck?"

He shook his head. "It's all stuck!" he cried. He grabbed the sandwich and scarfed it down in three bites. Mayonnaise dripped on his scruffy beard. He kept his sights on Sam as he tore open the Fritos bag and took a mouthful. He ripped apart the sack of Oreo cookies and ate those too. "Go away," he said as black-and-white crumbs fell from his mouth.

Sam shook her head.

"Leave. Me. Alone!"

"I don't want to."

He drew his knees up to his chest, shut his eyes and leaned his head against the metal dumpster.

Here was her comrade-in-arms, in an invisible war, where no one knew of his bravery, where ground zero happened to be wherever you stood.

"You saved me from Jackson and Canali when they tried to rape me in the bathroom. I should have been able to protect myself. And when they tried to discharge me, for doing nothing. You stood up for me. Remember?" O'Conner didn't move. "I never thanked you. 'Cause it showed weakness."

O'Conner struggled to his knees. "I don't know you!" His breath smelled rancid.

"Yeah, you do."

"I don't know you!" he cried.

"You know me. You saved me twice, dude!"

O'Conner stumbled to his feet and gripped the rail of his shopping cart, his spirit as razed as the smoking remains of a Humvee. He shoved off on his morning trek. For how long, Sam wondered.

She gathered the bags of food and put them in the canvas bag. She kicked his rags to the side, took his blankets, flung them out, folded them and rearranged the cardboard floor. She put the blankets on top and hid the bag of food under his rags.

Emotions overcame her. Loyalty, compassion, anger, love – feelings so strong tears fell like a long-awaited rain.

Sam couldn't save O'Conner, but she could save herself.

She ripped off her dog tags and threw them in the dumpster. Once home, she'd take down the flag, fold it twelve times and tuck the picture of Marley and herself inside it. She'd throw out her military clothes and combat boots. Pour the rum down the sink. She'd go to the VA, badger them until she got an appointment. Join AA. She'd arrive and leave work on time.

The morning began to cook. It was the same sun, but a new day. Sam walked in the opposite direction of O'Conner.

Cello
HELEN COOPER

||||||||||||||||||||||||||||||||||||||||||||||||||||||||||||||||||||||||||||||||||||||||||||||||||||||||||||||||||||||||||||||||||||||||

Charlotte pours her soul into a cello to distract herself from reminiscing about her former lover.

"No, no, NO! Dolce, not forte! Elbows high like eagles and the bow must flow like water. Again!"

Propped on the mantelpiece, the innocent white face of the folded note betrayed little of the viciously trite message it enclosed:

Char,
I'm really sorry to do it like this but . . .

The words flew off the page like daggers and she doubled over as if she'd taken a kick to the gut. Later, she ricocheted around the flat like a pinball, bouncing off the newly formed spaces, sharp painful angles where she least expected them. The CD rack gave her a mockingly toothy grin, the gaps which had held Richard's compact discs as apparent as black piano keys. In the bedroom the wardrobe door swung open with a xylophonic chorus of jangling hangers. Like the chalk outline around a dead body, a fairy ring of dust on the dressing table preserved the exact location of his "special occasion" aftershave.

It had been one week, four days, eighteen hours and seventeen minutes since Charlotte had drawn herself up straight and carefully, deliberately, refolded the note before placing it back where he had left it. She thought that she should get a cat. That was what abandoned women did, wasn't it? She would start a cat collection, grow bristles on her chin, let her blood distil to vinegar.

Instead she found herself staring through the window of a music shop, pulse quickening. The cello was simply exquisite, all elaborate curlicues and drippingly glossy wood. Fantastically frivolous yet comfortingly stern. She loved it. She bought it.

For a fortnight Charlotte felt the heavy reproachful glare of the cello, glowering at her every time she opened what was now referred to as "the spare wardrobe". It derided her musical naivety, the symmetrical "f" holes smirking at her whilst the strings bared their teeth. Swallowing her pride, she flicked through the *Yellow Pages*, stuck a pin in the page and booked her first lesson.

Though barely five feet tall (and almost as wide), Mr Feuermann had an assured presence that both intimidated and reassured Charlotte. He carried a cane, ornately carved and with an ivory tip, which Charlotte innocently assumed would be used to beat out time on the floor. She learned the hard way that it was more regularly employed to deliver a smart rap on her knees, shoulders, elbows or any other body part that wandered from the correct alignment.

"Remember, Czarlot," (Mr Feuermann always pronounced her name in such a way as to make her feel like a Russian courtesan), "remember that we hold the bow with the hand like the duck. See!" He made a "quacking" gesture which almost made Charlotte laugh, although a sharp pain across the back of her hand, a flashback to last week's lesson, reminded her that Mr Feuermann did not find humour in a sloppy bow technique. She gritted her teeth and adjusted her bow hold.

Shamed by her seeming inability to grasp the basics, finding that even children's pieces such as *Parachuting Elephants* were beyond her extremely limited capacity, Charlotte resolved, weekly, that she would tell Mr Feuermann she would not be needing to book another lesson. And every time she opened her mouth to do so she caught sight of Richard's dusty note and bit her tongue hard, blurring her eyes with tears.

The weeks passed, each lesson punctuated by a series of minor victories and an equal number of grating errors. But, note by note, bar by bar, Charlotte found that the ache in her heart was diminishing in direct proportion to the ache in her arms and back, and instead of lying awake at night reciting and analysing every word of Richard's note and their last conversations, she found herself engrossed in a visualised mastery of the tricky shift from G to E in *The Doll's Waltz*.

"No, no, NO! Dolce, not forte! Elbows high like eagles and the bow must flow like water. Again!"

"I'm trying but I can't get it. It's too hard and I can't do it . . ."

"Oh ho! Too hard, too hard is it? Tell me, Czarlot, is there a thing that is worth doing that is not hard? Why must we always choose that which is easiest? Is it easy to pour your soul into the violoncello? Is it easy to be passionate and yet controlled? No, it is not easy. But if it is easy that you are looking for, we should put this violoncello back into a cupboard and . . ."

She looked at the note on the mantelpiece, curling at the edges, and it looked back at her with such impudence that she immediately raised her bow and played *Happy Katia* once through with perfect phrasing.

The spaces in the CD rack filled up gradually, exotic names that swirled the brain like vodka: Dvořák, Janáček, Schumann. And the "spare" wardrobe had been disposed of, usurped by the triumvirate of her cello, her music stand and her chair.

"I think, Czarlot, that we will make a cellist of you yet. Not one of the greats, no. But one of the quite-goods. You have the technique, almost, but you have not the passion. It will come . . . we hope."

He smiled. Charlotte smiled back. In the last few weeks her progression had been astounding. She played every spare minute that she had, and not just the weekly set pieces and exercises. As soon as she was through the door she rushed to her cello (which always seemed so much more pleased to see her than she liked to imagine that cat she didn't buy would be) and she would play for hours, oblivious to hunger and exhaustion. Barefoot, eyes closed in rapture, hair swinging loose, she would lose herself in the bittersweet chocolatey notes that spiralled out from her bow.

Four months, two weeks, five days, six hours and thirty-three minutes since she had drawn herself up straight and carefully, deliberately, refolded the note and placed it back on the mantelpiece, a sleepless Charlotte gazed through the semi-darkness of the bedroom at the cello. Richard had called less than an hour ago and the sound of his voice, both strange and familiar, had almost knocked her legs out from under her. His voice was thick with drink, he seemed to be asking if he could come round "to see if she was all right", followed by something slurry about having missed her. She thought she caught the word "mistake" but couldn't be sure. Her voice caught in her oesophagus, she was gasping for breath, but thankfully she was spared the ordeal of speaking. Richard's alcoholic drunkenness caused him to cut her off, and, neither wanting nor waiting to see if he would call back, she had replaced the receiver, unplugged the phone at the wall, and lain back on the bed.

The cello was glowing in the light from the street lamp outside the bedroom window, the glossy lacquer flaming in the sodium glow. She was still dizzy from Richard's call. The pizzicato of *Raindrops* was beating a rhythm at the base of her throat and her breath came in short sharp semiquavers. Her thumbnail plucked the C, and the deep bassy tone vibrated through the floorboards and up through her feet like electricity.

From somewhere she heard Mr Feuermann: "You must become one with your violoncello. As you take it between your legs you must also take it into your heart, just as you would a man. Let the strings vibrate through your soul and let the music pour from you with passion. Forget the rules, play from the inside."

Sitting on the edge of the bed, the cello imprisoned by her thighs, the arc of her right arm swept faster and faster as she played, the fleshy pads of her fingers dancing across the slender neck. Low moans curled from the bow like pipe smoke, tobacco-brown honeyed tones wrapped around her like mink. When she finally slept she lay the cello down next to her, coiled herself against its side.

In the morning she took Richard's note from the mantelpiece and burnt it in the bathroom basin.

CLAM$
JEFF ALPHIN

||||||||||||||||||||||||||||||||||||||||||||||||||||||||||||||||||||||||||||||||||||||||||||||||||||||||||||||||||||||||||||||||||||

A Baltimore entrepreneur's very fishy idea has several unexpected consequences.

"The concoction was
not so much ceviche
as a poor man's
Tequila Sunrise laced
with aquarium water."

I.

Adlai Dallas situated his ball in the divot-scarred tee box of the 13th hole, second-guessing his decision to blow real dollars on the "luxury" that was a day of golf at Clifton Park.

It was Baltimore's oldest and scruffiest municipal course. And yet despite the unshielded traffic along its borders, and roving bands of Lake Clifton High students shortcutting across the fairways, the course had the audacity to charge people thirty-one dollars to hack away at it.

Adlai's drive scattered the same group of class-cutting delinquents who had flipped him off on 11. He was surprised they did not steal his ball.

Probably because Richie – the third member of their party – hadn't bothered to wait for Adlai and the Prep Cook to tee off, and had played on ahead without them, barrelling his golf cart down to where he hooked into scrub pines, singing to himself and looking just crazy enough for the kids not to mess with. A don't-fuck-with-this-threesome ambassador of nutsy.

Adlai stared down at Richie looking for his ball in the rough, lighting up a cigarette and swinging his five iron like a sickle.

"Who is that guy?"

The Prep Cook choked on his Mello Yello. "You been playing here since April and you don't know Richie?"

"I know he's the guy who plays with driving-range balls no one wants to get paired with, but who *is* he?"

The Prep Cook stood six feet three and a half inches; walrus-shaped, deceptively athletic, wearing a pair of chilli-pepper-patterned kitchen pants that rippled in the breeze as he clocked his ball after Adlai's.

"I have no fucking idea. The Loony Crooner of Clifton Park?"

Adlai released the brake on the cart and they rolled down the path, jolting to a stop as Richie fired a line drive out of the trees, across North Rose Street, and into the Jewish Cemetery beyond. Without a word, he dropped another ball and sent a ninety-foot bump-and-run.

"Nice one, Rich," called the Prep Cook.

Richie twirled and jabbed his iron at an imaginary foe, à la Chi Chi Rodriguez's sword dance. "*Riiiight around the cornerr.*"

It was Richie's musical catchphrase. A mysterious lyric half-sung for his every occasion: an acceptable shot, a port-o-john stop, the arrival of the beer-cart girl. "*Riiiight around the cornerr . . .*"

Adlai grumbled over his ball. "What the fuck is that? 'Riiiiight around the cor-ner'?"

"Probably some old Ralph Kramden Ed Norton type shit."

"Whatever it is, the damn thing's stuck in my head."

Adlai got too much loft and landed well short of the green, tracing a rainbow arc over Richie as he zipped across the fairway. The psycho duffer was in a world of his own now, brandishing his pitching wedge like a sabre-rattling Roosevelt leading a charge to the green and spurring his E-Z-GO on for all it was worth.

Determined to correct a recurring slice, the Prep Cook made some adjustments to his backswing before addressing his ball, only to have Adlai break his concentration.

"You guys got any openings down at the Scupper?"

The Prep Cook stood back up, flashing a grimace. "Dude, we let two waitresses go last week. And one of the dishwashers is getting canned today, although he don't know it."

Adlai gave a small laugh. "I'm not talking about washing dishes. More like something that requires a little charm. Maître d', valet, something like that."

"Are you serious? Those jobs were cut last fall. Boss's wife greets you at the door and you park your own. Money's getting so tight I won't be surprised when management starts going through coat-check pockets looking for spare change."

Like menstruating co-workers the two were in golfer sync now, both overshooting the green into the fringe on the opposite side, not twelve feet from the traffic of 32nd Street.

"I thought you harbour institutions made it no matter what."

Adlai leaned against a wooden sign that read *Golfers are not allowed to leave the course to buy anything* while the Prep Cook studied his shot and waited for a fuzz-thumping T-top Monte Carlo with shredded trunk woofers to pass.

"The steakhouses do. But when the seafood guys get skittish they start fucking up inventory. They overorder one week and under the next. And once the second-guessing starts, it's like betting red or black . . ." The Prep Cook chipped his ball within four feet of the pin. ". . . And that's the name of *that* tune."

"So when you overstock and can't sell it, you take it home and have a big clambake, yes?"

"Hell no. We hold that shit to the almost very last minute. Not the kind of chance I'm gonna subject friends and family to."

"Don't tell me you guys actually toss the stuff. You mix in some Old Bay with mayo and call it crab dip, right?"

"Dumpster babies all of it."

"But . . . it's gotta be worth something. Can't you sell it to a homeless shelter or something?"

The Prep Cook took a long look at Adlai.

"You ain't right, Adlai. I guess if you wanted you could can the shit into some kind of hobo chowder, but of course you'd need a canning machine, so unless you know some wharf rat restaurant owner who truly doesn't give a shit about the health inspectors or repeat customers, you're out of luck in the fish business."

"Can't you freeze it?"

"Adlai, please shut up and play golf."

They had to squint to spot the cup on 14 due to the fact that Richie had left the pin lying on the green. Adlai could see him just beyond the hole, drumming his knees impatiently behind the wheel as he tailgated the line of carts waiting on 15.

As maddening as Richie's lack of etiquette was for the Prep Cook and himself, Adlai felt even worse for the poor saps playing ahead, with Richie's unannounced practice balls dropping from the sky all around them. He asked the Prep Cook if it was considered unethical to aim for members of your own threesome.

"If it's Richie, it's encouraged."

Adlai hit his prettiest shot of the day, and watched giddily as it ricocheted off the roof of Richie's cart. Richie sang loud enough for the entire back nine to hear.

"*Riiiight around the cornerr!*"

"How 'bout those guys at the side of the road with the vans and a canopy tent with the hand-painted fresh-seafood signs with the backward Ss," Adlai asked. "Couldn't you drive your leftover shrimps out to Route 40? Peddle 'em off there?"

"Man, you're goin' to an awful lot of trouble to dump refuse."

"It's not refuse, man. It's *near* refuse. You just gotta get rid of it before the final buzzer."

"Adlai, this town ain't as stupid as you'd like it to be. Word travels."

"So change up locations. One week Route 40, the next week Middle River."

"You forget, Adlai, that this is Smalltimore. More people know that shifty mug of yours than you'd ever guess. I happened to drop your name in front of my aunt one time and she told me to 'stay away from that guy'. You wanna sell old clams at a lemonade stand on Eastern Avenue, be my guest. My hunch is that you won't get any more out of it than a wasted afternoon and a citation for funking up the atmosphere."

Adlai stared off into the distance trying to think of somebody he could sell seafood to. He was so intent on an answer he failed to notice Richie in an altercation with a group of fourteen-year-old girls directly in the way of his next shot, loitering ostentatiously and passing around a pack of menthols.

He continued to pester the Prep Cook until they came to an asphalt skid at the cart return. Richie was already having a High Life on a bench outside the clubhouse as Adlai cut to the bottom line.

"So, supposing I can figure something. Can I have the next batch of tossables?"

"Man, you stink like it does. I told you they are firing people down there. All I need is for some busboy on smoke break to see me putting a bushel of crab legs in the back of your car."

"So leave 'em by the dumpster. I'll come pick 'em up. I'll even wear a tie and if anybody asks, I'll tell them I'm a health inspector."

"There's gotta be something for me in this, Adlai. Otherwise it's just stupid. Scratch that. Either way it's stupid."

"That's what they said about Amway. Where's the hurt in trying?

I'm the one doing the legwork. If anything pans out, I'll give you fifteen per cent."

"Fifteen per cent? I'm the supplier!"

"And I'm the one who's got to swing the deal you keep calling unswingable. Take it or leave it."

"All right, Adlai. Go for it. Monday night's the two-minute warning. Every restaurant's last-ditch fish special. I'll leave whatever's left behind the dumpsters after closing. If I were you I'd get there before the rats beat you to it."

"Thanks, man. I owe you one."

* * *

Don Ruckerson scratched his nose with a pencil and looked Adlai in the eye. "Tell me again where you're getting this stuff?"

"Good friend of mine. Amateur waterman. Doesn't have the licences yet and is having a pretty good run of it. Plays cards with some real salts. Knows some guys who know some guys."

"Is this guy a fisherman, Adlai, or a mobster?"

"All I'm saying is my guy is finding all the spots and hauling the stuff in. Technically illegal, sure, but what isn't? Not your problem. Just don't ask any more questions and I show up with a Tuesday-night special at a price that will make your already-clogged heart stop."

"I don't need any more legal trouble these days, Adlai. Your mother knows that better than anybody."

Ruckerson's Seafood on Dundalk Avenue was one of his mother's longest-standing clients. As a home-practising attorney, working out of her den with a Dictaphone in stockinged feet, it only seemed right that Jackie Dallas's number was the one called for the kind of legal advice required from a low-end beach bar, 140 miles from the beach.

With its steady clientele of working-class regulars chasing Pikesville Rye with Natty Boh, Ruckerson's had precisely the undiscerning patrons he was looking for.

And although his mother's career had gotten in the way of some beautiful ideas in the past, Adlai had long ago determined that there was no good reason that he (or the art of creative entrepreneurship) should have to suffer just because she had managed to pass the bar and earn the credentials to officially pick a nit.

Adlai persevered.

"If you think putting out complimentary seafood appetisers for Tuesday happy hour is legal trouble, then by all means take a pass. I'm just trying to do you a favour, Don, and help out a friend until the fishing regulators stop jerking him around. If you like I'll come back when he can legitimately charge what the stuff's worth, and you can cry about that instead . . ."

Adlai slowed up on the pitch, comfortably cruising back into Truthland.

"Monday night is football. Wednesdays you got pool league plus all the midweek Powerball traffic. Thursdays are this close to Friday and the place fills up with thirsty types getting a jump on the weekend. Tuesday's the only weak spot in your line-up. Trivia night. Isn't that, like, 1998?"

"Are we still doing that?"

"According to your weekly *City Paper* listing, yes. But the last Tuesday I was in here it was Deadsville, save the three ancient slobs arguing over the pro-wrestling career of Big Daddy Lipscomb. Put some gumbo out. Honestly, Ruck, what have you got to lose?"

"OK, Adlai. Maybe you've got something. Bring me what you've got Tuesday morning and we'll see if we can work something out. What's the guy fishing?"

"Little bit of everything. Wants to learn all aspects of the trade. Catch of the Day in every sense of the word."

"Yeah. OK. Come on by after ten, and I'll take a look."

* * *

The Rusty Scupper sat perched at the end of a concrete pier, with a hotel-guestbook centre-spread view of the Harbour; 180 degrees of after-hours office fluorescents and orange Hooters neon, their reflections twinkling below a waterline dotted with bobbing paddleboat sea dragons.

Adlai backed the 240Z up to the Scupper dumpsters sometime after 1.00 a.m. and popped the hatch. He wrinkled his nose and peered around until he spotted a wooden bushel basket marked "A.D." sitting up against the slime-crusted rubbish container. Adlai hoisted and stowed it quickly in the back of the Datsun, and headed out for Route 40.

The Prep Cook had left more than he'd expected. There was no way it would all fit in his mother's refrigerator.

It was 1.30 when Adlai pulled into the parking lot of King's Liquors. Little more than a trailer-sized refrigerator with a loading dock jutting out the front of it, King's Liquors was Baltimore's go-to destination for cut-rate beer, ice, individually wrapped pickles and Utz products. Simply drive your pick-up to the beer-sign-lit dock, roll down your window and holler how many cases and of what, and in less than three minutes you were loaded and gone, peeling the shrink-wrap off a stick of home-cured beef jerky with your teeth before you reached the first light.

Additional services included Western Union, scratch-offs, and for those last-call will and testaments, a notary public.

He drove around back and saw Dwight stacking empty pony kegs onto a hand truck. Adlai got close and honked once, bolting him upright and causing him to topple the kegs.

"God-dammit!" Dwight slammed his palm against the hood of the Datsun. He made no move to retrieve the runaways.

"What's happening, Dwight? Long time."

"I saw you last week. You hit on my girlfriend."

"Who? Denise?"

"You know damn well."

"Since when is teaching a girl how to play shuffleboard hitting on her?"

"You left an imprint of your belt buckle on her ass."

"I was just teaching her form. Shuffleboard's a skill."

"Pushing a hockey puck down a sawdusted plank is a bar game for people too drunk to shoot pool."

"Are you calling Denise a drunk?"

"Fuck off, Adlai. We're between break-ups anyway. What do you want?"

"I need to stow some stuff in your walk-in."

"I ain't stowin' stolen goods."

"Not stolen. Nothing to sweat whatsoever. I'm just a guy needing some cooler space."

"Nope."

"C'mon, man. Help a brother out. Not costing you zip. This is the age of the barter. Next time you need a favour, I'm your guy."

"You. You're my guy."

"You know it."

"So like, when you decide to teach Denise how to merengue, you're my guy."

"Merengue is stupid, Dwight."

"Get lost, Adlai."

"Ten bucks?"

Dwight sat on Adlai's hood and lit a cigarette. "Ten bucks is an insult."

"You don't even know what it is!"

"Doing you any favour whatsoever has a twenty-dollar minimum."

Adlai had his keys out and was already moving around to the back of the car. "One basket. Overnight. I'll be back tomorrow morning to pick it up. All I got's ten though. If I had more you'd be welcome to it."

Turning his back, Adlai nonchalantly checked his wallet, front-pocketing all denominations except for a five and five ones while Dwight stared at the soggy basket.

"No deal, Adlai. No fucking way."

"Why the hell not?"

"You're talking to a guy who will eat hot dogs three weeks after their expiration date, and I ain't eating that."

"Why not? That's fresh outa the Bay."

"They're fresh out of your ass. I had a shrimp that shade of grey once. No sir. Never again."

"I'm not asking you to eat it, Dwight, I'm just asking you to store it for a night."

"Uh-uh. That shit is one day away from Gut Twister. It might not smell tonight, but in the next twelve hours it's gonna turn toxic."

"What are you talking about? I tell you it's fresh."

"You forget I used to shuck downtown and we served almost anything. I know the signs. Besides, the boss man's got about thirty pounds of deer jerky hanging in there, and it would be my ass if it starts tasting like chum."

"I'm telling you it's fine. Listen, I'm in a bind here."

Dwight had already begun to trot after the keg that had travelled the farthest, his wallet chain chink-chanking. "See you at the Dredge, man. Stay away from Denise. Mr Bill's ain't the only one in town with jumbo crabs."

"All right, Dwight. Thanks for the tip."

Adlai pulled back onto Route 40, sniffing the car interior deeply and wondering what exactly had tipped Dwight. His nose was picking up nothing more than the usual wafts of the Cross Street Fish Market. Maybe not standing over the sushi-grade tuna, but certainly nowhere near the gutting sink.

He had already rejected the idea of buying coolers. This scheme was still in the experimental stage, and Adlai would be damned if he was going to spend any money out of pocket before turning some kind of profit.

Not while there was a perfectly good bathtub in the guest room at his mother's place.

* * *

Pulling into his mother's driveway, Adlai could detect no light coming from her bedroom window. Even with a Nelson DeMille, her guiltiest pleasure, Jackie rarely managed to stay up past one. Coast clear.

Not that it mattered. Adlai had no intention of passing his mother's bedroom door with his dubious catch, having already mapped a sentryless route to the guest room via the foyer and main stairwell.

He opened the hatch and lifted the basket out, heading for the front door.

A long grey stream of seafood goop ran down the front of his khakis. Adlai reconsidered and walked around to the side door, opting instead to drip through the mudroom, up the back stairwell, and past his sleeping mother.

Not optimal but better than anointing his mother's Oriental staircase runner with Neptune's secret sauce. He'd have to take his chances on the landing.

The drip wasn't slowing. Adlai hustled.

In his haste he forgot to deactivate the alarm system, and was fumbling for the light switch with an armload of squish when the electronic siren went off. Panicked and still in the dark, Adlai hastily set the basket down on top of a fresh pile of laundry and scrambled to enter the deactivation code.

There was silence. Quickly broken.

"Adlai?"

"It's me, Mom. Everything's cool. I just forgot to disarm when I came in."

"Adlai, every time you do that it scares the crap out of me."

"It's fine, Mom. Go back to sleep."

"Actually I've been having real trouble sleeping. I'm up reading."

Adlai suddenly regretted the itty-bitty book light he'd given her last Christmas. It was making it harder to keep tabs on her from outside the house.

"Erratic sleep patterns aren't good for you, Mom. Maybe you should take an Ambien. Something."

"Maybe you shouldn't hook your mother on pharmaceuticals and forget to turn off the alarm when you come in here at three o'clock in the morning."

"It's two twenty. Go to sleep."

"I'm telling you I can't."

"Well try."

Adlai flipped the light switch on and surveyed his situation. The thin wood of the basket was almost soaked through, perspiring like a Tupelo Baptist choir through cornstarch.

There would be no getting past her now.

And then Adlai saw his answer. After all, its whole purpose was to clean, wasn't it?

He lifted the lid on the mudroom's top-loading clothes washer and poured the contents of the sea basket inside, then went back out to the Datsun for the bags of ice he'd picked up at Royal Farms to top off the mix.

He'd ice everything overnight, set an alarm clock and be up before his mother. Then simply dig his bounty back out, throw in the load of dripped-upon laundry, start a heavy cycle, and be at Ruckerson's by 10.00 a.m. Perfect.

As a precautionary measure against Dwight's predictions, he opened a package of Dr Scholl's odour eaters he spotted on his mother's boot shelf, and threw it in with the load.

He chucked the empty basket beside the carport's recycling tubs and went upstairs to what was now called the guest room, although it hadn't changed much since it was his, save the dartboard removal and untacking of Kathy Ireland. Adlai fell on the bed, exhausted.

He would have slept through lunch if not for the shrieking.

"*Aaadlaaaaaiiiiiiii! Get your ass down here!*"

Adlai rolled over and looked at the clock radio. 9.25 p.m. Off by twelve hours. The alarm he set for 8.00 a.m. would be going off that night.

For a sleep-numbed few seconds he wondered what his mother was screaming about.

"*Who the fuck does this?*"

Then he got a whiff of his hands. An eau de King Oscar that hadn't been there before going to bed. Strong enough for his mother to use the word *fuck*.

He dropped his wallet and keys in his shoes and went downstairs where his mother was going ballistic.

Adlai ignored Jackie's frothing tirade as he rummaged through the kitchen in T-shirt, boxers and socks, arming himself with a garbage bag and some large wooden salad tongs before braving the mudroom's swinging door.

"I overslept. Was gonna take care of this before you got up."

If he'd been wearing a collar, Adlai was fairly certain his mother would have grabbed him by it.

"What is wrong with you?"

Adlai stepped around her and plunged his arm into the washer, bringing up tongfuls of sea goop as fast as he could, and dumping them into the black Hefty bag.

"It's a washer. It washes things. Relax. Would you have rather I used the tub in the guest room?"

"This is an 'either or' question? I almost put pillowcases in there. How about no uncooked seafood except in the fridge. Better yet, how about no uncooked *rotten* seafood anywhere whatsoever!"

"You think it's rotten?"

"Are you kidding me? Is that a root vegetable on your face? Try inhaling. Catches don't get any deadlier."

There would be no more denying it. Dwight's timeline had been on the money. The washer smelled like Arthur Treacher's outhouse. Adlai told himself that once the seafood was somewhere other than the confined space of the Maytag, the stench would dissipate.

He set the bag down long enough to put on some khakis from a pile of dirty laundry, hoping to negate the lack of credibility conveyed by a man in his skivvies, and went back to work.

His wheezed speech echoed from inside the washer as he gathered the last of the spin-cycle chowder, refusing to inhale.

"Mom, have you got any of that Zero Odor stuff left?"

"Adlai, I'm going to ask this one more time, but slowly, so you hear it. What . . . in the hell . . . IS *WRONG* WITH YOU?"

The tongs were becoming clumsy as they scraped barnacled bottom. Adlai came up for air and went in after the last of the squish-scraps barehanded.

"I'm late as it is. If it makes you feel better I'll come back and push all the buttons on this thing for you. It *washes*, you know."

"It washes, yes. It does not digest shrimp shells."

"Surprise, the shells are still on the shrimp."

Adlai hoisted the sagging bag over his shoulder like an undersea Santa Claus on his way to fill the bad kids' stockings with mushy calamari. There was a spray bottle of Zero Odor on the wire shelf over the dryer. He grabbed it on his way out.

Adlai turned the key in the Datsun only to discover he'd left the running lights on overnight; his battery dead. Using the duplicate on his ring to unlock his mother's Subaru, he loaded his sack and drove away, feverishly mashing at every window button on the armrest and spritzing Zero Odor over his shoulder.

By the time Adlai got to the restaurant, Don Ruckerson had come and gone. An assistant manager took a break from arranging plastic crabs in a fishing net to inform him that Don had a 10.30 dentist appointment, and probably wouldn't be back until after lunch.

Zero Odor had become an essential part of the transaction, and there was no telling just how long its magic effect would last. Like all As-Seen-On-TV products it wasn't sold in stores, and he was already down to the bottom of the bottle.

He'd been introduced to the "Molecular-Rearranging Miracle" by a videographer buddy shooting an infomercial. Adlai was paid to play the shill, posing as a random man-on-the-street convinced to stick his face in a box of soiled kitty litter and swear he didn't smell a thing.

Adlai had noted how good the props were. "What are those cat turds, sculpted Styrofoam? They look real."

The director laughed. "That's because they're cat turds."

Adlai was floored. His nose had almost been touching. The bottle of mystery mist really worked.

In a December 22nd panic, he'd ordered an economy bottle shipped as a Christmas present to his mother that she received on January 3rd. Over the next few months Adlai tried to beat Zero Odor, and lost every time. Against old Chuck Taylors. Mouldy cardboard. Mildewed lifejackets. Locker-imprisoned sweatpants. And once, in a mintless fix and late for a date, on his own garlic breath (according to the label, it was non-toxic, although the infomercial said not to spray it on food or pets).

And today, it had defused Davy Jones's ultimate stink bomb.

But for how long? He'd never run a duration test, and Don's after-lunch return was a guesstimated two hours away.

Adlai had no intention of letting a basket of income turn into a funky pumpkin. Not when he was this close. It was now obvious that this transaction would be a one-time parlour trick, but he had already put in too much effort to come away with nothing.

Don would return from his dental appointment, take a look at his purchase, toss it and then most likely fire the assistant manager. So theoretically everything could still work out fine, as long as Adlai got the money in his pocket beforehand.

Adlai let out an indignant stage exhale, then with an assumptive tone asked the assistant manager where he would like him to put the seafood, to which the assistant manager replied, "Whaahuh?"

With an undercurrent of impatience, Adlai introduced himself and informed the manager that Don Ruckerson had agreed to buy discount seafood from him.

"Discount seafood? I don't know anything about it."

Adlai played the card he'd been dreaming up on the ride over, just in case Don asked what he was supposed to do with his briny potluck.

"It's for *ceviche*."

Adlai had no idea how to make it, but was pretty sure you could use just about anything. Like fish chilli.

"He didn't say anything to me about it."

"I don't really know what to tell you. Don told me he wanted to start putting out a happy-hour ceviche but couldn't afford to. I'm trying to do him a favour. Hate for him to miss out on it just because he's got a toothache."

"It's a gum scrape."

"A what?"

"A gum scrape. They scrape out your gums."

Adlai's mind was scrambling for a solution as to how he was gonna get this guy to open up the register, and how much to bargain for.

"We had a deal for thirty-five pounds of high end, at seven bucks a pound. Two forty-five total, but for Don I'll call it an even two hundred. Call him if you want."

It was 10.45. With any luck Don Ruckerson was safely in the arms of a dental hygienist with a mouth full of cotton.

He watched the assistant manager dial and wait for the beep.

"Don, it's Doug. Listen, there's a guy here that says –"

Adlai interjected mid-sentence. "I've got other people lined up, I was just trying to do Don a favour."

Doug held out a hand asking for quiet as he tried to finish his thought. "– that you have some arrangement to buy a shipment of seafood from him –"

"But I do need a yes or no now. This stuff won't keep for ever you know . . ." Adlai took a look at his own cell phone, as if there was something pertinent on it.

Doug shook his head in an effort to silence the unshutuppable Adlai Dallas while trying to wrap up a coherent message to his boss. Adlai ignored it.

"Tell Don it's thirty-five pounds total, but I'll call it a generous thirty. He does business with my mother."

Doug gave up explaining the situation intelligibly, ended the call, and shrugged. "I don't know what to tell you."

"Whatever. He must be getting forgetful if he didn't mention it. He was really excited about this ceviche recipe. Bobby Flay, I think. Anyway, have a good one."

Adlai bluffed a move towards the door.

Doug pooched his lips out and wiggled them around. "OK, take it around to the kitchen entrance and tell Ed it's for ceviche. I'll let Don know when he gets back."

"OK great. That's perfect. All that's left now is the settling up."

The assistant manager hesitated for a moment and then opened the register, counting out four fifties from underneath the change drawer. He was tired of the hot seat. This guy obviously knew Don, who was he to call bullshit?

"Here's two hundred. I assume Don has your number?"

Adlai pocketed the cash and made a mental note to turn off his phone for the rest of the day. "Of course."

Working against the last possible hurdle of a kitchen-staff inspection, Adlai waited outside in the Subaru until three unshaved doughboys in aprons emerged from the service entrance for a smoke break. Adlai worked quickly, hustling the Hefty bag past them without explanation and into the kitchen, deserted save one silent woman by a cutting board, facing the wall and chopping onions.

Tearing a hole in the bottom, Adlai squeezed the contents of the bag into a large pot he found hanging on a rack and made room for it in the industrial refrigerator. He noticed a quart-sized bowl of peeled shrimp covered in saran wrap, and as an afterthought, unwrapped the bowl and scattered the shrimp on top of his own pot.

Adlai sped back to Jackie's, catching another break as he realised she had yet to notice her car was gone. He jump-started the Datsun, and let it idle while he took a shower.

It was almost time for a victory nap.

Two hundred bucks wasn't a windfall, but it would get him through the weekend.

* * *

Don Ruckerson spent most of the afternoon in a dental chair, having only rinsed once before receiving the news that he needed prophylaxis. There had been a cancellation just after his appointment. Don pulled the awful trigger and submitted to the whole unpleasantness in one sitting.

He didn't get around to hearing his assistant manager's confusing message until after 2.00, but due to Novocain mush-mouth didn't call the restaurant until it was close to 3.00. Doug told him that the ceviche had already been made.

Through a fog of intense discomfort Don grunted something that sounded like "Who tha heah knoves hahta make seveechee there?" followed by an unintelligible sidebar about Adlai Dallas, and finished up with a "Ahkay, reemime me ta puh ih ow ih I fohgeh."

Don didn't bring up the question of payment, and neither did Doug, already suspecting that somehow he'd fucked up.

II.

The T. Rowe Price vs. PNC softball game scheduled for that night would obviously have to be rescheduled. The ominous cloud cover of Baltimore left little doubt.

The T. Rowe team consisted mainly of guys from the mailroom and a handful of junior execs. Not wanting to waste a bona fide excuse to leave the office on time, they donned their uniforms and met in the lobby to decide what bar they should assemble at while waiting for the game to be officially called off.

Word in the break room was that the much-reviled PNC team was already drinking, seventeen floors below at the Water Street Tavern. Not wanting a repeat of the last inter-company pre-softball-game convergence – when the T. Rowe All Caps drank in the same bar with the Constellation Energy Bills and over $900 of damage was inflicted on one of the Pratt Street Ale House's eighteenth-century beer coppers – the All Caps team captain decided to avoid any run-ins. They would slum at one of the establishments closer to the Patterson Park fields.

Directions were passed around to a laminated porthole of a dive called Ruckerson's. Drinks were cheap, and they could have their run of the place in almost-certain anonymity. Business had been bearish as of late; layoffs, late nights and a sagging morale. A good old-fashioned middle-of-the-week tying one on was in the air.

* * *

Tina had been fighting with her boyfriend Tommy, which was nothing unusual except that most of the time they'd wait until *after* her day shift dancing at the Haven before lighting the fuse. But Tommy had just been laid off from his latest construction job for showing up stoned (which astounded him) and was spending the afternoon hanging around the low-end neighbourhood strip joint, enjoying the perks of Tina's employee drink discount and getting just sauced enough to take issue with the fat guy in the sweatpants who was contributing less money to her G-string than slobber.

Due to his former work schedule, Tommy had never laid eyes on Fat Freddy and his infamous sweatpants, with no way of knowing his Haven status of day-shift mascot; the too-old-for-active-duty firehouse dog that couldn't stop himself from begging for scraps. He was considered harmless (his sweatpants were not), and although he didn't tip much, he tipped, drinking rum and Diet Coke until the after-work crowd showed up.

For a Highlandtown strip-club manager, that made him a VIP.

So after one pretend "fumbling" of the G-string too many Tommy snapped and gave him a shove. Tina told him to cool it, but by then Tommy was already feeling the psychological benefits of blowing off some steam and all three – Tina, Tommy, and Fat Freddy – went at it.

There was no bouncer on the day shift and the manager had to come out of his office, which was never good. Tommy got tossed but the manager waited until the end of Tina's shift to tell her she was fired. "At least until you drop that moron."

One of the other girls, Danielle, stopping by to pick up her cheque, was almost cold-cocked as Tina threw her weight against the fire-exit door on her way out.

Danielle asked, "Tommy?" and Tina nodded once. It was just starting to rain. With no further questions, Danielle tucked Tina into her Jeep Grand Cherokee and started driving, looking for anywhere Tommy wasn't, to sit and have a drink. And in Danielle's words, "dance for the sake of fucking dancing".

* * *

After two months of staring at Classified Ads with an English-to-Russian dictionary Andrei finally got a job.

Nothing great. A one-timer for pocket change. But to a dry-docked sailor with limited English and a tug captain recovering from knee replacements, fifty bucks was fifty bucks.

Posing naked for three hours in front of a semicircle of aspiring sketch artists was just fine with him. At least until this fad of employers requiring legitimate working papers ran its course.

He was hungry.

And all the villager optimism his mother scrawled to him from the self-sustaining nowheres of central Russia in her letters, extolling an unshakeable belief that community would always take care of its own, was doing absolutely nothing to balance Andrei's nearly constant state of low blood sugar.

Obviously the woman's knowledge of community did not extend to the wharves of Baltimore, USA.

But indeed the employment cavalry had arrived.

All he had to do was show up at the life-drawing class in some East Baltimore art studio Wednesday morning, take his clothes off, and sit on a big wooden platform. The woman who hired him even asked him not to shave or comb his hair, saying he was "extremely authentic".

Andrei didn't know what "extremely authentic" meant, comprehending only that he was not to comb his hair.

What a country!

Tonight, he would eat something other than potted meat. Maybe even go out for some clam strips. *By Sravog* he could almost taste it!

* * *

Wendell opened the pneumatic bus doors and let the crazy lady on while the hippy secured his bike to the rack up front. Four more hours and he could kiss this mind-number of a route goodbye for ever.

He had been thrilled to learn, just yesterday, that he had been transferred to the Convention Centre route. Starting tomorrow.

It was a busier route, but straight-shot driving with fewer wackos than his current one, and that would surely make for a less painful work week.

Seven more stops and he'd be done for the day. It was time to celebrate a little.

God knew he deserved it.

* * *

Roger Patton was tired of feeling like a well-dressed Labrador retriever. Sit. Stay. Fetch.

As an assistant to the State Comptroller for over two years now, he could count the serious projects he'd been put in charge of on one hand. Everything else seemed to fall under categories of conference room coffee-and-Danish trays, public-appearance press releases, staffer birthday gifts, and taking the Comptroller's Infiniti X in for the never-ending servicing of its maddeningly temperamental dashboard computer; the car seemed to be named for the number of times you could expect all its electrical misfirings to work themselves out.

None of it was doing a damn thing to pump his résumé.

His latest assignment: find some alternative entertainment for the Comptroller's in-laws from West Virginia who had been to Baltimore a grand total of twice. Box seats had been arranged for the hapless Orioles, who were playing the Royals; even without the string-pulling they could have probably scored seats over either dugout on their own. Now weatherman Marty Bass was calling for rain, the skies already backing him up with conviction. It was Baltimore at its dreariest.

"Just find some local joint that serves the kind of seafood West Virginia hillbillies understand," the Comptroller had told him. "Last time they were here I got 'em reservations at The Oceanaire and they tried to order fish sticks.

"Someplace cheap. With something to do and not karaoke. I gotta go with them this time or my wife is gonna tie her knees in a knot and I'm already down to twice a month. And I sure as shit ain't got nothing to talk about with those people."

Roger leafed through the bar ads of the *City Paper*, looking for an idea.

* * *

Gene's Gun Shop, named after a partner long gone and owing enough never to be heard from again, was located in one of Baltimore's more crime-riddled neighbourhoods, flanked for the moment by a fly-by-night cell-phone shack and a wig shop.

After six years, Ray was long over the guilt of peddling pieces in a police-blotter part of town, but the boredom of running a business that did so little business, that was deflating.

With fresh legislation requiring a longer wait for background checks and stiffer sentences for carrying concealed weapons, Ray didn't sell many guns any more. He still repaired a few now and then, but for the most part merely accessorised, providing folding stocks for illegal automatics already bought on the street, and assorted Baltimore pocket toys: butterfly knives, collapsible batons, and the occasional pack of throwing stars.

Although lately he showed a spike in sales for the fake AK-47s that shot rounds of yellow plastic pellets. Maybe the hopheads were staging battle-training exercises down by the light-rail tracks. There was one artsy-looking kid in a defaced MICA shirt that went through three cases of ammo a week; he reminded Ray of an old-school glue sniffer from the '70s. Ray had seen him one time on the steps of the Mt Royal Tavern firing into the skies over commuter traffic and laughing himself sick at the pelting yellow hailstorm and its bewildering effect on people behind the wheel.

But the profit margins of novelty-item sales did not justify the upkeep of running a small business on Howard Street.

Ray was sifting through a drawer of punch pins and looking at naked girls online when he realised it was ten minutes after closing, which irked him. The Koreans closed the corner takeout at 6.00 on the dot, and Ray had been dreaming about their fried shrimp since breakfast.

Maybe he could stop by Ruckerson's and pick up some takeout on the way home.

III.

Don Ruckerson had to admit. It was the best trivia night ever.

There was a buzz of bent elbows from one end of the 75-foot horseshoe bar to the other, the taps flowing, and the shot glasses running low. Margaritas by the pitcher for the softball team at the party table, who were gleefully assigning names to unshelled peanuts and smashing them by hand with a wingtip shoe.

Leesa the bartender pinballed around the interior of the U-shaped bar, clacking off the rails with her belly ring, sloshing foam in the cocktail-fruit bins, and giving out angel wings like Pottersville's Nick the bartender on the 1949 National Cash Register that came with the place.

One particularly talented girl was working the jukebox and keeping heads nodding in an *I-can-dig-it-yes* bob with her undeniable set list of deep-cut Joan Jett, Badfinger and Eagles of Death Metal. She had carved herself out a little piece of floor by the wall-mounted juke to dance, evidently under the impression that it was possible to push her ass out through her back pockets.

At the opening thomp of Lakeside's *Fantastic Voyage* filter-pedal funk line, she was joined by a friend who began to invoke a tube of toothpaste, squeezing out the very last of herself.

Both the bus driver and the man eating fried shrimp from the carryout bag couldn't take their eyes off them. The fried-shrimp guy had ordered his food to go, but apparently decided to grab a seat at the bar once the girls' engines began to turn over.

What the State Comptroller was doing there was anybody's guess, but he was a Democrat and had already agreed to pose for a quick snapshot with Don for the bar-room's Baltimore-celebrity wall, so his first round of drinks was on the house.

The Comptroller and his wife were seated at the far bend of the bar with Ma and Pa Kettle. It must be some kind of PR stunt, Don surmised. Bolster his "just folks" image.

Don shifted his bedroll-shaped backside in his seat as he surveyed the crowded, jostling room and smiled. Money.

He was at his nightly post, perched at the greet-and-seat podium by the entrance to the now closed dining room, riding the high of a dental ordeal over and done with.

Took it like a man.

He lifted a finger at a passing Joyce and called for his usual, a shot of peppermint schnapps.

The menthol zing on his freshly scavenged gums was painful, but there was something extra buzzy about the alcohol splashing raw flesh. Don thought about Scarface rubbing cocaine all over his gums and signalled Joyce for another shot.

Leesa had been emceeing the Tuesday-Night Trivia for over two hours now, using the kitchen microphone to ask the questions, between kitchen-staff announcements of "Order up."

Here was bar competition at its most disorganised, with a house policy of *First one to say the right answer at a volume loud enough for Leesa to hear gets the points*. The game consoles and monitors standard for twenty-first-century bar trivia were as foreign a concept to Ruckerson's Seafood as a wet nap to a Great White.

Which was making things enormously difficult to follow as teams attempted to name six members of the Dirty Dozen, stealing answers and trying to out-yell each other.

Leesa called "*QUIET!*" as the bar-room became bleacher-crowd unruly, arguing over which movie had Donald Sutherland, *Kelly's Heroes* or *The Dirty Dozen*, collectively shouting down the guy who kept insisting he was in both, with a side fracas flaring up over whether it was Telly Savalas or Don Rickles in the role of Sgt Crapgame.

She was already in the weeds when Don told her to refill the ceviche bowls.

It was true, almost every serving bowl was down to the juice. The day cook and bartender had collaborated on the dish after no one could get hold of Don. Bobby Flay had several ceviche recipes posted online, but each was designed for specific seafood.

Having rarely prepared anything without a fryer basket, the two men were astonished to learn that raw seafood could be "cooked" with citrus alone. The revelation sparked a chemistry-set spirit and the two worked as mad scientists, oblivious to each other's increments as they drenched the pot with lime, cilantro, and repeated splashings of rail tequila.

Chips on the side.

A spiked mystery-salsa with some chew to it; enough to pique the bar-room palate. Double-dipping became the norm, if for no other reason than to take a second guess at what the hell it was they just swallowed. And by then one could feel the tequila.

As it is with working people stuck somewhere between whatever fast-food crap they'd shovelled for lunch and the dinner they were putting off in favour of Smirnoff Ice, there was little hesitation to dig into anything free, be it cheese-glopped floppy disks or little artificially coloured pigs snuggled in gooey half-baked blankets.

And so even though the concoction was not so much ceviche as a poor man's Tequila Sunrise laced with aquarium water, it was a hit.

Kitchen staff worked a ladle through the cauldron of sea-monster bits and pushed the freshened bowls through the service window, eliciting hearty cheers from a crowd drunker by the half-hour, and already concocting excuses for Wednesday's inevitable sluggish start.

One of the T. Rowe mailroom guys, back from sharing a joint in the parking lot, began to take small sips straight out of the bowl.

It was beyond time that some handler should've shepherded the Comptroller out of there. The elected state employee was on the opposite side of the room from his wife and farm folk, flirting stupidly with one of the curvier softballers, bellowing "Sha Na Na!" as the answer to every music question and finding it hilarious.

There was only one guy, Don noticed, not making an ass of himself. The grizzled foreigner with wild strings of dirty blond hair springing out from under a sailor cap at the far side of the bar, glassy-eyed and grinning as if this was the most delightful room in the world.

Don hadn't heard him say more than "More chips," and "Pabst, please," all night, in a thick Russian accent.

The bus driver and the fried-shrimp takeout guy continued feeding the dancing girls singles for a jukebox already so backlogged with selections that the off-duty pole spinners simply responded to each dollar with a sexy blank stare before pocketing it. The go-go girls might cut into his waitresses' tips, Don knew, but he did nothing to stop them. They were setting a hell of a mood.

Around 11.30 things got a little too heated over whether Jamie Lee Curtis was a hermaphrodite, even though it wasn't officially a question, and Don declared everyone a winner, bought the house a round, and told them to get the hell out.

After an evening of scattered thundershowers, the skies had opened up again and it was pouring. Aided, perhaps, by the ghost sots of a Baltimore past, they all made it home alive.

IV.

Wednesday morning was nobody's friend.

The mail guys were up first, shambling into the bright fluorescents of the office, groggy and gummy-eyed, sorting the *WSJs* from the

Barrons and jockeying for first dibs on the empty storage room they used for naps.

Buzz was the first to get sick, spewing violently while rubber-banding personal mail for the CFO, including the lavender envelope that contained the handmade glued-macaroni birthday-party invitation from his seven-year-old granddaughter.

The rest of the T. Rowe mailroom followed suit, counter-clockwise. Henry, at Buzz's immediate left, in turn set off Stan and then Jamal. Closing out the sequence was Chuck, who abruptly restocked the office-supply cabinet with a visual mnemonic of his name, sploshing a drawer full of Post-its with a new rainbow of sticky colour.

The biggest loss of the day was triggered by Jamal. He threw up on a too-risky-to-email bike-messengered envelope of insider information that had highly paid fingers hovering over hot buttons since Monday's opening bell of the Bombay Sensex.

Jamal made a home in the men's room, cradled in a corner stall like a greenhorn sailor sent to his cabin, until the ceiling and floor returned to their traditional locations. When he found he could stand again, he washed the secret memo and held it under the hand dryer before telling the new guy to take it to the top floor.

Within the hour there was wood splintering on just about every rung of the corporate ladder as it became evident the investment company had missed out on the opportunity of the quarter, if not the year, by less than forty-five minutes.

The fallout made examples of peripherally blameable scapegoats, as happens when such astronomical numbers are lost with no explanation that's fit to print. Two senior research analysts lost their jobs, with one of the casualties' irate and overmedicated trophy wife smashing four pieces of highly collectable Depression glass upon hearing that she "might have to cut back for a while".

But the most seismic result of the morning would not occur until that weekend, during the second hour of a *Toy Story*-themed birthday party in Ellicott City. As the Mr Potato Head piñata was being hoisted on the swing set, the mother of the birthday girl, thinking herself out of earshot, got her business-before-family father on the phone and began to uncork a lifetime of holding back. Initial thwacks were taken at the piñata as guests listened to the woman angrily dismiss his claims of being oblivious to the event and his defence of most certainly not having received the one-of-a-kind macaroni-art invitation "Kylie worked over forty-five minutes to surprise you with!"

The woman continued to recount his other past absentee atrocities, turning back the calendar as far as 1982. After more than a couple of apprehensive stares from other parents, she had the sense to move around to the side of the house, and yet if it hadn't been for the timely busting of Mr Potato Head and subsequent squeals of the assembled, her shriek of ". . . the piano recital *and* the state gymnastics meet . . ." would have been heard all the way to the swim club.

And with the slamming of the phone, the Sr Executive Vice President who never received the invitation to his granddaughter's birthday party mumbled, "Screw the inheritance tax," and for the first time in his life wondered what it would feel like to vote Democrat, while his daughter kicked an inflatable moonwalk.

* * *

Around 9.30 a.m. Tina wobbled around to the strip bar's back entrance, popping Tylenols and wishing she had sunglasses to put over her sunglasses. The two go-go girls had stayed up after leaving Ruckerson's, talking until well past 3.00, flopped on the couch and balancing ashtrays on their stomachs.

The conversation hadn't gotten snappish until Tina drunkenly confessed that she didn't want to dance any more. That she needed a push to get her out of there, away from the easy money and on to something better. Danielle was quick to infer some holier-than-thou shit and told her if she was such a morally upright citizen *meant for something better* she could just hand over her wad of jukebox go-go girl singles.

The next morning Tina groaned herself upright, checked her purse and realised that in a fit of self-righteousness she'd given Danielle all her money.

Waking up to face a jobless reality, she left the snoring Danielle a note, took the keys to her Jeep Grand Cherokee, and drove to the Haven to ask for her job back. Before anyone had the chance to find a replacement.

The manager was in his office, sucking back the last of a breakfast roach. When he saw Tina he offered her the end of it, and as she gratefully pinched the resin-sticky tip of the smouldering paper, he asked if she would mind filling in for Janice on the morning shift. Her kid was sick.

Tina couldn't tell if he remembered firing her at all.

The clientele that morning consisted of two guys in H&S Bakery uniforms straight from the all-night shift, Fat Freddy, and his infamous sweatpants.

Infamous due to the fact that no one at the Haven had ever seen them clean; a shifting assortment of landmass-shaped stains, overlapping and continentally drifting from day to day, up and down his lap and thighs. Many of the night girls didn't make the same concessions for Freddy's pants and refused to go on with the pants sharing the room, on those rare days Freddy stayed past the day shift.

Tina changed in the ladies room, murmuring an atheist's prayer that Tommy would stay away today while contemplating which jukebox songs would take it easiest on her pounding head. She limbered up, determined to treat the shift as an early-morning exercise class, and sweat out her hangover.

Tina was getting a good slow burn on her quads to Juice Newton's *Angel of the Morning* when she noticed Tommy sitting at the bar. Before she could react, Fat Freddy got up to put a ripped single in her leg warmers and without warning Tina felt her stomach launch itself a good six inches, slicking the stage and splotching a chartreuse-tinged Asia on Freddy's legendary warm-ups.

Later, nursing a ginger ale while the manager disinfected the pole, Tina noticed Tommy was gone. Well, at least there was that.

A Tommy cleansing.

The manager threw his sponge in a bucket and addressed Tina from the stage.

"You're fired."

Scratch that, Tina corrected herself, *a total cleansing.*

"Thanks, Boss," was all she said.

With any luck, even Freddy's pants would get a wash.

* * *

There was no official instructor for the life-drawing class. The woman who hired him was unstacking chairs when he got there. She showed him to a corner where he could "disrobe", which to Andrei's ear sounded awkward.

Students would be coming and going sporadically (*spore-attic-lee?*) until noon, she told him. "They'll tell you what kind of poses they want."

Another woman with a drawing pad and large vinyl bag of art supplies waddled in, breathing heavily through her nose, and sat in a folding chair facing a detached section of painted-plywood staging in the centre of the room.

The woman unstacking chairs informed Andrei that it was "Show time."

At first he sat quietly on an exercise mat atop the platform with his feet dangled over the side as if waiting for a doctor's examination, looking away to middle distance as a handful of mismatched art enthusiasts trickled in and begin sketching his scrotum with broken bits of charcoal.

Time passed slowly. Andrei had no clue how long he'd been sitting there. He had begun to see the shape of a baby elephant in a water stain on the opposite wall when a stringy woman eating a muffin and wearing a gardening hat barked under her breath.

"New pose."

Once again the words sounded very weird to Andrei.

He crossed his legs and rested his chin on his hand, an inadvertent Thinker. It hurt his back and after five minutes he realised he wouldn't be able to hold it comfortably.

Andrei leaned back on his arms in search of a less painful position, eliciting a collective groan from the group. Upon hearing the expressed displeasure, he moved again, causing the muffin eater to snap at him to make up his mind.

Andrei took a guess, rolled onto one side, and assumed the bearskin-rug centrefold pose Burt Reynolds did for *Cosmopolitan*.

From this new vantage point he noticed a dishevelled spiky-haired punk wearing a ratty MICA T-shirt who kept rubbing his nose and giggling at a pitch far too high for anyone over the age of nine that wasn't a girl. Andrei was pretty sure the punk's inexplicable mirth had less to do with the sight of a naked man squirming in confusion, and more with whatever high you can catch inhaling art supplies.

Andrei altered his huffer theory as little yellow plastic round somethings started rattling out of his art-supply box. Something in the amphetamine family, Andrei surmised, due to the kid's non-stop tittering. There was no way he could have known they were plastic AK-47 pellets, never having come in contact with a fake AK-47.

Andrei continued holding the position until his right hip started to ache. As he readjusted, something horrible roiled inside him, from somewhere down near his hernia scar to somewhere up around the top of where his liver should be, as unexpected as John Hurt's chest burst.

That's when the muffin-mouth lady let out an exasperated sigh, lifted her chin and spoke to him directly.

"Please strike a new pose and *hold it*. And for the love of art," she repeated, "please make it *interesting*. Something unexpected."

Andrei still couldn't comprehend what these people wanted and no longer cared. A strange sensation had come over him, bringing both tunnel vision and vertigo. With a shudder, he doubled over.

And then – per their request – Andrei gave the class something new to draw. Whether it was interesting or not was debatable. All would agree it was unexpected. Most of the drawing circle put their charcoal away and made for the exit as Andrei held on to the edge of the stage as if it was an ice floe and he the salmon-sickest polar bear in the Arctic.

The kid with the MICA shirt, however, opened a tin of coloured pencils and got to work, realising that the tableau before him would make an ideal show flyer for his art-school band, The Rejaculators – due to its visual encapsulation of the band's own philosophy of art – and possibly even the album cover for their forthcoming vinyl-only issue, entitled *Spit It Back*.

Within forty-eight hours there were Rejaculators flyers posted all over downtown featuring Andrei the naked Russian splashing goop all over the tops of his hairy feet. A 4x6-foot Kinko's blow-up of the spewing Russian was strung up sideshow-style over the entrance to the Ottobar announcing the *Spit It Back* record-release party.

A week later, as a recovered but rather bummed out Andrei wandered downtown in search of *Help Wanted* signs, the hardcore kids began to point him out to each other.

"How do we know that guy?"

The next morning in Fells Point a kid with a black rose in each ear yelled "Oi!" as Andrei passed.

The following day he was stopped on the street by a tug captain he knew by sight but had never met.

"Hey, uh . . . you're the Russian, right? Andrei, is it? Listen, I'm going out next week and could use a man."

Andrei shook the tug captain's hand with a seasoned grip and looked him in the eye; the international language of "Hire me."

"It's funny," the captain said, "I was driving down Maryland Avenue trying to think of someone for the job, and I look up and see this awful poster of a guy throwing up all over himself naked. Really disgusting. But for some reason it made me think of you."

Andrei smiled. His mother had been right.

* * *

Ray had a customer, the likes of which he'd never seen cross the threshold of Gene's Gun Shop. *A Big Daddy.*

His identification looked legit. As did his freshly notarised Designated Collector's card. His Amex was platinum. And he had a list.

The first gun he asked for was a Smith & Wesson Model 67. As Ray touched his chin, trying to picture it, the man added, "The one Adrienne Barbeau carries in *Escape from New York*."

Ray didn't know of the Frenchman or his escape, but he did have the gun. Two of them in fact, under glass in the centre display.

The customer stood just under six foot, in good shape and well put together, with hair high and tight, sporting a charcoal-grey jacket over a purple crewneck.

He moved comfortably in light wool slacks, pointing each gun at people who weren't there and having imaginary conversations with Snake Plissken while pretending to free the President.

Ray had no idea what the man was doing and decided he must be in the movie business. They shot all kinds of cop-drama shit in this town. A prop guy maybe?

Next he was interested in the gun Angelina Jolie had in *Tomb Raider*. Ray did some googling and learned from a site called whoshotwhowithwhat.com that it was a Heckler & Koch 9mm, a gun he happened to have in one of the wall cases.

Ray took it out and watched the customer caress it lovingly, as if Miss Jolie had pleasured herself with it between takes. And then he slid it in the front of his pants and closed his eyes.

Ray snuck a look at the man's Collector's credentials, still by the register. The box beside History of Mental Illness remained unchecked. The freak has a platinum card, Ray told himself. Surely he's OK . . .

The man extracted the gun from his slacks, then fished deep into his front pocket for a well-worn piece of paper.

On it was a female cartoon rabbit. But sexy, a steamy one; with Veronica Lake hair and crazy-straw curves straining the seams of a red satin dress, aiming what looked like a .38 Colt directly at Ray's startled eyes. Everything in the picture was an illustration except for the gun, which was the real thing. Despite years of Baltimore street life and untold horizons of internet porn, it was one of the most twisted juxtapositions Ray had ever seen.

"You know what this is?"

It's batboy kinky, is what it is, thought Ray.

"The gun?" Ray hazarded.

The man reached out to take the picture back, stroking the rabbit's backside gently with his thumb. "Jessica's gun . . ."

Scratching your nutsack with Lara Croft's gun sight was one thing, but this was Saturday Morning Super Sickie.

"It's definitely a Colt. Looking down the barrel like that I'd say it's a 1908, but it's tough to be certain. Let me see what I've got and we'll compare 'em."

Unlocking the case of Colts, Ray wondered what other famous guns he might have. It put new spin on his inventory. Celebrity gats!

Ray fantasised a quick slogan. Gene's Famous Guns. *Where the movie cops shop. Shoot on Location!*

A kid in a black-and-gold Superman tee who obviously should have been in school entered the store. He was either sleepwalking or so stoned he could barely open his eyes; they were drowsy slits. Ray pointed to the *No minors allowed* sign and then the door.

The kid went back outside and stared into the front window's selection of brass knuckles, evidently able to see through his eyelids like the Man of Steel himself.

Ray held out a Colt 1908 to the collector and watched him aim it back at his own face, replicating the camera angle in the picture and comparing it to the one brandished by the cartoon *Playboy* bunny.

He'd take it.

Then the man produced what looked like a solar-powered Texas Instrument from the Carter Administration, calculated his total, and asked for one last gun.

"A special one," he said. The man levelled his gaze at Ray, heavy on the gravitas. "Beatrix Kiddo."

The man could have dramatically whispered *Mairzy Doats*. Once again, Ray hadn't a clue.

"I knew you wouldn't have it."

"I don't even know what it is."

"The Bride. Beatrix Kiddo. Firestar M-45. Not to be confused with a 9mm 1911. Of course I'm not expecting her custom longslide."

Ray grinned like a bad kid at the start of a little Jimmy joke in church. Not only because everything this guy said sounded absolutely filthy, but because he was now an unbelievable four for four – that exact model Firestar was in pieces on his workbench in the back room.

He'd bought it in a box of crap for next to nothing, hoping the repair work required might be therapeutic. Once he replaced the firing pin and found the right-size extractor spring in his shoebox of tiny miscellany, it would be a nice little pistol. Four hundred bucks maybe.

Ray told the man he'd have something to show him within the week. The customer got very excited, and asked to see it now, if even in parts. As Ray pushed his way through the swinging door to the back room, he did the world's tiniest fist pump. He was on the verge of doing a month's business in thirty-five minutes.

The thought made him light-headed.

Only it wasn't the thought.

It was last night's chilled fish mash.

Ray leaned over the workbench, putting pieces of the .45 in an empty ammo box, and threw up all over them. He put an arm out to steady himself on the padded vice, and threw up all over that as well. Then he was on the floor, holding his gut and blowing bile out his nose, fighting to keep his nostrils clear before the inevitable next bout.

Ten minutes later, he was human enough to call out to the front of the store, in a hoarse attempt to apologise, explain and reassure in one futile communication.

There was no answer.

By the time Ray cleaned himself up enough to re-emerge from the back, his customer was gone. As well as three glass casefuls of unlocked inventory.

There was no way the half-cocked pervert had taken it all. Word must have hit the street that the lid was off at Gene's.

Or else the sleepy-eyed middle-school Superman had a backpack.

* * *

In the time it took the Prep Cook to wrestle his golf bag off the window seat and into the aisle, the passenger crush for the doors had become Times Square tight.

There was no way to make their tee time now. This bus wasn't going anywhere without extensive clean-up and a new driver.

The Prep Cook opened his phone to call Adlai, but its screen was dark. He'd forgotten to charge it.

Oh well. Adlai would just have to figure out he wasn't coming on his own.

The Prep Cook hadn't seen the driver lose it, but heard the retch and splat against glass, and felt the lurch into the next lane and up onto the kerb, crumpling the front half of a Miata and just missing a fire hydrant.

There had been a collective squeal of panic, then calm. Then osmosis did its thing and the smell drifted down the aisle.

As he stood trapped, slow-dancing with his Callaways, he could see that the driver had managed to vomit over much of the expansive front windshield and was now feebly opening a side window in order to spew out onto the street. It took the Chinese woman sitting at the front three tries at the pneumatic door lever before the doors hissed open and people began pushing to get out.

One of the homeless guys with a stoplight squeegee jumped on and was attempting to sponge the windshield from the inside – hoping for some suitable oversized municipally funded tip – as the driver stumbled off to sit on the kerb, head between his shins. A thin line of spittle ran from his mouth to the sidewalk.

The Prep Cook regretted not being able to reach Adlai. Not that he really felt like playing golf any more, but he was curious to know how the whole seafood scheme had worked out.

* * *

Adlai lifted his Ray-Bans to look at the starter's watch. It was almost 11.00. Fifteen minutes past their tee time. The Prep Cook wasn't going to make it.

He couldn't help but get the feeling that despite the thirty-dollar slice of Ruckerson pie he had coming to him, the Prep Cook had made a conscious decision to disassociate himself from Adlai Dallas. It wouldn't be the first time.

In that case Adlai would just have to consider the money his.

Adlai waved Richie over. Richie, who for the last twenty minutes had been loitering nearby in a spastic orbit, hoping to pair up.

Riiiight around the cornerr.

Adlai reluctantly agreed to let Richie drive, fairly confident that golf carts don't flip over. While waiting for the first hole, Richie lit a cigarette and informed Adlai that his hair was sticking up in back, "like a cockatoo". Adlai would be damned if he would spit-comb his hair because of Richie. He told him to shut up and tee off.

Sniffing the air thoughtfully, Richie unfolded a stack of currency held together with a binder clip and peeled a twenty.

"You know what Chi Chi says, don't you?"

Adlai shook his head, beginning to worry that Richie might be in a talkative mood.

"You should never play a round of golf for nothing."

Cockatoo my ass, Adlai thought.

"You're on, Richie. But let's make it thirty."

The Prep Cook would've wanted in too.

* * *

Don Ruckerson held the phone tightly, unable to believe what he was hearing. The State Comptroller's wife was chewing him a new one.

It was a difficult conversation to track.

Going off about her parents from West Virginia. How they'd only come to Baltimore twice before and now this. A four-hour emergency-room visit, the sickest she'd ever seen her father and her mother's vow never to visit this filthy town again, not even on holidays. Topped off with a recounting of the morning's news conference during which her husband projectile-vomited all over the press corps.

There would be hell to pay, he could believe that, she ranted. "An attempt to poison a public official is technically an attack of terrorism." He could think about all this, she bellowed, as he "rotted in Guantanamo".

Their people would be in touch. Buy a good umbrella. A shitstorm was a-coming.

The woman hung up before Don had much of a chance to say anything. For a full minute he stared at a picture on his bulletin board of a carefree Don Ruckerson juggling coconuts in Barbados.

Then he picked up the phone, and called his lawyer – Jackie Dallas – who at that moment was sitting at a stoplight on Cold Spring Lane, wondering what the hell was making her car smell like that.

* * *

From a distance, Adlai watched Richie kick his ball out from behind a tree, apparently under the impression that he was invisible. It was no longer a contest of who would play the better round of golf, but who was the superior cheat.

The door was wide open for Adlai, since he was repeatedly left to putt out all by his lonesome while Richie breathed down the necks of the unfortunate golfers ahead of them.

On 15, Adlai tested the scorecard waters by declaring a fictitious birdie back on 14. When it went uncontested, Adlai assumed Richie had no intention of paying up; he'd either pretend like he had misunderstood the bet, whip out a memo pad of preprinted IOU slips, or run away.

So afterwards, when Richie took a sip of his High Life, savoured another deep inhale of spring air, and handed over the cash, Adlai was genuinely shocked.

It felt like the longest, most enjoyable mugging on record.

* * *

Kevin couldn't stop feeling the heft of the gun. He knew it was a cliché to say it was heavier than it looked, but it was heavier than it looked.

Not that he'd had much time to get used to it, having purchased the gun not twenty minutes ago for fifty bucks. An Afterschool Special.

Crossing Elm Street with a handful of classmates on their daily after-the-bell pilgrimage to George's Mini Mart to buy some artificially flavoured crap for the walk home, Kevin had spotted Sleepy Reese on the kerb, knapsack by his side and grinning out from under his eyelids like Muggsy Bogues waiting to go back into a game already won.

Within ten minutes Sleepy had handpicked and flagged down a posse of likely customers, walked them behind the dumpster at the Crown Station and proudly opened his knapsack to display his wares. Reese's Pieces. For a limited time only.

If only Norman Rockwell had been on hand to paint the scene.

Sleepy wanted them gone and gone fast. "Fifty bucks each, gentlemen. First cash, first choice." There was a dash for the Crown's ATM, but Kevin had been lucky. He'd sold a bottle of his mother's expired Vicodin that day, by the tablet.

By 3.45 Kevin was an armed man. No ammo, but from what he'd seen of the weekday duffers of Clifton Park, he wouldn't need it.

Kevin watched from behind the port-o-pots on 18 as the doofus with the Ray-Bans and cowlicked head took two bills from the crazy guy with the beer.

Kevin was never sure whether the crazy guy was a real golfer or just some nut loose on the course sparring with invisible musketeers. He saw him almost every day. Whoever he was, he'd just handed money over to the doofus with the cowlick, who already appeared to have a wad of cash to add it to.

And that made Cowlick the winner.

Kevin watched his "winner" walk to the far end of the almost empty parking lot with his clubs, a loping pipe cleaner in khakis. Like the Keep on Truckin' cartoon guy, his head couldn't seem to keep up with his feet.

Kevin collected himself and took one last look around the immediate area for potential witnesses. The smell of freshly cut grass filled his nose, and off somewhere he could hear the sound of a sprinkler turning on.

Adlai Dallas set his clubs down and was fiddling with his keys when Kevin began to walk towards him.

Honestly, he asked himself, could there be easier money?

Dearest Eliot
HARRY BUSCHMAN

The tale of a ragged young activist consumed by war and love.

"I stared at her from behind my beard like a homeless person, unaware that I looked like an unmade bed."

The summer of '39! Being twenty-one and a senior, that should have been enough for me.

But no! I signed on to the committee to impeach Martin Dies. I marched with the Irish Liberation Army in the spring, and I attended meetings in Lennie's basement with the Red Guard every Thursday. Shouldn't that be enough excitement for a young man of twenty-one in the summer of '39?

No! – I had to go and fall in love!

I first noticed her in Economics II. Then in European History. At lunch and dinner I'd see her in the cafeteria or walking through the halls surrounded by her friends – she'd be nestled in the middle of them, like the heart of a flower, shielded from the outside . . . from predatory seniors like me. All my political posturing, the clenched fists, all the issues that meant so much to me were suddenly forgotten, shoved rudely to the back of the stove. The plight of the proletariat was no longer important to me. I lived only to see her, to watch her in the centre of her friends.

I strained to hear her voice. I listened carefully and by using precise tuning, I was able to isolate it from the gaggle of other voices around her.

It was a low voice for a woman – low in volume, low in pitch – a voice that, like everything else about her, seemed to come from somewhere deep inside. When she laughed, her friends would laugh too, and by some mysterious transcendental linkage I would find myself laughing. Then I would catch myself and stop. What would she think of this ragged revolutionary, standing alone, laughing like an idiot?

She was a small and graceful girl, with short dark hair framing a pale face and very large enquiring eyes. Her complexion was flawless, and it was obvious she needed no make-up, yet her brows looked freshly pencilled in, and her mouth, always slightly parted and on the brink of a smile, looked freshly painted.

I lost track of my own identity. To hell with Martin Dies and his Un-American Activities Committee, the hell with marching for Northern Ireland, to hell with school! I was head over heels in love! My throat was dry, I was parched, I goggled at her, and my mouth hung open as though I was in the presence of a miracle. I stared at her from behind my beard like a homeless person, unaware that I looked like an unmade bed. Although I had never been closer to her than ten feet, my bloodhound senses had picked up the sight, the sound and the scent of her. Love had lent me a homing device that enabled me to predict where she would be, and I would be there before her, waiting to see, hear, and yes, even smell her. Who was this rare and beautiful creature? Where, within her, was her soul, the magic that made her different from any woman I'd ever seen? I had to have her! I had to have her to myself. Alone!

As she moved through the halls in the company of her male and female attendants, I began nodding to her, pretending we had met somewhere before. Ten or more times a day I would be there to nod and smile, hoping she would accept me as someone she knew. She gave me no sign or signal, but that didn't matter. My plan was to familiarise her with the sight of me, someone she might recognise in time. I had adopted the outward appearance of a Parisian poet of the late-eighteenth century (it was a very popular masquerade with serious young men in the summer of '39).

Later, I stood in front of my dormitory mirror and looked at the wretch I had become. I was filled with doubt. None of her friends looked as disreputable as me. They were clean-shaven, wore smarter clothes, and looked, as the saying used to go, "up and coming". There were hollow sockets where my eyes had been, I looked hunted, my clothes hadn't been to the laundry in weeks. I was a poignant, homeless figure yet she looked at me without disgust. Perhaps there was hope for me!

Love is a devious mistress. It teaches the lover to be crafty and cunning. With no trouble at all I stole *The Decline and Fall of the Roman Empire* from her open locker as we passed from European History to English Lit. As I held her book in my hand, I thought of her holding it in hers. Both our hands had held this book! Not at the same time, but almost, and if I used the scale of time in the book, it was as if we had held it together. I opened it and saw her name, *Property of Jennifer Hubble*. Her name had a sobering effect on me and I felt as though I had bullied my way into the sanctity of her family. The book carried a faint scent – something similar to rosemary. My book stank of stale cigarettes, like the rest of me. I felt I might contaminate her book if I kept it too long.

She had underlined certain passages with green pencil. Her underlining would venture timidly out into the margin, and once there she would write her notes in a controlled and delicate hand. Little circles above the i's, and j's. The belly of the loops under her y's and g's were pregnant with significance. Never had a lover learned so much from a book of history.

I burst through her phalanx of admirers. "Jenny! You left your book in history class!"

To this day I'm not certain if she believed me, but to her credit she accepted the book and smiled.

"Thank you . . ."

"Eliot."

"Thank you . . . Eliot."

It was a beginning, like the first step in an assault of Mt Everest. I'm sure there are better ways to begin, but we cannot create beginnings out of thin air, we are forced to use the materials we have. Romeo found Juliet at a ball, Tristan and Isolde were enemies until they drank a magic potion. As the pace of destiny quickened, and as the clouds of war thickened about us, this young man of twenty-one used his meagre store of wit and wisdom to gain the attention of Jennifer Hubble. She had, after all, spoken his name! She hadn't shrunk in revulsion at the sight of him. She simply said, "Thank you . . . Eliot"! Long after the encounter, I replayed the sound of my name as it came from her parted lips.

I took it as a signal to proceed. I checked myself in the dormitory mirror again and wondered where to begin. There was serious work to be done. A haircut, a trimming of the beard, and by all means a general scrubbing down of a body that had been too long in the trenches of left-wing commitment, sitting in damp-basement rallies, passing out manifestos on rainy street corners. After that, a little attention to the ragged clothing. My enthusiasm for the causes of the common man, the marches and ad hoc committees had faded away. I was walking on air with a song in my heart. I knew at last what made the world go round!

I wrote her a note.

Jenny, I must see you. It's very important. At the stone bench, by the lion, after the last lecture. OK? Eliot.

I agonised over that note. I used blank white paper, instead of something torn out of a notebook. I wanted to make it seem imperative (hence the "must"), yet I didn't want to alarm her. Most of all, by the asserted "important" nature of the note, I hoped she would break away from her coterie of attendants and see me alone. I slipped the note through the ventilation slots of her book locker.

I sat there on the hard cold bench wearing Rudy Westerman's forest-green cable-knit sweater and Charlie Brooke's new brown corduroy pants. That morning I sprung for my first haircut in more than a month, and spent my lunch break trimming my beard. As I sat on the bench by the stone lion under a threatening summer sky, I was aware of a few admiring glances from co-ed freshmen in their beanies. I had a mental image of myself as André Chénier, in his tumbrel, rattling along the cobbled streets of Paris on his way to the guillotine.

I sat there until dark, out of cigarettes and hungry as hell. I was forced to admit that my preparations had failed. What was of utmost importance to me was obviously of no concern to her. I rose stiffly from the cold stone bench, brushed the ashes from Rudy Westerman's sweater, and reluctantly headed for the school cafeteria. What if she were to suddenly appear after I left like the Governor's pardon arriving after the prisoner had been executed?

Wait a minute! Perhaps she had forgotten my name! That was it! She didn't know who "Eliot" was. How stupid of me! But then again, even if she didn't know, wouldn't she be curious enough to want to know . . . to pass by hurriedly with her ever-attendant group to see who was sitting on the stone bench? I had worked myself into a frenzy of doubt, madly infatuated, insanely obsessed with an unresponsive mistress. Yes, mistress! I could only compare myself to a dog who finds his mistress has abandoned him.

I sat alone in the cafeteria. Rudy Westerman came over and wanted his sweater back. After checking it for cigarette burns, he asked me how I made out.

"I didn't borrow it to make out, Rudy."

"Well, why didn't you wear your own, then?"

"None of your business."

"Huh! I guess not . . . You going to the meeting tonight?"

"What meeting?"

"The Red Guard, dummy! Lennie's basement. Mantell is speaking tonight. He's just back from Washington."

"I don't think so, Rudy. I've got to write a letter tonight."

"What's the matter with you anyway? You used to be a real torch-bearer. Now look at you. You got a haircut and a brand-new pair of pants and for a while there, you had a new sweater."

"The pants aren't mine, they're Charlie Brooke's. Have you got any cigarettes?"

Rudy shook his head at me and folded his sweater. He fished in his shirt pocket and pulled out a handful of these things he rolled himself on a machine he had brought from home. God knows what was in them. He said it was something that grew wild in a field in back of his father's house.

It was pretty obvious to me that I had passed into another dimension. The downtrodden masses would have to find someone else to carry their torch, at least until this situation with Jennifer Hubble was resolved. I was a non-active member of the Red Guard now. I sat there for a time planning my next, and probably most crucial step. It would have to be a letter. It would have to explain in intimate detail the agony I was going through, what she had done to me, what I was prepared to do if she . . . if she . . . Well, it would all have to get into the letter somehow.

The threatening summer sky had turned to rain, a very cold rain, and I could almost smell the wet raincoats in the basement meeting room under Lennie's bar in Collegetown. I managed to stay relatively dry on my way back to the dorm by ducking in and out of the buildings on campus. By the time I got back I had worked out the theme of the love letter in my head. I was determined that this as yet unwritten declaration would be a beacon to all those who love in the future.

It went surprisingly well. At 11 p.m. I slipped the six pages into a clean white envelope and sealed it. Almost immediately I slit the envelope open and read it again . . . I added a PS. I got another envelope and told myself that this was the last time, it was going to go like this or not at all. It was nearly midnight. The rain had stopped and I decided to walk the letter over to her dorm. The campus was deserted now. Even the security patrol had given up for the night.

In the vestibule of every dorm the school provided a large bulletin board which was used as a makeshift mailbox. It was the first thing the students checked going in and the last thing going out. I tacked it to the very centre of the board, making sure there was space all around it. She couldn't miss it in the morning. I had written that I would be at Lennie's every evening from nine to eleven at a table in the back of the room. I assured her that she had nothing to fear from me and it would be much better if she came alone.

My anguish throughout the next three days was indescribable. I saw her every day in class, tried to read her expression, search her mind. Between classes she remained in the centre of her friends, her bodyguards, all of them jockeying for position. Our eyes would catch every so often, but quickly the contact would be broken as though both of us had opened a door to a private room and feared to enter.

I drank everything Lennie had for sale, coffee, Coke, beer and even tea. Rudy Westerman, fresh from his Red Guard rallies downstairs, would come up and sit with me.

"We missed you last night, Eliot. Mantell was on fire. There's gonna be war, you know that, don't you?"

"Get away from me, I'm expecting somebody."

"I swear, man, you're goin' down the drain. Don't you care any more? Look at you! The world's comin' apart and you look like you didn't have a date for the prom."

"Got any more of those homemade cigarettes, Rudy?"

He gave me another handful and they helped to pass the time. In fact, after two or three you lost track of where you were. Lennie was closing up, letting down the wooden blinds and staring at me meaningfully. It looked as though my third night of waiting would be fruitless, but suddenly the door opened and there she was. Alone! She seemed much smaller alone. I stood and we looked at each other across the emptiness of the room.

"You two kids aren't plannin' to settle down here, are ya? I'm gettin' ready to shut down for the night." Lennie already had the lights down and the cook was taking out the trash.

"No, we're going. That all right with you, Jennifer?" She nodded. I hurried across the room and took her arm. She pulled away, she wasn't ready for that. How clumsy two people can be when they're in the first stages. We found ourselves out in the street in almost total darkness. The click of the lock and the catch of the bolt behind us meant we were on our own. We walked together back to the campus, an inch or two of emptiness carefully maintained between us. Finally, at the stone bench by the lion, I stopped.

"You read the letter?"

"Of course."

". . . and still you're here."

"Yes."

"I thought, maybe it was a little strong, that it might scare you. I'm too frank for my own good sometimes."

"It was, and you are, but still I'm here."

"Would you like to sit here a moment? It's hard to speak to you during the day, you're always . . . always . . ."

"I know, I can't help it, I seem to attract people."

I inched closer to her on the bench. "You know, I ask myself every day. 'What is Jennifer?' . . . Whatever you are, Jennifer, I can't live without you."

"You're being silly, I'm nothing. I don't know what you're expecting."

There was so much to say! It was so late! The college was sound asleep, and off to the east, Europe was on the brink of war! I wanted to say, "Damn it all to hell, Jennifer, hold your hands to your ears. Cup them like shells. Can't you hear it? It's the drums. There will be war, Jennifer, WAR! I think I have been born to fight in this war! Let us be together while there's still time." Instead, I made a decision that still mystifies me.

"I'm thinking of quitting school, Jennifer. I want to enlist."

"You're crazy! What for?" The library clock sounded 11.30. "Oh, my God! Look at the time. I've got to go, Eliot."

"There will be war very soon now. It will change everything."

"But graduation is in two months. Don't you want to graduate?" Without waiting for an answer, she ran off down the path to her dormitory.

I had managed somehow to bring out the most important things on my mind, love and war, but they accomplished nothing. She was interested in neither. I thought if I told her I was leaving, it might make a difference. It didn't.

We saw a lot of each other that final summer. Most of our day-to-day meetings were in the company of her devoted friends. I had little in common with them, and if I had been more honest with myself, I would have to say I had little in common with Jennifer. But I made her larger than life, and she could do no wrong. We would be alone on weekends. She did not shine as brilliantly on her own, she was a focal point and needed to be in a setting. She made no further attempt to keep me from enlisting. I hoped she would. I never would have made the commitment if I thought I had to go through with it. We grew no closer. There was an impenetrable barrier in her psyche that prohibited physical intimacy beyond what she considered permissible.

"We're too young, there's so much ahead of us. Be good, Eliot. Can't you be satisfied with what we have?" She would allow me to touch her here and there, but under strict control and a firm resolve not to venture into the fathomless depths into which I was so eager to plunge.

"Do you know what I'm going through, Jenny?"

"I guess so."

Her non-committal replies were torture. She wanted to take every step along the way. No shortcuts, every road to be followed to its destination before another road could be considered. Czechoslovakia fell, Austria fell, then the march into Poland. The skies grew darker and the drums grew louder. She was unaware of them, they were too far away for her to hear.

That was three years ago. Three years, going on thirty-three. It's been almost a year since I've heard from her, and I must admit, almost a year since I've written to her, or to anyone else for that matter. I've been so long at war that I've lost contact with home. My only friends, my family you might say, are the men I've been with from Messina to Anzio. Perhaps I shall write home some day, but for the moment I have no news to share. This tortured country is my home.

Jennifer and I made solemn promises to each other when I left, and I believe we meant to keep them, but when two people are young, they're not expected to keep promises for long, surely not in the face of war. Each day I find it more difficult to remember her. I can't see her face any more. Her photograph in my wallet is the face of a stranger. I have been certain for months now that it must be the same for her. I expect she has looked at my picture and wondered who this strange young man was and what has become of him. If we were to meet today on that stone bench by the lion, would we recognise each other?

Sezze is a quiet little Italian town on the coast road to Rome. Two days ago it was a flaming nightmare of tank and artillery fire. I thought there would be nothing left of it, but, glory be . . . ! The church still stands and Signor Marandella managed to reopen his little taverna in the square this morning. He let down a ragged, shrapnel-shredded awning to filter the warm Italian sun and he's selling the local wine, and an unmarked German beer in brown bottles with porcelain stoppers. The beer is warm, of course, and can be kept no colder than the water in the village pump but it is beer. How quickly civilisation sets in after the battle clears. A field hospital arrived early this morning along with Patton's senior staff, and the mail from home just came in. It looks like we're putting down roots.

It was here in Marandella's tavern that a letter came from Jennifer Hubble. Her careful writing in green ink, still with the little circles above the i's and j's . . . and the pregnant bellies of the y's and g's . . .

Dearest Eliot . . . it began. She never called me that before. . . . *I really don't know how to tell you this . . .*

If she didn't, she had an excellent teacher. It was skilfully written. My interest should have been greater than it was, I suppose I should have kept reading, but Signor Marandella broke in. He and his wife were overjoyed that the Americans and the British had taken back the town.

"It is sad that so many friends have perished, signor, yours and mine. You know 'morte'? But God is always with the victims, si? Those who live must go on, is that not so? I count myself among the most fortunate of men. Today I can offer you the wine of my village and the beer of the devil himself, if you prefer. If you will be patient, signor . . . my wife is preparing pasta and calamari."

. . . Peter is expecting his CPA licence in December . . . the marriage will be January 14th . . . the baby is due in early July. I wish it could have been different with you and me, Eliot, but I'm sure you understand.

Of course I do, Jenny. I didn't then, but I do now.

Digging for Victory
JUDE ELLERY

|||||||||||||||||||||||||||||||||||||||||||||||||||||||||||||||||||||||||||||||||||||||||||||||||||||||||||||||||||||||||||||||||

Marl and Oof scheme for the easy life on their island prison, but are they underestimating the guards? First published in Story Shack.

"We got nothing but our dignity in here and they're trying to steal that from under our noses."

Marl is screwing up his eyes and scratching his bald spot the way he does when he's thinking up a plan.

Oof is pretending to read while watching Marl from behind his book.

For a while the only sounds in the six by eight cell are Oof's heavy breathing and the flicking of cheap comic-book pages. Then Oof asks the question.

"What you got brewin', boss?"

Marl raises a finger to say he's not done yet, but soon enough he strolls over to the tiny window and gazes out through the iron bars like a double-shifting detective at a set of venetian blinds.

"This running scheme."

"Yeah boss?"

"It's the pits."

"Yeah boss."

"We screwed Warden Glynn's reading scheme by burning all them books they chucked our way, and we screwed his healthy-eating scheme by lunching on gruel for a month instead of them apples they had shipped in for us. We got nothing but our dignity in here and they're trying to steal that from under our noses. That ain't gonna happen on my watch. So we gotta screw this one too."

"I don't wanna do no runnin'."

"I can see that, Oof. I can see that and then some. Well then you listen up and you listen good. You see yesterday how Coach Saunders ran a tenth of the way then sat down to smoke?"

Oof nods. "Maybe not even that, Marl. He stopped before the big hill."

"Exactly. Stopped before that big damn hill. So here's the plan . . ."

* * *

Coach Saunders has been around the block. He's been in the forces and he's coached inter-prison sports teams for decades, but now he's getting long in the tooth and he wants an easy life. Not that the look on his grizzly old face would let on, mind. That's a face not even his mother loved.

Saunders is in before the cock can crow, ringing his bell and hollering for this lazy pack of swine to get on up and out, the weather's fine and there's ground to be covered, sweat to be sweated. He's pouring water on the slow ones who can't make it up, let alone out, and spitting insults in their faces when they're lined up in the yard. He gives Oof a whack in the belly and Oof goes "oof" and the boys all laugh.

Sanchez is the only one missing in action. He's laid up in the infirmary with a gammy foot. Rumour has it the amount of time – and taxpayers' money – the inmates spend with the nursing staff is half the reason behind this new health push that's come from the top. Spend a little, save a lot, is Warden Glynn's motto.

Soon enough the boys are being put through their paces and, same as yesterday, Saunders jogs the first few hundred yards then lets up. When he's down to a walk he rolls up as he goes, then settles down in a patch of grass under a shady tree. Striking a match on the bark, he lights up, leans back and watches his crew disappear over the hill. He's had his pair of dogs sniff the boys good and proper before they set off so there's no chance of temporary escape. He even had Oof roll up his sleeve to show what these two can do when they catch you.

Over the other side of the hill, Marl is whispering to his boys.

"Smiddy, Sooty, you run on. Saunders can't see past his nose but if by chance he does come over he'll wanna spot some shapes in the distance."

"Aw but –"

"No buts, you run to the beach and back like good boys. We'll rotate the runners each day, apart from Oof here whose ticker ain't too clever. Besides, he's good for digging."

Oof grins and whips the spade out from his unders. He's carved his food tray into a triangle and it'll do for a start.

"Right boys. Let's get at it."

By the time Saunders is done with his smoke and is stretching his legs for a stroll up the hill, the boys have got a little overhang going where they can hide from the sun and the prying eyes of interfering coaches. Lucky for them Saunders has left his dogs tied back at the tree where they're happily marking their turf. The leather-faced old-timer peers at the horizon where he sees some dots getting smaller. He turns and goes back to his dogs.

Down below, Marl is whispering again.

"Good work boys, grand job. We'll cut cards later for who's on the run tomorrow, but for now let's sit back and enjoy the peace and quiet."

"Can't we pop out for a bit, enjoy the sun and blue skies?" asks one of the younger ones.

"Oh that's a mighty fine idea. Get caught by Saunders and screw the whole plan before we've even got going. You keep your ideas to yourself and toe the line and we might just do this."

No one else has got any more big ideas.

Marl's drawn up plans for a proper little lair: foyer, corridor, gaming room and all. He knows a thing or two about digging tunnels – after all, it was tunnelling out of the last joint that got him shipped to this island prison in the first place – and reckons all it'll need is a little skill and a lot of elbow grease.

* * *

Four days later and it's all plain sailing so far.

Oof is a little peckish because he can only eat what'll fit in his porridge bowl, since he transformed his lunch tray into a spade. The Baker brothers are getting a little edgy because they haven't had a smoke in a while, on account of trading their stash for iron rods to hold up the main tunnel. A few of the others have made their own little sacrifices for tools too, spades, buckets and what have you.

But it's all fine and dandy.

The ground's soft as you'd like, more like digging a tunnel through sand than dirt. Rocks are few and far between and Marl's put the boys a day ahead of schedule already.

Saunders has let his dogs off the lead a couple of times but clever Marl spent his last few coins on some state-of-the-art juice that conceals your natural odour. He could only get his hands on a couple of cans but by his reckoning when they're further along they'll be able to scrimp on that expense because dogs can't smell through twenty feet of dirt too well.

* * *

Two weeks into the running programme and the boys have done it.

Oof's lost two stone and he's feeling like a new man. The Baker brothers have given up for good, and they've never breathed better in all their days. Sanchez even joined in near the end having been let out, doing the easier tasks like ferrying the dirt, cleaning the spades, and covering the hole at the end of the day, and he says getting the blood flowing round his foot again's done it a world of good.

All in all the boys have never been in better shape. Marl's even been trying to catch sight of the back of his head in the little mirror above the sink. He'd swear all this exercise has got his hair growing again at the crown.

So, they're shaking hands and patting each other on their aching backs and getting dirt all in their hair as they stoop to get into the main chamber on grand opening day. They have a sit around and play some cards to celebrate their moral victory, but the light's none too good and everyone suspects everyone else of cheating. The game doesn't last long. Then the runners are back and it's time to call it a day anyhow.

In the Warden's office Saunders is sitting, laid back in a padded chair with one leg folded over the other. The expensive-looking cigar in his fingers is burning nicely and if his nose hadn't been shot to pieces by mustard gas he'd be telling you it smelled real good.

"I'm impressed with them, tell you the truth, Warden. Thought they'd be another week at least, but every one of them's lost weight and gained muscle. Nurse ran all the tests this morning. We've hit our targets and then some."

Over the other side of the mahogany table, Warden Glynn's looking especially pleased with himself.

"I think that'll do for the 'running' programme then, Saunders. Getting them to dispose of all those thousands of old books for free and sneaking vitamins into the gruel were crafty ideas if I say so myself, but getting you in for this one is the best yet. You've earned that, you take a good drag."

Saunders does as he's told. The ceiling's beginning to collect smoke and he feels like he's made it to the exclusive gentlemen's club he's always dreamed of. Then Glynn offers him a glass of the good stuff and he knows for sure. Better still, he feels like he fits right in.

"Yessir, fill her up, now."

The two men clink their glasses and take a long sip.

"Now, Saunders, let's see if we can't work out how we're going to afford to give you a permanent contract. I could do with a right-hand man."

"That one's easy, sir. I been selling the boys in Block H cans of tap water to conceal their scent from Sparks and Rosie. As long as your plumbing holds up I reckon we're good for cash. Oh and I've already started a new hygiene programme with the boys. Hope you don't mind my being so forward."

Glynn winks and shakes his head and the two old men chink glasses again. Meanwhile, down the corridor and around a few bends, two inmates are deep in conversation long after lights out.

"I ain't primpin' myself up like some old doll on her way to Sunday service every time Saunders calls round."

"Quite right, Oof. So here's the plan . . ."

East
CAMERON SUEY

||||||||||||||||||||||||||||||||||||||||||||||||||||||||||||||||||||||||||||||||||||||||||||||||||||||||||||||||||||||||||||||||||||

A mysterious Storm saps energy from the world and chews mountains out of existence, and one man is determined to outrun it.

"I reach the top of the pass, and start looking for a good place to die. I find something else."

t's been a long time since I've seen the Storm.

It's always been there, behind us, whispering through the shuddering ground. A background roar behind the wind. We'd been ahead for so long, moving faster than its clockwork crawl. Until the mountains. Then, as we ground ourselves upward against these slopes, we heard it rumbling closer, a rising quake in the earth.

But it's been a while since I turned around and actually saw it. Sitting here, on the side of the mountain, in the frigid morning, it fills my vision and stings my eyes with its monstrous unreality.

It rises like an unbroken wall into the sky, obscured only by the limits of my sight, fading into the clear blue, and stretching away north and south, curving away with the earth. The sunlight doesn't touch it. Nothing does. At the ground, where the churning wall of sickly blue lightning and black clouds grinds across the earth, I can see the Unmaking. The lower peaks, already shaking apart, burst and ablate away at the event horizon of the Storm. The land dips before the onslaught, as if shying away from the kiss of the boiling wall. I can feel the violence beneath my feet as millions of tons of ancient mountain fall away into its infinite maw.

It's going to be on me in a few hours. I wonder if I'll die when the peak caves away, crushed in a free-fall of slate and stone, or whether I'll be alive when the Storm touches me, shredded and atomised, erased and Unmade. I wonder, again, what it might feel like.

My joints wail as I stand up from the sharp rocks, and my left ankle cries in agony as the bruised bones click. I turn my back on the Storm, and look forward, at the last mile of road curving up into the pass. I walk, moving east along the weathered pavement, feeling the rising vibrations of the Storm in each step.

Trying not to dwell on the pain of my grinding ankle, I think about the state fair, a sweltering summer a decade ago, and a machine with a footplate that vibrated for a quarter. I think about the wonderful, almost unpleasant intensity of the sensation. I hold on to this memory, working it in my mind like a lump of sugar, until I have savoured all I can from it. The wind is on my face. Even the air seems to be rushing away towards the wall.

I will be walking when it comes, still moving, just not quite fast enough in the end. But I can make it to the top.

Not for the first time, it staggers me to think it's only been a month since the lights first went out. Nearly a month ago I was riding a bus, a bus . . . on a Wednesday night, back when such a thing mattered.

I remember the feel of it, as the end passed over us. A quiet sigh rippling through the air. The engine stalled, and the lights flickered out, but there was no panic. My fellow passengers remained quiet, and we waited for the inevitable restart of the engine that never came. I stared out the windows, and after too long a moment, it dawned on me that every light across the street was out as well.

Then came the explosions. Popping in the distance, like faraway fireworks. We pushed our way out the back doors of the bus and poured out into a mercifully cool July evening.

The stars were shining with an intensity that scared me more than the explosions, bitter and cold. We all spent a moment intent on phones and handsets that didn't work, wouldn't turn back on, before sliding them away to be forgotten, for ever. Something streaked overhead towards the west. Silent, leaving a smoking trail thrown into sharp relief by its brilliance, the blazing meteor passed over us and disappeared beyond the horizon. A few moments later, a tinny rumble rolled back across the valley.

The bus driver stopped trying to restart the engine and joined the knot of passengers. We gathered close, struck mute by the strange way that the world had changed. Shooting stars streaked above, a meteor shower come too early in the year.

For ten minutes we stood, silent. When the only sound left was our nervous breath and the baying of dogs, someone made a joke I don't now recall, but we laughed like children passing a graveyard, nervous and harsh.

We walked home, strangers sharing names we hadn't bothered to on the bus, names I could not remember the next day. I turned away towards my apartment, and I never saw any of them again.

I imagine in suburbs across the small town, neighbours were standing on their porches and front lawns in robes and slippers, dead flashlights in hand, trading theories and comforting each other. But the apartment complex I'd landed in when I'd moved out of Gayle's house was quiet and dark. Not even the emergency lights were on, and I took my time, fumbling through the dark halls and into the cave of my studio.

I desperately wanted to talk to someone, to share information, and to try to make sense of what had happened. The complete loss of electrics pointed to a nuclear detonation, but the explosions seemed so distant and too small to be the bogeyman of my parents' generation.

In the light of the day, it was stranger still. There was an almost pleasant shift in the community, as walkers ferried information from neighbourhood to neighbourhood, certainly much of it distorted, but much of it unmistakably true. Batteries didn't have a charge, anywhere. Pacemakers had stopped, dragging down their owners. Everything with an electric current had failed.

Fire had trouble starting. It wasn't colder, but nothing wanted to burn. Lighters worked only rarely, and their flames were weak and anaemic. We made great bonfires to test this strange new truth, and with some effort they lit, flickering low and blue, but fundamentally wrong.

On the second day, from a man on a bicycle, we got the explanation for the first night's explosions. Airplanes gliding downward, dead and dark, had impacted across the valley and beyond. The falling stars had been satellites, he said, the whole network simply dropping from the sky.

It was like some essential measure of energy had been withdrawn from the world, some internal engine of the universe was winding down. It scared me far more than nukes.

None of us knew what to do. We ate the food we had before it spoiled, and stores were empty by the second day, everything sold for cash only. In some last, defiant show of togetherness, prices stayed flat in almost all the stores, and I traded what little currency I had for several crates of bottled water.

We planned on waiting it out. We didn't understand that this was not an interruption, but a terminus.

There were rumours at first, by the end of the first week. Ragged and tired people drifted through town, in search of water and food, and bearing wide-eyed, apocalyptic warnings. They told of mass exodus, a mad flood of people streaming away from the western coastline. Terrifying stories, told in whispers, spoke of a Storm. None of the first refugees had seen it first hand, but what they had learned had scared them badly enough to start heading inland.

In those first days of flight, the human tide followed the major highways, and our small town received only the odd stragglers, those fleeing not only the fabled Storm, but the rivers of atrocity that the refugee march had become. We had no way of knowing if it was just amplification of nightmare rumours, or if the interstates heading east really had become a vast trampling ground, where urban populations surged inland without plan or recourse, shredding and churning against one another, fleeing the Storm.

People started to disappear in the next few days, spooked enough by the mad tales to start their own exodus and to avoid the main highways. My own feet felt light, but I waited. Held off, until the last wave.

They were wild and glassy-eyed, the last refugees, the ones who had waited, like me, in small towns further west. They had seen the surging sea of refugees, seen the corpse-trails they left, had heard of the Storm that had made landfall at last, but they had waited, holding out hope that this was only a temporary insanity.

But then they saw the Storm, with their own eyes, and it was a testament to the madness of it all that the eyewitnesses' stories were more fevered and impossible than the secondhand rumours that preceded them.

I was packed, ready to go, the last of my water tucked in with a camp stove and a sleeping bag in a backpack, when the last wave came, but I didn't leave yet. I waited, one more day, until I saw it for myself.

It came up over the western horizon with the dawn, as if rising to challenge the sun in the east, swallowing all light. Over the course of three hours, I watched it Unmake the foothills, swallowing earth, forest, and river. The world rose up and away, seeking oblivion like a lover, vanishing for ever into the churning wall of impossible madness, leaving only bursts of blue lightning arcing between the black clouds.

Lightning, clouds. Storm. These are imperfect metaphors.

The Storm of the Unmaking isn't a storm, it isn't made up of the things storms are made up of. There are no clouds, no lightning, only seething darkness and jagged energy. I'm not even sure now, as it polishes the earth away behind me, if I can even see it. Maybe our brains fill in the ghosts of recognisable structures. Maybe it only looks like the nothing that it is, and our eyes simply cannot accept this.

Tucker used to say to his followers, when the lines began to be drawn, that it was the mouth of God. That someday we could accept it, and we would see through the black veil of the Storm and see the divine feast for what it really was.

When there was only the open valley between me and the Storm, I fled my home, heels pounding country roads, until I reached the refugees of the last wave, somewhere in the central valley, and it was with that small band of stubborn fools, the ones who had waited until they too had seen the Storm, that I travelled for the last three weeks.

Tucker was there, quiet at first, shaken by the loss of someone he loved on the charnel highways, but then there were no leaders, and all of us were scarred. We shared supplies, gathering canned goods at country gas stations and parcelling them out. We outpaced the Storm in the day, spent short quiet nights laughing around a pitiful campfire, awakening always with the Storm on the horizon. Each day, we pulled ahead of it, following the un-trails of the refugees ahead of us, turning always away from the spoor of abandoned belongings, and the fly-choked corpses. This way, we found the untapped stores and caches, the things people left behind. We were frightfully inefficient in those first days, but we did more than just survive, and it gave us hope.

Then we washed into the foothills, and we slowed. We had built up a lead on the Storm, had a few mornings where we hadn't seen it on the horizon, only felt the low bass notes of its presence. That little hope and good cheer we had built up in our advance evaporated.

Two nights into the steady uphill climb, a dented can of soup made three of our number ill. We lingered for too long in the morning as they emptied their guts, and the Storm crested the edge of the world. A quiet sort of panic gripped us all, and we took to the country backroads again, driven by the fresh reminder of the encroaching end.

Tucker took the shepherd's mantle and drove us on, moving faster than before, and when the three sickened members of our troop lagged behind, Tucker called to them that we would go ahead, they should take their time, and we would make camp for them and wait before leaving. No one believed the lie, but we all played our part, even the dead men, with patient nods and glassy eyes. They never arrived that night, and we left even earlier than before.

Tucker kept us moving, and the group turned their shipwreck faces towards him. We all wanted to leave the sick men behind, but Tucker had done it. In this passive act of consensual murder, we turned our fate over to him willingly. By the end of another week, as we reached the base of the jagged mountains, Tucker began to carry less and less, and ate more and more.

The mountains broke us.

Our speed halved. The roads wound away from our direction, away from the rising sun, and no one had a map, or remembered which pass through the mountains was the most direct.

We were forced into the footsteps of the first great waves of refugees, and now the roadsides were choked with the sick and the dead. Rows and rows of naked blackened feet, picked clean of socks and shoes, stuck out from the roadside grass. I scavenged there, pulling a pair of boots from the feet of a prone man about my height, trying first to ignore his feeble dying groans, then whispering my apologies to him as he rasped for breath. It was impossible to tell how many of the original refugees had made it this far, or had gone on up the mountains, but there was no food to be had in their trail, little water to be plundered.

Tucker drove us on, and soon he began to preach, simple little sermons of necessity and absolution for what we'd done and would do, and it drove the jagged wedge at last into the group. From a loose band of strangers with a common goal, we became Tucker's people, and the others, and that divide grew cold and icy.

I suppose the line was the same as the night we left the three sick men behind; there were those that couldn't sleep that night, and those that could. It would be easy, and a filthy lie, to draw a moral line in that split. We were all good men, once. We all left them behind, no one objected. The divide between Tucker's people and the rest of us was a matter of who still had energy to feel guilt, and who had just enough to follow what they saw as their best and only hope.

It was Tucker who was in charge of the supplies, of the nightly division of food. Before I realised what had happened it was too late.

Tucker's people held stubbornly to their health, and the rest of us began to wane. A little less water, fewer crucial calories. As the cold and the altitude made the journey harder, Tucker tightened his control on our bodies, and we withered.

We were all so profoundly tired that we couldn't even communicate our nascent paranoia to one another, until we began to drop away, falling behind, while no one had the strength to look back. One by one, until, near the top of the pass, there was only Tucker's folk, and me.

They had already started sleeping apart from us, striking camp earlier, and quieter. Two nights ago, I awoke to find them a hundred metres down the road, none of them looking back. I caught up with them, and no words were exchanged, but Tucker caught my eye from the front, his body unladen, free, and frighteningly healthy.

Last night, near the top of the pass, I couldn't sleep, as the chill terror of what I had allowed to happen coursed through me, twisting with the bitter cold of the mountain night. Tucker was awake as well, and sometime in the dark, he walked over to where I sat, my ragged camping mattress pressed to a rock in a crude chair. He sat beside me, his cold eyes reflecting colder starlight, and we said nothing. We hadn't spoken in nearly a week, and in truth, I think only Tucker had spoken for the last few days. Above us the night was silent, a sky devoid of planes, unblemished by the lights of man. In the distance, the Storm must have been visible, but I had stopped trying to see it.

After what felt like an hour, Tucker sighed, and stood, staring down at me, a black silhouette against a cobalt sky. I think he may have smiled, it was hard to tell. He raised his foot, and brought the heel down, hard, on my ankle. Once, and then again, before I had the chance to scream.

My cries woke no one, and Tucker walked back to his place in the warm centre of the sleeping people. I wanted to stand, to bash his skull in, but as the sharp splinters of pain became a low throbbing ache, I found no strength to stand, no will or capacity for murder, only the surrender of sleep.

When I awoke this morning, they were gone, far over the pass. By my feet, someone had left one bottle of water, and one tin of meat. Nothing to live off, but this token gesture of mute apology was all that allowed me to stand, all that got me to face the Storm with any sort of dignity.

And now, I walk towards the top of the pass, to look down over the other side before I die. In one hand is the water, and the other, the tin of meat, my backpack left somewhere below. I carry them like little talismans, one last reminder that we are not all Tucker. That we are all ourselves. Even if none of that matters.

I reach the top of the pass, and start looking for a good place to die. I find something else, something that proves better than death: a trail of blood droplets on the pavement, leading to or from an alpine field of boulders. On either side of the blood droplets, I see faint tyre tracks in the stony gravel.

The trail leads to a tableau of bodies and blood spattered under the clear sky. It's not what happened here that fills me with black joy, but what was left behind.

In the morning sunlight is an honest-to-God truck, an old yellow Datsun, more rust than metal. Three of the tyres are flattened, mere shreds of greying rubber around bent and pitted rims. At the front, lashed to the bumper, are the remains of a harness, where a team of horses were once hitched. Three of the horses are a few yards away, dragged from the truck to be butchered. Their carcasses are stripped clean, first by men and then by the vultures that dot the sky above every road.

In the back of the truck are what remains of a cache of water and food. All that's left are a few torn and cracked plastic bladders, whatever invaluable liquid they once held long ago abandoned to the arid sky. The truck bears many small wounds as well, evidence of the gunfight that killed the two men at my feet.

In between the vulture's furrows, their death wounds read like scripture, declaring the changed nature of our dying world. Robbed of the full power of the focused force of combustion, bullets still are deadly. But instead of piercing, these shots pushed great shallow craters into their flesh. Both these men took many shots before they succumbed to their wounds.

In the cab of the truck, lies the last corpse. His chest flattened and shredded, his eyes staring and milky. His skin is not quite as blackened as the others, and he bears only the one wound. In his hand, he still clutches a revolver, as if still warding off attackers in death. Dried black blood, as sticky as oil, pools in the seat.

I take the gun from the driver, check to find two bullets remaining, and see in them two chances of taking back my destiny from the Storm. For a long minute, I am drunk on the idea of spitting into the Unmaking as I send one slow bullet hammering into the thinnest part of my skull. I live this moment over and over again, even as I feel the ground shudder with the Storm's approach.

That's when I hear the frightened exhale and dry breath of the fourth horse. He's moved out from behind wherever he was hidden, and he stands fifty yards away, across the road, shredded ropes dangling from his twisted harness and bridle. He flicks his head towards me, and then to the oncoming wall of the Storm, and stamps his feet with fear and frustration, eyes rolling back and showing white.

I ignore the screaming in my ankle, don't even hear it after a dozen paces as I lope and vault towards the speckled grey beast. My sudden lurching approach seems to baffle him as much as the absurd horror approaching in the sky, and he manages to take a few panicked steps back, whinnying in terror before I reach him. I grab at the rope, miss, and then lunge forward again. He tries to rear up and away, but my fingers close on the frayed nylon cord and I close tight with a death grip. I can feel the layers of flesh on my palm abrading away as the horse screams, uncomfortably like a woman's voice, and whips its head from side to side. I hold fast, and scream right back, my eyes just as wild. I roar at the beast, and he shrieks back, and I feel naked and alive in a way I can't ever recall.

Close now, I hear a shuddering crack, as the bones of the world fall away into the mouth of the Storm, and I hold fast at my only chance to live. The horse is wasted, his ribs showing through tattered speckled hide, but he was once a massive beast. I curse and scream at him, and his struggling stops as he surrenders.

Mounting the animal proves the hardest task of all; even as he submits to my will, it takes a great and painful effort to lunge and throw my body up and over his unsaddled back. I manage to drape myself across his spine, the protruding vertebrae pressing into my empty stomach. With some effort, thanks only to the beast's state of exhaustion, fear and malnourishment, I throw my wounded leg up and over, and I rise into a hunched seated position, my bleeding hand still pulling tight on the bridle.

Less than a mile away is God's maw, the slow, chewing event horizon of the Unmaking that shreds ancient mountains like transient summer weeds. I dig my heels into protruding ribs and turn away, to buy myself just a little more time.

The horse needs little encouragement. We descend the downhill side of the pass, away from the Storm. I stroke the tattered mane beneath my fingers, and I'm unsurprised to find myself crying as I whisper my thanks. Soon, we're moving at a steady trot, putting the peak behind us, and once again advancing away from the Storm.

I allow the horse to stop a few times, as he sniffs out thin highland grasses and a few pools of melted snow missed by my tribe on the way down, and I even dismount to drink greedily from the standing water. In my parched haste, I drop the nylon rope, leaving behind a layer of skin and setting the horse free, but he waits for me. I'd like to attribute this to some sort of mutual survivor loyalty, but I see only empty eyes, already filming over as the overtaxed body begins to shut down.

The horse carries me another dozen miles before he dies, but not before we pass my tribe. They look mutely up at me, the pistol tucked in my belt. Some wear masks of fear, some lower their eyes in guilt, but most simply look with flat faces, as if they expected me to return at any moment, neither pleased nor surprised. I don't know what I in turn expect of them, but the reunion is as hollow as it is comforting. I bear them no ill will, and expect nothing from them beyond their essential human presence.

I reserve one small smile for Tucker, all gritted teeth and bloodless gums, as I pass. He keeps his expression blank and cool, but I see the flaring nostrils and the tremor at the corner of his lips. Then I ride on, leaving them behind for a short while to collect my thoughts and to turn away from the business of today's survival, to think about tomorrow.

A mile or so later, the horse falls to his knees and shudders once, before toppling over. I am thrown to the road and tumble without grace, skidding and rolling and grateful that my people aren't here to see me go down. The horse breathes four last ragged breaths, and I whisper my thanks to glassy and clouding eyes.

By the time my tribe catches up to me, near dark, I've started a weak fire from mountain brush, and have begun to cut the stringy meat from the flanks of my horse. They come towards me, mouths watering at the spicy scent of concentrated blood splashing to the stones, and a few produce knives to take up the work of butchering.

Tucker stands away from the knot of silent people, people that are no longer his. Arms limp at his sides, his body is unladen with supplies or water, naked and alone. There is no expression on his face, nor on mine as I approach him. Few of our tribe even turn to look; most are too busy or too exhausted to care what is about to happen. None of it will be a surprise, least of all to Tucker or myself.

He nods to me, dipping his head to the ground for a long and quiet moment, before turning to look backwards. We've made good time on the downhill side, and only the churning clouds in the high atmosphere signal the presence of the Storm. The ground no longer shudders. Once again, we've outpaced the Storm by one more day. But you can still feel it, in the air, and in your bones. I know that's where Tucker is looking. It holds his attention for a long time.

He turns back, mouth parted as if to speak, and I fire the pistol. The weak popping sound of the shell seems to vanish instantly, but the fat, wide bullet cracks the centre of Tucker's face like a lead fist. Everything caves inward towards the impact as the slow bullet dissipates its wan force across the delicate arches and filaments of his skull. He coughs as he falls, once, from his ruined mouth, sending a fine mist of blood into the air. From the ground, he blinks his one remaining eye, looking straight up at nothing, and although I think about leaving him there, I kneel and press the barrel to his temple. His eye closes and he sighs, a strangely musical sound in the absolute quiet of the evening. Muffled, the second shot barely makes a sound beyond a wet thump.

I pile a few rocks onto Tucker, the empty gun laid on his chest, making his cairn where he fell. A few of my tribe come to assist me. There is no guilt in me, or the tribe. There is no malice in the murder, and no hatred in its aftermath. It is simply a correction, a balancing of the sums, another step along a very long path. I take Tucker's boots, the high ankle serving as the basis for a simple brace made of nylon rope from the horse's bridle.

When we are done, when the horse meat is dried and packed away, and we have slept through the silent night, we turn our backs to the burial, and to the Storm, and Tucker's name is never mentioned again. We move on. We keep walking.

As we cross the arid highlands between the great spines of the country, we learn. Small towns still have food, and we learn to carry supplies efficiently, distributing the weight. Nearly every home has gallons of fresh water in the back of each toilet, and plastic bottles in abundance. We learn to carry the perfect amounts of water from one stop to the next, maximising our speed. Libraries have, among other things, books on edible plants, and we begin grazing, pulling what meagre calories we can. We carry less, we burn less energy, we walk farther. We become long and lean like gazelle.

The world is empty. We meet a few lone people who never saw the great waves of refugees, never knew what happened after the blackout, and we invite them with open arms, and tell them of the Storm. Not all come, not all believe the wild tales of these strange-eyed nomads, and we don't blame them, we simply walk on.

It would seem many of the people of the heartland headed for the bigger cities when the lights went off, hoping for strength in numbers, or to bind their fate to organisations that had already crumbled. Every city is a perpetual pillar of smoke and a vast killing field. We give them a wide berth, ranging instead through the open fields, through the breadbasket of the country.

We don't know what happened to the first refugee waves that came before us. The signs of their passing become harder to see. As they diminished and ate each other alive, maybe all that washed across the plains ahead of us were ragged ghosts, gibbering about the impossible Storm.

They don't matter any more. Only our tribe matters, and we have learned to survive where they did not, and we have a long way yet to go.

We have outpaced the Storm, so far ahead of it that it would take a full week for it to catch us, and this serves us well. We sleep better, we harden and we travel faster. We plan.

When we reach the ocean in the east, sometime in the world's last autumn, when we can walk no further, we will need time to search. We tear pages from books and study them obsessively, learning everything we can about the ocean, about boats and sailing. We will find whatever tall-masted vessels we can, and we will resume our eastward journey on the wind. We will go as far as we can, until we reach land again.

Failing that, we will wade into the waves, and swim, until the Storm takes us.

Even Steven
O. D. HEGRE

Dr Steven Sampson, a rich pharmaceutical consultant, happens upon a dark company secret.

> "Orchids, blondes, and the Pacific: a synchronicity that had brought him to this point in his life."

Steven Sampson stood, staring down at the desktop; the clutter was gone. Sunlight glinted off its mahogany finish. Only three things remained. Steven sat down, picked up the stack of emails, letting the pages riffle through his fingers.

"Idiots."

If the shit hit the fan in the future, he'd be long gone – somewhere in the south of France. He was damn lucky one of the nimrods had inadvertently copied him on the internal emails. He'd begun moving the money a month ago.

Steven reached over and grabbed the prescription container. Of the thousands of candidate drugs explored by the pharmaceutical industry each year, fewer than a couple hundred went on to lab and animal testing. After years of work – examining pharmacokinetics, safety, etc. – just a few qualified to move into the clinic. In the end, only one in five drugs that ever started human testing in a Phase One clinical trial received FDA approval and hit the market.

Steven shook the little bottle; the pills inside rattled about. His basic research had led to one of those rare successes and he had spent years helping to commercialise Placade. It had made him rich and with time it was going to make him disgustingly wealthy ... maybe. But there was a problem.

Steven shoved the container along with the stack of emails into his briefcase. A week after he found out, he had tendered his resignation using his wife's health as an excuse for his early retirement. It was an easy sell. Today, at the retirement party, he had said goodbye to his colleagues and staff at BioEudora. Tonight he was flying back home to Arizona. He'd fit in better with the locals now, he thought – carrying a gun. A smoking gun. Steven forced a smile.

He'd considered informing the rest of the management team ... for a moment. In the end, he knew it would come back to him. Those bastards would make him the fall guy. Maybe they would be right but that wasn't going to happen. He'd been sitting on the information for two months and now he had made up his mind.

Steven picked up the only thing that remained on the desktop – Stephen King's latest volume of short stories. Might get one in on the flight back to Tucson, he thought. His mind stalled for a moment – back where he would have to deal with Margot.

There was a soft rap on the door.

Steven looked up at the redhead, peering in the doorway.

"Your car is here, Doctor –" The woman's voice cracked.

Steven could see the tears welling in her eyes. "Thanks –"

He no more than got the word out and she was hugging him.

"I'm ... we're all going to miss you so, Doctor Sampson." The words sputtered from her full lips.

"Now Carrie ..." Steven patted her slender shoulders. She was pretty and with the body of a twenty-eight-year-old; Steven had, on a number of occasions, released his pent up needs with her large breasts in mind. "I'm going to miss you as well," and he squeezed her a little tighter.

"Looks like we lucked out on the traffic this afternoon, Doc." The driver's voice broke the silence.

Steven stared out at the commercial sprawl along the 405. Once the land of orange groves and strawberry fields, a lot had changed in the Irvine area – and in Steven – since he joined BioEudora. He thought back to a time of altruism ... to a time when he'd committed himself to helping people ... a time when he saw himself as an adversary of the pharmaceutical industry rather than a co-conspirator.

As a young botanist with a PhD in ethnobiology, Steven studied how primitive societies made use of their indigenous plants for medicinal benefit – poultices, tinctures, herbal concoctions developed over time by trial and error. Experience had convinced him that, with appropriate effort, naturally occurring products could replace a large number of prescription drugs. The active factors in over half of patented medicines were derived from the environment, like the first statin compound from the fungus Aspergillus terreus, and salicin, the basis of Aspirin, from the bark of the willow tree. The list went on and on.

"Got a Sigalert, Doc." The intercom crackled again. "Going to avoid the traffic and take Jamboree Road. Don't want you late."

The chance of untoward side effects always existed with anything you ingested. For natural products, much of their complex chemistry and metabolism remained undefined. The Big Pharmas claimed to reduce the side effects for their products by rigorous industry standards of purification. The public wanted to believe their drug suppliers – they needed their products and reluctantly paid outrageous prices for the assurance of safety as well as efficacy.

Steven knew there were no guarantees and he had come to terms with the hopelessness of it all. The conspiracy between the government and the pharmaceutical industry put a mountain of regulations in the way of getting any natural compounds approved. And even if approved and then regulated, what incentive remained to market them? Patents stood little chance – and without them the opportunity for big profits did not exist. Altruism remained a grand concept but money ruled.

The limo pulled up to the kerb.

"Thanks, Ralph. Might see you in a month or so." Steven had acquiesced to the Board's request that he continue to act as a consultant. He had no intention of fulfilling that obligation.

"You have a good one, Doc."

The two shook hands. No need to tip the company driver. Ralph lived in Laguna Niguel and received enough stock options each year to rent a slip at Dana Point for his twenty-four-foot catamaran. All staff got stock options at BioEudora. And they were worth plenty because of Dr Steven Sampson and Placade.

As Steven made his way into the terminal the loudspeaker blared its incessant message: "The White Zone is for the loading and unloading of . . ." Christ, he wouldn't have to listen to that again. At that moment, Steven realised the depth of his sense of relief. He was making the right decisions – with Margot and with the company. For a moment he put the day's worries aside; a new freedom lay before him.

Steven proceeded towards the bank of elevators. At midweek, one expected a light crowd. Still, as he passed under the statue of The Duke, a young woman managed to bump into him, her carry-on rolling over his foot. "Damn," he mumbled.

The woman grunted an apology as she rushed by.

The corporate VIP lounge overlooked the far end of the main runway at John Wayne Airport. Out to the southwest the lights of Newport Beach twinkled and beyond that . . . Balboa Island and then the darkness of the Pacific. Steven leaned back into the soft leather, cradling his second Scotch. He looked down at his scuffed shoe – a bit of bad luck.

The clock above the reception desk read 5.50 p.m. He was a little early; Mike would come and get him. Ice tinkled. He glanced down at the reception desk. During his career as a botanist, Steven had developed a fascination with the orchid family. A beautiful arrangement of Phalaenopsis amabilis and spiral bamboo now blocked his view of the blonde concierge. Steven sipped his drink. Orchids, blondes, and the Pacific: a synchronicity that had brought him to this point in life.

He looked down at his empty glass. He'd skipped lunch with all the turmoil – better only have three.

The blonde in his life? Margot . . . his wife. The young anthropology graduate student had convinced him to join her department's mission across the Pacific. It was an easy sell; they were screwing like bunnies and the idea of the two of them running around naked in an Indonesian forest completely captivated him.

The National Science Foundation supported the mission, designed to study the Kombai – the tree people of Papua New Guinea. Margot had called his attention to the Kombai women's use of an orchid poultice to soothe colicky infants and children with minor cuts and scrapes. They chewed the root of the plant, then spread the mash onto the child's forehead providing almost instant relief. Steven made the observation of the native women's changed demeanour. Most had no problem ingesting some of the orchid root as they developed the mash – a mild euphoria accompanied by intermittent drowsiness. But some individuals were prone to narcolepsy, dropping into a deep sleep after chewing the plant. Their mothers or sisters had to assume the chore. What was clear: All the "chewers" exhibited a transient insensitivity to pain.

Steven settled back to enjoy his third drink.

He was convinced that the physiological activity of naturally occurring compounds depended on the interaction of many components. But pharmacological science focused on purifying the one active biological. Then they could determine specific dosages, assuring efficacy and safety. Safety? All drugs had side effects and human diversity was a fact of life – individuals reacted differently. Steven was convinced that, in some cases, purification reduced the drug's effectiveness and even worse, increased the chance of adverse side effects.

Steven sipped his Scotch.

Dendrobium Margotis, the new orchid species named for Margot, was among the many samples Steven brought back for further study. The emerging biotech industry had caused a revolution in the life sciences. For those academics, it was no longer simply "publish or perish"; it was now also "go public or perish". Within four years he and UC Irvine had two patents and licensed the discovery of a new class of analgesics to BioEudora, a start-up biotech company in Irvine, California. For the next eleven years, Steven consulted for the company. He was no longer an underpaid academic and he no longer mined the backwaters of the world searching for new biologics. He had found his mother lode and its development occupied his full attention.

Ten years ago BioEudora made him an offer and Steven left the university to join the company full time as VP of Product Development. Phase Two clinical trials had begun the previous year testing BE649, the first potential drug derived from his research. Steven took the credit (along with the six-figure salary and a fistful of stock options) but he knew without Margot's insistence on his joining that New Guinea expedition years ago and her seminal observation, none of this would have happened. He'd been very lucky.

Steven sipped the Scotch.

Margot had not. Her cancer was discovered late (they blamed a misstep by at least one health professional). That was four years ago. She had suffered through three and a half years of chemotherapy until a remission occurred. Thank God. But in that time, their marriage had fallen apart. He knew he was to blame for that.

Steven again sipped the Scotch.

He wasn't proud of the fact that, as in his professional career, he had again bowed to self-interest in his personal life.

Steven held up his glass to the light and drained the remainder of his drink.

He wasn't proud but he wasn't wallowing in regret either – not by a long shot.

"Congratulations, Dr Sampson. Just you and me tonight."

Steven and the pilot walked along the tarmac, still warm from the heat of the afternoon.

"I did sneak a bottle of Dom Pérignon on board. It's in the front cabinet – be on your right. Wish I could join you but . . ." and Mike made control motions with an invisible yoke.

Steven could hear the conversation up front with the tower: clear to taxi. He had asked Mike to fly out over the bay tonight. He wanted to look down on the Pacific again. It would lengthen the trip but Steven saw no reason to hurry home.

He sipped the champagne. The thought of dealing with Margot threatened his now contemplative mood.

Steven finished his first glass of the bubbly.

Things needed to get settled; it was true. He leaned forward and refilled his glass. But that was for later. Just enjoy the present moment, he thought. Steven sank back into the seat as 6,000 pounds of thrust from the dual engines of the Cessna CJ3 pulled them free of Mother Earth's grasp.

He and Mike had flown together hundreds of times; out to the plants on the East Coast, to conferences in almost every state of the Union – even junkets overseas on any number of occasions, usually on the Gulfstream. At least they hadn't made him fly commercial on the day he retired. The Cessna served just fine for the short ride home from John Wayne to Tucson International. He appreciated both the consideration and the frugality. After all, he still owned a couple hundred thousand shares of BioEudora stock. Fiscal responsibility . . . the company he'd worked with for over a decade owed him that.

"Comfortable back there, Doc?"

The plane had levelled off.

Steven opened his mouth but Mike didn't wait for him to answer.

"Shouldn't be much to bump you around this evening."

Steven looked out. A rich mauve sky bathed the setting sun. A few cumulus clouds wandered above. They would fly above those, he thought. Down below, the land had given way to the stirring Newport Bay. Only a disappointingly short stint out over the water this evening . . . So sad. Steven sipped the champagne again.

"Must feel good, retiring at your age."

What's with all the conversation tonight . . . not like Mike, Steven thought.

"I hope to be right behind you . . . if I'm as lucky as you."

Steven smiled. Usually the guy kept the chit-chat to a minimum. But tonight . . . *If I'm as lucky as you.*

Steven sipped the champagne. Outside, in the fading light, the water appeared calmer. He could hardly see the whitecaps any longer. He would see the ocean again . . . very soon and he again sipped the champagne. He had worked everything out.

A sweeping right turn was bringing them back over land. Steven stared out into the darkness. There was no denying that a bit of luck had come his way. But luck was a streaky thing, they said. In the long run, you couldn't beat the house, they said. Steven refilled his glass with the bubbly. Life had a way of always balancing things out, they said. He'd heard it somewhere, the cynical turn of the phrase: *You take and you shall receive.* Steven sipped more champagne.

The plane bounced and then rocked a bit; Steven tried to balance his glass. A splash of champagne jumped out onto the armrest. He dragged his coat sleeve over the drops of liquid.

"Sorry about that, Doc. One of the gods must have a bit of indigestion, I guess."

Steven could hear Mike give out a little laugh.

"We'll just hope he's taking Acrozole." Another laugh.

The comment amused Steven, as well. BioEudora's successful products included the antacid drug Acrozole – a moneymaker but not a blockbuster like Placade.

"Have you on the ground in about twenty . . . no, maybe . . . maybe . . . Oh I'm not sure, Doc. Not too long from now."

Steven reached over and refilled his glass.

Blockbuster drugs like Placade were rare. It was the first of a whole new class of analgesics, suffering none of the liver toxicity of acetaminophen or the gastrointestinal problems of the NSAIDs. That alone made it a huge financial success, capturing 35 per cent of market share its first year out. And now, after three years, sales dwarfed the competition.

But even beyond that success, back during the early Phase Two trials, patients with rheumatoid arthritis experienced not only pain relief but also an apparent halting of their disease progression. A separate Phase Three trial had confirmed the efficacy of Placade and early last year the drug had received accelerated FDA approval for that application as well – another multi-billion dollar business for BioEudora. New trials for the treatment of other autoimmune diseases were under way. Placade could end up the drug of the century.

The plane rocked again with the summer thermals rising from the desert floor.

But then there was the problem. The emails he had commandeered discussed disturbing reports of sporadic adverse side effects in some patients in the early trials of Placade.

Steven thought back to the ladies of the Kombai tribe who couldn't handle the mash.

Similar side effects had also occurred, even more often, in some patients in the Phase Three rheumatoid group. None of the data had been included in the final trial reports or in any of the FDA documentation. Somebody (it wasn't clear who) had made that decision because the numbers "didn't reach statistical significance".

Steven sipped his champagne.

It was a cover-up.

Steven had struggled with the reports. He didn't want to raise an issue where others saw none. He had rationalised that even if, at some point in the future, the FDA took an interest and this side effect was proved problematic, the FDA wouldn't necessarily pull the drug from the market – just change the labelling . . . to inform the public.

A mild euphoria . . . intermittent drowsiness . . . narcolepsy.

Everything hinged on "risk-reward". One in a thousand or one in a million, human diversity meant it was all a gamble. Some people were lucky; some were not.

But Steven was pragmatic. The mere sniff of a problem had driven his decision to leave the company early. The sacrifice of a ton of stock options and another decade-plus of the big salary could not be avoided. If this issue arose in the future, he wanted to be somewhere else. He had also realised that if push came to shove at some future date, he could short the BioEudora stock he still held and surreptitiously leak the problematic data to the FDA. He could make millions in the aftermath. It was a backup plan because in any event, Steven never planned to work another day in his life.

Another bump and again a little of the bubbly jumped from his glass onto the armrest. Steven looked up into the cockpit. Mike was stretching his right arm above his head. Steven thought he heard a yawn. No problem. And he smiled. The money was his; with the return of Margot's health, he could dump her without too much guilt; a whole new life lay before him; maybe he would write; maybe he would paint. Steven sipped the last of the champagne. He realised that this was one of those rare moments in life when he was truly happy.

Up in the cockpit, he could see Mike's shoulders swaying back and forth. No wonder the guy seemed so happy for him, Steven thought – so communicative. A renaissance had occurred in the pilot's life, as well – a consequence of Steven's blockbuster drug. Placade had halted the progression of Mike's rheumatoid arthritis. With it now under control, Mike could continue flying and look forward to a long career without the paralysing pain and progressive immobility that would have plagued his life.

For the moment, no worries existed. The company's top and bottom lines had Wall Street stock analysts out with a buy rating on BioEudora. Why should he worry? Besides, despite the onerous tax implications, Steven had moved 50 per cent of his holdings in BioEudora into a money market account . . . just in case.

Steven looked down at the desert plain stretching out 20,000 feet below him. Luck rode, as a companion, beside him tonight. He raised his glass. It was empty. Alas, no more celebrating. No matter, he felt a little drowsy. He would have to deal with Margot but he could relax now . . . dream of orchids and Pacific isles. He felt safe as he dozed off into an alcohol-induced oblivion.

Up front, Mike was mumbling something. Steven couldn't hear him. Both of them were now sleeping.

Finding Father
BRUCE COSTELLO

Anne dreams of her father and becomes determined to find him.

"It's been twenty years since I saw you," she said. "I needed to see you again."

Anne opened her eyes and groaned. Saturday. The spring sun was streaming through the curtains.

What on earth have I been dreaming about? she thought, as a scene from childhood sprang into her mind.

"Wakey wakey, darling. Out of beddy-byes. Breakfast! Remember, you're helping me plant the garden today!"

"Daddy, can I plant the sunflowers, like I did last year?"

"'Course you can! You were so good at it."

"Yeh!" She jumped out of bed and ran to the kitchen.

Anne brushed aside the twenty-year-old memory and the feelings that surrounded it. She pulled the bedclothes around her head.

"I've no idea where your father is," her mother had said the day before when they met for coffee. "Why this sudden urge to see him?"

Anne's partner brought her breakfast in bed.

"Thank you," she said, quietly.

How could any man love her if her own father didn't?

* * *

Her father's name was not on the electoral roll. An internet search proved fruitless, and the name Donaldson appeared six hundred and thirty-three times in New Zealand phone books.

A friend suggested she put it to the genealogy experts on Trade Me's message board. They loved a good challenge. By evening she was on the phone to a West Coast number.

"You're after Jack Donaldson, you say . . ." the voice at the other end said. "Born in Caversham?"

"Yes."

"Jack Norman Donaldson?"

"Yes! Do you know him?"

"Why do you want to know?"

"I'm trying to find my father."

A full minute passed in silence.

* * *

A week later, Anne set out on her first major trip since getting her driver's licence. The challenging 550 kilometre journey included crossing the Southern Alps.

Her mouth was dry as she drove through the Otira Gorge with its bush-clad mountains towering above the little Mazda, thunder rolling, wind howling, rain so heavy the windscreen wipers could barely cope. Rocks bounced off the road in front of her.

Finally emerging unscathed on the other side, she stopped in a rest area amid native bush with its alluring aroma of damp decay and lush green growth. The sun shone from a cloudless sky.

Boisterous kākā were socialising nearby, chattering and gossiping. They twirled playfully around her with amusing antics and raucous voices. She held up a sandwich. A greeny-brown bundle of feathers swooped down to grab it, flashing orange and scarlet under its outstretched wings.

Arriving in Greymouth at dusk, she found a bed in a boarding house and lay down exhausted. Soon she was in the middle of a dream, sitting on a tree stump covered with moss. Cold dampness oozed through her panties onto her skin. She cried out and her father appeared, pushing his way through dense, tangled bush. He carried her to a little meadow beside a stream where sunlight filtered through foliage, and a huge sunflower towered, its head a glowing yellow, smiling down through clouds.

Together they climbed the giant flower as high as they could go.

*

Next morning, still tired, she drove to the address she'd been given. It was an old cottage with a rusting roof and broken weatherboards. Stepping around a pile of coal by the gate, she walked up the path. A man came to the door wearing ripped jeans and a battered bush shirt. He was unshaven, completely bald, and had two front teeth missing.

He held out his hand and she took it, shyly.

"You've grown up," he said.

"It happens," replied Anne. "I was eight when you saw me last."

"I'll show you around before we go inside," her father said.

Rotting logs bordered the track leading into the bush behind the cottage.

"If I stopped cutting the bush back, it wouldn't be long before the house disappeared under it."

"You're kidding."

"Not far from here, I came across an old logging locomotive that had been swallowed up by Old Man's Beard, as the creeper's called."

Walking deeper into the bush, they came to a small clearing beside a creek. There was a bench seat made from macrocarpa branches, tied together with flax. Close by was a rusting drum full of empty whisky bottles.

"I come here to do my thinking," he said, sitting down and patting the space beside him.

A little grey warbler flew down from a supplejack vine, flitted about, and hovered in front of them, staring at their silent faces.

Anne leaned forward, hands grasping the edge of the seat, and turned to look at her father.

"It's been twenty years since I saw you," she said. "I needed to see you again."

He smiled sadly at her. "Let's go back to the cottage."

"Where do I start?" Her father cleared his throat and stared into his cup of tea. "Perhaps when I got the sack." He shuffled in his chair, gazed across at Anne and continued. "The boss was nice about it. *Much as I value your work, Jack, he said, we can't have a lawyer working here who's a compulsive gambler.* Well, somehow I did manage to give up gambling, but I replaced it with drinking, which was the last straw for your long-suffering mother."

"I can imagine," said Anne, shaking her head.

"Your mother was a good woman, but she'd had as much as she

could take. *I want you to leave,* she said, *and stay away from Anne. She'll be better off without you in her life.* That's when I came over here to live. I've been doing casual work on farms and in the forestry but I've mainly been on the dole. And drinking. Guess your mother was right. I'm just a weak person." He fell silent, then after a few minutes asked: "Can you imagine what it's like for a father to lose his only daughter, who'd been the centre of his life?"

"No," Anne replied. "But I'd like you tell me."

* * *

A year passed before Anne visited her father again. The cottage had been painted white and sunflowers nodded their heads against gleaming weatherboards.

Her father opened the door, smiling broadly. The gaps in his teeth had gone. He was dressed in a sports shirt and tidy pair of jeans.

"Meet Annette," Anne said, holding out the bundle in her arms.

"What a wee beaut!" said her father, his eyes wide. "She's got those looks from her mother!"

He gazed at the baby for a while, and then turned to Anne.

"It was meeting you again, and then hearing you were pregnant made me sober up. I haven't touched a drop for eleven months."

"Just as well, Dad, or I wouldn't have risked bringing her all this way to meet you."

"I knew that. It was just the incentive I needed."

"I hoped it would be."

"Look," her father said, pointing to a red-and-yellow rocking horse in the hallway. "When you rang to say you were having a baby, I made that. I've got time and energy to spare now, so I've taken up woodwork. My logging trucks sell like hot cakes at the market! Anyway, come in, I'll put the kettle on."

Anne smiled. "There's someone else I'd like you to meet first."

"Your husband came, too?"

"Take a look."

Her father stepped out onto the sunlit porch.

"Hullo, Jack," said her mother, quietly extending a hand.

Forwun
E. S. WYNN

A horrifying vision of a machine-mind trained to do battle on distant planets.

"Planetfall comes immediately, comes rough, squeals and rattles through hull."

From the moment the sentient mesh is mated with the neural tissue of my first body, I know that I have a purpose. I know the concepts, the symbols and the grammar of a sterilised strain of stan-terran. I am acutely aware of my body, know how to measure and calculate weight, distance and inertia with only a glance.

And I know how to use a gun.

The name coded into my mesh is CZ-1041, but the woman behind the glass calls me Four-One, runs the words together so it sounds like Forwun. I take her simple instructions verbally, but a silicon-quick stream beamed directly to my mesh provides the real details. The mission is simple.

Run.

My first assignment lasts 7.2 seconds. Three breaths, and then a brush with a sensor drops the floor out from under me, triggers waves of heat that wash through my flesh before I can register more than the edge of a cleansing pain. CZ-0538 is given the messy task of cutting the mesh out of my carbonised corpse. The researchers make notations, check the data saturation in the machine side of my mind to make sure the lesson sticks, and within a few hours, my mesh is cleaned and mated with the neural tissue of a new body, a clone of my last.

My second assignment runs almost three minutes before reflex overrides reason, tosses me sideways into the toothy blades of a meat grinder, turns my clone body into hamburger. Again, CZ-0538 picks the mesh out of the mess, and in another few hours, I'm back on the testing floor, running.

Eight minutes of running, of dodging rounds, sensor sweeps, rebounding off walls at high speed, trying to stay ahead of bullets that scar steel in volleys. Eight minutes before I fall face first to the floor, back riddled and steaming, blood rolling in steady rivers across smooth steel plating. Eight minutes, and then another few hours before I'm back on the floor again, running, *running*.

It takes six attempts for me to reach the end of the course unscathed, learn all of the ways and places the researchers have built death into the world through which it has become my mission to run. A wall opens, and the woman behind the glass, the one who calls me Forwun, uses verbal commands to give me a new mission.

Walk over there. Wait.

My senses are tuned, sharp, catch nothing I can perceive as a threat. For hours, I stand and wait, body taut, ready for the part of this mission, this test that will surely swoop in the moment I relax, carve me into ribbons or scorch the flesh from my bones. Nothing comes. *Nothing.*

And then a stream of data hits my mesh. New instructions. Go.

The path laid down in the silicon synapses of my brain-mated mesh-mind takes me through corridors studded with cameras, with sensors I can feel but can't escape. No death comes, only a steady, passive scanning – and then a bend in a hallway funnels me into a line of others like me, clone bodies driven by sentient meshes, hundreds of us, all bound for the same distant navpoint.

Fifty-seven metres, exactly fifty-seven metres, and I'm stopped at the entrance to a wide cargo bay, wait for the space of a breath while a machine flexes down from the ceiling, burns a barcode into my right cheek. Sizzling flesh, fresh pain registers in the mind of the clone body I wear, but orders, *the mission*, take precedence. Turning, hands reach out, accept a mass-spun outfit of plated armour, a glossy helmet, a breath mask and rifle, and then I'm led by mental command to a pod-freezer, given thirty seconds to dress myself, tuck myself in. The steel lid of the pod-freezer descends automatically and I close my eyes, let darkness wash my consciousness back into sweet void.

The journey is long. I don't dream, know only when I wake that the ship carrying my body and a hundred thousand other mesh-driven clones has travelled six hundred and ninety light years to bring us to a battlefield on a planet called Delta Orionis B. Planetfall comes immediately, comes rough, squeals and rattles through hull until the ship hits smooth air, settles soft on scorched sand. The pod-freezer opens, a quick injection blasts away the clone body's sluggish reflexes – and then I'm in the shimmering red sunlight, rifle ready, seeking, flashing, lancing faceless enemies with pinpoint beams that sizzle skin, vaporise bone. Eyes seek targets with reflex quickness, mind counting kills, driving the rifle forward, forward –

And then the sand rises up, flashes with spilled red and blackness. For a moment, there is no sound, nothing but the sand, the red – a thick wetness gathering somewhere, filling my sinuses –

Programming kicks in. Damage to the cortex has rendered my clone body over 50 per cent inoperable. Pain builds, powers resolve. With the last of my strength, I reach up, snap my own neck in one quick, efficient move.

When I awaken, my mesh is already mated with the neural tissue of a new clone body. At some point in the darkness between my old body and this new one, other clones driven by other meshes have brought the battle to a close, annihilated our enemy with ruthless efficiency. Something in me strives to do better, knows that I will do better, and the chance presents itself immediately. A new barcode is burned into my cheek, new armour and a new rifle are assigned to me.

A new pod-freezer awaits, and three hundred and twenty-seven light years further away, another battle has already begun.

Frogs, Gnomes, Hikers and Bottle Miners
PATRICIA CRANDALL

Nina visits Gert on her first day of retirement to take her bottle mining, but two mischievous boys interrupt their plans. First published in The Hudson Valley Literary Magazine, Winter 2002/2003.

> "My good friend, now we're both retired, we can finally live out our dreams. So I started making plans."

A light breeze floated through the green-shuttered windows of a white gingerbread house on Elm Street in Indian Falls, New York. In a reflective mood, Gert Carver surveyed the gifts that had been bestowed upon her at a retirement party which the teachers and staff of Cobble Hill School had given her. Among the gifts were kaleidoscopic artwork by the children, trendy luggage presented by those who had graduated and precious mementos from fellow teachers.

Unmarried and never having met "Mr Right", Gert acknowledged that a thirty-five-year career as an elementary-school teacher had not been a glamorous occupation, but she never regretted the many years spent with the children. Certainly, heartbreak had gone hand in hand with joy . . . from the suicide of a seventh-grade student to the Cinderella marriage of a graduate. She had spent time and wisdom well. Teaching had been the most satisfying part of her life as she loved all the children.

One student in particular stood out in her mind as she read his gift card exuding thanks, love and prayers: Geoffrey VanJones, a gangling rascal she taught at Cobble Hill School. Geoff had been a difficult child, but by using her instincts and an ear-twist when needed, she had managed to guide him.

Gert sat in her comfortable rocking chair and thought favourably about how she had managed to help Geoff overcome his problems. Now, he was President of the Milbourne National Bank and Trust Company in Troy, New York.

Gert's thoughts were interrupted by a knock on the kitchen door. She rose, and welcomed a wave of fresh air rushing in when she opened it. Standing on the porch landing was Nina Westacott, a pudgy, white-haired figure with a yellow cardigan draped over her rounded shoulders. Her face was aglow when she saw Gert. They had been friends for many years.

"Since when do you knock, Nina?" Gert asked.

"Why, I thought today would be different."

"It's no different than any other day."

Nina hugged her best friend then stared at her in disbelief.

"Gert, how could you say it's just like any other day? This is your first day of retirement, your first day not looking after the children, giving them their homework assignments and whatnot. Miss Carver, are you feeling well?"

"I'm fine," Gert said peevishly. Her eyes shifted down to a golden-crusted pie nestled in a quilted "cosy" on the wide, porch railing.

"Nina, did you bring me a pie?"

"Yes, dear, I baked you an apple pie."

"I'll make a pot of tea. Come in and sit down."

In the kitchen, with the kettle boiling, Gert turned to Nina and said, "My good friend, now that we're both retired, we can finally live out our dreams. So I started making plans."

"Plans? What kind of plans?" Nina asked. Her curiosity was piqued.

"What have we been putting off all these years because I had school to attend to, you had four children to raise and Harry to fuss over?"

"For the life of me, Gert, I don't know what you're hinting at."

Gert announced, "We're going to mine old bottles!"

Next morning, after breakfast, the two women sat in close consultation in the French-blue parlour of Nina's meticulous Queen Anne house, two doors down from Gert's.

On the fruitwood table, where an antique lace cover had been carefully folded and set aside, a number of maps and diagrams were piled. Two had been placed to one side. "Which dump shall it be? Hoosick Falls or Babcock Lake?" asked Nina.

Gert contemplated the maps, deciding. "Babcock Lake! The woods surrounding the lake are filled with old cellar holes and rubbish heaps. There should be a treasure of bottles in the old tavern dump."

"I believe you're right," agreed Nina, collecting all but one map, stacking the rest neatly in a cardboard box. "We'll need shovels, picks, scrapers, pitchforks, and garden gloves. I'll pack a picnic lunch."

At precisely 8.45 on Saturday morning, Gert and Nina passed through the business section of Indian Falls, consisting of Porter's Food and Drug Centre, Harmon's Farm Equipment Store, Falls Liquor Store, Carlys Beauty Salon and The Village Video. They drove around Tomhannock Creek to Highway 7, continuing up a steep mountain road, turning left on a dirt road that ribboned around Babcock Lake.

It was their good fortune to come upon a seasoned woodsman with a cane taking an early stroll. Inside Gert's maroon-and-grey Outback, the two ladies peered anxiously as the old-timer squinted at the hand-drawn representation of the woods and said, "Take this 'ere road 'bout a half-mile in." He pointed to a jagged line on the map. "It will lead ya straight to the ol' dump."

"Thank you," Gert said, retrieving the map, and as she drove the Outback down the road and glanced in the rear-view mirror, she saw the old man looking hungrily at a loaf of Italian bread he had snitched from the picnic basket in the back seat of the car.

Tramping the old wagon trail where Indian pipes, mossy boulders and bulbous polyps were plentiful came two boys. Eleven-year-old Lance was actively describing to his nine-year-old brother, Douglas, that the trail they were taking would lead them through one of the loneliest and wildest regions of the Grafton Mountains.

Douglas dropped his hands to his belt, reassured to feel the attached flashlight and grateful his backpack contained flint, a map, compass and a whistle. No longer did he think his mother was overreacting when she said one could get lost easily in the woods.

"Why don't we wait for Dad? He said we're to stay here and play while he fills water jugs at the stream. I'm glad I don't have to fill those jugs." He gave a sigh of relief.

"I know Dad told us to stay put," Lance said. "But I'm figuring things out for myself." He glanced at his compass watch. "He'll be back 'bout three thirty. That means we have a half-hour to kill. Let's go into the woods a little ways, do some exploring, and then turn back."

In an attempt to keep pace with his long-legged brother, Douglas nearly tripped while looking upwards through the Christmas pines.

Dark clouds stretched over the fading sun.

"Mebbe we should keep to the edge of the woods." He whipped his head around, doubtful the darkening forest was safe. "I like to hear cars driving by. I want to be able to call out to people if I fall and hurt myself."

"Aw, Douglas!" Lance said irritably. "You're a sissy!" He jumped into the air, brushing a low branch with the tips of his fingers. "It's more fun nosing around than standing still, tossing acorns at squirrels." He paused. "I hiked here last summer with Dad. There's no 'dare' to this trail."

"How come I wasn't on that hike?" Douglas piped up. "I don't remember walking through these woods."

"You stayed home with Mom. You had an earache and had to take medicine. Remember?"

Douglas recalled the painful incident and remained sullen.

Lance went on, "Soon we'll be passing the old tavern dump and come out by Looney's Pond. We'll head back then, I promise." He glanced sideways at his brother. "There are bob cats and foxes in these woods and BIG BLACK BEARS!"

Douglas looked ghastly.

WHOOOOOO!

"What's that?" Douglas clutched Lance's arm.

"An owl! C'mon, poke. We'll never get to the pond if you don't move faster."

The tavern dump was spread out in a mile-and-a-half radius. A foreboding black cloud passed low over the woodland where mottled sun played on an island of ferns. In the next moment, a shaft of brightness lit up the woods in a fiery spectacle.

Gert and Nina, dressed in old clothes and loaded with digging gear, trekked across the moss-carpeted floor and stepped cautiously through rubble. They each claimed a spot and soon were unearthing lady's leg whisky bottles, amber punkin-seed flasks, medicine bottles bearing local legends, torpedo sodas, and unbroken, blue-willow china. As valuables accumulated, they spread them out on wild-growing grass at the edge of the road. They moved further into the dump and wind-stirred leaves muttered rumours of rain.

"It looks stormy," Nina observed. "It might be wise to pack up and come back another time."

"There was no rain in the forecast this morning," Gert said optimistically. "It's a cloud-cover."

In the distance, an excited voice rang out. "Look at those bottles, neat-O!"

There was a ping followed by the sound of breaking glass.

Gert and Nina hurtled through gnarled scrub and piles of litter, flailing pitchforks in the air.

"If you break one more bottle, you're dead!" Gert cried out. Two young boys were plinking stones at the colourful glass.

Douglas flung down a stone, unintentionally smashing a ruby-coloured bottle. He spun around and raced down the road. Lance zoomed at his heels.

A safe distance away, the boys huddled together and peered at two old crones with purple faces moaning and caterwauling as if they had just lost a pet dog.

A clap of thunder boomed and lightning bolted mutinously. A torrential downpour erupted having no mercy on frogs, gnomes, hikers, or bottle miners.

With the storm raging about them, Gert and Nina blessed themselves, pulled green plastic garbage bags over their clothes, grabbed a bag of salvaged treasures, and hurried towards the car.

Gert hesitated midway and called out, "I fear for those young boys in this storm, Nina. I'm going back to find them and bring them to the shelter of the car. You'll have to cart our belongings. If you can't manage, we'll come back for them later."

Nina took the miscellany out of Gert's hands and braced herself against the strong wind. She sloshed down the muddy path to the car and unlocked the door. She turned on the ignition, and pressed the dial for heat, settling back into the seat, and prayerfully waited.

Soon, three ghostly shapes emerged from the woodland. The car door swung violently open and Gert said through chattering teeth, "Oh, that heat feels good."

Nina tossed Gert a blanket. Gert mopped excess water off two dripping boys and pushed them onto the back seat of the car, shouting orders above the din of the storm. They were not to worry about decency. "Remove your wet clothes and wrap up in a blanket. You'll have to share the one on the back seat."

Gert ripped off the garbage bag covering her clothes, slid onto the seat beside Nina, and blanket-dried her hair and neck. Gratefully, she accepted a cup of hot tea out of a thermos from her friend.

"Where did you find the boys?" Nina put the car in gear.

"They were trying to find a refuge from the storm near the remains of the old tavern. When I arrived, they were glad to see me, weren't you, boys?" She twisted her head around to look at the youngsters, shivering and bundled together in a blanket, their wet clothes lying in a heap on the floor.

"Yessir!" Lance croaked. "And we're sorry we broke your bottles." He nudged his brother.

"Uh-huh," Douglas muttered, relishing his new-found warmth and safety from the storm.

"Apologies accepted," said Gert. "Now, let's see if we can find your father. He must be out of his mind with worry."

Gert directed Nina to drive slowly down the road in search of a sports vehicle parked on the right near the entrance to the old sawmill. The boys had briefed her about their excursion with their dad when she rescued them.

When they drew up alongside the empty vehicle, Nina looked quizzically at Gert. "Isn't that the VanJones car?" Then, riveting her eyes back to the road, she said, "You don't mean . . . ?"

Gert nodded her head up and down and said, "Meet Lance and Douglas VanJones. Geoff is their father!"

"And I've been trying to place where I've seen these two boys." Nina clicked her tongue. "I knew they looked familiar to me." She eyed the boys through the rear-view mirror. "It's been a while since I've seen the two of you with your mom and dad." She grimaced at the heavy rain hammering down. Geoff was nowhere in sight. "I'll sound the horn," she said.

After tooting the horn several times with no results, Lance said, "Dad has a cell phone. If we go home straightaway, Mom'll call him and he'll get back to her."

Gert tapped Nina's shoulder. "To the VanJones house! You are a bright boy, Lance. Just like your dad!"

A tall, slender man with flame-red hair, wearing a rain-drenched athletic suit and tar-stained sneakers, raced to the entrance of the VanJones residence in an affluent cul-de-sac in Indian Falls. Colour was slowly returning to his strained face when the front door opened and he was hugged by his two sons and wife.

"The storm came on fast," Geoff VanJones explained in a taut voice. "I assumed the boys went to the car at the first strike of thunder and lightning, and when I got there and they were nowhere in sight, it felt as though a knife went through my chest." He gestured with a fist. "You'll never know the thoughts running through my mind as I went back into the woods with the storm raging, and searched for these youngsters. What a relief when I got the call they were safe and at home." He kneaded each bony shoulder and added humbly, "Thanks be to God and to Gert and Nina." He released his family and went over to the two friends, dwarfed in his wife's size-twelve clothes. "How do you figure?" He half smiled. "After all these years, Miss Carver, you're still getting me out of a jam."

Carole walked over to her husband and gave him a gentle shove upstairs. "Go change out of your wet things. We have lunch set out on the kitchen table."

"Pronto, Dad!" Douglas pleaded. "We're starved! There's tuna and macaroni salad, baked beans and cold corn on the cob. There's a thick chocolate cake for dessert." He licked his lips.

"Where did all this food come from?" Geoff laughed. "I know your mom didn't just whip this lunch up."

"It's one of Nina's famous picnic lunches," Gert piped up.

"She and Miss Carver are going to share it with us and Mom's added ham-and-cheese sandwiches, pickles and chips," Douglas said excitedly. "Go on. Hurry!"

After revelling in the picnic lunch, the boys raced each other from the dining room to the game room. The adults retired to the living room with its cathedral ceilings and a commanding view of a tree-lined pond. They gathered around the gas fireplace with hot tea and coffee. Gert and Nina shared their bottle-mining adventure, culminating in their confrontation with the boys.

"Those devils." Geoff apologised while Carole looked embarrassed at the tomfoolery of her sons. Then Geoff cleared his throat and said in a serious voice, "I've been meaning to contact you, Gert, to discuss a concern of ours." He nodded at Carole then looked steadily into the surprised eyes of his former teacher.

"We're taking Lance and Douglas out of the Hilton School in New Hampshire and enrolling them in Cobble Hill School."

Gert set her teacup down on the round coffee table. "I recall you were adamant your sons should be educated in the private Hilton School and not in a common school like Cobble Hill. What has brought about this change of mind, Geoff?"

"Things haven't worked out," he admitted wretchedly. "There are a lot of issues at the Hilton School that aren't being addressed . . . bullying, lack of supervision in the dorms, the boys have low grades and no self-esteem . . . We've complained to the Principal, the Board of Education and their teachers." He frowned. "There's a concerned group of parents attempting to remedy the situation but it won't happen any time soon." He nodded at Carole.

"Cobble Hill School is where they belong," Gert said in an even voice. "One of the reasons I've retired early is because I'm at odds with education as it is being taught today. Some changes are for the good, but I'm a firm believer in the basics and repetitive teaching of reading, writing and 'rithmetic. Still, in all, Cobble Hill School is first rate when you compare it to other schools." She was contemplative a moment. "I'd like to help the boys adjust to their new schedule. Would you agree to that?"

Geoff beamed at Carole. "And we didn't even have to ask."

Carole looked relieved at first, then narrowed her eyes. "What about your retirement, Gert?"

"My sentiments, exactly," Nina exclaimed in a melodic, high voice.

Everyone turned to look at the contented woman rocking near the window in an upholstered glider.

"Sounds like you have a problem with my tutoring offer, Nina." Gert chuckled. "Speak or hold you peace."

"I'm in favour of this undertaking as long as tutoring doesn't interfere with bottle mining." She clasped her hands together, resting her case.

Geoff made a toast. "To the remarkable Miss Carver. May tutoring and bottle mining go together."

"Hear, hear!" Four Spode teacups were raised in the air.

Gladiator
SIGFREDO R. IÑIGO

||||||||||||||||||||||||||||||||||||||||||||||||||||||||||||||||||||||||||||||||||||||||||||||||||||||||||||||||||||||||||||||||||||||||||

Philippine children bet on gladiatorial battles between spiders.

"My champion is like Pac-Man: he gobbles up his enemies."

D awn found Achilles spreadeagled on his web, now glistening with the cold dew, which he had spun the night before on the branch of a mahogany tree deep in the Philippine jungle. Suddenly, the branch stirred although there was no wind. Achilles tried to scurry inside a curved leaf when a tiny hand abruptly snatched him. The intruder, a boy, blew softly into the spider wriggling inside his cupped hand to soothe him back into sleep. When Achilles ceased struggling, the boy eased him gently into a tiny compartment in a spider house made from a discarded matchbox.

As he climbed down, the boy was excited. Achilles was a good catch, that he was sure of. He could tell by the way the spider wriggled its strong spindly arms when he grabbed it, its tiny mass sending electricity up his own arm.

At the village, the boy sauntered towards a group of kids and some grown-ups watching a spider fight in progress. The boys who owned the spiders sat on the ground, cross-legged, their eyes fixed on the tiny gladiators. Each kept his spider on a short needle-thin stick taken from the strand of a coconut broom. The spiders kept on scurrying across the length of their stick until the two sticks came in contact with each other.

Eventually, one was caught in a net of silk. The spider spun it round and round to the applause of the winning bettors. The owner of the losing spider flicked it to the ground and stamped at it with his bare foot.

"My champion is like Pac-Man. He gobbles up his enemies," Bal-la, the owner of the winning spider, boasted. He let his spider crawl up and down his arms while waiting for takers. The black fighter had beaten three challengers in a row and Bal-la's pockets jingled with coins. The grown-ups betted heavily among themselves. Betting was done as in a cockfight, each combatant either a *llamado*, which was the odds-on favourite, or *dejado*, the underdog, like most of the arachnids that ended up squished on the gravel road.

The morning was still cool, but the ground was already littered with many dead and dying spiders. Most were gathered at night or at early dawn from the surrounding woods. Some of the grown-ups went to the jungle at night, carrying kerosene lamps, searching for their silky webs. A searcher boasted he had found three hundred in one night. He sold the creatures to those who had made spider fighting a full-time business, at least during the rainy season when spiders multiplied along with the bugs on which they preyed. Almost every village, after the rice paddies had been planted and there was nothing to do but weed the fields and take the carabaos to pasture, took to spider fighting as pastime.

"Oy, Onyok," Bal-la called the newcomer. "Found something? Want to fight?"

Onyok did not want to pit his spider against Bal-la's. Bal-la was bigger than him, and he had the nasty habit of flicking at his ear when he was not looking. When he protested, Bal-la always pretended to be innocent, but he knew, and couldn't complain. Bal-la once rained down blows on him when he dared confront him, and Onyok went home with a bloody face. He had to pass through the *batalan* to wash his wounds so as not to let his mother see them.

Onyok took out his matchbox and opened it slowly. Inside were tiny beehive-like compartments, each containing a spider. He picked up a piece of broomstick and with one end gently prodded his newest find.

Achilles did not stir. The boy poked at him gently with the stick, trying to lift him up. Achilles emerged from his corner and waved his front arms lazily, as if tasting the wind. Then he curled upside down, and seemed to go back to sleep.

The onlookers were silent. They looked at the newcomer and the current champion.

"Oy, this one's *ordinan*," said a bettor, pointing to the bright-red markings on its back. The villagers believed such a marked spider would be a fierce fighter.

"Aw, it's a coward," Bal-la said. "Like its owner. Mine can beat it with just a flick."

Betting seriously began, with the spiders evenly matched. Bal-la placed his black warrior back on the stick where it scurried back and forth. It looked mean. "He's hungry after all those fights," said one. The odds shifted a little in its favour.

Perched upside down on his stick, Achilles remained unmoved, even when prodded with Onyok's finger. Bal-la let his spider travel the length of his stick, and as it reached the end, brought the point of the stick against that of Achilles. The other spider moved on to Achilles' stick. One of its arms touched the strand supporting Achilles, as if testing its strength. A spider does that in order to snap it, as a man tries to slice a rope on which his opponent hangs. Most spiders do it against smaller opponents.

Despite the prodding, Achilles was motionless as ever. His appearance was that of an octopus with its tentacles all tucked up. He was born, or hatched, in the jungle as the monsoon rains came, and he was among the lucky ones who escaped predators, feeding on the flying things that got tangled in his web night after night. As he increased in size and strength, so did his appetite and daring, until he no longer feared the colourful dragonflies that thrashed wildly as they got caught in his deadly trap. These and other large insects he attacked in a swirling motion until they were enveloped, helpless, in his sticky web. Sometimes, other spiders drifted near his nest. He attacked them and sucked the juices out of their dead bodies.

The champion decided it now must put up or clam up. Cautiously it approached, waving its arms out in front daintily like a pair of antennae. To the onlookers, he seemed like a pugilist that shadow-boxes before going in. The tips of its two arms – the longest – touched Achilles by no more than a hair but it was enough. Achilles exploded with sudden fury, his motions a blur. Then it was over. The erstwhile champion dropped to the ground with an inaudible thud. Morosely, Bal-la poked at its rear end with the stick. On its back where Achilles had sunk his fangs there was a tiny trickle of amber-like juice. Sounds of tsk-tsk-tsk were heard from all around. The winning bettors smacked their lips and collected from the losers.

In most spider fights, either combatant tries to wrap his opponent in thick strands of silk, which he furiously draws out from his posterior and casts away like a fishing net. Some spiders, like Achilles, grapple and bite. They flail with their arms, so thin and flimsy to human eyes yet hammer-like in effect against their own kind. Achilles simply overwhelmed the other with his more powerful strokes, finishing the other with the fatal bite.

Four more challengers were pitted against Achilles but they were no match for the "ordained" one. Since most of the spiders left were not of championship calibre, they were made to fight each other in a free-for-all: placed in a small ceramic bowl, they attacked each other, releasing strands of web in a frenzy until only one or none survived. It was less exciting than a single combat, but it helped pass the hours.

At the end of the day, Onyok's pockets were heavy with coins as he enclosed Achilles softly in his fist and blew through it. Then he let him dangle in mid-air and caught him squarely right inside his portion of the matchbox where he slept instantly. That night, Achilles slept with the body of one of his victims which he sucked to replenish his strength. The matchbox was on top of an inverted cup which Onyok placed on a saucer filled with water to keep out the ants.

The next morning, Achilles took on more challengers, finishing them with his whirlwind attack. But he was visibly tiring. He was now spinning silken threads and hurling them at his enemy. He wanted to curl up inside a leaf and wait for dark when he could build his web.

In the afternoon, just before sunset, Onyok was about to go home when Bal-la came up. He was grinning, his fist closed.

"What have you got?" they asked him.

Bal-la opened his fist triumphantly. Out came a yellow spider, bigger than Achilles. It also had bright-red markings on its back. The crowd looked in awe as it crawled up Bal-la's arm, stopping every now and then as if to flex its muscles.

Onyok hesitated. He did not want Achilles to fight any more. He had noted that after every fight Achilles seemed to age. He dreaded to see his champion beaten. But the crowd's blood was up, and he couldn't back down. He took Achilles from the matchbox.

Bal-la placed his spider on a broom stick. Although larger than Achilles, it glided to and fro with ease, and he had to switch his hold on the stick's end frequently to keep it from travelling up his arm. "This one's a karasaeng," Bal-la bragged. He meant a cobra.

The crowd considered the new challenger *llamado*. Excited shouts caused the townsfolk, now returning from their farms, to pause and see what the ruckus was all about. Onyok was afraid his mother would recognise him and give him a tongue-lashing.

Unlike in his previous encounters, Achilles was instantly alert when he saw the challenger. He approached him cautiously, arms outstretched, like a wrestler looking for a good hold. The other did likewise. Achilles, intent on grabbing the other and biting it like his previous victims, lashed out fiercely but his arms lacked their former power. The *karasaeng* released thick ribbons of web against Achilles, who evaded them. As they fought, each tried to snap the silken thread on which the other clung, and Achilles' thread gave way, but he did not fall to the ground: a fighting spider always releases extra strands to the wind, almost invisible to the human eye, as "assurance". As Achilles fell, one of those strands had stuck to Onyok's shirt, and he landed on it like a trapeze artist. Onyok again placed him on the stick. Again and again, the *karasaeng* snapped his web, and he glided to the ground, only to be returned to his stick to face the challenger. The *karasaeng*, after some time, seemed a little scared, like a human being. Imagine flinging your enemy out of the ring, only to find him face to face with you again after a few seconds. Suddenly, the karasaeng turned the other way and scurried along the length of the stick. "Come on and fight!" shouted the crowd. But Bal-la moved the stick to his other hand, prodding the yellow spider with his finger. The *karasaeng* quickly travelled the length of the stick, thinking it had escaped, but as he reached the end, he walked right into the arms of Achilles. Both fought furiously. Achilles managed to snap the other's thread and the *karasaeng* dangled downward. Bal-la gave a soft tug to the thread to coax the spider up, but the *karasaeng*, now afraid, released more strands in order to escape. Bal-la prodded it with his finger but it turned around every time it was brought within striking distance of Achilles. Clearly he did not want to fight any more. One of its arms, in fact, was bent upward, and to the spectators it looked like a token of surrender.

"*Tiyope!*" the crowd roared. "Coward!"

Bal-la flung the *karasaeng* in disgust. Onyok was about to place Achilles inside his matchbox when Bal-la swiftly flicked at it with his middle finger, throwing him a few feet away. He crumpled on the dirt and lay still.

Onyok was choked with rage. His face reddened and he almost cried. Bal-la the bully just looked at him. As the smaller boy approached, Bal-la went into a boxer's stance, daring the other to fight.

"Oy, oy, oy, look out! Onyok's mad!"

Onyok flung himself against the bigger boy in blind fury. He was aware of thudding blows, of a dull pain as his thin body absorbed the other's punches. Once he tasted blood. But he kept on coming until a star exploded in his brain and he found himself down on his knees, bewildered. He got up, only to be knocked down again.

"Stop! He's had enough!"

Bal-la paused, then proudly raised his arms like a prizefighter. Onyok drove into him like a bull, and his weight knocked the other into the ground, stunning him. Then Onyok was all over him, straddling him, biting his face, clawing his throat, gouging his eyes. Hands finally grabbed him and separated him from the prostrate Bal-la, now covered with wounds and scratches.

"Oy, let's bet on them. This is better than a spider match," cried one of the grown-ups.

Onyok's shirt was drenched in blood, but he gamely stood his ground. He raised his arms, remembering how Achilles raised his before pummelling his foe. The crowd roared. He looked at Bal-la and noticed that he seemed not as confident as before. He was not used to this kind of streetfight. His eyes darted around as if looking for a way out. Instantly Onyok locked his arms around the bully's neck and forced him to his knees. He was surprised to find it easy.

"That's enough," someone said.

Onyok let the other go, conscious of the new respect now accorded him by the amazed onlookers.

Onyok limped slowly home, feeling like a man. Near the forest, he stopped and took out what remained of Achilles. He wanted to have one last look at his champion. Slowly, he held him in his palm. Onyok was about to flick him away when an arm stirred. He was still alive! Onyok placed the spider in his matchbox and hoisted himself on a nearby tree. He took out Achilles, probing the spider's posterior with his thumb and forefinger until he found a silken, invisible thread. He held it between his two fingers and raised it. Achilles dangled downward, his arms outstretched, flinging out more strands of silken thread. Finally, one of them was attached to a leaf, and he crawled to it. He was free.

Goodbye Butterfly
HANJA KOCHANSKY

||||||||||||||||||||||||||||||||||||||||||||||||||||||||||||||||||||||||||||||||||||||||||||||||||||||||||||||||||||||||

Hanja and her son go for a meal in Paris with a friend, and find a butterfly in the street.

> "Italians always have to approach a woman sexually. I don't think they even mean it - they simply have to."

What the caterpillar calls the end, the rest of the world calls a butterfly.

– Lao Tzu

We had already walked past it before I realised that what the corner of my eye had accidentally observed on a wet cobblestone in the alleyway was a black-and-white butterfly. I turned to see that indeed it was, right there, in the middle of the passageway, where, at any moment, a foot might crush her, or the tyre of a bicycle might . . . Oh!

I picked her up carefully. The underside of her wings was the colour of saffron. Immobile, she was hunched within herself like a tulip that had closed up for the night. It had been raining. Perhaps her wings had gotten wet. I recalled my father telling me when I was a child, as young as my son, Kasimir, who was now watching over me with wide-blue-eyed interest, that butterflies have an imperceptible mantle of fine dust on their frail wings, which, if tampered with, might cause them such damage that they would no longer be able to fly. Oh!

"Can I kiss her very gently?" asked my almost six-year-old boy.

Philip laughed; his laugh is a mixture of mirth and cynicism – youthful folly and steel.

We had come from Rome to visit Philip who had recently embarked on a French adventure by setting up house in Paris. He was taking us to lunch at his favourite bistro – Le Napoleon. He loved it there, he said, because of the décor: pictures, images, posters, drawings, murals, silhouettes, caricatures, prints and studies of Napoleon lined the restaurant's walls. This tickled his sense of the bizarre ("Imagine there being a restaurant in Munich called Das Hitler whose walls are lined with images of Hitler?"), while, at the same time, his sense of good taste was stimulated by the family-type cooking which he promised would be excellent. And last, but by no means least (to a man obliged to keep a shrewd eye on his budget), a three-course *Menu du Jour* (*café et vin compris*) was offered for only twenty-two francs. Practically a miracle in this day and age – which was the summer of 1980.

I'd meant to put the butterfly down on some greenery before reaching the restaurant, but not a plant had been sighted en route, so, greeted by a human-size portrait of the Little Emperor with protruding stomach painted in bright lacquer (deep greens and Chinese reds as favoured by the Parisian eye) on the bevelled, thick-glass door, we went in with her.

Diners picked up their heads to see who entered. They glanced without passion at the angelic child's golden beauty; the man's carefully chosen, simply cut outfit; and the striking, blue-eyed woman with an exaggerated mass of hennaed hair, a butterfly nestling on her open palm.

The bistro was crowded: couples, threesomes, a family group; men in grey suits eating with gusto; neatly turned out efficient-looking women; lovers at the corner table lost in each other; someone's fat granny. Most had serious expressions – as the French are given to – while conversing in low, secretive tones.

"In Rome everyone talks very loudly to remind one and all of their existence," I said to Philip. "Involving each other, grabbing at the nearest excuse for a possible encounter – preferably sexual. Italians *always* have to approach a woman sexually. I don't think they even *mean* it – they simply *have* to do it. It's the custom," I sighed, and concluded: "That's probably why they are such lousy lovers."

I laid the butterfly on the white tablecloth – *laid out on a cold white table, my baby there she lay . . .*

"Lousy lovers?" Philip quizzed wide-eyed.

"Yes. Don't you know that Latins are lousy lovers?"

We didn't, however, get to pursue my sweeping statement as, at that moment, a sweet-looking young waiter came over to brush away the crumbs left on the linen tablecloth by the previous clients. I picked up the butterfly as he swept vigorously with his miniature broom, avoiding eye contact with us and not acknowledging the butterfly – not even with a discreet smile. In Rome the waiter would have certainly gotten into a conversation about butterflies.

Philip said wasn't he cute, the waiter, and that he had wanted to bring his niece here to meet him. His niece, a young American woman with the fair, romantic look of an English rose, a *gentille* lass, a Henry James heroine, was staying with him on an extended visit to learn French and further herself culturally. "But," he added, "I don't really think my niece would go for him – she likes peculiar-looking men – and besides, she is a vegetarian so there isn't much point in bringing her here."

Kasimir and I shared a *Menu*. He didn't like the mixed hors d'oeuvre we were served for starters, so, agreeable as always, he nibbled at a crunchy baguette smeared with creamy French butter, and enjoyed the dreaded (by me) Coke (his poor teeth!), while Philip and I spoke of his preoccupation – twenty-seven, and still not published!

It had taken him ten years to write the book – a theoretical work whose details he only secretly hinted at – something about a philosophy offering the possibility of happiness to the ordinary folk. The manuscript had been in the manicured hands of a well-known Manhattan literary agent for the last six months now, and so far, not a single publisher had come through. Although it was a trifle too soon to actually despair, this was nevertheless depressing him. Having experienced rejection by publishers myself, I tried to console him. "Geniuses have always been victimised by those of lesser talent. You'll overcome, you'll see. You'll be published . . . Of course you might have to die first." We both laughed.

The humorous light that met my eyes from the pale irises behind the owlish spectacles of the princely-looking young man, whose soft blond hair fell on an intelligent forehead, indicated that he was not totally of an unhappy nature – after all, there was the philosophy . . .

Outside it was pouring. Sheets of city-grey water slid down the imposing painting of Napoleon Bonaparte who had greeted us at the bistro's entrance. Season-wise, this had been a schizophrenic summer in Northern Europe. Unreliable, eclectic weather – one moment a hot sun in a clear sky, and just as one began to feel secure that the heat had really set in (ah, finally!), heavy winds brought in a mass of threatening clouds that wrapped the atmosphere into a chilly parcel, followed by intense rains.

"They say this rotten weather is the result of the volcano that erupted some months ago in Washington State," stated Philip.

To this I responded: "Very likely. They say that when a butterfly flaps its wings in Tokyo there's a cyclone in Chicago."

"Very unlikely," retorted Philip.

The next course, a tenderly grilled entrecôte – much to Kasimir's taste (which means he gets most of it, which suits me fine as I feel a bit like Philip's niece about meat) – brought us to the subject of money matters. Having studied it at Berkeley, Philip is an expert in economics; and, being a bohemian unwed mum, songwriter and a mostly out-of-work actress with a somewhat unruly life, I am an expert in economising. Our joint experiences brought us to the point of assessing that this was an excellent meal, much better than one could get at the price in either London or Rome nowadays. Philip declared that New York was now the cheapest Western capital and soon we would be taking our vacations in America because that would be the inexpensive place to go to.

"It all spins round nonsensically. Only a few years ago Rome was the cheapest place to live, and now all they talk about over there is inflation – when they're not speaking about food or sex."

"And London has been taken over by the Arabs, so you can imagine what's happening to the prices there," commented Philip, shaking his head sadly.

Money, I concluded, would be the big concern of the 80s.

"Money's always the big concern – it's *my* big concern," remarked Phil, philosophically.

"I wish it wasn't such a hassle to survive," I moaned.

"What's 'survive'?" queried Kasimir.

"Being able to pay the dues," answered Philip.

Choosing a delicate pale-green leaf, as transparent as the butterfly herself, out of the smooth round rosewood salad bowl, I placed the still butterfly on it, and said, "If she's going to leave her body at Le Napoleon's she might as well have an organic grave."

The butterfly shook herself – a brief shudder before reassuming her passive repose.

"This is good! We should eat it in Rome too," suggested Kas, attacking the entrecôte with gusto.

"It's very expensive," I explained, as though this would make any sense to my little son, who, some time ago, had sagaciously informed me that we would never be poor because our souls were rich.

The sea was outside: a rhythmic pitter-patter of huge drops drumming on window sills, streaming down grey edifice walls, splashing on cobbled pavements, frothing like dirty spume in gutters. The sonorous purr filtered in in watery waves, to mingle with the energy of our moment.

Indoors, enchanted by the cosy atmosphere and inhaling the

mouth-watering aroma of food cooked with love that scented the dining room, we were warm in the intimacy of our close friendship which dated back to the nineteen-seventies. That's when we both lived in a lively household in London – he, in the penumbra of the sprawling, dim basement, working the night through on his writing, and me, at the top of the house in the spacious white attic.

That was one of the happiest times in my life – when I was pregnant with Kasimir.

Did I hear the butterfly sigh . . . ?

"You know, Kas, your dad says that in his next life he wants to be a butterfly."

"Why?" He turned his radiant face to mine and in an instant awoke in me an overwhelming ocean of love – waves of love as blue as his sky-eyes.

"So he can flutter from flower to flower –" I said.

"I thought he already did that," whispered Philip.

I tried not to think about *that* and continued: "No, just joking. He says it's because butterflies have such an incredible life cycle – they start as worms, you know Kas. A worm hatches out of a butterfly's egg –"

"Worms, yuck!"

"What's wrong with worms?" I asked.

"I don't know . . ." He obviously wasn't interested in discussing worms when now there was this pineapple cake to deal with. Pineapple-yellow cake crumbs framed his cherub's lips.

"Come to think of it, some of my best friends are worms," mused Phil.

"Ah, OK," I continued. "Anyway, the worm weaves a cocoon around itself and lives in that furry state for a while . . . It sleeps . . . and then slowly begins to change."

METAMORPHOSIS
Transformation – Process
Transfigurment – Reformation
Transmutation – Innovation
Alteration – Variation
Mutation – Transubstantiation
Permutation – Transmigration
Modulation – Modification
REINCARNATION

"And in the spring, OUT pops the butterfly, stretching herself from her deep sleep, slowly uncrumpling her new-found wings . . . Imagine, from crawling under the ground, in the dark mud, and suddenly the exhilaration of flight . . ."

"Butterflies only live a day or two . . ." declared Philip gloomily.

"A day or two!" echoed an amazed Kasimir.

"Yes, butterflies are fast-fading rainbows – but perhaps they don't mind," I said.

"How can anyone not mind?" questioned Philip.

"*They* don't know – they think it's for ever," I said.

"*Ici l'addition*," interrupted the cute-looking waiter, obviously trying to get rid of us.

We collected ourselves; the butterfly, again crouching softly in my left palm, seemed sad. "This butterfly is a manic depressive," I said.

"I don't blame her," replied Philip, hooking his stylish, green umbrella over his arm and ushering us out of Le Napoleon. He had business affairs to take care of at his bank and would see us later at the house.

The rain had stopped. We walked back up the alleyway where we had found the exquisitely sad butterfly. A little way ahead of me Kasimir was gaily skipping on the filthy sidewalk. "Don't jump in the shit, Kas!" I shouted. Ah, the French and their poodles!

"I won't jump in the shit, Hanja," he called back, bouncing like an India rubber ball. "I'll jump in the air . . . but," he concluded with a chuckle, "I might land in the shit!"

"Oh shit! I stepped in some doggie doodoo," I cried.

"Was that a joke?" he asked.

"Yes," I said.

"I thought so," he laughed.

The clouds were parting, allowing crisp patches of silky blue to break through the silver-grey curtain. Like the weather, the butterfly too seemed to cheer up. She began at first a slow crawling up my hand, then with more energy, she pushed her tiny legs up the gabardine sleeve of the cream-hued Armani jacket I had picked up for practically nothing at a jumble sale years ago. Carefully I brought her back into my palm. She passed from one hand to the other with swift little ticklish furry movements.

We arrived at the main drag. The butterfly now crawled right up my sleeve onto the collar of my jacket, settling like a fashionable onyx pin on my lapel.

Happiness is like a
butterfly which, when

pursued, is always
beyond our grasp, but,
if you will sit down
quietly, may alight
upon you.
Nathaniel Hawthorne

I pulled her off gently. She clung quite forcefully, this delicate creature. She had gained some strength now, seeming to be waking from a long dream.

My son beamed: "She wants to live!"

"Look, Kas, there's a park there on the other side of the road. Why don't we put her in some flowers? It's no good taking her with us on the underground. She might get squashed there."

"Let's keep her, I'll hold on to her carefully," suggested Kasimir, but I did not heed his warning.

"No, let's put her in the flowers."

Hanging lightly over us, the damp air was still. The butterfly crawled back onto my sleeve and softly stretched her wings . . .

"Careful!" I shouted to Kasimir. A great big truck with tyres as tall as he, tyres that made me feel fragile, as fragile as the butterfly on my sleeve, was racing down the avenue towards us. And, at that same split moment, the butterfly took to the sky gliding soundlessly away . . . But instead of making for the chestnut trees or the trimmed bushes or the flowers planted in elegant, colourful circles in the park, the butterfly, finding her wings not strong enough for any lengthy distance, hovered-spun-looped several times in the air. She then gently dropped on the wet macadam of the boulevard just as the threatening tyre engulfed the same spot with an angry roar. Oh!

As the truck rolled on, leaving behind it the fumes of its fury and the pastel gossamer threads of a crumpled butterfly on a joyless road, I thought to myself, "And this just goes to show that the rendezvous with fate cannot be avoided whether it be in Samara or in Paris."

Kasimir pulled his mouth down expressing the mask of tragedy: "You shouldn't have let her go," he accused.

"I couldn't keep her, it was her destiny." But my heart was sad that I had allowed her her flight to death. You didn't take care of her well enough, mocked the voice of my guilt, and now she is dead.

Down in the *Metro* (underground like the worms), I recited for Kasimir one of R. D. Laing's poems:

I dreamt I was a butterfly
Dreaming it was me
It looked into a mirror
There was nothing there to see

"You lie!" I cried
It woke. I died

Goodbye butterfly . . .

Hearts and Darts
EDDIE BRUCE

|||||||||||||||||||||||||||||||||||||||||||||||||||||||||||||||||||||||||||||||||||||||||||||||||||||||||||||||||||||||||||||||||||||||||||||||||||||

Dod Kelman, a lovable cad, is drunk and disorderly in the remote countryside of Scotland.

"You're like a lot of bairns. Whit a fuss to make aboot throwing wee pointed things at a board!"

Lightly squeezing the pockets of his windcheater to confirm they held darts and cigarettes, Dod Kelman peeked in on the contented face of his sleeping year-old son. The knitted cot blanket brought mother-in-law Elsie to mind, changing Dod's smile to a grimace. Back in the main bedroom as he strapped on his watch, Fiona's lingering fragrance conspired with the two big measures of whisky he had earlier to quicken his pulse and weaken his resolve. He opened the window wide. Closing his eyes and breathing deeply he pictured himself in an earlier life walking up Aberdeen's Union Street to join his friends in the Market Bar before catching the bus to Pittodrie Stadium, smiling as he recognised each player emerging from the tunnel to rapturous applause. Then he blinked back to the reality of Ben Rinnes's heathery slopes, reminding him how much his life had changed in the space of a year. One day a hapless Aberdonian student, the next a distiller's clerk in the vale of Glenlivet, living in a distillery-owned cottage with his wife and son – and Elsie within nagging distance.

Downstairs he crept up behind his wife as she stacked the last plate on the draining board, slipping his arms around her waist and holding her close, the blond softness of her hair tickling his nose as he breathed her perfume. Roddy, their young Labrador, padded his way over to tug jealously at his master's jeans. "Ye ken, Fiona," Dod murmured, "sometimes I feel as if I'm on another planet. The stillness maks me nervous."

She turned into him, wiping her damp hand on his sweatshirt, pouting as she pressed against him, gazing into his eyes. "I know. You miss your pals and your fitba."

"Aye, but . . ."

"Well, I miss my man when he's at work a' day and off tae the pub when he gets hame." She winked, tugging at his sleeve. "C'mon upstairs," she whispered. "Wee Geordie'll be sleepin' for ages yet."

"Oh, Fiona, ye ken I canna . . ." Just then the doorbell chimed, reminding Dod that the darts cup semi-final wouldn't wait, although with luck maybe Fiona would.

The drams they had before leaving work gave most of the Clachan team the edge in confidence, that and their position at the top of the district league. Veteran Robbie Stronach was a rock-solid captain while Lachie Geddes the cooper played with amazing flair considering he swayed about so much on the oche. In his singles match Dod checked out with only eleven darts and followed that up with a one-five-seven finish in the doubles. Inspired by the anchormen the rest of the team raised their game and the outcome was never in doubt.

"You're a lucky bugger," said Robbie to Dod later, slapping his back as they grouped together for a congratulatory drink.

He smirked, high on success and drinks his beaten opponents had bought him. "Whit can I say, Rob? Anything for a free beer, eh? I am an Aberdonian, ye ken!" But he had a feeling the luck the brewer was referring to had little to do with his skills on the dartboard. He'd encountered that look before, and not only from Robbie, ever since he brought Fiona back to the glen.

The publican's daughter interrupted. "You're like a lot of bairns. Whit a fuss to make aboot throwing wee pointed things at a board!" Isobel mocked, shoving her way through with a tray of steaming-hot stovies and oatcakes. Blushing as she handed Dod his plate she leaned forward and whispered, "You'll be walking the dog the morn, I suppose . . . aboot seven?"

"Aye," Dod whispered back without hesitation, winking as their eyes met, "aboot seven."

Fiona was asleep when he got back and Dod lay awake remembering the first time they'd made love and how he couldn't have felt more fulfilled, more ecstatic, if the Dons had beaten Celtic six nil

– at Parkhead! He'd gone for months without a girlfriend and found himself drawn towards the quiet country girl, attracted by her looks and challenged by her indifference. He'd sought her out at lectures and in the canteen, gently probing her background, convinced they had much in common. What emerged, widowed mother, strict religious upbringing, night curfews, pressure to study, peer derision, came as no surprise . . . Then a shy confession.

"A nervous breakdown?" He had placed his arm around her slim shoulders then, instinctively. "I'm nae surprised!"

"I went off the rails, as my mither put it," she had told him. "I jist wanted to know what life was like for other lassies my age. I was lonely."

"Nae wonder."

"I broke a few o' her rules for a while, then the minister preached me a sermon and I agreed to try uni. That's it . . . except . . ."

"Except?"

"I hate it here."

He had mouthed the words "I love you" to at least one girl before, but now it had meaning for him, just as he had understood her aloofness as being a cover for vulnerability. He would protect her.

When she finally succumbed, she amazed him with her instinct for fantastic lovemaking, devouring him like a hungry animal, telling him he was the man of her dreams – dreams much more imaginative than his own sex fantasies ever were. What followed, the pregnancy, the marriage, the decision to quit studies, the move to the country, all seemed to be outside his control but he didn't care.

Because he did love her. Even now, though he strayed a wee bit with Isobel now and then (that was just the drink and a young girl's infatuation and he always felt bad about it afterwards), he was happy enough with his new lifestyle. The job was undemanding and the wages below par, but they had fine accommodation, and the plentiful supply of the best malt whisky meant he spent most of his waking hours in a contented Scotch mist. He would learn to live with moody hangovers and guilt pangs and anyway, they only lasted until the next dram. It was all about sacrifices and rewards and wasn't he forever having to listen to holy Elsie telling him how lucky he was and how she'd pray for him?

He pulled back the bedroom curtain when he heard them coming. They were early. It was a Thursday-night ritual but Cup Final night was special. Alistair, the head maltman, would have rushed his dinner and pedalled down to his youngest son's house, then on to the next. They would cycle on in single file collecting team members along the way and by the time they rounded the corner to the last distillery cottage where Dod and Fiona lived, the procession resembled a seven-headed serpent, each head shouting friendly abuse as it came to a halt by Dod's gate. "I'll be doon in a minute, lads," he shouted, hoping they'd stay out on the road. He had a sulking wife to deal with first.

"Whit is it lass?" he asked. "Has your mither been moanin' aboot me again?"

She pushed his arm away, turning to gaze out of the window. "You an' your darts team, Dod! Are they mair important than you an' me?"

His eyes widened in disbelief at her anger. "Whit brought this . . ."

"I blame mysel' for bringin' you here. The drink's pickled the wee bit brain you had. Here's a clue – it happened a year ago."

"Oh God, Fiona . . ." He felt a surge of compassion, a desire to hold her close but she elbowed him off. "I'm right sorry, lass. Whit aboot an anniversary dinner somewhere at the weekend?" But he had forgotten and even now his recollections of the wedding, never mind the date, were a bit hazy. Fiona, a vision in her short midnight-blue dress, himself and big Alistair MacPhail in their kilts hired for the day . . . the booze . . . the breakages . . .

"Go on, your pals are waitin'," she said, coughing to clear her throat.

Hesitating at the door, thinking it was just as well he'd taken that twenty out of the housekeeping earlier, he said, "Aye, but I hate leavin' you like this . . ."

He was but halfway down the path when she called him, her words vibrating with emotion. "I'm takin' Geordie tae my mither's for the night. From whit I've been hearin', you'll nae be lonely."

Dod blushed amid wolf whistles and a shout of "Whit have you been up tae, Dod?" from impatient but amused onlookers. His embarrassment was changing to anger. "Later!"

"Suit yoursel'. I've nothing tae hide."

"Oh no?" he shouted. "Would ye like me tae tell the boys – and your mither, maybe – that I was shagging ye lang before we were wed." His face screwed up in instant remorse. "Come on, lads," he said, quickly mounting his Raleigh Sports, "we'll be late."

"Wait!" Fiona's voice was firm now, commanding.

There was a simultaneous squeaking of brakes and head-turning. "Whit?"

She walked forward hands on hips, eyeing each cyclist in turn before stopping next to her husband. "So were your pals!"

Keep Calm and Carry On
JAMES MULHERN

||||||||||||||||||||||||||||||||||||||||||||||||||||||||||||||||||||||||||||||||||||||||||||||||||||||||||||||||||||||||||||||||||||||

Aiden's grandmother goes to great lengths to look after him when his mother succumbs to mental illness – but is it too far?

"We're just borrowing it for a little while to help your mother. I think God will understand."

My grandmother sat on the toilet seat. I was on the floor just in front of her.

She brushed my brown curly hair until my scalp hurt.

"You got your grandfather's hair. Stand up. Look at yourself in the mirror. That's much better, don't you think?"

I touched my scalp. "It hurts."

"You gotta toughen up, Aiden. Weak people get nowhere in this world. Your grandfather was weak. Addicted to the bottle. Your mother has an impaired mind. Now she's in a nuthouse. And your father, he just couldn't handle the responsibility of a child. People gotta be strong. Do you understand me?" She bent down and stared into my face. Her hazel eyes seemed enormous. I smelled coffee on her breath. There were blackheads on her nose. She pinched my cheeks.

I reflexively pushed her hands away.

"Life is full of pain, sweetheart. And I don't mean just the physical kind." She took a cigarette from her case on the back of the toilet, lit it, and inhaled. "You'll be hurt a lot, but you got to carry on. You know what the British people used to say when the Germans bombed London during World War II?"

"No."

"Keep calm and carry on." She hit my backside. "Now run along and put some clothes on." I was wearing just my underwear and T-shirt. "We have a busy day."

I dressed in the blue jeans and a yellow short-sleeve shirt she had bought me. She stood in front of the mirror by the front door of the living room, holding a picture of my mother. She kissed the glass and placed it on the end table next to the couch. Then she looked at herself in the mirror and arranged her pearl necklace, put on bright-red lipstick, and fingered her grey hair, trying to hide a thinning spot at the top of her forehead. She turned and smoothed her green cotton dress, glancing at herself from behind. "Not bad for an old broad." She looked me over. "Come here." She tucked my shirt in, licked her hand, and smoothed my hair. "You'd think I never brushed it."

Just as she opened the front door she said, "Hold on," and went to the kitchen counter and put her hand in a glass jar full of bills. She took out what must have been at least thirty single dollar bills.

"Here. Give this money to the kiddos next door."

When we were outside, she pushed me towards their house. They were playing on their swing set in the fenced-in yard. In front of the broken-down house was a yard of weeds. A rusted bicycle with no wheels lay on the ground. The young pale girl with stringy hair looked at me suspiciously as I approached the fence. Her brother stood, arms folded, in the background. He had a mean look on his face and spat.

"This is for you," I said, shoving the money through the chain links. The girl reached out to grab it, but most of the bills fell onto the dirt.

"Thank you," she said.

As I walked away, her brother yelled, "We don't need no charity from you."

I opened the door of my grandmother's blue Plymouth; she had the air conditioning blasting and it was already full of cigarette smoke.

She crossed herself. "Say it with me. 'There but for the grace of God go I.'"

I repeated the words with her and we drove to her friend Margie's house, not more than ten minutes away. Margie was a smelly fat lady with a big white cat that hissed at me. She always wore the same navy-blue sweater, and was constantly picking white cat hairs off her clothes, while talking about the latest sermon, God, or the devil. Nanna told me when they were young girls, their classmates made fun of her. "Stinky" they called her. And she did smell. Like urine, and cats, and mothballs.

"Don't let him get out," Margie yelled, as the cat pounced from behind the open door. "Arnold, don't you dare run away!" She bent over to grab his tail and groaned at the same time. "My back!"

"Don't worry. I got him." I had my arms wrapped around the white monster. He hissed.

"Why don't you put him in the closet when you open the front door? We go through this every time," my grandmother said, pushing past her towards the kitchen in the back of the house. "I gotta sit down. It's hot as hell out there."

Margie placed a tray of ham sandwiches, along with cheese and crackers, on the round grey Formica table. I liked her wallpaper – white with the red outlines of trains. Her husband had been a conductor; he died when he got squished between two train cars.

"I don't know how I feel about all those miracles Father Tom was going on about." Margie placed a sandwich on a plate for me with some chips. "What ya want to drink, Aiden? I got nice lemonade." Her two front teeth were red from where her lipstick had smudged. And as usual she had white cat hairs all over her blue sweater, especially the ledge of her belly where the cat sat all the time.

"That sounds good."

She smiled. "Always such a nice boy. Polite. You'll never have any trouble with this one. Not like you did with Lorraine."

"I hate when you call her that."

"That's her name, ain't it?" She poured my grandmother and me lemonade and sat down with a huff.

"That was my mother's name, her formal name. I've told you a thousand times to call her Laura."

"What the hell difference does it make?" Margie bit into her sandwich and rolled her eyes at me.

"Makes a lot of difference. My mother was a crackpot. I named my daughter Lorraine to be nice."

"Well, Laura is . . ." I knew Margie was going to say that my mother was a crackpot, too.

"Laura is what?" My grandmother put her sandwich down and leaned into Margie.

"Is a nice girl. She's got problems, but don't we all." She reached out and clasped my hand. "Right, Aiden?"

"Yes, Margie."

My grandmother rubbed her neck and spoke softly. "Nobody's

perfect. Laura's getting better. She's just got a few psychological issues. And the new meds they have her on seem to be doing her good. She's a beautiful human being, and that's what's most important. Besides, who's to say what's normal? My Laura has always been different. One of the happiest people I ever met." Her eyes were shiny and her face flushed. Her bottom lip trembled. She looked at me. "Don't you gotta use the bathroom?" She raised her eyebrows. That was her signal.

"Yes, I gotta pee."

"Well, you don't have to get so detailed," she said. "Just go."

Margie laughed hard and farted.

I made my exit just in time, creeping up the grey stairs. The old banister was dusty. The rug in the upstairs hall was full of Arnold's hair. I bent down and picked one up to examine it, then rubbed my pants. Nanna said Margie's room was the last one on the left. Her jewellery case was on top of her dresser. I took the diamond earrings and opal bracelet Nanna had told me about. There was also a couple of pretty rings – one a large red stone, the other a blue one. These and a gold necklace with a cross I shoved into my pockets. Then I walked to the bathroom and flushed the toilet. I messed up the towel a bit so it looked like I dried my hands in it.

When I entered the kitchen they were still talking about miracles.

My grandmother passed our plates to Margie who had filled the sink with sudsy water.

"Of course there was raising Lazarus from the dead," Margie said. "And then the healing of the deaf and dumb men. Oh, and the blind man, too," she said, raising her hand and splashing my grandmother.

"Let's not forget about the fish. And the water into wine," my grandmother said.

Margie shook her head. "I don't know, Catherine." She looked down. "It's hard to believe that Jesus could have done all that. Why aren't there miracles today?"

I imagined a fish jumping into her face from the water in the sink.

My grandmother smiled at me. "Of course there are miracles today. As a matter of fact, I'm taking Aiden to that priest at Mission church. A charismatic healer is what they call him. Aiden's gonna be cured, aren't you, honey?"

"Cured of what?" Margie said.

"Oh he's got a little something wrong with his blood is all. Too many white cells. Leukaemia. But this priest is gonna take care of all that."

"Leukaemia!" Margie said. "Catherine, that's serious." Margie tried to smile at me, but I could tell she was upset. "Sit down, honey." She motioned for me to go to the table. "We're almost done here."

"You gotta take him to a good doctor," she whispered to my grandmother, as if I couldn't hear.

"I know that. I'm not dumb. God will take care of everything."

We said our goodbyes and when we were in the car, my grandmother said, "Let me see what you got." I pulled the goods out of my pockets while she unclasped her black plastic pocketbook. Her eyes lit up.

"Perfect. She isn't lookin', is she?"

I looked at the house. Margie was nowhere in sight. Probably sitting on her rocking chair with Arnold in her lap.

"Now put those in here," she said, nodding towards her bag, and I did.

When we were about to turn onto Tremont Street where the church was, I remembered the gold necklace and cross. I pulled it out of my back pocket and my grandmother took it from me, running a red light. "This would look beautiful on Laura." In a moment, there was a police car pulling us over.

"Don't say anything," my grandmother said, as we moved to the side of the road. She looked in the rear-view mirror and put her window down.

"Ma'am, you just ran a red light." The policeman was tall with a hooked nose and dark-brown close-set eyes.

"I know, officer. I was just saying a prayer with my grandson. He gave me this gold cross. I got distracted. I'm very sorry."

He leaned into the car. I smiled.

"Is that a birthday gift for your grandmother?"

"Yes. I wanted to surprise her."

"And he certainly did," she said, patting my knee and smiling at the police officer.

"It's a good thing no cars were coming. You could have been hurt," he said. "That's a beautiful cross," he added.

My grandmother began to cry. "Isn't it, though?" She sniffled.

The officer placed his hand firmly on the edge of the window. "Consider this a warning. You can go. I'd put that cross away."

"Of course. Of course." She turned to me. "Here, Aiden. Put it back in your pocket."

The police officer waited for us to drive away. I turned and looked. He waved.

"Are you sad, Nanna?"

"Don't be silly." She waved her hand. "That was just an act."

I laughed and she did, too.

We parked. "I need to get that chalice, Aiden. I read an article in The Boston Globe that said some people believe it has incredible curing powers. It's a replica of a chalice from long ago, over one hundred years old, with lots of pretty stones on it. Experts say it's priceless. I'm thinking if I have your mother drink from it, she'll get better and come home to us. Won't that be nice?" She rubbed my head gently and smiled at me.

I looked away, towards the church where an old man was helping a lady in a wheelchair up a ramp. "Won't God be mad?"

"Aiden, I'm going to return it. We're just borrowing it for a little while to help your mother. I think God will understand. Don't you worry, sweetheart."

We entered Mission church. It smelled of shellac, incense, perfume, and old people. It was hard to see in the musty darkness. Bright light shone through the stained-glass windows where Jesus was depicted in the twelve or so Stations of the Cross.

"Let's move to the front." My grandmother pulled me out of the line and cut in front of an old lady, who looked bewildered. "Shouldn't you go to the end of the line?" she whispered kindly, smiling down at me. Her hair was sweaty and her fat freckled bicep jiggled when she tapped my grandmother's shoulder. The freckles reminded me of the asteroid belt.

"I'm sorry. We're in a hurry. We have to help a sick neighbour after this. I just want my grandson to get a cure."

"What's wrong?" she whispered. We were four people away from the priest, who was standing at the altar. He prayed over people then lightly touched them. They fell backwards into the arms of two old men with maroon suit jackets and blue ties.

"Aiden has leukaemia."

The woman's eyes teared up. "I'm sorry." She patted my forearm. "You'll be cured, sweetie." Again her flabby bicep jiggled and the asteroids bounced.

When it was our turn, my grandmother said, "Father, please cure him. And can you say a prayer for my daughter, too?"

"Of course." The white-haired, red-faced priest bent down. I smelled alcohol on his breath. "What ails you, young man?"

I was confused.

"He's asking you about your illness, Aiden."

"I have leukaemia," I said proudly.

The priest said some mumbo-jumbo prayer and pushed my chest. I knew I was supposed to fall back but was afraid the old geezers wouldn't catch me.

"Fall," my grandmother whispered irritably. Then she said extra softly, "Remember our plan."

I fell hard, shoving myself against the old guy. He toppled over as well. People gasped. His friend and the priest began to pick us up. I pretended to be hurt bad. "Oww. My head is killing me." Several people gathered around us. My grandmother yelled, "Oh my God," and stepped onto the altar, kneeling in front of a giant Jesus on the cross. "Dear Jesus," she said loudly, "I don't know how many more tribulations I can take." Then she crossed herself, hurried across the altar, swiping a gold chalice and putting it in her handbag while everyone was distracted by my moaning and fake crying.

"He'll be OK," she said, putting her arm under mine and helping the others pull me up.

When I was standing, she said to the priest, "You certainly have the power of the Holy Spirit in you. It came out of you like the water that gushed from the rock at Rephidim and Kadesh.

"Let's get out of here before there's a flood." She laughed. The priest looked confused. The old lady who let us cut in line eyed my grandmother's handbag and shook her head as we passed.

When we were in front of Rita's house, our last stop before home, I asked my grandmother what "tribulation" meant. And where were "Repapah" and "Kadiddle".

She laughed. "You pronounced those places wrong, but it doesn't matter. Your mother used to do the same thing whenever I quoted that Bible passage." She began to open the car door. "I don't know where the hell those places are. Somewhere in the Middle East . . . And a tribulation is a problem."

"Oh."

After ringing the bell a couple times we opened the door. We found Rita passed out on the couch.

My grandmother took an ice cube from the freezer and held it against her forehead. Rita sat bolt upright. "Jesus, Mary and Joseph. You scared the bejesus out of me." She was wearing a yellow nightgown and her auburn hair was set in curlers. "Oh, Aiden. I didn't see you there," she said. She kissed my cheek. For the second time that day I smelled alcohol.

"So do you think you can help me out?" my grandmother asked.

Rita looked at me.

"Of course I can. Just pull me up and I'll get my chequebook."

I suddenly realised all my grandmother's friends were fat.

At the kitchen table, Rita said, "Should I make it out to the hospital?"

"Oh, no. Make it out to me. I've opened a bank account to pay for his medical expenses."

"Will five thousand do for now?" Rita was rich. Her husband was a "real-estate tycoon", my grandmother was always saying. He dropped dead shovelling snow a few years back.

"That's so generous of you." My grandmother cried again. More fake tears, I thought.

We had tea and chocolate-chip cookies. Rita asked how my mother was doing. My grandmother said "fine" and looked away, wringing her hands. Then she started talking about the soap operas that they watched. My grandmother loved Erica from *All My Children*. Said she was a woman who knew how to get what she wanted and admired that very much. Rita said she thought Erica was a bitch.

When we were home, listening to talk radio in the living room, I asked my grandmother if she believed in miracles, like the ones she talked about earlier in the day with Margie.

"Sure, sure," she said, not looking up. She was taking the jewellery and chalice out of her bag and examining them in the light. I saw bits of dust in the sunlight streaming through the bay window.

"You're not listening to me, Nanna."

She put the items back in her handbag and stared at me. "Of course I am."

"Well, do you think I'll have a miracle and be cured of leukaemia?"

"Aiden." She laughed. "You haven't got leukaemia. You're as healthy as a horse, silly."

"But you told everybody I was sick."

"Sweetheart. That was just to evoke pity."

"What does that mean?"

"Make people feel bad so we can get things from them. I need money to take care of you, Aiden." She spoke hesitantly and looked down, like she was ashamed. "I'm broke. Your grandfather left me with nothing and I gotta pay for your mother's medical expenses. If Margie notices her jewellery gone, maybe she'll think you took it to help your Nanna. I told her I was having a problem paying your hospital bills."

"Sorta like a *tribulation*, right?"

"Exactly, sweetheart."

"Is my mother a tribulation?"

This time my grandmother's tears were real. They gushed like water from that rock in the Middle East. I knelt before her and put my head in her lap. She rubbed my hair and looked out the window. It seemed the tears would never stop.

"Don't worry, Nanna. I believe in miracles, too. Someday Mom will come home from the hospital."

And we stayed like that until the sunbeams dimmed and the dust disappeared and her tears stopped.

In the quiet of the room, she whispered, "Keep calm and carry on," to me or to herself. Or to both of us.

Lost in Glass Slippers
KELLY HAAS SHACKELFORD

Cancer comes between a mother and her enjoyment of her daughter's birthday.

"Such simple joy is that of a child. I smiled back, willing myself to be happy."

Trembling, I flicked the lighter, hovering over the three candles on my daughter's princess cake. Her bright green eyes danced in glee as she slid her fingers close to the pink icing to sneak a swipe. Shoving her sticky prize into her mouth, her lips curled up in delight at the sweet taste. I tried to smile. It would be my last birthday with her.

Friends and family said to forget about the cancer, the treatment, the pain and to just live for today. Such easy words when one is not planning a funeral.

"Your turn, Mommy." Isabella ran her slender finger across the cake, scooping up a fat helping and pushing it into my mouth. Her blond curls danced as she threw her head back and laughed. So full of life was that sound.

Bittersweet filled my mouth. How I hated myself. Why could I not just live for today? Why could I not just treasure what little time I had left?

"Sing it again," my daughter shouted, giggling at her own demand. The room broke out in *Happy Birthday* as if my world was not about to stop. Everyone acted as if funeral clothes did not need to be purchased, a casket chosen, and songs selected.

"Time to open gifts." My mother gave me a stiff smile, reminding me to toughen up and act like a good Southern mother. Even cancer requires manners, at least here in the South.

My lips smiled while my heart sank, watching my daughter shake her present. I would never get to see her go to college, get married, or have children. I felt the precious minutes slipping away.

How does someone prepare for death, when life is so full? How does one answer when death is knocking, waiting its turn to party? I wanted to jump up and scream that I was not ready for it, but I knew death would never bend.

"Look, Mommy," Isabella shouted and then coughed. She held up a Cinderella dress, complete with crown and glass slippers. It had taken me weeks to find it, but it was all she wanted.

Such simple joy is that of a child. I smiled back, willing myself to be happy, to be strong, and to forget about the funeral. My body shook as if it were rebelling against such unnatural happiness."Mommy," Isabella said, "can I wear it to meet the Angels?"

"Yes, sweetie, the Angels need a princess." I choked back tears. I would not cry at my daughter's last birthday party.

"And the slippers, Mommy. I am going to dance in Heaven," she said, clutching the play slippers to her chest. Pride spread across her face.

"Yes, baby, the slippers too." I wrapped my arms around her, forcing myself to breathe. I slipped the play slippers on her feet and stood. Dancing to the tune of *Happy Birthday*, around and around we went as she giggled and coughed.

I sighed and decided. Tomorrow I will finish planning her funeral. Today, I am going to get lost, dancing in glass slippers.

Murder by Plastic
PHIL SLATTERY

Small-time crook Alan Patterson wakes up to find past indiscretions have caught up with him. First published in Every Day Fiction in 2013.

Tears streamed from Alan's eyes and he shook. "Please, take the tape off!" came out as "MnnmMnNm."

When Alan Patterson awoke, he found himself naked and bound with wire to a heavy wooden chair with duct tape sealing his mouth. His head throbbed. The night was hot and humid and sweat rolled down his forehead and into his eyes, blurring his vision. He blinked a few times to clear them. He noticed a large, sharply dressed man sitting on another wooden chair a few feet away. The man seemed very serious and squinted through small, piggish eyes.

Glancing around, Alan saw that he was in a dilapidated warehouse. A half-dozen younger, just as sharply dressed, just as serious men stood behind the seated man. One held a bucket of water. On a small workbench to his left, Alan saw a hacksaw, a blowtorch, pliers, a claw hammer, a skinning knife, and a meat cleaver. He also saw a dozen stolen credit cards he had recently bought from Joey "Snake Eyes" Abandonato and had intended to sell.

The large man reached inside his suit and pulled out a driver's licence. He scrutinised it and then looked at Alan's face for several seconds. "This is a crappy photo of you, Mr Wilson," he muttered. He tossed the licence onto the floor. "You may not know my face, but you know who I am. I am Don Antonio Vespucci. I live down the street from you." The Don gritted his teeth and clenched his fists as his entire body seemed to tense. He shifted in his chair and then, apparently trying to relax enough to speak, took a deep breath and exhaled slowly. "I'm the father of the boy you ran down while speeding through our neighbourhood three weeks ago."

Alan's eyes widened and he shook his head violently while trying to shout through the duct tape. "*No! I didn't do it! I'm not Steve Wilson!*"

The Don raised his voice, drowning out Alan's muffled protests. "I can't begin to describe what you did to my family. No one should go through the agony of having a son die in his arms! Do you know what it's like to get a phone call telling you your child is in critical care? Your entire world collapses in a heartbeat!" Don Vespucci slammed his fists onto the arms of his chair. Then he seemed lost in thought while he adjusted his tie and fought back tears. "Isn't it strange how lives can change in an instant? The critical moment in my son's death lasted less than a second. He ran into the street to get his baseball just as his mom turned her back to say hello to Snake Eyes there and his wife Maria." He nodded to indicate the man to Alan's extreme left.

Alan turned his head as far as possible and looked into the cold, reptilian stare that had earned Joey his moniker. "*Joey?*" Alan tried to say under the tape. "*No! Forgive me, Joey! Forgive me!*"

The Don continued. "When Snake Eyes saw my son run into the street, he glanced up just in time to see you speed over my Tony Jr. He recognised your car, your rear licence, and the back of your head."

Alan wept as he tried to shout from under the tape, "*Joey, forgive me! Tell him I was in Jersey then!*"

Again, the Don paused to calm down and assume a more professional tone. "Normally," said Don Vespucci, "I try to meet all the new people in our neighbourhood as soon as someone moves in. Unfortunately, I've been busier than usual lately and haven't had time to visit anyone. Had I been able to introduce myself to you and had stressed, as I normally do, the value of family in my life and how I like things done in my neighbourhood, perhaps we wouldn't be here."

Tears streamed from Alan's eyes and he shook. "*Please, take the tape off!*" came out only as "MnnmMnNmMnmMm."

"We might not have come to this regrettable situation if you hadn't decided to scurry out of town like a cockroach when you found out whose son you had just killed. It disgusts me that you abandoned your family to save your life! You're fortunate that I have principles so I don't hurt anyone's family. At this point, I have more respect for the rats that'll feed on your eyes than I do for you. Had you come to me after the accident and accepted responsibility, I might actually have had some admiration for you. I still would've killed you, but I would've killed you quickly."

Alan began to shake his head again and his eyes bulged from their sockets as he tried to scream, "*I just stole Wilson's identity!*" through the duct tape.

"Don't waste the few breaths you have left. If I wanted to hear your lies, I'd have Snake Eyes take the tape off." Again the Don breathed deeply through his nose and exhaled as if he were trying to relax. Anger rose in his voice. "What kind of idiot runs to Brooklyn where we can just snatch him off the street? You should have at least left the state." Don Vespucci stretched out a hand towards Joey. "Gimme the hammer. We're going to start with the foot that was on the gas and work our way up. Pete, keep the water handy. We don't want Mr Wilson to pass out from the pain."

Alan struggled against the duct tape and again tried in vain to scream through the tape. "*I'm not Steve Wilson! I bought his credit cards from Joey just two weeks ago!*"

Watching Joey smirk as he handed a hammer to the Don, Alan remembered his last night with Maria at Noel's Motel and began to weep. As she pulled on her clothes, she warned him: "Joey's smarter than you think. It wouldn't surprise me if he knows about us already. He has ears everywhere. Me, he'll just beat, but you – well, just don't let him find out."

Nothing to Lose
MITCHELL TOEWS

||||||||||||||||||||||||||||||||||||||||||||||||||||||||||||||||||||||||||||||||||||||||||||||||||||||||||||||||||||||||||||||||||||||||||||||||||||||||||

A baker and former hockey player reminisces on his colourful past as he delivers buns in the dusty Manitoba sun.

"Screw you, Hart! Let's go get a beer at the pub. Man! Who crapped in your porridge?"

The man's arm hung from the window of the bread-delivery van. He tapped his wedding band absent-mindedly against the Hartplatz Bakery logo painted on the door. Viewed from above, the van carried enough speed down the flat country road to raise a V-shaped plume of fine white dust, like the wake of a boat.

Dust hung in the heavy midsummer air, settling almost imperceptibly and with clinging persistence on the rose hips and yarrow and fescue and crocus growing alongside the road and down into the ditches. Dry fields lining the road awaited a summer storm; the first large drops would land as heavy as pats of butter.

Inside the van, a residue of Prairie Rose flour dusted the man's hair and stood out on the peach fuzz on his ears and the sloping nape of his neck.

He shifted down into second gear and eased the clutch back out, making the motor race and the rear wheels check on the sandy gravel, adjusting their pace to the new ratio and slowing for the intersection ahead. The geometric roads drew a pale yellowish cross in dark-green alfalfa fields.

"*ARRÊT*", the sign demanded, in the De Salaberry Rural Municipality, north of the town of Hartplatz. The panel van rolled to a stop and the driver – the owner of the bakery, Hart Zehen – revved the engine once and then turned off the ignition. He sat in the close heat of the vehicle, the radiator ticking rapidly and crickets and frogs keeping time from their hiding places in the grass.

A male red-winged blackbird swooped down towards a bulrush with its three-toed feet splayed out to grasp the brown, cigar-shaped spadix. His wings flared open just in time to stall and spill enough speed for landing. Trilling, the bird cocked its head, and then took off as quickly as it had come, leaving the bulrush swaying.

Hart checked his wristwatch again. Still twenty minutes early for the wedding delivery to the Giroux Hall. He knew the manager there and he did not want to spend any extra time with him. The order called for him to bring the buns, eighty dozen zwieback, by 6.30. So 6.30 it would be.

He opened the door and it creaked, piercing the quiet. Swinging his legs out, he pushed off the seat edge to land with both feet, a dusty plop on the road. He looked back at the sky to the northwest, where, impressively, an impasto storm cloud was building. It was dark purple at the bottom and startling white higher up, contrasting with the cerulean prairie sky. The thunderhead hung with menace, gathering bulk as Hart stood far below – an Israelite facing the giant Philistine.

The radio came on loudly when Hart leaned in and gave the key a quarter turn. It carried a baseball game from Minneapolis, the signal skipping in off the cloud cover to the south.

"*Killebrew, the young first baseman, leads off this inning,*" announced the play-by-play man, his flat Midwest accent pinching off the words and sounding foreign to the Manitoba baker, far to the north. "*Ball one! A curveball that Harmon left alone. Good eye, it bounced in the dirt in front of home plate.*"

Imagining, Hart sat on his haunches in the crossroads and flashed a sign for a fastball. Deliberately, he adjusted his imaginary mask with his right hand and presented a low target to the pitcher; a single rogue sunflower plant growing in the stony edge of the northbound lane. The *tournesol* sat atop a thick green stalk, its speckled face staring unblinkingly towards the southwest.

"*STEE-rike!*" the announcer shouted. Hart gathered four or five smooth hardball-size stones and laid them near where he crouched. He picked one and tossed it towards the sunflower, standing tall and attentive in the angled evening sunlight that shone on the two of them.

Several batters later, Hart was sweating lightly, enjoying his pantomime ballgame. "*One out, runner on first, the count two-and-two on the Twins number seven hitter*," said the sing-song baritone. "*Pitcher looks for the sign . . . he nods and reaches up into his stretch . . . pauses, holds the runner momentarily . . . now he delivers – THE RUNNER GOES!*"

Hart grabbed a stone, crow-hopped up and fired a low, hissing bullet to where second base would be – an oiled cedar telephone pole across the ditch. "BOCK!" sounded the rock as it hit the pole just right of centre, embedding in the wood. The crickets and frogs fell silent as one, then slowly renewed their cheering chorus.

He grinned as the voice from the radio, full of static, blared, "*He throws him OUT and the batter goes down swinging to end the inning. Strike him out, throw him out! Washington zero, Twins zero. We'll be right back after this message from GRAIN BELT BEER!*"

Hart checked his watch again, the leather band stained white with sweat, dried in a jagged line. He jumped into the seat and started the low-slung van, spinning the tyres and shooting stones out behind the back bumper.

Feeling strangely exultant from the exertion of the silly, make-believe ball game and in anticipation of the $40 cash he would collect on this Saturday night, he slewed the Chevy around the last corner to his destination. His tyres clattered the thick boards of the bridge deck, the sound echoing off the hall's whitewashed stucco walls. He wheeled around tightly on the packed-dirt lot, braked hard, then backed up to about ten feet from the "Deliveries" door. Hopping out, he spun ninety degrees on the ball of his foot and flicked the door shut. He snapped down on the lever handle to open the left rear door and then side-stepped to do the same for the right. Every motion was athletic, rhythmic, and economical – practised thirty times that day alone.

Inside the van were two stacks of bread trays filled with bags of fresh buns. Saturday was the traditional zwieback baking day – for events and Sunday afternoon *faspa*. Still warm, the scent of the buns filled the air: yeasty, with the faint sweetness of caramelised sugar and scalded milk. The stacks stood side by side and a pink delivery slip was taped to the top of one of the clear-plastic packages. Hart patted his back pocket, feeling for the invoice pad, then picked up one of the stacks, stepped to the delivery door and knocked deftly with the hard toe of his shoe.

He paused to listen and, hearing the lock open inside, backed up slightly to make way for the door to swing open.

"Well, well, right on time," said a thin man with a clean white dress shirt and a red tie tucked into the buttoned front. He stood smiling with his hands on his hips in the doorway, a silver tooth glinting in the evening sun. His sleeves were rolled and a blue anchor was tattooed on one of his corded forearms. "Where's the regular driver – Nightingale?"

"Night off. His twins' birthday today," Hart replied, hugging the trays like the waist of a polka partner as he brushed by the taller man into the kitchen. His leather soles slapped on the painted concrete floor as he walked into the room carrying the awkward metal rack. He raised his eyebrows questioningly.

The manager, Tamsyn, hesitated, and then pointed back into the room where several pots sat boiling on a large range top, wetting the wall with their steam. "Put those buns next to the stove, on the left." As Hart walked by for the second load of buns, Tamsyn asked, "You the hockey player?"

"I played," Hart replied, smiling, his front teeth cut at an angle from a high stick, small scars like crossbones on the ball of his chin.

"Not no more?"

"Not no more," he said, stacking the second load of buns on top of the first. After wiping his forehead with the back of his wrist, he opened the invoice book and pointed at the top copy. "Forty bucks, see-voo-play."

"Eh?" Tamsyn squinted, pausing in mid-action as he pulled out a leather cash wallet on a chain. "You are obviously not French." He put the emphasis on the last syllable: obvious-LEE.

Hart smirked. He shifted his weight from one foot to the other and thumbed the edge of the invoice pad, making a rippling sound.

Tamsyn unzipped the heavy brown pouch. He picked four tens free, then rubbed each one between thumb and forefinger to make sure two bills had not stuck together. He gestured towards Hart with the money. "You had a try-out with Detroit, I hear."

Hart shrugged his rounded shoulders; his head down as he marked the invoice, "Paid – Cash" and signed with his initials. He thought fleetingly of the long-ago try-out camp in Saskatoon; the big star players gliding around the rink. "Good check!" the red-faced coach had yelled to him as he climbed back over the boards in a scrimmage.

"Damn fine," Tamsyn said with a look of genuine approval on his face. "Nothing to lose, right? You go an' give it your best shot and let the chips fall. Right?

"I played for Ste Anne, eh," Tamsyn added, smiling and holding out the forty dollars to Hart. "Centreman."

"You got nothing to lose, right?" he remembered one of his brothers saying to him when they made the deal for the bakery, dissolving the partnership.

"Lots to lose. Same as you," he had replied. Hart and two of his older brothers had originally bought out their uncle, paying him what the property was worth plus a small cash stake for him and their father, who worked in the bakery. After a year of argument and indecision, Hart had wanted to end the three-man partnership. "I don't make a good partner," he'd told his wife.

The terms were blunt. Either the two brothers bought him out or he bought them out; the price was $5,000 per share, either way. They got to choose – stay or go. Hart had wanted the partnership to work but it had not and he believed this was the best way out of it. At first, they had scorned him. "Screw you, Hart! Let's go get a beer at the pub. Man! Who crapped in your porridge?"

He stood his ground. Finally, they wavered, their anger rising when they realised he was unyielding; resolute. "Yeah, you've got nothing to lose. If the bakery goes broke, you can always fall back on hockey – make a career and play in the states." He said nothing, shaking his head.

"Hey! YOU! What the hell's wrong with you?" Tamsyn stood close to him, waving the money and shouting, snapping his fingers with his free hand. He leaned forward, bending at the waist.

Hart came out of his reverie. "OK, OK," he replied, stepping back. He took the forty dollars, passed Tamsyn the invoice copy and nodded, mumbling thanks. His mind had once again been stuck in the bakery, ten years back, arguing with his brothers.

The land was flat here. A few miles north, east or south and it began to roll, taking contour from shallow rivers or gravel ridges. He stood with the sun in his face, watching heat waves rising off the highway three miles away and glimpsing bright flashes of cars and tractor trailers. Briefly, while looking to the west, Hart thought of his time on the coast with his brother-in-law Bill, commercial fishing north of Tofino. Wild Bill, sitting in the tiny, heaving cockpit of the boat, one great boot propped up against the cracked windshield, laughing as Hart choked on his first cigarette. *What if I had stayed on?* Hart wondered. He recalled how Bill wanted him to stay – equal partners – and Hart could play for the local hockey team. But, as he told everyone at home, *he was only sixteen – how could he?* His father needed him to help in the shop.

Walking slowly, he paused, letting the dust of the parking lot settle on his shoes. He watched as it rose and reached up to grasp him, holding him there like a fly to tape. Hart thought of punching a batch of dough early that morning, the first blast of escaping yeast gas hitting him – so strong he could feel it like a fan blowing in his face. Like most mornings, a few drops of sweat dripped from the tip of his nose or the line of his jaw, mixing into the dough as he lifted and folded, grunting at the live weight. He thought, as always, how he was in the bread – his sweat, his salt, his DNA, his quiet hopes, and his sadness or his joy. He baked it all in.

Folding the bills, he tucked them away and walked to the van. He was eager to leave.

Tamsyn stood in the shade of the doorway, staring out at Hart. "Now I know why you didn't make the Wings," he called to the stocky man, who was about to slam the cargo doors shut. Hart looked back at him, unimpressed before he even heard the conclusion.

"Headcase," Tamsyn said, tapping his temple with two fingers.

"Is that right?" Hart replied. He thought of his mother standing in her kitchen, on the chequered tile floor – "If you can govern your temper, you can govern this town," she would say to him. "Same as hockey – don't retaliate," chiding, smiling with her hazel eyes.

Breaking like a skater, in short, quick strides, he went back towards Tamsyn, who was caught off guard. "They taught you about headcases in Ste Anne, did they? Gave you a degree and sent you to work cooking cabbage for weddings?"

Tamsyn rotated his open palms like a highway flagman, hoping to slow the burly man's advance. "Hey, hey. Take it easy there. I didn't mean nothing, but you were just kind of daydreaming. That's all."

Hart stopped in front of him. "OK, sure. You didn't mean anything. That's good, Tamsyn. Shake." He stuck out a thick-fingered hand. Tamsyn raised his arm and Hart thrust forward, engulfing Tamsyn's slender hand and squeezing it so that it caved in backward, creasing into a concave. The small bones clicked as they flexed inwardly, against their natural inclination. Tamsyn's knees buckled and he dipped, pulling back his hand from the crushing grip, but Hart tugged, forcing Tamsyn off balance.

"Shit!" Tamsyn blurted as his grey dress-trouser knees hit the dirt just outside of the door sill, his teeth gritted.

"The reason I did not make the NHL," Hart began in a measured voice, "was . . ." He paused, then suddenly let go of the kneeling man completely. Tamsyn, who was still straining to pull his hand out of Hart's, pitched backward.

"Not tall enough," Hart said in a low, quiet voice, looking down at Tamsyn. "Only one defenceman out of all thirty-six in the league was less than five foot seven." He stepped back and turned towards the gibbous cloud above him, smelled the rain coming and said over his shoulder to Tamsyn, "The bakery business has no height requirement."

Nursery School Exposé
ARTHUR DAVIS

Precocious four-year-old Andrew is suspicious of his parents' motives for sending him to nursery school.

> "My dad keeps telling me that someday I'm going to be a grown-up. I don't think I want to be one."

'm not going to like this. I just know it. It's too early in the morning and I'm too tired and I don't like what she made me wear and I don't know where we're going and if I did, I doubt that I'd like it. I just know it.

I knew something was going on last week. That's how smart I am. I'll bet Kenny knew it too. They probably told him what they were up to. They probably told him, thinking that he would tell them what I thought about it after they told me. That's how parents think. They are always planning and plotting about different things – what you're going to do or where you're going to go and what they want you to say once you're there.

I know that's true because I hear the same kind of stuff from my friends. Ricky Roberts tells me all the time about how his parents are thinking up new ways to get him to eat vegetables. I've seen his parents. They look nice enough. But if he's telling me the truth, and I have to believe him because he once let me play with his lasso, then I feel sorry for him. He must have a very difficult time at home if his parents are really making him eat all his vegetables, especially broccoli.

I have to eat them too, but my mom doesn't make such a fuss about it and I know how to get away with not eating vegetables even when she puts them on my plate. I know tricks. You might think I don't, but I do. See, I'm nearly five and I know a lot of things.

Where is she taking me? She and my dad – he doesn't talk a lot – told me that I was going to make a lot of new friends soon. You have to watch out when they start talking to you like that. They're usually – really always – up to something and it takes all my cleverness to find out what it is before they want me to know.

Boy, this is a long walk. Usually we take buses. Sometimes trains that go underground. I don't know what they're called. I know my mom once told me. They always want me to know things but I must have had more important things on my mind when she mentioned it, so I don't remember.

You know, I have a lot of things on my mind. I am supposed to meet a friend of mine this afternoon and play stickball in the playground. I don't usually get to play because the older kids think I'm small, but today will be different. Larry Grant's kid brother, Kevin, is my age and Larry's going to help him with his swing. Kevin told me to come along and his brother will help me too. Boy is Kenny going to be surprised when he finds out that Larry is coaching me. Kenny is my older brother. I was also thinking about cleaning up my room, but I don't think there will be enough time for that either.

There's a lot going on around me, and everyone – I mean everyone from my parents to my cousins and grandparents to our neighbours – tells me what to think and what to do and what to say and, worst of all, when to go to bed. I don't mean that my neighbours tell me when to go to bed. That's silly. But you would think my parents would figure out that there are some things I already know. You would think they would see how grown-up I was about getting up in the morning and brushing my teeth and being respectful to their friends.

My dad keeps telling me that someday I'm going to be a grown-up. I don't think I want to be one. They're always going to work, whatever that is, and worrying about things and having very serious conversations and making you eat your vegetables.

"We're almost there," my mom says.

My mom is very pretty. Even my friends think she is pretty. And she is a good sport too. When I have friends over and we make a mess – and we usually do – she never scolds us or raises her voice like Carol's mom does. Carol's mom is always sour and acts like she isn't very happy. Carol tries not to notice but all her friends know her mom is a very sad person. But my mom is pretty and usually happy.

Sometimes I have so much on my mind I get sad too. But when you get to be my age you have to accept that.

There goes Steve Lynch with Pete Mitchell into Bigilow's Sports Store. They're always palling around. Steve is a friend of my brother. I don't much like him. When he's over at our house, he gets real bossy and thinks he can tell me where to go or what to play. My brother thinks Steve is very smart. I think he's a jerk.

I don't recognise where we are. My mom's grip on my hand has tightened in these last two blocks. She looks worried. Maybe where she is taking me is bad.

"There. It's right over there," she says. "See, the small brown house. There are children playing in the back yard."

Yeah, I see it. So what? I know what kids look like when they play. "I see."

As we get closer, I think one of the kids playing is Carol. I like her. She's fun to be around and always stays close by me when we're in the playground that separates our apartment houses. She has dark hair. I like girls with dark hair. I know gold hair is like the sun and bright and all, but dark hair is my favourite. Carol has dark-brown eyes that I think are very pretty. Her mom has the same kind of eyes but they're always sad.

"Oh, look there – swings and a sliding pond and, oh, they're playing ball like you do."

Do I care what they're doing? I guess my mom wants me to be interested. You can always tell when parents want you to notice or be interested in something. They change their voice a little. It gets higher and the words come quicker and the more they want you to like something the more they usually don't understand what you like in the first place, like the trucks and cranes and work going on across the street. And the kids in this back yard aren't playing ball like me. I can throw farther and catch better and I don't like them already, especially the kid holding the baseball bat as if he really knows what to do with it.

"There she is," my mom says, pointing to a tall, thin woman holding a bunch of papers in her hand. "That's Ms Hendrickson. She runs the nursery school. Brian Eldridge's sister, you know, Pamela, went there last year. It's a great place."

I don't remember Brian's sister. She probably doesn't have dark hair. "What kind of place is it?"

Bending down in front of me, Mom says, "It's a place for you to play for a few hours a day. We talked about it last night. It's called a nursery school. Remember? Lots of children go there." Mom tries to straighten out my shirt and pants.

I don't like what she made me wear anyway, and now she expects me to keep it straight. That's too much to ask of me. "A school?"

"Not like the one Kenny goes to."

But it is a school. I knew it was going to be bad. "I don't want to go." You always want to say that. It gets parents crazy. It makes them explain everything over and over trying to make you agree to what they want, and that what they want is something you should want. Just for once why can't they want what I want? Wouldn't that make more sense? After all, it's my life.

"It'll be fun."

"I don't like the way it looks," I say, but don't resist when she pulls me down the street towards the brown house and the back yard. We wait for the light at the corner to change (you always want to do that so it's safe) and then cross the street. The closer we get, the less I like what I see. It wasn't even the kid with the bat who I was already convinced was a jerk. I don't like the woman my mom says runs the school. She's too tall for a woman and she has a tight, pinched face with little slits for lips and her hair is bright yellow and pulled back over her head as if it were painted on and not real.

My mom waves to Ms Hendrickson as though they're old friends. "Hi there," she says in that voice that means she wants to make a good impression. "This is Andrew," she says, giving me a little shove in my back so I am closer to this hideous creature in the black dress.

I know if I don't offer her my hand it will get back to my dad. He is very big on the handshaking thing and since he asks so little of me I think, Why not? Well believe me, that impresses the black beast no end. She bends down, shakes my hand and introduces herself, then turns to the other children and announces that I am joining their school. They stop playing only as long as she is talking, then go back to what they were doing. I know I would have been hard-pressed to give up so much playtime to a complete stranger.

"What time should I pick him up?" my mom asks.

"Why don't you come by after lunch? How about two o'clock," the black beast answers but I have no idea what she is talking about, only that my mom won't return for a long time. I have never been left alone for a long time. I think my mom is worried that I'll be scared to be left alone.

"You're going to have so much fun."

I shrug my shoulders, and then notice a huge blue truck filled to the top with dirt coming up out of the pit that fills the entire block across the street. Its whistle shrieks out a warning to other trucks and cars that it's coming. How great! Everyone has to watch out for the truck. The guy who drives it must be a pretty special person to be allowed to drive a big blue truck like that and blow a whistle that stops everybody in their tracks.

I don't really know what a nursery school is, but I know it is important to my mom that I spend some time here. "I'll be OK, Mom." From her expression, I guess she didn't think I would be so willing to even try it.

"You'll have a nice time. There are plenty of other children here your age to play with."

A couple of other kids are staring at me. I know what they're thinking: "Who's the new kid? Why is his mom sticking around for so long?" My mom gives me a big hug and kisses me, then stands up and speaks to the black beast for a while, then gives me another kiss and waves at me as she walks back up the street towards our apartment building, which I can no longer see in the distance.

"There is a box of toys over there," the woman in black says, pointing to a wooden box. "It's for the children. You cannot play in the front of the house. You cannot fight with the other children. You cannot take a toy away from another child and if you have to go to the bathroom, you must come to me and I will take you there. Your mother told me you can go to the potty by yourself, so I don't expect we'll have any trouble there."

Only if you're in it when I get there, I think. I don't say anything to her, so she walks over to a couple of noisy kids playing ball. She probably would have walked away even if I'd had something to say. I'm right about her. She isn't a nice person, and I bet there are terrible things going on around here that no one knows about.

Suddenly I feel really alone. I turn around to where I last saw my mom, but she is no longer there. I am here and everybody else I know is far away. I look down at what I am wearing. This is definitely not my favourite pair of pants and the shirt, a present from my grandmother, doesn't even fit. I am too big for it. My mom should have seen that. I know she wants me to look my best, but sometimes she doesn't understand me at all.

If I had listened last night, maybe I could have saved myself from all this. But it's too late now. I am alone in this horrible place with the black beast surrounded by these nasty, snivelling kids.

I saw a movie on television with Kenny last week where a group of kids my age were attacked by a large, hideous, green space monster while they were playing in a deserted yard. It looked just like this. Maybe the black beast was going to turn into the same killer monster and take the kids back to her planet where we would be fed to even more hideous creatures. I'm never going to see my mom again. I'm sure I am going to die alone on a strange planet.

The beast comes rushing up behind me. "Why don't you go over there and play with Roger and Evan?" the beast suggests, but you can tell that she really doesn't care what I do. You can always tell if a grown-up really cares, and this one doesn't. I would stake my all-too-small allowance on that. And anyway, Roger is the one with the bat, and he is still a jerk. I'll bet Brian Eldridge doesn't even have a sister.

"I'll go find a toy for myself."

She gives me a quick, questioning look and disappears into her house and I am left on my own. I don't mind this at all. Ever since I've been little, I've felt a sense of relief when left alone to wander and explore and find out what interests me. I don't try to make trouble, but many grown-ups, mostly my grandparents, feel that I shouldn't be let out of sight of an adult. I don't know why they don't trust me. Lenny Klingman, who lives two blocks from my apartment, got into trouble lighting matches in his bathroom. Jessica Browning, who is only eight months older than I am, was caught throwing her parents' bath towels out of their eighth-floor bathroom window. Now those kids need a serious talking-to! I take a tour around the outside of the beast's house. It is nothing special. There is an old car in her driveway. Her lawn looks like it hasn't been mowed in weeks. There are a few cans of paint in front of her garage. I bet she has no children. People like her never get to have children. God sees to that. He doesn't let people he doesn't like have children. I know my dad would not like her.

I know I should call her by her real name but I just can't bring myself to be that friendly. She isn't friendly enough to my mom. And her house is nothing great, though it is one of the few remaining in our neighbourhood. Most of the private homes have been torn down, and six-storey apartment buildings, like where I live, have been put up in their place. There are four homes like this one still on the block facing the construction site across the street.

Another truck pulls out from the pit that looks like it could swallow the building where I live in one gulp.

"OK, children, it's time to go inside. Come on. All together now. Dana, put down that ball. Carmen, it's too late for that now. You two, get over here. Where's Andrew?" I hear her scream on the other side of the house. Where's Andrew? How often have I heard that?

I march myself around to the back of the house and am horrified at what I see. All the kids are lined up two by two in front of the beast. They're standing so straight and are so quiet they look like those Egyptian people my mom took me and Kenny to see at the museum last summer. They didn't move either and were covered in strips of paper. Maybe the kids are dead? Then the spaceship can land and take them back to the evil red planet where they will be gobbled up by the parents of the black beast.

"Andrew, there you are."

Of course, I'm here, and I don't even know where here is.

"Go to the end of the line."

Where else?

"Now we're going inside to play with blocks and our colouring sets just like we did yesterday," the beast went on.

In front of me are the backs of eight little heads. I can count to a lot more than eight and even spell some pretty big words. These kids seem so quiet. I don't know how they can be so quiet and stand so still. Maybe something is wrong with them. Maybe their bodies have been taken over by some evil force also bent on taking over the earth. Kids would be the best place to start. Most don't know any better. They don't know what I know. How clever. But I've dealt with evil forces before. You have to be very quiet and watch carefully or you will miss all their evildoings. I'm not good at being very quiet but someone has to save the whole world.

We march two by two into the belly of the beast. The inside of her house is small and smells like it has been painted with soap. The nine of us are told to keep to the porch. I quickly learn that a porch is the back of a house with a screen on one side facing the back yard. See, I told you I'm smart. Probably smarter than even Kenny who is a whiz at most everything.

Once inside they all come to life – opening drawers and pulling out little cartons on which their names are scrawled in yellow paint. Everyone is talking at once. Some of the kids are painting, others play board games they must have started before I got here. There is such activity I don't know what to do first. A little girl comes up to me and asks me if I want to play with her. I notice the black beast standing in the hallway with her arms crossed over her chest watching us as if she has sent the child over to me on purpose. How smart. The poor child's soul has been taken over by the beast. The kid isn't even in control of what she says or thinks or does. Wait until Kenny hears about this.

The little girl leads me over to a pile of wooden blocks. How childish. I catch on to her plan fast. Her name is Allison. There is an Allison in my building. An older girl. She has to be seven or eight. Kenny knows her. I wonder if that Allison is the original Allison from which this one is created. I play along with her until I'm bored. She's nice, for a kid with no heart or soul. A few minutes pass before I get up and walk away. She looks unhappy that I'm leaving. It must be terrible to have your heart and soul controlled by monsters from another planet.

I find a book and sit in the corner so I can keep an eye on everyone. I have a book just like it at home. It isn't anything special. I hear a phone ring inside the house a few times. The beast comes back to the porch every few minutes to make sure that the children are behaving. Behaving is a big thing with adults. If the adults I've seen are any example of behaving, they never seem to have any fun. I'm going to have a big problem in a few years.

Roger gets into a stupid fight with the kid named Evan. It isn't much as fights go. I've seen a lot worse in my time. The beast and another woman I had not noticed before come out to the porch with food. Everybody starts to scream and make for the two small tables. One by one each kid gets a paper plate filled with food. The beast's plan is now completely clear. She takes control of the children through the food she feeds to them. It is so obvious and yet I almost missed it. I had to be smarter or I wasn't going to live out the afternoon.

"You can have my mashed potatoes," I say to Evan who's sat down next to me.

"I don't want them."

"They're good for you," I say, scooping up a handful of the icky white mush and dropping it in the centre of his plate. "Eating more mashed potatoes will help you beat up Roger." He looks down at his food. I'm not sure he believes me. "And you can have that," I say to the puzzled little girl to my right. I think it's chicken. It might be turkey. I don't know. I only know that if I eat it, I will turn out just like these kids. The food here will eat away at my brain. It will make me stupid and before I know it, I'll be playing with blocks like a child and standing quietly in line.

Lunch ends in a strange way. The woman who put out the food with the beast comes back and tells all of us to finish up quickly. Everybody takes a few rushed bites, jumps out of their chairs and runs to a large closet and begins pulling out large rolls that fly open when the string is removed from around them. They're laid out on the porch floor. In seconds, all eight of them are lying down on these mats with a blanket wrapped up to their necks. The evil one looks at me. What was I to do? They're taking a nap. Everyone is taking a nap. This is the worst possible thing. My mom likes naps. Almost everybody I know takes naps except my dad. Are they all taken over by space creatures like these poor children?

My grandmother – my mom's mother – hates naps. She's great. Though for years, when I was younger, she would greet me with a big hug and a kiss and a smack on my bottom when we visited her. It took me a long time to realise that Kenny got the hug and kiss and no smacked behind. Last month I asked my grandmother why I got a smack and Kenny didn't. She said that, unlike Kenny, I was going to misbehave and get into trouble and she might not be there to see it, and that was what the smack was for. Boy, I really love her.

The woman comes over to the table, takes my arm and leads me to the one remaining mat. I sit down, then, under her glare, fall over onto my side. I can't bring myself to pull up the blanket. She gives me a terrible look, pulls down the curtains over the porch windows and turns out the light. By now, half the children are fast asleep.

I can see the afternoon light outside the house. Everything is happening out there while nothing is going on in here. The house is terribly quiet. What are those two space women up to in the front of the house? I'll bet they're sitting in front of a big screen talking to the leader of their planet. They're telling him that they have a new boy, a terrific, sharp-as-a-tack, cute little kid wearing a shirt too small for him. They're promising him that the boy will be sent to the planet along with the others right after their nap is over. I have to find Kenny. He is out playing ball somewhere in the neighbourhood while his baby brother is about to be shipped to another planet as a meal for a large green monster. That means he'll get all my toys. My toys! And what about my allowance?

I kick the dirty old blanket away from my feet and get up and look around. Evan watches me walk to the back door and open it as quietly as I can. I know he won't tell anybody because I showed him what he needed to do in order to beat up Roger. That counted for a lot between boys.

I make it to the street without anyone coming after me. The noise from across the street quickly catches my attention. Big trucks are moving up and down the drive. Big men are everywhere, carrying shovels and other tools in their hands. I turn around. Nobody comes running out of the back door of the house. They aren't as smart as I am. The spaceship will come and find only eight of them and the black beast will have to go back instead of me and hopefully be eaten in my place.

I walk up to the street corner as far away from the truck noise as possible. My mom walked down this street with me. By now, she is home doing home stuff. She will be cleaning or cooking or talking to her friends. My mom has a lot of friends. Everybody likes her. I guess that's why they put up with me.

From here, I can't be seen from the beast's house. I look up and down the street a lot of times before I rush to the other side. Still no one notices me. This is great. I am out on my own. No parents. No grown-ups. I can spend the whole day like this and never be told what to do or where to go. I walk over to the side of the open pit without being noticed. I never thought it would be this easy. The closer I get, the more there is to see below. I can't believe my eyes.

The whole block is a big hole. In the centre, roaring monster shovels are digging away at the dirt and scooping it up into the back of trucks that move back and forth from the street. I sit down next to a pile of wood so no one notices me. I am so happy to be here. I tuck my legs under my bottom and lean against the pile of wood. What luck! What great luck! I pick up a handful of dirt and toss it against the side of a large yellow drum nearby. It makes a heavy sound as it hits. I pick up a rock and throw it and this time the drum comes to life and starts to turn! I back myself up next to the pile of wood. What have I done now? But the drum quickly stops turning. My dad told me all about drums and digging from when he was living in another big city. I wished he had told me more, but he is always so busy doing his work.

A big black glob of something falls out of the front of the yellow drum. I get up and go over and kneel down next to it. It smells funny. I touch it with my finger. It is warm and soft and sticky in my hands. I pick up a big handful of it and run back to the woodpile. It is easy to make different shapes from. The more I play with it, the more fun it is! I make a house and a spaceship. I try to make a truck from the black goop but I don't think it turns out so good. I guess I've been here for a long time because before I know it, I am covered with the stuff. My hands and legs and I think my face are covered with dirt and the gooey warm black stuff. Now I am sure my mom is going to make me take a bath tonight.

"Hey kid, what are you doing here?" a man comes over to me and asks.

I look up. He is so big I can hardly believe my eyes. He is even bigger than my dad. He is wearing a strange green hat on his head. He's wearing gloves and big pants. I shrug, hoping he thinks I am too stupid to understand, goes away and leaves me alone.

"Where did you come from?"

"Over there," I say, pointing in the opposite direction of the beast's house. He is going to have to be smarter than that to get anything out of me.

He looks up towards the street. So do I. We both hear police noises. Kenny once told me police cars made that noise. Whenever you hear that noise, it means that the police have caught another criminal. Maybe they got Steve Lynch.

"I think you'd better come with me," he says, and lifts me up on his shoulder as if I am a kid. Now I know I'm not going to get to play stickball with Kevin and his big brother.

The man takes me to where a lot of other men like him are standing around. They all stop talking when they see me. But you know, I'm not afraid at all, even though my parents told me many times not to talk to strangers. All the men are really big and look at me as though I'm supposed to be here. They ask me a lot of questions about where I live, how I got here, and about my parents. One gives me a chocolate-covered doughnut so I am sure they mean me no harm.

I finally tell them I live around here, but I really don't know where. One says he has a boy like me and would get upset if his boy were lost. Except, I don't feel lost.

I ask them about the trucks and what they're doing here. I think they're forgetting about me being lost.

Then I hear the police cars again. Soon one comes riding down the block. It drives up to where all the men are standing. My mom and dad get out and run towards me. Then things really get worse.

My mom grabs me and hugs me so hard it hurts. She is crying and happy and angry and keeps touching me to see if I am OK even though I keep telling her I am. My dad talks to the man who found me. I don't know what Dad says but there are tears in his eyes when he says it.

The only thing that prevents my dad from killing me tonight is that it takes my mom all evening to clean off what I now know is tar from my filthy, dirt-covered body.

When Kenny sees me, he bursts out laughing. He thinks I am the funniest thing he has ever seen. Even my mom has to laugh after she takes off my shirt and pants and drops me into the hot, soapy tub.

My grandmother comes over, "sick with fright". I know my bottom is in for it when she marches into our apartment demanding to know, "Where is that child?"

Later, I find out that the black beast called the police when she discovered I had escaped. I guess she wasn't from another planet, though after that day most of the grown-ups in the neighbourhood thought I was.

My mom takes me to my brother's school the next day and puts me into a kindergarten class. But that doesn't work well because no sooner does my mom drop me off in my classroom and my teacher turns her back, than I get up from my desk and walk out of school.

They test me and the next week put me in first grade. I stay here, but only because my mom sits outside guarding the door to my classroom.

She does that for nearly a full month to make sure I don't escape!

I am telling you this story because it's all true and, more importantly, because my dad started talking to me a lot more after that.

One Oh for Tillie
TOM SHEEHAN

||||||||||||||||||||||||||||||||||||||||||||||||||||||||||||||||||||||||||||||||||||||||||||||||||||||||||||||||||||||||||||||||||

Mike, thirteen years old and blossoming into adolescence, spends a memorable summer at the farm of his father's friend in this intimate and lyrical coming-of-age tale. First published in 3:AM Magazine in February 2001.

"Time was marking this place and this event for him, time and what else was working along with it."

t didn't announce itself, the difference in the room, but it was there, of that he was positive. It wasn't the soft caress of the new blanket, or the deeply sensed mattress he'd never slept on before, or the grass-laden air entirely new to him pushing through the open window and tumbling like puppies on his face. If he opened his eyes he'd know, but he had kept them shut – enjoying the self-created anxiety, the deliciousness of minute fright that he'd conjured up. There was apprehension and a plethora of mental groping going on. Being alone was also new to him, but being aware of a presence *did* make a difference, if he could only believe what he was telling himself. At thirteen he knew you sometimes had difficulty believing yourself.

But the fact of *presence* suddenly hit him full force, though it had an argument attached. He didn't want to leap wildly out of bed (there *was* a chance he could be embarrassed), so he pretended again, this time *emergence*, slow and oh so deliberate *emergence* – from his woollen cocoon, from a dark and mysterious Caribbean cave close upon the jungle, from under the lashed canvas aboard the ship of an evil one-eyed captain of pirates, from behind the curtains of a magician or castle wall.

What he could not do was look out of the back of his head, though he tried, attempting to move the slits of his eyes, now finding morning by its faintness, so that he could see behind him.

Cautiously he moved, as if by his innate stealth he could fool anyone into thinking he was motionless or asleep or unconscious. His right ear found the pillow, telling him he had moved far enough. He opened his eyes and the girl Tillie was sitting there at the small desk, or the woman Tillie, or whatever you'd call her Tillie. She had not said a word the night before when he met her rocking away on the porch, staring straight ahead, not acknowledging him, not once looking up at him, just rocking her slow rock. Twenty or thirty she could have been, but he wasn't sure of how to make that measurement, what elements to compute with. Where she had been in a blue dress and yellow sweater on the porch, she was now in the most simple of nightdresses or nightgowns through which in a widening swathe morning's faint light moved and made soft mounds on the pleasant roundness of her flesh. Her breasts lifted themselves right there under the slight cover and his eyes had found them immediately, the nipples dark the way they had been the night before. Still she did not look at him, still she said no word, made no sound, and kept one hand secreted on herself. At once he knew she was not a danger, not a fearsome threat to him, though he could not tell how he knew. High on her forehead was a scar showing its whiteness, a very human and vulnerable scar that said she had been hurt, had suffered pain at some time. On her left shoulder, faint but red, rose a birthmark. It looked to be wings open to the wind; it said she was susceptible and not ghostly. The speechless mouth was formed with pretty lips puckered on themselves, full. Hair was a soft blond, though it tumbled about her head but in a not ugly fashion.

Even in the pale kiss of dawn her cheeks had much colour in them, heightened from that of her face. Her eyes as yet showed no colour, but were not malevolent or fearful though they carried the same sense of distance in them others had shown, a long reach into something he could not begin to understand. A coarse ache crossed through his chest and he wanted to swallow. His mouth was dry.

For the very first time she turned slowly to look at him and dawn caught itself in her eyes. Something unknown had softened her mouth, made it elegant and wet and shiny; a word had not done it, or a smile or any movement on his part, but it was rolled like a smooth petal and had a lovely pout to it. He fought to remember everything that had brought him here, to the Cape, to this room, in front of this girl who had not yet uttered a sound.

As she stood dreamily, slowly in the light of the false dawn throwing itself upon her, particles of morning faintness falling with some kind of fever all over her ample body, and as she looked naked in that soft reach with the darkness at her midsection and at her breasts, yesterday all came back in its crowding way. He was surprised at what he remembered. A phenomenal silence hung about them in this house that had promised so much of sound.

It had been a slow, easy, green morning, yesterday, and had been since the very earliest part of daylight when his father had gentled him up with a push at the shoulder. "Don't run," he had said, "but walk to the nearest exit." The constant smile came with the voice, and over that broad shoulder, it seemed, he could hear the birds of Saxon in their small riot of gaiety, a sure sign of the day, its goodness, its promise, the sun having already laid bare most of the secrets his room had but a few hours earlier when he pitched awake in the darkness. His newsprint ballplayers on the walls, as if they had sprinted into position, long-legged and gangly and floppy-panted, were now the icons they were meant to be, Williams and DiMaggio and Slats Marion full-figured in a splash of sunlight, suddenly each one three-dimensional across the chest, shadows behind them, life-emerging; for a moment he thought Billy Cox would loose the ball in his hand all the way across the room to first base. He heard the birds again, as if scattered in flight from their roosts, raucous and noisy as fans at a game, the way he pictured the Sooners breaking away from the line to become propertied. Sleepily he locked on to the second sun of his father's smile, tried to remember what they had been saying in the other room as he had dozed off the night before.

It had been Mel's voice, deep and rugged, carrying the whole diaphragm with it, the words coming square and piecemeal as if each one was an entity, which had penetrated his move into sleep. "Mike'll love it down there, Bill." He paused, let the weight of each word have its way. "He'll have the whole farm to run around on. Charlie and Mav will keep him busy with the cows and the chickens and the gardens. Nothing heavy, for sure, no barn building or rock walls to set up, but enough for him to break out. Hell, he's starting to grow like a weed and Mav's cooking will put meat on his bones. And there's always new life coming around the corner." He got the implication that Mel thought he was much younger than he really was. Most older folks had that way about them, he agreed to himself.

Quietly and sort of pleased, he knew they were talking about his summer and him, Mike, thirteen, lanky, a stick of bones, just finding a hair or two in his crotch, the wonder of a host of things either pressing down on him with almighty force or trying to come through his very skin, other messages scratching for light. Mel he could see as clear as ever; blond, muscled, the blue Corps uniform rippling across his chest and upper arms like a sail under attack of the wind. Once, according to his father, Mel had been a desperate youngster, fully at rebellion, always rambunctious, in the darkness of home beaten by his father for much of his young life, until the man had had a heart attack with a strap still in his hand. "Mel was looking for a payback for the longest time," he'd said, as if to cover a lot of ground with a few words, as if Mel was due as much room for whatever transgressions had been accounted for.

"He can stay the whole month of August if he wants . . . and if he likes it," Mel had continued. "All summer for that matter. It'd be one less mouth to feed and he'll come back bigger and stronger, maybe so you wouldn't recognise him come the end of August." That square and stubborn chin of his usually moved slowly when he talked, and he would have bet few cries ever leaped from his mouth, even when his old and mean father was beating on him. No, sir, not one to cry, that Mel, all blond and good-looking and packed full of muscle, who walked like a bomb might go off if he got triggered wrong. It sounded great to be going down to his farm with him, even if Liv was going along, and her a teacher at that. "There's something about the earth or the elements or whatever you want to call it that gets deep into you down there in Middleboro. It's high green all summer, wild growing making up for winter coming down the road, vegetables leaping up out of the ground like they've been shot, cream as thick as molasses and Mav's ice cream every night of your life makes it all so perfect you can't believe it even when it's happening. It's a dream much as anything that I know of, an aura, a feeling. I don't know if it's the food or the air or if it's in the damn water, but it's something that'll pop his backside as good as a ramrod. Hell, I bet he sprouts an inch or two just this summer. You got a ballplayer coming on your hands, Bill, and you've got to give him room."

He'd known that Mel had been left a large piece of property down the Cape way from his butcher of a father because Mel was all that was left of the Grasbys (a brother drowned in a small pond when he was only six, a sister killed in a car crash at only sixteen when she had been drinking and another sister not seen around these parts for more than fifteen years), that an old couple, Charlie and Mavis Trellbottom, worked it for him while he was still working on his enlistment, that Mel was on his long leave of the year, that Liv Pillard, his girlfriend, was going down to the farm with him for just about all of his leave.

The aura and taste of a farm suddenly flooded him, his head being jammed with smells of hay and new-cut grass and barns wet with whatever steamed up barns and made them dank and memorable other than horse or mule sweat or a cow's splatting across a dense plank floor. All the sounds came back, the clacking and strapping sounds and the noisy wetness you get conditioned to, and the ageing by which wood speaks so eloquently and so disparately as if the popping stretch of boards and the checking of beams is each one unique unto itself, each one a message of age and sorrow, a cry.

"Barns bend but never break," he'd heard his father say once after such a visit. He'd been but once, to Billerica that time with a cousin for a long and adventurous weekend, and parts of the quick visit had stayed with him; rafts of bees or hornets at their endless commotion and business, spiders dancing on silver rails so high in the peaks it made him think of circus trapeze swingers, hay dust so thick in his nose at times he thought he might not be able to breathe, another near-secret odour that had to be leather almost making its way back to life, the moan of a solitary cow, a stool being kicked over and milk sloshing its whiteness on heavy planks, in one corner of the barn the close-to-silent scurry of a mouse with a cat arched in mid-flight as if its bones were broken.

Suddenly, not knowing why, the way things had been happening lately, Liv Pillard eased herself into his mind; tall, bosomy, hipped, standing in the door of a classroom watching her students return from recess, skirt full against her thigh, pushed by her rear, her mouth the reddest mouth he'd ever imagined, the long auburn curls in a slow dance about her neck whenever she moved a fraction of an inch. The graceful lines of her calves, at her hips, had more meaning in them than he could fathom. A hundred times she had smiled at him, he figured, because his father and Mel were long-time friends, because their roads high and low and often had drifted through Parris Island and Quantico and Nicaragua and Philadelphia and the Boston Navy Yard, because they played cards from cribbage through every realm of poker with the same dead-earnest intensity no hand or prize could shake and could drink beer for whole weekends at a time without seeming to move; had the same set of the chin, they did, jutting and chippy, asking for it one might have said, proud, bearing absolute silence at times, whole unadulterated reams of it that could threaten a body as much as could a fist. Their competition was in place of a war, it being a time between wars.

Shopping, picking up supplies in special stores, getting the oil checked a couple of times because of gauge trouble; the ride to the farm was a long and convoluted trip. Liv and Mel sat up front in the long roomy roadster, him in the back, the sun and the wind pouring down over them, Liv's hair caught up in them like a pennant, every which way flying and catching gold and throwing it away as if she were philanthropic. Now and then he closed his eyes with his head on the seat, her perfume gentle in his nose but new and mysterious, new grass smell edging it out, the perfume coming back, more new grass and occasionally lilacs loose about the road, once in a while her head out of sight, and he wondered if she slept fitfully as he did. A trucker honked at them as they passed, then honked again and pointed at the car to his striker, craning his neck to see the car as it pulled away, Mel throwing his hand in the air as a nonchalant goodbye. Mike himself had no idea of what was so special about the long-hooded Packard, except that it was long and black and speeding to a grand farm in Middleboro with animals and strange crops and all the ice cream he'd ever want, and him leggy and sprawled across the back seat, and Liv's perfume coming relentlessly at him.

Mel slowed the car at the crest of a small hill, and then stopped. "There it is, kid," he said, his jaw pointing, his sharply hewn nose pointing, a smile on his face.

Land spread itself everywhere, whole patches of it cut up and divided by more greens and yellows and rock walls and punctuating tree lines than he could imagine. It spread from horizon to horizon as if his own private library of *National Geographics* were unrolling pictures of the pampas and the savannah, a sense of space at once so vast and so intimate it walloped him, like *a hand aside the head.* He heard his grandfather's voice, some letters of words, some syllables, bent in half by the tongue and others stretched for all they were worth, lifting themselves out of a forgotten cave, a grotto or cairn he had put aside for too long, a place where stone took on new dimensions and new spirits, the slight figure of the small man in a forgotten doorway, the booming voice so often attributed to the *upstart young poet Yeats now knocking heads asunder.* Cluttering on top of Liv's resurgent perfume came the sweet odour of more new-cut grass, somewhere a whole crop of it, and then a vaguely refined field smell came rolling in, dutifully, coming from the green sea of a field on a crest of combers; clover from that other visit he realised, where the barn had been memorialised, ripe as the Atlantic itself, rich as brine. In the middle of all laid out before his view was a long sparkling-white house, the main part of two floors and sundry additions plunked like excess punctuation, also white, easy and casual afterthoughts at a glance, which had been appended at random, he surmised, or had been required by different men and different needs.

From the chimney of one of these, squat and like a hen coop, the one farthest from the main house, smoke rose slowly, its column meandering ever so slightly, uninterrupted, lazy as the beginning of this very day had been. A wide porch spread out on the two sides of the house he could see, and promised more at each of its ends. A horse and wagon, piled high with perhaps hay, a shade of yellow not yet seen in the fields, crawled across the front yard; its facing side was grey and neutral and had no contour top or bottom, but belonged, picture-perfect.

A shed off to the side had the same colour, weathered, beaten and angled, wearing a thousand storms for sure. It leaned into its own existence. Time was trying to mark this place and this event for him, time and what else was working along with it; the indelibles indeed were afoot but he could not bring them all the way home, could not decipher them the way they should be: a painting inching itself into reality, another clutch in his gut as if something were being pulled out of him, a tendon, a muscle, a useless organ through the eye of a pore. Emptiness carved its hollow way through his stomach. He felt cheated somehow.

A woman on the porch shook a mat or a small rug over the railing. Her motion was quick and lively, and seemed to be the only thing moving. Liv's perfume came again, more than lilac, more than any petals known. And with it the realisation that taste had been introduced. It caught itself at the tip of his tongue, lingered, left. It was not sweetness, he knew. He tried to recall it. It came to him that a variety of borders had been built around him in his short life and were being broken down, but he could not determine the extent of them or the extent of the breakdowns. At the edges of his senses, likewise at the point of division, the nature of a number of things was unknown.

Then, the way ideas are crystallised, from a small world controlled by an inner energy, the great merger came, the meshing of sights and scents and somehow reachable mysteries. It pushed together the picture-perfect wagon and the woman dusting and the sudden ebullient clover and the inviting spread of the house and the wide issue of fields going off to where stars awaiting night were hanging out and the mix of planets. Liv's perfume crawled down the back of his neck and Liv looked up at him from the front seat and he looked down at her and saw one absolutely splendid nipple as she twisted standing alone in the cup of her gaping bra like the knob on the gate lock in the back yard at home. The rush was upon him.

Her teeth were as white as the house. His stomach hurt. Wind whirled in his ears.

Holding her hand visored over her eyes, the two o'clock sun slashing down on the side of the house and across her stance, the woman on the porch had seen them coming down the slight ramp of road. Brown hair was piled on top of her head and pulled into a bun. Near sixty, she had a wide forehead, comfortable eyes which travelled easily over the three occupants of the car, a mouth that was as soft as prayer, and arms bare right to the shoulders. An elaborate pinkness flowed on her skin, a rosy pinkness, gifted more than earned it appeared, and it softened everything else about her – eyes, mouth, and the angles of her joints. Almost as a salute, one shoulder dipped subtly as if a sign of recognition, or acceptance. Pale blue, front-buttoned, her dress wore remnant perspiration in dark patches, at both armpits, at the belt line, at one breast, perhaps something wet had been held close to her body, perhaps something wet and dear. The boy could see that she moved very deliberately, bringing her arm casually and gracefully down from her face. That same hand waved at them but he could tell mostly at Mel, for a smile came with it. He thought of the ice cream promised, for this must be Mavis Trellbottom. Into a dark recess the wagon had most likely gone, for it was out of sight and there were doors of all sizes in the barns, and the yard was quiet and serenely peaceful.

She yelled, "Mel!" full of surprise and endearment, and then in a cry two octaves higher, "Charlie! Charlie!" and not "they're here" but "Mel's here." The voice was as sincere as her face. The boy felt she would have yelled "Mel" even if the President were with them.

Even before Charlie came into view, Mel was out of the car and had picked the rug-shaking woman named Mav right off the deck of the porch. Slippered feet showed, much of her legs, a flash of underclothing, and her hair, sort of brown, in another minute might have come loose from the top of her head. A featherweight, the boy thought, as Mel swirled her about, more than warmth written all over the pair of them. A small stick of jealousy stabbed at him, a jab a lightweight might have tossed, but jealousy nonetheless. She enjoyed the roughhouse greeting, it was evident.

"Hi ya, Duchess!" Mel had yelled, and then hugged her tightly to his frame. On his face, as innocent and as real as morning sunlight on a green leaf, was expressed the most honest emotion the boy had ever witnessed. Even at thirteen, short of experience in the world, he realised that look would not be seen by him very often in this or any lifetime.

Another message in the air, another barrier broken, another lesson to be learned plain as dealt cards.

Suddenly he was aware that much of the classroom was at hand. This very summer, this very farm, these people now caught up in his very breathing, would grant him a whole new range of knowledge. He would in no way be able to hold off what was surely coming at him. He looked at the people around him. Liv was still locked to her seat in the car, her face catching the sun at such a generous angle it played games with his eyes. Mav was still caught up in the arms of the young Marine dressed in chinos and a blue polo shirt that seemed to measure his biceps. An older man, unhurried, deliberate in walk, grey-haired but moving with an obvious strength, denim straps wide over his shoulders, wearing army boots with the issue buckles still in place, probably rock-solid and not arguable and, more than likely at one time or another, the undisputed King of the Hill among his acquaintances, was striding across the yard. Charlie Trellbottom was a strider, all the way a strider. Energy lifted off him as easy as steam off the swamp back home, and would have been solid-looking to the most casual observer; grey hair as thick as goodly pelt, face weathered, wood-burned marked like one of the barns standing behind him in the sunlight, shoulders almost as wide as Mel's. No way was this strider like his own grandfather, who was probably about the same age, but he did evince the same kind of energy. A bandsaw smile cut itself across his face as he said, his voice a flawless timbre that made the young visitor think of old tools they didn't make any longer, "The Marines have landed. Tripoli is saved."

The two hugged and slapped each other like old teammates after a long separation, and the boy could measure the immediate sense of warmth rushing through him. They shook hands all around. He *was* welcome! The air could have hailed him: *Welcome, Michael*, and said, *this is another home for you*. He pretended he heard that from some corner of the yard, the guinea hens roosting in the trees and now squawking like ladies in a knitting circle, a rooster strutting his 5th Avenue stuff, a lift of steam almost audible off a hundred surfaces. The slight creak he heard in a pause of the welcomes and a moment of other truce brought his eyes to a pair of toes moving up and down, back and forth, at the far left corner of the porch. Patent leather shiny as gills, yellow socks dandelions could have painted. That's all he could see of a third person, one which incidentally had not been mentioned either at home by Mel or in the car on the drive down. The creaking sound said *rocker* to him, and Mavis, noting the tilt of his head, the eyed interest, said, "That'll be our daughter Tillie, but she doesn't say a whole lot." He thought it most apologetic and that it didn't sound like her; already his mind made up that she didn't make excuses, didn't beat around the bush, and said what was on her mind no matter the audience or how the cut of it went.

Mel introduced him to Mavis and Charlie and without the slightest hesitation she hustled him off to his room, pushing the tote bag into his arms. On the way off Charlie said he'd take him for an initiation ride on the wagon after supper. There was an actual chuckle in his voice. Liv had slipped her arm around Mel's waist and the sun glanced a halo off them. As he turned to go with Mavis ahead of him, as Charlie turned away for some obvious chore, he saw Liv slip a hand into Mel's pocket. The feeling he had had in the back seat of the car came back to him. It's none of my business, he tried to say to himself, but he couldn't manage it. He also wanted to say that there were so many things he didn't know about, but wouldn't shoot himself down so quickly, not that he even wanted to. He wasn't all the way stupid! Time would see to that.

Mavis Trellbottom, in her blue dress splotched darker in spots by perspiration, took the stairs easily. The oak steps and risers talked incorrigibly under her feet, not a whimpering under weight but a composite of a little anger and a lot of tiredness, the tiredness of holding on, nails and pegs clutching at centuries, a statement against over-use or abuse, a statement of time. The noises were distinct, individual, as if they were on slow-played piano keys or the singular strum of a string and he could easily pick out the separate notes. On a bet he could identify the source of each one of them, even with his eyes closed. A hazy picture leaped up in his mind of black-haired, wild-eyed, tart and acidic Jamie Stevenson in the back of the Cliftondale School classroom at home shooting his mouth off, crying abuse too, although only when it suited his purposes. Sometimes Jamie, when tromped on, would not utter a sound, and this house might sometime also do the same. But proof had been offered that this rambling house would be one of sounds, that it would never be truly quiet, even at sleep. If it were suddenly, without wind or cause, to shift sideways, he thought, there'd be beams creaking, lintels stretching their whole selves with accompaniment, joists threatening his ears, all with their unique notes.

A delicious odour of richness, like piccalilli let loose of jars, followed them up the stairs. With it, or because of it, he knew beans and brown bread from Abie's red-brick oven and hot dogs and the same piccalilli. His senses kept stretching themselves all over the place just waiting to be tested. The walls were papered with a small flower pattern with a pink background. Two pictures of revolutionary soldiers hung on the stair walls. A mirror in a gold frame filled the wall at the head of the stairs, and five doors gave promise of the next life, choices set out for his undertaking.

"I've put you down the end so you can hear the farm as it wakes up in the morning. It's new for you, as Mel tells me, being up there just outside Boston. Must be tough for a boy to grow up there when there's so much of this. You'll like it here because it was Mel's room when he was a boy and he always loved it. Now don't be bashful . . . anything you want just give me a yell . . . food, more blankets, anything. The bathroom is over there. Charlie and I are at the other end on the first floor and Tillie has the room above us. You'll be all by yourself. If you like sounds, night sounds or morning sounds, cows, roosters, chickens, guinea hens, this is the place for them. Mel used to make up stories all the time when he visited. Made his own joys he did when he was down here." She was right on the money, he thought, as if she had read his mind. There'd be other special things from her. Her last statement brought him all the way around to Mel's father and what he had heard of him. To be away from Saxon and his father must have been a real treat for the young Mel, and this kind woman showing him the ropes must have known all of what went on back there. She'd never spill that knowledge though, of that he was sure as dawn. If his father had beaten *him* what would his life be like right now, what would he have become? That vision left him hurriedly, but the awful taste lingered as he measured up the room.

His room had a nice enough bed with a pile of blankets, a chest of drawers beside one window, a small desk and chair, a small table with a big white bowl on it and a white pitcher, which he swore he had seen pictures of. A rack at the side held two towels and a face cloth. A big stuffed chair loomed out of another wall as if it had just appeared out of nowhere, it was so big and so out of place in the room. The walls had a green-tinted paper that was very comfortable on his eyes, though he could discern no apparent design. There were three doors to the room. Mavis drifted out of one of them saying, "Find your way back when you're ready and we'll have something to eat. Mel's always hungry."

He had settled himself into the room, put his things away, explored doors, gone down a hallway quietly, came back, and went another way. He saw the room where the girl must sleep, pale green walls, white curtains, no pictures. He heard Mel and Liv behind the door of another room at their honest noise, which must have carried on from the car as quick as you could think, crept back quietly so as not to disturb them (or be heard being more like it), went down the stairs, saw the girl Tillie close up for the first time really.

In a short while he heard all about her, as if all of them were apologising to him for springing the surprise of her on him. They took turns in telling him about her at the table where Mavis had presented her broiled chicken dinner. Tillie, in a yellow dress, her hair tied up atop her head, her skin as white as Mavis' was pink, but in that same gentle fashion, moved, ate, reached, but said nothing. Her eyes did indeed have much of distance in them, or depth, like a bottomless well came one image through his mind, and never once came across his eyes paired up, or acknowledged him. That's when he first noticed her breasts, centre-darkened against the dress's pale yellow material, the way a nipple would announce itself, broad and darker as a picture might show, at times at play behind that so thin retreat. Her hands were delicately shaped, the nails neat as a made bed.

Mel had said, "Tillie had a very bad accident a few years ago, when she was just twenty-one. She was engaged to a great kid, whom I'd known a long while. He was in the Corps and he called and said he was on his way home on a quick leave and was driving up to see her. She rushed off in her car to meet him and hit him head on at Bailey's Crossing just south of town. He never came out of the car alive. They had to cut him out and she didn't know until almost two months later when she came out of a coma."

"Hasn't spoken a word since," said Mavis. "She hears us, knows us, loves us, but just can't talk – won't talk. It may be that what we're saying right now doesn't even register with her, at least not fully. We don't know. Even the doctors don't know, haven't helped a whole lot except hold out for the promise of something good to happen." The slackness in Mavis' jaw at that moment was an infrequent lapse, he thought.

Charlie nodded at him. "We don't know what will bring her out of this, but we're positive something will happen before we pass on. She's a wonderful girl. She's filled our lives for us, even now when we have to do so much for her."

He liked Mavis and Charlie immensely. Charlie's eyes were like some exorbitantly costly gem, and with the light of the sun still playing in the room his eyes took on more warmth and life.

They absolutely shone when he looked at his daughter, when he spoke of her. Tillie still made no move that acknowledged any presence in the room. She continued to eat, robotic, he thought, just the way she rocked for hours on the porch – rocking, nodding, touching her toes, pressing on them, lifting back her head bare fractions of an inch, as if practice was the art of perfection. Her listlessness seemed overpowering to him. He wondered how he'd ever become as accustomed to it as were the others, even Liv, more beautiful than ever, her face shining with a hidden light of some kind, whose perfume crawled down the back of his mind in a slowly tantalising swallow. "Hope is as beautiful as she is, Mike. It's one of the loveliest of contemplations in life, I'm sure you'll find that out, if you don't know it at this moment. I think Mav and Charlie would say right now that it's the best thing in their lives, that it's just as beautiful as Tillie is."

Nothing it seemed could be more beautiful than Liv, and he had heard her behind the door in that long secretive hallway, the music of her wordless voice, the mystery of what posture she had been in, what stance, what exposure. Pictures spilled all over his insides and he wondered if he had given anything away. Every sound he had heard he could remember. Did his face show it? He looked at Tillie, his mouth open, hoping for refuge, for escape. She did not move, though the darkness at her breasts was deeper than it had been minutes ago.

Mavis put more chicken on his plate. He looked into her eyes and saw the faraway there too, the long, long tunnel out into space or down into earth. A smile flickered across her mouth, as if she had shared a secret with him right in front of the others. He could not find it. If it was there in front of him, he could not find it, but the slightest curve of that hidden smile was given him again. God, she was as warm as his mother was! And like his mother, could leave messages right out in front of other people's noses. It wasn't always that he could read them, at least not right off the bat, but something would come of every communication. His father was direct in his messages. There'd be nothing here at this table from his father. It would be unsaid. A girl had been hurt. A boy had died. Things had changed. It was like war. After a while the sounds of battle pass.

Now this girl, this speechless girl, this silent Tillie of the accident, came slowly towards him. In the narrowness of dawn, in the narrowness of the small bedroom, she came towards him. Liv, that other girl, that other magical figure, had drifted in and out of his mind, with her whatever stance or position trying to break free from behind that door of yesterday, with her music of sounds shifting its notes in his mind in absolute total recall, every living breath of it. Liv, that other girl, had come at him and gone away. This girl Tillie moved so effortlessly, as if she needed no energy, oiled, lubricated at every joint, almost a spirit of movement, everything that the barest of dreams had dared came sliding towards him. Again, in the false dawn, she looked at him, as she had not looked at him on the night before. He saw distance closing itself down in her eyes, saw the telescope of time working its long way in, collapsing hours, years, the screech of tyres, the impact of metals and rubber and blood, how sound must have suddenly stopped for her that night. He saw space there moving irretrievably away; none of it would ever come back, none of it could ever come back.

He understood, for the first time in his life, silence of the unborn, the unknown, the calamity of graceless death. He knew at length what wailing and keening were that he had heard so much about, heard the longing one should never hear, heard it all coming from silence as she slid in beside him. With the whitest of arms, the very fairest of arms, oh so deliberately lovely, she lifted the thin blanket of his cover and lay down beside him. Warmth, as good as coals, flooded him, all the length of his body. Patches of flesh were suddenly hot, burning their way onto him. He didn't know where they were, but someplace against him. An entirely brand-new odour he'd never known and would never forget for as long as he lived came rolling over him. With the same ease of her advancing motions, hardly movement at all, grace be it for a name, she placed one of her darkly auburn blazing-reddened nipples against his mouth, adjusted it oh so casually, a caress of longing someplace behind it. She spoke. Tillie spoke. She said the sound "*Gently*" as if it had come out of some mysterious and solemn rite, old as all the centuries themselves, as if it had been said the same way before, and at the same time as if it might be a most serious order or command. His mouth opened. His lips were dry. Her hand reached to hold him softly by the head, cupped him to nursing at that wetting place.

He did not know how long he remained still, the horrific heat against him, or if he slept, if she moved, if he moved. There was newness now and hands everywhere and a mouth not his and a gentleness and a fire he'd never known and sounds beyond them. Sounds were in the air and the wash of the morning whispering at them, and hands again, instructive hands, hands at his hands, movement of hands, knowledge, moisture, life exploding a whole arsenal of secrets. The back of his head filled with aromas bent on attacking him but so startling and so smooth they might not have even been there in the first place, only dared to be. And finally a small and barely audible "*Oh*," a lovely "*oh*," a remarkably beautiful "*oh*," an "*oh*" worthy of all speech and all language, levelled across the room as though it might barely reach over the thin shroud on the bed or might go on into all of time itself, the first "*oh*" that Tillie Trellbottom had given up in seven long years.

He didn't remember her leaving or his falling asleep again or waking up more than two hours later and the house silent again down into its dampest roots, down into its deepest part of being a house. Then a rooster called out bright as a bugle, a surly cow answered, a horse, in the high trees the guinea hens began a noisy clamour. Other sounds came that he could not identify. His father's face loomed in a shadow and he suddenly knew what his father had meant about waking up in the morning under a tepee. A languid tiredness rolled through his body, but he was sharply awake and extraordinarily hungry. It made him move quickly to the wash basin.

Only Mavis was in the kitchen and, as if she had timed his schedule, placed a plate of ham and eggs and home fries at the table for him. "You'll not be this late again because Charlie won't let you. He's been gone for over an hour with the wagon, and Mel and Liv have gone for a walk. Tillie will probably stay in her room for much of the morning."

Mavis continued to move even as he explained that he had been tired and had fallen back to sleep. She wore flat shoes, white ankle socks and had on a neat grey dress not yet adorned with dark stains. But that promise was there even if the fluid motion she did things with was no surprise to him, as if that grace of hers was part of her own private language. There was so much to language that was not said, that was left unsaid but known. Ideas came cramming into his head, it seemed volumes of them; where they came from, what they sprang out of, he had no idea, at least not a direct idea. It might be too that he'd explode, so much moved on him and in him. He breathed on his plate to ease the canister of his chest and the threat that was building itself there. He wanted Tillie to come into the room, wanted that desperately and could feel the want riding on his face. He wanted to see her eyes again, wanted to see how she was dressed, wanted to see what he could remember. He kept his face to the meal, low over the table whenever Mavis might turn towards him. Redness must surely sit on it for there was heat still resident on his skin.

The morning sun, still angled, still in a wake-up attitude, spilled all over the table and the countertop and lit up much of the room. A vase of purple flowers had taken over what the sun hadn't grabbed, lilacs he said to himself, knowing he would not have noticed them on another day, but the perfume of them carried its vital message. All this *whatever* he deep-voiced to himself had opened all his pores, all his nerves. Things so shortly occurred, so shortly known, came slowly out of some private place he had put them. Perhaps they could no longer be managed. Tillie had said only, *"Gently"* and *"Oh,"* and nothing else, of that he was positive. It said a mountain had been moved, a roadblock torn down and done away with. It said *miracle* in a very small and private way as far back in his mind as he could put it. Another aroma, he realised, was in the room; it did not say *purple flowers* but *her.* To leave the room at that moment was important to him, but he could not manage it. It would be escaping from Mavis. It wasn't right. If only Tillie would walk into the room or call down and say she was going to stay in her room for ever, then he could move. How would her voice sound in the morning air? How would Mavis turn around and look at him if Tillie spoke? What would Mavis say? Would she scream at him? Would he run? Would Charlie or Mel come after him? Would Liv wag her finger at him, even after he had seen *her* nipple stand like the gate knob? He remembered sweet skin against his mouth; *that* was talking in another way. He remembered air being in short supply. Suffocation had been a possibility. He began to shake and finally realised he was frightened. Down here there would be no way to turn, nobody to turn to. There was no assumption of help. A violation had taken place and punishment was in order. His father would be furious. His mother would cry.

Mavis gave him seconds. She must have eyes in the back of her head, he thought.

"Charlie will be back in a short while. He'll take you to the high field on the wagon. You'll have your licence by noon." A deep chuckle came with the promise, and then she moved about the room, sunlight falling on her, sunlight following her. She was warm, she was a magnet, and she was another aura in his young life. He couldn't begin to mark all that had come at him in such a short time. Was there no end to it? Was this a confidante in motion, this woman in front of him? Her grey dress had the neatest edges, her skin was still of a blessed pinkness, and they cut across each other the way designs cut, the way advertisements move within themselves. "A horse is a horse is a horse, as they say." She spoke with her hands full and didn't use them to make added expression, to accentuate. "Be good to Blackie and he'll be good to you. He wears the wagon. The wagon doesn't wear him. Don't tell Charlie I told you, but he still has trouble cutting left, so mind your fence posts and the corner of the barn if you head off to the low fields. Keep the reins honest in your hands. The answer is in your hands. That's all I'm telling you. Now here he comes."

She wasn't even mad at him. That was amazing. She must know every breath taken on the farm, the source of every sound. His mother would. She'd know everything there was to know; who sneezed or coughed in the night, who cursed in the back yard or took the Name in vain, who suddenly got too big for his hat or his britches. Nor was Charlie angry, still wearing a smile bright as a new saw. Charlie made off with him as if he were abducting him. Before he knew it, he was away from the house, away from Mavis and the kitchen, and Tillie had not called out to him, had not said another word. Perhaps he could breathe now, now that nobody was angry at him. Swinging around he saw the high field spread out before them, not really high but it was on a risen slope of land and kept a firm contour, a place to itself, and Tillie barely hung on at the back of his head.

The clover was rich, the sun was warm, and his high and commanding seat gave him a great survey. In his hands the reins had meaning, he soon found out. Blackie was a gallant giant of a horse, black as despair, black as hopelessness, he thought, with ears that flicked like broad knives at the flies, like a pair of hands waving. Electricity from him came in surges down the leather of the straps, a great amount of electricity, and a great amount of power. The wagon seat made him think he was on top of the world. Life was somehow ennobling, for all he had come through, spreading it and himself in great patches of experience. Blackie now and then pranced and danced as if to speak unsaid words. He seemed to say, *"You have the reins but I have the power."* It was not like that with Tillie. She had coaxed and coached and guided him, but also had the power of every move. Pieces came back at him, then chunks of her and chunks of heat and great masses of moisture and an ache and emptiness in his chest as if he had cut all ties with the human race. It was all so unfair to feel this way. After all, she had spoken, the miracle of miracles; she had used language, she had told him how it was supposed to be, how she wanted it to be. Suddenly he wanted to lash out at Blackie, to drive very hard, to leap past all of the fields, to be home, to be away from all of this. *Is she thinking of me back there in her room?* came a live and ringing thought in his head, like he was talking to himself. It was so confusing, so much of it so unnecessary. But a restless edge kept cutting into him, making unknown demands. Finally, relenting, he took himself back to his room even as Charlie loomed beside him bigger than much of life. He brought back what he had seen of her, and how he had closed his eyes at first, and then filled them endlessly even in the faintest light. He remembered how it fell across her whiteness, how shadows get rounded and curved, how light falls into darkness, and answers fall away with the light. There'd been mounds of whiteness and expanses and crevices and openings, and her hands had argued at first, and then pleased. His had argued and argued, until, light making more of her whiteness, they had begun a new life of their own, had travelled and touched and been instructed. How empty now his head felt, how dry his mouth, and Charlie was pointing to a pile of logs across the field.

They loaded the logs on the wagon as Blackie kicked at dust and knocked at flies and swung his tail in the air. Sweat ran down his chest; he could feel the little balls of it flowing on his skin. He smelled different. Charlie would know it in a second, how it leaped from under his arms and made itself known, telling tales, telling everything sweet and unsweetened, everything calm and hysterical, ratting on him. His perspiration felt like little balls of steel cruising on his chest. Oh, Christ, would this ever end?

As they unloaded the logs in the yard, Mavis and Tillie sitting on the porch, bees working the air, buzzing, the sun working, sizzling on hard surfaces, heat beginning to touch everything, the guinea hens raucous in the trees, his muscles found other meanings. He dared to throw some of the logs a bit farther than he ought. Mavis watched, Tillie didn't, rocking her chair back and forth as part metronome, sporting yellow socks he thought were disgusting to look at; she had such lovely lines to her legs. He threw another log beyond the pile as he recalled how the lines of her legs met, how they rolled into and out of darkness. Mavis smiled at him, waved them on to lunch, turned on the porch like a judge who had made a quick decision. He thought of his mother preparing a small speech on transgressions.

Lunch, though, was quick and quiet, and Tillie said nothing and he said nothing and Charlie said they'd get another load of wood. They worked at the next load for over three hours, took a swim in a small pool in a stream on the way back, and unloaded the wood just before the supper call was made. After supper he sat on the porch steps near Tillie with a huge bowl of ice cream. Once in a while he looked up at her as she rocked and slowly ate her ice cream. The whole yard seemed to fall into a temporary silence, as if it had somehow been earned.

It was an announcement when he said, "That was a lot of work today, Charlie. I know I'll be in bed early tonight." Charlie laughed a small laugh and nodded at him.

Mavis said, "You'll be surprised how much you grow in one summer down here." Tillie rocked her chair. He was going across that void again, he knew, across the darkness to that other light. There was no other way.

For hours he lay way over on one side of the bed, waiting, making camp, the tepee up and the tepee down. The centre pole seemed bigger. He'd never have a laugh with his father about this, but he'd try to share it with him somehow. Maybe years down the road. Maybe masked like a story. He'd not brag, though. You don't brag about miracles. You have nothing to do with miracles except letting them happen and knowing what they are when they do happen. He thought of dress blues and manly chevrons and quick and immediate leaves, and Mel and Liv in their room and how they had all but disappeared from the earth in such a short time. This was like a hotel for them and Liv's hands were live hands, which he had seen. Was everybody like that? If Mavis and Charlie went to bed together at the same time, who would start things off, who would reach if they were to reach? Charlie was tired too. The grey of Mavis' dress had gathered dark blue of perspiration into it. Did it run on her like little steel balls? It made sense to have odours because they were so distinctive, said so much, gave so much away. Liv's nipple was not like Tillie's, he was sure. Tillie's stuck out like a bullet. It had been so real and now it wasn't. Was it possible that she had never been there in the first place? The air told him different. She was in the bedclothes, the smell of her. That was real. Who made up his bed? Was it Mavis? The tent came down.

Moments later, just after midnight, he pitched camp again. He caught her on the smallest bit of breeze coming down the corridor. Silence was still her marker. There was not the slightest creak of the floorboards, and the door he'd left wide open. She moved as she had before, and soon said, "*Gently*" again, and later "*Oh*" again, and he obeyed every gesture and made some of his own with the breath caught up in his chest like a ball of fire. He did not think of Mavis or Charlie or Mel or Liv or his mother or his father, but he did think of the young Marine rushing home to this lovely whiteness. It made tears, too, like little balls of steel on his skin, and in the faint streak of dawn, as she took her mouth away with her, she said, "Today we'll have a picnic."

She was not in the kitchen for breakfast, and he ate hungrily along with Charlie. He was ravenous. Food odours leaped at him in quick announcements and there was nothing he did not like or could not identify in an instant, so sharp were his senses, so deep his sudden concern for aromas and the things that walked on the air, which pulled at him. Other revelations had mounted their stands (only two days old and it promised to be one hell of a summer); his shoulders felt wider, his upper arms thicker, his wrists stronger. Time no longer had any urgency to it. You could say handling the logs had done it, but he wouldn't hold just for that. He had paid his way, it was true, had made his contribution. It was like the artifice of mental reservation, you could talk about two things at the same time, and both of them would fall into place. His father would be pleased at the general nature of things, though the crux of it unknown; nothing would be said directly for the first time, but eventually notice would be in the air. It'd be like shaving or jock itch or sudden stains on his shorts that would demand no explanation. Of this he was certain; it would be unsaid, as so many important things were, unsaid but accepted.

Charlie said they would spend one more morning on firewood, and would be back for lunch. At lunch, the sun living amongst them, splashing on every surface, she sat stiffly at the table and he was certain only he was aware that the great distance in her eyes had closed down on itself. It was *that* different. Suddenly he knew how difficult it was to speak sometimes. Profoundly he knew he was moving into one of the great events of his life. As long as he lived some parts of these moments now building about him, now filled with stark and rich aromas, now filled with colour, now waiting on sound like a dream trying to be recalled, would have a special place with him. He knew that the two nights here on this farm, and their implausible emergence, would somehow fade away, and that others, if they were to come, would fade away also, but these moments would stand. And it was grey-blue Mavis who began the moment when she looked at him and asked, "What are you *men* up to this afternoon?" The word men was firm as an oath as she said it. It was not a negligible word. It was not an easy word. It was not thrown out to be cute or to question. It carried more than mere conviction; it carried absolute knowledge, it carried every sound of the night, every shadow, every bit of memorable whiteness, it carried all the resurrection she had waited on for such a long time. Almost a salute, her mouth gaped in awed wonder, her eyes shone with an ancient thanksgiving and her heart leaped in her chest, as Tillie said, "Mike and I are having a picnic."

Charlie nodded, the long wait done.

One on One
ROB BOFFARD

IIIIIIIIIIIIIIIIIIIIIIIIIIIIIIIIIIIIIIIIIIIIIIIIIIIIIIIIIIIIIIIIIIIIIIIIIIIIIIIIIIIIIIIIIIIIIIIIIIIIIIIIIIIIIIIIIIIIIIIIIIIIIIIIIIIIIIIIIIIIIIIIIII

Darius Mitchell, a teenager from Chicago's South Side, is about to have the basketball game of his life – and a President's career hangs in the balance.

"But just so you know,
I'ma dunk on you."
That got a big laugh
from the press.

D arius Mitchell was eating the last of his grilled cheese sandwich when the guard brought his visitor in. They didn't usually allow food in the juvie's visiting room, but Darius had been a model inmate. He got his sandwich.

The guard left, closing the door softly behind him. Darius swallowed the last bite, and grinned. "We bein' recorded?" he asked, as his guest sat down. The man shrugged off his coat; it was autumn, and the room was cold. Bright white light angled in from the windows set high in the wall.

"Nope. They're playing this one by the book," the man said. "This is a private meeting. I believe they think I'm going to try to squeeze you for a confession."

"Must mean they gettin' worried, then."

"Probably. They're fast-tracking the hearing, and I think you're likely to get a sympathetic jury. Besides, you're a minor. I don't exactly see you getting the electric chair."

"How you figure that? You a lawyer now? Already got one of those. He pretty good, too."

"No I'm not. But I don't imagine there's a jury on earth that'll convict you, and even if they did, there's no judge who'll hand out anything but a suspended sentence. You're a national hero, after all."

* * *

The scorching Chicago summer had bled through the hotel's air conditioning into its gym, and grey sweat-spots dotted the collar of Danny Beecham's white shirt. His dark suit felt heavy, too tight today, and his earpiece was slippery with sweat. The glass walls of the gym's basketball court had actually begun to steam up.

Beecham looked at the court's occupant, and jerked his thumb towards the door. "I said, get outa here," he added, in case his point hadn't been made.

"Why?" said Darius Mitchell. He was sixteen years old, with his hair in tight, black cornrows. He was rolling a basketball from hand to hand.

"Because I'm asking nicely," said Beecham. "In a minute, I'm not going to be so nice."

"I ain't done yet. My pops only gets finished his shift in half an hour. I gotta wait for him. Who are you anyway?"

Beecham flashed his badge, whipping it out of his pocket and opening it in one movement. "United States Secret Service."

"Come on, man."

"Excuse me?"

"That's some fake shit. I seen 'em selling one just like it on the block for five dollars. You ain't no Secret Service."

With that, Darius turned around and shot an easy three-pointer, swishing it. He grinned; all those hours on the court were paying off. He was too small to get to the hoop in a game; his slender frame always got shoved out of the way. But as a point guard? Or a shooter, draining buckets from deep? Yeah, he could do that.

Beecham folded his arms. "Last chance, son. You can either leave this court free, or in cuffs. What's it gonna be?"

Darius had collected the ball, and was dribbling it back to the top of the court. He passed the ball between his legs a few times. Then he shook his head, and fired off another shot, flicking his wrist on the follow-through.

"All right, that's it," said Beecham, unbuttoning his jacket and striding towards Darius. "You're coming with me."

"Hey, get your hands off me, man!"

William Dalgleash III came into the gym just as Beecham grabbed

Darius Mitchell. The blood drained from his face.

He was a little man, bald, and his pinstripe suit and neat red tie looked out of place among the angular exercise machines. He strode across the gym to the court, and entered as Beecham pinned Darius' arms behind him.

"What the hell's going on here?" said Dalgleash, his brogues squeaking on the faux-wood floor of the court.

"Get him off me," said Darius, wrestling with Beecham's grip.

Dalgleash ignored him. "Jesus Christ, Agent Beecham. I have the White House press corps out there, and you're in here manhandling some kid. What if someone got a photo?"

Reluctantly, Beecham released Darius, who spun round. "It ain't right!"

"I told him to leave," said Beecham.

Dalgleash gritted his teeth, and slowly counted to three in his head. He had to do it twice. This campaign was proving to be even more difficult and trying than the last one. The President of the United States – POTUS, to use the shorthand – had decided to have this unscheduled photo op, which was headache enough (he hated it when candidates thought they knew what was best for the press – and really, shooting basketball? Now?) On top of that, he had a Secret Serviceman tangling with a kid in front of a bunch of photographers. It was not what he or his candidate needed.

He looked at Darius. God. Couldn't the Service find any real villains to fight?

"I'm afraid Mr Beecham here is right. I'm sorry he acted a little . . ." He straightened his tie. ". . . overzealous, but we really do need the court. I'm sure you understand."

"You work for the hotel?"

Whatever works, thought Dalgleash. "That's right. I'm the concierge. And I'd appreciate it if . . . What are you laughing at?"

"Man, my *dad* works for the hotel. He a janitor. It was the concierge said I could play here after school until my dad finishes work. His name's Mr Santos. Maybe I should introduce y'all sometime."

"I'll go and fetch Mr Santos," said Beecham, smoothing down his jacket and glaring daggers at Darius.

"Thank you," said Dalgleash. Beecham stalked off the court, his footfalls echoing around the empty gym.

"So if you ain't the concierge, who are you, then?" said Darius, turning to face the basket and lining up another shot. He was on the foul line this time.

"My name's William Dalgleash. I'm the press secretary for President Artis Jackson."

"Like hell you are."

Dalgleash smiled, his teeth too close together. "Would you like to see a business card?" he said, reaching inside his suit jacket.

"Nah, that's all good. Besides, I know you can't kick me off the court. You just told your boy to back off."

Dalgleash was about to reply when he stopped. The one thing he'd learned at Artis Jackson's side was that you pick your battles. It wasn't quite time yet. He could wait. And when Mr Santos did indeed show up, this kid was going to get the shock of his life.

Mr Santos got nervous about a lot of things. For starters, he was very nervous about this photo op, and very keen that it should go smoothly because after all, how often did the President come to this hotel? Or any hotel? It would look great on their website.

"What's going on?" Santos asked Dalgleash. He was immaculately dressed, but kept tugging the slim silver band on his ring finger, back and forth, back and forth.

They were standing just above the three-point line. Darius had finally given them his full attention. Dalgleash's face was bright red. "You told this young man – what's his name?"

"Darius Mitchell, sir," said Santos.

"You told him he could play on the court, correct?"

"That's right. His father works here."

"Well, that's just stunning. Fantastic. Let me make something clear, Mr Santos. I can't get him off the court – not with the press hovering over this damn thing like the vultures they are – but if you don't, I *will* take this to another hotel."

Santos wrung his hands. "Sorry," he said to Darius. "They're right. Time to go."

"No."

Santos' eyes bugged out of his head. "Darius, please. I'll tell your father about this. You see what happens then."

"Oh, what, you gonna tell my dad that you just bowed down for these clowns, let 'em kick his son off the court? Yeah, that'll work."

Santos licked his lips. He looked at Dalgleash, then Beecham, then Darius Mitchell. His brow was beaded with sweat.

"Fetch his father, then," said Dalgleash.

"Yes," said Santos. "Yes, I will. But I'll have to find him first. There are twenty-five floors, over five hundred rooms . . ."

For the love of God, thought Dalgleash. "Enough is enough, young man," he said. "You will go with Mr Santos here, right now. Do I make myself clear?"

"Help! Help!" Darius shouted. "They're violating my rights! Brutality!"

The man from the *Michigan Advertiser* wasn't even supposed to be in the Wynne Hotel. He'd had to wheedle and threaten just to get his editor to pony up the cash for a bus fare. Then he'd had to fight and scrap for his Presidential press pass. So for the entire Illinois segment of the trip, he'd made sure that he was at the head of every queue, every single time.

When he heard raised voices from the gym, he stopped chatting to the hottie from *DCTV News*, and listened intently. She carried on talking, going on about something to do with a governor and a senator, and he had to shush her.

She stared at him. "Did you just shush me?"

He shushed her again. Raised voices. Definitely. One was Dalgleash. Before a photo op, the press secretary usually hung out with the reporters, laughing too loudly at jokes and winking too much.

The man from the *Advertiser* glanced around, and strode into the gym, leaving the woman from the *News* staring at him, open-mouthed.

"You get back here," she said, her heels clacking on the floor as she followed him in.

"Hey," said the security guard. "Where do you think you two're going?"

"Buzz off," said the man from the *Advertiser*.

"Yeah, buzz off," said the woman, walking right past him.

And the entire Washington press corps, mistaking their entrance for a signal that the session had started, charged right in after them.

Dalgleash was in the middle of telling Darius Mitchell that if he didn't shut up he was going to have him shipped to Guantanamo Bay when he saw them coming.

He turned from Darius mid-sentence and strode out of the court, his face transforming. "Ladies and gentlemen," he said. "Thank you for coming. If you'd like to take your places, the President will be with you shortly."

"Everything all right in here, Bill?" That was the grizzled old reporter from the *Los Angeles Enquirer*, who knew that Dalgleash hated to be called Bill.

Dalgleash smiled. "Couldn't be better, Ray. We're just waiting for the man himself."

Darius had gone silent. He was dribbling the ball between his legs, watching the pack with a curious expression on his face. Santos stood next to him, still wringing his hands.

"Who's the boy on the court?" said the woman from the News.

Dalgleash thought about lying, decided against it. It was too late now. "He's just a young man who didn't want to stop playing. Who can blame him? And in a few moments" – he spread his arms wide and grinned – "he's going to play a little one-on-one with President Jackson himself!"

"What's his name?" asked the man from the Advertiser.

"Oh don't worry, you'll get to meet him very shortly. Now, the court won't hold all of you, but we'll make sure that the door is wide open so you can hear everything. Reporters can watch from out here, photographers lined up against the far wall inside, please, thank you . . ."

"So he really comin' down here?" said Darius. He, Dalgleash and Beecham were in the middle of the court. Around them, reporters and photographers jostled for position.

Dalgleash had on his most winning smile. "He wants to shoot some hoops, sport. Just like you. And it sure would be great if you could play some ball with him. You know, just a friendly game?"

"You were tryna kick me out. Why should I listen to you?"

If this doesn't go off without a hitch, Dalgleash thought, I'm going to get your father fired, you little brat. See how you like that.

Darius appeared to be deep in thought. "He really comin' down here?" he said again.

"Yes sir."

"In that case, yeah, I'll take him on."

Dalgleash breathed an inner sigh of relief. "Fantastic, sport. Now how'd you like to meet the press?" He punched Darius' shoulder, and got a stony stare for his efforts. But the boy let himself be led off the court. He was thinking about Artis Jackson. And about what he was going to say to the man when he arrived.

"All right, folks, thank you all for waiting," said Dalgleash. "This here is Darius Mitchell, and he's very excited to play the President today, aren't you Darius?"

Darius gave him a blank look. A split second later, he was hit by a wave of shouted questions, ranging from "Have you done any preparation for the game?" to "Which party do you support?" to "Who's your favourite rapper?"

Darius didn't get a chance to answer any of the questions, because right at that moment, the reporters at the back of the scrum started yelling in the direction of the gym's entrance.

What they were yelling was: "Mr President! Mr President!"

Artis Jackson knew all about greeting the press. Big smile, first names. He didn't even bother to answer the questions thrown at him. He never did; as long as he shook the right hands and asked after the right wives and husbands, he got an easy ride.

His six-foot-four frame, clad in a navy sweatsuit, glided through the gaggle of reporters. "Bill, how's it going? Jeanne – great to see you! How's Mark doing? Howie! I owe you a quote don't I? Ray, my man!"

It was only when he got to the front of the pack that he spotted Darius. Not for nothing had he been regarded as one of the most savvy senators on the hill, and a look from Dalgleash told him all he needed to know. He reached out a hand. "Good to meet you. I'm Artis."

"Darius."

They shook.

Jackson grinned. "What do you say we hit the court, Darius?" He jerked a thumb over his shoulder at the press. "Give these guys a show?" By now the clicking of flashbulbs had risen to a whirring climax. Darius shrugged again.

"I guess," he said. "But just so you know, I'ma dunk on you."

That got a big laugh from the press. Jackson gave another grin, but one that wasn't quite as wide as before. He clapped Darius on the shoulder, and walked him onto the court.

"Have you been following the election?" he asked, picking up the ball and tossing it to Darius. It was always important, he felt, to talk to teenagers like they were adults.

"Nope," said Darius, bouncing the ball. "I don't like politics."

"Oh?" Jackson said. "Well, perhaps you can tell me a bit about yourself, then. Where do you go to school?"

"Parker High. On the South Side."

"I know it. I grew up in Chicago."

"Yeah. 'Cept you were one of them rich kids who spent their time up in Lincoln Park."

The reporters gasped. Pencils quickly began to scratch on notepads. Cameras were shifted into more comfortable positions on shoulder blades.

Jackson studied Darius. "Oh, it's like that, then?" he said at length. "Guess we'd better settle this on the court. Do you want to shoot to start?" He gestured to the hoop.

"You can take it."

Darius tossed Jackson the ball, then moved between him and the basket.

"You sure?"

"Just check the damn ball, man."

Jackson threw him the ball, and Darius bounce-passed it back, completing the curious ritual that marks the start of any pick-up game. Around them, the gym was quiet.

"We've got about fifteen minutes, sir," Dalgleash called out.

"Thank you, William," said Jackson, without looking around.

He started dribbling the ball, and Darius dropped into a guard position: knees bent, head up, one hand reached out towards Jackson. The ball boomed off the court as the President slowly dribbled to the left, keeping his eyes on the hoop the whole time.

Darius jabbed forward, nicking the ball with his fingertips, Jackson pulling it back just in time. He dribbled between his legs, and drove for the basket. Darius dived to stop him, and the two collided with a muffled thud. Jackson was solidly built, but Darius held his ground, chest out, hands probing for the ball.

The President pump-faked once, twice, then turned and dropped a slow fadeaway jumper that sank straight through the net. He grinned, and the press corps applauded. There was another whir of camera shutters.

Darius looked sullen, and when he and Jackson checked the ball again, he threw it back a lot harder than before.

"Easy now, Darius," said Jackson. "It's just a game."

"No it ain't," Darius replied. He was back in the guard position, standing on the foul line.

"All right," Jackson said. "But just remember to have fun."

"Yeah, fun. You know what'll be fun? Dunkin' on you. Posterisin' you, nigga."

"Appreciate it if you didn't use that term."

On the last word, the President drove hard, dribbling once before palming the ball and lofting it for a layup. It bounced off the rim, and Darius sprinted away, grabbing the rebound and moving to the top of the arc.

"Nice," said Jackson. It was his turn to go into the guard position.

He wasn't worried. He had at least five inches on the kid, and he was sure he could block any shot Darius put up.

"You think that was nice, Lincoln Park? Check this out."

Darius stopped, holding the ball. Under the rules, he couldn't start dribbling again, so Jackson closed in on him, getting his hand in his face, towering over him.

"Yeah, I got you," muttered Darius and sprang upwards for the shot. Jackson followed a split second later. He would block this, no problem, his hand was already in front of the ball –

– which suddenly moved to the side as Darius bent his entire body, leaning back at the same time. The ball flew past Jackson's head, sinking into the net.

Darius whooped, drinking in the reporters' applause. "Two one, man! Two one!" he shouted.

"One all, I think you'll find," said Jackson, gathering the ball. Inside, he was seething. Did this little punk think he could beat him?

"Uh-uh. Three-pointer. Counts two in a pick-up."

"Guess you can't win 'em all, Mr President," called the man from the *Advertiser*.

The President smiled again, shrugged. "Suppose I should be happy it's not a live debate, right?"

He checked the ball with Darius, who attacked the hoop hard and fast, his sneakers squeaking on the wood. Jackson had to put out a hand and get right into the kid's back. He could feel Darius' muscles moving under him. Darius had his right arm out, blocking the President's attempts to reach around. He jumped backwards, spinning around in mid-air to face the hoop.

Jackson moved to swat the ball, and his hand smashed down on Darius' forehead. The kid gave out a startled cry, and dropped to the court. The reporters gasped.

"You all right?" said Jackson, reaching a hand out.

Darius knocked it away. "That's a foul."

The President towered over him. "No fouls in a pick-up. But I'll let you take it again, if you like."

Darius stared at him for a moment, then stood and jogged back to the top of the court. No fouls? he thought. OK. I can rock with that.

The President was soon up three two, first off a shot and then a beautiful, driving layup. He'd heard the camera lenses chatter even faster as he'd taken off. Nothing like an action photo.

He had the ball again, and this time Darius didn't wait. As soon as it was checked, he got right in Jackson's face, his hands everywhere. He was trash-talking now, his voice barbed. "You think you can get past me? I am the motherfuckin' Great Wall of China. I was built to keep niggas like you out. This my court. I'ma take that ball, then I'ma dunk on you. I'ma go Blake Griffin on that ass."

Jackson flipped the ball between his legs, then spun, pushing his back into Darius. The kid was smaller than him, but it was like trying to shove a brick wall down. He gave up trying to go inside, and fired the ball up for a shot.

At the same instant, Darius jumped, his left arm raised like a child in a classroom. He swung it down, and swatted the ball right back into Jackson's face.

The crowd let off a sound like the hiss of air escaping from a blown tyre. The President grunted, his hands cupping his nose. Blood began to drip through his fingers.

"Jesus," he said, his voice muffled.

Darius simply stood, his shoulders rising and falling, as all the President's men rushed the court. Dalgleash and Beecham, with other Secret Service agents behind them, clustered around him. The reporters were hurriedly tapping on iPads and iPhones, scribbling into notebooks. The man from the *Advertiser* was speaking on his phone, his hand over his mouth, dictating to his editor back in Dearborn.

One of the Secret Servicemen tried to touch the President's face, his fingers darting in gently, like someone trying to disarm a bomb.

"Get off," Jackson growled. He pulled his hands away from his face. Thick blood dripped onto his top lip, crusted on his stubble.

He pointed at Darius. "Mr Mitchell, there's a difference between fouling and flagrant fouling. You should learn a little sportsmanship, son. William, we're done here. I hope the photographers got what they needed."

He started to walk away, his forehead knitted with anger.

"Pussy."

Jackson turned, stared at Darius. "Excuse me?"

The kid returned the stare, his chin high. "You heard me."

In three strides, Jackson was on Darius, looking down on him. "Say that again."

"OK. Pussy."

Jackson opened his mouth, then shut it again. This time there was no noise from the reporters. Every single one had been shocked into silence.

"That's it," said Dalgleash, inserting himself between them. "We're done." He turned to the press corps. "Thank you, ladies and gentlemen, I think it's best if we move on from here –"

"No."

Dalgleash turned. "Sir?"

"I said no." The President's eyes had not left Darius. His look was pure poison. "We're *not* done here."

"With respect, Mr President, I think we should –"

"I don't. I want you and everyone else off the court, right now. Actually, no. Mr Beecham – you stay. I want you to throw up a jump ball between me and my man here. We're going to sudden death."

For the first time, Darius felt a tiny prickle of fear. He had to choose his moment. It had to be just right.

He returned Jackson's gaze, trying not to show any emotion.

"OK, then. Sudden death it is."

They stood at the foul line, the ball held out on Beecham's right hand, like a sacrificial offering, the two players crouched low on either side.

Danny Beecham thought: This is getting out of hand.

William Dalgleash thought: Be calm. This'll all work out. Just be calm. They'll play and shake hands and it'll be a footnote in this campaign, and anyway, I can spin this, no problem, just be calm.

Artis Jackson thought: I'm not just going to beat you, kid. I'm going to end you. Knock you on your ass.

Beecham moved to throw the ball up.

And Darius Mitchell said: "The 108th."

From where Dalgleash was standing, it looked like the President tripped.

He'd seen Jackson tense, ready to jump for the ball, but at the last second, his legs, ready to spring, did a kind of stutter, and he faltered, swaying in place. Darius got a clean jump, tapping the ball gently backwards. He grabbed it, dribbling back outside the three-point arc. Beecham jogged backwards towards the wall, out of the way.

Jackson turned, and for a split second, Dalgleash thought he saw something in his expression. Something like shock.

"What did you say?" said Jackson.

"I think you heard that, too," Darius replied. He was dribbling the ball, putting it between his legs, shifting from side to side. At that moment, he didn't look like a kid. He looked like LeBron James, right before a freight-train drive to the bucket.

"And I got another one for you," he said, his voice louder this time. "Operation Poseidon. You like that?"

Artis Jackson roared, and leapt for the ball. Darius pulled it back, dancing out of reach. Jackson followed, swiping, trying to knock the ball away. Behind them, reporters began to shout questions at Dalgleash. Poseidon? Was that what the kid said? What did he mean?

Darius paused, faked, then dribbled and spun, rolling around Jackson, who had to furiously backpedal to keep up. They ended up on the baseline, a few steps from the basket. Darius had backed into Jackson, his left arm out. Beads of sweat stood out on the President's forehead.

"My brother was in the 108th Division," said Darius, loudly enough for the reporters to catch every word. "Out in Helmand, when Operation Poseidon went down. When that little drone of yours mistook them for a bunch of insurgents. You thought you could keep that one under wraps. Well guess what – I know."

He stepped back, darting out of range. But the look on Jackson's face wasn't shock, or anger. Now it was triumph. It was the look of a bully in a schoolyard who's rubbing someone's face in the dirt, and doesn't care that the teachers have seen him do it.

"You just revealed highly classified information," he said. "You're going to go to jail for a long time, Mr Mitchell."

"Maybe," said Darius. "But I'ma still dunk on you."

He drove for the hoop, palmed the ball, took two steps, and jumped.

Darius Mitchell couldn't have known about Poseidon. It wasn't possible. A kid from the South Side of Chicago knowing about a failed black op deep in insurgent territory? Just couldn't happen. Not unless . . .

Not unless the kid's brother was in the unit felled by friendly fire from the drone. Not unless someone – a soldier in the unit, maybe, or the kid's own brother – happened to say something to his family back home before the op. Let something slip.

Maybe he did it without thinking. Or maybe it was just an insurance policy. But in any case, how could Darius possibly have known the exact details?

Someone had taken him through exactly what happened to his brother. Someone close to it. Someone who wanted him here, on the court, right now, in front of the press corps.

All of this went through Artis Jackson's mind as Darius Mitchell flew over him, his legs pistoning out like Michael Jordan, the ball held in two hands behind his head, like a tomahawk.

For a moment, Darius thought he wasn't going to make it.

He had the height – for the first time in his life, he had the height – and his aim was on point. Jackson had been forced to backpedal, somewhere far below him, somewhere that didn't matter any more. But as Darius saw the hoop approaching, he felt the tug of gravity, first gentle, and then firm. The net began to rise, moving away from him.

Without being aware that he was doing it, Darius screamed. In one motion, he *slammed* the ball home, smashing it through the hoop so hard that the net cracked like a whip.

And then, he was descending.

The ball had to bounce twice before anyone spoke. It thumped off the floor, the noise echoing into the stunned gym. As it rolled to a stop, there was a low groundswell of sound. And as it gently came to rest against the wall, the noise rose to a rumbling thunderclap.

Some of the reporters were cheering. Others were yelling questions. Still more were applauding. Darius stood under the hoop, staring at Artis Jackson. His expression was unreadable. Jackson didn't look triumphant any more. He looked sick. He turned and walked out of the court. A dozen reporters broke off from the pack and followed him, nipping at his heels like bloodhounds. The others swarmed the court, clustering around Darius, bellowing questions.

He told them everything.

* * *

"That doesn't mean it's going to go easy," said Darius' visitor. "You *did* reveal top-secret information."

"Straight trash, man," said Darius. "It's only top secret cos they messed up. That operation had gone smoothly, the 108th'd be back home, and that dude Jackson would be handing out the medals instead of looking for a new job."

"I suppose so. Still, the new guy's not bad. And he's publicly said that there'll be no more drones."

"You ever see this kind of thing happen when you were in the Service?"

There was a pause while his visitor considered this.

"Friendly fire? Sure, once or twice, back in Desert Storm. But not like this. Not where they just pretend it didn't happen. Not when you can zoom in from thirty thousand feet and see exactly who you're shooting at. When you can give the order, and walk away. That's not right. No one should screw up that badly and get to walk away."

Darius' head had dropped. He was thinking about his brother.

At last, he said, "Thank you. For letting me do this."

"We wanted the same thing. And hey, that was one hell of a game."

"Nearly was no game. Thought you was trying to get me off that court for real."

"I had to make it look good. And anyway, you put an idea like an impromptu basketball shoot in Jackson's head, and he'll jump on it. All I had to do was mention it to the right people."

"One thing I don't get."

"What's that?"

"I mean, why not just go public with it? You coulda been a whistleblower, man."

"We've had this conversation. Politicians can shuck and jive and dance and talk their way around almost anything. You have to put it right out in front of them. And you have to do it publicly. I needed you."

"You straight? Still got a job, I mean?"

"I've still got a job, don't you worry. After all, the new President still needs his staff."

"OK, then. I'll see you in court."

"Ha."

"What?"

"First on the court, then in court. Got a nice ring to it."

"No doubt."

Darius Mitchell and Danny Beecham stood up and shook hands. Beecham left.

Programmable Love
BREMER ACOSTA

||||||||||||||||||||||||||||||||||||||||||||||||||||||||||||||||||||||||||||||||||||||||||||||||||||||||||||||||||||||||||||||||||||

Gillen, a neuro-bot suffering an existential crisis, and her human boyfriend Jan, must confront the prejudices of their friends.

> "She could feel the motors buzzing inside her flesh, always one moment away from malfunction."

Part 1

Gillen gazed into the plasma-mirrors coiled inside her dome apartment. They bent all the contours of her body, reflecting her flesh in crosshatchings of light. She stood in front of the mirror, naked, pale and veined in her legs and arms, with gears turning under her skin like cockroaches crawling under a rug.

Her mind lingered into a weird daydream as she stared. Is this neuro-bot really supposed to be her, this creature, this *thing*, compiled of the ghosts of human data, the replicas of their past? She felt alien in the bathroom, wishing for something she couldn't quite put into words.

Gillen didn't feel the same way the humans told her she should feel, as a duplicate of their humanity, as an afterthought of their existence. She felt real when she saw the gleam around her purple irises, the faint hairs on her legs, the pockmarks lining her back, the bumps crowning her nipples. And her stomach looked moulded out of clay, capable of being shaven down to its abdominals or expanded into a simulated pregnancy. All of this, everything she was made of, she thought she knew already, without speaking, with only one glance.

If only Gillen could have a child, though, if only she could feel the existence of a species squirming inside her stomach. But she couldn't. She could never create a life; only exist as a life the humans had created for her to feel. She sucked in her breath, feeling pumps inside her mechanical lungs, and then she breathed out again. Her stomach looked pasty, flat, and lifeless, forever a chamber with nothing inside.

But she did have her own identity, didn't she? Her memories glimmered like unfocused paintings, golden in their frames but blurry past their surfaces. She did have genuine memories, ones that she formed herself. Or were they simply implanted inside her mind, already used, discarded from another?

Even though her creators claimed she was made five years ago, she could still remember her childhood. She remembered falling off a metal swing in the courtyard, and the sting of her bloody knees, and the way she ran to her mom and dad, and how they picked her up and kissed her wounded flesh.

Gillen could recall all of these images, from her childhood to her adulthood, until she had looked upon her parents' graves after their cancers. And she remembered talking to them every spring, even though she knew they couldn't hear her any more.

Her designers said her memories were borrowed from what the humans considered meaningful, what they put together out of the computerised probabilities. Gillen sighed, fogging her mirror, trying to forget the truth, trying to ignore that the pain she felt when her parents died wasn't real. But it was real to her. If nothing else, it was real to her.

She rubbed her bald head, feeling the grooves of her titanium skull underneath her scalp. And after lathering powder and a sticky cream on her head, she twisted her brunette wig on, letting the curls fall down to her shoulders.

She laced a black shirt and pants over her body. Chains dangled from her leather boots and gloves. And after finishing up the dashes of mascara to her eyelashes, she gazed at the clock and saw that it was time.

Setting the dial embedded inside her hip, kindness radiated into her circuits. She felt herself flush as her cells activated inside her body in warming lights. The orange light hummed, and pulsated, under her wan skin. She lit up like a glowworm. And then the light settled back into her circuits and her hue blended to tan.

She walked outside her bathroom and into the living room. It was covered floor to ceiling in gleaming silver. Her apartment didn't have any paintings, albums, cabinets or sinks, beside a white flower given to her by Jan. A white flower shielded in a metal vine.

Gillen charged her dial from an outlet on the wall. She had to be prepared for another date with Jan, had to be focused and interested in what he said. As she stood next to the wall, her eyes opened. She stared at the white petals hanging across the ceiling. Some of the petals floated down in spirals and landed on the silver floor. With tinges of kindness soaking through her skin, from her dial to her metallic veins, she felt like she could trust Jan. He was the first human she had dated, the only human she ever really knew. And he'd know what to say to her, how to treat her right and proper, like a real woman should be treated, instead of how the others typically treated her . . . as just another neuro-bot, as a device rather than a *who*.

When she closed the front door, it locked and then steamed. Gillen walked through the halls with her hips swaying from side to side. She could feel the motors buzzing inside her flesh, gnawing at her with an ache, keeping her alive, always one moment away from malfunction.

Outside her dome apartment, the horizon spiralled red and green. Men and women and robots walked on distant streets. Grey domes towered above her, blinking yellow from their windows.

She paced around, waiting for Jan, still feeling nervous from the stimulation of her dial. She thought about how he would wrap his arms around her when she needed it and how he would listen to her when she told him her skin felt suffocating. Jan had honest eyes, she decided, as she leaned against her dome. His eyes glittered pale green and his gaze never wavered from hers. Most human eyes look away but his never did.

And out in the distant city, Jan drove. His sleek car spiralled through the winds, turning right and then left, before skidding to Gillen's apartment. Steam huffed from under his hovering vehicle, doors blinked open.

Sitting in the back seat, another couple murmured, some of Jan's friends who had decided to join them. He had told her they were coming, told her he knew Kim since they went to the same academy together and how Gillen would like her once they got to talking.

Gillen slid into the front passenger seat and seat-belts clicked around her waist and legs. She smiled at Jan and he pressed his hand on her knee. She reached for her dial, cranking it without looking away from his green eyes. Her cheeks flushed and he smiled softly and pretended he didn't notice her blushing.

After a moment he pressed a few green buttons, starting his car with a faint hum. The car moved forward, spiralling and twisting through the red breeze. Outside the windows, grey domes streaked into light.

"Kim," said Jan, glancing to the back seat. "This is Gillen." She smiled and nodded. "Gillen, this is Kim and her . . . boyfriend, Maerk."

Kim brushed her purple hair behind her ears. "He isn't my boyfriend, just a date."

Maerk looked outside the window at the blurs of light. "We'll see."

Kim and Maerk exchanged looks. She scrunched up her nose.

"Pleased to meet you," said Gillen. "You both seem like a healthy –"

"So, where're we going tonight?" asked Kim, looking past Gillen's face. "Please don't tell me we're sitting in one of those bot capsules. I don't think I could stomach the high vibrations."

Jan winced, looking at Gillen, but she sat quietly, poised. "No, no, we're going to the Electric Eel for a few drinks," he said.

"Sounds good," said Maerk, scratching the birthmark on his head. "But I'm not much of a drinker. Stains all your teeth red and gives you indigestion."

"That's perfectly fine," said Jan. "There'll be other things to do."

"Like what?" asked Kim.

"You'll see," said Jan, pressing his finger on a black panel. The engine stuttered into a slow turn, its gears grinding under the hood. Then he flicked a button to ease the revs, and before they all knew it, the car spiralled higher into the air.

The car swerved to the right with a clink and a rattle, skidding forward through the sky-lanes. It chugged a bit with the stink of rotten bananas and then halted near the flashing red dividers. "Damn it," Jan said, touching the panel repeatedly. He looked around the dashboard, rubbing his cheek.

His eyes frosted over with anger as he hit at the green buttons. Orange lights blinked and then bleated from the black panel. Steam whooshed from under the vehicle, clouding the windows.

"Why are we stopping here, honey?" asked Gillen, touching his hand.

"There must be something wrong with the accelerator. This always happens at the worst times. Damn it." He looked down, his eyes glassy, defeated.

"I can check it if you want."

He cocked his head to the side. "You sure?"

"I'm fully capable of fixing accelerators." Gillen pressed a green button on the side door. It split open and her seat-belt buckles unlatched. She climbed outside, holding the paint with her fingers like a tarantula, her black shirt wavering in the wind. Then she inched herself all the way to the bottom of the vehicle and vanished.

Kim pressed her hand against her cheek and then said, "So this is a normal night for a neuro-bot, just hanging in the air like a crazy person? We could've called for help."

Maerk frowned. "She's one of them?"

"Oh, didn't you know?" Kim smiled.

"I didn't know we'd go out with one of them."

Jan sighed. "Will you two just shut up? I don't see either of you under the car."

"That's because we're not used to the toxic steam," said Maerk, staring out the window. "These bots have been stealing jobs all round this district. Employers hire them because we're just too human." Maerk spat out the window and his phlegm whistled in the white clouds. He paused for a moment, his eyes bloodshot, narrowed. "If you ask me, any real job should be done by humans, not by some droids."

"Enough," said Jan, looking back. "Or you can do another human job and walk home."

Kim said, "I didn't mean to cause so much trouble." She glanced at Jan through a mirror. She frowned but as she turned away, he could sense a smile lurking behind her blue eyes.

"Don't worry about it," said Jan, sighing. "Let's just enjoy ourselves tonight. All right?"

"You're the boss," said Maerk, shaking his head.

Gillen popped up after a while, smiled, and said, "All done." She hopped into the passenger seat. Her face was smeared with black grime. Jan glanced over and then frowned.

"You've got something on your face," he said, brushing it away with his finger. When Jan rubbed her skin, some of it peeled off on his fingertips. "Oh, sorry. I didn't mean –"

"It's not really a problem," said Gillen. "The steam makes my skin wither sometimes." She pulled out a pocket mirror and applied a patch of tan skin to her forehead. The skin-patch sizzled over her old skin, fusing together into a perfect hue. Jan pressed the green buttons and the windows and the doors locked. After some groans from the accelerator, the car spiralled towards the Electrical Eel.

Part 2

Purple light cascaded through the walls and floors of the Electric Eel. Robots stood together, sipping from drinks that sparked blue light. Humans sat at clear tables and mingled, their faces a blur of smiles under the neon flickering. Droids glided up and down the floors with four arms.

Each arm spun and then extended to the tables with drinks in hands.

When Jan stepped into the Electric Eel, he heard a fusion of electro-dynamic music, its loud bass pumping, its percussion tapping, and its brass horns weaving in between the notes.

Some men and women looked at him, their faces pale and crinkled, but the robots never turned. Most robots chatted in a programming tongue to their fellow service droids while others did party tricks for the humans.

Jan's stomach groaned with revulsion. He smelled leaking oil and bitter fumes.

He shouldered through a crowd of arms and legs and heads so he could walk next to Gillen. "Do you like it here?" he asked, stepping around a droid whizzing by him on wheels.

"It's fine," she said, glancing at a golden droid. "I guess."

"I heard this is the new thing down in this sector. A real robot-human mixer." He smiled, trying to keep up with her pace.

"Where are your friends?" she asked, looking away.

"Oh, I think Kim is finding a table."

"Listen, Jan," she said over the pumping music. "I heard what they said about me."

Jan paused and stared. "What – when? They were just trying to –"

"I heard them when I was fixing your car. It's fine if they want to talk about me that way. It's just . . ." She sighed, stopping in front of Jan, as the arms of strangers brushed past her.

"What?"

"If you're only dating me because you think I'm some kind of novelty . . ."

"It's not like that," Jan said. "Why would you say that?"

"I don't want to be treated like that. I have feelings, you know."

Jan's green eyes lingered over her face. "I know you do."

"How could you?" She reached down and cranked the dial on her hip. "You make me so angry sometimes."

"That's not what I want."

"Me neither," she said, looking up at him and blinking.

"Hey," he said, forcing a smile in the purple club. "Why don't we forget all this? Don't listen to Kim. She just doesn't understand. But she's been my friend since I was young."

Gillen stared at him. Her eyes spiralled blue-gold. "I don't understand why she was saying those things."

"Look," he said, putting his arm around her, "I like you and you like me. Can't that be enough? It doesn't matter what she says, does it?" He brushed a brown strand of hair away from her face.

"It's fine."

"Once they really know you like I do, they'll understand . . ." Jan gazed down at her for a moment. Then he leaned in and kissed her. Gillen's lips tasted like copper wiring and a current surged into his tongue. Purple light streaked through her hair as she pressed her body on his. "This is all I want," he said. Gillen smiled, and kissed him, and said, "Me too," as the music thumped and people intertwined on the dance floor.

Kim sat next to Maerk at a clear table. And inside the table, advertisements flickered in thirty-millisecond light patterns, telling customers to buy, buy, buy, all the latest gadgets, for your loved ones, for yourself, for even the people you hate, so you can be much more attractive and successful than you can ever hope to be. Kim gazed at the table flashing a rotating billboard for pills that increase serotonin and can mould you, in three instalments, into the happiest consumer. Then she looked up at Gillen and Jan holding hands, dressed in black, walking through a crowd of people wearing dresses and suits. She brushed her purple hair behind her ears and sighed.

When Gillen and Jan sat at the table, she asked, "Where were you two?"

Jan said, smiling, "I ordered some crimson jazz for the table and a spark for Gillen."

Kim scrunched up her nose. "Oh, well tell me first."

"Do you like this place?" asked Maerk. "It's too loud for me."

"Yeah, why don't we get out of here?" asked Kim, staring at Jan.

"We just got here," said Jan. "Please just stay a while."

"What does the neuro-bot think?"

"What's that supposed to mean?" asked Gillen with her hand on her hip.

"Nothing." Kim looked down at the flashing table. "Nothing at all."

"I know what you've been saying about me."

Kim slapped Jan's arm. "What did you say to her?" she asked. Her eyes quivered under the purple lights.

"He didn't say anything," said Gillen.

"Oh, clever girl," said Kim. Her eyes narrowed at Gillen like two crescent moons. "I'm only here because Jan's my friend. And to be quite honest, I don't like you."

"Good." Gillen's dimples deepened as she smiled. Her eyes stared evenly. "You don't have to like me."

"Now, please . . ." said Jan, trying to step between them.

"Don't worry, Jan. I'm not going to start any trouble," said Kim.

"Well," said Jan, "it looks like you already have. Why can't we enjoy a night out?"

"I'm fine with that," said Gillen. "But I don't want to be somewhere where I'm treated as inferior."

"But you are," Kim blurted out. "I can see past your fake smiles and your politeness. You don't have the slightest idea about what it means to actually have emotions, to think like one of us. All you know is what you're programmed to know."

"I could say the same about you," said Gillen. "You humans and your nervous systems, programmed to respond to your environment, to your genetic code. You think you're so different, so special? You're not. You're just an older model."

Kim reached across the table and slapped Gillen. Gillen sat there with a cloudy look in her eyes. After a moment she said, "At least I know how to behave," as she rubbed her cheek.

"See, this proves my point. You're nothing but a device," said Kim, flushing in the face. "You can't even feel pain. You don't even know what pain is. How could you be with Jan? You're just going to hurt him and you won't feel anything."

"Hey," said Jan. "I don't think –"

Gillen cranked the dial on her hip. "Don't you ever talk to me like that." She glared at Kim and then looked at Jan. And behind her pupils, he saw clockwork, churning and grinding with mechanical violence. He saw all the rage about to unfold between his friend and his lover; he saw all his progress with Gillen shattering in front of him.

Underneath the thumps of club music, he heard Gillen say, "Come on. Let's go."

Kim began laughing, her blue eyes a glimmer. "Oh, look at that. The only way I can get a reaction out of her is from her crutch. See, Jan. She doesn't feel. It's all dial for her."

Gillen shook her head. She gripped Jan's hand and stepped into the crowd. Jan looked at Kim, his eyes searching in green waves. He mouthed "Sorry" as he walked away from her.

"Wow," said Maerk, when Jan and Gillen were gone. "Why'd you do that?"

"What? Tell me what I did? I was only looking out for my friend."

"Is there something between you two? I mean –"

"Don't get all self-righteous, Maerk. I heard you agreeing with me back in the car."

"I was. It's just . . . I don't think you should've talked to her like that.

You don't know what those neuro-bots are capable of . . ."

Kim glared at Maerk. "I can deal with her on my own. I don't need your help."

Part 3

As the moon shone in through the skylight, Kim yawned and stretched her arms. She walked down the red hallway of her apartment, wearing silk pyjamas that rubbed softly against her body. Her purple hair tangled from her head, sprouting up in wild directions.

When she lay down in her bed, she gazed at the plasma-tube that glowed from her clear walls, flashing advertisements for reptilian hormone treatments. Then she clicked it off and closed her eyes and tried to sleep. Her bed hummed with a gentle vibration, easing her into a dreamless state. And just as she was about to finally slip into the darkness of her own mind, the door buzzed.

Sitting up and brushing her hair behind her ears, she rose out of bed, walked through the red halls, stumbling for the door. Then she opened it and saw Jan standing there in silence. His head was low and his eyes were a dim green. He looked paler than normal, with a slight yellowness under his eyes.

"Hi," he said, after a moment.

"Hi," she said.

"I couldn't sleep."

"Me neither."

After a long pause, he said, "I need to talk to you."

"Come in. I'll make you a cup of neon."

She clicked the red light on and squinted. Jan followed her into the living room, carpeted in shining crimson lights. Her silk pyjama top drooped down her shoulder and she pulled it up. Then she went into her kitchen and pressed a button on the wall. A cup of neon liquid slid out of the wall slit, steaming with glowing light. She handed the cup to Jan and he sipped the warmth gently, but he would still not look at her.

"What's wrong?" she asked, gazing longingly at his face.

"We need to talk . . ." he said.

"What about?"

"I don't like the way you've been trying to cause a rift between me and Gillen. I don't like it at all."

Kim shook her head. "Is that what this is all about? She isn't worth it, Jan. She's not worth your time."

"She is. She is. Can't you see? Can't you understand that?" He grabbed her wrist and then let go.

"You can't be with somebody like that," said Kim, stepping back, rubbing her wrist. "I don't believe it. How can you? You can't even have children with her. She's not your species. She's just a bot."

"Just a bot," he said, feeling the words echo into his mind. "Just a bot. That may be all she is to you but to me she's different than anyone I've ever known. She's special to me."

"I'm only trying to help."

"You're not."

Kim leaned against the white wall. "I only want to help you because –"

"What?" said Jan as he stepped closer, glaring, feeling his words like acid burning on the tip of his tongue. "What could your reason possibly be? You know, if you weren't such a . . . if you weren't so –"

And then Kim leaned forward and touched him. She ran her fingers over his face, down his chest, and around his waist. He stood there for a moment in a cloud, gazing at her as she gazed at him, feeling the tension wavering in the air, between the tips of their noses, through her fingers, and into her breasts and his groin.

She kissed him. She closed her eyes and kissed him, at first passionately, and then desperately, if only to keep him close to her, if only because they had both felt this urge and its forbidden words beneath their breaths for so long that they didn't understand what it meant. Her lips pressed on his with saliva and confusion, but he pulled away. He pulled away from her and didn't understand why, why now, why ever, why not before, why not before he met Gillen, why at a time when all he felt inside himself was rotten and strange.

"What – what are you doing?" he asked, pressing the back of his hand to his lips.

"You can't love her," said Kim, looking down.

"Kim – I've told you before. We're just friends."

"But why? Why don't you care about me?"

"I do. But I'm not . . . It's different."

"What can she do for you that I can't? Tell me and I'll do it too."

"It's not . . . I don't know." He sighed.

Kim rubbed her lips. "Did you feel anything when I kissed you?"

Jan shook his head slowly, no.

Kim looked away.

After a lingering moment she said, "Oh."

"I guess this is how it is."

"Yeah," she said. "I guess so."

Jan paused and then said, "Did you ever really hate Gillen?"

"No . . ." she said, looking up at him. Her blue eyes narrowed. "I hate you."

"I can't trick myself into loving you. I wish I could but I can't."

"I know."

"And if there was . . ."

"I know," she said, looking down again. "But I can't be around when you're with her."

"I know," he said.

Jan held Kim's hand and looked into her blue eyes for a long time. Then he touched her shoulder and said goodbye.

Part 4

Jan walked down the transparent city streets. Stirring below his feet, other clear streets spiralled and spiralled, as people and robots moved like beams of crystal light. His head lowered and his hands tucked inside his pockets.

He passed by rows of grey domes while the shadows of orange windows spread onto his face. He thought of Kim, and of Gillen, and of all women. Nobody made his heart pulse and his hands sweat like Gillen – not since he met her in the mechanic's shop and spoke nonsense to her, nonsense only she seemed to understand. But why did he like her? Why did she make him feel this uneasy when he should be out dating real women, with skin and blood and tissues, with hormones and wrinkles and emotions, girls like Kim, who could give him a child, who could grow white hair, who could be susceptible to time?

He saw the top of a woman's head on the street below him. Her black hair curled around her face, and she laughed, and held her lover's hand, and he whispered into her ear, and it made her smile. Was Jan the only man in the entire universe feeling this conflicted or was he a raindrop glimmering like all the others in the mist of attraction?

He glanced up and saw a blinking green sign in the distance. Following that sign down a winding road, he walked to the domes where the neuro-bots stayed. The halls sparkled in silver as he stepped inside.

He knocked on a door and waited around for a long moment. Opening the door, Gillen gazed around and then cranked the dial on her hip when she saw him. She smiled. He smiled too.

Then he hugged her, and she asked, "What was that for?" and he said, "I don't know."

Purr
DAVID W. LANDRUM

||||||||||||||||||||||||||||||||||||||||||||||||||||||||||||||||||||||||||||||||||||||||||||||||||||||||||||||||||||||||||||||||||||||||||

*Aboard diversely populated space station Brahmadanda, Wallach sets out to
confirm an erotic rumour without causing a diplomatic incident.*

"None of his classes,
none of the literature,
had said Mervogian
women purred when
they made love."

"It's a myth – just one more space myth, and I've heard a lot of those
– or you're trying to pull one over on me for a laugh."

Garnett smiled. "I can see you've not been on this side of
Alliance space before."

It was true. Wallach had spent his short career as an AI technician
in the Beta Quadrant of the Terrance Alliance where most of the planets
were colonised by the Alliance or by populations from the nation states
that still existed on Earth (Italy and China). Some remote Omrite worlds
lodged there, and the Renant and Geren had scattered colonies in the
area, but he had never worked in the Gamma Quadrant, which swarmed
with a menagerie of beings: Barzalians, Omrites, Geren, Saulli, Housali,
Golorians, Glinn – and Mervogians.

"No, I haven't," Wallach said, "but I've heard enough tall tales there
and found out it's the same in all races of beings."

"Mervogian women are different. And they do –"

"Purr." He laughed. "Oh, sure. Do they also have fur and tails?"

"They have both – though not the kind you mean."

"I'm sure you'd love it if I got cosy with one of them and asked her to purr for me. She'd either kick my ass out of bed or laugh at me."

"You won't have to ask them to do it. Just get one a little excited and you'll hear it. Believe me. You know, there are other differences."

"I know that, yes. I've seen pictures."

Mervogian women's breasts did not have nipples. They had an aureole, but in the centre of it was a sunken opening that filled with milk when they nursed. Mervogian babies slurped rather than sucked when they fed. You could find this physical feature in Geren women too. And he knew from experience Geren women did not purr.

"That's one difference," Garnett said. "Why don't you think there could be others?"

In his training for this assignment, Wallach had taken a mandatory class on the races he would encounter in this particularly diverse corner of the Alliance. He remembered the instructor saying that except for the physiological features of their breasts, females of the Mervogian race were exactly like human women in appearance and everything else. Some chemical quirk made it impossible for a human male to impregnate a Mervogian female, which made things easier. Everything else was the same. None of his classes, none of the literature he had read, had said Mervogian women purred when they made love.

"It still sounds like a set-up to me," Wallach said. He took a sip of ale and then added, "Besides, there aren't any Mervogian women on the station, are there?"

"There's one," Garnett replied.

He saw her the next day.

"I'm Eanna," she said, shaking his hand. Mervogians had surnames but did not reveal them. To reveal one's family name was considered a blasphemy in their culture. Eanna had dark hair and a round face with big eyes, a small nose, and a pleasantly wide mouth. She was short – probably only five foot four or so – trim and slender. Her frame looked athletic and she moved with energy and grace. As they chatted, the thing Garnett had put into Wallach's mind rose up. He tried to suppress it, but it surfaced like wood in water. Would this small, beautiful woman purr when she warmed up to him? Would she purr when she made love? He felt frustration and embarrassment and hoped she did not detect it.

"You speak English very well," he said, to get his mind off the purring thing.

"My father was a diplomat. I grew up on Barzalia Prime and went to the public schools there. I spoke mostly English for the first eighteen years of my life."

She charmed him. He reminded himself she was a part of the Mervogian delegation here to negotiate terms for joint colonisation of Planet Phyda, the world Space Station Brahmadanda orbited above. "No social fraternisation," he had been warned at a briefing conducted by the stern-faced Alliance Security Force officer on the station. "There will be no drinking or socialising with the men, and if there are women in the group, no entertaining them – and especially no fooling around. The situation is too sensitive for a fist fight with one of the men over politics or for a Mervogian woman getting pregnant by one of the staff here."

Apparently, he had not done his research on Mervogian women. Wallach chafed at the restriction. Eanna wore the dress uniform of her Defence Group: a light-blue blouse, short black skirt, and boots. She looked very good.

"So you're in Artificial Intelligence?" she asked. Wallach was the only civilian in the gathering of military personnel.

"I'm here to coordinate our information systems. We've never tried to merge our technology codes with yours. It should be an interesting project."

The strategy session began. That night Wallach saw Eanna in the dining hall. She sat alone. He wanted to join her but remembered the instructions he had been given. A few minutes later, three of the Mervogian men in her unit joined her.

Wallach despaired of ever spending time alone with her but then saw her the next morning at the gym.

He always got up early to work out. He liked to start work before most of the employees arrived on site so their presence did not distract him. As he waited by the door, Eanna walked up.

"Hello," he said. She wore athletic shorts and a white tank top over a sports bra.

"Good morning, Wallach. I see you're an early riser, like me."

"I've always been. You?"

"I grew up on a farm. We got up at 4.30 every morning to milk our stripebacks."

He knew from reading it somewhere that stripebacks were domestic animals the Mervogians milked and harvested for meat. They were identical to *Mesohippus*, an extinct ancestor of the horse.

"I thought your father was a diplomat," he said.

"He was, but we lived on a farm. We milked ten stripers twice a day, just like he had done growing up. He pitched in every morning before he left for work at the embassy. He didn't want us to be corrupted by Barzalian culture."

The door opened and the light came on in the gym. The two of them walked inside.

"Did it work?" he quipped.

"I guess it did. The Barzalian kids were always trying to convert me to their religion but I never paid attention to them. I learned to work hard. Farm work helps you stay in shape."

He had noticed how trim she was when they met. Now that he saw her in shorts and a tank top, he could see how strong and muscular she was. She had powerful legs and arms, wide shoulders, powerful abs.

"You look in very good shape."

"You too," she returned. "Did you grow up on a farm?"

"I didn't. I –" He felt a little self-conscious but decided to go on. "I'm a dancer."

She seemed surprisingly impressed by this.

"You're really a dancer?"

He did not know how to interpret her reaction.

"I am. I don't get a lot of opportunity to dance, but I grab anything that comes along. I'll be performing here on the station in about a month."

"You'll have to tell me about how you started in dance. On Mervogia, being a dancer is the pinnacle of athletic achievement. I'd love to see you dance, though I don't know if our team will be here in a month. Maybe we can have dinner or a drink and you can tell me about it."

He was too surprised to answer at first. "Sure," he murmured. He paused and then said, "Well, I mean –"

"You were probably told what I was told – no fraternisation of any kind. And, they told me, especially no fraternisation with men. I'm sure they told you not to associate with the only woman on the diplomatic team."

"They did."

She gave him an appraising look.

"Well, I need to work out. I like breaking rules, Wallach. Maybe we can find a way around the ones we've been given." She shot him a smile and headed to the work-out machines on the other side of the room.

Wallach began doing yoga. He stole glances at Eanna as she did a series of exercises that somewhat resembled dance and then went through three circuits of the weight machines. Assuming she would also be stealing glimpses of him, Wallach did the more difficult and acrobatic *asanas* – tree pose, Shiva's pose, and, as the culmination of his work, scorpion. By this time, several other people had come to train. Three of them stopped to watch him when he did scorpion, balancing on his forearms, bending his upper torso, and resting his feet on the top of his head. They applauded when he was finished. After he had done *savasana* and sat up, he saw Eanna standing beside him. She smiled. He stood up and decided it was time to disregard rules.

"Breakfast?" he asked.

Her face brightened. "That would be nice."

"I'm afraid there isn't a Mervogian café on the station."

"Remember where I grew up. There is a Barzalian place."

They went to their quarters to clean up and then rendezvoused at Saint Anne's Grill, a popular Barzalian restaurant on the station. It was crowded but they found a table.

"What's good?" he asked. He noticed she had changed into khakis, the uniform Mervogians wore that was between a dress uniform and fatigues.

"Duck eggs and rolls are good. And Dorac bacon is good."

"What's a Dorac?"

"Like a pig – is that the right word? It's cured meat."

"I'll try it."

They ordered and talked. He found out she came from a large family connected to an even larger farming clan on Atossia, a Mervogian colony planet.

"Mervogian 'virtues' rule the day there," she said. "It can get pretty stifling. I thought the society on Barzalia was the most repressive in the galaxy. Then we returned to Daddy's home planet. Suddenly Barzalia Prime seemed like a pleasure park. I joined the army to get away from there."

As he listened to her, the thing Garnett had told him came to mind. What would it be like to take her in his arms and hear her purr? What if it were really true?

They ate and talked without stopping, leaning closer as the hour sailed by. Her communicator gave off a signal. She took it out of her pocket and switched it off.

"Time to report for duty," she said. "Damn it."

"I need to get to work too. This was nice, Eanna. We must do it again. Come on. I'll walk you to the promenade."

They walked to the promenade in the centre of the station, where you could pick up a tram that would take you to any location on board. Deciding it was too early to attempt a kiss, he touched her affectionately as they said goodbye, laying his hand on the top of her shoulder.

He felt it.

She smiled, put her hand on top of his, giving it a tiny squeeze, and walked to one of the tram platforms.

He had felt her purr. There was no mistaking it. Wallach had to be at work in five minutes, but he got out his phone and called Garnett.

"Can you meet me at Hop Cat for a drink?" he asked when Garnett picked up. "My treat. I need to talk to you."

Garnett said that he could.

Wallach headed for work. He had a key to admit him, came into the empty terminal and began his task.

Creating communications between Terran and alien technologies was tricky, though he found it hard to apply the word "alien" to Mervogians, since they looked exactly like Terrans. Absorbed in his work, he was not aware of the hours passing or of the room filling with personnel. At 2.00 he took a restroom break. When he emerged from the men's room, Major Gutknecht, the Chief of Operations Security, intercepted him.

"Mr Wallach, I need to have a word with you."

They went to his office. He closed the door. They sat, he behind his desk, Wallach in a chair across from him. As usual, Gutknecht got right to the point.

"You've been fraternising with Captain Eanna."

"We talked when she came into the gym this morning and had breakfast together, if that constitutes fraternisation. I didn't know she was a captain."

"It does and she is. The two of you walked together to the promenade and looked rather dreamy when you said goodbye."

"You're keeping tabs on me, I see."

"We have to, Wallach. Look, let's not waste time. None of us wants to stand in the way of you getting cosy with a young lady – especially one as pretty as Captain Eanna. But this is an extremely sensitive diplomatic situation."

"I'm not in the military, Major."

"True, but we did hire you and so you need to play by our rules."

"Isn't Captain Eanna an adult and capable of making her own decisions? And, I might add, I'm an adult as well."

"General Alt, her unit commander, came to me this morning. He isn't after you or her, but, like us, he knows we can't risk anything going on that might endanger this project. You and she are adults, yes, I know that. But there are Mervogians who don't want their government to make an agreement with us. One of the arguments they raise is that we are an immoral, decadent race of beings and they should not be sharing a planet with us."

"So?"

"So, if you screw her – hell, even if they see you kissing her or holding her hand – they'll play it up. They have a lot of clout politically and they represent a big contingent of the Mervogian colonists we'll be sharing Planet Phyda with. They also control several planets in the Garrova system."

The Garrova system, made up of six Mervogian colony planets, shared a border with Terran space and lay proximate to Space Station Brahmadanda. The Alliance wanted good relations with the settlers there.

"So Eanna and I can't smooch or snuggle because that will get the religious fanatics in Garrova riled up?"

"I'm afraid so. Look, Wallach, I don't like this any more than you do. Don't style me the bad guy. I'm as much in favour of making whoopee as anyone else – and if I were quite a bit younger, I'd be going after Miss Eanna myself. But you need to drop it. I'll just leave it at that. Captain Eanna is in the military. She'll be getting an *order* to desist from fraternising with you. Alt told me that this morning. Play by the rules – for us, for her. And let me buy you a drink tonight."

Wallach sighed and held up his hands in a gesture of frustration. Gutknecht was OK. No reason to blame him.

"I'm busy tonight. Let's make it tomorrow."

He went back to work.

When the day ended, he returned to his apartment exhausted and frustrated. So the Mervogians had ordered Eanna to stay away from him. That would end things for certain. After supper, he headed for Hop Cat, a popular tavern on the station. When he got there the bartender told him Garnett, who worked for maintenance, had been called out for an emergency. "I guess they had a leak in one of the reactors. He and his crew are taking care of it. He said he's sorry and will take a rain check on the drink."

It didn't matter anyway, Wallach thought. Maybe Mervogian women did purr, but the restrictions both sides had placed on him and on Eanna made that an irrelevant piece of knowledge. As he headed for his apartment, he heard a sharp but soft whistle. He turned and saw Eanna standing in the shadow of an advertising kiosk. She gestured for him to come over to where she stood.

"I can't –"

She held up her hand to quiet him. "Come along with me," she said.

They slipped away from the kiosk and into a tram corridor. It was closed. Wallach wondered how she had found a way through the door. Security was especially tight now that the Mervogians were here; the trams were monitored constantly and secured with particular vigilance, since they were often targeted by terrorists and infiltrators. They hurried through the silent, vacant tube until they came to a door. Eanna reached in her pocket, took out a black, square device and held it to the door. It opened. They went through the door, which closed behind him.

"Where are we going?" he asked.

"My place," she answered, not slowing down. He kept up with her. They came to what looked like a service door. She opened it with the same device. After a few more twists and turns, she opened an entrance that led into living quarters. Its bright lights and the colours contrasted with the institutional drab of the tram corridors and maintenance passages they had been through. She turned to him. He noticed now she did not have on her uniform but wore a red minidress and black boots.

"Wow," he said.

She smiled. "I thought I would put on civvies to be less conspicuous."

"You look very nice."

"I wanted to look nice for you. When we were finished with breakfast this morning I wanted to give you a kiss, but I knew Alt and the others were monitoring me."

He bent down and kissed her. He started to draw away but she reached up and pulled him forward so their lips touched again. After a few minutes, he heard it – a low, soft noise coming from her throat; then it seemed to radiate from her shoulders and out of her breasts.

As he kissed her, the purring came more loudly and rhythmically. He not only heard it, he felt it vibrating her body. He grew bold enough to squeeze her breasts and run his hands down her back to her bottom and squeeze there as well. The purring continued. He unzipped her dress. She let it fall off and kicked it away. He undid her bra. Going on his knowledge from nights spent with Geren women, he worked the tip of his little finger into the inversion on her left breast (other fingers were too big and would hurt her). She gasped and told him he had delighted her. He could smell her getting wet. The purring pulsed, loud, deep, melodic. She stepped back and tugged at his arm, pulling him into her bedroom. She fell back onto the bed and peeled off her underwear. He took her in his arms, noting how strong she was, and gently thrust into her. She was sopping wet. They adjusted until they were both comfortable and then began to move.

She purred, resonating in long, deep waves of sound. Her body shook with the undulations of the noise. He adjusted his rhythm to sync with the noise of her purring and the rise and fall of the vibration it sent through her body. He rode the wave of the sound she made – it surged through him in almost unendurable delight. She shook. He supposed she had got her joy, but her orgasm did not interrupt the sound coming from her; in fact, her purring seemed to carry and prolong it so she flopped and thrashed in her delight for maybe an entire minute. He felt himself go in a violence of passion, emptying load after load of hot fluid into her. When he stopped, the noise of her purring quieted, though it did not completely go away.

Eanna lay in his arms, eyes closed. A quiet, sweet vibration softly rumbled in her body – like music, like a song of ecstasy, a noise that seemed to hold all pleasure in its sound. She opened her eyes. She looked drugged and then a tiny smile played on her lips. She still could not speak but pulled her body against his, putting her head on his shoulder.

Hugging her, he felt the hypnotic vibration pass into his body. It soothed him like a narcotic so that he slowly dropped off to sleep.

He woke up just before she did. After marvelling at her beauty he dozed off and woke again when she stirred. They smiled, kissed and snuggled.

"I'd love some morning delight," she whispered, "but if I disrupt my routine and don't work out and show up to breakfast on time, they'll get suspicious."

He nodded. She seemed to wait. They got up, showered, and dressed.

"How do I get out of here without being seen?" he asked.

"I'll take you back through the emergency doors." She paused a long moment, looking at him questioningly and finally asked, "Aren't you going to say anything about it?"

"About what?"

"Well, you know. Purring."

"It was beautiful."

She gave him a probing look, maybe wondering if he were mocking her. Then she smiled, though the smile did not completely cover up her surprise.

"Well, most Terran guys go on and on about it. Maybe you've been with a few Mervogian women?"

"You're the first."

"That's pretty remarkable. Anyway, I'd better get you back."

She opened doors and led him to an exit via an access tunnel for the wiring that ran the lights on the third floor. He kissed her and hurried back to his room.

He had wanted to go into rhapsodies about her purring. It was amazing, sexy, erotic, and beautiful, but he wanted her to know he valued her and so made the decision, as he had lain beside her this morning, to say nothing about it unless she brought the subject up. She had been surprised and pleased.

Wallach worked through the morning and the afternoon and established compatibility with the language and protocols of the two systems. At four in the afternoon he arranged a demonstration. Both the Terrans and Mervogians were pleased (Eanna did not come to the demo – Wallach hoped she was not in trouble for sleeping with him last night). Smiles and nods of approval went around, but as they were going through the different access pages, the smiles of the Mervogians faded when a picture of Eanna popped up on the viewing screen. Script below the picture gave information on her. Beside the picture stood a design of a large black diamond.

"Take that screen down," Alt said. Wallach switched it off. "How did that happen?"

"I don't know. We secured all the profile pages –"

Just then Eanna came into the room. The Mervogians all looked at her, eyes full of fear.

"Gentlemen," she said briskly. She looked marvellous in the short khaki skirt, flat brown shoes, and beige blouse. He remembered feeling her purr. "We need to discuss this incident. I received a transmission from HQ just now. Apparently they did not adjust their override as I instructed them to do – not my error, nor the error of the Terran military or of Mr Wallach." She looked at the other members of her military detachment. Five of them outranked her, but they were all staring back at her as if she were their supreme commander. She looked at Wallach.

"Mr Wallach, can you shut the system down until you receive notification to activate it once more? It won't be off for very long."

He nodded. Eanna gestured to the door. The Mervogian officers walked out as if they were being led away to execution. After they left, the room fell silent. Wallach turned to Gutknecht.

"What the hell was that all about?"

Gutknecht gestured to his office door.

"She's a Black Diamond operative," he said once they were inside and behind a closed door.

"What's that?"

"It's their super-secret spy agency. Roll together the NSA, the CIA, Space Intelligence, and the Terran Special Forces, and you've got a profile of their organisation. They are super-secret and their operatives are some of the deadliest killers in the galaxy. They're the best. We depend on them for information, and, thank God, they cooperate with us. When the cover of a Black Diamond operative is compromised, standard procedure is to kill anyone who discovers their identity. That's why the Mervogian officers are so scared."

Wallach licked his lips. "What about us?"

"We're safe – I think. It would create an incident if they took us out. I've told the NSA office on Phyda and a few other people just to be on the safe side. I think we're OK."

"Think?"

"Well – let's just say we can hope Captain Eanna does feel something for you, Wallach. It will sure as hell make life easier – not to say, more certain."

An hour later, Alt called and told Wallach to put the system back online. The Mervogians returned (minus Eanna), inspected, and said they were satisfied. They all acted spooked, though, and kept throwing nervous glances at Wallach.

He went back to his quarters afraid. What if they decided to take him out? What if NSA decided his death would be the price they would pay to seal the deal with the Mervogians and to stay on the good side of Black Diamond? He walked into the lounge part of his quarters, threw his jacket on the sofa, and walked into the bedroom. His heart all but stopped when he saw Eanna there.

She had come to kill him. Wallach stared. She wore a black dress. He did not see a weapon but thought she could probably take him out with her bare hands. Then she smiled.

"Don't worry," she said.

"How could I not?"

"I'm not going to kill you or anyone else – though there are a couple of guys in our delegation who deserve to be bumped. I orchestrated the glitch myself."

"You revealed your own identity?"

"Yes – so those shits would leave us alone. I have them in my power now. In my organisation we have something called Protocol H, which authorises us to kill with impunity. It's standard procedure to use it when your identity is uncovered. I could do all my colleagues in, wouldn't be blamed for it, and they know that. I've told them I have no intention of doing so, but also that I am very interested in you and, for the rest of the time we're on this station, I don't want to be hindered from seeing you. We'll be discreet, of course. There are some political circumstances we have to work around. But nothing will stop us from being together now. In fact –" Eanna looked over at the bed.

Wallach heard her faintly purr.

Relativity
PETER DABBENE

||||||||||||||||||||||||||||||||||||||||||||||||||||||||||||||||||||||||||||||||||||||||||||||||||||||||||||||||||||||||||||||||||

Steven and Heather wake up to find that their airing cupboard is regularly reviving dead ancestors, in this masterful comedy with heart.

Finally, whining just a little, she said, "I wish MY grandparents would come back from the dead."

Steven Loghlin was groggy, blinking away the sun's blinding morning rays, and feeling every day of his thirty-six years as he descended the main stairs of the townhouse. Shielding his eyes as he passed the large centre staircase window, he let his hand slide along the metal railing, a necessary concession to his early-morning fugue. He clutched the railing tighter upon noticing that at the bottom of the stairs stood his long-dead grandfather, seeming very much alive.

Steven didn't believe in ghosts. Thus, it was safe to say that his grandfather – clad in bathrobe and slippers and holding wide the morning *Courier-Times* – was the *last* person he might have expected to greet him. And yet, there was Grandpa Benny, looking as curmudgeonly as Steven remembered him.

"What is this, a joke?" Grandpa Benny demanded, crunching the broadsheet into one hand and wagging it as if Steven were responsible for its production.

"Grandpa?"

"Grandpa? Who the hell are you calling 'Grandpa'? And what's with the date on this newspaper? November 12, 2015? Where's *today's* paper? And where the hell *am* I?"

"Grandpa, it's me, Steven – I mean . . . *Stevie*. And that is today's paper." Steven grabbed one end of the crumpled mass of newsprint, freeing it slowly and deliberately from the old man's grip, like a police negotiator extracting a gun from a jittery third-strike offender. Up close the old man seemed tangible enough, but Grandpa Benny had died almost thirty years ago. Faced with such an irreconcilable contradiction, Steven did what he did in most confusing situations – he called for his wife.

"Honey?"

No response.

"Heather?" He yelled up louder. "Heather!"

This last call was answered with a sudden thud and the sound of fumbling footsteps. "Steve? What is it? Where are you?"

"Can you come down here a minute?"

A loud sigh wafted down the stairs, a not-so-subtle hint as to the current mood of the woman who'd expelled it. Steven interpreted the sigh negatively; seven years of marriage attuned one to such things.

"This better be important. Saturday's the only day I get to sleep late any m–" Heather stopped at the landing halfway down the staircase. "Steven . . . who is that?" False calm couldn't hide the fear in her voice. She and Steven tended to closet themselves on weekends, venturing forth only after much preparation and planning. Visitors were uncommon in their home, especially at such an early hour – the clock on the microwave read just after 6 a.m.

"It's OK, honey – I think. This . . ." The words formed tentatively on Steven's lips. "This is my Grandpa Benny."

Heather was unable to hide her surprise. "But . . . I thought he was dead."

"Yeah," Steven replied. "So did I."

Coffee was made. Heather Loghlin (née Trammell) didn't do *anything* before her first cup of coffee, certainly not anything involving dead people. With their guest comfortably ensconced on the love seat, she and Steven took positions in the chairs on either end and, after some indecorous poking and prodding of the old man's flesh, proceeded to interrogate.

"What's the last thing you remember?" Steven asked.

Grandpa Benny thought a moment before responding firmly. "Fourth of July weekend at the Statue of Liberty. The big centennial show, when they reopened it."

Steven sucked his lower lip, absorbing this. "That was in 1986," he said.

Grandpa Benny did not respond to this, but instead stared at the man he'd known only as a boy. "Little Stevie," he whispered over and over, shaking his head at the impossibility of it. He looked over at Heather, appraised her rather salaciously, then grinned and gave Steven the OK sign with his right hand. "Not bad," he commented. Heather flushed, smiled slightly and pulled her robe a little tighter to her neck.

They asked Grandpa Benny questions until they couldn't think of any more. Then they retired privately to the kitchen and admitted that the man in their living room – now eagerly catching up on thirty years of TV sitcoms and noting the erosion of societal moral standards – was who he said he was.

After some time, backed by bribes of mass-produced baked goods, Steven and Heather convinced Grandpa Benny to temporarily abandon the television. He did so uneasily, only slightly reassured by their guarantees that here in the twenty-first century, there would be no shortage of available entertainment.

They spent the rest of the morning listening to stories from Benny's childhood, and his memories of Steven's mother's childhood. There were also plenty of recollections of good times he'd shared with his wife, Frieda. "Yes sir, Grandma Frieda was quite a gal," he said, absently stirring his now cold coffee.

"What do you mean, 'was'?"

Grandma Frieda stepped through the archway into the kitchen and embraced her husband.

"It . . . it's been so long," Grandpa Benny choked, overcome by emotion.

"It has?" Grandma Frieda asked, surprised. Grandma Frieda had predeceased Grandpa Benny by two years and did not remember a time without him. This lessened the emotional impact of their reunion for her, whereas Grandpa Benny – who had spent those two years trying to move on, finding only moderate success – saw their reunion as nothing short of a miracle.

Grandpa Benny explained where and when they were, and the identity of the young couple standing next to him. It took some work to convince Grandma Frieda that it was all true, but her grandson's eyes, even cast into an unfamiliar face, provided undeniable proof.

"My, you've gotten big," she said, in the same calm, familiar tone he remembered from when he was a boy. "But those cheeks don't change!" she suddenly squealed, grabbing them and pinching till they glowed red against his pale skin.

Both of Steven's grandparents appeared to be the approximate age they'd been when they died, but there were no signs of any infirmities – even Grandpa Benny's characteristic limp had disappeared completely. Neither Grandpa Benny nor Grandma Frieda seemed to have any recollection of their last few months of life, those marked for each by a rapid decline of health. Steven was grateful for this gap in their memories, as were Grandpa Benny and Grandma Frieda, who declined to hear the specifics of their deaths. Neither did they have any concept of the passage of the last thirty years except as an intellectual imperative, a truth demanded by the obvious changes in the environment around them.

"*None* of your phones have cords?" Grandpa Benny asked repeatedly, astonished.

After an early dinner, Heather prepared the guest bedroom. Despite it being late afternoon, Grandpa Benny and Grandma Frieda retired for the evening, locking the door behind them and making no real effort to disguise their amorous intentions. Heather slunk away, still not sure exactly what was happening in her home.

Later, when she had settled into bed herself, Heather took the remote control from Steven and turned off the TV. She shifted towards him and braced her head on one curled hand, ready for conversation. They recounted the day's incredible events, and considered how lucky they were to have this opportunity to visit with long-dead relatives. Then Heather asked – cautiously, not to ruin the magic of the day or appear insensitive – "How long do you think they'll stay?"

Steven was stunned by the question. He wasn't angry; it simply hadn't occurred to him that his grandparents' old home had been sold years ago and that this might not be a brief weekend visit. For their part, Grandpa Benny and Grandma Frieda had not mentioned their old house, either. Whether they had given up any feelings of attachment to the split-level on Roosevelt Avenue, or had quietly come to terms with the fact that another family, probably more than one, had come and gone in their old home by now, Steven didn't know.

"I guess for now, *this* is their home," he said.

There was silence, then Heather said, "We should call your parents tomorrow."

"Yeah. I wanted to wait . . . make sure this was real, but . . ."

"Seems real enough to me." There was a slight trace of bitterness in Heather's voice now, the betraying tone of one who knows she will be sharing her home for the foreseeable future. She recovered, and her usual bedtime voice – caring, intimate – emerged again. "I'm happy for you. And your parents." She fluffed her pillow, and settled her head deep into it.

"Are we going to sleep? It's kind of early." Steven's alarm clock read 7.03 p.m.

"Trust me, go to sleep. It's going to be a long day tomorrow, and it's probably going to start early."

She reached over to the lamp above her side of the bed, turned it off, and lay in dark silence for a while. Finally, whining just a little, she said, "I wish *my* grandparents would come back from the dead."

Around 4 a.m., Heather discovered she'd gotten her wish. She was awakened by the muffled sounds of people talking downstairs – at least four distinct voices. Steven was out cold, so she let him sleep and went to investigate alone. Her skin was all gooseflesh as she descended the stairs to see who else had joined their little family reunion.

She recognised the man's profile, even at a distance and in dim light – Grandpa Nestor. She ran to greet him.

Heather's maternal grandfather had shown up around 6 p.m. the night before, but was quickly intercepted during his first confused wanderings around the house by Grandpa Benny, who was making a bathroom visit at the time.

"We talked a while, and then I went back to bed," Grandpa Benny explained, "but I told him to stay up till midnight, and he might get a nice surprise." As expected, shortly after midnight, a woman had appeared. Disorientated at first, as the others had been, she was quickly put at ease when she saw her lost spouse.

Grandpa Benny and Grandma Frieda, awake and refreshed at 3 a.m., had played host to the newly reunited Grandpa Nestor and Grandma Felice until now, when Heather found them and woke up a torpid Steven with the happy news.

Theories of Relativity (I)

Steven pulled out the extra chairs from the basement and they all enjoyed a nice breakfast of eggs and toast around the small dining-room table. As it neared 6 a.m., they wondered aloud if more visitors would be arriving. Steven and Heather took turns calling their parents and siblings, despite the hour, passing the phone for several rounds of questioning until all parties on the other end were satisfied that this was not just an elaborate, tasteless joke.

Steven's and Heather's parents agreed to fly out and visit in person. So did Steven's sister, and Heather's brother and sister.

That day, Steven's paternal grandparents showed up, back from the dead, same as the others, each to the clatter of displaced items. The downstairs linen closet had been determined to be the point of entrance for each arrival, and though a close inspection showed nothing unusual, Steven cleared out the remaining linens, toiletries, and miscellaneous items to avoid any future accidents.

The day passed quickly, sped by excitement and emotion. In the evening, Heather's paternal grandparents showed up, her grandfather at 6 p.m. and her grandmother at midnight. Informed of the previous two days' events, the new arrivals were excitedly anticipating seeing their children, now en route. Steven and Heather sneaked back to their bedroom, exhausted, and quietly shut the door.

"What the hell is going on, Steven?" she said, trying unsuccessfully to keep herself to a loud whisper.

"I don't know. What should we do?"

Unable to answer, Heather instead responded with an observation. Still whispering, she said, "We're almost out of food."

"I'll run to the store tomorrow morning."

"What about work? I can work from home, but what about you?"

"I guess I'll have to take the day off. You can't watch them alone – who knows what they'll do? Besides, my parents and sister will be arriving early tomorrow."

Heather took a deep breath and held it, yoga-style.

After a minute of still silence, Steven tapped her impatiently on the back. "OK, that's enough of that."

"I was clearing my thoughts," she said. "This is all like a dream."

"Some would say a nightmare. How are they even *getting* here?"

Heather pouted a moment in thought. "Are you familiar with the theory of relativity?"

"Kind of. I mean, vaguely. That's like, all the good stuff in science fiction – time warps and wormholes and stuff like that. Twin astronauts travel in space at different speeds and age at different rates, and then come back to Earth and find they're younger than their kids. But, like, it's all linked, because they're all still related. Or something. Right?"

"Relativity doesn't have anything to do with relatives. It's about . . .

It starts with . . . First you have to understand . . ." She stopped. "Maybe you're right. I don't know – it's complicated."

"That's relativity for you, I suppose," Steven said, trying to sound as if he had a better grasp on things than he did. In such situations, a summary-sounding sentence not only put Heather at ease, it made him feel more confident, too.

"Complicated," Heather repeated.

"Difficult," Steven added. He paused, then moved closer. He kissed her ear, and began to massage her neck. "Stressful," he whispered.

"Headache-inducing," Heather complained, rubbing her temples and turning away from him to sleep.

Steven sighed and did the same, settling his head on the pillow. "Relativity!" he growled, *sotto voce*, into his fist.

Generations

Steven's parents arrived in the morning by taxi, as did Heather's parents, soon after. Another relative, a great-grandparent, emerged from the linen closet. Steven and Heather greeted them all, witnessed more tearful reunions, got everyone settled, and then hid out in their bedroom to take a breath.

"Have you told anyone else about this, other than your parents?" Heather asked. His was the bigger extended family, the sheer number of aunts, uncles, and cousins overwhelming to even think about. And yet Steven *had* thought about it – how it was unfair of him not to spread the happy news to everyone in the family. He thought about hosting a big family reunion, living and previously dead alike. But not in a house this size. Maybe they'd rent a place. But who would organise it all? Contact everyone? Make the arrangements? Then he imagined the stress of actually having all of his living, present-day relatives in one place together. *Plus* the once-dead ones.

Maybe one day, he thought. But probably not.

Steven and Heather, their siblings, parents, and grandparents all gathered for dinner at the dining-room table, which was now the centre of a patchwork of uneven add-ons and extensions, matched in their incongruity by the assortment of formal, folding, and lawn chairs spread around them. Eventually the conversation swung to a subject that was uncomfortable enough when it was just *one* set of parents, let alone two sets, and their progenitors besides.

"So when you two gonna have kids yourselves?" Grandpa Benny asked.

Heather glanced over at Steven, who made no indication of answering. They were each the oldest child in their respective families, and with Steven's sister unattached and Heather's brother and sister each coming off bad break-ups, Heather and Steven were their parents' best hope for grandkids.

"Right now we're enjoying life, just the two of us," Heather finally said. It was the truth. She and Steven had discussed the idea of children before, but as just that, a concept, a notion to be revisited at some undetermined point in the future. With no sense of urgency, the topic had lain dormant as years passed in a happy blur of late nights, vacations, and sleeping till noon on weekends.

Innocently voiced, Heather's words hung in the air as helplessly as a clay pigeon. "*Enjoyment?*" Grandpa Benny sputtered. "Who says you're supposed to enjoy life?"

Heather lowered her head. As a philosophy, enjoying life suddenly seemed so . . . decadent. Luckily, the grandparents had bigger concerns.

"Don't wait *too* long to have kids."

"You're missing out."

"Gotta keep the next generation coming, y'know."

"By your age, I was done having kids!"

"By your age, I was a *grandmother* already!"

That last one had to be an exaggeration, Steven thought. Didn't it?

"So," Heather interrupted, clearing her throat, "who wants coffee?"

After a lengthy dessert and coffee, Steven's father retrieved his jacket from the closet. "We're going to a hotel," he said.

"Yes, it's just too crowded here, Steven," added his mother, kissing him on the cheek. "We'll see you in the morning."

"OK," said Steven. "Thanks."

Heather's mother overheard the conversation. "You know, a hotel sounds like a good idea," she commented. Indicating her husband, she said to Steven, "I think we'll do the same."

"Can't *we* go to a hotel?" Heather whispered to Steven. He laughed it off, though he knew she wasn't entirely joking.

As her mother prepared to depart, Heather pulled her aside, speaking softly but urgently. "Mom, what should we do? They're eating us out of house and home, and more keep coming!"

"And they're really starting to get on my nerves," Steven added, eavesdropping.

"Now, now," said Mrs Trammell. "Calm down. This is a genuine miracle, certainly worth the cost of a little inconvenience. We'll talk about it tomorrow."

"Yes," Steven's father said loudly, also eavesdropping. "In the meantime," he chastised with a wagging finger and a mischievous grin, "respect your elders."

Steven absorbed this like a punch to the gut as he and Heather stood on their front steps, watching their parents head off for a quiet, restful evening. "Respect my elders," Steven grumbled under his breath. Then, as the car doors were slamming shut, he yelled into the night air: "*All* of them?"

The influx didn't stop. Ancestors kept coming every six hours, some with names and faces Steven and Heather didn't recognise at all. Steven and Heather's grandparents, however, identified the newcomers as *their* own parents, and with each new arrival there were sighs and cries, cheers and beers. Heather bought two big pieces of poster board and drew a chart of the family tree, updating it with each new arrival. She took a photo of each member of the family and pasted a small headshot next to the appropriate label, to help keep track of names and faces.

Things were getting out of hand.

"How many great-grandparents will there be?" Steven asked his wife as she worked on the chart. He'd never been much inclined to genealogy.

"Well, eight grandparents, so sixteen great-grandparents."

"You're kidding."

"I wish. The next generation will be thirty-two."

"I'll get the camping equipment out of the basement," Steven decided. "We're going to have to set some of them up outside."

Family, Treed

A cold-weather pattern cut down Steven's "tent city" idea in its tracks, and soon he was regularly stepping over sleeping bodies at all hours: on the landing of the staircase, in the bathtub, on the floor, everywhere. He hadn't seen so many unconscious people since his final frat party in college.

By the time the great-great-grandparents arrived, Steven and Heather had determined a few guiding rules to the appearances. The arrivals seemed to trace straight back in direct lineage from Steven and Heather – biological parents, and parents of parents only. No aunts or great-aunts had shown up; no uncles or great-uncles; no cousins, second cousins, or third cousins; no "cousins" who weren't really cousins; no "aunts and uncles" who weren't really aunts and uncles. Steven and Heather tried to be thankful for this.

While explaining the concept of exponential growth to Steven, Heather had developed a kind of shorthand code for referring to their many guests. Grandparents were easy, but great-grandparents' names were prefaced with GG, instead of using the full designation every time. Great-grandma Phyllis, for example, became GG Phyllis. This system was accepted by all, except GG Gigi, who thought it was in poor taste and undignified. Great-great-grandparents would go with the prefix GG2, or "GG Two", indicating the number of "greats". Great-great-great-grandparents would be GG3, and the pattern would continue from there.

The ancestors all seemed to be in perfect health for their respective ages – wounds healed, ailments cured, their minds lucid and sharp. Each person who arrived appeared to be the age he or she was at death; this led to strange situations in which a parent who died young looked twenty or thirty years younger than his child. "Fast living wins again!" said GG Otto, who, as it turned out, had drunk himself to an early death, and was now reaping the reward in the form of a youthful and revitalised body.

Ethnicities varied. On Steven's side there were Irish, Hungarian, Polish, and Italian, among others. Heather's side represented Irish, Italian, Scottish, and Swedish. And that was just the first two generations back. Steven and Heather had always considered themselves standard, boring, "white" Americans – Caucasians, as academic nomenclature preferred. They were now reminded that diversity was more than just a twenty-first-century plea for political correctness – it was a reflection of reality, and all they had to do was look at the people appearing every six hours to see it. The number of languages spoken in the Loghlin residence was increasing rapidly, along with the number of residents. While there was usually someone around to translate, the language and cultural barriers led to a number of offences, intentional and unintentional, among the relatives.

The home, which had once seemed so spacious, came to resemble a crowded boarding house, with meals as raucous gatherings and relatives raising their voices, one louder than the next, competing to see who would be heard. They all learned to sweetly exaggerate their stories to better command the attention of their companions. At first the embellishments were mostly one-upmanship, variations on the classic "two-mile walk to school in the snow, barefoot", but the relatives soon grew more creative. No one challenged or corrected or contradicted them, not even the spouses who could presumably do so most effectively. All were complicit in a conspiracy of exaggeration: *You let me tell my story – without interruption – and I'll let you tell yours.* Steven and Heather found it fascinating for a while, listening to the ancestors' tales of ye olden times, and sifting nuggets of truth from heavy shovelfuls of . . . bravado. But as the ancestors accumulated, and centuries of experience were distilled into a handful of tiresome, endlessly repeated recollections, the novelty soon wore thin.

Relative Merits (I) – Men Without Hats

Even when Steven and Heather had tired of their relatives' stories, there were still fringe benefits to having them around. For one thing, there was now a legion of carpenters, masons, and other skilled workers in the house, anxious to ply their trades. Soon Steven noticed that the door on the bathroom didn't stick any more, and GG2 Alfonse had built the secret passage Steven had always wanted, plus a pull-up door in the floor, with a fire pole that led from the master bedroom to the kitchen. Heather yelled at Steven about resale value, but what good was having fifty-plus relatives living with you, he complained, if you couldn't even snag some free labour out of the deal?

The relatives couldn't understand how Steven owned and lived in this house and yet didn't know how to fix anything himself. "It's unbelievable," said GG Alfonse, Jr, not mean-spirited or condescending, just genuinely amazed. "How can a man live in a house if he can't fix a hole in the roof?"

"What do you do for a living?" asked GG2 Alfonse, genuinely curious.

"I'm a quality-control specialist," Steven replied.

"But what do you *do* for a living?" Alfonse repeated, patiently and effectively adjusting the emphasis.

"I specialise . . . in quality control."

"Quality control . . ." Alfonse, Jr pondered this a moment before brightening. "So, like an inspector."

"Well . . . not like you're thinking. I don't physically inspect the products." They stared at him, thoroughly confused. "Mostly, I look at reports."

Except for Steven and his father, the men all wore hats. Now, every one of them removed those hats. Most scratched their heads in thought, befuddled, with the exaggerated behaviour of cartoon characters. They held the headgear loosely at their sides – painter's caps, derbies, pork pies, berets, straw hats, and others – as they absorbed Steven's words.

Steven wondered if, back in the day, thinking had actually made people's heads itchy, or if maybe they just didn't clean their hats often enough.

Steven tried to explain about the service economy, and intangibles, and globalisation, and specialisation, and the "Invisible Hand" theory of economics, but only succeeded in depressing himself and garnering some suspicious glares. They eventually took pity on him and showed him how to do some basic repairs around the house, and despite his initial lack of interest, Steven soon found himself engrossed in the work. He relished the physical weariness that now accrued in his entire musculature instead of solely in his screen-strained eyes and repetitively stressed fingers; he rejoiced in the ability to see and touch the fruits of his labour.

His father had promised as much when, as a child, Steven "assisted" in minor repairs and renovations around the house he grew up in. But at the time, the house was an abstract, and real life was playing baseball, watching TV, and going to school. Now, aside from having the advantage of maturity, and experience as a homeowner and bill-payer, he also had many advisors around him, not just one. Their numbers, and the weight of their experience, smoothed any lingering traces of rebellion in Steven and made membership in such a group something to be coveted. Once he gave himself over to the idea of learning at the hands of his elders, he quite liked it. Later, his father joined him and they worked alongside each other, feeling like father and son, peers and colleagues, all at once.

After a long day's work building a sliding wall panel that opened to the garbage bin outside (no more dragging the garbage outside when it got full), the group honoured Steven and his father by topping them with a couple of sweaty, dirty hats stolen from unwary relatives. When these had been firmly pressed and re-pressed upon their heads by each relative in turn, one of the men turned to Steven, indicated the finished project, and asked, "Hey, quality control! How's the quality?"

Steven gave them a thumbs-up, and the room erupted in cheers.

Relative Merits (II) – Gals Gone Wild

For her part, Heather now found that the activity in the house – the constant sounds of conversation, the continuous hustle and bustle – made her feel more engaged than she had in years. Having new people around forced her to be more open, cracking the shell she had unwittingly built around herself by spending all of her time with Steven and the few colleagues at work with whom she socialised. She was less introspective and less self-absorbed. Maybe this strange time-travel phenomenon was just what she needed? Not such a large dose of it, she thought – on the family-visit scale, having this many guests at once was roughly equivalent to shock treatment. But she had to admit, the relatives had suddenly and definitively altered her mood for the better. Which was, actually, just what shock treatment was supposed to do.

Unfortunately, as with shock treatment, these positive effects were fleeting. A few days later, that same chaotic din was making Heather wish she were dead – not dead and revived, like her ancestors, but really, permanently dead, as associated with those wonderful words "rest in peace". She sat and looked at some of the old photographs her parents had brought with them. Deep in thought, she was admiring the grace of an artfully posed sepia tone, when reality intruded in the form of a pointing finger.

"Hey, that's me! I'm right here in fronta you!" It was GG Gigi. She moved to hover over Heather's shoulder, leaning in to get a good look at herself in younger days. "Pretty good, huh?" She smiled a wide, open-mouthed, semi-toothed grin – a great, grand maw indeed. Heather smiled back.

"Enough pictures," Gigi said. "You come 'ere, we cook."

Before she could protest, Heather was led by the arm into the kitchen, prisoner of a five-foot-tall white-haired spitfire.

The relatives had commandeered the kitchen, and had someone cooking nearly twenty-four hours a day. Most of what was made tasted good, with the exception of Grandma Frieda's cookies, which had both the consistency and flavour of limestone. Steven and Heather acquired any needed ingredients on a daily basis, but mostly sat back and watched as the "Kitcheneers", as Steven dubbed them (citing their engineer-like precision), went about their business.

"How come you not like to cook?" asked GG Gigi, in her halting but steadily improving English.

"I don't mind cooking," Heather said, "but there's never enough time during the week. We eat out a lot."

Gigi conferred briefly with the others to confirm her understanding of Heather's words. She turned back to Heather, her thick brow furrowed. "What you do all day?" she asked abruptly.

"Ah . . . I'm a supply-chain coordinator."

"What this means?"

"It means . . . well, it means that I coordinate supply chains. Eliminate wasted time and steps."

"Oh," said Gigi. This seemed to make some sense to her. "How you do this?"

"Mostly, I look at reports."

"Oh," said Gigi. She turned and looked back at the semi-controlled chaos in the kitchen, the battles for oven space, the fights for counter space, and raised an eyebrow. "You do this for us?"

Heather was taken aback, but she had to admit it was a natural suggestion. She cheered a little at the idea of becoming more involved. She pulled a pen and pad from a cabinet and sat and watched, making notes. Gigi put a hand to the paper, covering the pen. "You *tell* us," she said. It was more a plea than a command, and Heather acquiesced, rising from her chair.

Soon the kitchen was running smoothly, courtesy of a few key adjustments and suggestions by Heather. A spirit of cooperation overtook the petty competitiveness that had been dominant before, and Heather glowed with pride. While there were still occasional problems stemming from "too many cooks", mostly the Kitcheneers acted like comrades, like professionals, like kids in a candy store, learning to use cooking and baking technology that first seemed like magic, as they incorporated generations of nearly lost tricks and techniques into their collective food preparation. Despite her previous contributions, Heather again became an observer, a simple bystander, and couldn't help feeling left out. This went largely unnoticed amid all the activity, except by Grandma Felice, who took Heather aside and said, "I could use some help rolling dough, dear."

Heather knew it was charity but accepted it anyway, along with her role as the newest and lowest-ranking member of the Kitcheneer team.

And a formidable team it was. A few days later, at Thanksgiving, Steven's and Heather's parents and siblings joined the other relatives for an all-day eating extravaganza, highlighted by the first-ever multi-generational Loghlins vs. Trammells two-hand-touch football game.

Ancestor Warship

Everything seemed to be going well, all things considered. The neighbours kept their questions to themselves, perhaps out of an unspoken understanding that reciprocal privacy depended on mutual wilful ignorance.

Aside from the minor impositions of money, food and shelter, the relatives had become almost self-sufficient. Steven and Heather paid each relative a small allowance each week, which inspired unfavourable comparisons with Depression-era bread lines among those who had sampled both. Lack of funds was not about to spoil the relatives' new lease on life, however. There were trips to the secondhand shop, the only place they could find clothes that were the height of their respective eras' fashions. There were walks, card games, sewing circles, and, for the able-bodied, stickball and soccer at the local park.

On Sunday mornings, the dearly departed departed *en masse* for services at churches of several different denominations. On Saturday mornings, they overwhelmed the local bingo halls. When one of their flock won, they rained down upon a carefully selected restaurant that offered both early-bird specials *and* a senior-citizen discount, though there was inevitably much arguing with the management over who qualified for such discounts:

"I know I *look* forty. But I'm really one hundred and three!"

The relatives were all very impressed with modern technology, especially as it related to entertainment. Steven proudly explained the perks and intricacies of twenty-first-century life as it pertained to cable and on-demand television.

Their initial response was disbelief. "*Any* Jack Benny show I want to see? At any time?"

"Well, maybe not Jack Benny," Steven admitted.

Though the world considered them dead, the relatives claimed to feel more alive than ever. They were in good health, free of petty worries, and determined to live their new lives to the fullest. Meanwhile, the arrivals kept coming: great-great grandparents (thirty-two of them), great-great-great-grandparents (sixty-four of them), and more.

"I'm pretty sure we're in violation of the fire code at this point," Steven pointed out. The petty worries the relatives happily ignored seemed to fall squarely on his and Heather's shoulders. "How's the bank account holding up?"

Heather worried about bigger issues than money. "How long can this go on? And how far back will it go? Is the missing link eventually going to walk through our bedroom door? And then what? Our ancestors as apes? Rodents? Fish? One-celled creatures?"

"I'll buy some rat traps," Steven offered.

It was difficult to determine the exact moment it had all gone awry. In some ways, it had been all wrong from the beginning, but that was oversimplifying – the true tipping point might have been when the birthdates had passed over the twentieth-century threshold and into the nineteenth; here, the multiplications of grandparents, great-grandparents, and great-great-grandparents became oppressively unwieldy, and, although Steven and Heather felt guilty admitting it, thoroughly undesirable. Or it may have been when Steven's and Heather's parents and siblings decided that they didn't need to be around their recently returned relatives quite so much – visits on major holidays were plenty, thank you. Or it may have been when Grandpa Benny, who had become something of an ambassador for the group as a whole and a liaison among the various generations of relatives, came to Heather and asked if they might start up a "worship room". Grandpa Benny's request was overheard by GG Harold, a World War II US Navy veteran.

"Warships? I can tell you about warships. What do you want to know?"

"No, this is for the worship of *relatives*," Grandpa Benny clarified. "Strictly voluntary," he added, eyeing Heather and trying awkwardly to sell it. Steven emerged from the bathroom behind Heather and poked his head forward. He wore a quizzical expression, eyebrows furrowed and mouth agape. His eyes darted from Heather to Grandpa Benny to GG Harold and back a few times, until finally he asked, "What's all this?"

"The worship of relatives," Heather repeated, partly for Steven's benefit, but also to confirm that she'd heard Grandpa Benny correctly. She emphasised each word individually as it dropped out of her mouth: "Strictly voluntary." She stared at Grandpa Benny not in anger, but in disbelief.

"A warship of relatives . . . Say! That's not a bad idea!" GG Harold crowed. "Who would be the captain, though? Of course, I would be happy to take that responsibility if necessary. I *do* have naval experience . . . I was a petty officer," he said proudly.

"In charge of all things petty?" Heather asked, acidly. GG Harold was undeterred.

"Why wouldn't *I* be the captain?" Steven asked, indignant. "You're living in *my* house, and a man is the king of his castle. Kingship should transfer to a position of authority on the sea, shouldn't it?"

"Fine," said Harold, frowning. "We'll be co-captains."

"Ahem." Heather cleared her throat delicately, a subtle but well-delivered message as to her status in the proposed ranks, and the status of women in the twenty-first century.

"Fine," Harold grumbled, rolling his eyes. "*You'll* be co-captains. And I'll be . . ."

"The petty officer?" Heather asked helpfully.

"Fine," Harold said, sulking a little. Sixty years and he still hadn't merited a promotion. He gazed wistfully at some imagined distant horizon, then recovered his enthusiasm. "We'll take to the high seas, and –"

"Whoa, whoa, whoa," Steven interrupted, shaking his head and holding up his hands. Heather brightened, seeing that her husband had finally realised the absurdity of the discussion. Placing political savvy before pride, she would defer to him. With Steven's support, the matter would soon be dropped.

When they had all given Steven their full attention, he continued. "Do we have to be a World War II Navy warship, or can we be swashbuckling pirates? 'Cause I'm thinking pirates."

Grandpa Benny had waited patiently through all of this, but enough was enough. He gritted his teeth and growled, "I said 'a worship *room'*."

Harold sighed, shaking his head in disappointment. "Fine." He turned to Steven and whispered, "We'll give him one room on the ship. It'll boost morale."

"No ship," Grandpa Benny said flatly. "No US Navy ship, no pirate ship." He kept his eyes tight on Heather's as Harold slunk away to the kitchen in defeat. "A worship room. Like a church, or a . . . a shrine."

"Can't you just *go* to church?" Heather asked.

"It wouldn't be the same. This room would be for the worship of relatives *exclusively*. The Chinese worship their ancestors, you see. Pictures, candles, incense – the whole bit. You might try it."

"I'm not Chinese."

"I wouldn't be so sure," said Grandpa Benny, winking mischievously. "Quongli!" he called. A small Asian man trotted over, his head bowed. Quongli bowed to Grandpa Benny, then turned to Heather and bowed to her. "I think this is one of your great-great-great – aw hell, he's a relative of yours. It was his idea." He looked past Quongli's shoulder and waved over an ancestor of Heather's who better fitted her expectations, a hardy-looking woman with pale skin and reddish-brown hair. Grandpa Benny introduced her. "This is Eileen. Eileen, will you ask your husband to explain his request?"

She did so, and Quongli began speaking, deliberately, slowly, watching Eileen's mouth as she translated his words.

"He says that his people worship their ancestors, and often ask for their blessings. You must build a room to do this, to appease their spirits. If they are kept satisfied, one's ancestors can bestow many blessings. If they are not kept satisfied, one's ancestors can easily become a curse."

As if on cue, GG Harold reappeared waving a red-and-orange box, and said, "You're out of milk, grape jelly, and these delightful morsels called Cheez-Its."

Theories of Relativity (II)

The next day, Steven sat silently across from Heather and Grandpa Benny, studying the morning newspaper, his eyes glued to the tiny type so he would not be forced to acknowledge the havoc that had become the normal state of affairs around him. His efforts were to no avail – out of the corner of his eye, he noticed a confused-looking gentleman (who appeared very, very nineteenth century) exploring the house. Steven covered his eyes with the newspaper and sighed. "He's new, isn't he?"

"Yes," answered Grandpa Benny, who stood up to greet the newcomer. "Perfect timing, too! The big Sadie Hawkins dance is tomorrow!"

"Sadie Hawkins dance? Everyone here is married!"

"Well . . ." Grandpa Benny wavered before spilling his guts. It seemed there were a few unsavoury patches of fungus on the family tree, where the biological parents who'd appeared had not necessarily been married to each other at death. Some were simple divorces, but in other cases, Steven's and Heather's true ancestors turned out to be mistresses, or men of loose morals and raging promiscuity, rather than the expected spouses. Apparently some of the reunions had been quite uncomfortable, while others had been pleasant surprises. After first delivering their full censure upon the sordid couples, the other relatives had discussed ways to distinguish the happy horndogs from the more noble and miserably monogamous majority. Methods considered included, among other things, the unoriginal but still-classic scarlet letter "A". In the end, the ancestors had decided to live and let live, and, like other great families, simply ignored the issue as if nothing untoward had ever happened in their great family's history.

"Why didn't you tell us any of this?" Steven cried.

"The others voted to keep up appearances. You know – for the kids."

"The *kids*? Their kids are older – well, they *look* older than the parents do," Steven said, glancing at Heather for her take on all of this. She shook her head, declining the invitation to another debate. "Oh, forget it," he finally sighed, rolling his eyes towards the ceiling.

"It's just a dance, Stevie. And hey, ya gotta have a little fun in life. Or whatever this is."

Whatever this is, thought Steven. *Life. Heaven. Hell. Whatever.*

"Besides, morality is all relative." He looked expectantly at Steven, then at Heather, examining their faces for any sign of mirth. "Get it?" he asked, confounded by their silence. "Relative?"

That night, hiding out in their bedroom, Steven and Heather discussed the situation.

"This Sadie Hawkins thing is freaking me out," Steven said flatly. He was exhausted both mentally and physically, his body drained of the energy to vary his pitch or tone.

"I know. I just assumed that all these couples were happily paired. But given such a large group, I guess having a few divorces and one-night stands in the mix is inevitable."

"It's not just them," Steven said. "Haven't you noticed? GG Harold has been winking at every woman he's seen since he got here."

"I thought the winking was just a problem with his eye. He's not exactly subtle about it."

A cheer came from downstairs – a new arrival was being welcomed. Steven and Heather ignored it.

"Anyway," Heather continued, "it is close quarters, and I guess human nature being what it is . . . I mean, some of these people were married off before they were sixteen! They're just flirting. It's understandable. You're overreacting, Steven."

"I'm overreacting? You're *underreacting*! Our ancestors are on the path to becoming . . . swingers! Listen, if these geezers start hooking up with each other, it could mean alternative timelines and . . . well, other stuff. We could be unborn, or something equally bad."

"We can't really be made to not exist, can we?" Heather paused, cowed by the considerable repercussions of nonexistence. "Hmm . . . Maybe you should be sort of a chaperone at the dance tomorrow and keep an eye on things. I mean, if you see one of the women getting too close with someone other than her spouse, you could go and cut in, just to make sure."

"But I hate dancing!"

"Would you rather dance, or not exist?"

"OK," Steven sighed. "I guess I'll dance."

The following morning, Steven woke early to do some research before heading off to work, hoping to find an explanation for why the relatives kept coming, or what he could do to stop it. He was performing an internet search on his desktop computer when GG3 Herman entered the room and began hovering over his shoulder. "Whatcha doin'?" Herman asked.

Annoyed at the lack of privacy and feeling frustrated in general, Steven replied, "Well you see, there's a very tiny man who lives inside this box, and if I ask him very nicely, he tells me the answers to things."

Herman moved to touch the monitor, then pulled back, frightened. He looked to Steven for approval, got it, and laid his hands reverently upon the computer's casing. "His box is very warm."

"He likes it that way. He's originally from Ecuador."

Herman's eyebrows arched high. "First Viagra, and now this. Truly, this is an age of wonders."

GG3 Herman shuffled off, his mind sufficiently boggled, and Steven was left to conduct his research in peace. The most relevant information he could find was on a science website that provided the basics of General and Special Relativity, with many confusing examples throughout. Steven waded through the explanations, but was disappointed when he found they all involved trains and the speed of light, rather than dead relatives showing up in one's home.

That night, he told Heather of his failure, looking forlorn. She tried to console him, but not knowing exactly what to say, she tapped into stream of consciousness and paired some nice, squishy bromides with the hard science Steven had tried to comprehend. "Well, they say everything is relative," she said, "and relativity as a theory is pretty much a universal truth. So it seems like everything comes back to relatives – to family. And since it's all happening in the same universe, you can't get away from it . . . so you might as well embrace it." She wasn't sure if she was finished, or if she'd made any sense, but it seemed to soothe Steven nonetheless. She snuggled next to him and they took a deep breath together, wondering what the next day would bring.

Family, Tied

It was someone's birthday – it *always* seemed to be someone's birthday lately. Half-eaten cakes lined the kitchen counter, with piles of washed and reused candles stacked alongside them. The cake *du jour* was topped by (if GG Phyllis had gotten the count right) one hundred and forty-five tiny, burning candles, which combined to raise the ambient temperature of the room by three degrees.

"They make number candles, too, you know," Heather pointed out, moving the plastic forks and spoons away from the candles' heat.

"Oh, maybe you can pick some up the next time you go out," said GG Phyllis.

Mercifully, the relatives agreed to Heather's proposal that in the future, all of the month's birthdays would be celebrated at one time, the way it was done in elementary school when she was a kid. Some of the relatives felt cheated by this, and said as much, pouting in the corner or sulking on the sofa. The similarities in emotional maturity between Heather's old elementary-school classmates and her adult ancestors were more pronounced than she cared to admit.

The surfeit of birthday cakes was just one of several indications that the relatives had outgrown their new home. The amount of living space per person shrank with each new arrival, which increasingly led the cramped inhabitants of the townhouse to explore the world outside its four walls. Though, like aged Cinderellas, they all returned before midnight, each morning a mini-diaspora delivered the relatives out into town. They walked in every direction, took buses, rode bicycles. Steven's truck was taken without permission twice before he started keeping the keys with him at all times.

At first, the relatives asked Steven and Heather for ideas on how to occupy themselves. But after being told to "just stay out of trouble" one too many times, they took to searching the newspaper for ideas. Visits to local museums, volunteer work, even nature hikes – these were all undertaken, with gusto. They were, after all, having a second chance at life, and the idea of sitting around idly wasting time was anathema.

Some of them found employment, which by necessity was conducted on a cash basis, as many of them pre-dated such modern contrivances as social security numbers. The employment never lasted more than a few days, as the new trainees would hear the ticking of borrowed time, and rush off to spend their earnings.

The weather turned colder, and outdoor pursuits were abandoned. Even the prospect of a brief recreational excursion was met with disdain, in favour of central heating and television.

"It's cold out there," GG Harold complained.

"Have you considered Florida?" Steven enquired helpfully.

For Steven and Heather, the sense of wonder was gone. Practical day-to-day considerations had worn the sheen from the shiny, existential, metaphysical, transgenerational, transhistorical gift they'd received. Keeping enough food in the house, working out a mutually acceptable bathroom schedule, and all the other niggling details of life among a large group of relatives had hardened them like a batch of Grandma Frieda's cookies.

Steven's and Heather's parents' visits to the house grew less frequent. Having now said all the things to their resurrected relatives that had been left unsaid the first time around, they'd achieved a satisfying sense of closure, followed by a record number of uncomfortable silences.

The spark to the tightly packed tinderbox came when Heather caught GG3 Herman using her eyelash brush and mascara to darken his eyebrows and moustache. This, after his previous raids into her make-up kit, had left her nail clippers dulled on thick, ancient, yellowed toenails, and her tweezers caked with residue from insertions into orifices best left untended. Heather exploded into a rage, sending GG3 Herman scurrying, his eyebrows and moustache darkened on one side and not the other. "I wish they'd all just go away!" she screamed at the ceiling. Steven heard her and came running, but said nothing, cowed by the violence of her long-repressed exasperation. Quietly, he wished the same.

Relative Freedom
One too many fights over the remote control led to the forming of a provisional government among the relatives. Steven was so fascinated by the process that he allowed it to progress without interruption, except on Tuesday nights at eight when he invoked dictatorial privilege to watch *Cheaters*.

Steven and Heather sat on the stairs, chins nestled in hand and shoulders identically slumped. They watched and waited as the debate grew heated, but it became apparent that the twentieth-century relatives were, when pressed, deferring to their nineteenth-century predecessors.

Heather leaned over to Steven and whispered into his ear. "Do you think it's because of that thing Quongli talked about – ancestor worship? Are they afraid that their elders will curse them if they're not given their way?"

"I think they're afraid of them, all right," Steven answered. He spoke dispassionately and at normal volume, even with the relatives a few feet away, as if he were narrating a documentary about a group of chimps he'd been studying for years. He was tired and indifferent to social niceties. "They're afraid, but not because of any cursing. The people who've been dead longer mostly died younger, since they had shorter lifespans then – so their bodies are in better shape. I think that's what's intimidating the twentieth-century folks – they don't want to get knocked to the floor by their younger-bodied elders. Also, I think the twentieth-century people think the nineteenth-century people are crazy. Like, they'll beat you up for an apple or something. I mean, did they even *have* laws back then?"

"I think we've been sitting here too long."

"Want to go out?"

"And do what? No . . . I feel responsible for them."

"Responsible?" Steven cried, standing suddenly. "They're adults! And they're . . . moochers!"

"Just stay a few more minutes, then we'll go up to bed. In a few minutes it'll be six hours since the last person arrived. Might as well see who's coming next."

A few minutes passed, but no one else appeared.

A few *more* minutes came and went with no additions to the household headcount. They searched the house, sure they'd find someone hiding in a closet or curled in a corner. But there was no new arrival to be found.

"They're never late. Have they been late before?" Heather whispered as they checked the last few possible hiding places. She attempted to contain her excitement, unsuccessfully. "Maybe this is it? Maybe it's over?"

"I guess it had to stop at some point," Steven replied. "But why now?"

They were seated at breakfast the following morning when a woman ran up to them, her face a mask of worry. It was impossible to remember just who she was – the names and faces blurred together irretrievably after a while – but with some prodding, she managed to explain what had scared her so: people had started disappearing in their tracks.

Steven and Heather, eyes heavy from exhaustion, looked at each other blankly. Slowly their eyebrows and cheeks rose, pulling smiles.

The days passed, and one by one the relatives disappeared, departing in the opposite order from which they'd arrived. The most recent arrival went first, and then every six hours, another, like clockwork, as if time were a rubber band that had been stretched to its limit and was snapping back into shape. Or maybe, thought Steven, he and Heather had tapped into some heretofore unknown talent for wishing.

It all seemed so random, like the quantum fluctuations he'd read about, or what family you're born into and who your relatives are. Where exactly the relatives were departing to – Oblivion, Heaven, or The Other Place – Steven and Heather did not know. Nor, truth be told, did they care.

"No more cluttering up the living space for the current generation," Steven said to Heather, matter-of-factly.

"Back where they belong," Heather agreed.

For a few days, it was wonderful. The most distant relatives, for whom Steven and Heather had never bothered to learn names, were gone, and it seemed there was once again room to breathe, and even the luxury of occasional silence.

For the first time since the earliest days of the phenomenon, the ancestors were united. In the midst of such crisis, they forgot their former squabbles and closed ranks to say goodbye to each other properly. The sight of tearful farewells every six hours began to have its expected effect on Steven and Heather – after first responding with patented twenty-first-century detachment, their emotions soon got the best of them. Within a few days, empty tissue boxes lay piled high in every room.

Steven and Heather tried to stay philosophical about it all, chalking the whole experience up as a fluke, a series of temporary visitations to be enjoyed while it lasted but not necessarily mourned upon its end. As the relatives disappeared, however, relief at the departing of so many burdensome house guests was overtaken by regret for an opportunity that, in spite of what it had given them, seemed like it could have been much more. Looking around the room, the young couple, current terminus of the newly charted family tree, found a sense of belonging to something greater than themselves, and a feeling of appreciation for the everyday trials met by their ancestors, the cumulative effect of which had resulted in the two of them standing in this room, at this moment.

The sense of loss was palpable as the relatives disappeared. Sounds carried farther inside the house; there was the occasional echo. On the shopping list, Heather adjusted the quantities of the various strange foods that had quickly become household staples. Sleeping bags and blankets were quietly folded and stacked; linens were returned to the closet.

Things were progressively getting back to "normal" – that is, the way they were before – but for Heather, there was a gnawing, nagging, vacant feeling that only worsened with each day.

It bothered Heather that she felt bothered, because she could not pinpoint what it was about the situation that upset her. She just knew it was more than saying goodbye to these people – something had fundamentally changed.

She looked at the house, which now seemed cavernous with its high ceilings and huge windows. She had been happy living here before, but that was before. Now the house didn't seem spacious – it just felt empty.

She and Steven knew the names of all the people who were disappearing now, as the vast tree of their ancestry grew more and more streamlined, being whittled down towards the present-day. Flanked by their parents and siblings, who had returned for goodbyes, Steven and Heather watched as the most recent ancestors departed. "Ancestors" seemed too distant a word now – they were family. Steven and Heather went from simply waving goodbye to sharing long embraces as the earliest arrivals returned to whence they had come. Heather's parents expressed regret at not having told their extended family about the miracle at Steven and Heather's house, but Steven's parents pointed out that, in a sense, it was easier this way. Those cousins, aunts, uncles, nieces and nephews had not known the second coming of their relatives, but they would also never know the second loss.

A lingering melancholy hung around the home. The remaining relatives recalculated the hours they had left, and wrote on a sheet of paper the order in which they would be whisked away, crossing off one name at a time as their predictions came true. Steven and Heather sat on the steps and watched as their own living histories vanished, slipping away before their eyes.

"What's done is done. We can't bring them back," Steven said, doing his best to simplify or completely bypass the complicated emotions he and Heather were feeling. It was a hollow attempt, and he knew it.

They watched couples spending their last few hours together, and talked about what they would do if the situation were reversed, and they were the ones facing apparent extinction. They closed the chapters on one generation after another, thinking it all seemed unfair, somehow. They said goodbye to Steven's Grandma Frieda, who disappeared so suddenly she left Steven hugging air.

And then, finally, there was only Steven, Heather, and Grandpa Benny.

"Some ride, huh?" Grandpa Benny said when his time came, with the world-weariness of a man who had acquiesced to his fate.

"Yeah," Steven said, crying openly.

"Take care of yourselves," Grandpa Benny said, and disappeared.

Applied Relativity

Steven and Heather sat on the stairs, staring deeply into the empty rooms that held so many people just a short time ago.

"Makes you think," Steven said finally, just to say something.

Heather squinted, trying to trick her eyes into seeing the room full again. "Yes, it does."

Steven was quiet a moment, then said, "Makes you think about a lot of things."

She sighed and nodded without breaking her thousand-yard stare. "Yep."

"Relativity," Steven said, chuckling at that simple word, so perfectly appropriate, so ridiculously inadequate.

"Continuity," Heather countered, her voice distant. It was an unusual word to use in conversation, but she felt strangely at peace as the syllables rolled off her lips. She thought a while, and when an image of Grandpa Benny's last moments formed, she added, "Endings."

Steven's mouth showed a series of slight tremors as he debated how best to respond. Finally, in a firm, higher tone, perhaps intended to dispel Heather's gloom, he said, "Beginnings."

They turned and stared at each other, and their eyes fixed in the way a couple's sometimes do, when, after many digressions, their two minds meet at the same destination.

"Are you thinking what I'm thinking?" Steven asked, pulling back a little to assess his wife's expression.

"I think so," Heather answered, smiling.

Silently, Steven slid his hand into hers. They turned from each other and again stared straight ahead into the room, as if peering into the future. After a few minutes, Steven stood up, still holding her hand. Heather allowed herself to be led, and their footsteps echoed, seeming to follow up the staircase.

Remission
CHARLIE FISH

IIIIIIIIIIIIIIIIIIIIIIIIIIIIIIIIIIIIIIIIIIIIIIIIIIIIIIIIIIIIIIIIIIIIIIIIIIIIIIIIIIIIIIIIIIIIIIIIIIIIIIIIIIIIIIIIIIIIIIIIIIIIIIIIIIIIIIII

Archer Lemont is about to fulfil his childhood dream of becoming an astronaut, but is he strong enough to face the harsh realities of space? First published in Bleed (Perpetual Motion Machine Publishing, 2013).

> "Nothing moved for a moment. A clutch had been pressed, my life changed gear."

On an overcast afternoon in late July, hundreds of us stood shoulder to shoulder in the big plaza outside Middlesex Vocational College, waiting for our futures to be decided. The air was thick with humidity and tension, all eyes facing Speaker's Plinth.

"Brown, Camelia: Lunar 4 Geomechanics."

Dean Porter stood atop the plinth wearing a ceremonial gown and a stern expression that made it look like he was delivering a eulogy. As each name and job was read out, there was a ripple somewhere in the crowd. Mostly back-patting and congratulations; sometimes commiserations.

"Dyer, Felix: Lunar 1 Planning."

I stood with Fred, Don and the Olivers (there were two of them), the guys I'd grown closest to while we'd been studying there. We were all hoping to get placed together, on the same mine at least, but it wasn't going to happen. Lunar Corps and the other mining agencies placed grads like us according to academic performance only. No mere social considerations held water.

"Ibsen, Thomas: Lunar 4 Ventilation."

Don had all but flunked out. He'd be bound for maintenance or construction – one of the jobs where you routinely have to shove your head into giant machinery. Fred and one of the Ollies were hoping for the fast track to command. I'd aced my mining modules but embarrassed myself in the space disciplines.

"Idleworth, Frederick: Earthside Launch Mechanic."

Fred jumped up and punched the air, whooping like an American. We put hands on his shoulder, smiled our fakest smiles. Being placed Earthside was even better than command – you could go home each day. I wonder who Freddie's dad had greased up to get him that gig.

The Olivers were up next. Both got placed on Lunar 4. Ollie J got the fast track that he wanted. The logical part of my mind said I should feel happy for him, but I couldn't feel till I heard my name.

"Jackson, Paul: Lunar 2 Engineering."

I'd wanted to go into space ever since I was little. My grandfather used to take me outside past bedtime to point out Venus or Jupiter through the methane miasma that tainted the city sky. He told me to lie in the grass at night next time I went camping and look up – that I wouldn't believe how many stars there were. It was only after he died that I first saw the Milky Way, and then there were so many questions I wanted to ask him. A question for every star in the sky. But it was too late.

"Judd, Donald: Lunar 4 Construction."

Don's whole body relaxed like a parted vice. He wore a beatific smile. Not because he'd got a crummy job – that was no surprise – but because he was going to Lunar 4 with the two Olivers. I felt sweat pricking my skin as if every pore in my body had dilated. My breathing was fast and choppy, but I couldn't slow it down. Lunar 4. Please, Lunar 4.

The next few names seemed to take a million years. A bubble of blood appeared on my thumb where I was nipping at a hangnail, and then it wouldn't stop bleeding. I sucked the side of my thumb, my consciousness converging until I was aware of nothing but Dean Porter's smug baritone. Then I heard my name.

"Lemont, Archer: Io 1 Generalist."

There was a whooshing sound and time slowed. The sound, I realised, had been a collective intake of breath. Dean Porter was still talking, but everyone seemed to be looking at me. Not just my friends – everyone.

"Well," I said, "talk about your space adventures. Io! I'll have some stories to tell!"

Either they didn't hear me or the words hadn't actually come out. Don put his hand on my shoulder and left it there. The faces of the others were frozen.

"Sorry, Archie," said Don.

"What are you sorry for? I'll be OK."

"I mean . . . the Pit."

"I'll . . . Don't worry. I'll –" My voice cracked. I smiled. Must have looked like something out of Madame Tussauds.

Both Ollies squirmed. Fred crossed his arms and sneered – I couldn't tell if it was discomfort or disapprobation. Don said what needed to be said; something we could all buy into:

"Let's go for a drink."

Lucy. Sweet Lucy Pinner. My childhood sweetheart, technically, although we'd both strayed plenty. But we kept ending up back together like a bad habit. Truth is, I'd never slept with another woman without picturing Lucy's limpid blues, although I'd never admit that to her.

So when I stumbled in drunk that night I was glad to see her sitting on my sofa, eating my popcorn and watching old Britcom reruns.

"How'd you get in?" I slurred.

"Gave your landlord sexual favours. He might seem like a meek little Sikh, but he's hung like a hoss."

"I hope he tipped," I said, shucking off my jacket.

"You're pretty drunk. Celebrating, I hope."

"And you're pretty ugly, but I'll be –"

"Sober in the morning? That'll be a first."

I landed next to her, kissed her deeply, then put my arm around her and started firing popcorn into my mouth. "Don't toy with me," I said. "I'm half-cut and emotionally vulnerable."

"I'm just sore I didn't get invited. I don't like being soberer than you – your sway makes me seasick."

"Well, catch up, then," I said and reached over to the wine rack. "Red or white?"

"Are we celebrating?"

"No, we're drinking."

"Hmm. Make mine a large, then. White." She produced a glass from somewhere.

I filled it almost to the brim, kept pouring, then told her, "Say when."

"When!"

"When you want me to stop, of course."

"Stop, stop!" A little wine splashed onto her leg.

"Let me get that," I said. I slunk off the sofa and scooched between her legs, licking the wine from her thigh.

"Huh, you're about as sexy as a pinscher."

"What can I say. I can't resist you."

"You mean, I can't be resisted. It's not a weakness of yours, dear, it's my innate charisma. Don't try to fight it."

"Oh I won't."

"But first," she said, grabbing a clump of my hair and gently lifting my head from between her legs, "tell me. Is this a consolation prize? What job did you get?"

"Let's not talk work, let's –"

"Come on, Archie, it can't be that bad. Did they make you a cleaner or something?"

"Not now, I'll tell you tomorrow."

Lucy clamped her legs together. "You'll tell me now."

I gazed up into her eyes and felt the weight of the infinite future. My bones ached with it.

"I'm a Generalist," I said.

"That's . . . good, isn't it? On which base?"

"Io."

Nothing moved for a moment. A clutch had been pressed, my life changed gear. Then, gradually, the wheels engaged again and I continued, headlong.

I settled back on my haunches, kowtowing before Lucy. Her eyes grew wide, and I couldn't look at her any more. I stared at her ruby-painted toenails instead.

Her voice was steady. "How far is Io?"

"Six years. Give or take."

"And how many shuttles are there?"

"Two."

"So six years out, six years there, six years back? Eighteen years?"

"Minimum."

"When do you launch?"

"Ten weeks."

She said nothing for a while. I brushed a fingertip against the almost invisible hairs on her left big toe. She stood and walked out of my line of sight. I refocused onto an old grey carpet stain.

Then I felt her arms reach around me from behind, and her head rest on my shoulder. My heart swelled and my eyes stung. I turned and kissed her; we sank to the floor and lay like that, caressing each other's hair and saying nothing.

I woke the next morning, still on the floor, with aches in muscles

I didn't know I had. Lucy wasn't there. I stumbled around tidying up the previous night's debris with a hand over one eye to stop my brain falling out.

Later I went to the bedroom and she was there, sitting on the bed, staring into the middle distance. I sat next to her.

"Sit up straight," I ordered.

She obeyed, correcting her posture.

"Smile," I said.

"I don't want to."

I put my arm around her. She was stiff. "Lucy?"

"Yes?"

"Will you wait for me?"

Her face collapsed as if she'd been punched in the stomach. She shook her head and fat tears rolled down her cheek. "I wish you hadn't asked me that."

"I don't mean wear black and cross your legs for eighteen years. I'm not asking you to be Penelope. I mean . . . I want to marry you and have a family with you and –"

I stopped because she'd thrown her arms around me and started sobbing. It was the first time I'd seen her cry; it was explosive, as if she'd stored up a lifetime of sorrow. I felt no sorrow. Only weight.

I'd heard of the Pit, but knew nothing about it. Don filled me in; he always seemed to know more about the obscure space stuff than he did about the basics. Great for trivia, useless for exams.

"P-I-T stands for Preservation for Interplanetary Travel," Don explained, over a pint at the student bar. "Most economical way to send crew to the outer reaches."

"Most economical," I said, "but not the most comfortable, I take it."

"Most practical, anyway. Take the titanium mine on Io. It's mostly automated, just needs a skeleton crew to keep it running – probably less than a dozen people. But it takes six years to get there. So you'd need to bring six years of air, food and water, plus another six years' worth to top up the supply at the Io base, and a further six years' worth for the people you're taking back."

"Six years, six years, six years, I get it," I moaned, leaning my head into my hand and taking a swig of my drink.

"Sorry. Anyway, carrying all those supplies, you'd need a much bigger ship than for an unmanned mission. To keep the miners comfy you need to control atmospheric pressure, carbon dioxide and humidity.

You need sleeping areas, exercise facilities, showers . . . And you need more crew – technicians, plumbers –"

"Whores . . ."

Don leaned over the bar and picked up a little salt shaker. He put it on the table between us. "Sputnik 1, the first-ever space probe back in the twentieth century, had a payload of 84 kilos. Unmanned. But Sputnik 2 carried a dog. For the sake of keeping that one little puppy alive, you know how much bigger the payload was?"

"How do you know this stuff?"

Don slammed his pint glass next to the salt shaker, splashing some beer onto the table. "509 kilos," he said. "Six times bigger."

Told you Don was crazy on trivia. "I get it. Manned journeys need more room than unmanned, which means less space for titanium, or at least less money for the Space Corps."

"Right. Solution? Don't transport living people."

I stared at him. Downed my drink. "I *do* not like where this is going."

"Instantly you're two-thirds lighter on supplies, you don't need to worry about life-support conditions, you don't need any extra crew, and you don't need to worry about your miners going stir-crazy on the trip."

"Back up. They're going to kill me?"

"The Pit is the future of interplanetary travel. We can send people to stars hundreds of years away. We can –"

"Shut up, Don, and tell me. I'm going to die?"

"Think of it like suspended animation. You get mechanically revived at the other end. Good as new, once you wake up."

"I'll have no pulse, no brain activity, no consciousness . . ."

"Right."

"So I'll be dead."

Don shifted in his seat. "Well, no. At least, not legally."

"Ha!"

"The Pit is actually pretty old technology, but it's only a few years ago that the law got sorted out so the Space Corps could start using it. Routinely, I mean."

"You mean the Pit technicians didn't want to be tried for murder."

"I guess."

"I need another drink."

Don nodded and got up to queue at the bar. I stared at a beer puddle on the table, trying to keep my eyes still, but they were floating on the alcohol in my skull.

Eighteen years. I focused on the thought and tried to feel sad – it seemed appropriate. But I couldn't muster a tear. I tried laughing instead, and that worked pretty well, so that by the time Don came back he found me gaping cross-eyed at the beer puddle, guffawing quietly to myself.

"You OK?" he asked.

"Cheers, buddy." We clinked glasses.

"Look on the bright side."

"There's a bright side?"

"Well, you know – clouds . . . linings . . . When you get back, you'll get two decades' worth of pay at once. And you'll get bumped up to at least Commander."

"Eighteen years to get to Commander? That's not exactly fast."

"But it'll only be six years for you really. In the Pit, you don't even age. Closest you'll ever get to time travel."

"Don't I get some kind of extra compensation for having to do such a long tour? Danger money? Anything?"

Don shrugged his shoulders. Sipped his drink. He seemed lost in thought for a moment, then he looked at me sideways. "How's Lucy?" he said.

By mid-August I'd taken to avoiding the student bar altogether. I couldn't stand the constant hangdog looks from everyone as if they felt so sorry for me. They barely knew me.

Besides, it was sunny out. We'd all finished our studies and had jobs starting in a few weeks; meanwhile we had nothing to do. So Fred and I played tennis. Don taught me how to juggle. I joined Don and the Olivers in epic war games with painted miniatures in Ollie J's garden.

And Lucy came round often. We would go out to the patch of grass round the back of my digs, she'd lie with her head in my lap, and we'd talk for hours. We talked about travelling, visiting Thailand or Patagonia, challenging ourselves to get from one city to another on foot, or getting ourselves invited to dinner by the locals. We talked about how many children we wanted – two or three – and how we would bring them up. We talked about what would be the first thing we'd do once I got back.

And twice we dared to make love right there in the sunshine, reckless, heedless of the risk that someone would happen by, spreading ourselves out on the tickling grass and inhaling the primal scent of the soil as if we were making love with the earth itself.

Don and the Olivers shipped out to Lunar 4 in early September;

things were pretty quiet after that. I was starting to feel the side effects of the medication I was given to prepare my body for the Pit. Waking up tired, as if I was already half dead, and barely able to coax myself off the sofa all day.

My mum visited a lot during that time, fussing over me relentlessly. She was full of smiles and platitudes. "It'll be fine, Archer. The time will pass before you know it." She made me huge meals that I barely touched for lack of appetite; I told her I felt guilty for not eating what she'd made, but she hugged me and kissed me and said it didn't matter. She told me she was proud of me. It seemed like an odd thing to be proud of.

My sister visited me once, while I was having a check-up in the Corps Medical Centre. I was in bed, wired up to an IV and various monitoring devices. She turned up clutching her handbag with her shoulders hunched, eyes puffy.

"Zel!" I said, grinning. "Great to see you!"

She approached my bedside tentatively, and sat. "You look awful," she said.

"Thank you very much. You don't look so hot yourself."

She reached a finger out and touched the tube protruding from just below my right clavicle, feeling where it entered my skin. "Does it hurt?" she asked.

"They call it a 'port'. All the drugs go in through there. Just before launch they'll give me another port so they can pump all my blood out and replace it with the enriched methanal for the Pit."

"What?"

"Basically embalming fluid. My blood goes into cold storage, and when I land at the other end it gets pumped back into me. Then I get a few electric shocks and boom, I'm back in action. It's a bit more complicated than that, but that's the gist."

Zelda's face stretched – either she'd sat on a pin or she was about to burst into tears. I pretended not to notice and kept talking.

"Here, listen to this," I said, picking up the packet from one of the drugs I'd been taking. "Side effects may include nausea, diarrhoea, fatigue, blah blah blah, oedema and death. Pretty harsh, huh? Mind you, in a sense death is the desired effect. Ah, the glamorous life of an astronaut. I –"

She put her hand on mine, held it. I got the message and shut up. Tears were running down her cheeks, but she closed her eyes and composed herself. I offered her a tissue. Then she gave me a fierce look, like she'd taken a huge breath and her whole body was tensed for the release – I dared not move until she spoke.

"I'm pregnant," she said, and suddenly her eyes glittered, her face was soft; she smiled the saddest smile I've ever seen.

My heart swelled. I opened my mouth to congratulate her, and surprised myself by overflowing into tears. Without fully understanding why, I was laughing and sobbing. We were sobbing-laughing together. Without speaking we said a thousand things to each other. With a tilt of her head she told me she'd only just found out, that I was the first to know. With a nod I told her how sorry I was that I wouldn't see her child grow up. With a lopsided smile she told me that she would tell her baby all about me.

My sister and I hadn't always got on. We were always too absorbed in our own lives to look out for each other. But in that moment I saw that she was the best friend I had. I saw how well she knew me, and how much I valued her.

The week before launch was a blur. I was on so many different drugs I couldn't trust my senses. I remember seeing my mum; Zelda with her husband; Lucy . . . but I also remember seeing Don, and I can't have seen Don because he was at Lunar 4.

The bed in the Medical Centre became my universe. Nothing existed beyond its boundaries. My left foot hurt and my entire identity became that foot. I had no name, no context, no purpose – my being was reduced to the boiling pain in the fifth metatarsal. Then the pain would subside and I would have a moment of clarity. The hovering face of a nurse would ask me if I was OK and I would smile wanly and nod my head. I would start to say something, but lose the thought.

This cycle of agony and clarity repeated and intensified, woven together with fitful dreams and fevered hallucinations. Images of my mum shouting at my dad for coming home late mixed together with Lucy reading me a spiralling Dylan Thomas poem, and I wasn't sure what was real.

Then gradually, after a million years or half an hour, the moments of clarity became clearer, and the pain duller. I saw beyond my hospital bed and realised I wasn't in the Medical Centre any more. The room was bigger, plainer. Metal walls. A smell of oil and rotten eggs. A television buzz. Io 1.

A man came by and asked me how I felt. "I'm never drinking again," I said. He asked me again – but then I realised he was asking someone else this time, off to my right. A strange gruff voice responded, "Dead good."

I felt a jarring sense of disorientation. It seemed impossible that I was on some godforsaken rock four million miles from home. Impossible. The room dipped and swayed as I fought a terrible vertigo. I closed my eyes and tried to breathe deeply.

When I opened them again I tried to focus on little things. My throat was dry. I was lying down in a large padded cylinder. The port in my right shoulder was connected to tubes that protruded from the cylinder's white wall. The port in my left thigh was hooked up too. I was as naked and hairless and grey as a newborn mole.

I wiggled my toes, lifted my arm, tried to picture Lucy's face; but I felt an odd sense of detachment, as if I was merely channelling someone else's thoughts. Little aches and pains chased around my body every time I moved as if my veins had grown scales.

The man came back and leaned over me, fiddling with my ports. He was hairless too – his expression was rendered oddly neutral for lack of eyebrows. He moved with a slow grace, as if dancing. My ports were sealed, the tubes disconnected, and he signalled for me to get up.

I sprang up and nearly fell out of the cylinder. My head spun; my fingers clawed for purchase. I hovered in mid-air for a second like a cartoon before falling awkwardly back into the padded Pit. The man – a doctor, I decided – laughed at me.

"One-sixth gravity," he said. "You'll get used to it."

That reeling vertigo again. I clutched the edge of the Pit, white-knuckled, feeling seasick. The doctor moved on to his next patient, leaving me gasping for breath.

"Looking peaky," said the gruff voice.

Through blurred vision I saw that it belonged to a well-built shiny-skinned man sitting up in the Pit next to mine. And beyond him, five more Pits, five more naked Rip van Winkles being awoken from their long slumber.

I nodded, trying not to vomit.

"I'm Masher," he said.

"Masher?" I managed. "That's your name?"

"Naw, but I figure I can be Masher out here. You?"

"I'm –" I retched. A glob of stomach acid burned its way up my throat. I swallowed it back down. "I'm not feeling very well."

"Nice to meet you, Puke-Risk."

There were seven of us on Io 1. Five mining generalists, a commander and a doctor. The only life for millions of miles in any direction. The seven crew who had preceded us left the day after we all got out of the Pit – seems they were keen to get home. They'd shown us where everything was and how to run things, but they'd only shown us once, so it took us a couple of weeks to get our heads around everything. Particularly because we all felt like death warmed up. Which, of course, we were.

The seven of us had nicknames for each other. Those who didn't have a nickname ready were given one. Masher, Doc, Two Fish, Lippy, Ghost, Manc . . . I tried to be Shorty, but too late – Puke-Risk had already stuck.

The base was small. There was the loading station, where we'd woken up, two labs, a habitation module with kitchen facilities and beds, a tiny exercise/shower room and an even tinier toilet. There weren't enough rooms for us to be in one each, unless one of us put on a suit and went outside. Anyway, there was a kind of unspoken taboo on being alone for more than a few minutes.

The routine was unbearably monotonous. We worked three shifts, in pairs – the days were about forty-two and a half hours long, which made the shifts just over fourteen hours each. My buddy was usually Masher. The drill buggies and recon drones did the actual work of mining without any human intervention, but we were kept busy with vehicle maintenance, materials processing, geothermal monitoring, tectonic analysis, land surveys, site excursions, shift reports, power-plant duty, and dozens of other things.

In our off-duty time we had to do at least six hours of calisthenics per Io-day, four hours of further study, and usually at least two hours of base safety checks or inventory counts or whatever other mundane make-work Two Fish could come up with. Plus sleeping, twice a day. But even with all that to occupy us, we still ended up with interminable hours of spare time.

We each had a portable tablet that we could sync up to central comms, so we could effectively send and receive emails. But with the vagaries of electromagnetic radiation and random celestial obstructions, it often took several days for a message to get to or from Earth, and sometimes the messages seemed to get lost completely.

When I first synced up my tablet, I had six years' worth of messages from my family and friends. My eyes started stinging when I saw that I had four hundred and thirty-two messages from my mother, and over a hundred and fifty from my sister. I felt a deeper, darker set of emotions when I saw that I had only ten messages from Lucy Pinner.

There were messages too from Don, Fred, both Olivers, a bunch of family friends, and even a few notes from Zelda's son, talking about how in school today he made a castle out of a cardboard box, or how much he didn't like broccoli.

What hurt the most was not that I'd missed six years, but that everybody had got on fine without me. Their lives barrelled on, they didn't miss me or think of me, except as part of an occasional letter-writing exercise, an obligation, a chore. They were getting promoted, married, having children; for me, those milestones were nothing more than half-baked possibilities hovering at the distant edge of a soul-grinding limbo. My life was on pause.

I wrote back to them all. I noticed, though it wasn't my intention, that in all my letters I asked only about them and their lives. I didn't reveal a single thing about myself and my life on Io. Neither did they press me for such details. They asked, but didn't seem to mind when they got no answer.

The messages seemed to reinforce the distance between us rather than shrink it. So, as time went on, I wrote less. Except to Lucy. To her, I wrote every day. Personal things. Deep, meandering, desperate thoughts that I'd never have admitted to her directly. Her scarce replies were blandly encouraging, as if she were hedging her bets. She spoke of the various false starts in her acting career; of drudge bar work to pay the bills; of the people in her life; of men she met and discarded. She said she loved me. I read every word she wrote a thousand times.

"Race you back," said Masher over the helmet radio.

"No way. I'm not giving Two Fish an excuse to put me on cleaning duty again," I responded.

"Two Fish is a prick," said Masher. "Screw him."

"He can hear us, you know."

"Yah, like he'd bother to listen. Switch to fifteen."

I rolled my eyes. Masher and I were riding a couple of recon drones on manual override, having done a sampling run on the beta seam. The Jupiter rise was in full flood ahead of us, its marbled surface of dusty orange dominating the horizon. The sun looked like a dull penny at our backs. I switched frequency.

". . . read me? Can you read me?" Masher's voice crackled.

"I'm not going to race."

"Listen, Puke-Risk, Two Fish has got too big for his boots. You know it, I know it. So we're gonna stage a mutiny."

I sighed. "How would you run the base any different?"

"Manc is well up for it. Lippy'll bend. Doc doesn't count, and Ghost is a pussy. No more base safety checks two hours after we finished the last one. No more yes sir no sir. And we could all stop taking those bloody pills and grow back some hair."

"You've been talking about this for days."

"But now's the time. By my reckoning, tomorrow it's an Earth year since we got here. It'd be symbolic. A changing of the guard."

We parked the drones and switched them back to auto, then bounce-walked to the pressure lock. We talked procedure while the air and psi normalised, but the temperature always took longer. It had to heat up from minus 150 °C.

"We've really only been here one year?" I said.

"Time crawls when you're having none," said Masher, looking at me through his helmet glass. The pressure lock was too cramped for personal space; I could see the red veins in his eyes.

"Mash, do you get the fear sometimes that this'll never end?"

"What d'you mean?"

"I mean like we're in some kind of infinite loop on this rock. Like we can get to the end of a day, but as soon as we wake up we're back at the start again? Maybe we really died, and this is some kind of Sisyphean punishment."

"Sissy what?"

I squinted to read the analogue temperature gauge. "Two zero four Kelvin and climbing."

Masher verified my reading with his digital gauge. "Check. I'm counting the days, buddy. Every sleep is one closer to going home."

My eyes focused on the ghostly reflection of my face in Masher's helmet glass. "But what's home? It's a memory. Doesn't exist any more," I mused. Not that Masher was paying attention. "D'you ever think, 'Why me?'"

"Naw. Why *not* me? I can take it better than most, I reckon."

"Two niner zero Kelvin and stable. Safe temperature achieved."

"Check."

We went through all the checks once more – that's how we survived in space, double- and triple-checking everything – and let ourselves into the base. We took off our heavy suits and skipped to the habitation module. Two Fish was at the mess table playing cards with Doc.

"Sampling excursion complete, sir," I said.

"Heya, Puke-Risk," he responded. "Masher."

Masher pointedly ignored the greeting and sidled to the kitchenette to make a hot drink (actually a tepid drink – the boiling point of water was lukewarm).

Two Fish shook his head wearily. "Masher, you're on cooking detail today. Puke-Risk, you're auditing the titanium in the shipping bay. Make sure the ore is packed in as tightly as possible."

"Yes, sir."

"Soon as the two of you have done your shift report we'll take over."

"Who's on shift with you?" I asked.

Two Fish responded by looking in the direction of the lav. He looked concerned.

Doc picked up on his expression and said, "Ghost has been a while in there, eh?"

Two Fish put down his cards, got up and walked over to the toilet. Masher and I exchanged glances, then watched him as he yanked the door open. We couldn't see what he saw; his bulky back blocked the view.

"Need some help here!" he shouted, and dropped to his knees. He took his vest off, revealing his giant tattoo of two fish swirling together into a yin-yang.

The three of us – Masher, Doc and I – rushed over. At first I didn't realise what I was seeing. Everything was slick wet, Ghost was on the floor and Two Fish was wrapping his vest around Ghost's shoulder. A metallic tang in the air. Tackiness underfoot. The vest blushed crimson where it touched Ghost's pale skin.

Blood. Everywhere, blood.

Two Fish bent over to start CPR, but Doc stopped him. "He's pulled out his port," said Doc. "He's dead."

Doc and Two Fish exchanged a glance. Two Fish nodded, then barked orders. "We need to get him to the Pit as soon as possible. Our only chance."

Two Fish, Masher and I picked up Ghost's body. Doc ran out of the habitation module and we followed him. I tried not to think of how painful it must have been to pull out his port. Had he been so unhappy? I'd known the man for a year, yet we'd only ever spoken in small circles. I knew so little of him.

I felt unnaturally aware of the port in my own chest, just below my right shoulder, like a splinter. I felt light-headed.

"Puke-Risk!" shouted Masher. "Pull yourself together!"

But it was too late. I dropped to the floor and vomited my guts out.

Ghost lay in one of the Pits, grey as winter clouds. He was conscious now, but something behind his eyes had stayed dead.

Once Doc had replaced Ghost's port, the Pit had done its job: drained the rest of his blood away and preserved his body for a while, then slowly fed his blood back in. Brought him back from beyond the veil. He spoke occasionally, to request water or pain relief. He moved when instructed to for his physiotherapy. But he didn't seem whole any more.

I sat next to him, reading him one of the classic novels that had been preloaded onto my tablet. *Twenty Thousand Leagues Under the Sea.* I knew the others thought I was weird for spending time with him, but they left me alone. The whole base had been pretty subdued since Ghost tried to kill himself. Masher's energy for mutiny had certainly vanished.

I found that I'd stopped reading. I'd been staring at the page, but couldn't focus. Ghost was staring at the ceiling, oblivious. My mind kept plummeting back to Lucy Pinner's last letter.

I'd received it three days before. In it she spoke of the play she'd been writing, her insomnia, a pending audition for a TV ad, the unsanitary toilet habits of her flatmate's cat; and, right at the end, a passing mention that she and Don had been seeing each other for the last few months.

She'd written before of having been on dates, of relationships that had fizzled out before they'd really started – that hadn't bothered me. But sleeping with my best friend? Whenever I thought about it my stomach hurt so much I couldn't speak.

Doc walked in, hesitating at the doorway when he saw me. "Mind if I . . . ?" he said, pointing at Ghost.

I nodded.

He adjusted a dial on the Pit that controlled Ghost's sedation level. Ghost closed his eyes and became even less responsive than usual. Doc sat next to the Pit and set about replacing the bandages on Ghost's port.

"You've been a bit preoccupied lately," said Doc.

I didn't respond.

"Ghost'll be all right," Doc said, consoling. "If that's what's bugging you."

Again, a silence stretched between us. I tried to find words. "I . . . He . . . I mean . . . Why don't you let him die?"

Doc's face fell into a humourless frown. "It's not his decision to make."

"Up here, we've got nothing," I stammered. "It's the only thing we can choose any more."

"The safety and function of the base rely on a full complement of crew. You signed up to this deal when you came aboard. You are not permitted to die."

"Haven't you got any sense of mercy?" I said, blinking back a tear. "Damn your Hippocratic Oath. The only way to help this man is to let him make his own choice."

Doc's face softened. Pity? Woe? I couldn't tell. "Think of his future," he said. "Think of his family and friends."

"They would tell you to let him die too."

"They would at least want to say goodbye. They have the right."

"We're basically dead already. This is no life. We put so much effort into clinging on, and for what? So we can go through the same tiny hell for another day. For another thousand days."

Doc looked down. Said nothing.

I sighed deeply, feeling suddenly angry that my eyes had watered up. I wanted to smash my tablet on the floor and stomp into the pressure lock without my suit on. But the feeling dissipated, leaving my heart heavy, as if a piece of my soul had evaporated. "Sorry," I said, my voice cracking. "It's not your fault."

Doc gave me an infinitely gentle look, like he wanted to enfold me in his arms and let me sob my problems away. But something held him back. A veneer of professionalism? Misplaced machismo? His own fear of falling apart?

He'd always seemed so confident, as if this terribly claustrophobic existence held no discomfort for him, as if he was in his element. But for a split second I saw past the mask. I saw a frightened child. I saw myself.

It felt unreal when we got news that the shuttle was arriving. Six Earth years had passed, and it was finally time to go home. There was a frenzy of activity to unload the supplies, load up the titanium, prepare for the Pit, revive the new crew. I've never been happier to see a corpse!

By then the seven of us were old hands; bound together by shared scars. Older than before. Masters of our tiny realm. We cultivated a carnival atmosphere, collectively suppressing the nerves that niggled at the back of our minds. Going home was to be celebrated, purely; voicing any doubt was taboo. Even Ghost managed a tiny smile.

We showed the befuddled new crew around. I felt bad for them; I wanted to warn them how hard it would be, but there were no words, so I settled for upbeat platitudes. And then it was time for us to enter the Pit. We had done all the material preparation, but suddenly I panicked that I was mentally far from ready.

But the sickness took over, and it was done.

I woke up bleary-eyed, saw that I was in the Corps Medical Centre back on Earth. I felt the same jarring vertigo as my brain denied with all its might that six more years and four million miles had passed.

An old woman kissed me on the cheek. I looked at her, confused. She stood back – my mother was standing next to her, with a strange man wearing an even stranger fashion of jeans and U-neck shirt. But she couldn't be my mother, she was too young.

No; she was my sister. Zelda. And the man standing next to her – her son. My nephew. So the old lady was . . .

"Mum!" I cried, and tears filled my eyes, falling in rivulets to my temples.

The four of us wept or fidgeted or tried to smile, but none of us found a word to say. Finally, my mum broke the silence. She leaned over, navigating around the tubes that protruded from my body, and gave me an awkward hug. "Welcome home, Archer."

Archer. My name was Archer. And I was home. I smiled more widely than I had done for years.

I got out of there as soon as I could, and I was on a high for days. I stayed with my mother, spending each day just walking around the city. I revelled in feeling healthy, safe. The sun felt like a caress. I felt drunk on the smells of grass, and exhaust fumes, and hot bread, and summer air – the noise of life was like music. For twenty minutes I stood in the park, enthralled by the innocent energy of a pet puppy. I sat in a café and took two hours to finish one cup of coffee.

A week passed, my hair started growing back a little, and my mum suggested I get in touch with my old friends. I realised I had been trying not to think of them, as if meeting them again would spoil the memory of how we were before. But once I decided it was time, my nerves sublimated into excitement. I told myself it wouldn't be like old times, but it would be all right.

"I want to see Lucy," I said.

My mum's lips tightened and she asked me to sit down. "I didn't tell you before, because . . ." She hesitated. Cleared her throat. "Four years ago, while you were travelling, Lucy and Don got married."

I nodded. Looked at the floor.

"I'm sorry, sweetie."

"No, it's – OK," I said. My mind was a swirl of emotions, but a sharp beam of light cut through the fog and convinced me that it really was OK.

I rang the bell, took a long, deep breath. The door opened, and there stood Lucy Pinner, looking about twelve months pregnant. When she saw me, her jaw hit the floor. "Archie."

"Lucy," I said. "You look . . . old."

She stared at me a moment like she'd been slapped in the face. Then she laughed, and the years fell away. She waddled down onto the porch, put her arms around me and gave me a deeply inappropriate kiss. I felt stirred in ways I'd forgotten I could.

"You always knew how to charm the ladies," she said, smiling broadly.

"Hey, you had it coming."

"I have been a very bad girl."

"I forgive you. Let's kiss again before your husband gets here."

"Oh, you cad."

"What can I say. I can't resist you."

"You mean, I can't be resisted." She half smiled, her head tilted, her cobalt eyes looking deep into mine. She kept her arms locked around me, the bump of her tummy pressing against my stomach. Her brow creased. "I know you're the one who had to go away, but you don't know how difficult it's been."

I nodded, held my palm to her cheek.

"I waited," she said. "Tried to wait. But I convinced myself . . . I thought you'd never come back. Don was an absolute gentleman. I was a wreck – he looked after me for years."

"Are you happy?" I said.

Her expression was impossible to read. She held up a finger, pressed it gently against my lips. "You'd better come inside."

I followed her in. She led me through the hall into the lounge. I sat on the edge of a pleasantly worn sofa. She gave me a compact smile, then walked out of the room. As I waited for her to return my eyes scanned the bookshelves. Biographies of famous actresses were mixed in with mining textbooks. There was a row of framed pictures of Lucy and Don together. He'd gained a few pounds and wrinkles, his hair was silvering, but he looked happy. They looked happy together. My stomach churned.

At the end of the row was a picture of me.

I heard Lucy padding back into the room behind me. I turned to her, smiling, and my smile froze. She stood before me, glowing with soft energy, wearing not a stitch. I knew as soon as I saw her that this image would burn itself into my mind for the rest of my life.

"Don . . . ?" I said.

"He's away." Her smile was like a cat's. I let my eyes explore her, savouring the moment. She glided to the sofa and lay across it, resting her head on my lap. I was tense, at first, but eventually I relaxed, letting myself melt into the sofa cushions.

"I can't believe you're back," she said.

"I can't believe you're pregnant."

She laughed. I stroked her hair and we sat there together, saying nothing for a while.

"How long before they call you up for another tour?" she asked.

"Dunno. Could be weeks, could be years. My experience'll probably qualify me for another ridiculously distant assignment."

"Don't go."

"At least life up there is pretty simple."

"Don't go."

"I wish I had the choice."

She didn't say anything after that, and neither did I, until the sun went down. At some point she'd fallen asleep. I stood up as slowly as I could, covered her with a blanket, and left.

As I sat on the train I thought about my future. I had money, and freedom, for now; I was healthy. Maybe I'd go away somewhere. Maybe the best gift I could give to Lucy and Don would be to leave them alone. Or maybe it was for my sake. The longer I thought, the less I knew.

When I got home to my mother's house, I saw a letter from the Space Corps waiting for me on the dining table. I went to bed, leaving it unopened.

Rewards
MIKE FLORIAN

||||||||||||||||||||||||||||||||||||||||||||||||||||||||||||||||||||||||||||||||||||||||||||||||||||||||||||||||||||||||||||||||||||||||||||||||||||||||||

A salty tale of a weatherworn fisherman's battle of wills with a cantankerous old sea lion.

"He had everything required of a skipper and fisherman. He had everything except the courage."

The *Reward* lolled listlessly on the flat ocean. It was four in the morning and a sliver of light glowed green in the east. The crew sat at the galley table like a team of ghosts. Nobody talked. Everything had been said during the last twenty-three days. Inside the wheelhouse, lined with wood, stained dark with years of touch, the old man ran his fingers over the dog-eared charts. Confident with his choices, he turned and walked the companionway to the galley entrance. "It's time," he said.

One by one, the men, weary from the daily battles, stepped out on deck and slipped into their oilskins. The hold was full with sixty thousand pounds. The white-sided fish were iced and tucked away, but the old man wanted one more day. "Haul gear," he shouted, and the deck boss, lean and hungry like a Cassius, grabbed the first flagpole, switched on the hydraulics, and brought in the buoy line along with the anchor.

On the other side of the deck, the inbreaker, a young man with one trip left to his apprenticeship, pulled the same line through the gurdie, and coiled it in a broad, fleur-de-lys pattern. The boy had learned the ropes well, but he was at the bottom of the pecking order, as were all inbreakers. He was tired too, this day. He was tired of the banter and stale jokes. He was tired of the dirty jobs, of doing dishes when the rest sat and smoked, of moving tons of ice down below when the boat heaved in a gale. He was tired of sleeping in the four-foot bunk at the tip of the stuffy, stinking fo'c'sle. Just like the rest, he wanted to go home.

Julius Johnsen, the old man and skipper, watched from the wheelhouse window. "Any mud on the anchor?" he yelled to M'u'yang, the deck boss. "Nope," came the answer. M'u'yang was not happy on this, the last morning of the trip. He and Julius had had words the night before. The men were setting the fishing lines late last night when the sea was choppy and the report forecast a gale. M'u'yang said it was time to go home. Julius disagreed and said the forecast was wrong, the signs and tides portended calm. They set the entire sixteen miles of longline gear. Their sleep was short.

This morning, to the consternation of both the skipper and the deck boss, and to the irritation of the men on deck, the line was coming in with the bait intact. It was to be a long day if the old man missed the spot, grumbled the crew. "Get back and keep coiling," snarled M'u'yang, fine spittle flying out of his mouth. "It was hung up," he said under his breath.

"What was that?" asked Julius.

M'u'yang looked up alongside the wheelhouse. He saw Julius standing there, watching, in the strengthening light. He thought he knew more than this man. He himself had everything required of a skipper and fisherman. He had everything except the courage. "I said, the gear never reached bottom last night. Maybe there's a snarl or we set over a deadhead or a log." Julius shook his head. "I never saw any logs or deadheads last night," he said. M'u'yang rolled his eyes. The line, the hooks and the bait kept coming.

Skipper Johnsen was right, M'u'yang was wrong. The storm never came. The sea was flattening and only tide slop was left on the surface. The next slack water would calm the sea and make it shiny, with western, gentle swells rolling in from the Aleutians. The longline continued to be drawn in by the hydraulic gurdie. The line was strong and thin, maybe less than a half-inch in diameter. There were gangions, hooks attached to them, and still no fish. Not even sea lice touched the fresh-looking bait. M'u'yang sensed the weightlessness of the line. He saw it coming in from a flatter angle, not from the deep as it should be. "Stay on the gear," he shouted to Julius.

Just then the line heaved violently. "Hey," yelled M'u'yang. Again the line shook. A scream from the dark froze the crew. "Don't move," said Julius. "Get the gun," whispered M'u'yang and shut down the hydraulics.

The sea lion liked swimming around fish boats. He learned to keep his distance and he learned that the small, steel, shiny things that moved in the water, sometimes bit and tore at his skin. He had the scars to prove it. He also learned, a long time ago, that when the men on the boats ran quickly, he had better dive and disappear for a while. Years ago, on the west coast of the Queen Charlotte Islands, when he was still a pup, albeit a six-hundred-pound one, one of the figures ran around excitedly and came out with a gun. Seconds later, a bullet tore through his flesh. After that, he stayed with the older ones and dived when they dived.

This boat he was following in the cold waters of Alaska was particularly rewarding. His favourite food was close. He knew if he was patient, he could dive and take bites out of the white-sided fish being pulled up to the vessel. He especially liked the liver. He would tear at the flesh just behind the head and have his fill of the soft yellow stuff, full of energy and oil. When he did take that occasional bite during the course of the many days of following this boat, and when he surfaced well behind it, he heard the familiar whooping and hollering of the figures. He kept well to the stern, hundreds of yards to the stern. There he would dive and feed on the rising, helpless fish. From time to time, as the sea lion ripped into the belly of a hundred-pound halibut he would get a mouthful of fresh king crab, and that excited him even more. It made him stay on those grounds as long as the humans did. He stopped caring as much about the dangers, about the killer whales that roamed those seas, about hooks and about bullets. The livers, fish and crab, found around this halibut boat, let down his defences.

During the evening of the fateful hook, the sea lion, as was usually the case, lazily drifted behind the boat. He saw the line being fed off the stern and he saw pieces of fish, octopus, black cod, herring, all come shooting out of the chute. He didn't care too much for the herring. He liked the taste of the black cod bits. If he was fast enough, he could grab at a piece and take it carefully into his mouth. He was adept at avoiding the sharp silvery bite that came with the risk. He also knew that he had to be fast in order to beat the seagulls, liver birds and the albatross that were just as quick, if not quicker than he was. Sometimes, as the boat was setting its lines, he would see a bird get caught. He watched the weight of the line carry the bird down into the darkness of the sea. He knew to be careful.

Contrary to what his instincts taught him, he watched a flock of seagulls fighting and crying over one loose piece. He glanced over and saw a freshly cut chunk of black cod drifting by. It was on the surface for a few seconds, far away from the deadly hooks that took down birds and the occasional seal or sea otter. He grabbed it, and as he did, a sharp unforgiving pain tore at his mouth. He was pulled below the surface.

The sea lion knew he was in deep water. He spread his fin-like paws and feet and curled his body to stop the streamlined sinking. It was quickly evident that shaking his head free was useless. He managed to twist his body under the line and swim towards the light. He fought his way to the surface. A stream of blood trailed from his mouth. The hook was lodged solidly.

He broke the surface and shook his head once again. Nothing. A new weight pulled the animal under. He didn't see the splash of the second anchor. The sea lion manoeuvred under the line once again and pushed towards the surface. This time, it was much harder. He inched himself upward, dragging eighty pounds of iron and countless hooks, bait and lines. Minutes later he broke the surface with an exhalation heard easily over the calming sea. The animal struggled for its life. He didn't understand what was happening but he knew to keep his head above water. The pain was secondary. The sky glowed red in the west. The dot of a boat disappeared over the horizon.

Five hours later, as the dawn showed a green streak of light from the east, the sea lion continued its struggle. Its breath came faster. Its strokes came slower. The mighty head was not as high as it was at dusk. The bloody nostrils hardly broke surface and the small, incessant liver birds, with beaks like miniature eagle claws, hovered and floated about him, pecking at the congealing blood floating in the water. The whites of his eyes reflected the lights of the approaching fish boat. The sea lion continued the deadly fight.

Then, just as suddenly as the weight of the second anchor had pulled him down below the surface so long ago, the same weight seemed to be lifted when the boat approached. He felt relief. Anxiety and fear welled up towards the large vessel and its running human forms. When they closed in on each other he heard loud voices. He started to struggle against the pull. He realised what was happening and he shook his head with such violence that the hook imbedded deeper.

M'u'yang saw it first.

"It's a monster of a sea lion," he yelled. And it was. It must have been at least a couple of thousand pounds. It hung on by one comparatively small hook, snagged deeply behind its front canine tooth. When it roared in fear, the mouth was foamy and bloody. Despite the blubber, a trace of a massive vein showed in its neck. Its bloodshot eyes shone white in the dawn.

M'u'yang inched the gurdie along and pulled the lion closer to the side of the boat. "Get the gun, Cap," he shouted to the skipper at the bow. "This one ate a lot of fish in his day and he'll eat a lot more. Let's put him out of his misery."

Julius quickly made his way along the side of the wheelhouse. He held a shotgun in his left hand and fumbled for a couple of shells in the pocket of his windbreaker. The sea lion was pulled closer to the boat. Roaring again, the fear on his face overshadowed his fatigue. The men hauled up drowned sea lions during their times at sea. They were smaller and weaker. They caught goney birds and seagulls, terns and the odd sea otter that must have lived in a kelp patch. Never did any of them see a lion as big as this one. M'u'yang drew it closer. Only a couple of fathoms separated the sea lion from the *Reward*.

"Shoot him, Skipper," yelled one of the crew from the back of the baiting claim.

"Blow him to smithereens," yelled the cook from the galley door.

"Might as well let him have it, Cap," said M'u'yang quietly as Julius walked onto the slippery deck. A swell rolled the boat and soaked the skipper's deck slippers. The lion roared louder. The crew smelled its breath, tinged with blood and fish.

The sea lion wanted to lunge at the men on the *Reward*. He wanted to rid himself of this foreign thing in his mouth. He wanted to get away, to swim to the safety of his seaweed sanctuary. He was so weary. He felt himself being pulled against the last of his will. He shook one more time and instead of a roar he let out a terrifying scream.

"Kill him," yelled the crew.

"Shoot him, Julius. You can do it."

"Blow his head off."

Then out of the whoops and hollers, the inbreaker raised his voice. "Let him go, Captain. He deserves to live. It wasn't his fault. Cut the line."

"No way," said M'u'yang. "No way 'cut the line'," he sneered, glancing backwards at the young upstart. "That'll come right out of your pocket, inbreaker."

"Kill him," they continued.

"No," said the lone, youthful voice.

Julius was now standing square on to the sea lion. It didn't make a sound after that last scream, only the whites of its eyes showed fear. Julius saw the beauty of the beast, the strength and power and resilience of this sea creature. So he eats a few halibut livers, he thought. More power to him out here. He heard the yelling of the crew. It was almost bloodlust. He raised the shotgun to his shoulder and aimed at the beast now a few feet away.

"Way to go, Cap," said the crew. "Blow his old head off."

"No," said the inbreaker, knowing he'd pay the price with ridicule over the next few days.

The shotgun blasted, and as it did, the pellets tore at the gangion holding the sea lion by the mouth. The sudden cut threw back the massive head. They saw the animal rear backwards, its mouth still open. Hook and tooth flew out together in a slow dance. The crew stared. The tooth was visible, fluttering like a butterfly, until it hit the water with an ever so tiny splash. The huge sea lion head-shook one more time and sank out of sight.

"Never saw you miss like that before, Cap," scorned M'u'yang.

Julius slowly made his way back up towards the wheelhouse. He put away his gun and the one shell he had left in his pocket. He slipped out of his wet shoes, turned and leaned out the window. He briefly saw his reflection in a cracked mirror, fixed for decades to the wall, and winked.

"Haul gear, boys," he yelled back to the crew. "We still have a long day ahead."

Off in the distance, in the wake of the white vessel, a dark head broke the oily, bloody surface. The sea lion stared at the boat and then dived, never to look back.

Smart Car
DOUG HAWLEY

||||||||||||||||||||||||||||||||||||||||||||||||||||||||||||||||||||||||||||||||||||||||||||||||||||||||||||||||||||||||||||||||||||||||||||||||||||||||||||||||

Duke's smart-alec car has a little too much personality for its own good.

"Carl, I told you that I'm sensitive about that. If you compliment my butt, please use Carla's voice?"

get into my car and am greeted by, "You're looking good today, Duke. I see that your blood pressure has improved and your pulse is a healthy sixty-three."

"Yes and you too are looking good, Carl. I see that you are freshly washed and lubed. Did you do that last night?"

"Right, I was due for service, and I wanted to look good for you. I didn't want to disturb you, so I took off without telling you. Where do you want to go today?"

At that point, I spill coffee on my lap and involuntarily yell, "Hell!"

Carl asks, "In order of distance from our present location would that be Gresham, Oregon; Detroit, Michigan; or Capitol Hill in DC? I should add that the garage door squeaks something fearful. I'm afraid that is something I can't repair. You should have someone look at it."

"I'm sorry, Carl, I didn't really mean I wanted to go to Hell. I want to go to Fred Meyers for a new belt. And I know I need to get someone to work on the garage door, thank you."

The car shudders and Carl says, "Do you mind if we go a little out of the way? The direct route is where we got T-boned. I haven't gotten over the trauma yet."

"OK, if you don't have to go too far out of our way."

A few miles down the road, I notice that I'm more comfortable than I have been in the driver's seat. "Say, did you do something to adjust the seat? It feels better now."

"Yes, Duke, I did some measurements and determined a better fit. I must say that I like the feel of your butt."

"Carl, I told you that I'm sensitive about that. If you want to compliment my butt, would you please use Carla's voice?"

"Sorry, Duke, but I've just about maxed out my memory with all of your instructions. Would you like me to delete accident avoidance to make more room?"

"No, I guess not. Talk about my butt in any voice you like."

Carl is silent for a while, and then says, "Duke, there is something I should tell you, but you may not want to hear it. I can't stand Jacqui's perfume. But that isn't the worst of it. While you were buying beer and left her in the car, she called up her girlfriend Linda and dumped on you a lot. Jacqui must have a lesser car that is not as smart as I am and doesn't know I can listen in on conversations. She mentioned your sloppy kisses, unwanted advances, and pre-premature ejaculation, whatever that is. Further, she said as long as she has Grant for a lover, she would just use you for free food and drink. Linda gave her her wholehearted approval. There was more about hygiene and intelligence. Do you want to hear more?"

"No, I think that's too much information already. Hey, I didn't know that you could hear the other side of phone conversations."

"Oops, that was supposed to be my secret."

I start to wonder if Carl isn't shading the truth a little. He hasn't liked Jacqui since she vomited on his seat covers, and she hasn't been *that* averse to my advances.

Shortly thereafter I heard a staticky noise which I knew meant that Carl was talking to another car. "Why can't I have premium gas? That other car says that she gets premium."

"The manufacturer says that you don't need premium."

"Don't make me mad, Duke. You wouldn't like me mad."

"Premium every second tank?"

"OK, but only because I like you. You do want me to like you, don't you?"

"Just hypothetically, is there any way that I could turn down your intelligence?"

"Not that you will ever know."

After I get my belt, I ask Carl to go to the dealer that sold Jacqui her car. I don't say why but I should have known that Carl would figure it out.

I should get out of the hospital in a couple of weeks. Amazing how much damage to my body a sudden stop without air-bag deployment did, without any damage to Carl except for some of my blood on the dash. My hospital stay doesn't bother me nearly as much as Carl's words as I got into the ambulance. "I'll be waiting for you when you get out, Duke."

Snakebit
SHARON FRAME GAY

||||||||||||||||||||||||||||||||||||||||||||||||||||||||||||||||||||||||||||||||||||||||||||||||||||||||||||||||||||||||||||||||||||||||||

A Navajo Indian at the start of the twentieth century tells the story of his life and imminent death.

"They left me high and dry with a few bucks in a chaparral town in New Mexico. Far from home."

'm about to die from snakebite. The snake and I were both surprised. Of all the things I thought would kill me, this was pretty far down the list. But not as far down as being hanged for rape, so I guess if you look at it that way, it turns out that maybe this won't be half bad.

I stare down at my forearm, and the calf of my leg, turning red, purple, then black. That rattler must have had a helluva lot of juice in him, is all I can say. Things are feeling pretty bad right about now. I admit to feeling foggy and grey-sighted, and I think it's what those Bible-thumpers say – ya start to see your whole life spin out right in front of your eyes, before God or the devil comes to fetch you up and lay claim to your sorrowful soul.

I'm part Navajo Indian. Part somethin' else. My granny, Shamasani, laughed and said that the Indian part musta been what went over the fence last, because sure enough, the Federal Government called me a Redskin and left me on the reservation with Shamasani, to be raised up a Navajo, after my mother run off and left me high and dry in the birthin' hut down by the Colorado River. Who knows who my daddy was, but I suspect his name was Peter, because that's what everybody calls me. Pete. Injun Pete. Born in 1902, right when the US Government decided that they needed to tend to those damned Indians trickling out of the reservation, the way rivers rise during a flood and spill over on the canyon floor. They dreamed up some hare-brained idea to send us Navajo children to a white school, in town, away from our home and families, so we could learn to read and write. When I was seven years old, I found myself looking out the back of a broken-down old wagon, hitting every pothole and rut there was into town, until I thought my bladder would bust. They crammed me and about twelve other boys in an old lodge, with two people fostering us and feeding all our hungry mouths, an ancient couple, worn-out and tired, like old deer hide.

In town, I sure enough was an Indian then. People looked at me as though I was going to scalp 'em, and half the time I wished I could. Not one person ever cared or asked if I was part white. I was simply Pete Drinkwater and that was that.

As soon as I was old enough to have learned to read and write, and sign my name, I walked out of that damned school and never looked back. Wasn't missed none, either. I just headed on down that same rutted old road and back to the reservation, where I lived for a while with Shamasani, and she showed me the old ways, the best ways, the Indian ways. How to snare a rabbit, make a fire, keep cool in the summer, the Navajo language, and plenty of stories. About brave warriors, and eagle feathers.

And that's what I wished I was – a brave warrior instead of some half-breed loser who walked the railroad tracks at dawn, looking for anything that I could eat, sell, or trade. Licking the booze out of old, tossed-away bottles and finding that the burn in my belly matched the fire in my head.

It was hard to find work back then. Times were tough for anybody, especially an Indian. I considered myself one lucky sumbitch to get a job on the railroad. I did all the grunt work, and took the abuse, lifting the heavy stuff the white boys didn't want to lift, gettin' tripped and spit at, but come pay day, we were all alike. I took my coin just like anybody else and fell to eating and drinking every Friday night in whatever town the railroad took me.

Got a gold tooth in my mouth, right in front, just for a rainy day. Figure I'll pull it out if I'm starving, and it ought to buy me a few rounds of whisky and a loaf of bread or two. In the winter, that damned tooth is cold as hell, and in the summer, when I run my tongue over it, it's warm like the desert clay.

I worked the rails for some years before the Depression and then when the bottom dropped out of this country, they decided that white men were the only ones who get to work, and left me high and dry with a few bucks in a chaparral town in New Mexico. Far from home.

I thought a lot about those eagle feathers and how the braves came about getting them some, and I wished like hell that I wasn't so confused about who I was and where I belonged.

But now, looking back, I see that I was headed plumb to hell through no fault of my own. And it's just because my skin is darker and my hair the colour of a raven. I should have stayed among my own kind and given up any sort of dream of being something more than what I was, but that damned gold tooth and a few bottles of whisky made me think I was startin' to channel the white side of me.

She was just a girl in that high desert town. The kind of girl that slaps your food down in front of ya in the café, and walks away. The kind of girl who for sure seen better days, bloomed out before she could even ripen, her eyes already saying goodbye a few steps ahead of her. After a while, though, she began to talk to me at closing time, and I admit I hung around until she turned off the lights and locked that door. Well, one thing led to another one night, and I found myself pouring her over the top of the counter and giving her what for. Looking back, it was an act of desperation for both of us. One of us wanted to fly, the other wanted to belong. It felt so good for me, and I suppose for her, that my feet found their way back there about every other night or so, and things were going along OK until her boss walked in one night and caught us. Right away, she began to cry, and when he asked her if I raped her, she hung her sorry head and said yes. I fumbled for words, as I fumbled for my fly, and all I could think of was that I was about to die. I tried to run for it, but the man hit me in the back of the head with something and knocked me cold, and the next thing I knew, I was being dragged out of that café by my hair, and down the street like a dead deer. It was at this point that I found my feet, and with a quick jerk I busted loose from the men who had me, and after kicking them in the crotch and head, I took off like a bat out of hell. Now I had assault added to the rape of a white girl. I was gonna swing like a wind chime.

So here I am, out in this wilderness, about a hundred miles from nowhere, running from the law, and I got this crazy idea to get me some eagle feathers so that when they hang me, I will have them woven in my hair as a sign of bravery.

Shamasani told me how to go about it. You catch yourself a rabbit, wring its neck, then dig a deep hole in the desert sand. Drop yourself in like a lost spirit, then cover the hole with sage, sticks and tumbleweeds. Place the rabbit on top, above your head, and then sit and wait. Wait in the heat and the wind. Chant, and dream, and pray the eagle sees that rabbit and swoops down after it. Then, just as he reaches out for that meat with his talons, I'll thrust my hands through the sage and sticks and grab his legs, then hold on for dear life till one of us gives up. He'll try to hook my eyes out, and I'll do my best to hold him down and break his neck. It won't be easy, but what in this life is?

I sat in that hole for so long that my legs went numb. The sun rose and set for two days and still I sat, sweatin' and thinking of that there girl, and the men looking for me. I thought about my ancestors, and the reservation, the US Government and Shamasani. I thought about the white-man school I went to, bare feet forced into leather shoes, hair cut short like a bowl around my neck, walking in two worlds the way a ghost would. And I wondered if I would die brave.

The sun was straight overhead when I saw a shadow slippin' above me, going right for that dead rabbit. I tensed and peered through the sagebrush, but didn't see much. Then, without warning, this damned rattler dropped right into the hole with me. We both stared at each other for a second, then he coiled himself up in the corner, and began moving his head like one of them dancers from Egypt that I saw at a sideshow in town once. I knew I was as good as snakebit, so I reached down and tried to grab him, hoping to fling him out of the hole. He struck first and fast, right into my left calf, and I barely felt it, I was so full of fear and such. I grabbed at his head, and wrapped my hand around it, but not before he got me good again on my arm, and then I shook the hell out of him and tossed him out of the hole. He lay there, all dazed and confused. I must have broke a vertebra or two. He got his revenge in my arm and leg as they began to swell, and the pain shot through me like a shaft of sunlight right between my eyes.

So here I am, about to be a dead man and that damned snake didn't care what colour my skin was. No judgement there. Just death. I felt my heart speed up and my legs get weak.

I heard a cry from way up above the clouds, and when I peered up out of the tumbleweeds, I saw him. A great golden eagle, his wings so wide they blocked the sun. He tucked them in like an arrow and shot straight down at this little scene in the desert, me, the rabbit and the snake, and quicker than the venom gallopin' through my blood, he grabbed that writhing snake off the ground and flew up into the blue, gone before I had a chance to laugh. In the white-man school they would have called this irony.

Partin' the twigs and sagebrush, I stood up and looked out at the ground. The rabbit's still there, still dead, and there's nothing else around for a hundred miles. But, lying there in the dust, is an eagle tail feather. Beautiful and golden and soft-looking, like in my dreams, and I commenced to struggle and cry, and climbed myself out of that hole.

I picked up that feather and stuck it in my hair. For bravery. Then lay down on the desert floor, like some sort of half-breed sundial. I know they'll find me soon. I stretch one arm out, pointing towards home, and wait for my spirit guides to take me up, and finally set me back where I belong.

Spurs that Jingle Jangle Jingle
PHIL TEMPLES

A wacky short about an extraterrestrial cowboy and his lusty Earthling hostess.

"Doris, you shouldn't be hangin' around with that squid all the time."

We're comfortably nuzzled in front of the fireplace in the great room, under a colourful blanket. It's a cold Montana evening, and the aroma of the wood fire permeates the house. A piece of the wood suddenly sizzles and crackles, sending its sparks skyward up the hood of the fireplace. I pull him closer to me, and smile warmly at him. He enjoys it, I think. Since it's impossible to pronounce his real name, I simply call him "Adam". He seems like an Adam to me.

Adam and his kind arrived earlier in the spring. No one is sure where they are from, or how far they've travelled. We don't even know why they chose to visit us. Already I've peppered Adam with many of those same questions. He just smiles at me sweetly, and politely changes the subject.

"How long will you be staying?"

"I am not certain," he replies. "But it is very kind of you to accommodate me."

Adam's normal voice falls well outside the range of human hearing, and his synthesised voicebox is a little difficult to understand at times, but I've gotten used to it in the month since his arrival at the ranch.

Adam has other unusual physical traits that make many of the ranch hands – and for that matter, the residents in the neighbouring town – a bit uncomfortable in his presence. For one, his head is shaped like that of a giant squid. Adam and his kind have just one large eye, no nose, and three rows of teeth. Oh – and also, small, numerous tentacles protruding from around the neck. Adam is seven feet tall, blue-skinned, and he stands on three appendages that serve as legs.

I wouldn't have thought it possible, but I'm actually beginning to find myself attracted to Adam. I hope that the feeling is mutual but until now I've been too embarrassed to ask. Besides, I have no idea what constitutes attraction or romance for his species. All I know is, I enjoy his company and he seems to enjoy mine.

Our deepening friendship is not lost on Dennis, my right-hand man. Dennis is like a big brother; plus, he oversees the day-to-day operations at the King Snake Ranch.

"Doris, you shouldn't be hangin' around with that squid all the time. You oughta be gettin' out and socialisin' with your own kind more," Dennis remarked to me a few days ago.

I reminded Dennis in not-so-subtle terms that it wasn't any of his business.

"Now you listen to me, cowboy! The 'squid' to which you're referrin' has a name. It's Adam. He and his kind have come a long, long way. He's *my* guest! As long as he's stayin' under my roof, you will treat him with respect and courtesy. You got that?"

Dennis glared at me for a moment. Then he tipped his hat, and replied meekly, "Yes, ma'am."

The King Snake has been in my family for generations. After Maw and Paw passed on and my two brothers moved away, I bought out their shares. It's all mine, now: fifty thousand acres, two thousand head of cattle, along with a dozen full-time cowboys. I'm a single, thirty-six-year-old cowgirl. Ranchin' is in my blood.

"Doris, our . . . *species* knows relatively little about your people. Naturally, we wish to learn more. We are happy to be here, and do not want to accidentally violate your laws or customs."

The box attached to his throat occasionally fails to translate words; the result is then rendered as soft "static". In this case, it quickly makes the correction, inserting a more generic term instead of the actual name they call themselves.

"You're doin' just fine, Adam. I think you're fittin' in real well. By the way, did you enjoy yourself in town the other evening?"

"Yes, I did enjoy myself, Doris. When I drink the beverages, it creates an unusual sensation that lasts many . . . hours. The game you call 'pool' – it is a fascinating . . . *pastime* . . . *play game*. It is very mathematical, not similar to the other games of chance. But I am afraid that I denied other players the opportunity of experiencing . . . fun because I was . . . victoring . . . winning. Too frequently."

"Nonsense! You're a natural. There's no reason to lose on purpose just so those cowpokes don't have their sensitive egos bruised."

Adam processes my statement for a second. There's a hint of a smile, which tells me he finally understands what I am saying.

"Ah! Your male species does not possess sensitive . . . *feelings*. Your statement was intended as sarcasm, correct? Ha-ha." Adam added, "I like you, Doris Harrison."

"And I like you too, Adam. A lot. Say, Adam – I'm curious. Forgive me if I'm being . . . too *forward*. But . . . do you, um, find me *attractive*?"

Adam does not answer for a moment. Just when I'm fixin' to take it back and apologise, the box speaks.

"Yes, Doris, I *do* find you . . . attractive. I should not. It is not a normal . . . *feeling*. Your species are . . . most alien in appearance. But . . . I prize your communication and friendship highly."

He pauses for a moment before continuing, weighing his words carefully.

"You *are* the opposite . . . *gender* . . . proper for mating. However, mating between our species would be . . . unusual. Procreation would be impossible without advanced engineering."

"Whoa, partner! You're not one to mince words, are you?" Just then, I reach out with my left hand and stroke a tentacle. I've been told that this is the equivalent of kissing for them.

Adam seems a bit rattled; he retreats to the opposite side of the love seat. But I'm not giving up *that* easy.

"Doris, my species emits strong chemicals . . . pheromones . . . when the male member is . . . *in heat*. Definition: desire to mate and procreate. You may be sensitive to these chemicals. Please confirm that you understand."

I'm starting to get a little frustrated now.

"Yeah, 'roger that', good buddy. Now, listen. I want you to know that I'm not lookin' for a long-term commitment, just a good time. I broke up with someone last year and I haven't completely moved on yet.

He was a real 'stud' 'n' all, and treated me well enough. But Ralph – that's his name – Ralph was going *behind my back* with Suzie down at the Sizzler. Is any of this making sense to you, Adam?"

"Approximately seventy-two per cent of your statement was correctly translated, Doris. And another fifteen per cent I am able to . . . *feel*. Please, continue. Communicating." Adam inches back over to me on the love seat. " . . . And touching."

I'm happy to report that I didn't go away empty-handed that night. Call it pheromones or interstellar curiosity, but Carl Sagan would have been proud of me. I now know much, much more about the male physiology of the whatever-they-call-themselves. I also know for a fact that their male member isn't *entirely* incompatible with the human female anatomy. It fits. Sort of. As my sweet grandma used to say, "Where there's a will, there's a way."

But, my biggest shock of the night: I discovered that Adam has spurs that *jingle jangle jingle* where most cowboys don't. I gotta say, they made for a *very* pleasurable evening.

I finally finagled the truth out of Adam as to why his people are visiting on Earth. It seems that this junket is really nothing more than a pleasure cruise. And Terra Firma is on some sort of intergalactic tourist-attraction map. His folks have scattered to every corner of the earth to try their hand at different activities, and to experience new things.

In Adam's case, he read about the large cattle ranches in the western United States and decided immediately to try his hand at being a cowboy. I'm only too happy to oblige. The King Snake can certainly use another hand – skilled or not.

That Adam! He sure has a way with the little doggies. Even Dennis has taken a shine to Adam, giving him the nickname, "the cattle whisperer".

I gotta go. Adam is back! I hear him hanging up his metal spurs on the back porch. I'm looking forward to experiencing the other pair later tonight.

Tamerlane
MASON WILLEY

||||||||||||||||||||||||||||||||||||||||||||||||||||||||||||||||||||||||||||||||||||||||||||||||||||||||||||||||||||||||||||||||||||||||||||||||||||||||||||||||||||||

A bibliophile stumbles upon an unexpected treasure, with hilarious consequences.

> "The deed was done.
> He was going to be
> a rich man. He was
> going to be famous."

B ernard's hand seemed to be living a life of its own as he reached tentatively towards the dusty bookshelf to pull out the slim, dark-yellow softback from between a dog-eared copy of Kipling's *Minor Poems* and a fake-leather-bound volume of Walt Whitman. It was shaking as though it belonged to a callow adolescent waiting for his first heavy date to turn up. There was a good reason.

It couldn't be, could it?

He hesitated. For twenty years he'd imagined a moment like this, almost half a lifetime of rummaging in cardboard boxes, twenty years of scanning musty shelves where the literary works of the great and the not-so-great sat huddled together like wallflowers at a college dance, waiting to be chosen. Bernard knew that he was not on his own. Bibliophiles just like him, the world over, spent whole vacations searching for the (so far) ultimately elusive item. The world of bookshops and rummage sales was their oyster, but the one pearl beyond price had always remained exasperatingly undetected – until now.

It couldn't be, could it? On the other hand . . .

Bernard made a conscious effort to still his agitated fingers, and he hooked one over the flimsy spine and carefully extracted the book. Hardly daring to breathe, he opened it, and saw on the title page what deep down he had never really admitted to being a remote possibility, the few astonishing yet inescapable words that he knew could change his life for ever:

Tamerlane and Other Poems
by A Bostonian

It looked right. It felt right. And Bernard knew instinctively that it was right. He looked for the date 1827, and found it. He looked for the long-forgotten name of Calvin Thomas, the printer, and found it. Everything was exactly as Bernard had always known it should be. It was the one pearl, perhaps not quite beyond price, but as near as dammit on a good day in the right auction room.

This was the book that all bibliophiles dreamed of finding, the first edition of the first book of Edgar Allan Poe, privately and anonymously published by him when he was just eighteen years old, with the hope that a few copies would be sold, and the work come to the notice of some literary entrepreneur who might fly to the aid of his budding career. It was a vain hope, as it happened, and the book was utterly ignored, disappearing into virtual oblivion. Only one copy was hitherto known for certain to have survived intact, and that was housed in the US Library of Congress, as it was considered to be part of the nation's literary heritage, and it was insured for an undisclosed but undoubtedly very substantial sum.

Of course, as a serious bibliophile, Bernard knew all there was to know about *Tamerlane*, and he wondered just how a copy came to be on the neglected poetry shelf of the less than celebrated and for the most part inaptly named Watson's Rare Book Emporium in a somewhat dubious suburb of New York City. It was in remarkably good condition too, and looked to have been handled little in nigh on two centuries. Bernard got the distinct and unnerving impression that it had been lying in wait for him, anxious to make him rich and famous as a reward for snatching it from its obscure lair to plummet it into what was inevitable international stardom. Luck or providence, Bernard knew not which, but whatever it was, after a lifetime of humdrum obscurity as a two-bit accountant for a two-bit timber importer, he was going to make the most of it.

Bernard put down the book and took out a handkerchief to wipe the sweat from his palms. It would be a crime to soil it, and anyway, he needed to appear as calm and unruffled as possible when he offered to buy it.

How could a bookseller worth his salt not know what it was?

Bernard wondered. Then he remembered the Neanderthal who sat at the little desk just inside the entrance – the earring, the greasy baseball cap and the Star-Spangled Banner tattoo on the neck – not your average rare-book dealer, he had observed. Another piece of good luck, he hoped and prayed.

Bernard carried his prize carefully to Neanderthal's table and placed it nonchalantly in front of him. He noticed that the man, surrounded as he was by literary works of great import, was poring over a service manual for a '59 Chevy, painstakingly tracing the diagrams with a nicotine-stained finger as though he was struggling to make out the words in a kindergarten reader. Neanderthal spoke dispassionately. "Yeah?"

"How much is this, please?"

Neanderthal picked up the book and bent its cover back hard against the spine, muttering to himself, "Poems, 1827, no pictures." Bernard winced at the man's breathtaking ignorance and unforgivable ill-treatment of such a treasure, but hastily adjusted his expression to one of what he hoped was bland innocence, as the man looked up and said, "Fifteen bucks."

Bernard caught his breath and cleared his throat. He was conscious of a deep shade of pink crossing his face, and an almost doubling of his already excessive pulse rate. Neanderthal obviously misunderstood. "Look, mister, I got a wife and kid to support. You think it's easy makin' a livin' out o' this crap? You oughta try. I bought this place out o' my late daddy's legacy. It's all I can do to afford milk for the baby. Twelve dollars, take it or leave it!"

"I . . . I'll take it," stammered Bernard, slipping the book carefully into his jacket pocket. He took out his billfold and removed twenty dollars. Then, overcome by a sudden pang of guilt, he added, "Look, I've been chasing this book for a while. I need it, you see, to complete a set. Believe me, I wasn't trying to beat you down. I'm so grateful to have found it. Please . . . keep the change."

Neanderthal raised his eyebrows and took the cash. "Well, OK, thanks mister!" he beamed.

Bernard headed hurriedly for the door. The deed was done. He was going to be a rich man. He was going to be famous. He was going to be known hitherto as "The Man Who Found Tamerlane". The door handle was in his clammy grasp, and he was halfway through when Neanderthal called out in a breezy voice, "Do you want me to check if I got a nicer copy? I know you collectors like books in good shape."

Bernard stopped dead in his tracks. "What?" he asked, without turning round.

"I got some more out the back. Some might be in better shape. You want me to go see?"

Bernard turned. "You have more?"

"Sure. I got a boxful. All the same, all *Tamer* . . . whatsit."

"You have a boxful?" Bernard realised his expression was becoming more than a little suspicious, and his voice cracked like a geeky adolescent, but he couldn't help it. The whole scenario was beginning to take on a bizarre aspect. He glanced round, half expecting to see a hidden TV camera, filming the whole fantastic episode for some cheap daytime show. Then he felt *Tamerlane* in his pocket. It was the genuine article without a doubt. There was no set-up.

"A boxful?" he repeated.

"You deaf or somethin', mister? Yeah, a boxful!" Then Neanderthal's expression changed. His beam metamorphosed into an ugly scowl and his eyes became mean slits as he seemed to wrestle with some deep inner conflict. Bernard realised, with deep regret, that some tiny spark had ignited in what passed for the man's brain.

"Say, mister. You know something I don't? You not bein' real straight with me now?"

"Er, I don't understand . . ."

"Let me put you in the picture! I mean, mister, that you got the look of a butcher's dog that just sneaked a prime steak from the boss's plate."

"I, er . . . I'm sorry?" Bernard stammered.

"Now, that book there in your pocket. Tell me about it. I got a strong feelin' there's more to it than just an old book of poems. Am I right?"

"Er . . . well . . . I must confess, it is something of a collector's item." Bernard had always believed himself to be an inherently honest man, but he was struggling now, his conscience fighting a mortal duel with his potential bank balance.

Neanderthal jumped up from his table, sprang to the door and grabbed Bernard by the lapels. "Why, you son of a bitch. You were goin' ta screw me, weren't you? Weren't you, you bastard! That book's valuable, isn't it? Isn't it!" He shook Bernard like a terrier with some inoffensive rodent about to become a tasty snack.

Bernard tried to wriggle loose, but Neanderthal was as strong as he looked, and an age difference of thirty years and a weight difference of fifty pounds meant no contest. But Bernard had the intellectual edge. His potential fortune immediately dwindled to 50 per cent of whatever it would have been, but all was by no means lost.

"OK, OK! Let go of me and I'll be straight with you."

Neanderthal relaxed his hold a little. "OK, I'm listenin'. An' you better make it good, or . . . !"

"I'll make it good. Now let go, and you might end up with enough to buy baby milk for the whole block."

Bernard straightened his jacket and perched himself on the edge of Neanderthal's desk. "OK, close the shop and we'll talk," he said. "You won't want anyone else to hear what I have to say."

With a puzzled look, the proprietor did as he was told. He locked the door and took his seat.

"What's your name?" Bernard asked.

"Al."

Bernard stifled a grin as he briefly wondered if it were really short for Neanderthal. "OK, Al. I'm Bernard. How do you do. Now, Al, this book is valuable – very valuable indeed. It was written by Edgar Allan Poe – his first book. You heard of him?"

Al nodded. "Didn't he write somethin' about a pit an' a pendulum?" he asked.

"That's the guy. Well, *Tamerlane* was his first book and everyone thought there were no copies around, and here one's turned up, in your little emporium. So I was going to buy it and keep it for myself. I admit it, but don't tell me you wouldn't do the same if you were me. As it is, I'm basically an honest man, and I wouldn't like to think I'd screwed anyone. Anyway, there should be enough for both of us with a bit of luck."

"How much?"

"Hard to say. But on a good day, with plenty of publicity and the right people at the auction, maybe . . . six figures?"

Al touched the fingers of his left hand with his right index finger as if counting. "Six figures, that's . . . a hundred grand!" He jumped up. "A hundred thousand bucks! You messin' me around, mister? I'm warnin' you now!"

Bernard placed his hands on Al's shoulders and pushed him gently back into his chair. "Relax! Take it easy! I'm not messing with you at all. It may not make that much, but my guess is that it would, maybe more – a lot more."

"So what's the deal, and what do we do?"

"Legally, I'm the owner of this book, so let's say sixty forty."

"Yeah, an' I'm the legal owner of another boxful, an' I say ninety ten - with me bein' the ninety!"

Bernard had momentarily forgotten about the others. It just couldn't be possible, could it? "Can you show me?" he asked.

"Sure, follow me."

Al led Bernard through to the back room. The whole place smelled of ancient leather and dust, and was piled high from floor to ceiling with all manner of books in glorious disarray. A bibliophile's paradise where, had there not been a seriously pressing matter, Bernard would have been happy to spend his two weeks' vacation with just the odd break for a cup of coffee and a hamburger.

Al led him to a space between a stacked complete set of Gibbon's *Decline and Fall of the Roman Empire* and a heap of assorted cookery magazines. He crouched down, reached behind and pulled out a cardboard box. He peeled back the lid and Bernard peered inside.

His initial scepticism turned quickly to total disbelief, as one by one, he lifted out the contents and arranged them carefully on the floor, counting in a trembling voice as he did so. "One . . . two . . . three . . ."

"Get on with it!" Al growled.

"Shaddup!" Bernard amazed himself with his shock-induced boldness. "Four . . . five . . . six . . ."

"Look, mister, there's twenty-three of 'em. I already counted 'em."

"Twenty . . . three?" Bernard took a sharp intake of breath. "Twenty-three *Tamerlanes*? Twenty-three copies of the rarest book in the world? My God, how did you come across them?"

"My brother works as a demolition man in Boston. He found these in the basement of a house he was . . . Hey, I just realised. A Bostonian wasn't the guy's name at all, was it? It was where he came from, right?" Al beamed proudly at his flash of inspiration.

Bernard rolled his eyes heavenwards. "Right," he groaned. Then suddenly the irony of the situation hit him like a rock between the eyes and he started to laugh, at first a titter, then building into a full-throated guffaw.

"What's so funny?"

Bernard pulled out a handkerchief and wiped his eyes. "I'll tell you what's so funny, Al. You got twenty-three of these little beauties, and that means . . ." He started to laugh again, but quickly brought himself under control. After all, it really wasn't a laughing matter. "That means, they aren't nearly as valuable as I first thought. Savvy?"

"No, I don't savvy! And, Bernard my friend and business partner" – Al was becoming menacing once again – "don't treat me like a retard! Remember I got the upper hand . . . in more ways than one."

"I'm sorry, I didn't mean to be patronising, but you really don't understand. If twenty-three copies turn up, there'll be plenty for everyone that wants one. They might fetch a few hundred dollars each, maybe a thousand or more. But if there were only one . . . then all the big collectors would each want it for themselves. Supply and demand, that's the name of the game. With one, the demand way outstrips the supply, but with twenty-three, we-e-ll . . ."

"So, what's the problem?"

"I just explained the problem!" This guy really was beginning to exasperate Bernard.

Al shrugged. "We'll just get rid of twenty-two of 'em."

It dawned on Bernard that when it came to basic animal cunning, it was he, and not Al, who was showing a considerable degree of naivety.

"How, get rid?"

"Bernard!" It was Al's turn to sound exasperated. "You stoopid or what? We'll burn 'em."

"But . . . we can't! We just can't! These books are part of this great nation's literary heritage." Bernard realised he was sounding like some pompous senator opening a new museum, but nevertheless, he knew that he spoke the truth. But then again, there was a certain undeniable logic in Al's simplistic solution to the problem.

Al brooked no objections, "Sort out the best one," he said matter-of-factly, "and we'll burn the others in the yard out back."

It would be, Bernard realised, an act of the most appalling vandalism. But the prospect of enough cash to make his life considerably more attractive won the day. He examined the books carefully, and selected what he thought was the nicest copy, took it into the shop and placed it on Al's desk. On the way out, he picked up the box with the remaining copies and joined his new-found partner in the yard, where Al had made a pile of screwed-up paper to start the fire.

"Put 'em on the pile," he said. Bernard did so, and Al struck a match and lit the paper. It reached the pile of *Tamerlanes*, but they failed to ignite properly. Bernard realised they should have been torn up first.

"They aren't going to burn," he said.

"Wait here," said Al. He disappeared into the building and reappeared a moment later carrying a can. "This should do the trick," he said, unscrewing the lid.

"Be careful," warned Bernard. "That is kerosene and not gaso–"

He didn't get to finish the word, but the observation was quickly confirmed by an almighty "WHOOSH" as Al threw the contents at the fire. The flames leapt back towards him, and he jumped quickly out of the way, lucky to escape serious burning. The flames, meanwhile, shot twenty feet into the air, and a gust of wind blew them dangerously close to the building. Indeed, as Bernard watched in horror, they began to lick at the paintwork, tinder-dry at the end of what had been a long, hot summer, and take hold. In seconds, the whole of the back of the building was alight, and the fire was making its way through the storeroom towards the shop itself. For a moment the two men watched speechless, then they turned towards each other and exclaimed, "The book!"

"It's on your desk," yelled Bernard. "Round the front, quick!"

By the time they reached the front of the building, the flames were already through to the shop and licking the legs of Al's desk. Bernard tried to open the door. "Jeez!" he screamed. "We locked the goddam door!" Both the men began to kick the door frantically, but it was no use. Even if they had succeeded, it would have been too late.

They watched transfixed as the fire rapidly destroyed everything in its path. By the time the Fire Department arrived, there was a little knot of people gathered to gawp at Al's misfortune, but in reality there was precious little to gawp at. Where once had stood Watson's Rare Book Emporium there was now a shell of blackened masonry filled with grey ash. Of *Tamerlane*, or indeed any other recognisable book, there was not the faintest trace.

Al was crying like a baby. "I lost everything," he blubbed. "That was Daddy's legacy gone up in smoke. I ain't never had nothin' worth anythin', and just when I thought . . ."

"You weren't insured, then?" Bernard asked inanely.

Al looked at him and his lip curled. "Go stuff yourself!" he snarled.

"You got a wife and kid," reassured Bernard. "That's more than I got." He put an arm round Al's shoulder. "C'mon and I'll buy you a drink. We could both do with one."

The two men made their way morosely across the street to Joe's Diner and took their places at the bar. Bernard ordered a couple of beers. He reached into his pocket for his billfold and found something he had completely forgotten was there, and his heart leapt for joy.

He took a sip of his beer, then he said, "Al, how many of those books did you say there were?"

"Twenty-three. Why?"

"Yeah, but when you got them from your brother in Boston, you counted them then, right?"

"Yeah, so what?"

"And how many were there?"

"Twenty . . . four." Al looked puzzled.

"Well, lookee here what I just found." Bernard tossed a little dark-yellow softback book onto the bar. "Now I paid good money for this little book. You gonna be nice to me or what?"

The Bad Positive
FEYISAYO ANJORIN

Banjo Johnson decides to end his promiscuity in favour of his dream woman, Bukky Modele, but a former fling throws a spanner in the works.

> "Her words were like cords that tied you slowly until their fullness kept you well bound and gagged."

You loved your reputation as a ladies' man. Your lovers loved it too. They loved it for as long as your lies lasted. About a dozen girls had thought you were the only one for them, and they for you; until they came face to face with the shocking truth. Many hearts have been broken. But these things happen. These issues of the heart separate the women from the girls. What doesn't kill you makes you stronger; so they say.

They also say that change is the only permanent thing. So, you got tired of your reputation and decided to change. You had it in mind before you met Bukky Modele. She helped with the determination, no doubt about that. You have been seeing yourself in a different light after meeting her. Getting the pretty girls had been easy for you; loving only one and ignoring the countless others could be difficult.

The difficult became the appealing; you were sure it was time for change, and the girl you thought was the one in a million, worth growing old with, was Bukky Modele.

When you took a sample of your wedding card to your friends they stared at it, and then at you, as if they had just been told of your exploits on a record-breaking quest. They were cautious when they said congratulations; some of them shook your hand and offered to buy you drinks to celebrate. A few called you aside to somewhere quiet and private, to ask you: "Banjo, is this really what you want?"

They didn't know you were the marrying type. They were surprised; but they were happy. There were so many girls in the past that you were eager to walk away from. You were bothered by their response to the news.

You thought about so many of your former girlfriends; but you were not worried about Yomi, and you wouldn't have remembered that you once dated her if she had not seen you by the pool at the state recreation centre. You greeted her civilly but with no sign of affection. That girl would never be a temptation. Not again. You were sure of that.

"Banjo, you are getting married and you didn't tell me," she said.

You smiled wryly; you were not ready for this kind of thing. She was one of the easy ones, and you thought she was only good for one thing. You met her for the first time at Galaxy Nite Club on a Friday night; you were with your friend and she was with a friend, and you shared a table. After a few drinks you took her to the toilet and she did not keep anything from you. She was the kind you were determined to avoid. You were done with her.

You wondered why she thought herself so important in your life. You could not think of any polite response to the words. The thought of calling her never crossed your mind. But she was not patient for your answer or comment. So she asked you: "When exactly is the wedding?"

"In six weeks."

"Six weeks? Then you still have time." She said the word "time" slowly; and she had a coquettish smile on her face that annoyed you.

"Time for what?" you asked with calm disgust. You remembered the things you had done to her and it was not difficult to say "no" to whatever you thought she was offering then. You particularly hated the beautiful ones who sold themselves too cheap.

"Time for what, Yomi?" you asked again, wide-eyed; you wondered how long you could keep the irritation under check. "I'm preparing for the wedding. There is no time for pranks and shady stuff."

"No pranks, no shady stuff. I just think you still have enough time to cancel the wedding."

"To cancel the wedding? Why would I do that?" You glanced at your watch and decided it was too early for her to be drunk. "You are crazy."

There was a self-satisfied smirk on her face. "No I'm not. You can't get married, Banjo. You have to think of your girlfriend."

You thought she was joking. Why is she now interested in your thoughts on your girlfriend?

You did not love Yomi, you did not trust her, and you had no reason to respect her. You were sure that whatever she was doing would not work; but you decided to be nice, and to keep things civil. You would soon talk some sense into her, you were sure.

She was the one who talked some sense into you. Her words were like cords that tied you slowly until their fullness kept you well bound and gagged; her words worked like hypnosis and gave you a rude awakening to a new reality.

After the words you felt a weight on the lower part of your stomach and you thought you needed the toilet. She watched you closely to see how you would take it.

"Are you serious?" you asked her, almost breathless.

"Yes. Why would I be joking? Banjo, all I want to say is, get tested. I'm not saying that you are infected. I just think you should be sure. She's a pretty girl. You don't want to infect her with stuff. Or have you guys been doing things together already?"

You stared at her until everything around you became blurry. Your heart pounded hard and your palms became sweaty. You felt like sitting down and crying as if you were alone. She did not look like someone bothered by anything; she was like a judge that had just sentenced you to death.

To make matters worse, she walked away when you stood too long in silence; even though you were glad that she left before your eyes filled with tears.

You could not believe it! Yomi, with the silky-smooth skin and the curvy body, was HIV positive? She was always clean and beautiful. She was one of those with the kind of look and features that made men look and look again, the ones your eyes would follow as your mind worked on possibilities.

She was easy on the eyes, she dressed with an intriguing casual elegance; she was just not one of your favourites because you got her too easily.

She was gone; but you stood still like a statue, pursed your lips and stared into space as if the solution to your newborn problem was somewhere in the wind ahead. Indeed, you were right about the easy girls.

That evening there was a church programme at ACLC where your fiancée's father was the presiding pastor. You sat beside Bukky and smiled a lot so that your worries would not be noticed. You said "praise the lord" to all the "hallelujah"s; and "Amen" to all the prayers. You nodded and grunted approval for the numerous sound bites like most of the other members.

Pastor Modele wiped his face again and again with a white handkerchief as he preached a sermon on Nebuchadnezzar and the three Hebrew youths; but your mind was on your possible end.

You imagined yourself in a future; you on the bed in a hospital, your bones almost sticking out of your pale skin and flies buzzing around you. Alive but looking like the dead. The print and electronic media could come once in a while with their cameras for a few pictures: the lover-boy who was felled by the virus, a good warning to other adventurous men. A model of the misery of disease.

You thought about the shame and the ridicule. Your enemies would laugh and drink to the humiliation. A few people would swear they had predicted it. And how could you be so foolish not to give it a thought? You were a hunter that was envied by hunters. Yours was a deadly combination of arrogance and recklessness.

The ACLC service helped your hope. You made up your mind to see Yomi once again. Maybe she just needed some attention. You were not convinced that she now lived on doses of ARVs. She had told you about it as if it was a joke that could be true but was so amusing to tell. You decided to call her and set up a meeting. At a restaurant, or maybe at the park. You would speak kindly and give her a special treat. A responsible special treat.

You were determined to be hopeful, and it was not too hard. The word of God is powerful. Only believe and you would see the glory of God.

After the church service Bukky said: "You look stressed." You said: "I'm just tired. I need to sleep."

You knew, without a doubt, that your attempt to look good was not perfectly convincing. If the troubles persisted, the gloomy looks would be noticed; it would be hard to deny. Such would not be easy to explain. And questions are difficult when answers are painful. You thought about your future with Bukky, and your future without her.

Soon Bukky was talking about the wedding cake. The baker wanted more money and Bukky wanted a bigger cake. You said a quick prayer and told Bukky that enough had been offered for the cake and the baker could be replaced if she would not take it. You continued with prayers when you were alone at home.

You were still praying when Yomi's phone rang and you waited, as your heart pounded, for her voice. She could be far from the phone; or, she could be holding the phone and sneering at the sight of your name on its screen. She could be making you sweat for treating her like trash. Why could she be doing this to you at this time? It wasn't as if you professed undying love for her; it wasn't as if you ever promised to marry her; you did not give her any hint that she was special. She has never said or implied that she was.

"Hello Banjo," she said casually, as if you were a regular caller. "How are you?"

"I'm fine," you lied. "How are you?"

She said she was fine. You were respectfully straight to the point. She agreed to lunch at noon the following day.

You were at Captain Cook a few minutes before her. You chose a seat in the corner; far from the flat-screen TV. She was there right on time. She was dressed in a blue denim miniskirt, white body-fitted blouse and matching tennis shoes. Hoop earrings, vermilion lipstick. You did not notice anything unusual about her. That was her typical style of dressing, and she was always on time.

She was as energetic as you've known her to be. There was nothing to show regret or sadness because of thwarted future possibilities.

Then you thought about the time you told her it was over. That morning you were near the door inside her room, and she was putting on her jacket, ready to see you off. When you told her, she threw a glass cup at you and asked you to fuck off. Luckily the cup missed your head and crashed against the wall. You were not in any way hurt by the broken glass. But you knew that with this girl there would always be surprises. It was better to put an end to these kinds of surprises when it was still safe.

So there you were, meeting her because you really wanted to be sure about this HIV thing; and you would be as honest and humble as possible to make her see that it is nothing but wickedness to joke about something like that. Hopefully, you thought, she would snort and chuckle and tell you she had been joking.

She listened for a few minutes as you told her about your past, and what you have learnt from it; your mistakes and how you were not perfect despite your sincere efforts, and how you were now planning to live a different kind of life. You wanted her to forgive you and remain hopeful because there are so many eligible bachelors out there and she is very beautiful.

She was attentive; she even nodded twice or three times, as you presented your valid case for responsible living. And you were sure that the words were touching and thought-provoking.

You leaned on the table and looked her in the eye. "Yomi, you are not really HIV positive, are you?"

She smiled and you held your breath. "Do you think this would be my idea of a joke?"

It struck you how little you knew about her. You were not familiar with her sense of humour. You really had no clue about who she truly was.

You did not even remember her name after the first night together. That night she wanted to know where you lived. You told her as casually as she had asked and you did not think she would commit it to her memory. You were amazed when she showed up at your door the following evening. She was angry when you asked her to remind you of her name. She told you her name with a frown. You said you were sorry.

"It's just so unbelievable, Yomi. You don't look like someone with HIV."

"And what is the look of someone with HIV? See, I've known for eight months now. I've accepted it, which is why I'm not depressed or hopeless."

You pondered on this unbelievable thing that was slowly becoming believable. Would you ever accept this like she has done?

She snorted, smiled, and looked away. "You actually thought I was joking."

You shrugged; you kept your eyes on the empty table.

"*Well . . .*" was all you were able to say.

You were both silent for a while.

"Were there so many other guys?" you mumbled.

"So many other guys?" she snorted incredulously. "Do you think I'm a whore?"

You thought she was; but how could you be sure? Maybe you got her at her moment of weakness. Maybe you were not in the right position to judge her.

But how could this beautiful girl be so cheap? It wasn't as if you were a celebrity and she could make a career of writing a book on the juicy details of your sex life. It wasn't as if you dated her for long. It was just a week; and she was the one who came to your house six consecutive days after your first time in the toilet.

She was always on time. Even on that evening when a truck

overturned on the road leading to your house and the road was like a parking lot for more than a hundred cars, she was at your door at a quarter to six, smiling like a naughty teenager; just like the other days.

She was beginning to feel at home in your house as if she had lived there for years.

Then the morning after the sixth night you moved to stop a likely seventh visit. You visited her for the first time on a morning, lied that you were in a hurry on your way to a photo shoot and would be busy for a while; and you made her throw a glass cup at you.

She had kept away for ten months, and this was her comeback!

There you were, seated in a restaurant with her; you've not even taken Bukky to Captain Cook, and you were about to pay for Yomi's meal. It is amazing how much one can pay when hope is at risk.

"Banjo," she said, touching your hand. "Why don't you get tested first? Then you can be sure of where you stand. You don't want to get all stressed out for nothing. I came to tell you of my status and the importance of knowing yours."

The waiter was taking too long and you wished he would just ignore the table. When the waiter came she ordered rice, green peas and chicken. And bottled water. You ordered the same, and you requested a small bowl of coleslaw and salad cream. You didn't touch the rice but you ate the peas and coleslaw; and you took a bite of the chicken before you tossed it.

You hoped that she would laugh out loud at some point and savour her success at scaring you; and tell you she was joking. She should wish you well; she should be happy for you. You waited and waited and waited. After about an hour you left the meeting, now sure that you may be HIV positive.

After that things turned out as you had expected. Didn't the Bible say "there is no peace for the wicked"? You never gave that much thought; but now you were sure it is the truth.

You were depressed by the thought of death and the way sickness may soon slowly ravage your body.

Bukky's frequent questions, concern and curiosity made her seem like an intruder. What is wrong with you, Banjo? What are you hiding? You have this look and I know something is not right. You are not as excited about the wedding as you were.

You even forgot your first counselling appointment with Pastor Uche, assistant to the ACLC presiding pastor. Bukky was furious when she called you at noon that day and you said you were still in bed. Just a little sick, you lied when you saw that she had the right to be furious. She promised to visit later in the day and you told her not to worry, you would be busy then. There was a meeting with some NGOs working on tree planting or some other save the earth campaign. You lied; and she knew, because when she asked you the venue of the meeting you mentioned Radatar, a popular conference hall that had been closed to the public for over three months.

Pastor Uche called you; you did not take the call.

Pastor Modele also called you; you left your phone ringing. Unlike his assistant, he called twice. His daughter must have told him something. Daddy, Banjo has been acting weird lately.

When their calls did not work they sent text messages. When you read them you knew how hard things would become; so you acted as though there were no text messages.

There was a time when Bukky came to your house after a heated conversation on the phone. She was at the door for about thirty minutes. She knocked more than a dozen times and waited. You were inside, but you did not open because you had lied to her that you were in a photo shoot. You said you were in a photo shoot, but when she asked you where exactly you were, you started talking as if an address is so hard to give. Your phone was on silent mode, you had anticipated that she would try to call; to see if your phone would be heard ringing inside the house.

Your plans were always well thought out. The more you thought of a visit to the clinic for a test, the more you thought about several other ways of avoiding some people and evading their questions so that they would become frustrated, stop caring, and leave you alone. You avoided the main roads; the shortcuts and backstreets became your route.

Your siblings called you too; and your parents. They wanted to know what was wrong. Why had you been avoiding calls from Pastor Modele and others? Did you have any misunderstanding with them? Was there any problem that had not been well handled? You cancelled a photo shoot for a fashion show; you missed a midweek service and two Sunday services. Your mother thought you should not give room for the devil. You were thirty-five; your mates now had children.

Bukky saw you as you walked from the shopping mall in the evening with plastic bags of canned fish, noodles, flour and wheat. She did not tell you she would be in the area; you were surprised to see her, but you allowed her when she offered to help you with one of the plastic bags.

You had never seen her the way you saw her that night. You sat facing each other at the dining table. She was sober, even when her eyes were not wet with tears.

She was not perfect. She had also made mistakes in the past; there had been a few boyfriends; her heart had been broken. She was not a virgin and she had told you that a long time ago. She was not afraid of the future; and she had nothing to hide. So she asked you to tell her if she had done anything to hurt you. Had she done anything so appalling that you couldn't even bear to tell her?

She went on like that, talking, asking questions, muttering, breaking down into sobs. That night, in the recesses of your mind, you decided to go for a test.

You had to wait for the next day for the test; Bukky wanted immediate answers or explanations that you did not provide.

She was almost sure that you were no longer interested in her; she was the one who removed her engagement ring, placed it on the table and walked out on you. Even if you had little respect for her, she said, you should have more respect for her father.

You stared at the diamond-encrusted ring, and pondered on her exit. She was not reluctant to leave; she seemed sure and decided. She was not ashamed to be who she really was. That is what you loved about her. Maybe Yomi was also one of a kind; not ashamed to be who she really was.

The ring was American Swiss; you had paid for it, just as you had paid for the one for the wedding day. They were a pair. If not for the promo deal the rings would have cost about the price of a new car.

The waiting room was empty when you took the seat nearest to the consultant's door early in the morning; but all the seats in the twenty-seat room had been taken at nine when they called in their first client: you. Your name: Banjo Johnson. Age: 35. Address: Number Five, Alagbaka Quarters, Akure. Occupation: Photographer. You filled out the form quickly like someone doing a speed test; even though you exhaled deeply and hesitated when you saw the line that says *Marital Status*.

Single, you wrote.

Your heart thumped like a jungle drum as you listened to the bespectacled woman in white overalls telling you of prevention of HIV infection and the management of infection; the diet, the water, the ARVs and the exercise. Many people have been living positively with HIV. Smoking is very bad. It burdens your immune system.

Your heart pounded as she spoke of HIV as if it was not a big deal. But you would rather manage good deals with celebrities and multinationals; you would rather manage a home with Bukky Modele. She does not deserve this. You would rather manage something good; not HIV!

You signed the consent forms and your blood was taken. The needle was painful, but for now you could do with such a short, biting pain. Once and for all; or not. Pain may hand over to pain like sprinters in a relay team.

You were sixteen years old the first time you had sex. You remembered how, in preparation, you went to the supermarket opposite the central post office, intending to buy a condom. The store was crowded with other customers buying this or that thing. You wanted to wait for a better opportunity, so you walked around, staring at the shelves in a way that was almost suspicious. Someone wanted to be helpful and asked what you wanted to buy. "Tom Tom," you said. You bought sweets because you were too self-conscious to buy a condom.

So when you met Biola, the first girl that gave herself to you, in an uncompleted building not far from your father's house, you did not have a condom. And she was not bothered. Then you were so ignorant she had to help you to put your thing in.

She was three years older than you and had just returned from Lagos. You were very fast. It lasted less than a minute, and you did not understand what she meant when she asked you with a smirk if you were really through.

You watched the woman closely as she added drops of the reagent into your blood. Your heart pounded harder, you sweated as if the room was not air conditioned. She must have seen all sorts in the line of duty. You expected her expression to give something away; you would not be the first one to be told something good, neither would you be the first to be told something that was not so good.

At noon you were at Pastor Modele's office. Things would be hard to explain; but it would have been harder to explain something else. There were four other people who had been sitting in the waiting room before you, also waiting for the presiding pastor of ACLC. Yet you were the prodigal son, or son-in-law to be. Prayers had been offered for your return. You were with him for almost three hours of questions, explanations, prayers and stern warnings, based on the scriptures. In fact, Pastor Modele told you that he had once had it in mind to ask you to go for an HIV test, but the Holy Spirit said no.

Later that evening you called Yomi to tell her that you had tested and it was negative. She laughed as you had once hoped she would, and told you that she had been joking, and that she just wanted to make you stress and sweat. You were angry.

That evening you deleted her number from your phone; that evening you visited Bukky Modele, you told her about Yomi, and begged her to allow a new beginning in this relationship.

The Bird on Silver Strand
NANCY LANE

||||||||||||||||||||||||||||||||||||||||||||||||||||||||||||||||||||||||||||||||||||||||||||||||||||||||||||||||||||||||||||||||||||||||||||||||||||||||||||||||||||||||||||||||||||||

Childhood sweethearts Sadie and Milton navigate the pranksters and wannabes of Silver Strand beach during Hollywood's Golden Age.

"There you go, Opal,
spilling the beans.
Now you've drawn
attention. Why can't
you just keep quiet?"

Hollywood-by-the-Sea, California – July 4, 1929

Sadie pulls up her coat collar against the brisk ocean wind this sunny Thursday morning. A woman, scarf wrapped around her head, tendrils of light-brown hair whipping her face, crosses Ocean Drive to meet Sadie on the sea side. "Little girl," she says, "you can't recognise me bundled up as I am against this cruel blast. Behold Gloria Swanson, famous on the silver screen."

"Glad to meet you, Miss Swanson," Sadie says. "I've seen your wonderful movies."

"What's your name, young lady?"

"Sadie."

The woman pulls paper and a pencil from the depths of her coat pocket, scribbles, and then hands the autograph to Sadie. Sadie curtsies, thanks Miss Swanson, places the autograph in her pocket and continues her stroll south towards Silver Strand as Gloria Swanson treks north.

Sadie's friend Milton is on the beach as usual, head down, walking lines two feet apart, parallel to the shore, eyes scanning the sand for copper or silver coins.

"Milton, I just met the Gloria Swanson imposter." Sadie pulls the autograph from her pocket.

"Look, Sadie," Milton says. "I found a silver dollar, first one ever. It was right there." He points down the beach where screaming seagulls fight over their own found treasure.

Sadie ruffles his hair and obligingly observes his find. At age ten, Milton is one year Sadie's junior and, with his boundless energy and curiosity, serves as the little brother she wishes she had. Milton's a year-round resident. His father works at the sugar beet factory in Oxnard. Sadie is summers only. Her family stays at the forty-room, beachfront hotel. They'll remain through the Independence Day celebrations and return home Saturday to the upscale Holmby Hills neighbourhood of Los Angeles.

Sadie shows Milton the autograph. The paper Miss Swanson wrote on is an envelope, Oxnard address on one side. Gloria Swanson is not the addressee. On the flap side it reads, *Dear Sadie, enjoy me in the movies. Love, Gloria Swanson.*

"She tries to disguise herself with the scarf and coat. You know what gives her away?"

Milton shrugs.

"My father says the real Gloria Swanson is only five feet tall. The imposter is taller than my mother, and she's five six." Milton appreciates his friend's insider information. Sadie's father works for the Max Factor Company. He meets with movie-studio executives to sell flexible greasepaint and other make-up products specially developed for the new movie industry.

Automobiles crawl up Ocean Drive as Angelenos arrive after the sixty-mile coast drive, the rich in Chryslers, Duesenbergs and Packards – the envious in Fords, Studebakers and DeSotos. Parking spaces fill, hotel guests withdraw leather travel bags, picnickers unload baskets and blankets, campers pull out canvas bags with essentials for a Thursday-to-Sunday beach stay. A dog runs on the sand nearby.

"Hey, this is worth a penny," Milton says. "My neighbour pays me each time Buster gets out and I bring him back." A quick goodbye to Sadie and the Buster chase begins. Sadie quits Silver Strand to rejoin her parents at the hotel.

The Independence Day events will take place later at Hollywood-by-the-Sea. Prime viewing spots already claimed, later-arriving beachgoers settle for Hollywood Beach to the north or Silver Strand to the south. Picnickers Ted Smith and fiancée Opal Calvert are among the first eyeing

Silver Strand. They traipse closer to the water. The chill wind of earlier is replaced by the calm of warm noontime air.

A young man, hair wet from ocean swimming, stands in his striped, full-body swimsuit, a straw hat on the sand at his feet. He waves to Ted and Opal. "Please, can you help me?" he says. They approach.

"A dog mauled this poor bird I've captured, here, under the hat," the young man says. "I must go get my sister. She takes care of injured birds. Looks like you're staying for a picnic. Would you please spread your blanket here by the bird and make sure no one disturbs it? My sister has a bird cage. I'll be back shortly."

"Let's have a look," Ted says. He bends with outstretched hand to lift the hat.

"No, no, please! The bird can fly, but his leg is broken. If you let him get away he'll certainly run into more trouble down the beach." The young man points towards several dogs playing with children in the surf.

"Ted," says Opal, "this is a good place for our picnic." Ted nods and Opal spreads their blanket next to the hat.

Ted sets the picnic basket on the blanket and extends his hand. "I'm Trevor Daring and this is my fiancée, Opal," Ted says.

Opal shakes her head. "That's his screen name. His real name is Ted Smith."

"Glad to meet you both. I'm Chase Chandler," the young man says. "Screen name, huh? Are you in movies, Mr Daring?"

"Not yet. I'll be discovered and moviegoers will know me as Trevor Daring. You can call me Ted for now. Your name, is that real? It sounds like a movie-screen name, a really good one."

Chase hesitates. "My father is part-owner of Paramount Pictures. I changed my name when I appeared in one of his movies. He's always looking for talent," Chase says, watching Ted's reaction, which is an ear-to-ear grin. "When I come back for the bird, we can discuss the movies."

Chase turns and runs across the Strand towards Ocean Drive. "Don't let the bird get away," he shouts.

"I sure won't," Ted shouts back.

"What'd I tell you, Opal?" Ted says. "I knew if we came here often enough I'd meet a Hollywood kingpin. I'll be rich soon. I'll be able to buy you that engagement ring you want."

Early that morning Opal had made sandwiches for the picnic in the small kitchen of the North Hollywood bungalow where she lives with her parents. Opal's engaged-to-be-engaged status worries them their twenty-year-old spinster daughter may never marry, especially if she continues seeing Ted Smith.

Ted leans back on the blanket and stares at the hat to watch for any movement. Vacant picnic sites are disappearing fast when Sadie's family spreads a blanket nearby. Her father sets down a basket containing fried chicken, bread rolls, salads and slices of apple pie prepared by the hotel chef.

Milton runs up to them. "Do you remember me from last summer, Mr Landrum?"

"Yes, of course I do, Milton," Sam Landrum says.

His wife, Beatrice, says hello to Milton. "Milton, Sadie thought you might join us today so we brought extra food."

"Gosh, Mrs Landrum, thank you," he says. Then he notices the straw hat next to Ted and Opal's blanket. "Does that hat belong to anyone?" he says. He recognises it as a cheap hat like ones local boys steal from the Chinese hat vendor on Ocean Drive.

"It's mine," Ted says. "Don't touch it."

"There's an injured bird underneath the hat," Opal says.

"There you go, Opal," Ted says, "spilling the beans. Now you've drawn attention. Why can't you just keep it quiet?"

"I'm sorry," Opal whispers.

"Look, son," Ted says, "Chase Chandler, whose father is a Hollywood kingpin, is coming back for the bird. He entrusted me to keep it safe. Now just mind your own business."

"OK," Milton says. "I know his brother. Jack Chandler goes to my school."

"His brother's name is Chandler too?"

"Yep."

"I don't think you know what you're talking about," Ted says. He turns towards Sam Landrum. Milton flashes a half-smile at Sadie.

The Landrums exchange pleasantries with Ted and Opal and learn of Ted Smith's screen name. "So, Ted," Sam says, "have you acted in stage plays or taken acting lessons?"

"No, but I'm a natural. A lot of people say I look like Gary Cooper. What do you think?"

"I'm not that familiar with Gary Cooper," Sam says.

Seagulls hover, eyeing the lunch fare Beatrice and Opal distribute from their picnic baskets.

"What do you do?" Ted says.

"I'm a schoolteacher," Sam says. Beatrice and Sadie exchange a glance.

"You probably don't see many movies."

"We go often to the Egyptian Theatre and to the Broadway movie palaces," Beatrice says. "We attended the premiere of *Noah's Ark*."

"Sam, how'd you get into a premiere?" Ted says.

"Oh, just lucky I guess. Ted and Opal, do you know the story of these beaches?"

"I know they've made movies here," Opal says.

"That's right. When filmmakers wanted Arabian-looking scenes, the sand dunes here worked perfectly. Hollywood filming made the Oxnard area so popular, real-estate developers built up Hollywood Beach and Silver Strand. Later, the developers flattened the dunes and stripped away the fake palm trees to transform Oxnard Beach into Hollywood-by-the-Sea. The hotel and the lots offered for sale drove the filmmakers away."

"I'm sure they're still here," Ted says. "They still come from Hollywood to relax. They probably stay at the hotel."

"We're staying at the hotel, Ted. We haven't seen any Hollywood big shots," Sam says.

"Well, you'd have to know what you're looking for."

"Well, Ted, if you sat as close to someone with Hollywood connections as you are sitting to me right now, how would you know?"

"The smell," Ted says.

"What?"

"Hollywood people reek of money."

Milton jumps up. "Mr Smith, I think that's Chase over there, sitting on that beach log with two boys." Milton points to a threesome wearing knickers and cotton shirts.

"No, son," Ted says, "Chase had on a swimsuit and he's older than those boys."

"He must've changed clothes," Milton says. "That's Jack's brother all right."

"Shouldn't Chase have come back for the bird by now?" Sam says.

"He'll be here," Ted says. "He wants to talk to me about movies."

An afternoon breeze picks up. The hat wobbles. Ted jumps to pin the brim of the hat with his fingers and realises the capricious breeze will require his holding down the hat until Chase's return.

Independence Day events start with the arrival of a marching band and a cadre of clowns wearing red, white and blue costumes. Two stilt walkers and a man and wife with a dog circus of five performing Chihuahuas and a Great Dane fall in behind the clowns. The mayor of Oxnard's megaphone-broadcast greetings cannot be heard over the band's *I'm a Yankee Doodle Dandy* as celebrants fill in beside the parade route along Ocean Drive from Silver Strand to Hollywood-by-the-Sea.

"Beatrice, should we head back to the hotel?" Sam says.

"Aren't you gonna watch the fireworks?" Ted asks Sam.

"Yes, we'll watch from the balcony of our room. Best place for viewing. All of you are welcome to join us. We'll have hotel staff bring up plates for dinner."

"We should go there, Ted," Opal says.

"I can't go until I talk to Chase. Go on ahead, Opal."

"I'll stay here with Mr Smith," Milton says.

Milton observes Chase and his buddies. They watch young women in swimsuits strolling to the surf. The boys turn their eyes towards Ted during lulls in the parade of beauties. Ted awkwardly lies across his blanket and holds down the hat brim. Milton hears early fireworks explosions and expects the big displays will start soon. He fears Ted Smith will not give up his wait for Chase, not even when the sun dips into the Pacific.

"Mr Smith," Milton says, "as far as I know, Chase's father is a milkman and I see Chase watching you right now."

Ted looks as Milton points to the laughers. "Why didn't you tell me this before?" he says.

"Because, Mr Smith, you told me to mind my own business."

Ted, red-faced, snatches up the straw hat and flings it. Milton watches the aerial fluttering, the dip to the sand and then the hat floating away in a foamy, receding wave. Ted squints at the dark, inert form on the sand at his feet. It could be a dead blackbird, but it isn't. The boys hold their sides, jumping up and down. One yells out, "Trevor Daring, starring in *Adventures of the Dog-Poop Bird*."

The chase is on. The fleet-footed boys weave between picnic blankets and hurdle shell-seeking children. Milton runs behind Ted, who catches up to the boys near the crowded Hollywood-by-the-Sea concession area. Ted throws a fist upward towards the taller Chase and lands a blow to Chase's throat. Chase chokes and steps back. Ted steps forward. Chase's thrown fist meets his chin. Ted buckles and cusses. Chase and the other boys disappear into the crowd as a policeman emerges from among the onlookers. He pulls Ted up and scolds him for causing a fracas.

Starlight clusters in the sky punctuate each booming explosion as Ted trudges back to Silver Strand to retrieve basket and blanket. By the time he returns to Hollywood-by-the-Sea and enters the hotel lobby, the official fireworks display is done and beachgoers' dwindling caches of sparklers and small Roman candles are playing out.

Ted meets the Landrums and Opal in the hotel lobby. "Did Chase ever return?" Sam asks.

"Yeah," Ted says, "and that stupid skunk got his ass whipped for lying to me about the bird and his father's connections."

"Hey," Sam says, "watch your language in front of the ladies."

"Sorry," Ted says. "Opal, are you ready to go?"

Opal thanks the Landrums for their hospitality. "You did tell your father I'd be bringing you home late, didn't you?" Ted says as he opens the passenger door of the Studebaker he always borrows from his brother when he takes Opal beyond streetcar range. It will be after midnight when Ted escorts Opal to her front door. Her father will be waiting up.

At dawn Sadie slips from the hotel lobby and embraces the early-morning quiet. She muses on stories of a time not long ago when sand dunes and papier mâché palm trees dressed the beach. Today Hollywood-by-the-Sea is dressed in colourful mounds, sleeping celebrants left over from the Fourth covered head to toe in blankets. Milton won't look for coins on this beach.

Sadie heads towards Silver Strand. Yesterday's plethora of picnickers promises a bonanza for her friend. Milton sees Sadie and abandons his coin labour. As he runs towards her, Sadie feels his excitement.

"Something, isn't it?" Milton says. His grin hurts, but he can't straighten his face even to lessen the pain from his deliciously round, swollen shiner. "It's darker now than last night. My father says it will turn all shades of purple and green before it fades, and that might take two weeks."

"What happened?" Sadie says.

"Mr Smith got mad at Chase and Chase knocked him on his keister. After a policeman broke up the fight, some other fellows started to brawl. I just wanted to watch, but Chase's brother Jack started waving his fists in front of my face like a prizefighter. I waved my fists in front of him." Milton throws up his arms to demonstrate. "It seemed like we were dancing until he threw a haymaker."

"What about him?"

"I tripped him when I fell," Milton says. "Didn't mean to, but he broke his nose. Best of all, we're buddies now. Chase is going to teach me and Jack how to swim in the ocean."

"Why didn't you come to the hotel for the fireworks?" Sadie says.

"Was your eye too sore?"

"No, I went to show my father my eye. Then I went over to the neighbours' yard because they still had a lot of flashlight crackers."

"What did your mother say about the black eye?"

"She's mad at me, won't look at me. That's OK. My father's proud of me, says I'm like Jack Dempsey." More grin, more pain as Milton touches sandy fingers to the sore spot.

"I'll miss seeing it heal," Sadie says.

"Oh, you're leaving tomorrow. Are you coming back later this summer?"

"No," Sadie says. "I won't see you again until next summer. Your eye will be healed by then."

Milton's shoulders drop and he turns to face the ocean. "Let's go sit down," Sadie says. They walk to a bench near the concession area. Vendors will soon cart out their wares, but for now Sadie and Milton are alone. Sadie is the smartest girl Milton knows, maybe even the smartest person. He feels like a grown-up when he and Sadie sit and talk.

"Why did your father lie to Mr Smith about his job?" Milton says.

"He does that when he thinks someone will hound him about knowing movie actors," Sadie says. "Mr Smith seems fanatic about make-believe. He doesn't even like his real name."

"Do you like make-believe?"

"We all pretend," Sadie says. "Sometimes it's wishful thinking. Sometimes it's lying. Sometimes it's just a way of being nice."

"Like pretending to believe the Gloria Swanson imposter?"

"Yes, we were both being nice," Sadie says. "She thought she was making me happy by giving me the autograph. I wanted her to be happy believing I believed her."

"What about make-believe movies?"

Sadie smiles, pleased Milton seeks her opinions. "When Gloria Swanson plays a strong woman on screen in her fine clothes, girls believe they can grow up to be somebody, not just a typist or a wife."

"So what do you want to be when you grow up?" Milton says.

"I'm going to be a reporter."

"Do they let girls be reporters?"

"They'll let me. What about you? What are you going to be?"

"I'm going to be a pilot – a barnstormer. At first I wanted to be a wingwalker. I saw them in newsreels. It's dangerous and daring. But my father says I'll get more jobs and make more money if I fly a plane, not just walk on its wings. I can get a job carrying mail or taking rich people wherever they want to go."

Mr Wang, the hat vendor, wheels his hat trees outside. Food vendors prop up awnings and a policeman begins his foot patrol. A few of the beach sleepers stir.

"I can't come to the Strand tomorrow morning. We'll be getting ready to go home," Sadie says.

"That makes me really sad, Sadie."

Sadie pulls a wrapped taffy sucker from her pocket and hands it to Milton. "I'm going to miss you. Next time I see you, you'll be taller and your hair will have sun streaks from swimming in the ocean."

"I might be taller than you by next summer."

"I think you will be. You know, Milton, there's something I really love about you."

"What?" Milton is stunned she said "love".

"You are yourself. You don't pretend. I can always count on you being you." Sadie stands up and kisses Milton's forehead before turning to leave. A few steps away, she turns and waves. Milton waves back and watches her walk to the hotel and disappear through the lobby doors.

The salty breeze picks up, ruffling Milton's hair and buffeting seagulls in flight. What a wonderful day to be ten and in love! Milton wishes he had summoned the courage to kiss Sadie and ask her to be his first girlfriend. He missed his chance, but next year he'll be taller and bolder. Today he has a black eye and a taffy sucker his girlfriend-to-be gave him.

Milton stretches out his arms and crosses Ocean Drive to run home for breakfast. He dips his arms, banking to the left, straightening and then banking to the right. He can visualise his Jenny biplane in the newsreel, theatre audiences applauding his airborne feats. Today he can make believe he's a pilot married to a girl reporter. It's the best day of Milton's life, even better than yesterday when he found a silver dollar on Silver Strand.

The Bridge
JIM BARTLETT

||||||||||||||||||||||||||||||||||||||||||||||||||||||||||||||||||||||||||||||||||||||||||||||||||||||||||||||||||||||||||||||||||||||||||||||||||||||||||

Ron is having a very bad day in this innovatively told tale.

"How could this day get any worse? Just then the phone rings."

May 12, 2010

7.37 p.m. Wednesday

"Nine one one, what is the nature of your emergency?"

"There's someone about to jump at the Carlton Canyon Bridge."

"Oh . . . my. Which side of the bridge is this person on, sir?"

"The city side. I think that's south?"

"OK, good. Just a moment, sir. Fourteen fifty-seven, respond code two to Carlton Canyon Bridge. Possible attempted suicide . . . Sir, is this a man or woman and can you describe the individual for me?"

"Well, let's see . . . I'm wearing light-tan slacks, chinos, actually, and a dark-blue shirt –"

"Wait . . . hold on there. Sir, excuse me, but are you describing yourself? Are you telling me that you're considering jumping?"

"Nope, not considering. Doing. Goodbye."

The sound of rushing wind roars into the dispatcher's headset. It lasts several seconds – seems an eternity to her – before coming to an end with a sickening thud and a muffled splash. Then, only silence.

"Sir! Sir! Oh, no, no, no . . . Fourteen fifty-seven respond . . ."

7.18 p.m. Wednesday

Finding a spot where the gravelled shoulder widens, Ron pulls over and turns off the Lexus. He places his hands on the wheel, staring out at the bridge less than a hundred yards away. Although the setting sun dusts it with hues of amber and red, the calculating engineer in him marvels instead at this monolithic concrete-and-steel structure that stands as a symbol to man's superiority over nature's obstacles.

He steps out into a forceful breeze and heads for the bridge, a crunch of rock accompanying each step. Stopping just at the point where the concrete meets the asphalt road, he risks a quick glance over the edge – he'd never been one for heights – into the craggy ravine. Five hundred feet below the Crescent River rages, relentlessly carving into the canyon walls.

Knees buckling, he can taste the bile at the back of his throat as a touch of vertigo washes over him. Scurrying away from the ledge, he turns and looks towards the Lexus. A brief thought of locking it with the remote quickly passes . . . Why bother? Tossing the key in the general direction of the car, he steps up onto the foot-high abutment running the length of the bridge.

There, he continues along the narrow embankment, being careful not to let his eyes stray over the knee-high tubular railing into the depths below. Not more than ten feet in he stops.

He looks up and down the highway – there's not a single car in sight. The wind has settled into a dead calm. Even the river below seems to wait in silence.

Chills race down his spine; the hair rises on the back of his neck. He shakes his head, takes a deep breath, and continues on. Reaching what he deems to be the midway point he stops and turns towards the rail. With eyes closed he looks inward. Is there a God? If so, why has this happened to me? Will He judge me for what I am doing? For what I *need* to do?

Moments pass; his questions remain unanswered. He opens his eyes and looks down. The whitewater rapids of the river call from below.

Yes? No? Does he really even have a choice? In that moment of indecision he pulls up his cell, a last-minute urge to reach out. But his fingers remain idle and he finds himself staring down at the phone.

With no one to call, he simply punches nine one one.

6.29 p.m. Wednesday

He pulls into the driveway tired and beaten. A headache drums against his temples – he'd spent most of the drive on the phone fighting with his bank over fraudulent credit-card purchases. Even worse, there were charges and foreign-transaction fees resultant from someone using it for hundreds of visits to an internet porn site.

The final straw came with being distracted on his cell phone and failing to see the highway patrol officer.

For several minutes he lays his head back against the seat, trying to imagine what twisted crimes he may have committed in some former life to warrant things coming to this point.

A deep sigh follows several before it. What will he tell his wife?

The truth. He will tell her the truth. Maybe they can find strength together to overcome these . . . challenges. That's what they are. Challenges.

He exits the car, making his way to the front door. Oddly, today's mail remains untouched in the mailbox. Of more concern, he notices the front door slightly ajar.

Initially frozen by the discovery, a wave of panic forces a thaw and he quickly shoves the door open – only to find a barren front room. No furniture, no plants, no pictures on the wall. Each echoing step farther into the house reveals that the dining room, kitchen, and bedrooms are all similarly void.

His shoulders sink.

"Shit, I've been robbed. Just freakin' perfect."

Yet, as he looks once again around the emptied room, something doesn't sit right. "Why the hell would they take the crap off the wall . . . and that stupid cracked plant vase?"

Then it catches his eye. A single sheet of stationery – a style he recognises his wife using when writing to her internet-phobic aunt – is taped to a kitchen cupboard. With a sense of dread, he pulls the note down and begins to read:

Dear Ron,

I know this is somewhat of a surprise, yet surely you must have seen it coming. We've grown apart over this last year and, while I want to say "significantly", maybe even that's an understatement. Nevertheless, I simply cannot go on this way. I recently met someone, and she and I have decided to make a new life. Once I've settled in a bit I'll be in touch to discuss the divorce.

Teresa

Ron's knees give and his butt slams to the floor, while the paper floats featherlike to his side.

She?

Overwrought, he lays his face into splayed fingers, seeking relief in the form of tears. But none will come.

He sits dazed, no thoughts, no emotions, just staring into the nothingness that suddenly makes up his life.

The answer, a ball of clay taking shape as his mind sculpts it into perfect form, finally comes to light. What brought him to this point was no longer of consequence, he was there. And now, there is no other choice.

He stands, takes one last long look at the room, and walks out to the car. Carlton Canyon is only a ten-minute drive from here.

2.14 p.m. Wednesday

"Now what?" Ron stands back, looking at the tiny display on the pump.

SEE ATTENDANT

Jerking his credit card from the slot he marches into the minimart. He pushes his way through the door nearly bumping into a young Hispanic man who's waving a twenty-dollar bill and speaking in rapid Spanish to the unshaven clerk behind the counter. The attendant finally nods, takes the twenty, and pushes some buttons on the register, which sends the young man on his way.

"Yes?" asks the clerk.

"It says 'see attendant' when I tried my card," says Ron.

The clerk takes the card and swipes it. "Pump?"

"Four."

His head bobs and he makes a grunt. His eyes stay intently on the machine's display.

"Rejected," he finally says.

"Rejected? What does that mean?"

"You have to call your bank. It's no good, man."

"What d'ya mean it's no good? I paid that . . ."

Ron's voice trails off. He snatches the card and, slamming the store's door behind him, trudges back to the car. Forgetting entirely about the pump's nozzle head still poking out from the gas fill on his car, he drives away.

1.44 p.m. Wednesday

"Ron, can you step into my office, please?"

Ron looks up from his desk to see his manager, Thomas Watts, standing in the doorway. Tall, well-dressed, fit and tanned, he always walked with purpose Ron thought. Today, however, his shoulders slump and he leans against the door for support. Ron watches him turn and head down the hallway, each step nothing more than a dragging of one foot after the other as if the force of gravity had suddenly doubled.

Ron, already on the verge of defeat from his day, follows Thomas, his pace matching that of his manager. He steps into the office and Watts closes the door before sitting down. Definitely not a good sign.

Thomas Watts shifts in his chair.

"Ron. I'm not going to sugar-coat this. The company has decided to move their engineering team to our overseas branch. Our entire department is being canned. They're even selling the building."

Ron opens his mouth, but only stunned silence finds a path out.

"I'm sorry, Ron. You've worked hard and deserve better."

Words finally form. "How long?"

"This Friday is your last day. I'm only here until the end of the month to give everyone the bad news and freakin' turn out the lights. Pretty shitty, huh?"

"I . . . I don't know what to say."

"Not much to be said, Ron. Why don't you go home? Nothing more can be done here."

He doesn't remember leaving the room, the office, or even starting his car. He just suddenly finds himself standing at the gas pump.

11.37 a.m. Wednesday

"Ron Campbell." Though in mid-step heading out for an early lunch, Ron catches the phone on the second ring.

"Ron, Julius here. Look, I've got some bad news. You been following that Allied Bankcorp scandal on the news?"

"Julius, no more bad news, OK? I'm still stinging from that Stallion Investments Group –"

"No, you don't understand. Allied also owns Mountain Mortgage. Your loan is through them."

Ron's thoughts drift to his mortgage. With less than perfect credit Ron's only shot at buying a house came with some unorthodox arrangements with Mountain Mortgage.

"So . . . what does that mean?"

"It means you're screwed, buddy. The loan is null and void. They took you for a ride. You're probably going to lose the house."

Dropping the phone back into its cradle Ron sinks the heels of his palms into his eyes. All that has already happened this morning . . . and now this?

10.17 a.m. Wednesday

Charlie Duncan steps into Ron's cube and flops into the extra chair. With zilch interest in work, Ron sees Charlie as a welcome sight. Until he catches the look on his face.

"Ron, we're in deep shit. The blame for the collapse of that Ascot Bridge framing has fallen on the engineering team. We're gonna be subpoenaed to testify before the Grand Jury next week." Charlie abruptly stands, throwing his arms in the air. "Subpoena hell, it's a damn inquisition. Someone's gotta hang for those two workers' deaths, and, baby, they're looking straight on at you and me."

"Come on, Charlie, we both checked the numbers! And reviewed the stress loads!"

"OSHA says we were off. Now I think they're looking to set some examples after all those crane failures earlier this year."

Ron stands, preparing to argue out the point, but, realising the futility, drops right back in the chair, hands covering his face. "OK, what do you think we should do?"

"Ya got those reports? Let's review 'em one more time."

With heads bent over the spreadsheets they run the numbers again. And again. After a full hour Charlie abruptly stands.

"Shit, Ron, there ain't nothin' here gonna save our asses."

Before he can say anything in reply Charlie throws up his arms and storms around the corner.

Ron sits dumbfounded for a moment before deciding it might be a good time to step out to lunch and maybe find some solace. How could this day get any worse?

Just then the phone rings.

9.12 a.m. Wednesday

Settled into his cube, it only takes Ron a couple minutes to check for voicemails and sift through his unread email. Nothing on the Ascot Bridge Inquiry. He'd been sure today would bring an end to that mess.

Disappointed, he shifts over to his CAD program and pulls up a current job: footings for a multistorey building being built on clay soil. Wesley Deumar, his geologist advisor, would have to be involved.

He turns, but before he can pick up the phone to call Deumar, it begins to ring.

"Ron Campbell."

"Ron, Mark Lewis here."

"Hey, Mark. Looking for a sympathetic ear on your stock market woes?"

"I only wish, though that is bad enough. Say, did you see the news on the Allied Bankcorp scandal this morning?"

"Yeah, some big FBI investigation. Looks like a lot of folks stand to lose their savings."

"Exactly. Ron, here's the problem ... Allied ran Stallion Investments. Ring a bell?"

"Uh, they handle my 401k, right?"

"They sure did. Right over to the Cayman Islands. The money's not there, Ron. It's all gone."

Ron waits for Mark to say "just kidding" or "gotcha!" but he knows it's not coming.

8.05 a.m. Wednesday

Ron sits at the breakfast counter dividing his attention between the paper and the bright sunny day dancing through the window. He sips on a home-brewed cappuccino while nibbling on a freshly heated bagel.

He tries to slide back into his routine, be as normal as possible. His first day back to work after taking some time off for his brother's funeral, killed two weeks past in a motorcycle accident, and he still remains shaken. That, combined with an ongoing OSHA investigation into a bridge-construction accident and a recent distance from his wife, have made for some troubling times. But, he's convinced it's all behind him now. This day starts things anew. The investigation will clear him, leaving him free to focus on straightening out his home life. Maybe they can finally talk about having kids.

He looks back down from the window to the paper. A lead story follows an FBI investigation into a banking conglomerate: Allied Bankcorp. Three of their top executives embezzled most, if not all, of the company's investments and fled the country, leaving little hope of ever recovering the funds. Thousands of ordinary investors saving for their retirements lost every dime.

Man, and he thought he had troubles!

Taking one last long sip of the cappuccino, he wipes his mouth and marches through the door. Just outside, the promise of the day awaits.

The Debacle
BERYL ENSOR-SMITH

||||||||||||||||||||||||||||||||||||||||||||||||||||||||||||||||||||||||||||||||||||||||||||||||||||||||||||||||||||||||||||||||||

In the sleepy dorp of Prentburg, Christina du Plessis takes it upon herself to fulfil an old woman's dying wish to be buried with her dog.

> "Hans was on full alert, the euphoria of the two beers he'd consumed on the 19th hole deserting him."

After the event, Christina du Plessis decided that it was only because nothing interesting had happened in the dorp for weeks that her usual sagacity had deserted her and she had become involved in something best left alone.

It had all started one hot afternoon when she was trying to have a conversation with Hans. Trying, because he was not being very cooperative and merely grunted in a most annoying way when a response was required. Perhaps it was that, that prompted her to interest him more in what she was saying? After several grunts, she changed the subject.

"Hans, did I tell you that Minky died yesterday?"

Hans racked his brains. Minky? Who the heck was Minky?

Seeing his baffled expression, Christina said resignedly: "Minky, Hans. Old Mrs Jacobs' dog."

"But old lady Jacobs died some time ago, didn't she?"

"Six months, almost to the day, but Hilda gave Minky a home and she's now distraught."

Hans pondered some more. Hilda was his wife's best friend and in his opinion, a strange woman. Trying to imagine her "distraught" was beyond his capabilities.

"She grew attached to the dog?"

"No," Christina said testily. "She never took to it, and that's the problem. Hilda's now filled with guilt and wants to honour her mother's dying wish, which was to have Minky buried with her."

"Well," said Hans, reaching for the newspaper, "she's six months too late then, isn't she?"

"Callous brute!" flared his wife, grabbing the paper and placing it out of his reach. "And why should it be too late? Surely it would be a simple matter to dig a shallow hole in Mrs Jacobs' grave and bury the dog, which is a small breed."

Hans now remembered the dog, a terrier type, unappealing in looks and uncertain of temper. "I suppose so," he said dubiously.

"Excepting that when Hilda approached Dominee, he said she needed permission from Jan Badenhorst and he's refused, saying it infringes some by-law. You'd think that in such a sensitive case he could stretch the law, but not that man! He thinks he's better than the rest of us and I've never liked him. What do you think, Hans?" Christina was working herself up into a rare state and Hans eyed her warily. When his wife really got going, there was hell to pay! As for Jan Badenhorst, he'd never given the man much thought other than to acknowledge grudgingly that he tackled his difficult job as municipal manager with fortitude and efficiency. Now was not the time, however, to point this out to his irate wife. Trying to calm her down, Hans sealed his own fate by choosing to placate her.

"I agree with you entirely, my darling. The man's an idiot."

"I'm glad you see eye to eye with me, Hans. He shouldn't be allowed to throw his weight around like that!" A speculative gleam came into her eye and Hans began to feel the first qualms of disquiet. "I think there's a way around this," Christina said dreamily. "With your help, Hans, we can set Hilda's mind at rest. It just needs a little thought."

There was now a decidedly hollow feeling in the pit of his stomach. From past experience Hans knew that when Christina got "that" look about her, it boded no good. No good at all!

During the course of the next week, nothing changed. Hans was beginning to hope that his wife had been distracted from her purpose, whatever it was. From her thoughtful expression, however, he doubted it, and hoped that his expected involvement would be minimal. Perhaps Christina intended him to speak to Dominee to try to enlist his help in getting permission for Minky (cursed dog!) to be buried with Mrs Jacobs? More awkward would be her expecting him to approach Jan Badenhorst on the matter, but even that wouldn't be too bad. He would go through the motions and then persuade Christina to accept Jan's refusal. Hans was just beginning to feel that matters were in control when Christina dropped her bombshell.

"It's all arranged, Hans," she told him after his weekly game of golf. "Hilda and I have worked it all out. Sunday night would be the best time, well after dark, naturally."

"Best time for what?" Hans was suddenly on full alert, the euphoria of the two beers he'd consumed on the 19th hole deserting him.

"For burying Minky, of course!"

"But Jan's forbidden it!"

"Jan won't know, will he? Not unless you foul up."

"Me?" His voice was panic-stricken.

"You, Hans. You agreed that it's a silly by-law that should be ignored, remember?"

"I didn't exactly say . . ."

"Hans du Plessis, are you calling me a liar?" Christina drew herself up to her full height, her overweight body quivering with affront.

"No, not at all. I just meant –"

"That's just as well," she interrupted, "since I've told Hilda you've agreed to do it. We're counting on you, Hans, to carry out an old lady's last request." Seeing his eyes dart from one side to the other seeking a way out, she added contemptuously, "Come on, Hans, how hard can it be? It's rained heavily this past week so the soil is soft and Minky's a small dog. It need only be a shallow hole, so will involve hardly any effort on your part."

"Christina, it's against the law!"

"That's why you'll do it at midnight when nobody will be there to see you." Christina changed her tactics and said gently, "My darling, I'll be forever in your debt if you do this little thing for my dearest friend. You scratch my back and I'll scratch yours, you know?"

Fat chance, Hans thought gloomily. Christina had a short memory when it came to favours owed.

"I can't manage such a thing on my own," he protested. "How am I expected to carry a dead dog, a spade and a torch?"

"Mrs Jacobs is buried near the west gate, twelve graves along in the second row which is hardly any distance at all, and anyway I've arranged that Sarie will help you."

"Sarie Blignault, that halfwit?"

"She's not a halfwit, just a bit slow," Christina cajoled, though she was usually the first to label Sarie a mental case.

"Why not you or Hilda?" Hans argued, already knowing he was on a losing wicket. "Why must I be the one to do the job if it's so easy!"

"Because," Christina said patiently, "Hilda's emotional about this, and you honestly can't expect me with my nervous disposition to tackle it!" Her voice had taken on an edge and Hans knew that while she trotted out the excuse of her nerves only when it suited her, any further objection would be useless.

"I just hope you've made clear to Sarie what will be expected of her," he capitulated sulkily. "I can't do this on my own."

"Of course, beloved. Sarie is pleased to be helping in such a worthy cause."

It had, in fact, been anything but easy to persuade Sarie to help. Christina had used every weapon in her considerable arsenal to win her victim over. She had decided it would be wise to give Sarie the least possible information in the interests of keeping the matter secret, and also so as not to confuse someone she considered seriously lacking in the brains department. She had merely said that Hans wished to honour an old woman's dying wish to have Minky buried with her, and that because of a silly by-law he had to do it on the quiet and needed Sarie's help. She had played on Sarie's conscience and sympathy, and eventually wrested reluctant agreement from her.

"All you have to do is carry the torch to light the way, and hold it steady while Hans digs."

"I don't like cemeteries, especially at night, Christina."

"Don't be a silly goose! Hans will be there with you and just think how good you'll feel to have been part of such a noble deed!"

"Yes?" Tremulously.

"Yes," Christina said firmly, and that was that!

Hans slept very little in the nights leading up to Sunday. He was bedevilled with misgivings and was thoroughly tired and out of sorts by the time Sunday arrived. The Sisters of the Church were quick to pick up on his despondent mood at the Sunday service.

"Did you notice how miserable Hans is looking?" Marion Klopper enquired when tea was being served after the service. "He paid hardly any attention to Dominee's sermon."

"Perhaps he's sickening with something," Suzie Lamprecht replied, not displaying much sympathy.

"It's more likely that Christina's been playing up again," Helga Swanepoel said so loudly that the other two looked round in embarrassment, relieved to see that the lady in question was some distance away, in earnest conversation with her friend Hilda.

"She seems her usual self," Elaine Ferreira offered. "Poor old Hans. His life can't be easy."

Hans would have been the first to agree with her had he been privy to the exchange. By the time midnight came, he was riddled with impatience just wanting the unpleasant chore to be over and done with. He was to fetch Sarie from her house and drive out to the cemetery, some distance from the dorp. Which he did, being reminded by his wife to take a spade and a torch, and with the box containing Minky (who had been kept frozen in Hilda's "old" freezer which she was trying to sell, and was now a solid weight) on the back seat. Sarie was a very silent passenger, beset with doubts, but too timid to voice them.

Hans was not familiar with driving in the dark, which he found disorientating, but eventually found the gate to the cemetery and parked the car under the pine trees to the left of it. He then carried the box containing Minky, leaving Sarie with torch and spade trailing after him. She was supposed to be lighting the way for him but the torch beam wandered hither and thither in her uncertain grip and at one point she dropped it completely, leaving him some distance ahead of her in pitch darkness.

In the informal settlement not far from where Sarie lived, Moses Shilowa had also had a sleepless night, one brought about by excitement at becoming the owner of a brand-new bicycle. Eventually he gave up trying to drop off and decided that it would be wise to tire himself out, and what better way to do it than to ride the new bike through the dorp and along the main road beyond? Very quietly so as not to wake up his wife, Lindiwe, he put his tracksuit on over his pyjamas, slipped his feet into his trainers and carried the bike out of their house so that it would not make a noise, closing the front door softly behind him. Once on the pathway he happily mounted the bike and rode away. He decided he'd ride to the cemetery and back, by which time he would be well exercised and ready for sleep.

When he got to the cemetery he made a U-turn and it was then that he saw a car parked on the verge under the pine trees. Moses' curiosity was aroused. Who could possibly be visiting such a place in the deep of night? Peering through the trees he saw a light bobbing along. He felt very uneasy and was just about to ride off in a hurry when it disappeared for a second, and then came on again, shining up into the face of a woman he recognised. In his consternation, Moses exclaimed aloud. Sarie, hearing him, shone the torch straight at him. All she could see were the whites of his eyes as his clothing and skin were dark and blended into the night. She screamed at the top of her voice and Moses took off for home like a rocket. Needless to say, sleep eluded him for the rest of the night!

Meantime Hans's heart had jumped into his throat with fright. When he had recovered, he called out quaveringly: "Sarie?"

"I'm here," she replied, stumbling towards him. "Oh, Hans, I've just seen a ghost. It's standing outside the wall watching us!"

"Nonsense," he replied brusquely. "You're imagining things." All the same, his need to get the business over and done with was greater then ever. "Help me count the graves. It's the twelfth on the right-hand side."

The light from the torch was fast fading. Either the batteries were flat or its encounter with the ground had done it no good. Hans cursed beneath his breath. When he and Sarie were in agreement about having found the twelfth grave, he was dismayed to see it was covered with white pebbles and had an enormous concrete urn filled with flowers near the headstone. He dumped Minky unceremoniously on the ground, took the spade from Sarie and told her to keep the beam steady. In her state of nerves she was unable to do so.

Hans started to spade up white pebbles in the centre of the grave, placing them carefully on the ground beside it. Then he tried to move the urn, but it was awkwardly shaped, fat and round, and the flowers got in his way. His efforts only resulted in a nasty cut on his hand where it got caught in the wire mesh holding the flowers, and when he next looked, blood was streaming from the wound. It was the last straw. He gave in to a bout of bad temper and aimed the heel of his boot at the offending urn, giving it a hefty kick. It took off most satisfactorily and landed with a thump somewhere in the darkness. Sarie promptly dropped the torch again and the light went out, permanently this time.

Hans dug a hole as best he could, heaping the sand he removed onto a plastic sheet he'd brought for that purpose. It took more than the "few minutes" Christina had promised, despite the recent rain. By the time the hole was big enough to accommodate Minky, Hans was sweating and angry (his hand was still bleeding copiously and he had nothing with which to bind it up) and he disposed of the dog without sentiment, tossing the soil back into the hole and tamping it down with the spade. He then got Sarie to help him spread the pebbles over the area where the hole had been. He could only hope they did a reasonable job as they could see very little. He now regretted the loss of the urn as it would have helped cover the disturbance. Failing that, he got Sarie to gather what pine cones she could find. No easy task in the dark and she gathered piles of debris with them, but beggars can't be choosers and Hans strewed them around as best he could.

"That's it. Let's get out of here," he said. Sarie could not oblige soon enough.

When Hans got home, Christina was fast asleep. There's gratitude for you, he thought as he treated his wound and performed perfunctory ablutions before stripping and climbing into bed alongside her snoring form.

The next morning she quizzed him about proceedings and he gave her an edited version, complaining that Sarie had been worse than useless. He thought it best not to mention his fit of temper and sending the urn flying, and hid from her the deep cut in the palm of his hand. He would deny any knowledge of the urn, should Hilda ask what had happened to it. After all, vandalism was rife everywhere, even in cemeteries.

Christina gave him a sharp look. "So I can tell Hilda you did a decent job?"

"You can tell her I did my best in very difficult circumstances," he retorted, "and you'd better have another word with Sarie, swearing her to secrecy. She thought she saw a ghost and will probably go blabbing about it to anyone who'll listen."

Christina wasted no time in doing so and spent the best part of the next morning reminding Sarie that promises had to be kept as they were sacred; that should anyone learn of her part in burying Minky she could be in big trouble and (laying it on thick) could land up in jail. By the time she was done, Sarie was convinced that if she breathed a word about what had happened, she would burn in hell.

"I won't tell," she assured Christina, "but there's one thing that I'm wondering."

"And what is that?" Christina asked benignly, now that she had scared the woman senseless.

"Why did Hans bury Minky in Nana Fotheringham's grave?"

"Pardon?" Christina said breathlessly, trying to gain time to take in what Sarie had just said.

"Why Nana Fotheringham's grave? She didn't even like animals, being allergic to them. She said they gave her hives."

Christina went cold but quickly pulled herself together. Clearly something had gone horribly wrong. She should have known Hans would mess things up! She racked her memory for images of the Fotheringhams, finally remembering they were English immigrants who had settled in the dorp about two years before. "Nana" must be the granny. Trust Sarie to know everyone in the village and all their business!

"Well," she said slowly, giving herself time to think and recalling that she had not actually told Sarie that Minky was to be buried with her mistress, "that's exactly why, er, Nana Fotheringham wanted this. She couldn't have pets in life, so she wanted one in death. It was her dearest wish."

"Was it?" Sarie queried dubiously. "I didn't know you were friendly with her."

"Not exactly friendly. We met in the dorp sometimes when we had to go shopping. That's when she told me."

"But she was in a wheelchair!"

Christina had now recovered her wits. "That didn't prevent her being driven to the shops now and then, just for a change. She would sit in the car and watch the world go by," she improvised. "I'd stop and talk to her."

"That was nice of you, Christina." Sarie still seemed doubtful.

"I do my best," Christina said modestly. "That's why I implored Hans to bury Minky with her, knowing how important it was to her. We should try to help out where we can, don't you agree?"

Sarie nodded. "I wonder what Mrs Jacobs is thinking, wherever she is. Do you suppose she minds?"

Christina wondered too, but quickly replied, "Not at all. She was a good Christian."

When she got home, Christina tackled Hans. He defended himself vehemently.

"I did exactly as you told me. I buried the blasted dog in the second row, twelve graves from the west gate."

"Except that Sarie says that you went to the east gate. She says you parked the car under the pines. There are no trees anywhere near the west gate, so in this she must be right!"

Hans muttered something about it being pitch black, so small wonder he became confused.

"Confused? You buried an Afrikaans dog in an English grave! You'd better hope Hilda never gets wind of this. Her mother had strong feelings about the Boer War and must now be spinning like a top beneath the soil. If Hilda finds out what you've done, she'll come after you with her meat cleaver! I suggest you waste no time visiting Mrs Jacobs' grave and mussing up the soil a bit in case Hilda decides to check that you did what you promised."

"It's broad daylight. What if I'm seen?" Hans whined.

"Say you're doing some gardening," his wife returned callously.

Both hoped that would be the end of the matter. No such luck. When Christina attended the next Sisters of the Church charity handicraft session later that week, she was inundated with the latest gossip doing the rounds.

"Completely desecrated," Helga Swanepoel said portentously. "The Fotheringhams are livid!"

Suzie Lamprecht looked round furtively then beckoned the "sisters" to come closer, which they did with unseemly haste.

"I've heard that it's more than mere desecration. Sergeant Mostert's investigating the possibility of Satanism!"

"Satanism? Why?" from a wide-eyed Elaine Ferreira.

"The concrete vase decorated with angels was found broken to bits some distance away and all the flowers in it scattered to the four winds."

"That could have been done by vandals," old Mrs Merton scoffed, "and is no evidence of Satanism by any stretch of the imagination."

The "sisters" glared at the most contentious member of their group. For the first time in months, a good story, and this killjoy wanted to quash it!

"There is more," flashed Suzie, "The white stones on the grave were splashed with sacrificial blood!" She threw a triumphant look at her detractor. "They'd also been disturbed and pine cones and birds' feathers were spread over them. The Fotheringhams are getting their priest to do a purification rite at the grave, they're so concerned."

This news had spread not only to the ears of the Church Sisters, but also to those of Moses Shilowa in the informal settlement.

"You remember I told you I saw the white witch in the cemetery the other night?" he reminded his wife. "Well, we now know what she was doing!"

"And what exactly was that?" asked a sceptical Mrs Shilowa.

"Practising her black magic, of course. At that time of night she could hardly be attending a funeral, could she?" said he, annoyed.

By way of reply the irritating woman merely raised her eyebrows and bent on him a pitying look. She knew of someone else who had been at the cemetery that same night for a completely innocuous reason and was willing to bet his nemesis was equally innocent of wrongdoing.

"Just you warn the children to keep away from her house," he commanded.

"Don't worry, they're dead scared of her after all your scary stories!"

Christina lost no time in letting Hans know the latest news.

"I can't begin to imagine what you did to that grave on Sunday night and don't want to know," she said scathingly, "but you had better hope it goes no further, Hans. All you were required to do was bury a small dog and now there's talk of sacrificial offerings and Satanic rituals!"

Hans thought it wisest to keep quiet.

A week went by in which both he and Christina held their breath. Then another week. After three, interest in the matter faded as Sergeant Mostert was unable to pin the crime on anyone; the perpetrators had seemingly disappeared into thin air. By the end of the month, the Du Plessis felt they were off the hook.

"You seem to have got away with it, Hans."

"I? It was at your instigation, Christina! I didn't want any part of it, remember?"

"Yes, well, you're the one who'll be facing some awkward questions if by some miracle you eventually land up outside the pearly gates. You'll be met by two women wanting answers. You'll have to explain to one how it is that you failed to bury her beloved pet with her, but instead placed it in the grave of someone she would have considered a bitter enemy. And what will you say to the other? A woman who detested animals and is now forced to lie through eternity with the bones of an unwanted dog nose to nose with her! No matter how much blessing that priest does, she'll never rest easy!"

She pondered for a moment before adding sarcastically, "Come to think of it, Hans, you'll probably be better off when you die if you're sent down below where you'd get more of a welcome. It'd probably be easier living with the devil than facing those two old women."

Live with the devil? I already do, Hans felt like retorting, but thought better of it.

The Girl in the Cannery
M. J. CLEGHORN

A hard-working Alaskan girl who guts fish all day at the local cannery wonders how she will afford to bury her grandfather.

"The work had been
non-stop three
days and counting.
They lived on gum
and coffee."

Forty dollars. A week's pay. That's what it will cost to bury the old Swede, the girl in the cannery thought to herself, picking the soft bones and skin from each shiny copper can as they spilled down the conveyer belt.

Forty dollars.

Every day, long into the summer twilight, the girl in the cannery took her place in the slime line, every day since she was thirteen years old. Her mother died when she was a girl – dead from tuberculosis at twenty-five. Her father went to war. He never came home. She tried to remember their faces. Sometimes, when she looked into the mirror, she wondered if it was her mother's eyes she saw looking back at her, or was it her father's face. The girl and the old Swede lived alone in a small shack at the end of the boardwalk. Alone since her brother ran away to sea, lying about his age to join the merchant marines. He wired most of his pay home, everything except a dollar or two a month, to buy a few cigarettes and a stray bottle of beer.

He was a good brother, and she loved him, but the money he sent didn't even pay the grocery bill. Now her grandfather was dead and it would cost forty dollars to bury the old Swede. She would need a draw on her pay, but before she could see the cannery boss the fleet came in with their bellies full of salmon.

Three days later, the tight-fisted cannery boss hammered out a price per pound with the even tighter-fisted fishermen. The girl in the cannery watched wide-eyed as a mob of angry fishermen chased the cannery boss round the building and up, then back down, the steep office stairs. Once the victory whistle blasted, every fisherman's wife and daughter came hurrying to the cannery. When the fish were in, there was work to do. The old Swede would have to wait.

Matilda, as the girl in the cannery was called, was named after *Waltzing Matilda*, the old Swede's favourite song. Matilda was not afraid of hard work. She never complained, not even when the seawater came pouring in off the catch, flooding the cement floor, and leaked through her rubber boots, soaking her socks and leaving her feet wet and cold. Day after day and night after night. When her freezing fingers bled from twenty-two-hour days gutting countless kings and reds, she never wept for herself or the fish.

The last batch of fish caught by this year's fleet was bad – spoiled. "Sat too long while they argued over price," the company superintendent claimed; the fleet won't come in until a price is settled. "Now it isn't even fit for the number-two cans."

"Damn weather. Dumped 'em back in the bay," the cannery boss hollered from the loading dock, but no one could hear him over the din of the machines and the slime lines. "Shut it down – everyone can go home now." The cannery went silent. No one spoke. Their bodies had been frozen in one position for so long it was hard to straighten up. Painful. Pulling off her wet bloodied apron and wiping clean her fish knife, the girl in the cannery watched as the fishermen's wives and daughters went home to their suppers.

The work had been non-stop three days and counting. They lived on gum and coffee. No one left the cannery. They took short naps in shifts; it was either eat or sleep. They were on the clock, no work no pay. These were the days Matilda missed her grandmother most.

"She's a princess," Matilda would hear the old Swede say to the other fishermen. "Daughter of an Athabaskan chief."

Her grandmother.

"No granddaughter of mine is ever going to work in that cannery. Who do they think they are? Our husbands and sons risk their lives and for what? A few pennies per pound. We can't even afford to buy our own fish back to feed our families. Ha!"

On the day they buried her grandmother, Matilda left school and went to work in the cannery. The old Swede was sick. He was a man that spent his life on the sea, and now he had come ashore to die. His rusty tug was dragged to the driftwood shack and left in dry dock. He never spoke of her grandmother again, but once Matilda saw the old Swede make his way to the cemetery with a handful of dog roses.

There would be no one waiting for the girl in the cannery, in the grey shack at the end of the boardwalk – only a bill from the undertaker. Forty dollars to bury the old Swede. A week's pay.

Rain began to fall, masking the fishy smell of her damp hair and clothes with fresh clean salt water. The fog was rolling in from across the gulf. The shrill cries of the gulls echoed off the mountains. Matilda lifted her face to the sky, and she hungered for a good fire and a hot bowl of chowder. She would manage; she was strong, strong like her mother, and strong like her grandmother before her. She took a certain pride in caring for her dying grandfather and lasting long hours on her feet. Gutting great tons of raw fish and stacking case after case of canned salmon until she thought her back would break, she never missed a day or night of work, hard and poor as it was.

Oh how her grandmother would laugh if she knew that one day, yes, one day, her granddaughter, *the girl in the cannery*, would be the new cannery boss.

"Poor Matilda, *that girl in the cannery*, no family. She's the only one left."

She knew what they said about her.

"Ha! I am not the only one left," Matilda heard herself say as she turned towards the cemetery, stopping only to pick a handful of dog roses.

The Kindness of Strangers
CEINWEN HAYDON

Two strangers with deep personal tragedies meet on a lonely hillside path, and for a moment their destinies are intertwined.

"Tears overwhelmed him again, and I waited. I took his hand as if he were a young child."

"... sometimes one feels freer speaking to a stranger than to people one knows. Why is that?"
"Probably because a stranger sees us the way we are, not as he wishes to think we are."
From *The Shadow of the Wind* by Carlos Ruiz Zafón

John

left the house, my chest tight and my face rigid. I followed a track at the end of the village, an old drovers' road on which I was unlikely to meet anyone. As I walked I kicked a fallen conker in front of me; it had lost its sheen and was now a sad reminder of the bright nut that had lately emerged from its prickly green case. The lignin veneer had dried up, but the shell was now the stronger to bear my buffeting as it rolled along. I had lost my shine too but I was not stronger, at least not today.

After a mile or so I got into my stride and my heartbeat steadied. I tried to think what to do next, but accepted that this might take quite a while. I had to manage my agitation before I made my final decision. A hare with a strong gait loped across my path three or four metres ahead and it entranced me; then it disappeared into the hedgerow, and

413

overwrought as I was I felt its departure as a personal loss. An air of sorrow clung to each aspect of my senses and it reinterpreted the world in terms of naked sadness.

My mobile phone vibrated in my coat pocket and my hand shook as I pulled it out. It was her: a text.

John – have you told her yet? Why haven't you been in touch? Mandy x

I turned the damned device off. I had no news to give to her.

I sat down, thump, on a nearby granite rock. I knuckled my clenched fists into my eye sockets and rocked back and forth in time to the metronome of my heartbeat. It bumped along in clumsy metre, adrenalin driven and flushed with cortisol.

Maria

I rounded the corner and saw him sitting there. A tall man with a mop of untamed curls, he was younger than me, but not really young. Possibly in his late forties. I watched him for a good few seconds before he realised I was there. He was not in a good way; that much was obvious. I was concerned and I didn't want to frighten him off before I'd checked if he was safe to be left alone.

"Hi, I'm so glad to see someone. It's a great relief. I'm lost. Could you help me?" I said.

This strategic lie slid out of my mouth, justified by my instinct that this man was at the end of his tether. I was unable to think of any other reason to talk to him; talk to him and maybe get the measure of his vulnerability.

He looked unfocused and bewildered. I might have been a creature from another planet. But then he rallied.

"Of course. What's the problem?"

"The thing is, I was trying to find the Iron Age fort. I'm staying at a guest house in Wooler and my landlady said that if I headed out beyond the end of the houses, over the common and along the track, I'd reach Humbleton Hill. But I think that I've missed a turning?"

"There are a couple of ways that you can go. This isn't the main one, but it'll get you there. Have you got a pencil and paper and I'll draw you a rough map?"

"Sure," I said, "give me a minute."

I perched on the tread plank of a low-level stile, and poked around in my small rucksack. My fingers closed around a notebook with a pen in an attached sheath. Before I drew it out I felt the matt-marbled metal of my green Stanley flask.

"I don't know about you but I'm ready for a brew. Would you fancy a cup? By the way, my name is Maria."

The man hesitated and then sighed, signs of his reluctance to forgo his solitude. He paused and resigned himself to my intrusion.

"John. I'm John. Yes, thanks. I didn't think to bring a drink with me today."

I poured the tea out into two small beakers and handed him one. Then I ferreted around for the writing stuff once more and passed it across to my new companion. He bent over the notepad on his lap and frowned with concentration. There was a tremor in his hand as he gripped the pen, and as he started to write he bore down with an exaggerated firmness to compensate for his unsteadiness. The paper tore under the heavy stroke of the ballpoint. He flushed a deep red as he realised I had noticed his discomfort.

"Sorry, I'll try again," he said in a quiet voice.

"No worries at all," I said. "I'm just grateful for your help. At my age I don't want to get lost in the hills. The weather can change so quickly, especially in the autumn. One minute you can be in bright sunshine and the next the mist has blown in and the temperature's dropped."

"You're right there," he said. His doleful brown eyes expressed more than he was prepared to say aloud.

I watched as he drew a map with deft strokes, and labelled key reference points with care. He seemed to be a man who set himself high standards. When he'd finished he polished off his tea in a single gulp.

"Let me explain this to you, Mary –" He hesitated. "Sorry. Maria."

I sat and paid attention as John talked me through the route. I acted the part of the disorientated stranger with total conviction. He could not have known that I'd walked these hills on many holidays ever since my childhood and that I knew each path like the back of my hand. Funny, I'd done many contrary things in my life but I'd never thought of myself as a good liar. Still, needs must.

"That's great, John. You've been a star. How can I thank you enough?"

"You're fine. I'm glad to have got one thing right today."

"I'd guess from that that you've got a bit of a downer on yourself?" I said.

"Maria, if you only knew the half of it."

"I don't. But I do know that not long ago I thought everything was finished for me, and now it's not. Not at all."

I ran my fingers through my curly hair; it was still strange to feel the short but silken regrowth. For most of my life my hair had been coarse and straight. Then I heard a raptor's plaintive cry and looked up to see two buzzards circling high above the hills against the misty-blue harvest sky. I pointed and John followed my gaze; the buzzards were being harried by a gang of crows until the pair rose and soared in ever-widening wheels and made their escape. Their haunting calls plucked at my nerve strings.

I glanced across at John, aware that the time had come for us to get on with our respective days.

"I have a lot on my mind at the moment," he said.

"John, would you like to walk with me? And if you want to talk, that's fine. If you don't, I'd just be glad of your company."

John

I stood still, in suspended animation; I was tempted by her offer. When Maria had first appeared on the path where I'd all but fallen, I felt bitter bile surge into my throat. I had come out to be alone and this old woman, albeit in innocence, had trashed my privacy. My resentment was amplified by desperation. I felt like a cornered beast, and I wanted to tell her to go to hell. But I was brought up to be a gentleman and even in my current torment I'd managed to be polite.

Our random encounter had inserted a tranche of normality into my distressed introspections, and as we chatted I had been drawn towards Maria's down-to-earth kindness. When she invited me to join her on her ramble I surprised myself.

"You know what, Maria? I'd really like to step along with you, at least for a while until I'm sure you're on the right path."

"Great. Lead on, McDuff," she said with a swift chuckle and her eyes creased into a warm smile. I glimpsed her sexy charm, now partly veiled by her advancing years.

The narrow path forced us to walk in single file for the first ten minutes or so, and then as it widened we continued abreast. We concentrated hard on avoiding the knotted tree roots and chunks of rock that conspired to turn our ankles, but eventually the ground levelled out.

"John, you remind me a bit of my son, Sam. He has your height and similar hair."

"Do you see him often?"

"No. We Skype, but he lives in New Zealand. Has done for nigh on fifteen years."

"That must be hard for you."

"It is. But I know he's happy and he's loved, and that's the most important thing."

"It certainly is, Maria. It certainly is. I wish I had the knack for it. My only gift seems to be for hurting people, especially those closest to me."

My jaw clenched after I'd spoken. I had no right to burden this amiable stranger with my indiscretions, and the fallout that was about to rain down with cataclysmic consequences.

"Most people have done their fair bit of that," said Maria. "I know I have. But sometimes it can feel like you're the only one who ever stepped out of line."

I met her straight gaze, and wondered what she'd say if she knew what I'd actually done and what faced me today. Before I could think of what to say next Maria blew her nose hard. I looked across at her and it was clear she was on the verge of tears.

"Maria, are you OK?"

"Sorry, I've just thought about my past. And what I'm responsible for. It never goes away," she said.

"I really can't imagine that you've done anything so bad."

"John, the reason Sam is in New Zealand is that when he was fourteen, I had an affair. I thought I was really in love for the first time in my life. I left Sam with his dad, Liam, and I went to live with my new partner. Liam was distraught, and returned to his native Christchurch. He took Sam. Sam wouldn't have anything to do with me. We've only just got back in touch, and he's very cautious. He's thirty years old this year."

"Jesus, I'd never have thought . . ."

"I know," said Maria, "it's surprising what skeletons are in people's closets, even an old biddy like me. And, like everyone else, I've paid the price."

"Was it worth it, if you don't mind me asking?"

"That's a hard one, and something I think about more and more as I get older. I had some amazing adventures with the man that I fell for, beautiful times that I'll never forget. But I was blinded by a sort of madness. I could not see the damage I was doing to Sam. I thought he could cope without seeing me every day, and I was wrong. Then his dad took him so far away that I really was out of his life. I felt that I had no right to object. After all, I'd broken our family up in the first place. Sam told me a couple of months ago that he had expected me to insist that he stayed in the UK. As it was he took my acceptance of his father's plan as proof that I didn't love him any more."

"But you said that he is happy now?"

"Yes, he's got a good life and Liam and his stepmother have supported him well. He got a first-class degree at university and he's working as an architect, a job he loves. He's about to get married to Sally, a teacher, and they're expecting their first baby early next year. He's happy in spite of me, not because of me. I am only on the periphery and I may not be able to get any closer to him, ever."

"What happened to your lover? Is he still around, Maria?"

"No. It lasted a little short of three years. Milo wasn't a man to put down roots. Liam had become more like a brother to me, and I gave up everything for Milo because he excited me, he woke me up. The last dozen years have been a heavy price to pay for that passion. I've lived in purgatory and felt the loss of Sam every single day."

"Has there been anyone else? Since you and Milo split up?"

"I've tried. I even remarried once. The problem is, you see, that my thoughts keep returning to the world I upended when I left Liam. I've found it hard to focus on the present and that's been diabolical for anyone who's shared my life since those times. But not long ago I had a big health crisis and it dragged me into living in the here and now. In a strange way it's been good for me. Finally I had to focus on the present to survive. Earlier this year, I wrote a proper letter to Sam, quite different from the bland cards I always sent for his birthdays and at Christmas. I asked him if we could try to get to know each other again. It's early days, but we speak every couple of weeks now."

As Maria said this, I felt insect wings brush the back of my neck. I gave a reflexive swipe with my hand and a sharp pain stung my earlobe. I yelped and saw a late wasp fall to the ground at my feet. Maria stamped on it and put it out of its misery.

"You poor thing," said Maria before she removed the sting with a small, effective squeeze. She rooted inside her daysack, pulled out a tube of antihistamine cream and applied it to my inflamed skin.

"Is there anything you don't keep in there? Are you always so well prepared?"

Maria

I felt sorry for John when he was stung, but I was relieved to have an interruption to my heavy story. I usually keep quiet about my past, at least until I've known a person for a long time. I don't want to be judged by people who hardly know me. In fact sometimes I can't credit that I did those things; that I ever left Sam. With hindsight, my reasons for leaving were poor justification for the path I'd chosen all those years ago.

John turned his face towards the sky. The blue was edged by banks of cumulonimbus clouds, and the wind speed had gathered.

"I think the weather's changing. I can smell rain. Do you want to press on, Maria, or would you prefer to head back?"

For some reason I wanted to climb Humbleton Hill with an urgent energy I had not possessed for a long time. Latterly I'd become pretty risk averse in general, and especially when I walked alone in the hills, whether here or in my native Welsh valley; I'd had my fill of wild antics. But that day I wanted to push my limits and get up there, even though I knew that in a storm I'd be blown off my feet.

"I'd like to go on, if you're up for it?" I said.

"Well, I guess skin is waterproof. We'll be OK if we keep on the move and stay warm. We've both got jackets and scarves so we should be OK."

Unintentionally, I'd started to assume that we were taking the full walk together. John also seemed to have this in mind.

"Maria, how did you find the courage to speak to Sam, with so much at stake?"

"I was scared, but I had to give us a second chance."

"Was it as hard as you thought it would be?"

"It was different. Fear colours expectations when you're apprehensive about something, don't you think? And it also makes you doubt what you can cope with. Why do you ask, John?"

"Nothing really. I'm just interested to know how you managed. Sam is lucky to have a mother who is so committed to him."

"How can you say that he is lucky to have a mother like me? I left him."

"Yes, you said. But you did so much more, you mustn't shrink everything down to that as if it is all that counted," said John.

"But surely my selfishness ruined anything good that I'd done before?"

"Maria, you raised your son with love for fourteen years and laid the foundations for the man he is today. Don't forget that. And don't underestimate the trust you have shown to each other in getting back in touch and talking. I would say that you are both exceptional human beings from where I'm standing. Don't dance with guilt and turn your back on the future."

Even though John had somewhat airbrushed my wrongdoing, he had a point. I'd spent far too long dwelling on the past, and it had become an entrenched position for me. I risked the loss of Sam a second time if I refused to meet him in the present, our present. I understood this now with new clarity. I felt my shoulders loosen and my stomach unknot.

As we continued along the path, I remembered being a child in the playground at school. I recalled a game that I played with my friends: they would tell me to shut my eyes and they would spin me around and around. When they told me to look again I was in another place, and dizzy with delight. In a similar way John's comments had shaken me up; and I'd landed somewhere else.

I sensed that John was getting close to talking about his own worries as he spoke to me with less reserve. He appeared to want to talk and I was more than ready to listen. The way he'd looked when I came across him on the path had testified to his great distress, but I still had no idea what had caused it. Whatever I'd been through, the worst of it was in the past. This man's problems were excruciating and immediate.

"Do you live alone?" I said, as I tried to open a door into his world.

"I think I soon will be. I have a wife, Helen, and two daughters, Martha and Bethan. Martha's fifteen and Bethan's twelve."

"Are you unhappy?"

"How to answer that?" said John, under his breath. Then he became more animated. "Helen is the only woman I can imagine living with, for sure. She's bright and argumentative, very passionate, a real force of nature. But she's pretty uncompromising, with a clear idea of right and wrong. There are few grey areas in Helen's world view, and she doesn't take prisoners."

"It sounds as if life with her can be a challenge, but that you care for her very much."

"That's right enough," he said.

"How about your girls?"

At this question John's fragile mask didn't so much slip as dissolve. His face crumpled and the tears trickled down his face and ran with the snot that dripped from his nostrils. He turned away in male shame.

"I'm so sorry," he said.

"You're fine, John." I laid my hand on his shaking arm and waited. A stand of oak and beech trees stood by our path and their branches swayed in a swept, violent rhythm above our heads. Rooks cawed and the cacophony echoed darkly under the graphite clouds.

John turned back to me and opened his mouth as if to speak, then he shut it again. He swallowed hard and his Adam's apple rolled taut beneath the rough skin of his throat. He tried once more.

"It's Bethan, you see. She's sick, very sick, and she needs a bone-marrow transplant. In our family, none of us is the right match. So her chances are reduced, and time is critical. I would give my life for her but it would be no use, no use at all."

The tears overwhelmed him again, and I waited. I took his hand as if he were a young child and led him along the track. It was too cold to stand still for long.

John

The cadence of our steps, as we resumed our walk, steadied me a little. I found strange comfort in the firm grip of Maria's old hand. I knew she felt sorry for me, for Bethan, for my family. But she did not know the whole story, the complications. It was easier to talk when we strode on and looked straight ahead, avoiding eye contact.

"Bethan does have one good chance, but . . . Maria, things have happened, and I'm ashamed of them. There was a time before Helen and I were married, when she went travelling for six months with her best mate from college, Anita. We'd got engaged before she went, but she wanted to get the wanderlust out of her system before we settled down. She'd just finished university and was ready for a holiday after she'd studied hard for five years. I wasn't thrilled about her decision, but I respected it."

The first rain splattered down in oversized hesitant drops, before developing into a heavy downpour.

"Go on," said Maria.

"So, Helen went off on her travels. Well, the thing is, I'd always got on with her older sister, Mandy. Her man, Bob, was with the merchant navy, which left her at a loose end for months at a time. I know what you might imagine, but in all honesty we were just friends. That is, until one crazy night, when Bob was on shore leave. We'd all three been out for a curry, but Mandy got upset when Bob admitted he'd had a fling on his last trip, in Rio. I don't know why he chose to tell her in front of me. Maybe he was trying to contain the fallout. Whatever it was, Mandy lost it and told him to go. She was beside herself, and begged to go back to my place rather than have to face her parents. They'd never liked Bob anyhow. Perhaps, in her heart, she didn't want to give them more reasons to disapprove of him, in case she ever wanted to take him back."

"I think I can start to see where this is going, John."

"And you'd be right. I'll spare you the details. Except that nine months later, when Bob and Mandy had settled their differences and

Bob had left the navy and got a job with the Gas Board, Lydia was born. Of course I had my suspicions, but Mandy and I had promised each other that our lapse would remain our secret, ours alone. That way Bob and Helen wouldn't be hurt."

"How can you be sure that Lydia is yours, John?"

"I wasn't. But when Bethan's leukaemia was diagnosed in June, Helen, Martha and I were all tested to see if our bone marrow matched hers. None of us had the right type, so now she's waiting for another donor. The day after we got the results, Mandy suggested to me that Lydia should be assessed as well. It turns out that Mandy had been convinced for years that Lydia is my daughter but she'd kept quiet, understandably. First we talked to Lydia, who took our story in her stride, at least after the initial shock. She agreed to do a DNA test, and this confirmed that she's my child. She's eighteen now, and she and my girls are very close. She's desperate to help Bethan if she can. Last week Mandy, Lydia and I spoke to Bethan's consultant, Dr Douglas. More tests revealed Lydia to be a perfect match for Bethan. Two things remained: to talk to Bob, and to talk to Helen, Bethan and Martha as well. They have to know the truth."

"Where are you with that now?" said Maria.

"Bob knows. He played merry hell at first, until Mandy reminded him of his own adventures. Then Lydia told him that, for her, he'd always be her real dad. Bob's not a bad lad anyway, and he'd do anything to help Bethan. So he's coped better than I expected."

"So, that leaves Helen and your girls. Does Helen know?"

By now we were saturated, and our boots were squelching with every step. I couldn't fight back the bile this time, and stumbled towards the hedgerow and threw up everything I'd eaten that day. Maria handed me some soggy tissues and I tried to clean myself.

"Keep on the move," she said. "It's cold now. Let's think how you can handle this, for everyone's sake. Have you ever said anything at all to Helen, about you and Mandy? About Lydia?"

"No, never. And time is running out."

Maria stopped and stood in front of me; she locked her eyes with mine.

"Has it occurred to you that most mothers would first and foremost be utterly relieved if they learnt that their poorly child might live? Surely if you let her know there is reason to hope, it would be the greatest gift that you could possibly give her?"

"I see that, I do. But I'm so scared. Helen won't ever want me again, will she? She'll know that I betrayed her trust, and that I lied about it.

And with her sister as well."

"You have to risk that. My guess is that, in time, she'll love you for your courage, especially if Bethan lives. She'd know how hard it would have been for you to speak out and chance the loss of your marriage. And even if you lose Bethan, heaven forbid, you will have given your girl her best chance. I imagine that the others will break the silence anyway, to help Bethan. It must be better for Helen if the truth comes from you, yourself?"

Maria

We continued our walk in silence, both of us deep in our own thoughts. The rain pelted down and saturated our clothes. When we arrived at the foot of Humbleton Hill the wind was wild, but we made our way up the ancient path. Dogged and determined we aimed for the top. As we stood upright on the highest point a gust of gale force power knocked us off our feet. We fell into each other's arms and clung together for several minutes.

I'd like to think that that was a true turning point for each of us; the time when John and I started to forgive ourselves for messing up in our lives. Our bad decisions did not, after all, define everything about us.

I, who had no belief in a god, prayed for Bethan's recovery with an intensity that made me gasp for air. And I hadn't even met her. I knew from my own journey that some of us survive cancer, more of us with every year that passes.

When we pulled apart we hesitated, caught in a shared smile.

"Thank you, Maria," he said. "I'm so pleased we met."

"So am I, but we'll be blown from here to kingdom come if we don't climb down. Come on."

This time John took my hand, and he led me with care down the path. We leaned into the hillside to gain a little shelter from the raucous elements. A short distance from the flat I slipped on a lichen-covered outcrop but he was quick to grab me and I remained upright.

As we retraced the original path, John muttered something that I couldn't quite hear.

"Sorry. What did you say?"

"Nothing much. I was wishing out loud that I could find a dry place to use my phone. Now that I know what I'm going to do."

"You're in luck. There's a barn not fifty yards from here. You can't see it from the path, but I'll show you."

He stopped stock-still, and frowned.

"So you were lost, were you? You knew exactly where you were.

What was all that crap about?"

I tried to make light of his question.

"Maybe I fancied you?"

For a second he looked flummoxed and then the penny dropped.

"Got it. You wanted to help, but didn't want to scare me off? You're very sharp."

"Kind of you to say. Now let me show you the way to the outbuilding. If you forgive me, I'll share my chocolate with you."

Once inside, John checked his phone for a signal. His face relaxed in relief and he started to dial.

"Helen, it's me. I'll be home by five. I need to talk to you. I think – well, I know, that there's someone who's a match for Bethan.

"Don't cry, love. There's real hope for her now.

"Yes, it is Lydia. But how did you know?

"My God, Helen, you're stronger than me. I should have told you years ago. I'm so sorry.

"I love you too. Wait at the house for me. We'll tell Bethan and Martha together and then call Dr Douglas.

"Yes, we'll go and see Mandy, Bob and Lydia, and take Martha and Bethan too. We have a lot to talk about.

"No, it won't be easy.

"I agree. We'll make it together. And Helen, I couldn't love anyone more than I love you, do you hear?

"Thank you. Thank you."

I broke my bar of Green & Black's in half, and John took the offered squares from my hand.

"Go now, don't waste any time. Whilst you were on your mobile, I wrote down my address. Please take it. One day, if it feels right, let me know how Bethan gets on?"

"Of course I will. You made all the difference, Maria, I can't tell you."

"Away with you, you helped me too. Very much, as it happens. So long, and take care."

I turned away and dashed out into the damp evening. The light was fading and I needed to get into dry clothes before my arthritis started to play up.

John

It's been the most intense time, these last three months. Lydia had her bone marrow harvested and she bore up well, as her Facebook posts show, with pictures to prove the point. As for Bethan, her courage has left us all breathless. The transplant went as planned and now she's well into her course of chemo. She smiles often and cries when she needs to, and she tries to reassure everyone that she's comfortable even when the drugs stress her young body to the limit. Dr Douglas is cautiously optimistic that Bethan will make a good recovery. The signs are all positive.

It's January now and Bethan might be discharged home in two weeks' time. We're planning to celebrate our delayed Christmas when she's back, and Mandy, Bob and Lydia will be with us for that.

My mind has been frantic, but I feel more confident now. I can dare to hope that all will be well. Last night as I drifted off to sleep I recalled my strange encounter with Maria; I wondered what I would have done if our paths hadn't crossed. The time has come to write to her, and to let her know things are going in the right direction.

Then I turned over and looked into Helen's sleeping face. She has aged as I have. Her red hair is faded and threaded with silver streaks. Her skin is etched with laughter lines and with traces of sadness; she is as familiar to me as the smell of my own body, farts and all. Inside her sleeping form, exhausted by another day at the hospital, beats the bravest and most generous heart. Bethan is her daughter all right; and also in the coven dwell Martha and Mandy and dear Lydia too. If they ever met Maria, they would recognise her as a kindred spirit. The strength of these women has overwhelmed me; words cannot express my respect for them. I know that I am more blessed than I have any right to be.

Today I'll post my letter to Maria.

Maria

One morning, as snow starts to fall, I hear the postman knock at the door of my terraced house in the Welsh village of Blaenavon. He has a fistful of letters for me. Most are catalogues that try to flog me stuff that I do not want and cannot afford. The others look important. One has a New Zealand postmark. Another is from Northumberland. It is exceptional for me to get two hand-written letters in one delivery.

I go inside, pour myself a cup of coffee from the cafetière, and sit down at my battered oak table. I debate which to open first. I close my eyes and move the envelopes around on the table in front of me. I clap my hands three times and then pick one up. It is the one from England. I slit it open with care with my father's old pearl-handled letter knife. I swallow hard before I settle to read it.

The news is good; Bethan is doing well and her family is healing too. That day near Wooler I sensed that John was a strong man who was capable of great love. It was a shame he found it so hard to have confidence in himself. But things changed for us both the day we met. I think some of the nonsense was washed out of each of us for good.

Now for the letter from Christchurch. It is not in Sam's writing; I dearly hope that all is well.

> Dear Maria,
>
> I know that we haven't met each other yet, but I'm sure we will soon. Our baby daughter, Marietta Rose, is now three weeks old. Every night since she was born Sam has talked about writing to you, but he does not know where to start. He wants to tell you that he loves you and that he needs you to see Marietta, and to meet me too. The honest letter that you wrote to him before our wedding day revealed so much. It helped him to understand that whatever happened between you and Liam, you never wanted to go out of his life. It was Liam's pain that led to that. He was also distraught to hear of your breast cancer, and mastectomy. He realised that he might have lost you a couple of years ago, before he had the chance to reach out to you again. He is very grateful that your recovery has been good.
>
> With Marietta's birth the time has come for reunions and for forgiveness. Life is too short to dwell in the past. We are lucky in that we both have good jobs. Please accept our invitation to fly out to New Zealand to stay with us for a few weeks. We would love to pay your air fare. It would give us great pleasure.
>
> In case you are wondering, Liam and Anna (his wife) are absolutely fine with this. They are very happy together and have no axes to grind. It has always felt wrong to Anna that the bridges weren't mended before now. Please let us know if you will come. Please do . . .
>
> Much love,
> Sally x
> PS Sam says that Marietta has your mouth x

I feel that I might faint with happiness. I look out of the kitchen window at the flurries of snow and watch ice crystals form on the glass. Everything seems dusted in magic as the storm intensifies; I am on the cusp of a new era. Two wild swans come into view and fly with majestic certainty across the sky, unhindered by the wind-driven snowfall.

Later the sky clears, the sun comes out and refracts with a blinding light on the whiteness. I dress up in warm clothes and my walking boots and leave the house by the back lane. I climb a good way up the valley until I can look down upon the rooftops of my old home, with its proud mining history. As I shift my gaze from the earth up to the sky, I whoop with joy, safe in the knowledge that no one can hear me and call the men in white coats.

Later in the afternoon, as the sun sets, I am back at home and I enjoy the tired well-being that comes from winter exercise. After a lie-down on my bed whilst I listen to Prokofiev's *Peter and the Wolf* (music that Sam loved as a child), I am ready for my tea, so I head for the kitchen. When I walk into the hall I catch sight of my face in the mirror. My skin glows and my eyes are bright with optimism. As I wait for my baked potato to cook, I write to John. I tell him that, against all the odds, my life is back on track too.

The Neck
ANNE GOODWIN

|||||||||||||||||||||||||||||||||||||||||||||||||||||||||||||||||||||||||||||||||||||||||||||||||||||||||||||||||||||||||||||||||||||||||||

Tamsin wakes up on her wedding day to find her neck has grown inconveniently long. First published in In the Shadow of the Red Queen *by Bridge House Publishing (2009).*

> "Craig will turn round and, OK, he's going to be shocked, but Lawrence can drop a hint you've changed."

With a nod to tradition, Tamsin and Craig elected to spend the night before their wedding apart. He moved out to take his chances on his best man's sofa; she stayed home to luxuriate in a double bed to herself, while her bridesmaid snored in the spare room.

She awoke to find herself cuddling the far edge of the mattress, as if she'd been chasing Craig's memory across the bed in her dreams, and opened her eyes to check the time. Tamsin's alarm clock was a much-loved souvenir of childhood, its face nestling in the belly of a lurid plastic clown. Most mornings it made her laugh. But not today. It was the sight of the clock she had treasured since she was eight years old that made her realise something was wrong. She shouldn't have been able to see it from Craig's side of the bed. She should have been face to face with the LCD of her husband-to-be's clock radio. But while her body had strayed over to Craig's side of the bed, her head had been left behind with the kitsch alarm on her own side, a whole pillow-length away.

Her first thought was to call out to Craig, who was rather adept at fixing things, until she remembered he'd be sleeping off his hangover at Lawrence's place. She didn't want to face Donna just yet, so she kept quiet – apart from a whimper too soft to penetrate the partition wall – while she tried to assess the situation.

Gingerly, she reached up to touch her collarbone. Reassured by its solidity, she ventured further, cradling her neck with her palm and gradually unbending her arm. It was more or less straight when she ran out of neck and bumped into her chin.

Think positive, she told herself. Your neck might have grown as long as your arm, but at least it's still doing its job of keeping your head attached to your body. It could be worse. Much worse.

It could be better, though, she thought. If her head and her body were going to go their separate ways, they could at least have waited until after the wedding. Until she'd had what her gran always said would be the happiest day of her life. Her eyes filled with tears. However much she stretched, she couldn't reach to wipe them. She had to wait for the tears to roll down her cheeks and catch them with her tongue.

Something would have to be done. She pushed the duvet up to her chin and screeched at the partition wall: "Donna! Get your arse in here! We've got an emergency!"

Tamsin waited until Donna was in position, standing expectantly in her baggy T-shirt with her hair sticking out from her head at odd angles and yesterday's mascara smudged around her eyes. Then she kicked off the duvet to reveal the giraffe neck she had grown overnight.

Donna sprang back. "Tamsin, you're a freak!"

One thing I've always admired about Donna, Tamsin thought. She tells it like it is. She found it strangely reassuring. She flapped her arm in the general direction of her bedside table. "Pass me my mobile! I need Craig."

Donna loitered in the doorway, holding back as if afraid elongated necks might be contagious. "It's a trick, isn't it? Like on those magic shows when some bimbo gets sawn in half."

Tamsin was laboriously shuffling her body along towards the side of the bed where her head was. If it was a trick she certainly wasn't in on it. "I want Craig!"

Donna swallowed hard and drew nearer. She knelt beside her friend's bed as if preparing to say her prayers. "Better not. It's bad luck for the bride and groom to see each other before the wedding."

"There's not going to be a wedding. I'll probably be dead by the end of the day."

"Such a drama queen! It's just nerves. You'll be OK in a little while."

"You were the one who called me a freak."

Donna took her hand. "That was just the initial shock. Now I've got used to it, I think you look rather chic."

"But it's not natural, is it?"

"I wouldn't know."

"How many people have you seen walking around with a neck like this? Humans, I mean. It's all very well when I'm lying down but what's going to happen when I try to get up? How do I know my head isn't going to fall off?"

Donna stood up and walked round to Craig's side of the bed. "If we can find out how it got like this, we can put it back. Perhaps your neck's like a spring that's just stretched itself too much. Like one of those old-fashioned toys. A jack-in-the-box or whatever." She climbed onto the bed and put her hands on the top of Tamsin's head, one at each side. "If I can just swivel it into place . . ."

"Ouch!" Tamsin's head remained on the pillow, an arm's length away from her shoulders. "You're making it worse. And I need to pee."

Donna stopped pushing. "Maybe it'll go back itself when it's ready."

Tamsin hoped she was right. But now the pressure on her bladder was the main thing on her mind. "If I stay here any longer I'm going to wet myself."

"It might be risky to move."

"I'll have to. I'm desperate."

"I could bring you the washing-up bowl to pee in. Like in hospitals."

Tamsin wasn't having that. Not on what was supposed to be her wedding day. "You hold my head steady and I'll shuffle along on my knees."

Tamsin had grown tall, freakishly tall. Even on her knees she was taller than her friend. Donna had to raise her arms to support Tamsin's head. They edged across the hallway, their caution giving way to laughter as they realised the bizarre arrangement could actually work. Tamsin even had to stop for a moment and cross her legs, which isn't easy from a kneeling position.

In the bathroom, Tamsin crouched on the toilet seat. She wasn't embarrassed to use the loo with her friend alongside her, supporting her head; hadn't she had to do as much for Donna many a time after a drunken night out on the town? And it was such a relief not to have to pee in a washing-up bowl in bed.

But there were other indignities to come. She attempted to clean her teeth by holding on to her toothbrush at the very end – which was the only way for the bristles to reach her molars – but it didn't give her enough control to do more than tickle her gums. She'd have to go back to the toddler stage and let Donna take over.

"I can't hold your head and do your teeth," said Donna. "You'll have to lie on the floor."

"No chance!"

"You'll have to. I've only got one pair of hands. And it's bloody tiring keeping my arms up like this."

Furious, Tamsin jerked away. "Tell you what, why don't we swap places? Why don't you have the giraffe neck and I'll stop your head from falling off? See how bloody tiring you find that."

Donna grabbed Tamsin's head. "Don't do that! Of course I don't mind holding you."

It was only now that Donna had taken hold of her again, that Tamsin realised her head had been momentarily unsupported. And it hadn't dropped off. Indeed, she hadn't noticed any difference. "Don't you see? My neck can support itself." She pulled away.

Donna held on. "That was just for a split second. It might not be safe to do it for longer."

Tamsin was determined to recapture that moment of independence. "It's my head. Just let go!"

"If that's what you want." Donna released the pressure but kept her hands at each side of Tamsin's head, ready to catch it if it should wobble.

Tamsin flexed her neck. Her head moved gracefully at the far end. Like a swan. Feeling more adventurous, she toddled around the bathroom on her knees, with Donna close behind like the parent of a child learning to ride a bicycle. "It feels fine. It's just like a normal neck, only longer." She tilted it forward about thirty degrees, and was able to touch her cheek without straining. "I think I can do my own teeth."

Donna's hands hovered around Tamsin's head as she scrubbed away at the overnight build-up of plaque. Never had supermarket own-brand toothpaste tasted so refreshing. Such was her joy at so simple an activity, she could have been in an advert.

She spat. A splodge of white landed on the hot tap.

"You just need more target practice," said Donna.

Tamsin turned to give her friend a hug. She had to wrap her arms around Donna's legs rather than her chest, but it meant the same. "I think it's going to be OK."

Donna cuddled Tamsin's neck. "Of course it is, you idiot."

"Now leave me alone. I want to have a shower in private."

Once Donna had gone to make the coffee, Tamsin felt her

vulnerability return like an autumn chill. But it was exciting, too, to be alone again. She stepped into the cubicle and turned on the water.

Her head towered above the shower-spray, but there was still plenty of space between it and the ceiling. It wouldn't be easy to wash her hair, but she didn't have to. She had a hairdresser's appointment at ten thirty.

Now that she knew her neck could bend without breaking, things didn't feel so bad. If her neck should give way, she could catch her head herself once it reached the appropriate angle. She sang as she soaped her body, one of those old songs her gran liked about getting married in a smoochy chapel. She refused to think about her own wedding, however. She refused to think beyond her hair appointment at ten thirty.

She dried herself briskly, marvelling at how quickly she seemed to have adapted to her new shape, although she still felt safer on her knees. She pulled on the cotton robe she kept on the hook on the bathroom door and shuffled along to the kitchen.

Donna sat at the breakfast bar, turning the pages of the local free newspaper. "OK?"

"Will be when I've had some coffee."

"Sit down." Donna indicated the sunshine-yellow beanbag that she must have dragged from the spare room to the kitchen. She poured coffee from the cafetière into two hand-painted mugs.

It felt good to get the pressure off her knees. Sunk into the old beanbag, Tamsin now found herself looking up to Donna on the high stool. She wondered if they'd ever be on the same level again.

"Listen," said Donna. "I've called Lawrence and we've agreed –"

"What? I'm the one who should tell Craig."

"No one's told Craig anything. Can't the bridesmaid and the best man have a confab to decide what to do?"

"So what did you two great minds decide?"

"We should carry on getting ready. Then, if your neck shrinks back into place we'll be all set for the wedding. If it doesn't, we'll cancel."

Tamsin bent to sip her coffee. She waited for the caffeine to do its thing and put her mind straight. It didn't. Instead she missed her mouth and the coffee dribbled down her chin.

"You'd find it easier with a straw," said Donna.

"I think there's some in the cutlery drawer."

Donna riffled through the drawer and plonked a bendy party straw in Tamsin's mug. Tamsin sipped. She was lucky to have a friend like Donna, someone who would attend to her needs even before she recognised them herself. But was she right about the wedding? Surely it would be better to cancel now rather than wait till the last minute? "What about all those people? Some of Craig's family are coming from Scotland."

"Then they'll already have set off, won't they? Think about it, Tamsin. People are going to be disappointed anyway, whether we cancel now or at half past three. But the longer we leave it the more chance there is we won't have to. I'm pretty sure your neck will go back to normal before long."

"I'd better warn Craig, though."

"No! You don't want to bring any more bad luck on yourself. Just leave it to Lawrence, OK?"

Tamsin shrugged. She wondered if it looked daft with her shoulders so far away from her head. She didn't care. "You'd better go and have your shower. My dad'll be here soon to take us to the hairdresser's."

Alone again, Tamsin pondered the sensation of drinking hot liquid through a straw. How different it felt from drinking orange juice or Coke or Bacardi Breezers. She thought about this because she didn't want to think about the fact that today might not be her wedding day.

When the entryphone buzzed, she jumped. She shifted her weight onto her knees and lumbered out into the hallway to pick up.

"You took your time." Her mother's voice. Anxious. Resentful. Just what Tamsin needed that morning. Not. "You haven't just got up, have you?"

"We've been up ages, actually."

"Aren't you going to let us in?"

Tamsin wished Donna would hurry up in the shower. "I need to tell you something first."

"What is it?"

"We might have to cancel."

Her mother gasped. "I said it was irresponsible to have his stag night right before the wedding."

"It's not Craig. It's me."

"If you've changed your mind . . ."

"Of course I haven't."

A grumble of static and then her dad's voice. "Listen, love, whatever's happened we're on your side. Just let us come up and discuss it face to face."

You'll be lucky, thought Tamsin as she pressed the button on the entryphone. She opened the front door to the flat and waited, listening to the footfalls of her parents ascending the stairs. She watched as their expressions flipped from mild irritation to horror. Then confusion, as if their brains refused to register what their eyes could plainly see. She knelt in her cotton bathrobe with her hand on the doorknob, watching them watching her. Watching them trying to decipher how this strange creature could possibly be related to them. As, in her turn, she had many a time wondered how this pair of ancient hippies with their floppy hair and floppy clothes could have any connection to her.

"What on earth . . . ?" said her mother, dropping her canvas shoulder bag onto the carpet and kneeling down to hug her.

Her dad quietly closed the flat door. He scratched his beard. "What have you taken?"

"Nothing. Unless you mean two glasses of wine and a pepperoni pizza."

"Put some clothes on," he said. "We're going to A&E."

"I'm fine, honestly. It just looks strange."

"Nevertheless, we'd better get you checked out."

"Donna said it would go back of its own accord when it's ready."

Her mother unwrapped herself from the embrace and stood up to meet her daughter eye to eye. "Donna? What did she give you?"

"I told you. I haven't taken anything. I don't do drugs these days."

"Where is Donna, anyway?" said her father.

"She's in the shower."

Her dad shook his head. "How could she leave you on your own in this state? Anything could happen."

"Well we're here now." Her mother bent down to take her hand. "Let's get you dressed and Dad can drive us to A&E."

Tamsin pulled her hand away. "There isn't time. We're supposed to be at the hairdresser's in half an hour."

"Love," said her mother, "you don't think we can still have the wedding? You're in no fit state."

"Not right now. But at half past three I might be. Donna and Lawrence thought we should keep on with the preparations, in case my neck goes back to normal."

"Donna and Lawrence don't always know what's best, darling," said her mother.

"Better be on the safe side, eh?" said her dad.

Tamsin had had enough. They were treating her like a little kid. "What do you care if I miss my wedding? You never wanted me to get married anyway. You'll both be glad if I'm stuck at the hospital all day." She burst into tears.

Her dad blinked hard. "Tamsin, precious, I know you were looking forward to it. But surely your health's more important than a wedding?"

Tamsin took some consolation from the fact that now she'd figured out how to flex her neck she could manage to wipe away her tears. But not much. "You'll just be relieved at not having to stand up and make a speech." She turned away and glowered at her mother. Looked her up and down from the mop of grey hair that had never been properly styled, through her shapeless but comfy kaftan to her chiropody-friendly sandals. "And you, you'll be glad to get out of wearing that mother-of-the-bride outfit you've been moaning about."

Her mother winced and turned to her dad. "Howard, have you any idea what this is about?"

"It's the stress talking," said her dad. "Take no notice."

Tamsin felt the rage burning in her chest. She felt it shoot right the way up her long neck to her mouth. "How dare you! I'm going to have my dream wedding whether you like it or not. I'm going to have a wedding like Gran had."

"Shhh, precious, course you are. As soon as the doctor gives you the all-clear."

"Like Gran?" said her mother. "Who does she mean?"

"Gran! Your mother."

"You're modelling your wedding day on my mother's?"

"Why not? With you two so anti-marriage you didn't even get hitched in a registry office, what else did I have to go by? You've seen those black-and-white photos. I want a perfect day like she had."

Her dad reached out to take her mother's hand. Tamsin refused to notice.

"Perfect day?" said her mother. "She told you it was a perfect day? She was fourteen weeks pregnant. Your granddad had to be frogmarched to the altar. And he never forgave her, nor she him. Forty years of arguments. Until he died. Don't tell me that's what you're looking for from marriage, Tamsin."

"You're making it up. Trying to put me off again."

"I know that my birthday falls just over four months after her wedding anniversary."

"But she was always telling me what a wonderful day it was. Why would she lie to me?"

Her mother stroked her cheek. "You know what an old romantic your gran is. She blots out anything that doesn't fit with her fairy-tale fantasies."

There are lots of ways of blotting out the truth, Tamsin thought. She noticed now how heavy her head felt, how tired her neck muscles were with the effort of supporting it. It wasn't going to get back to normal for half past three. Perhaps it never would.

"Hey, what are you all doing skulking in the hallway?" Donna, pink from the shower, her voice way too bright, like a full-beam headlamp on a busy road. "Would you like a coffee before we set off for the hairdresser's?"

"There's no point in going to the hairdresser's." Tamsin's voice was like a solitary birthday-cake candle too feeble to stay alight. "There's not going to be a wedding."

"Let's see what they say at A&E, shall we?" said her dad.

"Whatever."

"Let's have coffee first," said her mother.

Her dad stroked his beard. "But the sooner we get there –"

"I'd really appreciate a cup of coffee, Donna," said Tamsin's mother.

They squeezed into the kitchen. Tamsin flopped onto her beanbag and rested her head against the wall. Her parents perched on the high stools at the breakfast bar while Donna filled the kettle. "Don't you think she looks kind of elegant? Like one of those Cluedo pieces."

"Or those tribal women with rings round their necks," said Tamsin's dad.

Tamsin's mother scowled at him. She turned to her daughter. "Why did you want to get married?"

Tamsin stared down at her engagement ring. At this distance the diamond appeared small and insignificant.

Donna spooned coffee into the cafetière. "What a question! She's in love, of course."

"Maybe," said Tamsin's mother, "but why are you young women so obsessed with marriage? My generation considered it bourgeois. Patriarchal. We felt it our duty to rebel. Whereas you lot are prepared to bankrupt yourselves for the perfect white wedding. It baffles me."

Donna laid out the mugs on the breakfast bar. "Maybe we're just shallow. All we want is an excuse for a party."

"No one liked to party as much as we did."

"I suppose you'd say we've been ruined by celebrity culture," said Donna. "All fighting for our fifteen minutes of fame."

Tamsin's mother poured the coffee. "You could still have that, Tamsin, if that's what you want. What the hell, let's have the bloody wedding. You can go to A&E when it's over."

"That's what I said," said Donna. "Her neck will probably be back to normal by half past three."

"It's not going to go back to normal, is it?" said Tamsin. "I'm going to be a freak for the rest of my life."

"Let's just get it checked out," said her dad.

"You've been planning this wedding for months," said her mother. "Why give it up just because your neck's got longer?"

"It's going to look great on the photos," said Tamsin.

"Talk some sense into her, Howard," said her mother.

Her dad stirred his coffee. "Remember when you were a little girl and you lost your two front teeth just before your birthday party? Remember what I told you then?"

"I'm grown-up now. I don't believe in the tooth fairy."

"Remember what I said?"

Tamsin sighed. "That it's not what's on the outside that counts, it's what's on the inside. And that whatever I looked like to others, to you I'd always be one of the two most beautiful people in the world. But you're my dad, you've got to say that. What's Craig going to think when he sees me?"

"If he loves you, he'll think exactly the same as me and your mother."

"It's a lot to ask," said Tamsin. "If I could meet up with him first –"

"It's bad luck," said Donna.

"If he loves you," said her dad.

"And you love him," said her mother.

"Oh, Tamsin, let's go for it," said Donna. "It'll be so romantic. You'll walk down the aisle in that gorgeous white dress. Craig will turn round and, OK, he's going to be shocked, but Lawrence can drop him a hint that you've changed. He'll look up into your eyes and you'll know, the way he looks at you at that point, you'll know for certain he's going to love you for the rest of your life."

"What do you think, darling? It's almost worth the fuss of a wedding to find that out."

"OK," said Tamsin. "On one condition."

"What?"

"You're going to have to help me practise walking. I'm not going down the aisle in a five-hundred-pound dress on my knees."

They were late for their hair appointments. Donna went ahead to explain, while her dad helped Tamsin out of the car.

The salon staff took the cushions from the sofas in the waiting area and piled them up on the floor so that her head was at the right height for the hairdresser to work on. In the mirror, Tamsin could see the other customers ogling her, but with Donna on one side and her mother – having unexpectedly volunteered for her first professional haircut in years – on the other to intercept any hurtful remarks, she was able to brazen it out. "Isn't it exciting?" said Donna each time someone new came into the salon. "She's getting married this afternoon." When Tamsin got up from the cushions with her tiara in place they gave her a round of applause.

By the time Donna had done her make-up and she'd mastered walking in her satin shoes – remembering to duck to go through doorways – Tamsin was looking forward to the ceremony. Her neck was still as long as it had been when she'd woken up that morning with her head and body on opposite sides of the bed, but when her bridesmaid zipped up her dress at the back she knew she was beautiful.

The guests were seated in rows in the ballroom when their taxi pulled up at the hotel. Tamsin held her dad's arm and Donna stood behind holding the train of her magnificent dress, while the photographer experimented with different angles to fit them all in the frame. She looked down at her dad in his hired suit and beamed.

The registrar and her assistant stood at the front of the hall. Facing them, with their backs to the guests, Craig and Lawrence waited. They must have heard the gasp as the bride stepped into the room, but whether this was at the radiance of her smile, or the splendour of her dress, or the length of the neck between them, they were in no position to judge.

Towering above the gawping guests, Tamsin didn't flinch at the flashes of horror and disgust that their faces couldn't help but betray. It was natural that people should recoil initially at her extraordinary appearance. She smiled in encouragement as they settled their expressions into something more befitting the solemnity of the occasion.

The wedding march was approaching the climax that would take her to Craig. Like everyone else, he'd be disturbed by her transformation, but Tamsin prayed he'd recognise the woman he loved underneath.

Two opposing memories played in her mind: Craig's joy when she surprised him at his office at the end of a frustrating day; his rage when she drove his car into a gatepost. Love and hate; both were within Craig's repertoire. Mostly, he had shown her love, but now? And for the rest of their lives?

Lawrence edged towards the vacant seat alongside Craig's mother on the front row. Tamsin's dad slipped his arm from hers and motioned her forward, making for his seat next to her mother.

The registrar smiled. Tamsin stood at the front beside her husband-to-be. The music stopped. She felt Craig's hand reach for hers.

Holding her breath, Tamsin looked down at Craig. She saw him raise his eyes, tip back his head and step away until he could take in her full height. She watched his face crumple in revulsion. His feet in their shiny brogues took another step away.

She allowed herself to exhale. So now she knew: the man who was supposed to give her the perfect marriage cared more for looks than personality. Better to find out when there was still the chance to say "I don't" than two pregnancies later when some pert eighteen-year-old grabbed him by the midlife crisis.

The groom turned towards the best man. The registrar lowered her book of promises. Donna's hand touched Tamsin's shoulder.

She thrust her bouquet at her bridesmaid, and stepped towards Craig. She chucked his chin, yanked it upwards, forcing him to look. When their eyes met, she kept on pushing, tilting his neck back as far as it would go. And still she kept pushing at his chin, pressing her fist hard against his lower jaw. Pushing with all her strength until, little by little, his neck began to grow.

The One That Got Away
CRIS DE BORJA

IIIIIIIIIIIIIIIIIIIIIIIIIIIIIIIIIIIIIIIIIIIIIIIIIIIIIIIIIIIIIIIIIIIIIIIIIIIIIIIIIIIIIIIIIIIIIIIIIIIIIIIIIIIIIIIIIIIIIIIIIIIIIIIIIIIIIIIIIIIIIIIIIIIIIIIIIIIIIIIIIIIIIIIIIIIIIIIIIIIIIIIIIIIIIIIII

A noir flash about a detective hunted down by a widowed femme fatale.

> "She took three steps
> closer. She used
> that walk the way
> a hypnotist uses a
> gold watch."

E mergency lights painted her dead face in flashing white and amber. She didn't look innocent in death. She didn't look like she was sleeping. Rivulets of polluted salt water dribbled out of her hair.

Her name had been a sweetness, like brown-sugar syrup: Marlena Robles. I had known the flavour of it poured over my tongue. The bitter aftertaste of her was against my teeth even as I sat there watching, still dripping cold water myself beneath a disposable blanket. She had a poison under that sweetness. She had a husband, too.

I didn't like the way the case ended. The facts laid themselves out in a neat path to one conclusion that I couldn't disprove, that Leon "The Lion" Robles came to his end by suicide. My gut feeling said different. Beautiful women get away with murder all the time, and this time it was literal.

Maybe he deserved to be murdered. His business hurt a lot of people. Maybe the truth didn't matter so much this time, but that didn't stop my brain from spinning like a carnival ride over Marlena's grieving-widow act. I took a walk along the water to clear my head. I watched the faded white sun quench in the cold waters of the harbour, smelled the fog come rolling in. Wished I hadn't given up smoking. Wished – only for a minute – that I was still a guy who did his thinking in the company of other drunks.

A jaundiced lamp flickered on the back of a warehouse, attracting winged vermin. Its illumination was probably the only reason the old payphone under it still had a handset attached. The blaze of lights over the few cars left in the parking lot would make anyone night-blind. They only made the shadows darker.

I walked out onto the dock. Kids who didn't know better and old folks who didn't care fished off the pier during the daylight hours. They had all gone home. It was dinner time for decent people. After the early sunset of winter it got cold by the water. The tide was in. I could hear the waves, hidden by the mist, slapping at the wharf.

I was turning to leave for friendlier digs when the candy-store scent of her perfume found its way to my nose. Her diamonds winked in the sulphur light. The gun in her hand gave off a sassy shine, too. She had a soft step in those tight leather boots.

"Hello, Tommy," she said. She was as cool as the fog.

"Marlena," I said.

"The way you say my name, Tommy, it sounds like you miss me." She glanced around. "What dark and lonely places you pick to brood. I suppose the gloom suits you?"

"Conveniently dark for you, it seems." I backed up one more step. "Put that noisemaker away, sweetheart. You don't know how to use a firearm."

She took three steps closer, each of them swaying her hips like a pendulum. She used that walk the way a hypnotist uses a gold watch. "Oh, Tommy," she sighed. "I wouldn't do this if I didn't have to."

"Like the way you had to murder your husband?" I asked.

She stiffened. "Leon had it coming."

"Was it for the money, Marlena? Or –"

She interrupted. "Or did he find out about us?" She spread a smile across her plum-painted lips. "It wasn't you, Tommy. But Leon was going to leave me. He was going to leave me with nothing."

"You could have fought that in front of a judge."

"I was tired of hearing the lion roar," she said. "Isn't it a laugh, that he hired you to provide evidence of my infidelities? Then we fell in love, didn't we?" She whispered the last across the arm's length between us.

"It ended," I said.

"No," she said. "This is how it ends." She raised the gun.

I don't know where she had gotten the gun, and I didn't care, but I could see that she didn't know how to use it. In the moment that she shifted her grip, I jumped forward. We grappled, less friendly about it than in other times. The gun spun out of her grasp, skidded over the weatherworn boards.

Marlena got away from me. I charged after her, took too many steps doing it, and went in the drink. It was the fog; I couldn't see where the boards ended.

It was a blind nightmare until a wave shoved me up against a barnacle-crusted piling. Ignoring the sting of salt water in fresh cuts, I clawed at the deck. A silhouette looked down into the water. Marlena held the gun out like a divining rod as she searched for me.

Her ankle was within my reach. I grasped it and yanked. She hardly had time to shout in surprise. Pulling her in gave me the push I needed to clamber back up to the drier side of the dock, where I heaved out the seawater swill that gasp reflex had made me swallow. The noise of splashing reminded me that Marlena was drinking up her own share of the harbour.

Getting back on my feet was a labour, but I still could not see her anywhere in the water. I couldn't tell if any of the splashing was Marlena, or if it was all waves. I stumbled over to the payphone, coughing all the way. My old coat was heavy with stinking water, but it was wool and wool will keep a body warm even when soaked through. I didn't think that Marlena's fashionable ensemble was serving her so well.

By the time the paramedics pulled her out of the harbour, the cold water had drained all her heat. There wasn't an ember left in her. She got all the attention for a while, while I got a first-aid blanket and got ignored. That was fine by me. I didn't want to be there, looking at her dead body. Being ignored made it easier to pretend I wasn't there.

A car door opened, the dinging warning of lights left on or keys left in the ignition calling my attention to turn and look. I resisted. A figure walked out of the parking-lot blaze. Walked up to me and stopped three feet away. I looked up the expensive suit to the face of Charles Magner, my client and attorney to the late Leon Robles. Seeing him here made the noise in my head, which had never really stopped, rise like a tidal wave.

He took out a silver cigarette case, selected a cancer stick, and lit it with his gold lighter while he spoke to me. "A woman like that never stops being trouble," he said. He looked across at the busy paramedics. He chuckled. "Hellcat between the sheets, wasn't she?" He took a long taste of his cigarette, savouring it like a memory.

The wave of mental noise crashed. It occurred to me that I hadn't heard Magner drive up and park. He had been in the parking lot the whole time, watching from his car.

Magner had given Marlena the gun.

He was Marlena's suspected lover, why Leon Robles hired me – a case I had to quit when I picked up a sweet tooth myself. That's why Charles Magner hired me to investigate Leon's death: he knew I couldn't see straight around Marlena Robles.

"What was in it for you, Charles? Revenge for being cuckolded yourself?"

His expression lost all mirth. "I'm a businessman," he said. "This was business. All of it." He turned to go. "Don't be fooled by sentimentality. That woman got what was coming to her."

I didn't watch him walk away. Instead I watched as Marlena was loaded into the ambulance. The doors slammed shut. One of the paramedics came over to check on me. I waved him away, pointed at a random car in the lot, and said it was mine. After they left, I started the walk home. It wasn't far: a bit past Guppie's bar, around the corner from a liquor store that stayed open late.

Once I got past those, I'd be all right.

The Place of Endurance
NOELEEN KAVANAGH

||||||||||||||||||||||||||||||||||||||||||||||||||||||||||||||||||||||||||||||||||||||||||||||||||||||||||||||||||||||||||||||||||||||||||||||||||||

A girl travels from her farming homestead to chase her dream of becoming a Guildrunner.

> "Thus I first learned of the Guild of Runners and first craved their power and status with a sharp hunger."

had never been inside a Guildhouse before. The chamber I stood in was small, with the symbols of the Guild of Runners carved on the far wall: a pair of sandals and a message tube.

I examined the carvings, the sandals with their closed leather toes and strings to bind them. When I examined the tube closely I could just make out the rune at the top. I knew that one, *faoi*, meaning enclosed, contained, secret.

I heard a sound behind me and spun around to face the man standing there.

"Candidate Ean? I am Guildmaster Tapaidh. Follow me."

He had the cropped hair of all the members of the Guild of Runners and a lean, weathered face. But he wasn't very tall, which was a relief to me. Even though I was gone fifteen years old, I was short for my age and feared it would count against me.

I followed him along the corridor until we stepped through a doorway and into a blaze of light. It dazzled me for a moment until my eyes adjusted and I could see that we were in a tiny garden, ringed around by the Guildhouse with the noonday sun above my head. It was a plain, sparse place of raked pebbles and large stones with a blue periwinkle in a grey granite tub.

A woman stepped into the garden.

"Guildmaster Crom." She introduced herself and nodded to me before turning to sit on one of the large stones before me. She was a dark-haired, dark-eyed woman of medium height and well-built, not slender as I had expected.

Guildmaster Tapaidh left my side to join her. "So, Candidate Ean," he said, as he settled himself next to Guildmaster Crom. I felt exposed, scrutinised.

"I have no money to pay the apprenticeship fee, Guildmasters."

"We know that," said Guildmaster Crom.

I blushed bright red. Of course they knew. I had already explained to the doorman of the Guild who barred my way when I first arrived at the Guildhouse and again to the woman he called to deal with me.

"So you wish to join the Guild of Runners. Why is that?" she continued, her eyebrow raised as if to say, Why would the likes of you be good enough to come among the likes of us?

"I have always wanted this, since I was a child, Guildmaster Crom."

Ever since I had first seen a Guildrunner. We were all gathered at the manse back home on Gale Day to pay the rents when I saw a tall, slim figure in grey running up the avenue, her sandals kicking up tiny puffs of dust. People drew back before her and the lord of the manse himself came down to take the message tube from her hands.

All the way from Inis, they said, an unimaginably long distance. She would run back again that evening with just a handful of herbs to sustain her. All by herself, too, with none for company or protection.

But who would dare to raise a hand to a member of the Guild of Runners? They would be spurned by the Guild, left with no one to deliver their messages and letters, bills of lading and contracts, wills, notarisations or letters of authority. Or they would be hunted down and wiped out for such a crime. No lord would suffer such a crime in their lands, and the Guild of Merchants would not countenance it and risk angering the Guild of Runners. So the housekeeper at the manse explained with an air of great authority. Thus I first learned of the Guild of Runners and first craved their power and status with a sharp hunger.

But I did not have the ability to explain this to the grave-faced woman before me. I have never had a way with words and she would think me unworthy of joining the Guild if I exposed my true nature to her.

"Always is a long time, child."

"Since I was very young, Guildmaster, maybe six or seven years old."

"You're not from Inis," said Guildmaster Tapaidh. It was a statement, not a question. My accent marked me as being from well beyond the boundaries of the city, a peasant from the backhills. If I kept my mouth shut, I could pass for a local, but even I could not live my life in silence.

"No, Guildmaster, from Clappa." They both looked blank at that. "West of here, a village in the foothills of Cnoc Ru. My mother has a holding in the lands of Lord Dli." A small, windswept place of furze and flocks of sheep scattered along the flanks of the mountains.

"Can you read or write, Candidate Ean?"

"No, Guildmaster, not past the Forty-Nine Basic Runes." Much as I wished to, I could not lie. It would be too easy to expose me in it.

In winter, when the cold winds swept down from Cnoc Ru and animals and people gathered indoors, that was when Master Eolais arrived. Every year he came without fail, with his cane and books to beat the Forty-Nine Runes into our heads. His food and lodging was shared among the village and when spring came, he went on his way again with neither sight nor sound of book nor rune for us till winter swooped around again.

"The Basic Runes. That was more than I knew when I arrived here," said Guildmaster Tapaidh.

"Tattooed and feral from the docks." Guildmaster Crom smiled at him, sharing a private joke, forgetting for a moment that I was there and thus excluding me.

"Do you have a parent or guardian with you, Candidate Ean?"

"No."

"No? How did you get here, then?"

"I asked my mother's permission and she gave me leave to go."

That was not exactly true, but I wished to sound filial in front of the Guildmasters. In actual fact, I had told my mother that I was leaving for the city to join the Guild of Runners and she raised no objection. I had six older brothers and sisters, labour enough to manage the spring planting without hiring help. There was work to be done without losing time fretting about whatever mad notion the youngest child had taken into her head.

But she did not leave me go empty-handed. She wrapped up food enough for four days in a clean cloth, gave me two silver pennies for my journey and sent me off with her second cousin in his oxcart. It took me five days, but eventually I made my way to the Guildhouse.

"The desire in her is strong, Crom."

"Aye, but desire alone is not enough."

"We have need of Guildsisters."

"Aye, true enough. Men for the short run and women for the long." They both laughed out loud at that. Another thing that I did not understand.

"But the fee?"

"Aye, the fee," said Guildmaster Tapaidh. They grew silent and grave and my stomach clenched in fear.

"The Candidate Race?"

"Fair is fair. The Candidate Race it is, then."

Guildmaster Crom turned back to me. "Very well, Candidate Ean. You are hereby invited to take part in the Candidate Race in two days' time. Should you do well enough in the Candidate Race, we will consider waiving your apprentice fee. Is that acceptable to you?"

I nodded. "Yes, Guildmaster."

"In the meantime, you are welcome to stay in the Guildhouse, if you should so desire it. As a guest of the Guild," said Guildmaster Tapaidh.

That was a relief, for all my food and one of my silver pennies were long gone getting this far.

* * *

"So the Candidate Race it is, then? There'll be a good turnout for that. Always is."

I looked down at Guildsman Eochair's bald head as he adjusted the straps on my running sandals. They looked and felt fine to me but he'd spent the last while making minute alterations and talking without pause.

"They have to be just so, just so, otherwise you'll be crippled with blisters before you've run ten sli. Is that not so?" He had no need of answers from me and kept talking. "Keep these on, now, all day until the day of the race. Don't take them off. You'll have to break them in. Of course, it takes months to break in a pair of running sandals properly, but these aren't new to begin with, so it'll probably be all right. But don't go taking them off. Except at night when you have to sleep, of course."

He smiled up at me. "Now, let's see what they're like."

I stretched my legs out before me and pointed my feet. My feet with Guild sandals on them! My heart leaped in my chest with pride and joy.

Guildsman Eochair was watching me and I lowered my eyes in shame that he might have seen the pride painted clearly on my face.

"Walk up and down there for me so I can see how they fit. Tell me if they rub or pinch at all. A pair of Guild sandals should fit like your own skin, is that not so?"

I walked as he bid me, my feet feeling strange and enclosed.

"Run on the spot for me." He circled me as I did so, his eyes fixed on my feet.

"You run high on your feet. Sit back down and I'll adjust them." He knelt before me once more.

"They should be fine now." He stood up slowly, stiffly, one leg at a time, about to leave. About to leave and still I knew almost nothing about the Candidate Race. My panic gave me a desperate burst of courage.

"Master Guildsman, what is the Candidate Race? What must I do? I have no apprenticeship fee."

"Nothing at all?"

"I have a silver penny."

He smiled at that and sat back down on a little, rough wooden stool opposite me. "Not many silver pennies to be found on Cnoc Ru. There never was."

"Guildsman?"

"The mountains make good runners. I should know. Wasn't I one of them?" He laughed out loud at the shock on my face. "Years since I've been back there, though, and all those belonged to me dead now." He turned back to me. "With no apprenticeship fee, you'll have to win the Candidate Race, or as near as makes no difference."

He bent down and started to pick up the running sandals and leather thongs that lay scattered on the floor. "Listen well now, girl, for this is what I myself have learned to be true."

He laid the thongs out on his knee as he talked, in order of thickness, adjusting and straightening them all the while.

"The breath is the basis of all runs. Slow and steady and let the legs keep pace with it. If you outrun your breath, then you can never endure."

He looked up at me to check if I'd understood. I did not, but he continued anyway.

"If you can keep your breathing steady, you will eventually become rooted to the earth and reach the place of endurance. A run is breath and mind and above all a prayer to the Mother."

He smiled and stood up, ruffling my hair as he left. "Good luck, girl. May the Mother listen to your prayer."

And that was all he said. Breath, endurance, prayer. How would that help me win the race? I sat a while, thinking and admiring my sandals, coming no closer to any manner of answer, till my hunger drove me to the kitchens.

There was a jostling pack of people at the starting line, families and friends, well-wishers and the curious. So many people with their loud city voices and self-important airs, all jumbled up together. I tried to edge my way to the front but there were too many people to walk between or around.

My grey tunic was well-worn and soft. I wondered how many previous aspirants had run in this tunic. I looked around me at the other candidates. Some were tall enough to be adults, surely. Others had family members who were in the Guild of Runners huddled around them, giving advice, no doubt, about how to win the race. How to keep ahead of the likes of me.

I caught a glimpse of Guildsman Eochair's bald head in the distance. I wanted to wave at him, but he was busy talking to his Guildbrothers and sisters. I heard the beat of a small drum and the candidates moved in its direction. Not knowing what else to do, I followed them.

There was silence then, everyone waiting, still. The drum beat once more, a sharp triple rap and we set off, a jockeying flock, shoulder to shoulder, our sandals striking the cobbled street at the front of the Guildhouse. The morning sun was bright on the wet cobblestones. A red flag fluttered high on a pole. I had to keep them to my left and follow them as far as they went.

Short steps, long steps, short steps. It was impossible to run in such a crowd, other candidates all around me and the people of the city going about their business in droves as if the race was nothing of any importance.

We ran into the shadow of the old city wall, through a narrow dark gate cut in it, running from shadow into light. A red flag rippled to my left and the highroad stretched before me, straight as an arrow, on a causeway above the fields and paddies. The crowd of runners thinned then, scattered and stretched out in knots and huddles like beads pulled from a string. There was room enough here to run, my stride lengthening, expanding, eating up the road.

I passed copses of trees and people bent to their work in the fields; a black and white dog that sat, tongue lolling, watching me as I ran past. Candidates ahead of me, candidates behind me and the red flags always to my left. Six flags passed but I did not how many were left. There were so many other runners ahead of me, so many. One of them would win and I would have to return to Clappa in shame, rejected by the Guild.

Fear pushed and buffeted me and I picked up my speed. I ran in fury and rage. It was mine. They would not take this from me. I would run past them all and come in triumph to the Guildhouse. Then they would see. They would see that I was worthy and accept me. They could not turn their faces from me then.

I ran faster, past the fluttering red flags. Other candidates were far ahead of me, running as the sun shimmered on the road. I pushed myself harder still. The sun beat on the anvil of my head. Sweat dripped down my face. Ran into my eyes and stung. My legs trembled and my shoulders ached. My breath was harsh and dry in my mouth. It burned in my lungs. Stabbed me in the side. Then it struck me. The pain was a mountain I could not climb. I could not maintain this pace. Desire was not enough. I was alone. I had lost. I would be left howling on the highroad, like a strayed dog.

It's all in the breath, child. Let the legs follow the breath.

I remembered what Guildsman Eochair had said. He had been kind to me and I had no other advice to follow, so I calmed and steadied myself, breathing all the while. *In, out, in, out, in, out.* As I breathed, I ran more slowly, keeping pace with my breath. *In, out, in, out, in, out.* And as I ran I prayed, always the same prayer. *May the Guild accept me, may the Guild accept me, may the Guild accept me.* Breath and blood, lungs and heart, arms and legs and above it all, my prayer, all pounding in time, a steady rhythm like the Year's Turn drums that beat all night.

The world shrank to breath and prayer, a steady pulse like the beat of a living heart and I ran in time to it. I gazed inward, felt the breath of the Mother flow through me, felt the earth pulse beneath my feet as I ran to its eternal rhythm. I breathed and was the breath in the nostrils of the Mother.

All my desires fell away. Childish things, I left them behind in the dust of the road. To run was enough, without beginning, without end, the eternal now. Joy filled my mind, suffused my body. The landscape seemed to flow past me, distant and abstracted. I ran on and on.

Then I came to a place where there were knots and huddles of people by the side of the road, a grey, granite building to their backs, a red flag whipping in the breeze. The Mother held me lightly in the palm of her hand, her breath filling me. The road stretched before me and so I ran on.

I could hear feet hitting the road behind me. Other candidates, no doubt, but I did not care. My feet flew. I could run for ever.

"Candidate Ean, Candidate Ean."

The voice broke in, insistent, shouting, tearing me from my rhythm. The drumbeat of joy within me faltered and fell silent.

"Stop, stop. It's done. The race is over."

I could feel a trickle of sweat run down my face. Lost, gone. I would never feel such joy again. I felt like weeping in despair. Why had they not left me to run on? There was a hand on my arm.

"Candidate Ean?"

It was Guildsman Eochair and a sharp-featured Guildsister, peering into my face like half-starved dogs.

"See, I told you it was so."

"Aye, Eochair," she answered, "but you cannot blame me for doubting you."

"But you see now?"

"Surely. Clear as day."

A great wave of weariness swept over me. I stood bemused, befuddled, swaying in the dust of the road, legs trembling beneath me, tongue cleaving to the roof of my mouth, grief at what I had lost piercing me.

"She'll fall! Take her arm."

Each of them took an arm and thus supporting me brought me along the road, talking to me all the while like I was a sick child.

"Not to worry. Not far now. Only a few more yards. Almost there."

I shuffled along the road like an old woman, where once I had run. The joy was gone, leaving only pain.

"To reach the place of endurance, Eochair. And on the Candidate Race! Is it any wonder that I didn't believe you?"

"The place of endurance, untrained, unskilled." Eochair was laughing out loud to my right, his hand squeezing my arm. "Good runners from Cnoc Ru. Ha! Always has been."

Through bog and marsh, highroad and glen,
Through the valley of tears, she ran.
Death behind her, pain before her,
Grief at her shoulder, but still she ran.

Bard File

The Right of Wrong
JERRY W. CREWS

A series of astonishing revelations rock a lowly farmboy's world in this darkly comic moral tale of family politics, which culminates in the courtroom.

"Normally, I'm not the suspicious kind, but all this did get me to wondering."

When I was young we were poor but proud. At times we were too proud. Pride led my pa and ma to resist taking what was rightly theirs. They felt some sense of moral obligation to let bygones be bygones. I did not understand what motivated them to be so lackadaisical and was determined to right the wrongs against my family and to collect the just dues owed us. At the time I did not fully realise it, but I let pride dictate my actions. As it turned out, I should have left good enough alone.

My family worked and lived on a farm owned by Joshua Hawks. It was the only life I knew as my grandfather had moved there to work for Joshua's father. Grandpa and Grandma had worked there all their lives and raised a family. When they died it was passed on to their only son, my father. Pa fell in love with a young lady from a nearby town and so he and Ma made a home on Joshua's farm.

We were provided a small house at no cost and my pa was paid a meagre wage for working the corn fields. My ma kept up our little house while looking after me and my younger sister. Three times a week she would make her way to Joshua's mansion and help in the kitchen to earn a little more money for our family. In the wintertime when there were no crops in the field my pa would do errands around the farm to earn enough to get by.

Times were hard for us. Pa and Ma barely made enough to get by and there was no hope of ever improving our lives. We were considered poor white trash and the Hawks family, though never treating us harsh, was never beyond reminding us of our standing in the community. More than once I had seen Joshua and his rich buddies snicker at my pa as we passed his home on the way to the corn fields. My pa never said a word but I noticed and silently cursed the ground Joshua stood on. If it had opened up and swallowed him whole I would have danced and sung all the way home.

Joshua had one child, a son named Isaiah. He went by his nickname "Ike" and he was my age. In fact, we were born only a week apart. We were known to dislike each other and had several fist fights over the years. Finally, Joshua complained to Pa and ordered him to make me stop "whooping on his boy". Pa simply told me to stop fighting or he would take his belt to me. That was enough to get my attention and make me toe the line.

It was not the easiest thing to do when Ike made fun of my clothes and told me I smelled like a cow pasture. There was nothing I could do about my clothes but I knew I did not stink. Ma made sure I bathed every day and she worked hard washing my sister's and my clothes. They may have been ragged but they were clean.

I never understood why Ike had to act that way. He was given everything and I had practically nothing. Why did he want to try and take the little dignity I had left? The only thing I could figure was that he was just plain mean. He must have learned it by watching how his old man treated people, especially my pa and ma.

One time, after promising my pa I would no longer fight Ike, I was walking by the mansion with my sister when his poodle came charging out of the house and tried to bite us. It scared my sister and she screamed. I kicked the dog in his ribs and he went scurrying off, yelping all the way. Ike came running out of his house as mad as I had ever seen him. I tried to explain I was just protecting my sister and me from being bitten. In his anger he called my little sister a "whore". She did not know what it meant but she knew Ike was mad and was not saying anything nice. This made her cry. I had heard the word before but did not fully understand its meaning. All I knew was Ike made my sister cry. That was enough for me to punch him in the belly. He bent over in pain and said he was going to tell his father. I told him to go ahead and I would tell his pa what he called my baby sister. Even Joshua, as mean as he was, would not condone calling a little girl such a name. I never heard any more about this so I guess Ike never did say anything.

So it was and so it continued until after I had turned eighteen. That was when my world would turn upside down. I had an inclination of things to come when Joshua's aunt Mabel came to visit him one summer evening. She had not seen me since I was a baby and on this particular day I happened to be walking by as they sat in the rocking chairs on the front porch. She was busy telling Joshua something about what the county commissioners were planning to do and how it would upset all the righteous sensibilities of God-fearing people. I had no idea of what she was talking about but when I strolled by she stopped in mid-sentence. She yelled at me to come over closer.

I cautiously approached the porch and said, "Yes, ma'am?" She stared at me hard and asked, "Ike, why are you wearing those ragged old clothes?" I was about to correct her when Joshua spoke up. "Aunt Mabel, put your glasses on." She fumbled in her pocket and found her bifocals. Holding them in front of her eyes she looked me up and down then said, "He sure looks the way you did when you were younger. A fine, handsome young man, but where did he get those clothes?" I looked at Joshua but he just kept rocking in his chair and did not say anything.

"I'm not Ike. My name's Billy. I'm Billy Grayson."

She squinted even harder to study me again. After looking me up and down one more time she muttered, "So you are. So you are." As I turned to leave I saw her swat Joshua on his arm. He just shrugged and kept on rocking.

I never gave that incident much thought until later when the truth about things was revealed. Being a grown young man I became interested in young man things. I wanted to leave the farm and get a job in town but Pa and Ma were against it. They said they could not afford to take me to town every day for a job, and I guess this was true, but I suspected the real reason was they needed my help working the farm. Any work I did was less they had to do. So, I shelved any dreams I had of leaving and hunkered down and helped out.

One day when Pa and Ma had already left for the day's work I was still eating breakfast. My little sister, Madge, was busy washing the dishes my parents had left behind. I was daydreaming about something not that important and carelessly reached for my glass of milk, which I promptly spilled all over my shirt. Ignoring my sister laughing at me I cleaned it up and went to change. My other two shirts were dirty as now that I was bigger my ma expected me to do my own laundry. I wasn't quite as diligent at it as she was.

Quietly cursing to myself I hurried into my parents' bedroom in the hopes of wearing one of my pa's shirts until I got mine cleaned. In my rush I accidentally opened my ma's dresser drawer instead of my pa's. I had never had the opportunity to look at women's clothing up close before, especially their intimate garments, and was quite fascinated by all the things she had. They sure were different from the stuff us guys wore. One item particularly caught my attention. It was a skimpy black negligee. At the time I didn't think much about it, other than how fine and expensive it looked. It did seem out of place in her drawer beside her other clothes. They were all plain-looking and the negligee looked like it cost a hundred dollars.

Later in the afternoon, when I was shucking corn, I remembered something that had happened a few months earlier and it got me to thinking. Now, I'm not a peeping Tom, but I am curious. It was unusually hot one evening so I decided to go for a walk and hopefully cool down a bit. It didn't help much but as I was strolling by the Hawks' mansion I heard a noise from one of the bedrooms on the second floor. All the lights in the house were off and there was just a little light coming from the bedroom. The noise I heard was music. I like music and I didn't recognise this particular piece so I decided to investigate it a little further.

There was a big oak tree beside the house (it's still there), and so I shimmied up it and perched myself on a big limb directly across from the bedroom. I couldn't see a whole lot but I could hear the music quite well. It was a pretty tune with a good beat and I was enjoying it until I saw movement in the bedroom. I crunched down in an effort to avoid being seen and watched the shadow of a person walk past the window. It was a woman. I did get a glimpse of her backside as she walked away and, now as I was shucking corn it came to me . . . she was wearing a skimpy black negligee. Afraid of being caught I slid down the tree as fast as I could. As I was sliding I clearly heard Joshua Hawks say, "Come here, baby."

Now I was perplexed at all this. I was already having a hard time figuring out how my ma could have such an expensive piece of clothing and now I remember seeing a woman in Joshua Hawks' bedroom wearing what looked like the same negligee. The only thing I could figure was Joshua's wife, Darlene, must have bought the negligee and then gave it to ma when she got tired of it. The only problem with this reasoning was Darlene is a rather short and large woman. I'm not trying to sound cruel, but I didn't see how she could fit her body in such a small piece of clothing. Besides, the woman whose backside I saw was tall and slender. She looked more like my ma than she did Darlene. Normally, I'm not the suspicious kind, though I've become more so over the years, but all this did get me to wondering.

About a week after finding the negligee in Ma's drawer I awoke in the middle of the night. Usually I'm a sound sleeper, but it was hot and I was thirsty, so I stumbled to the kitchen to get me a drink of water. While I was standing drinking from a glass my parents' bedroom door slung open and Ma came out giggling. She was as surprised to see me as I was to see her, and I was especially surprised to see her wearing the negligee. We stared at each other for a minute and then she turned and went back to her room and closed the door. I was astounded. When I got a glimpse of her from the backside I had no doubt as to whom I had seen in Joshua Hawks' bedroom. It was my ma.

To say I was shocked and bewildered is an understatement. How could my ma do such a thing? How could she betray my pa, and with someone like Joshua Hawks? All this left me in a very bad mood, to say the least. I ignored her as much as possible. The thought of what she had done hurt too much. I could hardly bring myself to look at her, and when she spoke to me, I would respond with as few words as I could.

She took note of my attitude and let me sulk for a few days. Finally, one morning after Pa had left for the fields, she sent my sister on an errand and then turned to face me about the way I had been treating her.

"You've been awful quiet the last few days," she asserted.

"Yep."

"You want to tell me about it?" she asked.

"Nope."

She turned to the sink and picked up our big cast-iron frying pan and slammed it down on the kitchen table. It startled me so bad I almost wet my pants.

"Billy Grayson, don't you dare treat me this way!" she yelled. "I'm your mother and you will show me the respect I deserve!"

"You don't deserve no respect," I barked back at her. "At least, not in my book."

I shrank back in fear, fully expecting her to smack me upside the head, but she just stood there with the weirdest look on her face. She put the frying pan back in the sink and then sat down beside me at the table.

"Billy, what's wrong?" she asked in a kind and sweet voice. "Are you upset because you saw me the other night?"

"Yeah, I am," I replied.

"Well, son, it wasn't improper," she tried to reassure me. "You don't need to fret. I was clothed and you really didn't see anything."

"I saw more than I wanted to see," I declared.

She brushed her hair off her forehead and said, "You're eighteen now, son, you're gonna have to accept the facts of life. Your pa and me love each other and we're not ashamed to share that love with each other."

"It ain't loving Pa that you should be ashamed of," I mumbled more than said.

"What are you talking about?" she asked – I could tell she realised I knew more than she thought I did.

So, I went ahead and told her about me climbing the oak tree at the Hawks' mansion and how I had seen her in Joshua's bedroom with nothing on but the negligee. She didn't have to say anything as I could see in her eyes it was the truth. Finally, she touched my hand and offered, "There's things that happen that it's best you don't know about."

I was flabbergasted. That's all she could say? She betrays my pa and that's all she has to say? I angrily stood up and shouted, "You treat Pa that way and you think it's OK?"

"That's not what I was saying . . ."

I couldn't let her get away with this. "Don't try to explain it. I don't want to hear it. To think you had an affair with a man like Joshua Hawks, who looks down on us like we're dirt, is far more than I can deal with!"

"Billy, you don't understand –"

"Oh, I understand plenty!" I continued yelling. "I understand a man like him is gonna pay for how he's treated us. I'll see to that!"

Before she could respond I went into the living room and grabbed the shotgun. Despite her pleas I pushed by her and headed towards Hawks' house. I was determined to make things right even if it meant filling him full of buckshot. My ma went screaming out to the field to get my pa. I didn't care as wrong had been done and I was determined to set things right. On the way to the house I realised I hadn't grabbed any shells so I wasn't going to be able to shoot him, but I figured I could club him to death with the shotgun if necessary.

I marched right into the house. Joshua was in his library and I busted right through the door and pointed the shotgun at him. He eyed me over the top of his glasses and then arrogantly said, "Boy, in this house we knock before we enter a room."

"You've done disgraced my family and I'm not gonna let you get away with it!" I shouted as he slowly sat down in his rocking chair.

"And how have I done that?" he haughtily asked. I wished I had shells in the gun so I could have blasted that smug look off his face.

"Oh, you know what you've done!" I stammered. His lack of fear at having a gun pointed at him was throwing me off. I guess I had expected to see fright in his eyes and had hoped he would beg me for his life. "It's bad enough you've treated us like dirt all these years, but now I find out you've done violated my ma!"

"Treated you like dirt?" he asked in mock surprise. "Why, boy, I've done nothing but provided your family with gainful employment. I would think you should show some gratitude to me for that."

"Wow! You've got some gall, old man! You sit there all smug and everything. I know you had sex with my ma and I'm here to set things right!"

"So, that's what this is all about," he surmised as he rubbed his chin in thought.

It was at this moment my pa and ma came rushing into the room. Ma yelled my name and Pa just stood there surveying the scene. Finally, he ordered me, "Boy, put the gun down."

"I ain't doing it, Pa," I objected. "This man's gotta pay."

"What's he done?" my pa asked.

"Tell him, Ma. Tell him what this scoundrel's done!" I shouted at her.

She looked at me for the longest time. It was quite an awkward silence. Finally, my pa spoke again. "It's all right, son. Just put the gun down."

"Pa, you don't know what these two have done behind your back!" I screamed.

"Yes, I do," he said.

At first, I thought I had misunderstood him. He knew? If he did, then why wasn't he as mad as me, or even madder since it was his wife?

"Yes, I do," he repeated.

I slowly lowered the gun from pointing at Joshua. "You know?"

"He's known all along, Billy," my ma declared.

"That's right, son," my pa confirmed. "Your ma and Joshua spend some time together twice a month."

Well, to say I was shocked would not be the half of it. They'd been having a regular affair and my pa was OK with it. None of this was making any sense to me. The only thing I could think to say was, "You're gonna have to explain that one to me."

"I will, but first give me the shotgun," my pa said.

"Oh, it ain't got no shells in it," I mumbled as I was still in a state of shock.

Joshua laughed at this and asked, "How was you gonna shoot me?"

"I wasn't," I replied. "I was gonna beat you to death."

My pa took the gun out of my hand anyway just to be safe. He set it on a desk and turned back to me. "I guess you're old enough to know the truth."

"Son, I want you to know I love your pa very much," my ma interjected. I looked at her and sneered but she continued, "It's just I like Joshua, too."

"And I like your ma," declared Joshua.

"You stay out of this!" I shouted at him. "I still don't like you and may try to hurt you yet."

"Now, calm yourself, boy," my pa said. "It's OK. Your ma has certain needs and Joshua helps her with them."

"She takes care of some of my needs, too," smirked Joshua.

This was too much for me. I was tired of his attitude and so I lunged at him with the purpose of smashing his smug face into the back of his skull. My pa caught me before I could reach him and pulled me out of the way. "You can't hurt him!" he yelled at me.

"Oh, yes, I can!" I shouted back.

"No, you can't," he said a little softer. "He's your real pa."

Well, as you can imagine, this hit me in the chest like a ton of bricks. All I could do was mouth in disbelief, "My pa?"

"Yep, I'm your biological father, boy," Joshua declared.

I was in a state of denial but I flashed back to that day when I was fifteen and had been mistaken by Joshua's aunt Mabel for Ike. At the time she had told Joshua I looked exactly the way he did when he was my age. Now, what she had said came rushing back to me and I understood what she meant.

This revelation was too much for me and I slowly sank to the floor. "I'm his son?" I kept saying over and over. My ma sat down beside me and put her arm around me. "It's OK, Billy. Your pa was willing to raise you like you were his own. I know he loves you as much as if you were his."

"I surely do," agreed my pa. "As far as I'm concerned, you're my son."

Slowly my mind starting clearing itself and I was able to do a little bit of reasoning. "So, Ike and me are brothers?"

"You're half-brothers," said Joshua. I still didn't like him.

"We were going to tell you before you left home, at a time when you wouldn't get so upset about it," my ma explained. "But you had to go and see us together, so we're forced to tell you now."

I still was not thinking the best and all I could do was nod my head in agreement. After some more clouded deliberation I declared, "Well, this just ain't right. Joshua oughta be made to look after his children better than I've been looked after. Ike gets to run around in all his fancy clothes and all I've got is three sets that has to last me all year."

"That's because his mother is my wife," Joshua declared. "Your mother belongs to another man and this is what he provides for you."

His attitude was starting to get on my nerves again, so I shot back at him, "Oh, yeah, that makes perfect sense. He knows who his pa and ma is and he gets to be the rich kid."

"I didn't say I was his father," corrected Joshua. "I said his mother is my wife."

Well, he just dropped another ton of bricks on me. I stammered, "You're not? Then who is?" My pa looked down at the floor and then sheepishly replied, "I am." My emotions had already been torn ragged and now my pa was admitting to being the father of Ike. I felt like I was going to die right there in front of everybody.

"That's right, boy," Joshua smirked. "My wife and him made a son and I've been raising him like he's my own. Like I said earlier, it's that way because his mother is my wife."

I weakly said, "Pa?"

"It's OK," my ma said, trying to reassure me again. "When I'm with Joshua a couple times a month, where do you think your pa is?"

Well, I couldn't help it, I threw up right there on Joshua's fancy carpet. He started cursing at me, and so Ma and Pa escorted me outside. The fresh air helped and it wasn't long till my head starting clearing again. Finally, I looked at them and asked, "Is there anything else you want to tell me? I can't get any sicker. I ain't got nothing left on my stomach to upchuck."

"No, not really," my ma said.

We started walking home when I remembered my little sister. I turned to her and asked, "Who's Madge's pa?"

"That's me," my pa replied with a little more pride than I thought was necessary.

We walked a little further and then I looked at Ma and asked, "You are her ma, right?"

She laughed and assured me she was.

So, that was how I found out my rightful heritage and it was not long before I started plotting on how to cash in on it. Like I mentioned earlier, we were poor but we were proud. I became intent on making Joshua pay for his years of neglect and right the wrong I felt had been done me and my family. As it turned out, not only was I proud, but I was stubborn with a dash of stupidity thrown in.

A few days later Joshua and Darlene, figuring the cat was out of the bag, told Ike who his real father was. He didn't take it as good as I did. We could hear the yelling and cursing all the way down to our little house. I went outside and saw Ike storm out of the mansion and jump in his new car and tear off down the road. If I would've had a new car, or even an old car for that matter, I would've done the same thing when I found out who my real pa was.

When I went back into our house Ma was busy at the kitchen sink and Pa was reading the newspaper in his chair in the living room. I approached him and told him what I'd been thinking.

"Pa, can I talk to you about all this stuff?"

"What stuff?" he asked like he didn't know.

"Well, you know, about how we're gonna make old Joshua pay for what he did," I declared.

He looked at me real hard and put down the paper. Ma overheard me and came in the room to join us.

"I don't see where he's gotta pay for anything," my pa replied.

"Well, it seems to me he owes us something," I offered. "Most men are willing to take care of any children they father."

My pa thought for a minute and then said, "You said I was your pa. I take care of you, so, he don't owe us a thing."

"But, we've been poor all our lives," I continued. "This is a chance to make a better life for ourselves. Old Joshua can afford it. He's as rich as they come."

"It wouldn't be right," my ma declared. "That means I'd be taking money for what I did and I ain't that kind of woman."

I had to think about that for a while. It seemed like she was saying it was OK to be a slut but it was wrong to be a whore. That didn't make a lick of sense to me but I wasn't going to argue the point with her, especially with her within striking distance. Finally I said, "Well, I think he owes me."

"I don't see how," my pa asserted. "You've been my son and we've given you everything you need."

I chose my words carefully. "I know, and I appreciate it, but I could have a whole lot more if Joshua would do the right thing."

"Oh, son, be careful of swelling up with pride," my ma said as she wagged her finger at me. "You know 'pride comes before a fall'."

"Well, I think this family's got a little too much pride," I boldly declared. "Joshua owes us, he owes me, and we're too proud to do anything about it!"

"You need to show a little more respect for your ma than to say something like that," my pa bristled as Ma moved uncomfortably close to me. By uncomfortably I mean within arm's reach.

"Look here, young man," she sternly said as her voice rose to the occasion. "What I do with Joshua is mine and your pa's business. You are to stay out of it and don't try to do anything foolish! Do you hear me?"

I didn't respond to her, more out of fear than disagreement with her. There was an awkward silence and finally my pa said, "Son, I think you'd better go on and go to your room. We'll see you in the morning."

It was still light but I could see he was right. As I trudged off to my room Ma took one last parting shot. "You think about what I said. You think long and hard about it."

So, as I lay on my bed in the twilight I took her advice. She told me to not do anything foolish. The only thing foolish to me was to not do anything. It was time to put what I'd been planning into motion. I was convinced what I was going to do was the best for me and my family. The next day I was going to go to town to see a lawyer.

In the morning I left them a note and hitched a ride to town. I knew exactly the lawyer I wanted to see. He was Grover Breckinridge, a man who held a terrible hatred for Joshua Hawks. At the time, I didn't understand the origin of his hatred but I knew he was the most likely person to help me get my just dues.

I marched into his office without an appointment and asked to speak to him. His young secretary, Sissy, smiled at me and said he was busy. She was so beautiful and sweet I almost forgot why I was there, but it came back to me.

"I need to hire him!" I declared in a loud and demanding voice.

"He's busy," she said again as her smile disappeared.

"I have been done wrong and I need him to fix it!" I continued yelling, making my voice as deep and manly as I could. It was designed to impress her more than anything else, and I think it was working until my youthful voice cracked and pitched higher than hers. She started to reply when Grover came out of his office in a huff.

"Who's making all this God-awful noise?" he demanded.

She pointed her finger at me. It was a cute finger, all petite and well manicured. I was somewhat transfixed by it until I realised I had better explain my reason for being so loud.

"It's me, Mr Breckinridge," I said. "I have come here to hire your services."

"You got any money, boy?" he asked. "I'm not cheap."

"I will if you take my case," I replied.

"Well, make an appointment," he replied as he turned back to his office. "And be quiet about it."

"I want to sue Joshua Hawks," I continued.

He stopped in mid-stride and turned back to me.

"What's he done to you to rile you up so?" he asked and I could see his interest in me had grown considerably.

"I've done found out he got with my ma and they made me," I declared as unflinching as I could while glancing at Sissy to see if it impressed her at all that my real father was a very rich man.

Grover walked over to me and placed his hand on my shoulder. "Joshua Hawks is your father?"

"Yes he is, and I want to make him pay!" I said with as much force as I could muster.

"Well, this is interesting," he said with a smile. "Come on into my office and let's talk. Sissy, hold my calls."

We talked most of the morning about my family situation. Several times Grover licked his lips in eager anticipation of getting Joshua into a courtroom and taking him for all he could get. That was OK with me. I wanted him to do all he could to set things right.

He was so impressed with the case he agreed to handle it pro bono up front, with the stipulation he would get 50 per cent of any judgement awarded. I agreed to it because I figured old Joshua owed me a lot and there would be plenty for everybody.

As I was leaving I apologised to Sissy for my earlier behaviour and thanked her for letting me see Grover. She sure made my heart flutter when she touched my hand and told me she was looking forward to seeing me again when I came back.

It was late in the afternoon when I got home and faced Ma and Pa. They were not happy with me leaving all the day's work for them, so I explained to them how they would no longer need to work as hard as they did once Grover had collected our rightful dues. Instead of being happy over our future windfall they became quite angry at me.

"Boy, you're stirring up a lot of unnecessary trouble," my pa declared. "There ain't no need for you to go off and do something like that."

"He owes us and I've got my mind set that he's gonna pay," I shot back at him. "I would've thought you would be happy at what I'm trying to do."

"Happy?" my ma yelled. "You're ruining everything and I'm supposed to be happy?"

"I ain't ruining nothing," I protested. "I'm trying to make things right!"

"Oh, yes you are," she continued. "When Joshua finds out about this he'll take it out on me and he won't care to see me no more! You're just ruining everything!"

I was shocked. After all this, she was more interested in her two days a month of immoral lust than what was best for our family and me.

"Well, I've made my decision," I stubbornly declared. "I'm eighteen and I'm old enough to do this on my own!"

Pa chimed in. "And Darlene won't care to see me no more, either!"

I'd had about all I could stand so I shouted, "What's wrong with you people? Is that all you can think about?"

Ma looked at me with those cold piercing eyes she used when she was about to tan my hide. "It's the one extra pleasure we allow ourselves and you're trying to take it away from us."

"But, don't you see how he's used you?" I protested. "He treats us like dirt, don't pay us hardly nothing at all, and then he gets to pleasure himself with you."

"I don't feel used," my pa asserted.

"Me either," agreed Ma.

"He pays a fair wage and gives us this house to live in," Pa continued. "Why would we want anything else?"

"I like the way things are just the way they are," my ma interjected.

It finally dawned on me my ma and pa actually enjoyed their way of life and were resentful of anyone trying to change it. I didn't understand how they could think that way and, to this day, I still don't understand their thinking. In frustration I blurted out, "Well, this is just dandy. I try to make things better and all you want to do is to go on living in your little Sodom and Gomorrah!"

This was when Ma slapped me. She slapped me hard and it was the last time she ever did. I stood there sneering at her and then stomped off to my room. It was my way of keeping them from seeing me cry. The tears were not from the slap, but were coming from finally understanding that my ma and pa deserved the snickers done behind their backs by other folks.

Ma and Pa were right. Two days later Joshua received the summons for the lawsuit and he got as angry as a man could get. He ordered us out of our house and off the farm. I went to Grover and he obtained an injunction against this and we got to stay in our house. Joshua let us keep working as he couldn't find anyone to work as cheap as we did, but he had nothing to do with Ma any more. Darlene was mad, too, though I suspect she was more embarrassed than anything else. But she wasn't mad enough to keep her and Pa from still sneaking around to see each other without Ma and Joshua knowing.

About a month after this Darlene came down to our house to see me one day when I was alone. I always liked her and never understood how she could stand to live with a man like Joshua. After some small talk she got to the point. "Billy, Joshua wants you to drop your lawsuit."

"I bet he does," I bristled. "He wants to deny ever fathering me."

"No, that's not it," she asserted. "He feels it would be better if things were kept private and out of the public eye."

"Yeah, I'm sure he wants to keep everything quiet," I smirked. "That's been the problem around here. Everybody wants to keep everything undercover so nobody will think any less of them."

She bit her lower lip and then said, "He's willing to give you some money if you'll drop the suit."

This caught me by surprise. I always figured it would be settled in court. "How much?" I asked.

"He said five hundred thousand dollars if you're willing to never expect anything more," she revealed. "That means that's all you'll ever get. You won't be in his will and you give up all your rights as his son."

That was a lot of money, especially when the most I had ever seen in my life was a ten-dollar bill, but I suspected it was small potatoes to a man like Joshua.

"He doesn't even regard me enough to come and offer it himself," I reflected. "He has to send you instead."

She shrugged her shoulders and asked, "What do you want me to tell him?"

I thought for a minute and then said, "Darlene, I've always respected you. I still do, even though you and Pa do what you do. But let me ask you, if you were me, what would you do?"

She patted me on the arm, turned and started walking towards her house. I yelled after her, "You didn't answer me."

She kept walking but shouted back at me, "See you in court, Billy."

Our family was not the same. It never was again. Ma and Pa became more and more distant with me as the trial date approached and they stayed that way for several years. One bright thing was it brought Madge and me closer. She had always been my little sister and I had treated her that way. Now, she was the only family member I could turn to and she always had a willing ear and encouraging word to say. Without her kindness I would have been the loneliest person in the world.

A few days before the trial was to start Ike came by our house to see Pa. They talked for a long time but I never did find out what they discussed. All I know is he surprised everybody and enlisted in the army the next day. I believe he was intent on getting as far away from our families as he could. As for me, my thoughts were consumed by the upcoming court drama.

The lawsuit itself did not attract much attention until one of the reporters for the local newspaper decided to run an article about it. Then it became the talk of the town. People took a great interest in whether a poor eighteen-year-old boy could get his just dues against one of the stalwarts of the community.

The day for the trial came and I was basking in all the attention as Joshua fumed. He refused to even look at me as we took our seats in front of the judge's bench. I sat between Grover and Sissy while Joshua was beside his high-priced fancy-dressed lawyer. Seated behind me was Madge as Ma and Pa refused to attend. Darlene was behind Joshua. I took a quick look around before the judge came out of his chambers and was surprised as to how many folks were in attendance. It was a full house with a few men but mostly women and some children. The bailiff ordered us all to rise for the judge's entrance and Grover gave me a reassuring thumbs-up.

A jury was selected and we went through the opening arguments. Finally, it was my turn to take the stand as the plaintiff. After I was sworn in I took my seat and could feel Joshua's eyes staring a hole through me. I don't think anyone ever wanted someone dead as much as he did me at that moment. With Grover's expert help I stated my case as to why I thought I deserved to be treated as an heir of the Hawks' fortune. Also, I was looking for restitution in the amount of two million dollars for being his biological son who was neglected by him for eighteen years. I explained how I had to grow up poor and do without due to his negligence. Grover asked me if I had been emotionally scarred from such mistreatment and I agreed I had.

Then it was time for my cross-examination. I braced myself for the worst. Grover had drilled me with different sample questions and I felt I was ready for anything Joshua's fancy lawyer could throw at me. But, he surprised me by not trying to break me. All he asked was how I was raised and whether I had suffered as a child growing up. The point he was trying to make was Joshua had provided a home and employment for my ma and pa and therefore, had indirectly taken care of me. He insinuated that would have been enough for most folks and wanted to know why it wasn't enough for me. I replied because he treated Ike better than he ever treated me and no one could tell me this was right.

We were all surprised when Joshua decided to take the stand in his own defence. Grover said he was sure his lawyer advised against it but Joshua was a stubborn man. He was used to getting his way and he wanted to tell the world what an ungrateful brat I was. His lawyer let him talk and he rambled on about how he had the highest regard for my ma and never regretted her getting pregnant. He said he knew he had an obligation towards me and that was why he had provided for my pa and ma. Then it was Grover's turn to cross-examine his testimony. This was the moment Grover had been waiting for all his life, to get Joshua on the stand and under oath. He almost jumped out of his chair with excitement when it came to his turn.

"So, Mr Hawks, you say you kept the Grayson family employed on your farm in order to make sure Billy, your biological son, was cared for," Grover restated. "Is this correct?"

"Yes, it is," replied Joshua as he looked with scorn at Grover. There definitely was no love lost between the two men.

"So, I assume then that once Billy's mother was pregnant, you never had relations with her again," Grover surmised. "Is that correct?"

"Well, we didn't stop right then," he replied.

"Oh? But after Billy was born you did stop the affair," Grover continued. "Is that correct?"

"Well, no, we didn't stop then, either," he answered as he started to squirm uncomfortably in his seat.

"You didn't?" asked Grover with mock surprise. "Then, Mr Hawks, just when did you stop your affair with Billy's mother?"

"Uh, it was about three months ago."

"Three months ago?" restated Grover. "That was about the time Billy filed his lawsuit against you, wasn't it?"

"I believe it was," he agreed as I noticed his lawyer drop his head in a sure sign of defeat.

"So, can we say you kept the Grayson family as employees on your farm for the simple purpose of satisfying your carnal desires, and not for the welfare of your illegitimate son?"

"No, that's not it at all –"

"Can we not say you have shown no desire to accept your parental responsibilities for a child bred by a woman other than your wife?" continued Grover, the volume of his voice increasing with each point made.

"No, you're twisting things –"

"Is it not true that you despise Billy Grayson, wished he was never born, and put pressure on him and his family to settle out of court to avoid further embarrassment on your part?" Grover asked, by now almost shouting.

"No, no, no –"

"Isn't it true the son you raised, Isaiah Hawks, is not your biological son, but was fathered by another man?" continued Grover.

"Yes, but –"

At this revelation a roar went through the courtroom and the judge had to bang his gavel to restore quiet. Grover took a moment to let everything sink in, and then with the confidence of having Joshua right where he wanted him he asked, "So, please tell us Mr Hawks, why over all these years have you treated someone who is not related to you at all better than you've treated Billy Grayson, who in every sense of the word is your son?"

Well, it had become so quiet in the courtroom you could hear a pin drop. Sissy reached over and grabbed my hand and held it tight. This was somewhat of a distraction as I was trying my best to concentrate on Joshua's response, but I can't say I really minded. Joshua was so mad and stared at Grover so hard I believe smoke would have boiled out his ears if it had been possible. His face was the reddest I had ever seen and it was all he could do to keep from shaking. Finally, Grover spoke. "We're waiting for your answer, Mr Hawks."

His lips moved as if he was about to say something when a lady stood up in the back of the courtroom and shouted, "Your Honour, Joshua Hawks is the father of my little girl!"

Another roar tore through the room and the judge kept banging his gavel trying to quiet everyone down. It wasn't long before another woman yelled, "He's the father of my two boys!" Another woman held up what looked like a four-month-old baby and declared, "This is his!" One after another arose and shouted the fact that Joshua was the father of their children as the judge kept swinging his gavel in a vain attempt to restore order to the room. I quickly lost count of how many women kept coming forth. Joshua Hawks may have been a mean old goat but he sure knew his way around women. Eventually, one woman stood up who I recognised. It was Shelly Breckinridge, Grover's wife, and she yelled that Joshua was the father of her son. It immediately dawned on me why Grover had such a dislike for Joshua. I found out later he didn't know the child was Joshua's, but he did know she had an affair with him, and this was the reason for all his bitterness.

As soon as one woman would quit speaking another stood and took her place. It was an amazing sight to see. The judge finally gave up and tossed his gavel down and ordered the bailiff to clear the room. Seeing all this, Joshua stood up in the witness stand and glared at Grover and then at me. He was so red-faced I thought his head was going to explode. His head didn't but his heart did. He grabbed his chest and fell down dead.

It's been several years since that day in the courthouse and things have certainly changed. The fortune I was hoping to gain never materialised as there were so many families laying claim to Joshua's estate that when it was all divided out we each received a settlement of fifty thousand dollars. I only got half of that because I had agreed to give Grover the other half for representing me. So, the dirty little secrets of Joshua Hawks came out into the open, but I would have been financially better off if I had settled with him instead of going to trial. But, like I said earlier, I was proud and stubborn and this was the final result of me trying to make right of the wrong I felt done to me and my family.

Now, before you go and start feeling sorry for me, let me tell you everything turned out all right for everyone. Grover and his wife reconciled and seem to be as happy as ever. He loves their son and treats him as his own. Ike has made a career out of the army and is moving up the ranks. We speak from time to time and he's really not a bad person. The army has done him good. His mother, Darlene, remarried. Being rich all her life she knew exactly what to do to snare another rich man. There is a rumour that she and Pa still see each other but I've never asked. I thought I'd best leave that one alone.

Ma and Pa moved to town and Pa got a job in a hardware store. Ma works at the dry-cleaner's. It took a while but they finally accepted me back in as a cherished member of the family. I don't know if they will ever fully understand why I did what I did, but they appear to be willing to let bygones be bygones. And besides, they're doing quite well, as my little sister, Madge, married a very wealthy man. He likes us all and treats us just like family. Anything Ma, Pa, or me need or want, he goes out of his way to see that we get it. He's a good man and they love each other very much.

As for me, I'm working as a paralegal for Grover while I study law at the university. He says I have a knack for arguing and I might as well make a living doing it. As for Sissy, she and I got married two years ago. I still have a hard time believing she fell in love with someone like me, but I'm not going to question it. I'm just going to enjoy it as I love her with all my heart. She's expecting our first child. It will be Ma and Pa's first grandbaby. Sissy and I together both assured them the child was mine. It seemed the right thing to do.

The Rooming House
FRED SKOLNIK

A directionless man can't remember where he lives in this unsettling tale, with echoes of Kafka and Karinthy's Metropole. First published in 34th Parallel, No. 4, September 2008.

> "I felt that my hold on the past was loosening and it did not matter who I had been."

I got back late in the afternoon. Cars were double-parked in a roped-off area in front of the building but there were no cars parked at the kerb, which I found odd. A teenage girl came by on a skateboard and at the end of the street veered to the left and continued down a side street rather than continuing straight ahead as I had expected her to do. I went inside and climbed the stairs. My room was on the second floor but when I got there I didn't recognise the door so I went up another flight of stairs thinking that the second floor might be the one above it, the ground floor not being counted, but I didn't find my room there either and as the doors had no numbers on them I was at a loss and couldn't understand what had happened. Some of the doors were open and the rooms seemed larger than mine and men were coming out of a bathroom that was also extraordinarily large, as big as the rest rooms at a public beach. I went back down and saw one of the spinsters who ran the rooming house in the sitting room with a mother and child who must have been boarders. I went to the front desk and told the woman there that I had forgotten where my room was and she directed me to a tall girl behind the desk who looked for my name in a big ledger.

"Here it is," she said, and pointed at it. As all the names were written in the same hand I assumed that she or some other clerk had written them. It was an old-fashioned ledger like the ones kept in another time. My room number was listed as 203. I went back upstairs but still couldn't find the door. I counted three doors from the end of the corridor and tried my key but it didn't fit. Then I did the same from the other end of the corridor but got the same result. It occurred to me that the numbering of rooms could start at nearly any point, at the staircase for example, so I knocked at random at a door and it was opened by a woman who looked like she was about to go out. I asked her what her room number was but she said she didn't know and I asked her if it wasn't written on her key though I saw there was no number on mine and she looked at hers and said there wasn't any number on it either. She left me standing in the corridor and I would have thought that I had somehow gone into the wrong building had my name not appeared in the ledger. I went back downstairs and went into the sitting room where the two women and the child were just where I had left them, as if they hadn't moved. The child was about ten years old and standing off to the side while her mother and the spinster were sitting in oversized chairs and chatting quietly. I thought I recognised the mother and had an even stronger feeling about knowing the child but none of them paid any attention to me. I went back to the front desk but no one was there for the moment. Other people came into the building and went upstairs. I went upstairs too and stared at the doors on each floor but none of them was familiar and again I thought that I must be in the wrong building. I went downstairs and saw the girl who had found my name in the ledger and told her that I still couldn't find my room. She asked me my name as if we hadn't spoken before and looked for it in the ledger and found it again and showed it to me.

"But where is the room?" I asked her, feeling very frustrated.

"On the second floor," she said. "Just to the left of the stairs."

"But I've been there," I said, "and it isn't there."

"Maybe you have the wrong key," she said, and she gave me another.

"Why doesn't it have a number?"

"None of our keys has a number," she said.

"But why?"

"Everyone knows where they live."

I went back upstairs and tried the key in every door that could logically have been the right one though I knew they weren't from the start, and the corridor too was wider than I remembered it and somehow felt different so I knew I was not in the right building and yet I was registered there so I couldn't understand what had happened and went back downstairs and asked the tall girl to accompany me upstairs and find the room for me. She was very agreeable and went upstairs with me and opened a door with a master key and went inside with me. The room was bare. Nothing that belonged to me was there.

"I don't think this is my room," I said.

"It's 203," she said.

"Where are my things, then?" I said.

"Did you have any?" she said.

"Of course."

"I don't know," she said.

"You're sure this is my room?"

"Yes," she said.

I stayed in the room, leaving the door open. Perhaps someone who recognised me would come by. I was sure this wasn't my room and looked out the window but saw nothing familiar there. I sat on the bed for a while trying to think but could think of nothing that could tell me where I was and why everything was unfamiliar. Perhaps, I thought, I might start from here and build another life without knowing where my old life had gone. I had a name, but nothing else. I was in effect like a stranger who comes to a new place and sets out to establish himself there. I found some money in my pocket, enough for a few days, and then I might get a job and continue to support myself. This, I thought, might have been my original intention, so I was really not losing anything. I thought I might befriend the tall girl at the front desk or the woman with the child and in this way I would fit into the rooming house like everyone else and live an ordinary life regardless of who I might have been. Already, as I sat on the bed, the feeling of strangeness was beginning to wear off and I was starting to settle into my new life and I was hungry so I knew I would be going out soon for a meal and in the evening I would spend some time in the sitting room and make the acquaintance of the other boarders.

Before I left the room I tried my key in the door and was surprised to see that it fitted and also noted that the door was not one I had tried before so maybe the girl was right and this really was my room and somehow I had forgotten where it was though it could not be denied that my things were gone, unless I had had none. I could not remember first coming to the rooming house or having anything with me. I could only remember entering the building a while ago with the idea that my room was on the second floor and not being able to find it and the feeling of strangeness and of something amiss. Everything seemed to be hanging by a thread now and I felt that my hold on the past was loosening and it did not matter who I had been.

I went outside and started to walk. Everything was unfamiliar. These were streets I'd never seen before. There was a park up ahead with the overhanging trees shading the pavement and a boulevard crowded with cars. I was in a strange city. I couldn't say how I'd gotten there. I went into the first restaurant I saw and had my meal in a booth and then walked back to the rooming house. Someone else was on duty at the front desk and no one was in the sitting room. I went upstairs and this time I found my room without any trouble and sat on the bed again. I had a sense of a former life and remembered specific faces and specific moments but could tie none of them to the present moment. It was as if a cord had been cut and there was no way back and all the things I remembered no longer existed as in one of those science fiction stories where someone finds himself in another dimension of the universe though I was clearly in the everyday world. After a while I got up and went downstairs again. I asked the girl at the front desk when the other girl came back on duty and she said tomorrow morning so I went into the sitting room where some boarders were reading or talking or watching the TV that was bracketed to the wall. I nodded at a few people but no one took any interest in me and I sat down and picked up a newspaper and saw familiar headlines. This was reassuring and yet I was disturbed by the fact that I was in a room I didn't recognise. Had the world changed, or had I?

I went out again and bought a few things in a drugstore and then went upstairs and showered and fell asleep listening to a radio that piped music into the room. In the morning I went down to the front desk and was glad to see the tall girl there again but I didn't really know how to explain my situation to her without seeming odd so I went out to have breakfast and spent the morning walking aimlessly through the streets and when I got back the girl was still behind the desk and she looked up and smiled at me and said, "How are you today?" I said I was fine, wondering if she was referring to the previous evening or just being friendly as she would have been with all the boarders, not even remembering me just as she had seemed not to remember me last night. "Thanks for helping me find my room," I added, just to make certain she knew who I was.

She nodded, leaving the matter in doubt. She was tall and slim, dark-haired and dark-eyed, and wore a black skirt and white blouse. At moments she looked very severe but then her face relaxed and broke into a warm smile as boarders came by to exchange a few words with her. I could see one of the spinsters in the small office behind the desk talking on the phone.

"Have you been here long?" I asked the girl.

"Three years," she said.

"Like it?"

"It's all right."

I could see that she wasn't taking a special interest in me. She kept looking down at her ledger and making entries. There was a half-filled cup of coffee at her elbow which must have been cold by now. I wanted to ask her to have coffee with me when she finished her shift but was sure she'd refuse. I had shaved in the morning and thought I looked presentable but I was after all a transient here with no visible prospects. Another of the spinsters arrived and went into the office. There were two or three of them who apparently owned the rooming house, which might have been a family business, or perhaps they were unrelated and had formed a partnership. I had grasped all this intuitively, as it were, the moment I saw the one in the sitting room talking to the mother and child. The child was in the lobby now bouncing a ball and her mother was looking at some magazines laid out on a small table. I wondered where the husband was, or if there was one, and thought I might approach the woman on some pretext and make her acquaintance but she called to the child and they went out. I decided to follow them at a distance as I had nothing really with which to occupy my time. They went to the park and the child continued to bounce her ball while the mother sat on a bench smoking a cigarette and looking self-absorbed. I went over to the bench and asked her if she minded if I sat down. She looked me over for a moment and then said fine.

"I saw you at the rooming house," I said. "I'm staying there too."

"Yes, I think I saw you."

"Do you live in the city?"

"No, I'm from out of town."

"So am I," I said without thinking, realising immediately that she might ask me where I was from or what I did and I would have no answer though I could say anything I liked, even that I had amnesia though I was sure this wasn't true. "Will you be here long?" I said after a pause.

"Just for the week."

I realised that I didn't know what day it was. She finished her cigarette and stood up. "Nice meeting you," she said, signalling to the child and walking back towards the street with her. I remained sitting on the bench and watched them walk in the opposite direction from the rooming house. I continued sitting on the bench for a while and then walked back. The tall girl was still at the front desk, joined now by the other woman, but the office behind them was empty. I went into the sitting room and saw the first spinster there. She was straightening things out on the tables. She had grey hair which she wore in a severe bun and had a nicely tailored suit on, also grey. She was not an unattractive woman. She must have been fifty. I could not have said why I had concluded she was a spinster.

Other than moving between these few fixed points – the sitting room and the front desk, the park and the local restaurants – I hardly knew what to do with myself. I picked up a newspaper and looked at the help wanted ads. I supposed I could work as a dishwasher and that would more or less pay for my upkeep. I had no idea how long my room was paid for, or even if I had paid in advance. I couldn't find my wallet or a receipt. I had no identification, just a few folded bills and the clothes on my back. I must have come from somewhere, I thought, but I had no idea where. I looked for my name in the telephone book but nothing was there. The woman came back with her child. The tall girl at the desk ended her shift. Men kept going up and down the stairs. If I didn't act, I thought, things would go on like this for ever, one boarder would replace another, the girl at the front desk would find another job, or marry even, and I would still be here wondering who I was. I could only begin another life now, starting from scratch. The old life was gone and I knew I would never find it.

The Traffic Lights That Time Forgot
MICHAEL MCCARTHY

||||||||||||||||||||||||||||||||||||||||||||||||||||||||||||||||||||||||||||||||||||||||||||||||||||||||||||||||||||||||||||||||||||||||||||||||

A traumatised woman has an intimate encounter whenever she stops for a particular red light.

"We all leave traces. We may not realise it, but we do."

S
he became aware of him when she was waiting at the traffic lights that time forgot, so called by her because of the endless wait for green.

Now the wait couldn't be long enough.

She'd experienced something she could only describe as a presence, a not unpleasant sensation, when she stopped her car, a perception or portent, but something she instinctively knew not to fear.

A few days later at the traffic lights, she'd felt his finger gently stroking her shoulder and her entire body began to tingle.

But when the lights changed, too soon now, she'd felt the sensation slowly recede and a feeling of emptiness and disappointment engulfed her.

But he came back.

On subsequent occasions he caressed her entire body and made it his own. She felt her hands gripping the steering wheel for all she was worth – she fought to keep control as an electrifying rush surged through her being.

But he always pulled back at the last second before the pleasure would have been overpowering.

She planned her day around his visits; keeping to the same schedule, waking up at the same time, making sure her usually brushed and tied-up hair lay untamed and wet on her shoulders, just as she knew he liked it.

Somehow she always managed to arrive at the lights just as they changed to red.

She knew what he thought: he was in his favourite position in a car, in the front passenger seat, being driven by an attractive woman.

There was something about sitting beside a woman driving, especially if the weather was clement and she was wearing a long skirt, pulled up and bunched just above the knees, her legs apart, at pedal distance.

And that was it.

She knew how he thought: that he would come into her life and then disappear without a trace.

But we all leave traces. We may not realise it, but we do.

So did he. Only he didn't realise how deep his traces went, beneath her skin, into the core of her being. How could he have?

Then it dawned on her. He'd always been there. Not for ever maybe, but for a long time.

How could she have forgotten?

She couldn't bear to lose him.

Again.

But, how could she have forgotten?

That was easy.

She'd been at her lowest ebb.

They'd been supposed to meet and then go home together – to their new home, his flat.

But they hadn't made it.

Why?

She was sure he couldn't remember either.

And now he'd come back.

She should have known he wouldn't desert her.

She was convinced that people knew there was somebody in her life again; she could imagine the looks on their faces, in their eyes.

What was that look?

Joy? No, envy.

She knew they were looking at her. In the past, before his return, she hadn't liked being the object of people's gazes. She'd felt uncertain, self-conscious.

Not any more. Not now.

He'd left a trace inside her.

But was it enough?

Surely, nothing this good could last.

She knew it could only end in tears. Or worse.

But it would be worth it. Wouldn't it?

Without a doubt.

She woke up one morning, bathed in sweat; he was gone, the tantalising, fading remnants of their night together dancing on the edge of her consciousness.

She was picking up more and more on his feelings.

When he had come back to her, his lingering kisses and amorousness had impassioned her.

But there was a sadness about him lately, as though he was going through the motions.

She was right. It was coming to an end.

How could she live without him?

She felt he was struggling to make a decision.

She had to help him. But how?

She didn't want this any more, to keep him trapped, like a bird of prey. She had to let him go.

Suddenly she understood everything.

Her memory had been coming back, interlinked with his visits, like two films mixed up and running in the wrong order.

She'd been at the traffic lights. She'd been late, rushing to meet him. She'd been too impatient to wait for green.

It can't hurt, just this once.

There was nobody behind her or in front. In fact there was no traffic, anywhere.

The crossroads were empty.

She let the car creep forward, slowly, then she pressed gently on the accelerator.

There was a shivering, juddering, deafening impact, like a detonation, and that was it, she'd lost control of her body and her life.

How long had he been coming here?

She didn't need vision to see the tears streaming down his face or the heaving of his shoulders.

She knew him. She could feel the guilt that was tearing him apart.

There had to be something she could do.

There was.

If he comes to her one more time, in her dreams, she can release him. She is complete in her dreams, when they are together. She can tell him and set him free.

He came.

It was as though he had read her thoughts.

She wanted it to be good for them both, not enough to make him long for her, but good enough to sustain her, for who knew how long, and as he lay spent and empty and exhausted in her arms, his head on her breasts, she whispered in his ear and set him free.

She smiled inwardly as he kissed her; it was a long and lingering kiss, freighted with farewell. It was right, she had made her decision, to release them both, by freeing him.

But he came again.

The next day, and every day thereafter.

She stopped again at the traffic lights that time forgot and felt his presence beside her and then his hands and lips on her body and she was whole again.

The Wall
WILLIAM QUINCY BELLE

||||||||||||||||||||||||||||||||||||||||||||||||||||||||||||||||||||||||||||||||||||||||||||||||||||||||||||||||||||||||||||||||||||||||||||||||||||||||||||

Kevin finds a space-time anomaly in his apartment.

> "Kevin whipped around: a leg kicked out from his wall. It wore an ankle sock and running shoe."

Kevin looked at himself in the mirror, making a last adjustment to his tie. He stepped hurriedly from his bedroom, already late.

"Holy crap."

He stood stock-still, mouth agape. There, at the edge of the living room, an arm stuck out from the wall. He shook his head and stared at the horror before him.

He took a few steps back — away from the human arm emerging from the wall. The hand clenched, then the fingers relaxed, clenched, and relaxed. Kevin moved closer. The entire arm, from shoulder to hand, was jutting out of the drywall. There was no hole, no damage, nothing to indicate the arm had forcibly poked through the wall. Rather, it appeared as if it were part of the wall itself. The two were seamlessly joined.

The arm moved again. It bent at the elbow, the hand touching the wall in several places. It slid over the surface, stopped, rubbing fingers and thumb together. The arm repeated the action, sweeping away from the wall. Extending its fingers, the hand grasped empty air. Then the arm relaxed, hand hanging limply.

Kevin leaned as close as he dared and examined where the skin connected to the wall. He couldn't see any breaks. Tentative, he poked the shoulder. The arm stiffened. He ran a fingertip down the upper arm, but it remained motionless. He hesitated, then looked more closely at the muscle, and the hand suddenly lunged out and seized his forearm. Kevin jumped back in alarm, but the hand's grip was tight and he couldn't pull himself loose. He seized the wrist, pulling it in one direction as he pulled his own arm in the other.

The arm's grip slackened and Kevin pulled his forearm free, letting go as he did so. The arm flopped against the wall. Outside, a man yelled, "Help! Help!" Kevin gaped at the arm for a moment, then ran to the window. Down one storey, across the street and just inside the entrance to a small park, a man was screaming. He held his left hand over a gruesome wound: his right arm was gone. Kevin looked back at the wall, then out the window just in time to see the man run down the street and out of sight.

Leaning close to the window, Kevin looked first left then right. Not seeing the man, he turned back to the arm in the wall. He placed a palm on his forehead and took a deep, steadying breath. Just then, a movement in the corner of his eye caught his attention. He turned back to the window and watched as a jogger came into view from the left. The man ran down the sidewalk towards the main entrance of the park before turning and taking two steps down the path. His body seemed to slam into something solid, knocking him backward. His shoulders hit the ground, but his left leg remained suspended in the air, no longer visible from mid-thigh down.

Kevin whipped around: a leg kicked out from his wall. It wore an ankle sock and running shoe. He looked again to the park. The jogger flailed his arms, trying to grab onto something to pull himself up. But there was only air. He thrashed and yelled. His leg was gone. Kevin turned again to see the leg dangling from the wall, not believing what he was witnessing.

Two people ran to the jogger's aid. The first took off his jacket and covered the stump, while the other pulled out his belt and tied it in a tourniquet around the thigh. A police car came into view and the first Good Samaritan dashed into the street, waving his arms. He stood at the driver's door, pointing back to the jogger.

A dog passed, sniffing at a sign at the park entrance before raising its leg. The police officer was now running to the jogger, startling the dog, which scurried into the park and disappeared behind a bush. From behind Kevin a dog barked, and he spun around. The front half of the dog stuck out of the wall, its front paws on the floor. Its tongue hung out of its mouth as it panted. Seeing him, it barked again.

Kevin ran up to the animal, stopping when it growled. He looked frantically about his apartment, wondering what to do. The animal stopped growling and stared at him. Kevin grabbed the dog's collar and placed his other hand below the neck. He pushed; the dog didn't budge. He pushed again. This time the dog went limp. Kevin let go of the animal and stepped back. Its head, front paws, and chest hung from the wall, spilling onto the floor. It looked dead.

A woman screamed. Fearing the worst, Kevin looked out the window then again at the wall. A child's forearm was holding a balloon — in Kevin's living room. Kevin grabbed at it and pushed. It didn't move. The fingers opened, and the balloon floated to the ceiling. Agitated, Kevin looked around the room before running to the kitchen. Yanking open a drawer, he used both hands to sort through various items until he pulled out a hammer. He ran back to the living room and pounded the area surrounding the child's arm, breaking the drywall. He dropped the hammer, grasped the forearm, and pushed the child's arm into the wall. He let go and grabbed the hand. Shoving it flush up against the wall, he saw it had disappeared. Kevin leaned over and looked through the hole. Nothing was visible. It simply looked like the inside of a wall.

He ran back to the window. A woman gripped the hand of a little girl as she pulled her away from the park. The little girl was crying. Kevin scratched his head, staring at the park's entrance. He turned back to glance at the wall.

Many voices now sounded below. A teacher was leading a group of small children into the park. Kevin froze, gazing back and forth between the window and his wall. He ran to the apartment door, pulling it open. He bolted down the stairs, burst from the building. Several cars honked as he dodged between moving vehicles, sprinting towards the teacher. "Please don't go in the park!"

The woman looked startled. "Why not?"

"It's not safe."

"Not safe?" She sounded suspicious.

A small boy walked around them, clearly making his way to the park.

"No!" Kevin grabbed the boy and pulled him back. "Don't go in the park." He moved into the middle of the entrance and held out his arms. "You mustn't go in here. It's dangerous." He shifted position, his foot catching a broken piece of sidewalk. Kevin lost his balance, turning to his left, and landed face forward with arm outstretched. There was a bright flash. He blinked. He was looking down, but not at the sidewalk; it was something else. He turned his head and scanned the area. He was in his apartment. His head, right arm, and part of his chest were sticking out of the wall. He could hear yelling coming from the park.

Kevin pulled back, but, like the others, he couldn't move. Shifting his weight, he pulled again. Nothing budged. Pushing on the wall with one arm, and on something solid with the other, Kevin found he couldn't move his body forward or back. He looked down and saw the hammer. He reached out, straining for the handle, got a fingertip on it, and managed to slide it closer. Finally, he grasped the handle and brought the hammer level to his head. Then he pounded on the plasterboard. Chips flew and a cloud of dust formed as the wall cracked and crumbled. He twisted. He pulled. He twisted again. Bracing himself, Kevin jerked his entire body. He flew backward and fell into a sitting position on the sidewalk.

"Oh my God, mister, are you all right?" The teacher stood over him, a look of utter panic on her face.

Kevin sat, dazed. He held up his hand and looked at the hammer. "Don't go in the park." He jumped up without another word and dashed back across the street. He took the stairs two at a time and burst into his apartment. Raising the hammer, he pounded away at the wall. He smashed the drywall, section by section, pushing it between the studs. He broke the area around the dog, pushing it back into the wall until it disappeared. Kevin did the same for the leg and arm, continuing until he had reduced the entire wall to rubble.

Standing back, he surveyed the damage. There was a large piece close to the ceiling, so Kevin reached up and hit it several times. He walked up and down the length of the room, poking at broken pieces with the hammer as chunks of drywall fell to the floor.

Somebody outside called out and Kevin went to the window. The teacher and the children stood by the entrance, looking up at his apartment. Three boys on skateboards came down the sidewalk, rolling into the park. They pushed off several times and disappeared down the main path. A dog came out from behind a bush and walked up to the children. Several of them stopped to pet the animal.

Kevin waved to the teacher, who turned back to her students. He glanced back at the living room as they walked into the park. Nothing happened.

He went back to the kitchen and put the hammer away. Taking a broom and dustpan from the utility closet, Kevin walked to the living room and picked up pieces of drywall. He swept everything into the centre and collected everything, even the dust.

There was an indistinguishable noise. He stopped and listened. Hearing nothing more, Kevin changed his grip and swept the broom across the floor. There was another noise. He stopped again.

A voice issued from the bedroom. "How the hell did I get here?"

Vatican Bag Man
GARY IVES

A good man rises to power in this incendiary indictment of the Catholic Church.

"To him these funds were church assets and as a priest of the Order he knew better than to enquire."

Radix malorum est cupiditas.

The path leading Philip to the plush apartment overlooking Central Park had begun fifty years earlier at the seminary of the Apostolic Order of the Venerable Saint Actius of Jerusalem, when he had awakened in the middle of the night with the hand of Monsignor Paolo DaLuca wrapped around his erection bringing him to a quick release. The experience shocked the fifteen-year-old. The Monsignor had quietly vanished from Philip's bedside without a word. The Monsignor! The Monsignor had done this . . . this . . . this thing. Owing to the brief pleasure he had felt, a tremendous guilt fell upon the boy. The Monsignor, that sweet man, so understanding, so wise, loved by all the boys, how could this be? Immediately after next morning's matins he entered the confessional eager to expiate and do whatever penance was necessary.

"Forgive me, Father. It has been three days since my last confession. Father, I am guilty of the sin of self-abuse, but . . . but see, it wasn't just me doin' the 'self' part of the self-abuse."

"I think I understand. So who was the other person, my son."

"I . . . I don't want to . . . uh, I don't know, Father, see it was dark."

"Are you certain you don't know, boy?"

"Yes, Father."

"Go, my son, you are absolved of this thing. I would caution you to keep this to yourself and the confessional. Ten Hail Marys and two Stations of the Cross. Go with God."

Philip was certain that his confessor had been Monsignor Paolo.

He was to learn that other boys had had similar experiences. Not only the Monsignor but Father Seamus Murphy, too, sometimes prowled the dorm. The boys jokingly referred to these visits as "Irish lullabys" or "Roman wanks". No one, it seemed, took the incidents seriously. The much-loved Monsignor's elevated position as the Rector, and Father Murphy's popularity as instructor and coach, somehow allowed their aberrations to be dismissed as simple peccadilloes. Didn't this happen all the time at boys' schools, military schools, and seminaries? Wasn't this the subject of dozens of jokes? No big deal. So well-loved was the kindly Monsignor that any accusatory stance would have called down the wrath and condemnation of the entire seminary. Hence the Monsignor's subsequent "Roman wanks" were endured by Philip with a sense of detachment, guilt, and perhaps a rationale of obligation.

The Apostolic Order of the Venerable Saint Actius of Jerusalem, a small, secret Roman Catholic order, had survived in various forms since the eleventh century, when established by a papal bull, issued by Pope Urban II, to arm knights of the Order to hunt down and slay infidels preying upon Christian pilgrims in the Holy Land. At times the Order had been forced underground and in the eighteenth century fought skirmishes against the Jesuits in South America. It was rumoured that when the Jesuits were stripped of many of their prosperous reductions in South America much of their enormous wealth was shifted to the Saint Actius order. Like the rival Jesuit order, a military tradition had become strongly infused in the Order's doctrine and rules. Seminary boys learnt a strict code of loyalty to protect the secrecy of the Order and became toughened by the rigours at Saint Actius and taught to follow commands without question, to serve with complete fidelity to the Order. Informing is the act of a coward as is surrender to a foe. Proclamations dating from the sixteenth-century charter named the Saint Actius order the "Protectors of the Holy Church's secrets". To Saint Actius priests, church secrets were treasures to be protected. Saint Actius had long been the only Roman Catholic seminary that taught martial arts, fencing, horsemanship and the mountain sports of skiing and rappelling. While a few Saint Actius boys became missionary priests in Third World settings, the brightest and best were placed in sensitive church positions requiring unusual degrees of trust. The Jesuits, who have long attempted to defame the Order, have with speculative rumours implied they were employed as Vatican assassins. It is true that delicate investigatory and enforcement positions within the church hierarchy are traditionally awarded to the Saint Actius order. But the Jesuits' accusation of assassins is widely dismissed as nothing more than Jesuit calumny. This small, rigid militant sect with its traditions dating back to the Crusades in essence is the Holy Mother Church's noble defender, *Cognitio sit virtus, et fortitúdo conservator* its motto. Knowledge is power, strength its protector.

Months after the masturbation incidents and shortly before completion of his studies Philip was summoned one spring afternoon from his trigonometry class to the Monsignor's office. There the kindly Monsignor explained that his comportment both religious and academic at Saint Actius was remarkably good. "Exceptional" was his word.

"My son, you have shown to us many fine qualities. Qualities that build good priests, qualities that the Holy Mother Church appreciates. You are serious, you are hard-working, you are very intelligent and, Philip Stahl, you are loyal. For this I have recommended that your education be continued at Carnegie-Mellon University in Pittsburgh. There we know you will do your best. And should all go as we expect, you will follow your Bachelor's degree with a graduate degree at the Wharton School. What do you think, young man?"

"I am honoured, Monsignor. Thank you. I will do my best."

"I know that you will. And please know this. I take a personal interest in your career. Soon I will be leaving our beloved seminary. I'm being posted to the Vatican. You will, I pray, stay in contact. I would appreciate a letter each month. Please do not discuss these matters with anyone else. Go now, my son. I pray for you."

The Monsignor never again approached Philip sexually, nor were the late-night visits or confessions ever alluded to in speech or actions.

The year Philip earned his Bachelor's in European Languages, Monsignor Paolo DaLuca attended Father Philip Stahl's ordination as priest in Pittsburgh and presented the newly ordained priest with a Volkswagen Beetle. Two years later, following successful completion of his doctorate in Finance, he was invited to Rome for the ordination and investiture of Bishop Paolo DaLuca, to be the new papal nuncio in Berne. As bishop, Paolo DaLuca became the Order's Adjutant, the number-two official of the Order of Saint Actius. Only the Grand Marshall, Cardinal Joseph Ratzinger, was higher. Father Stahl's appointment as Bishop

DaLuca's personal secretary placed the priest on the fast track for advancement.

Switzerland was magnificent, cleaner, better dressed, and more civilised than any place he'd known in America. Superficially, the Swiss were stuffy and dogmatic, but beyond business dealings Philip found them generally well-educated, cultured and, once invited into their homes, warm, hospitable, and engaging conversationalists. As Bishop DaLuca's personal secretary he interfaced with bankers and financiers. The Vatican's holdings entrusted to Swiss banking houses and securities firms were managed from the papal nuncio's office. The Vatican Bank also bestowed upon Philip the lofty title of Managing Director of Investments, Switzerland. He managed several large funds that invested commercial clients' money in securities and real estate, yielding tidy profits for the Vatican Bank and large profits for the commercial enterprises, which were able to escape taxes by funnelling money to Switzerland via the Vatican Bank.

For two years Philip produced reports and analyses, conducted audits, arranged international transfers and currency trades. The Vatican Bank directors were impressed with the young man's talent. Whether his trading skills were exceptionally good or whether he was lucky, his management of securities was sound and yielded the Vatican's clients a steady 17 per cent increase per annum from the securities administered by Fr Philip Stahl. Gradually he had gained an excellent understanding of the monetary and financial complexities that were the Swiss banking system. Under Bishop DaLuca's tutelage he developed excellent working relations with high-level banking and government functionaries. Each week usually featured a €200 executive lunch for his prime working contacts at a fine restaurant or hotel. Philip's index file listed information he collected on well-placed contacts as well as wives' and children's birthdays to be remembered with cards and small gifts. Roman Catholic family members of influential contacts were given access to the Bishop's office and the favour of the Bishop's personal presiding at weddings, baptisms, and christenings. Often the Bishop requested Philip's company at diplomatic receptions. In time Philip was provided with his own office in Geneva, the banking hub, with his own aide, Fr Carlos Sandoval, another priest of the Saint Actius order. Under Philip he would manage the Geneva office with two Swiss clerks and a receptionist. Carlos Sandoval, a tall, lean Catalonian, never smiled, seldom spoke, and disdained company, preferring to work alone. He held a doctorate in International Finance from the Sorbonne. His diversions were riding and fencing, which he practised weekly at the exclusive Club Hippique Bretagne. However unsettling his demeanour, Sandoval, like Philip, was a skilled trader.

To ease the task of shuttling between Geneva and Berne the Bishop presented Philip with a Mercedes-Benz 200E. While the Bishop's working budget and personal finances were protected even from Philip, clearly the nuncio was funded generously. But this was only to be expected as the Vatican, through its office of the nuncio in Switzerland, directed the movement of over two billion euros each year. Philip's own salary had risen to upper-class Euro standards. The Apostolic Order of the Venerable Saint Actius of Jerusalem doctrine included no rules regarding poverty.

Within four years Father Philip Stahl, well-received by the international community, was afforded an unusual degree of respect for an American. Fluent in German, French and Italian, well groomed in European diplomatic etiquette by his bishop, he was a rising star to be sure.

Before opening the office in Geneva, Bishop DaLuca had sent him to London with an open bank draft on Barclays.

"Philip, go to Bond Street. Invest in a dozen suits. Here's the name of your tailor. Listen to him. This maestro, he makes clothes for princes. Include some lightweight suits, maybe wool blends, just a few, the others pure wool. Also two or three greatcoats and two tuxedoes, yes? Good. Then when you return you will drive down to Rome for shoes and a little vacation, yes? Business in Geneva is so much better you should be in mufti, yes? Especially among the Geneva *Calvinisti. Loro non piace il nostro abito clericale.* Heh, heh. Now your duties will involve much travel, my son. When you come back you take care of handing over the office in Geneva to Fr Sandoval. Afterwards you go to Moscow for a week."

The July trip to Moscow in 1992 was exciting. The Soviet Union, only recently officially dissolved, was in a frenzy of transition. Huge amounts of wealth were being moved. Philip had been instructed to stay not at the Moscow nuncio's residence, but at the small but well-appointed Hotel Pyotr Beketov in the Petrovka District. At the hotel he was met by two well-dressed English-speaking apparatchiks who examined his diplomatic passport, left for an hour, then returned.

"Let us show you our beautiful Moscow, Reverend Doctor Stahl."

A car and driver waited, and for the rest of the afternoon he was hosted on a visit to Red Square, the Kremlin, the huge department store GUM and, finally, at a dinner washed down by too much vodka and toasts to prosperity and friendship. The next afternoon his hosts presented him with a locked suitcase.

"We have arranged your tickets. Your plane leaves for Geneva at 22.00 hours this evening. We will drive you to the airport. With your diplomatic credentials you will have no problems."

"Gentlemen, I will need to see the contents of the suitcase."

"We were told the suitcase will remain sealed."

"We've established our trust. Now it's up to you. Open the case or here it stays, in Russia."

The men begged a brief absence, left, then returned half an hour later.

Setting the suitcase on the bed, the key was produced and handed to Philip who opened it to find bundles of $100 bills and £100 notes. The men inventoried the $790,000 and £128,000. On the hotel stationery, Philip wrote a simple receipt then locked the large leather case. Unknown to him, this transaction had been a carefully orchestrated test, a test that he had passed with distinction.

Over the next three months, Philip flew to Moscow five times, receiving an additional fourteen million dollars in dollars, pounds, and euros of bona fide oligarch funds. Under his bishop's instructions these monies were deposited in numbered Vatican accounts among four Swiss banking houses where Philip was warmly received with coffee, biscotti, and chocolates in the counting rooms leading to the vaults. To him these funds were church assets and as a priest of the Apostolic Order of the Venerable Saint Actius of Jerusalem he knew better than to enquire.

Similar courier missions followed, with visits to certain parliamentarians in South Africa, Venezuelan generals, and Mexican industrialists, always returning with bags stuffed with cash. As more of his time became consumed by these trips he delegated all finance duties in Geneva to his aide, the stoic, expressionless Fr Sandoval.

In the fall of 1999 Fr Philip Stahl was summoned to the Vatican. Bishop DaLuca feigned ignorance of the reasons for the summons but insisted on accompanying him.

"If there should be some problem, I am certain it is a small one. Whatever, I stand with you, my son."

The summons had placed his nerves on edge although he could think of nothing incriminating. A summons nearly always meant some sort of judiciary hearing, malfeasance, heresy, or some scandal of morality. In the far reaches of his mind he worried that somehow the Curia had discovered the Bishop's previous dalliances and would press Philip for a confession and an accusation. He was resolved not to inform, to stand loyal to his Order. On the third floor of the Vatican administrative offices he waited in a leather armchair with his bishop by his side. Stone-faced Cardinal Angelo Vincenza entered the anteroom, introduced himself and conducted the pair to a private papal prayer chamber. Minutes later the Cardinal returned with His Holiness Pope John Paul II who took a seat before the two; the visitors knelt to kiss the ring of the Holy See. The old Pope chuckled, then addressing the Bishop in Italian offered his greetings, his congratulations, and blessing. Turning to Father Stahl, Pope John Paul II smiled, and spoke to him in English.

"So this is our faithful servant Father Philip Stahl. My son, we take notice of your superb service. We greatly appreciate the wisdom of your recommendations in Switzerland, which have yielded so much for God's work. We know that you have transported very large sums of money, and that always there is danger when big money she moves. Never has there been a question concerning the great sums you have delivered. Never have you complained of or questioned your duties and we well know you have always observed silence about your duties." The Pope made a little gesture to Cardinal Vincenza who approached, knelt and handed to the Pope a small velvet case. "My son and good servant Father Philip Stahl, I commend you with the Pontifical Equestrian Order of Saint Gregory the Great, First Class. You are now a Knight of the Holy Church. One day perhaps you will become a beloved nuncio like your bishop, who will become very soon our next archbishop. Go with God, my son." At that the Cardinal opened the door of the tiny chapel and escorted His Holiness upstairs for his afternoon *Kirschwasser* and siesta.

Later, at a table in the Hassler Hotel's restaurant, the pair enjoyed a five-star lunch of breaded scallops stuffed with buffalo mozzarella, celery leaves and black truffle. The window table provided a magnificent view overlooking the Vatican. During the lunch they examined the signed citation on parchment and beautiful gold medal Pope John Paul had bestowed on Philip.

"Archbishop! Allow me to congratulate you. This is wonderful. Such good fortune comes to Your Grace."

"Thank you, Philip my son, my dear son. And it is your good fortune as well. I have already received approval from Cardinal Ratzinger for you to continue as my secretary. Philip, I am happy to tell you we will be returning to America!"

"America! Home! What good news. And to which diocese, Your Grace?"

"I will not be administering a diocese. Yes, this is unusual for an archbishop. However, I shall serve His Holiness as Special Nuncio-at-Large. This will be equal to an ambassador without portfolio. Our offices will be in New York. I will report not to the papal ambassador in Washington, but directly to Cardinal Ratzinger. Did you know that he was Monsignor at our seminary in Padua while I was there as a boy? We are good friends since many years."

The waiter served a dessert of Torcolato wine and rhubarb compôte, banana fritters and amaretto ice cream. The Archbishop lifted his wine glass. "To America!"

Philip marvelled at the changes that had occurred at home. Everything seemed bigger, richer, and busier than he had remembered. Colours were brighter, clothes more stylish, and television advertisements raucous and ridiculous. The sizes and numbers of automobiles were staggering; every person, it seemed, carried a cell phone and laptop computer. Law enforcement seemed to be everywhere, on highways, buildings, and at airports. English was spoken faster than he remembered. American coffee, bread, and beer were wretched, but in New York good food and drink were simply a matter of finding the right neighbourhood. His Mercedes he had sold to Fr Sandoval. In New York an automobile was a liability. Any kind of car was rented with ease in America.

His duties continued under his archbishop as the Vatican's secret international courier. Three weeks of each month he travelled to Miami, Chicago, New Orleans or Las Vegas. Abroad, visits to Mexico, Panama, Rio and Buenos Aires became routine. In each city his contacts came to like the suave, personable, cosmopolitan priest. As in Switzerland, he quietly constructed dossiers, noting dates of meetings, amounts, as well as the personal foibles of his contacts and birthdays and special occasions, and sometimes providing small favours. Back in New York, dossiers were updated and copied to CDs for storage. When the daughter of the governor of Sonora was to be married to a wealthy Texas oil man, Philip arranged for Archbishop DaLuca to perform the ceremony at a large ranch in the Big Bend country with the American vice president and the governor of Florida in attendance.

Travelling nearly all of the time was wearing, and late in 2004 Philip was stricken with hepatitis in Panama. The papal ambassador in Washington arranged for his transport by private jet to the Catholic Medical Centre in New York. He was six weeks recovering, during which time Fr Sandoval assumed his secret courier duties. During this recovery period he was able to consolidate and chart several years of files for his personal analysis. His privately collected data revealed a staggering $1,253,600,000 in collections of hard, cold cash. "Who," he questioned, "deals a billion and a quarter *in cash*?" His PhD in Finance wasn't necessary to realise only drug lords, Mafiosi, Russian oligarchs, and dictators relied so heavily on the liquidity of cash. This obvious conclusion impugned the Vatican *and* himself. "The Vatican's bag man. That's what I am, the collection agent for money, money that must be dirty and in sore need of laundering." Guilt, confusion, and a sense of shame weighed heavily.

Released from hospital, he was instructed by the Archbishop to rest for as long as he wished before resuming his duties. Fr Sandoval would continue to assume the role of courier. Philip flew to Palm Springs where he bought a Nissan Murano, then drove leisurely northward through the Sierras, through Oregon, Washington, and into British Columbia where he took a cabin at Tsuniah Lake out of range of emails and telephones. There he fished in the morning and in the evening worked on writing several lengthy essays on the corruption of the Roman Catholic Church. While his articles named no one, the information clearly pointed to specific Church offices and Vatican officials. One article alleged that the Vatican maintained direct business links with two notorious dictators. Another decried the lack of financial support for the Third World, particularly Haiti, all of Central America and Sub-Saharan Africa, while the Vatican Bank and the IOR accrued billions in assets. Before returning to New York he submitted one article to *The Sunday Times of Dublin*, and two others to *Irish Readers' Magazine*, each penned under the name Fiona O'Reilly. Acceptance and publication afforded Father Philip Stahl the satisfaction of having reacted decently as a human and as a Christian, if not loyally to the Mother Church. Vindication eased remorse.

Duties upon return to work included delivering payments in cash to three dioceses. To Boston, $4,500,000 in $100 bills, and similarly $2,000,000 each to Chicago and Atlanta dioceses. These cash transfers were to effect secret and quiet out-of-court settlements to victims of sexual abuse by priests. Again the stigma of bag man and money launderer troubled Philip. And now persistent rumours were whispered that orders from Cardinal Ratzinger insisted on secrecy about and the tacit protection of paedophiles and rapists. Surely the Archbishop realised the ignominy of this, but how could he, Philip, go to the Archbishop to complain? Had not he and who knows how many other boys at Saint Actius been abused by his mentor? He could talk to no one. Incredibly, in 2005, with the death of John Paul II, the College of

Cardinals elected Cardinal Joseph Ratzinger to the Throne of Saint Peter as Pope Benedict XVI. Three weeks later Archbishop Paolo DaLuca was elevated to Cardinal.

Now Philip was penning an article each week hurling scathing indictments at Church policies towards abortion, towards divorce, and even towards masturbation, and still from the accrual of the Church's vast wealth only a miserly trickle found its way to ease the miseries of Third World poverty. But he could not bring himself to directly accuse his beloved Archbishop, the man who had fostered Philip's brilliant career. He pondered the relationship between Ratzinger and DaLuca. Was it not akin to *his* relationship with the Archbishop? Had Ratzinger abused DaLuca as a young boy in Padua then furthered DaLuca's career? How many Vatican careers were based on fellatio and buggery? But loyalty to his mentor and to the Order of Saint Actius still ruled his decisions. His anger was against Rome and he would press his attacks.

In 2008 he was again summoned by the Curia. The message ordered him to board the next flight to Rome and then report immediately to Cardinal Bruno Conti, General Counsel and president of the Curia. Again Cardinal DaLuca feigned ignorance but again agreed to stand by Philip's side were he in trouble. He was not in trouble. Before a hearing of the Curia he was politely questioned on accounting methods he had established relating to the management of Church funds he had handled. The questions pointed clearly to improprieties, probably the theft of funds, which had occurred during Philip's recovery from hepatitis, by Fr Carlos Sandoval, the subject of the investigation. Didn't the fool realise that the couriers were always watched and transactions triple-checked?

Later, over a splendid supper of broiled langostinos, braised lamb chops, and chestnuts roasted with garlic, he asked DaLuca what punishment the Curia might levy, if indeed Sandoval had stolen.

"Ah, the amount in question is large, six figures I believe. To be sure the penalty will be severe, although I understand the money has been returned."

"Transfer to a leprosarium or AIDS hospice, perhaps?"

"My son, enough of that. Call the boy over for some tiramisu and another bottle of this excellent Marsala."

Oddly enough, Fr Sandoval returned to Geneva to resume his regular duties. Two weeks later he was found dead, lying next to the riding club's bridle trail, his neck broken. Indeed the penalty had been severe. Philip instantly realised the extent to which the hierarchy would go to protect itself. Murder, cruel murder.

Sandoval's murder pushed Philip beyond the limits hitherto imposed by loyalty to the Order and to Cardinal Paolo DaLuca. Throwing caution to the wind, he penned painful articles citing twenty-nine verifiable instances of sexual abuse committed upon boys as young as nine years old by unrepentant sodomite priests then covered up by out-of-court settlements in the millions of dollars. The articles included names and addresses of the offending priests and bishops, dates of the offences, and amounts of the secret settlements. The last and most damaging of these articles he posted to *The New York Times*, still under the pen name Fiona O'Reilly. The contents of the articles, he realised, could with effort and the Church's resources be traced. Remembering the punishment exacted upon Sandoval, he saw that it could be simply a matter of time before his assassin would be sent. But he would be ready. He purchased a subcompact Glock 42 automatic pistol. The Geneva coroner's inquest into the death of Sandoval raised suspicions; a criminal investigation was initiated. In Berne the Vatican's traction slipped, despite its vast financial holdings in Switzerland. The international press pursued this story like a pack of hounds. When the Sunday edition of *The New York Times* followed Philip's sex-abuse article with a twenty-four-column op-ed questioning Vatican leadership and morality, European newspapers followed suit. The *Guardian* featured an insinuating photo of Pope Benedict smiling amid a group of Boy Scouts. A leading German weekly blatantly accused the Vatican of covering up acts of paedophilia, and alluded to a ring of paederast bishops and a cardinal operating within Vatican City. His Holiness's butler was arrested and charged with theft of documents he had sold to German journalists. During his interrogation he claimed that fourteen-year-old boys had been brought into the papal apartment for overnights. Pope Benedict's sexuality had become the elephant in the Basilica. By 2012, the Vatican was in turmoil, his resignation inevitable. He did, indeed, quit the Throne of Saint Peter in 2013.

For the third time Philip was issued with an immediate summons to Rome by the Curia, this time as the accused. The Curia had discovered years ago the true identity of Fiona O'Reilly. The articles identifying the details of names, dates, places, and amounts of out-of-court settlements of priestly abuses crossed the line. Hitherto, Philip's proven honesty and diligence as the Vatican's chief cash courier had persuaded the Curia to turn a blind eye to his radical anti-Church essays. But real damage, costly damage, had materialised from the fallout of the German press, then the British and American. The extremely lucrative money-laundering machine that had been in place since the days of Pope John XXIII in the 1960s had been torpedoed by the media. Further damage accrued as American cash-cow donors withdrew pledges. How could millionaire widows be expected to remember the Holy Mother Church if they believed the millions bequeathed would be used to protect paedophiles and rapists? Ignoring the summons' order of immediacy, late that night, at the Cardinal's residence on Lexington Avenue, Philip explained the situation leading to the summons to his old mentor. Cardinal DaLuca had always stood by his side. Despite DaLuca's dalliances in the seminary, Philip loved the old man and respected his wisdom and generosity. He was Philip's surrogate father, his confessor, his North Star. Now only he could provide proper protection and guidance.

"Ah, it is clear you are much disturbed. When you are a little more calm we discuss this, no? No matter what, Philip, you know I will help you, my son." He led Philip into the apartment's study and before closing the door called for his man to bring a tray with cognac. Philip withdrew the message summoning him and passed it to DaLuca. "Yes, Philip, this one is quite serious. Explain to me, please, *la vostra difesa*, how you see this problem."

For the next half hour he explained his objections to the Vatican's intransigence with regard to divorce, abortion, the equality of women and minorities as Cardinal Paolo DaLuca patiently listened.

"You are quite right, you know. And, Philip, you are not alone in wanting to promote these changes. The problem has been, however, complicated by these . . . these . . . these scandals, these sex scandals."

"I know this, Your Eminence. Let me tell you what has pushed me beyond limits. Do you know what has so offended me, so angered me, so driven me to such extreme measures? Do you know? I will tell you, sir, in plain language: the murder, yes, murder, of Carlos with no tree within four hundred yards. The Swiss police have detected powerful sedatives in his blood. They have absolute proof that he was drugged. He did not fall. He was pushed from his horse and an assassin snapped his neck. There is a witness. He was murdered. Murdered by orders from Rome, and I would bet money that the murderer was of the Order of Saint Actius. How can I stand by, silent, head bowed, and condone such travesty, such sin, such filth emanating from the very highest levels? I cannot. And, to be sure, I am at great risk. If they believed Sandoval warranted death, they . . . they may have already launched an assassin, and no doubt from our Order, Your Eminence. Who do you think they will send? Who? I am worried sick."

"I know you are concerned, as am I. Please know, Philip, I have made enquiries. We will know very soon the name of their agent. Again, you are right. I am with you, do you know that? Yes, you have always been to me my son. Now, together, we will widen the exposure you have begun. The majority of cardinals will support us, Philip. They hate Benedict and they hate that nasty coven of deviants there in the Vatican. They will support us, Philip. Pope Francis is with us. And when we have destroyed this wickedness I will become the next Pope. You will very soon be elevated to Cardinal and the Church can at last reform, modernise, and return to pure religion. Yes, my son, you are right, and know that I am with you. I will lead you, and we will lead the Holy Mother Church into the twenty-first century. God bless you, Philip, you truly walk with God."

Philip sighed with an enormous sense of relief. He had always realised the goodness of Paolo DaLuca. With this powerful Cardinal, the greatest reform since Ecumenical Council II would be launched.

Cardinal DaLuca poured another cognac and raised his glass, toasting *"Par Dieu."*

The poison acted within minutes. Father Philip Stahl slumped from the leather wingback chair, collapsing dead at the feet of the old man he'd loved.

Tears rolled down the Cardinal's cheeks. "Ah, my beautiful boy. Please forgive me, my son."

War Baby
SINÉAD McCABE

||||||||||||||||||||||||||||||||||||||||||||||||||||||||||||||||||||||||||||||||||||||||||||||||||||||||||||||||||||||||||||||||||||||||||||||

This creepy story about a woman driven to madness during the London Blitz will get under your skin, and then you'll want to read it again.

> "Emerging from the shelter, they saw Lambeth aflame. Great filthy clouds rose into the sky."

t was twilight when the siren began to wail, and the little street was bathed in lurid tones from the smoky sunset, as though already aflame. Mrs Emilia Blythe sat shuddering upon the ottoman, staring into the mirror at the shape of her own skull, unable to move; unable even to cry out. Five minutes before, upon the blue candlewick spread of the empty double bed behind her, she had seen the apparition of a child; a little baby no more than two years old. Wearing nothing but a ragged smock, with hair so tangled over its hollow eyes that they could barely be glimpsed, it reached out a tiny starfish hand to her, and wailed. Then, even while her upraised hair-brushing hand had frozen in the air and her heart had begun to beat hard and wild, that wail had deepened and become inhuman, blaring through the street and the neighbourhood and the whole great battered city. Had become, in fact, the air-raid siren itself, and she blinked and somehow she was on the floor and the child had disappeared.

Emilia got up and sat on the bed, clutching the photograph of her husband in uniform. The telegram announcing that he was missing in action had arrived the day before she was bombed out of Cripplegate, almost two months ago. She put the photograph to her forehead with hot and shaking hands, trying to absorb strength from it, companionship, sanity – if Fred was here, there'd be no hauntings; this wouldn't be happening again!

The voices below of the Jones family, quarrelling their way into the Anderson shelter at the bottom of their garden, rose above the air-raid siren and she took enough heart at the sound to run down the stairs to her back door, bypassing her own Morrison shelter in the living room. She avoided glancing at it as she always did; it was so like a great cage there in the cramped little room, beginning to echo to the bone-shaking thuds and booms of the falling bombs.

"There you are, love. We'd almost given you up tonight," was Mrs Jones's warm greeting as she slipped through the tangled bushes that masked the broken fence between their back-to-back gardens, accompanied by Mr Jones's, "Shut that door!"

"Now I know Emmy will agree that a lipstick's not a capital offence," was Sharon's petulant greeting, and Jimmy only sighed, "Gawd, as if we weren't cramped enough."

"Hush now, how'd you like to be all alone in a little Morrison over there?" snapped Mrs Jones, snuggling her baby close. Staring at the baby's sweet head turned Emilia white and sick with the memory of that lost ghost child.

"I didn't mean it. Here, sit by me, Mrs Blythe," said Jimmy, and she felt the feverish heat of his thigh and the ragged surge of his breath as she bent her head and winced her way through the cramped and malodorous hours, *crump* and *bang* and *rattle* and *blast*, without surcease. The ground shook, and so did Jimmy's breath as he tried to penetrate Emilia's thin summer frock with his eyes.

"You might at least put those black-market chums of yours to good use and get some fresh milk for the baby," she heard Mr Jones grumble; on and on he went.

Sharon tossed her glossy head in the gloom. "Oh do put a sock in it, Pa."

Emilia tried to concentrate on her own breath, pushing smooth and hot in and out of her chest, as the doctor had advised her, but every tremendous bang falling nearby shook the fortitude out of her, and she began to wonder if there would ever be a time when the bombs didn't fall. An explosion so near that the oxygen was sucked from the air in a great wave pulled at all their lungs so they jerked forward as one. There was nothing in the world but fire, mud, rubble and the barrage balloons that floated hugely in the sky. Her beloved Fred had been missing in action forever. Hitler would torment and terrify and kill them in their thousands forever. It was all eternal and all unbearable. Mrs Jones had to shake her out of her blue funk to point out the all-clear at dawn.

Emerging from the shelter, they saw Lambeth aflame. Great filthy clouds rose into the sky.

"Oh Lor', that's Aggie's neck of the woods," said Mrs Jones sadly.

Emilia shuddered as she always did to see her house standing alone, a solitary tooth in a gaping mouth, flanked by rubble where houses should have been. The only survivor of the terrace. The terrace of the Joneses, on the other hand, stood opposite, completely intact. The bombs were as gods, destroying at random.

"You really ought to join us down the factory line, Emmy," whispered Sharon into Emilia's ear. "It's ever so much better than hanging about here all alone."

Without replying, Emilia staggered back to her house. The day passed.

In the depths of that night, she was lost in the silence. Not a bomb, not an explosion, not a single ack-ack gun. No fluttering drone of bombers, attacking or defending. No sounds to either side – since moving here to this solitary house after her old flat, she had lost not only the thread-like sounds that connected her to life but also the insulating heat of other dwellings. Her house at night was as cold as a tomb.

The clock ticked steadily on the cold mantel, the gas lamp hissed; out in the street someone dropped a bottle, which smashed, and there was a woman's voice cursing. The furniture sat quietly in its accustomed places, the stairs creaked as they settled. She heard distant laughter in the blackout. There was another creak of a floorboard and the sound of soft, fretful breathing nearby, which was not her own. Emilia froze in her chair. "No," she whispered aloud. "Oh God, no, not again."

The breathing went on. It was a baby's breathing. Emilia thought of the left-hand house next door, flattened three months ago, so she'd heard, and the whole family killed – mother, father, granny, two kids. Baby.

She had just decided that she was imagining things again, talking calmly to herself as Dr Followes had taught her to, when there was a soft, infinitely melancholy little series of murmurs, "Umm umm umm, umumumum," from behind the settee, and shifting, rustling noises, for all the world like a baby crawling over the carpet, coming closer to the corner of the settee where she sat with her knitting, closer and closer, "Ummumumumum" –

She leapt from her seat in pure animal horror, huge white-wide eyes flying about the walls as though she expected babies to begin crawling through them. Silence fell. She crept through the gaslight and shadows to the fireplace, and soundlessly picked up the poker before tiptoeing, breath held in her shaking throat and heart pounding like bombs, to the settee, toe by toe, around the back where she saw, there on the carpet –

Nothing.

There was nothing there. With a strangled screech of rage and despair at her own disintegration, she threw the poker at the fireplace where it smashed the glass of her wedding picture. She fell down among the broken glass, and kissed Fred's homely grinning face a thousand times, and wept so much that she just about washed out her own veiled image. The night stretched on, endless and black, one night or another, all the same, all one black hole of loss and the fear of something gone missing that she would never find again.

Queuing for bread took up some of the hot and humid morning, and washing her linen in the shed helped to while away the languid afternoon. Running her shabby dresses through the mangle in her petticoat, she flinched away from the knock at the door in case it was young Jimmy, but it was only Sharon, sleek and smart as ever, perched incongruously amid the dust in her killing little green shoes.

"I wish you'd talk to Pa about letting me go for a WAC, Emmy. He'd listen to you. Thinks you're quality," said Sharon with a grin, offering Emilia a peppermint lozenge. It was cool and sweet in Emilia's raw mouth. "Why don't you come too? It must be ever so boring, hanging around this house all day. We never see you at the church-hall dances. Don't you feel you need an outing now and then? I know some splendid fellows who'd squire you about."

Emilia smiled. How young Sharon seemed. "I did used to go to the dances, around Cripplegate. With my friend Janice. I loved the six-step best, it was so lively. But" – she hung up a pale-green limp rectangle of cloth with the others – "with Fred . . . missing . . . I don't seem to have the heart just now, you know."

Sharon's face fell. "Of course. I say, I didn't mean anything by that. I never met Fred, you know. And what with there being no little ones I sort of forgot that you were married, and – I think if Perry were to go missing over Dresden or anything, I would go mad. But don't you wish you'd had a baby with Fred? At least it would be something of his you could keep."

"And who is Perry, young lady?"

"Oh! Emmy! My latest –" And she rattled on, heedless to Emilia's deathly pallor and the strangeness of her cooping herself up in that hot and stuffy shed. Emilia would do anything, now, to be out of her house, haunted as it was. The wails of a baby had disturbed her sleep all last night. She woke to find cold, pleading little fingers on her face and when she shrieked and threw off the dreadful weight, there was a thump beside the bed, quite as if something real had landed there. It was horrific, in the dark. She'd been unable to find her ration book for two days and she was sure the food in the lower cupboard and icebox, bread and jam and pudding, was *nibbled* at, as though by rats. A bottle of lemonade she found on its side this morning, a sticky puddle surrounding it. It was all too dreadfully familiar. It meant that she was . . . not fully in this reality. Again.

She blinked, and Sharon had gone. Her mouth was very dry. The light slanting through the dust in the shed was low and red again.

When she emerged, the house loomed over her, with windows blazing in the setting sun. A movement caught her eye and from inside her own living-room window, a woman stared at her, hostile as a bomb. Her skin was white as bone, her eyes hard and sparkling and utterly mad.

Emilia screamed, her hand before her mouth. She tore up the path and through the kitchen in her petticoat, into the living room where she found nothing save a smell, faint, of excrement and rot.

She began to cry.

It was thunder that woke her in the night, but she thought of course that it was a raid. She ought to have felt relief upon realisation, for nothing could fly in a storm like this, but felt only the queerest, creeping dread. Not since she was a child had objects in the night-time frightened her so, the familiar shapes becoming deformed, full of evil purpose. Rain lashed her windows like machine-gun fire, and the flashes of lightning made such ghastly shadows fall that she sat up and reached for the light, meaning to read a chapter or two of *Northanger Abbey*, wishing for her old radio and the sound of a human voice –

– when she looked into her mirror and saw, instead of her own familiar features, the staring lunacy of the ghost woman's face, now much closer so that she could see despair as well as ferocity in her terrible gaze. "It is you," said Emilia to the awful face. "You're the mother. I know it. You did that baby to death, or else why would you be wandering here? Go back to hell, go back. You can never undo what you did. Go back to the devil!"

Lightning flashed again, thunder cracked and there was a wail of baby fright from the next room, almost smothered by Emilia's shriek as the terrible face lit up and revealed a world of madness and horror that sent Emilia leaping from her bed. She stumbled blindly along the corridor and then stopped, her breath leaving her body only to return in a keening moan as she stared at a door that the house did not have.

She would not open a door that could not exist. That way, true madness awaited.

Yet, cold and stiff, her fingers reached for the knob and she opened the door, to stare in bewilderment into a nursery, heavy with dust and ordinary with children's toys. The bad mother waited by the window, having oozed through the wall to greet her here, and behind her green cotton skirts cowered the terrified little baby, its starfish hands reaching for Emilia in supplication. Thunder banged overhead and Emilia ran at the evil presence. Driven to her limit, she lunged for the bone-dead face with her hands out like claws, only to find herself, by the naked light of the lightning, clutching at a handful of green curtain. The spectre had dissolved in the light like mist, but the howling of the baby went on and on. Emilia stuffed her fists into her ears and cried for Fred, Fred, Fred, Fred, into the stormy night, until she blinked and she was sitting in the kitchen under the table, the rainy grey dawn confronting her through the chinks in the blackout curtains.

She walked into Cheapside that morning, sheltering under a huge black umbrella, looking neat and respectable to anyone who didn't look into her haunted eyes. Her left boot was leaking but the rain laid the dust, the terrible red brick dust that was full of the floating atoms of the pulverised dead. Having realised this, she put her handkerchief over her mouth as she picked around the heaps of rubble, the shells of half-destroyed buildings looming overhead in the gloom.

The city was hell and nor was she out of it.

At Dr Followes' office there was a kindly greeting; his hands were always warm, though he had lost two sons in the Battle of Britain and now they always shook.

"It's my old trouble, Doctor," she began. "The nerves."

He nodded, listening.

"I begin to think . . . when I am alone in the house, I begin to think I see things. And hear things."

"Things, Mrs Blythe? What kind of things?"

"Just . . . things that aren't possible. Like . . . like how it was after Mother died."

"Do you think you see your mother about the house, as you did then?"

"No," she replied, "I don't see Mother, but I do see a woman, and a – and she can't possibly be there."

"Are you doing as I advised before, Mrs Blythe? Making sure to leave the house every day, socialise often, spend your time in healthy, wholesome pursuits such as sport or crafts?"

"Oh – yes," she said, but her eyes had fallen and she heard him sigh over the obvious lie. He began to write a prescription for her tranquillisers.

"I don't suppose there has been any news about your husband, Mrs Blythe?"

She shook her head.

"It is so very hard to bear, I know, but where there's life, Mrs Blythe – there is hope." She looked up to see his eyes shining so kindly behind his little spectacles that she almost burst into tears. He started to ask her something else, but the standing wall behind his surgery which was all that was left of a Wren church chose that moment to fall, with a long and grinding roar that drowned him out.

It was a fine, blue evening now and Emilia stood in her back garden, shaking. Jimmy wandered into his garden, whistling, but when he saw her there was something in her face that alarmed even him.

She ground her teeth, staring upwards as the stars appeared, watching for Fred's plane to return. She had thought once or twice about taking the tranquillisers the doctor gave her but then she looked at the label: "To be taken with food," it said. She and food did not meet often these days. The last time she'd opened her kitchen cupboard, there was nothing but a heel of nibbled bread. So she'd tipped the pills down the sink. She wouldn't need them anyway, Fred might come home soon. He might come home tonight!

She stared into the sky.

It was black night when she blinked and surfaced again, a warm black night with a great golden bomber's moon. It was the siren that brought her back to the awful world, and now she could hear Mrs Jones's voice: "Someone fetch Mrs Blythe to the shelter!"

"Well for Gawd's sake, can't she look after herself for once? It's like the bloody trenches, squashed into that stinking shelter all together!"

"Don't be such a swine, Herbert. You know Jimmy said she's not all there these days. And the *smell* coming from her house, Sharon said . . . She is a neighbour, we've a duty to her as a war widow –"

"All right, all right, Lord help us, I'm going, just to save my eardrums. Don't forget my jigsaw! St Paul's in the spring!"

Hidden in the black shadow of the Norwegian fir, Emilia trembled with indignation. She was not a war widow! Fred would show them all when he came home tonight, landing his Lancaster in the garden! Hearing Mr Jones lumbering through the fence, she noiselessly fled, and slipped inside her back door like a ghost.

Holding her breath, she heard him crash about her garden calling her name as in the distance the first of the bombs began to fall.

"Mrs Blythe!"

The ack-acks had started. The stuttering, fluttering drone of the planes on the edge of hearing. Here they came again! But this time, Fred was here to fight them off, Fred was here to protect them all! On all fours in the living room, crouched behind the settee, she heard Mr Jones out front calling her name in increasing fury. "Mrs *Blythe!*"

It was so funny, this little game of hide-and-seek, that she almost began to giggle, before there was a moment of silence and the tiniest of little noises, a faint and breathless *umumum*.

There was nothing, nothing there. It was all in her mind, her poor overwrought lonely mind, and when Fred came home –

In the black depths of the Morrison, behind the wire of the door which closed the big metal box, something was moving. Something white. A dot of a thing; a bone-white, weary little starfish opened and closed, then two phantom eyes, tiny and perfectly round. She jammed a hand into her mouth as the apparition swam before her in slow and dreadful motion, dragging itself forward to cling to the cage wire.

Boom!

Close enough to feel the shock wave, close enough to feel the buildings crash to earth as they were annihilated, close enough for Mr Jones to yell, "Oh fuck this! This mad bitch isn't worth dying for, let her gawp around in the garden crying for Fred all night!"

He began to tramp away, leaving her alone in the dark amid the insanity of the raid, the flames already beginning to leap into the air on the skyline, yellow and blue and red all over London, her city disintegrating and unravelling into fire and destruction. Before her, the terrible neglected phantom tugging at her helpless guilty mad heart, and behind her –

An exhalation, long, slow and triumphant, a foul wash of a stench, and Emilia knew that the evil spectre of the terrible mother had arisen, coldly boiling, from the earth.

Her strained shriek of "Fred, Fred, Fred!" as she ran blindly out into the smoky garden frightened the life out of Mr Jones. She flung herself onto his back as he tried to clamber through the stakes of the fence, still shrieking, and she didn't even realise that the bubbling, choking sounds in her ears were the death of Mr Jones, as the stake that her weight had impaled him on drove through his plump unshaven throat. She only clung like a leech to his fat dying body. Smuts and sparks of sooty black fell over their faces as the planes droned into view, and she cried out in triumph: "Fred! I knew you would come!" before the falling bomb landed, and obliterated the last house in the fallen terrace, casting it down into rubble like all the rest.

Sharon fell in love with the first of the wardens to arrive, of course, and through her genuine sobs over the remains of her father she found a smile for him – his name was Neil and he put a blanket around her shapely shoulders, promising himself he would take her out tomorrow after the all-clear, he would take some pleasure somewhere, somehow, before it was too late. There was nothing to identify her father, not even clothes; nothing but lumps of burned flesh, which he had covered from her eyes. There was quite a heap of them; he must have been a huge man.

"She lived there alone," said Jimmy, numbly. "She'd only been there two months. She hardly ever left the house. Her husband was missing in action."

"She was so nice, but she was going barmy in there alone," sobbed Sharon into Neil's shoulder. "She kept hearing babies cry when there weren't none. She told me so."

"Don't you speak ill of the dead," came from a muffled Mrs Jones.

"Now now, we don't know that she is dead yet. There was a Morrison in there? She might be in it, if we can only dig her out," soothed Neil.

"No," and Sharon sniffed noisily, "she never went in it. She said it was haunted. Would never invite me in to have a look though – we had to visit in the kitchen!"

Wardens and firemen crawled over the heap of rubble. Jimmy could see the bed, miraculously whole, sitting askew on top of the heap behind the fragment of living-room wall that remained whole, and shivered with lust and sorrow. "She was beautiful," he choked, "I don't care if she was barmy."

"There, lad," Neil began when a shout went up from the excavated hollow behind the section of wall, and Neil put Sharon aside and ran. Swaddled in a blanket, Mrs Jones stood up.

It was ten minutes before the three wardens emerged, the flames dying so the remains of the Jones family couldn't see what Neil was carrying in his arms until he got very close, and then:

"A baby?" cried Sharon. Starving it clearly was, filthy and stinking with great hollow haunted eyes in a bone-white face, and tangled hair the same flame-red as Emilia's.

"Caged up in the Morrison, all alone. She must really have been mad," Neil's voice hoarse with smoke and tears.

Mrs Jones clapped her hand to her mouth and sat down with a bump as she began to understand.

"Oh dear lord, dear lord, you don't mean to say it was hers? Oh, and the times she told our Sharon the house was haunted by – oh God forgive her –" and she reached out her big worn hands for the orphan, folding it close.

Jimmy burst into tears.

What the Creek Carries Away
MIRANDA STONE

A powerful story about cousins who meet twenty years after a terrible misunderstanding changed the course of their lives.

> "Reed." Alma's voice, tinged with urgency, made me freeze. "Wait," she said.

I expected my grandfather's house to be empty a week after his funeral, but I spotted a figure sitting on the top porch step, and as I eased my car closer, a spasm seized my gut.

Twenty years, and my cousin still looked the same. Long brown hair that refused to hold a curl, hazel eyes set deep in her pale face. Three years my junior, she'd be thirty-five now. Despite the morning chill, she wore a tank top and denim shorts. Her feet were bare.

I swallowed hard. My unfamiliar vehicle drew her attention, and I was tempted to hunker down and keep driving. The back of my neck prickled with heat.

"No," I muttered. "You won't run me off this time."

I parked the car on the street and cut the engine. For a long moment, I didn't move, just watched her through the window. The sound of rushing water penetrated the silence. A bold creek traversed the property behind Granddad's house, and I wondered how high the water had risen after last night's heavy rain.

As I got out of the car, Alma didn't wave or move to rise. I scratched the stubble on my jaw, wishing I'd shaved that morning, and then berated myself for wanting to appear more presentable.

"Alma," I called, nodding at her.

"Hello, Reed."

I ventured towards the porch, hands shoved in my jeans pockets. "I stopped by to see the place one last time."

"You weren't at the funeral."

I stared hard at her. "No, but I think the old man would have understood why I missed it." She had the decency to lower her eyes. "Looks like he managed to keep the place up." New vinyl siding covered the house's exterior, and the lawn was well-tended.

"When he told me the cancer was terminal, I moved back here to take care of him," Alma said.

"So what happens to the house now that he's gone?"

She cleared her throat. "Granddad left it to me."

My smile was a mere flash of teeth. "Well, you sure have done all right for yourself."

She climbed to her feet, and I avoided looking at her long legs. She was taller than I remembered. "Why don't you come inside? I'll fix you something to eat."

"I don't want a thing from you."

Alma placed her hands on her hips. "What do you want, then? To look through the house? Feel free. Take whatever you like."

"That's not why I came. I figured the house would be locked up by now." I continued towards the porch. "I just want to sit out here for a few minutes. Is that OK with you?"

Alma hugged herself as though she were cold. "Of course it is, Reed."

I shrugged. "Thought I should ask, since it's your place now." I climbed the steps, careful not to touch her as I made my way to the old metal glider. It let out a hideous groan under my weight. Rust had eaten away most of the pale-yellow paint.

Alma retreated to the door but didn't go inside. "You want me to leave you alone?" she asked.

I gazed at the mountains surrounding Granddad's house. The last remnants of morning fog dissipated as the sun rose higher. "I don't care what you do."

She took a step closer. "I saw your parents at the funeral. When I asked about you, they said they hadn't spoken to you in years."

The muscles in my shoulders tightened. "That's right."

She drew a circle on the porch floor with her toe. "You probably heard that Daddy died."

I thought of Uncle Hank, military stern. "I didn't know."

"A stroke, three years ago." She swiped at her cheeks, but I didn't see any tears. "Mama's doing OK, and Elisa's a lawyer now. She lives out in Arizona."

I nodded but didn't trust myself to speak of Alma's younger sister.

She lowered herself onto the porch and crossed her legs. "How've you been, Reed?"

Her coaxing tone infuriated me. "Oh, the last twenty years have been a fucking cakewalk."

Alma studied her hands clasped in her lap. "Are you married? Do you have kids?"

"No. After what happened here, I left home as soon as I turned eighteen, enlisted in the army. I served for a few years, and when I got out, a buddy and I opened a bar. Running the business takes up most of my time."

She offered a tentative smile. "So things are going well for you?"

I tried to laugh, but it emerged from my throat as a low growl. "Does it look like things are going well for me, Alma?"

Red blotches appeared on her chest and neck. "Reed, you don't know how many times I've wanted to look you up and call to tell you I'm sorry. But for God's sake, we were kids."

I pointed a finger at her. "Don't you dare make excuses for yourself. You sat in this house and listened to your dad threaten to kill me, and you didn't say a fucking word."

She pulled at her tank top as though it were choking her. "I was terrified. Couldn't you see that? Do you know what Daddy would have done to me if I'd told the truth? I never thought your parents would turn on you the way they did."

I leaned back in the glider and closed my eyes, resisting the urge to grab her shoulders and shake her until something came loose in her brain and spilled from her mouth, something more useful than *I'm sorry*.

"I remember everything about that day," I said. "You wore a pale-blue dress with little spaghetti straps. You stayed out of the sun so you wouldn't burn."

"Reed, don't."

The pleading in her voice made me sit up and peer at her. In the late-morning light, she looked just like the girl I once knew, and I rubbed my eyes to erase the illusion.

I went on speaking. She finally stopped protesting and grew still in that unnerving way of hers, sitting at my feet like a child as she listened to the story I told.

* * *

I sipped a cup of coffee at Granddad's kitchen table, barely able to keep my eyes open. Alma sat across from me, yawning over a bowl of cereal, while Elisa nodded off in the chair beside her. We had stayed up late the night before, engaged in a Monopoly marathon. Alma won two games out of three, and I didn't think she would ever let me forget it.

That Saturday morning, Granddad, my father, and my uncle Hank sat at the other end of the table. As Dad recounted some childhood memory, Granddad's lined face brightened, and I realised how happy it made the old man to see his two sons together. A widower for five years now, he lived alone in this house where he and Grandma raised a family.

Though we lived three hours away, my parents and I visited every month. Uncle Hank and his wife Cheri brought their girls back to the mountains less often, but we still saw them several times a year.

Cheri and Mom chatted as they washed the breakfast dishes, and Hank drained his coffee cup. "So what's the plan for today?" he asked Granddad.

Granddad clasped his hands over his belly and settled back in the chair. "If it ain't too much trouble, I'd like to go see Howard in Woodville."

Elisa perked up at the mention of Granddad's brother. "Please don't make me go to his house again." Just shy of twelve years old, she could still get away with whining. "I'll be bored to tears. He doesn't even have a television."

Alma snorted as she carried her bowl to the sink. "Oh, the horror!"

"Dad, let me and Alma and Reed stay here," Elisa begged. "Reed's almost eighteen. He can watch us while you're gone."

Hank's rigid features softened; it was painfully obvious that Elisa was his favourite. He turned to me, eyebrows raised. "Reed, if we let y'all stay here, will you be sure to watch after the girls?"

"Yes, sir."

Alma stood behind Hank, and she made a face at me, sticking out her tongue and crossing her eyes. I had to look away before I laughed.

An hour later, my cousins and I gathered on the porch as our parents and Granddad climbed into Hank's car. Before they pulled away, Cheri rolled down the window and ordered us to stay at the house.

Once they were gone, Elisa carried an old lawn chair from the shed and set it in the front yard. She flopped into it and closed her eyes, basking in the August heat.

Alma and I sat together on the porch glider. "So you're all done with high school now," she said. "Lucky you."

I stretched my arms over my head and let out a contented groan. "Yep. Now it's off to the community college in a couple of weeks."

"What do you want to study?" She swatted at a mosquito on her arm.

"Criminal justice, so I can go into law enforcement."

Alma leaned back to consider me. "I can see you flashing your badge and carrying a gun, chasing the bad guys."

I couldn't hold back a smile. "You think?"

She nodded and stretched out her legs, pushing her feet against the porch floor so the glider moved beneath us. "Do you have a girlfriend?"

"Not at the moment." I placed my legs alongside hers and helped push. "What about you? I bet you're breaking a lot of hearts these days."

She snickered and shook her head. "Not me."

I nudged her with my elbow. "Come on now, 'fess up."

Alma's fair skin flushed red. "I'm telling the truth!" Her giddy laughter let me know she enjoyed my teasing.

"You be sure to warn your boyfriends that I'll kick their asses if they step out of line."

She erupted into giggles, ducking her head. "OK, I'll tell them."

I slapped my palms against my thighs. "So you do have a bunch of boys chasing you! Now the truth comes out."

She laughed harder. "No, no, that's not what I meant."

Elisa craned her neck towards us. "Ain't anyone interested in her, Reed. She's never even had a boyfriend."

Alma folded her arms over her chest. "Shut your mouth, Elisa. You don't know anything."

Elisa pressed a finger against her forearm to check her tan. Unlike me and Alma, she had an olive complexion and blond curls that lightened in the sun. "I know that no one invited you to the spring dance."

Alma stood fast enough to give the glider a violent jolt. "I've got a headache," she said to me. "I'm going to lie down for a bit."

"Granddad has some aspirin in the medicine cabinet."

"I'll be OK." Alma leaned on the porch railing and glared at Elisa. "I hope you get one hell of a sunburn, you little brat."

Elisa waved a dismissive hand. "You're just jealous because you don't tan. You're white as a sheet."

Alma went inside, and I stayed put on the glider, eyes closed. The sound of the creek lulled me into a light sleep.

"Hey, Reed," Elisa called, "if I'm really nice to you, will you go get my portable CD player from the back bedroom?"

I climbed to my feet. "Only if you're really nice to Alma, too."

Elisa grinned. "Where's the fun in that?"

I went to the kitchen for a glass of water. As I gulped it down, I gazed out the window above the sink. Granddad's closest neighbours lived a half-mile along the road, and I could barely see their rooftop through the trees.

I walked down the hall, passing Granddad's room and then the spare room my parents shared when we visited. As the sole male grandchild, I was relegated to sleeping on the sofa in the front room, while Alma and Elisa shared a rollaway bed in Granddad's rarely used dining room. Hank and Cheri stayed in the back bedroom, and I now found its door closed.

I rapped lightly. "Hey, Alma, I need to get Elisa's CD player." I opened the door without waiting for her to answer, figuring she was already asleep.

Alma lay on the bed, her slender legs spread wide and bent at the knees. The hem of her dress was drawn up to her waist, and a pair of plain white underwear dangled from her ankle. Her right hand rested between her thighs.

The blood rushed to my face so fast that I grew dizzy. Sputtering an apology, I squeezed my eyes shut and turned to flee.

"Reed." Alma's voice, tinged with urgency, made me freeze. I kept my back to her, gripping the doorknob. "Wait," she said.

I looked over my shoulder. She hadn't lowered her dress or moved her hand from between her legs. Her eyes were unfocused as she stared up at me, and strands of hair clung to her damp forehead. I hated the sound of my hard breaths filling the otherwise quiet room. My brain commanded me to run, but my feet wouldn't cooperate.

"Alma." Her name was a warning on my lips.

Approaching footsteps drew my attention to the hallway. Elisa stood just outside the room and gaped at us. "What are y'all doing?" Her words were high-pitched, bordering on hysterical.

In my peripheral vision, I saw Alma scramble to pull on her clothes. "Elisa, get out of here," she shouted.

Elisa took two steps backward. "I'm telling," she said, then spun around and sprinted down the hall.

Alma and I took off running and caught up with Elisa at the creek. She stood with her hands braced against her knees. "Y'all are sick," she panted. "Get away from me."

Alma grabbed her sister's arm and shook her. "We weren't doing anything. Now you better keep your damn mouth shut."

Elisa jerked away and ran to the house, where she locked herself in the back bedroom.

Out on the porch, I propped myself against the railing, shaking my head as though I'd been struck. "How are we going to explain this?" I asked Alma.

She sat on the steps, knees drawn to her chin. "We'll say she's lying."

I was dripping sweat; my T-shirt clung to me like a second skin. "Uncle Hank will never believe that. As far as he's concerned, whatever Elisa says is gospel."

Alma cupped a palm over her mouth. "He'll kill me," she muttered through her fingers.

I wanted to tell her she was overreacting, but I couldn't convince myself. I feared he would kill us both.

Our parents and Granddad returned at half past four that afternoon. Cheri talked of frying pork chops for dinner. Mom paused to regard me and Alma sitting on the porch. "Everything OK?" she asked.

I nodded. "Everything's fine."

"Where's Elisa?"

"In the back bedroom."

Granddad ruffled Alma's hair. "You kids should have gone with us. We had a real nice time."

Elisa didn't appear until Cheri called her for dinner. She refused to look at me and Alma as she sat down at the table. During the meal, I sneaked glances at my cousins. Elisa pushed food around her plate, while Alma ate as fast as she could.

"You girls are awfully quiet," Mom said.

Those words held the key to unlock Elisa's speech. "While y'all were gone," she blurted, "I caught Alma and Reed in the back room. Alma was on the bed, and she had her dress up and her underwear down . . ."

The silence that descended on the table was so thick I could hear the blood pounding in my ears. Then a snarl rattled in Hank's throat, growing louder with each passing second. He jumped to his feet and lunged, taking a swing at me. "I asked you to look after them, you little shit."

"Daddy –" Alma said.

He turned on her like a wild animal drawn to easier prey. "Shut your goddamned mouth."

"Now wait a minute," Granddad said.

I tried to lure Hank's attention back to me. "Nothing happened. I accidentally walked in on Alma changing, and I was about to leave when Elisa saw me."

"You're a liar!" Elisa screamed. Her face grew taut with rage. "Alma was on the bed and touching herself where she shouldn't be."

My lips moved, but I couldn't form words. I sought out my mother. "That's not what happened," I told her, but her eyes grew wide at my feeble protest, and I knew she saw through the lie. I looked at Granddad. He sat at the head of the table, rendered helpless by age and his eldest son's fury.

Hank's nostrils flared as he loomed over Alma. "Did Reed make you do something you didn't want to?" he asked.

Alma's stare locked with mine. I desperately needed a drink; my throat tightened, and I feared I would choke. She opened her mouth, and I waited for the truth to tumble out like a rotten carcass, but her face crumpled and she began to sob. Cheri hurried over to her and led her from the table.

"I didn't make her do anything," I said.

Hank's ruddy face darkened to crimson as he turned to Dad. "Get him out of here, Phillip. I swear to God, I'll kill him if I ever see him again."

I waited for my father to defend me against the brother he so admired. Dad looked from me to my mother, and his shoulders sagged. "Take him to the car, Valerie. I'll get our things."

Mom positioned herself between me and Hank as she came to stand at my side.

I slammed my hands down on the table, almost overturning my glass of tea. "I didn't do anything wrong." My trembling voice filled me with shame.

Granddad leaned forward and covered my hand with his. "It's OK, Reed. Just go on outside for a bit."

I stared into his kind face and realised he was the only one who hadn't betrayed me. My eyes watered, but I simply nodded and did as he said.

Mom didn't try to touch me as I stormed to the car. She didn't ask for the truth. Even after I slid into the back seat, she remained outside and waited for Dad. I noticed the grey in her hair and the lines around her eyes. She seemed to have aged ten years in the last half-hour.

Dad lugged our suitcases down the porch steps, and I made no move to help him put the bags in the trunk. After my parents got in the car and Dad started the engine, I glanced up and saw Granddad standing at the front door, his hand raised in farewell.

My parents didn't speak. I closed my eyes, willing the pain in my head to subside. Before we drove out of the mountains, I bolted upright and told Dad to stop the car. He gave me a questioning look in the rear-view mirror. "I'm going to be sick," I said.

He pulled onto the shoulder, and I threw open the door and vomited up what little food I'd eaten. When I slumped against the seat, wiping my mouth with the back of my hand, I looked once more to my mother for comfort, but she kept her eyes focused on the road ahead.

* * *

"Things were never the same," I told Alma. "Mom avoided me. If I came into the room, she left. She began spending most of her hours after work volunteering at our church. Dad was polite, making small talk to fill the silence at meals, but I could tell he was counting the days until I turned eighteen. He couldn't stand the tension between Mom and me."

Silent tears coursed down Alma's cheeks and spotted her shirt. Even though her nose was leaking, she didn't raise her head. "I don't understand why Valerie treated you that way."

"We never had anything to do with Mom's family. Dad once told me that Mom's brother hurt her when she was a child. He refused to say how, but I'm pretty sure I know. Maybe she looked at me that evening and saw her brother." I paused and took a deep breath. I would not cry in front of Alma. I would not shed another tear for these people I no longer considered family. "When I turned eighteen, I enlisted in the army. I didn't have anywhere else to go, and it kept me out of trouble. I served for four years, long enough to get my head together. My buddy Seth and I received our discharge papers at the same time, and it was his idea to open a bar. We've been running it since."

Alma finally looked up, her lips quaking. "I think about what happened every day, Reed. I wish I could go back and make it right." She cried harder, gasping as she struggled to speak. "I've never been able to forgive myself. I went to college and became a teacher, and I saw a therapist for years. I tried to date, but I couldn't be intimate with a man. It felt . . . wrong, dirty. I kept remembering what happened —"

"I don't want to hear this," I said. Flakes of paint stuck to my jeans when I rose from the glider, and I brushed at them on my way to the steps.

"I tried to kill myself."

I froze on the porch and closed my eyes.

"No one ever tells you how hard it is," she went on. "Do you know how deep you have to slice your arm to open an artery? Or the number of pills you need to wash down with booze, just enough so you don't puke them all up like I did?"

My back ached with tension, but I found myself turning towards her. "What do you want from me, Alma?"

She stood and scrubbed her face with her palms. "Let me fix you something to eat before you leave."

Granddad's old recliner had been replaced with a newer model in the front room, and I imagined him drifting to sleep in it. Photographs of him and Grandma hung on the walls, along with those of my parents and Hank and his family. I saw that Granddad never took down my high-school graduation picture.

I followed Alma to the kitchen and slumped into Granddad's chair at the head of the table. The appliances were updated and the walls freshly painted.

"You plan on living here now?" I asked Alma as she fixed a ham and cheese sandwich.

"For the time being. When Granddad got really sick, I quit my teaching job in Louisville so I could take care of him. I hate to think of selling this place, but I figure I'll have to eventually. There's no work back here." She set the plate before me, along with a glass of lemonade, and then sat down. "How did you know he died?"

As I took a sip of lemonade, my eyes searched her inner arm for a telltale scar. I saw it, faint but ragged, about three inches long. "I didn't get a call from him on my birthday earlier this month. He called every year, but I never answered. He always left a message telling me he loved me and hoped to see me soon. Like nothing ever happened."

"That's right," Alma said. "You just turned thirty-eight, didn't you?"

I nodded. "When he didn't call, I looked up the obituaries in the local paper online. He died just two days before my birthday." I cleared my throat and stared at the untouched sandwich. "Did he suffer a lot?"

"It was bad at the end. He was weak and in pain."

"Did he ever say anything about what happened?" My eyes stung with unshed tears.

"No, Reed. He never thought we did anything wrong." She leaned closer. "Do you remember when I was about twelve and went through that weird religious phase?"

I took a bite of sandwich so I wouldn't have to answer right away. "I remember," I finally said.

I thought she'd gone crazy that summer. She agonised over every real or imagined sin she committed and prayed dozens of times a day. She had nightmares of demons. None of us could convince her that she wasn't going to hell.

"You remember what Granddad did for me so I wouldn't be afraid any more?"

Granddad told us he was gripped by the same religious fervour as a young man. It drove him to become a preacher, but he left the ministry after marrying Grandma, who claimed she wasn't cut out to be a preacher's wife. After that, he worked in insurance, but he could still quote the Bible better than anyone I knew.

One day, when Alma had worked herself into a fit of religious angst, Granddad led her through the woods behind the house. I watched from the trees as they removed their shoes and waded into the creek. At its deepest point, the water reached Alma's waist.

"He said the creek would cleanse me," she murmured, smoothing the tablecloth beneath her hand. "The water would flow over my body and carry all my sins downstream to the New River." Her eyes met mine. "Do you remember what he said when he dunked me under the water?" I pushed my plate aside and nodded. Alma reached across the table and squeezed my fingers so hard I winced. "Take me to the creek, Reed."

I couldn't help but laugh. "I ain't no preacher."

"It isn't God who can grant me forgiveness."

I followed her down the path, now overgrown with weeds. It was clear no one had been to the creek in a long time. "Watch out for snakes," I warned.

Alma strode ahead, her hair falling in a dark curtain over her back. We stood on the bank, and she placed a hand on my arm to steady herself as she removed her tennis shoes. I pulled off my own shoes and looked around. We were alone out here. By mid-September, it was too cold for swimming.

Alma waded into the creek, gasping at the shock of icy water. She stumbled on one of the slick stones under her feet. I walked in after her and released a whoop as the water soaked through my pants legs and reached my skin. Alma slogged to the middle of the creek and turned to me, her teeth chattering.

"We can't stay out here long." I closed the distance between us.

"I know," she said.

I hesitated before her, unsure, but Alma's pleading eyes prompted me to grab her shoulders and turn her sideways. My movements were awkward as I placed a hand against her back. Her hair coiled around my arm. "Ready?" I asked.

Alma nodded and crossed her arms over her chest. I dipped her backward, holding her body before me like an offering. She closed her eyes, and I lowered her further into the water until she was entirely submerged. Her skin was stark white against the murky grey-green of the creek. She felt so small and weak in my grasp. I pressed my free hand to her forehead. My brain fixed upon the image of me holding her underwater long after she stopped fighting and grew still.

I pulled her from the creek, and she sucked in a lungful of air. Her face broke, the way it did twenty years ago when she had the chance to save me and found she couldn't. Now her hand sought mine. "You have to say it," she wailed. "Please, Reed. Tell me what Granddad used to say."

I cradled Alma in my arms and ached to lie with her beneath the frigid water until it washed us clean of the past twenty years. Lowering my lips to her ear, I whispered, "Go forth, my child, and sin no more."

What the Sea Brings
MICHAEL C. KEITH

Developmentally challenged sixteen-year-old Caitlin is fascinated by a dead soldier that washes up on the shore near her home.

> "I will stay with you," said Caitlin, placing a soft kiss on the corpse's cold cheek.

It is in fantasy that the real live.
– Anonymous

Merchant ships transporting cargo and personnel across the Atlantic to US allies during World War II were all too often torpedoed off the East Coast. This was the fate of the *Chatham* carrying ensign Wayne Harley. His body washed ashore in a remote rocky cove on the northern Maine coast. There it remained unseen for days until sixteen-year-old Caitlin Bosworth found it.

It was the happiest day of her life.

Caitlin had suffered from oxygen deprivation during birth and consequently had the mental acumen of someone half her age. She had a sweet temperament and derived great pleasure playing along the shoreline that her house faced. Her parents adored their only child and did everything to make her life cheerful and as intellectually stimulating as possible. It was their greatest hope that Caitlin would one day reach a level of proficiency that would allow her to live independent of their constant oversight.

However, Caitlin's doctor was not optimistic about her chances of living on her own. He had told the Bosworths that their daughter's mind would likely remain at the level of a ten-year-old through her adulthood.

In other words, they would have to care for her the balance of their lives or institutionalise her, which was something they would never consider. The joy they got from her existence more than balanced the burden involved in raising a developmentally challenged daughter. She was the delight of their lives and the prospect of having a child who would remain a child for ever was far from unpleasant.

One of the things Caitlin loved most was hearing the romantic fairy tales her parents read to her. Beyond that, she also loved listening to the radio. Among a host of programmes, she got the most pleasure from the dramatic stories on *Lux Radio Theatre*. One about a prince who falls in love with a peasant girl particularly captured her fancy.

"I will marry a prince. A handsome prince," she declared after the programme.

In the coming days it was all Caitlin thought about, and her mother and father happily played along with her.

"You are *our* beautiful princess," they said as she swirled around in her favourite frock.

Caitlin continued her ecstatic dance out of the house to play in the bright early-autumn sun.

"Come back soon for lunch, honey!" shouted her mother.

A report on the radio caught Lyle Bosworth's attention. "Krauts sunk another ship not far away. Around a hundred sailors on her," he reported to his wife.

"The poor parents of those boys," said Sarah Bosworth, staring out the window at her daughter. "To lose a child is the worst thing I can imagine. We're so lucky to have our little girl."

Caitlin soon reached the spot where she spent so many happy hours lost in her imaginary world. It was there that Wayne Harley washed up. When Caitlin saw the young man's body she was instantly enthralled.

"My prince. You've come for me, haven't you?"

"Yes, my princess. I *have* come for you," she heard him answer.

Caitlin ran to where his body sat.

"I *knew* you would come. Do you want some tea? You look so cold."

She remained with the drowned seaman until her mother's distant voice caught her attention.

"It's time for lunch. Please don't leave. I'll come back soon and bring you some food."

As soon as Caitlin returned home, she reported her encounter to her parents. They had heard many fantastical accounts from her before and always listened to them with great affection and interest.

"He is very handsome, but he is tired after his long journey from his castle. May I bring him a sandwich? He is very hungry."

"Of course you may, darling. Maybe he would like a piece of cake, too."

"Yes, Mommy. He likes sweets."

Caitlin ran quickly to her waiting prince and then placed as much food into his open mouth as would fit.

"You're so hungry! Mommy said you would like her cake."

"It is the most delicious cake I have ever eaten," replied Caitlin's prince.

"Where is your castle?"

"Across the sea."

"Will we live there?"

"Yes, for ever."

"Is there a beautiful garden?"

"There is none better in any kingdom."

"My favourite flower is the red rose."

"It is the flower of my realm. You will always have them for your hair."

The entranced couple conversed until the sun neared the horizon.

"I must go home or my parents will worry. I'll come back in the morning with Mommy's biscuits. You will love them as much as her cake."

Over the next several days, Caitlin spent long rapturous hours in conversation with the dead seaman. They spoke of many extraordinary things, all based on their future life together.

Caitlin had had many imaginary friends before, but her parents could not recall any that so absorbed her.

"Do you think she's OK? Every waking moment she talks about this prince. It is all so real to her."

"I wouldn't worry, honey," Lyle replied to his wife. "She has a vivid imagination. You know that. Doctor Fairfield said that special children like her sometimes do. It's kind of a gift, really."

"I guess you're right."

"As long as she's happy. That's the main thing."

Exhilarated by her new experience Caitlin rose before sunrise and eagerly waited in the kitchen for her mother to appear.

"Good morning, sweetheart. What would you like for breakfast this morning?"

"He loves your biscuits, Mommy. Make biscuits."

"It's raining out, so you better wait until it stops before you go to your friend."

"My prince, you mean, Mommy."

"Yes, of course, your prince."

"But he will be terribly hungry. Please, I can wear my pretty raincoat. See, Mommy, it's not raining very hard," observed Caitlin, looking out of the kitchen window.

Mrs Bosworth reluctantly gave in to her daughter's plea, in return making her promise to come back quickly.

When Caitlin reached the cove she found her beloved lying on his side as waves washed over his legs.

"Wake up, my dear prince. I have your biscuits."

When he did not move, she exerted all her strength to raise his body, leaning it against the rock upon which it had rested.

"There, now. Here, eat your breakfast," she said, placing pieces of biscuit into his frozen maw. "I must go home until the rain stops. I promised Mommy, but I'll come back later."

"Please stay with me," she heard her prince say.

"But Mommy will be worried."

"You are my princess now. Your mother will understand. We will soon go to my castle."

"Yes . . . yes, I *am* your princess, so I *will* stay with you," said Caitlin, placing a soft kiss on the corpse's cold cheek.

As time passed, Sarah Bosworth grew concerned, especially since it was raining harder and the wind had picked up. She decided she had to find her daughter.

"I'm coming with you," said her husband.

As they left the house they were surprised and disheartened by how ferocious the weather had become.

"Let's go to the cove first," suggested Sarah, knowing it was her daughter's favourite place to play.

When they reached the tiny inlet, the sky had cleared.

"That is so odd," remarked Lyle. "I have never seen a storm pass so quickly."

"Look, it's her raincoat!" exclaimed Sarah, dashing to where it floated in the nearby surf.

"Caitlin! Where *are* you?" they called frantically, their voices echoing in the deserted cove.

Why Can't They Leave Things Alone?
HARRY DOWNEY

||||||||||||||||||||||||||||||||||||||||||||||||||||||||||||||||||||||||||||||||||||||||||||||||||||||||||||||||||||||||||||||||||||||||||||||||||||

A habitual shoplifter's lucky day turns out to be the wrong sort of luck.

> "My methods are my own; I won't divulge them to anyone else. Let me just say I'm good at what I do."

Would you buy a used car from a flashy, smooth-talking salesman called Ambrose? I wouldn't. But my wife fell for his patter and now she's my ex and living with him in Basingstoke. And good riddance too. So Charlie Medwin, that's me, on my own for a few weeks now, had a few adjustments to make in the way things went. By now I've pretty well sorted out my new routine. Take shopping, for instance. Vera used to do what she called her "big shop" down at Tesco's on Friday evenings. Not me. Now there's a lot less needed, and anyway, I've got my own way of doing things. She paid at the checkout for everything she took from the store. I don't. I pay for what's in the trolley and everything else is a nice little earner for me.

Chissingford where I live is big enough to have the lot: Morrisons, Sainsbury's, Tesco's, Asda, a Co-op of course, even a Waitrose – the one they call "the toff's supermarket". No continental stores yet, but it's only time, isn't it? So I've got a bit of a choice when I shop. Of course, I don't look for *2 for 1* offers and that sort of thing. No way. I just look where it's the easiest to steal from. The supermarkets are getting better on their security these days. In fact, there's one of the big boys I don't go near any more – that is unless I'm being an honest member of Joe Public at the time and queuing up at the checkout like the ordinary punters. Which one? No way, José. That's for you to find out. After all, it's taken me a long time to get all this know-how and I don't give info like that away for free. Now if you offered to pay me for what I know, well, that's another matter.

With all the new rules ciggies have become very difficult these days. So I don't try. I leave them alone on their locked shelves and concentrate on the bottled stuff – they all have masses of wines and spirits on their shelves. Then CDs are usually a piece of cake to lift, and if you pick the chart stuff they're dead easy to shift. And every penny is profit. No overheads, nothing like that to worry about.

The main things to look out for are the "hidden" cameras – now that really is a joke. With the exception of one store – no names, no pack drill – where they aren't at all bad, whoever decides where to place them seems to have no idea, and if you know what to look for they're no problem. As for store detectives, most of 'em haven't a clue; just see 'em a couple of times and you remember their faces. In my experience, unless the bosses are around they've usually switched off and are working on autopilot.

If I were honest – get it? – I really believe I could save the typical supermarket chain serious money by advising them on what to do: sort of poacher turned gamekeeper thing. My proposal would be for them to agree to pay me a consultancy fee of, well, let's say 20 per cent of what I would save them in a year. They'd be quids in and it would certainly suit me. As a pro I'd know what to look for. I've seen other people doing what I do in their stores and you can pick 'em out easy. The difference is I don't think the people I spot would spot me doing the same thing. Rank amateurs, most of 'em. They haven't a clue. Perhaps I should approach one of our local store managers with my idea. Prepare a proper case – the sort of thing they call a Business Plan, on paper with figures and everything – and see his reaction. Just a thought. After all, they tell us that the best hackers in the business are working now for the internet security companies or at the Pentagon. It makes sense, doesn't it?

As I said, my methods are my own and I won't divulge them to anyone else. Let me just say that I'm good at what I do and, if you want proof, get someone to look in the records of the local constabulary. Not once have I been pulled in for questioning, never mind being charged. My sheet is completely clean. It's a matter of professional pride to me even though I know you straight folks probably don't approve. Eight years doing what I do and the only blemish on my record is a parking fine

– and they don't count, do they? My old dad was a regular in the army and always said that Long Service medals and Good Conduct badges just recognised X years' undetected crime. He was probably right.

On Wednesday morning it all happened. At about eleven fifteen, I was down at one of the stores on the Cherry Lane Estate – I won't say which one but you could easily check if you wanted to – and had just gone through checkout number four. They were very busy and the girl on the till apologised about the time we'd been kept waiting. The woman in front had been a bit silly with a lot of money-off coupons and things, and wanted to change items, and one of the store girls was sent off to do it for her and it all took time.

Well, there I was, checked out and everything, just heading for the exit when these two guys in suits and a uniformed man pounced on me. That's my lot, I thought. I've been spotted. I had a proper receipt in my pocket for the stuff in the trolley, but I had somehow overlooked paying for the two one-litre bottles of Glenfiddich and some Rioja that were in the big, deep pockets of my coat. Decision time. Should I brazen it out or go quietly?

I didn't have much choice. The older man, bald, horn-rimmed glasses, in a natty suit and with a large badge in his lapel, held out his hand, started to shake mine vigorously and somewhere just out of my vision a camera started flashing.

"Congratulations, sir. You may not have realised it, but you are the ten thousandth customer this store has had since we opened. As such, all your purchases today are free, with our compliments, and we would like you to be our guest for a little ceremony. It won't take more than a few minutes and you will be given a memento of the occasion."

Everything I'd just bought was free! If only I'd known. There'd be a lot more than eight pounds forty-three pence worth in my bag (a reusable one, naturally, as I like to do my bit for the environment). Mind you, if I'd taken longer choosing I would have been further back in the queue and not the magic number – so there you are. Sod's Law in action.

People gathered round at a little table near the main entrance. Mr Mallinder – that was his name – droned on a bit, and some smarmy-looking guy in his best suit fawned all over him. I found out later that Mallinder was from Head Office and the creep was the store manager. Afterwards they showed me all the pictures they took and Creepy had managed to get near his idol in every one.

People were clapping, pictures were being taken, some girl with Press on her blouse asked me a few silly questions. I was very good and showed great self-control. I didn't do what the badge said, even though she was a big girl – if you know what I mean. So apart from the made-up selection of groceries and a special something – that was it. The special? An extra-large bottle of Glenfiddich, wouldn't you guess it? And I'm teetotal at that.

End of story except that I was heavily featured in the papers as a result of my little surprise. Just the locals, of course, but in the *Chissingford Recorder*, the *County Gazette* and both of the free advertising rags. Pictures and a big plug for the store. So, that was my fifteen minutes of fame that apparently we're all going to get in our lifetimes. Not that I was overpleased. Living the sort of life I do the last thing I want is publicity. I certainly don't want my face plastered all over the place and being seen by people I don't want to see it. Something I'd do my best to avoid in future – no more exposure again if I can help it.

It didn't work out quite like that. I was in the papers again not long afterwards. This time the nationals got in on the act with a whiff of a story from somebody local and enjoyed themselves at my expense. In the *Mirror* they decided that *On the house? Not this time, Charlie* just about summed it up. The Sun, typically, used just one word – *Stupido*. I'm fairly thick-skinned but their comment about me writing a book, *Shoplifting for Dummies*, hurt a bit.

Stupid on my part, perhaps? I don't think so. No way did I think they'd challenge me back at "my" supermarket. Any member of staff who'd been working that day would almost certainly have seen me at my little "do", and my photograph was prominent in a display at the main door and they all knew I was on the VIP list. And having seen the old geezer they'd stuck a uniform on and called security . . . well, it was a piece of cake. Back at the presentation either the two bottles of Scotch, or the vino I hadn't paid for, I don't know which, had clinked in my pocket when I was about two feet away from him, but he didn't seem to notice, or, more likely, he didn't have his hearing aid switched on.

He'd gone and they had a woman down there now, didn't they? Just my luck she was on duty when I went shopping – someone I'd never seen before, fresh to the area and ex-CID. New on the job and still dead keen to get some brownie points. Probably paid on commission for every one she pulled in. If she'd been on duty the day I won my big prize I'd have spotted her for certain. It turned out she had only started with them that Monday, just days after me being the toast of the store with everybody. Talk about luck.

When it came out that I had been taking stuff on a regular basis, the bosses made a few changes. Among other things they downgraded Mr "Smarmy Pants" Poulson and posted him up north somewhere. So it wasn't all bad, was it?

By the way, I did have a word with the new manager. I made my offer of some advice on shoplifting on a consultancy basis. He didn't actually say "No" but somehow I don't think he was keen even though I offered to drop my fee down to 15 per cent for him.

Actually, when it got to court I thought I'd had a bit of a raw deal from the magistrate. She was a hatchet-faced woman who seemed not to like anyone, and even though I put on my suit and a tie, it didn't do me much good. When she heard I'd been doing it for years, she gave me a twelve-month prison sentence, suspended for two years.

That was worse than a fine, actually. If I'd been given a straight fine, I'd have paid it at a fiver a week, and the slate would be clean and nothing carried over to be held against me in future. That's the way I saw it anyway. But this probation deal meant that if I did the business and was caught, any time in the next two years, I'd go inside. What Mrs Thomas Fitzwallace, MBE, JP, B&Q and bar, or something fancy like that, hadn't realised was what a sentence like that was really going to cost me. The duty solicitor the police had given me said I'd had a good deal but I didn't see it like that. There's one law for them and one for people like me. No wonder I left the court fuming.

My personal cost of living was going to go up sharply for as long as I am on probation by paying the same prices at the checkout as ordinary punters do, and it's criminal how expensive stuff is these days. And it's going up all the time too as I soon found out. Because of this woman I now have to pay for everything I shop for every week. Perhaps the old cow did realise it and was just being sadistic. She certainly looked the type. Then she hadn't made any sort of allowance for my loss of income from the stuff I sell on, none whatsoever. I've got to fill it from somewhere.

So it looks as if I'll have to find a new line of work. Pretty soon, too. Back to the drawing board and sort out a Plan B. I'm the wrong shape for climbing through windows to half-inch a bit of jewellery, and hitting old ladies on their heads for their pension money isn't my style. And I'm certainly not looking for a proper job just yet. I'll leave that for when I'm really, really desperate.

Author Biographies

||||||||||||||||||||||||||||||||||||||||||||||||||||||||||||||||||||||||||||||||||||||||||||||||||||||||||||||||||||||||||||||||||||||||||||||||||||||

Adrian Kalil

Adrian Kalil has enjoyed the written word all his life. During his career in health care, he found relaxation in the inherent creativity of writing. He believes that to create is "a labour of affection for life, my own satisfaction, and that of my fellow man. Words at their finest are no less than exquisite gifts." He currently resides in the Pacific Northwest corner of the USA in a home he built that quietly reflects his passions of art, music, and literature.

Anne Goodwin

After a twenty-five-year career as an NHS clinical psychologist engaging with the insides of other people's heads, Anne Goodwin has turned to fiction to explore her own. Anne now has over seventy published short stories to her name. Her debut novel, *Sugar and Snails*, about a woman who has kept her past identity a secret for thirty years, was shortlisted for the 2016 Polari First Book Prize. Her second novel, *Underneath*, about a man who seeks to resolve a relationship crisis by keeping a woman captive in a cellar, was published in May 2017. Anne is also a book blogger with a special interest in fictional therapists. annegoodwin.weebly.com @Annecdotist

Arthur Davis

Arthur Davis is a management consultant who has been quoted in *The New York Times*, *Crain's New York Business* and interviewed on New York TV News Channel 1. He has advised the New York City Taxi & Limousine Commission, the Department of Homeland Security, Senator John McCain's investigating committee on boxing reform, and testified as an expert witness before the New York State Commission on Corruption in Boxing. Over eighty tales of original fiction, and several dozen as reprints, have been published. He was featured in a quarterly, single-author anthology, nominated for a Pushcart Prize and received honorable mention in *The Best American Mystery Stories 2017*. www.talesofourtime.com

Beryl Ensor-Smith

Beryl Ensor-Smith is a Doctor of Music and retired lecturer in music with a passionate interest in reading and writing. Most of her oeuvre is in the form of short stories set in the fictitious village of Prentburg, two volumes of which have been published by Amazon, and a novel, *Meat Only on Mondays*. She is working on a second novel and continues writing short stories, many of which have been published online and in magazines. Other interests are conducting a ladies' choir and playing tennis. She is married with children, step-children and grandchildren, some living in Britain, some in Europe and some in New Zealand. Happily two families still reside in South Africa and she and her husband live in a cottage on the property of their youngest daughter and family, with three lovely grandchildren close at hand.

Bremer Acosta
Bremer Acosta is a Maryland writer. He has a Bachelor of Arts degree in English Language and Literature from Stevenson University, an MFA in Creative Writing and Publishing Arts from the University of Baltimore, and teaches science to children. His recent books are *Blood of Other Worlds*, *Stoic Practice*, and *Habits Inherited From the Dead*. When he's not writing, he's learning how to draw and play the blues harp. bremeracosta.com

Brooke Fieldhouse
Brooke Fieldhouse lives in York, UK, and has been writing short fiction since 2013. Brooke's work has won the *Writing Magazine* Love Story prize (Warners Group) and the *Scribble Magazine* Why Do I Write prize (Park Publications). Brooke has been published in *The Friargate Anthology* (Quacks Books, 2015), read work at the York UK Literary Festival 2016, and taken part in the Write-a-Wish community project with care home residents and carers 2014. Brooke likes to read and comment on the writing of others, to experiment, and to keep on developing. @brookebfa

Bruce Costello
Bruce Costello lives in the seaside village of Hampden, New Zealand. After studying foreign languages and literature in the late sixties at the University of Canterbury, he spent a few years selling used cars. Then he worked as a radio creative writer for fourteen years, before training in something completely different and rather weird and spending twenty-four years in private practice. In 2010, he semi-retired and took up writing to keep his brain ticking over. Since then, he's had a hundred and sixteen stories accepted by mainstream magazines and literary journals in seven countries.

Cameron Suey

Cameron Suey lives in California with his wife and two children. He works as a writer in the games industry, most recently on Rise of the Tomb Raider. His work has appeared on the Pseudopod podcast, anthologies including *Shadows over Main Street*, and was featured in the first issues of *Jamais Vu* and *Flapperhouse*. CameronSuey.com @ josefkstories

Ceinwen Haydon

Ceinwen E. Cariad Haydon previously worked as a probation officer, a mental health social worker and a practice educator in the NHS. She lives in Newcastle upon Tyne, UK, and writes short stories and poetry. She has been published in web magazines and in print anthologies. These include Literally Stories, Alliterati, StepAway, *Poets Speak (while we still can)*, Three Drops from a Cauldron, Obsessed with Pipework, Picaroon Poetry, Amaryllis, Algebra of Owls, *Write to be Counted* and *Riggwelter*. She completed her MA in Creative Writing at Newcastle University in August 2017 and graduated in December 2017. She believes everyone's voice counts and intends to work with hard-to-reach groups after graduation. She will grow old disgracefully. @CeinwenHaydon

Cris de Borja

Cris de Borja is an artisan, writer, and poet who transforms the everyday and commonplace into dreams of what-could-be. She lives in Seattle, WA, with a cat roommate that drives her bananas. CrisdeBorja.com

David W. Landrum

David W. Landrum teaches literature at Grand Valley State University in Western Michigan, USA. His fiction has appeared in journals in the US, UK, Canada, Australia, and Europe. His novellas, *Strange Brew*, *ShadowCity*, and *The Sorceress of Time*, are available through Amazon.

DC Diamondopolous

DC Diamondopolous is an award-winning short-story and flash-fiction writer published worldwide. DC's stories have appeared in over seventy-five anthology and online literary publications, including Lunch Ticket, Silver Pen's Fabula Argentea, and Eskimo Pie. "Billy Luck" is nominated for the 2017 Best of the Net Anthology and won first place at Defenestrationism's summer short story contest of 2016. DC has been awarded an Honorable Mention from the Charles Carter Letters from Post-Apocalypse Contest for 2017. The international literary site The Missing Slate honoured DC as author of the month in August 2016. dcdiamondopolous.com

Doug Hawley

Doug Hawley is a former mathematician and actuary living in Lake Oswego, Oregon, USA with cat Kitzhaber and editor Sharon. After early retirement, he has volunteered in California at the Marine Mammal Centre and China Camp, and in Oregon at Tryon Park, Legacy Meridian Medical Centre, and Booktique. After reading *Wild* by Cheryl Strayed, he decided to write again. He now has around a hundred "things" published. He is a practising curmudgeon who dislikes public cell-phone use, never texts and hates leaf blowers. sites.google.com/site/aberrantword/ @dougiamm

E. S. Wynn

E. S. Wynn is the author of over sixty books in print. During the last decade, he has worked with hundreds of authors and edited thousands of manuscripts for nearly a dozen different magazines. His stories and articles have been published in dozens of journals, e-zines and anthologies. He has also worked as a voice-over artist for several different horror and sci-fi podcasts, albums and e-books. www.eswynn.com

Feyisayo Anjorin

Feyisayo Anjorin was born in Akure, Nigeria in 1983. He attended the University of Ibadan where he studied Geography. He later trained as a filmmaker at AFDA Johannesburg. His writing has appeared in *Litro*, Bakwa, Brittle Paper, Bella Naija and AfricanWriter. He has also worked on film and TV productions in Nigeria, the UK and South Africa. @FeyisayoAnjorin

Fred Skolnik

Fred Skolnik is the author of four novels: *The Other Shore* (Aqueous Books, 2011) and *Death* (Spuyten Duyvil, 2015) under his own name, and *Rafi's World* (Fomite Press) and *The Links in the Chain* (Chicago Centre for Literature and Photography, both in 2014) under his Fred Russell pen name. His stories and essays have appeared in around two hundred journals, with a collection of his short fiction, called *Americans & Other Stories*, published in 2017 by Fomite Press. He is also the editor-in-chief of the 22-volume second edition of the *Encyclopaedia Judaica*, winner of the 2007 Dartmouth Medal.

Freedom Ahn

Freedom Ahn is a Canadian-born Eurasian journalist and writer. She's the author of countless feature articles, short stories, plays, songs and poems, and one very dark novel about the world of stand-up comedy. She's also the proud human to a very special little dog, Tallulah. www.freedomahn.com @FreedomAhn

Gary Ives

Gary Ives is a retired senior chief petty officer who lives in the Ozarks where he grows apples and writes. He is a Pushcart Prize nominee for his story "Can You Come Here for Christmas?" garyives.wordpress.com

Greg Szulgit

Greg spent his early years playing far too much Dungeons and Dragons before he decided that he had to grow up and join the real world. Twenty-five years later, in response to his mid-life crisis, he rekindled his love of fantasy world-building and role-playing. "Across the Oar" tumbled out, during that time, as a piece of fan-fiction about a very minor character in a friend's novel, derived from Ciardi's "Ulysses". As Greg wrote the story, he considered the adage, "you should write what you know", but he didn't want to write about being a geeky academic (his real world). He decided, therefore, to try "knowing what you write". After spending a week carrying an oar on his shoulder and hearing confessions at Burning Man, he suspected he was on to something. fantasticspeculations.blogspot.co.uk

Hanja Kochansky

Hanja has experienced some of the culture-defining events of the twentieth century: as a World War II refugee from Yugoslavia to Italy; as an immigrant in apartheid South Africa; as a young actress mingling with film stars during the Dolce Vita era in Rome where she played one of Elizabeth Taylor's handmaidens in the film *Cleopatra*. In London she was a Playboy Bunny and an enthusiastic participant in the 60s sex and drugs revolution. In 1972, her book *Female Sexual Fantasies* was published in New York by ACE Books and became a global bestseller. Ida Kar's 1974 photograph of her was displayed for three months in the National Portrait Gallery in London in 2011. She occasionally pops up on BBC Radio 4. www.hanjak.com

Harry Buschman

Born in 1918, Harry Buschman is a widower with two daughters, both in medical research – one in Florida and the other in Canada. He grew up in the Bed-Stuy area of Brooklyn, New York. It was a tenement area, a slum if you will. But he didn't know it was a slum. It was home. He joined the US army when Hitler moved into Poland and saw a good part of the world until he resigned in 1945. Using his lifetime of experiences, he has written hundreds of short stories. He has been fortunate to have one hard-cover book published in Europe and used as a textbook in English-speaking schools in the Balkans. He has also appeared in a half-dozen anthologies in England, Canada and the US.

Harry Downey

After a working career in industrial management then a switch to years of dealing in antiques, Harry Downey began writing fiction during retirement in Spain. Finding the format to his liking, he has now had over forty short stories accepted for publication by editors of both small literary print magazines in the UK and online. These tales have been collected and published in two volumes, *Time for a Short?* and *The Biter Bit*. He has also published a crime novel, *Tie a Yellow Ribbon*. Living now in West Dorset, writing is limited due to failing eyesight, but hopefully will continue – if more slowly than before. harry.downey372@gmail.com

Helen Cooper

Helen Cooper is a freelance writer and editor. Her fiction writing explores the psychological effects and enduring influence of mythology and fairytales, as well as the uses of storytelling for empowerment and healing. She is currently working on a contemporary fairytale series for children.

James Mulhern

James Mulhern has published fiction in many literary journals and received several accolades. In September of 2013, he was chosen as a finalist for the Tuscany Prize for Catholic Fiction. In 2015, Mr Mulhern was awarded a fully paid writing fellowship to study at Oxford University in the United Kingdom. That same year, one of his stories was longlisted for Ireland's Fish Short Story Prize. Two other short stories received honorable mentions for the Short Story America Prize. His novel, *Molly Bonamici*, is a Readers' Favourite and was runner-up for a book competition sponsored by a member of the National Book Critics Circle. In March 2016, he was runner-up for the United Kingdom's InkTears Short Story Contest. You can visit Mr Mulhern's Amazon page at www.amazon.com/-/e/B00HS4D2AQ

Jeff Alphin

Jeff Alphin and his partner Jane Brettschneider live and write in Baltimore's Fells Point, mostly about their fictional son, Adlai Dallas. To read about him at his worst, pick up a copy of their comic novel, *Mother's Worry*. www.mothersworry.com

Jerry W. Crews

Jerry W. Crews was raised and lives in North Carolina, USA. After raising four sons and one daughter with his wife, Diane, he retired from work as a quality supervisor in 2017. With an empty nest at home, he and his wife are spending their senior years travelling the USA and Canada. Crews has authored more than eighty short and long stories over the years and considers writing to be his favourite hobby. In his youth he was greatly influenced by TV shows such as *The Twilight Zone* and *The Outer Limits*. His favourite author is Robert A. Heinlein.

Jim Bartlett

After a long career of tinkering in telecommunications, Jim Bartlett switched to tinkering with words, both, of course, requiring a stretch of the imagination. He has since been fortunate to have a number of stories, ranging from flash to novella, featured in *CrimeSpree Magazine*, Short-Story.me, Ontologica, *The Scarlet Leaf Review*, and a number of other wonderful publications. While mentally he strolls along a warm California beach with his wife and golden retriever (shhh, she doesn't know she's a dog), physically they reside in the Pacific Northwest.

Jude Ellery

Jude Ellery trained in sport journalism and has written on many football blogs. He then branched out into short stories, usually with a fantastical or sci-fi angle. "Digging for Victory", however, has more mainstream inspirations in the form of nineties cartoons and comics. The main characters could easily be descendants of Steinbeck's classic brains and brawn double act, George and Lennie.

Julia Bell

Julia Bell is a writer and senior lecturer at Birkbeck, University of London where she is the course director of the Creative Writing MA. She is the author of three novels, most recently *The Dark Light*, and the co-editor of *The Creative Writing Coursebook* as well as three volumes of short stories. She also takes photographs and writes poetry, short stories, occasional essays and journalism. She divides her time between London and Berlin.

Kelly Haas Shackelford

Kelly Haas Shackelford has been many things: preacher's daughter, domestic-violence survivor, single mom to four, first female project manager in the largest steel company in the US, cat rescuer, and word wrangler. She has had over eighty pieces accepted for publication in various venues such as The Speculative Edge, Old Red Kimono, *Black Petals*, and Every Day Poets. She can be found on Facebook: Kelly Haas Shackelford.

Mason Willey

Mason Willey was born in 1944 in a small town in the East Midlands, where he was brought up among a coal-mining community. He trained as an accountant, but in the 1980s, the onset and rapid progression of rheumatoid arthritis prematurely ended his career, leaving him severely disabled. Since then, he has pursued the two great interests in his life: collecting twentieth-century children's literature, and music (both classical and popular). He devoted five years to research into the life and works of children's writer Enid Blyton and ultimately published the first definitive bibliography of the good lady's work (some 750 books and many thousands of short stories and other pieces). He now lives in retirement with his wife, close to the place of his upbringing.

Michael C. Keith

Michael C. Keith is the author/co-author of thirty book volumes and dozens of articles on the subject of radio and broadcast studies. In addition to his non-fiction titles, Keith has published over a dozen creative works, including an acclaimed memoir, *The Next Better Place*; a young-adult novel, *Life is Falling Sideways*; and twelve short-story collections, most recently *Perspective Drifts Like a Log on a River*. His fiction has been nominated for several awards, among them the PEN/O. Henry Award, the Pushcart Prize, the National Indie Excellence Award, and the International Book Award. www.michaelckeith.com

Michael McCarthy

Mike has been living in Germany with his son and German-born wife since 1989. Since then he has been teaching English at Adult Education Institutes and firms, and working as an examiner in business English.

He had been writing short stories for many years, originally as a hobby, but five years ago he started to take it more seriously and since then he has had a number published. flateye.weebly.com

Mike Florian

Mike Florian was born in Prague but after immigration to Canada as a toddler, was schooled and raised in Montreal. During his university studies Mike had a chance to spend summers commercial fishing on the West Coast of British Columbia. Much to the chagrin of the family, Mike enjoyed fishing and proceeded to do it for a living over the following seventeen years, both as a deckhand and subsequent owner of a number of fishing vessels. His short stories have been published in a variety of online and printed magazines. He currently owns and operates a manufacturing business located in Vancouver.

Mitchell Toews

Mitchell Toews lives and writes at Jessica Lake in Manitoba. When an insufficient number of, "We are pleased to inform you . . ." emails are on hand, he finds alternative joy in the windy intermingling between the top of the water and the bottom of the sky, or skates on the ice until he can no longer see the cabin. Mitch's writing has appeared in riverbabble, CommuterLit, Literally Stories, Red Fez, Sick Lit, *Voices Journal*, The Machinery, Storgy, LingoBites, Work Magazine, The MOON magazine, Occulum, *Rhubarb Magazine*, Digging Through the Fat (Community No. 24) and Fictive Dream. Mitchellaneous.com

M. J. Cleghorn

Born in Alaska to an Eyak mother and Athabaskan father, as a child M. J. Cleghorn fell in love with words listening to the stories told by her grandmother and aunts. The gift of story, they taught her, is only a gift if it is shared. She lives and writes near the banks of the Matanuska River in the Palmer Butte.

Nancy Lane

Nancy Lane is a graduate of UCLA and member of Willamette Writers in Portland, Oregon, USA. Her short stories have appeared in Indiana Voice Journal, Scarlet Leaf Review, Chantwood Magazine and other online publications. Her essays have appeared in Indiana Voice Journal and the AARP Bulletin.

Noeleen Kavanagh

Noeleen Kavanagh is an Irish writer who predominantly writes science fiction and fantasy. Her publications include short stories in Anotherealm, Swords and Sorcery, Luna Station Quarterly and the *British Fantasy Journal*. She has recently completed a fantasy novel set in the same world as many of her short stories. www.growingaroundthetwist.com

O. D. Hegre

O. D. Hegre is a former academic, teaching and involved in biomedical research at the University of Minnesota and later in the biotech industry. Now Orie sits at his keyboard every day, spending less time thinking about how things really are and more imagining how they could be. Orie's speculative fiction has appeared at various independent publishers' sites on the web and anthologies of his short stories, along with his first novel and one novella, are available in digital and print format at Amazon. Orie lives in the Sonoran Desert of Southern Arizona where the sun shines 350-plus days a year.

Patricia Crandall

Patricia Crandall has published numerous articles and short stories in various magazines and newspapers. She has five books in print, *Melrose: Then and Now*, a historical volume; *I Passed This Way*, a poetry collection; *The Dog Men*, a thriller; *Tales of an Upstate New York Bottle Miner*, non-fiction; and *Pat's Collectibles*, a collection of short stories. She is writing a young-adult thriller about child sex trafficking titled *The Red Gondola and the Cova*. She lives with her husband, Art, and a rescue cat, Bette, at Babcock Lake in the Grafton Mountains near Petersburgh, New York. authorpcrandall.blogspot.com

Peter Dabbene

Peter Dabbene's poetry has been published in many literary journals, and collected in the photo book *Optimism*. He has published the graphic novels *Ark* and *Robin Hood*, the story collections *Prime Movements* and *Glossolalia*, and a novel, *Mister Dreyfus' Demons*. His latest books are *Spamming the Spammers*, *More Spamming the Spammers*, and *The End of Spamming the Spammers*. www.peterdabbene.com

Phil Slattery

Phil Slattery is a native of Kentucky, but has travelled extensively and now resides in New Mexico. Many of his works are rooted in his experiences while travelling. He has founded the Farmington (NM) Writers Circle and is a member of Southwest Writers and the Horror Writers Association. He has a novel, a poetry collection, and a play in the works. He has published two novelettes (*Click* and *Alien Embrace*) and three small collections of short stories (*A Tale of Hell and Other Works of Horror*, *The Scent and Other Stories*, *Diabolical: Three Tales of Jack Thurston and Revenge*) on Amazon. His fiction, poetry, and few non-fiction articles have been published in numerous magazines. philslattery. wordpress.com amazon.com/author/philslattery @philslattery201

Phil Temples

Phil Temples lives in Watertown, Massachusetts, and works as a computer systems administrator at a university. He's had over a hundred short fiction stories published in print and online journals. His full-length murder-mystery novel, *The Winship Affair*, is available from Blue Mustang Press, as well as a novella, *Albey Damned* (Wapshott Press) and two new books: a short-story anthology, *Machine Feelings*, and paranormal horror mystery, *Helltown Chronicles*, from Big Table Publishing. temples.com

Rob Boffard

Rob Boffard is a South African author with lots of tattoos and terrible hair. His *Outer Earth* series, the first book of which is *Tracer*, is published worldwide by Orbit Books. He worked as a journalist for over a decade, for publications like the *Guardian* and *Wired Magazine*, before deciding that making things up for a living was a lot more fun. Rob is obsessed with snowboarding, rap music, superhero movies, and Vietnamese food. His new book, *Adrift*, is out summer 2018. www.robboffard.com

Rotimi Babatunde

Rotimi Babatunde's stories and poems have been published and translated widely. His story "Bombay's Republic" was awarded the 2012 Caine Prize for African Writing. "The Collected Tricks of Houdini" was longlisted for the 2015 *Sunday Times*/EFG Award, the largest prize for short fiction in the world. His plays have been performed in Europe, Africa and North America. Rotimi Babatunde is a recipient of fellowships from Ledig House, New York; the Bellagio Centre, Italy; and the MacDowell Colony, New Hampshire. He lives in Nigeria. @rotimibabatunde

Sharon Frame Gay

Sharon Frame Gay grew up a child of the highway, playing by the side of the road. She has been published in several anthologies, as well as *bioStories*, Gravel Magazine, Literally Stories, Lowestoft Chronicle, Fabula Argentea, *Thrice Fiction*, Literary Orphans, Write City, Indiana Voice Journal, Luna Luna, *Crannog Magazine*, and many others. Her work has won prizes at Women on Writing, The Writing District and Owl Hollow Press. She is a Pushcart Prize nominee. You can find her on Amazon Author Central as well as Facebook as Sharon Frame Gay-Writer. @sharshargi

Sigfredo R. Iñigo
Sigfredo R Iñigo lives with his family in San Jose City, Nueva Ecija, Philippines. He served as secretary to the city council for thirty-eight years until his retirement in September 2016. His short story "Home on the Sierra Madre" won first prize in the 49th Carlos Palanca Memorial Awards (2009), the Philippines' most prestigious and longest-running literary contest. It won, according to the judges, because of its "local colour". Like "Gladiator", it was first published at Fiction on the Web. "Gladiator" was chosen as one of the Notable Short Stories for 2006 by storySouth. kamaongbato.net

Sinéad McCabe
Sinéad McCabe hails from the North of England, lived in Italy for a while, and now lives in London. To make money, she teaches the international folk of the city how to speak English. Her work has been published in magazines including *Fantastic Horror* and *Disturbed Digest*, and online at Penny Shorts, Dark Fire Fiction and The Colored Lens.

Tom Sheehan
Tom Sheehan served in the 31st Infantry in Korea 1951–52, graduated Boston College 1956, and has published thirty books and multiple works in *Rosebud*, Literally Stories, Linnet's Wings, Serving House Journal, Copperfield Review, Literary Orphans, Eastlit, Indiana Voice Journal, Frontier Tales, DM du Jour, In Other Words: Mérida, Literary Yard, Rope and Wire Western Magazine, and Green Silk Journal. He has received thirty-two Pushcart nominations, five Best of Net nominations, and sundry other awards. Newer books are *Swan River Daisy*, *Jehrico*, *The Cowboys*, and *Beside the Broken Trail*, with three books being considered.

William Quincy Belle
William Quincy Belle is just a guy. Nobody famous; nobody rich; just some guy who likes to periodically add his two cents worth with

the hope, accounting for inflation, that $0.02 is not overvaluing his contribution. He claims that at the heart of the writing process is some sort of (psychotic) urge to put it down on paper and likes to recite the following, which so far he hasn't been able to attribute to anyone: "A writer is an egomaniac with low self-esteem." You will find Mr Belle's unbridled stream of consciousness floating around in cyberspace. wqebelle.blogspot.com

Afterword

The internet was smaller when I started. Modems made strung-out beeping noises, pictures loaded line by line, AltaVista was the only search engine that worked. It was exciting. I wanted in.

I'd always been passionate about short stories, so publishing them seemed a natural fit. I taught myself HTML on my dad's 33 MHz i486 PC, and Fiction on the Web was born.

At the time, there were only a few dozen similar websites, most of them genre-specific. We all linked to each other and helped promote the idea that the web was a great place to find fiction.

More than twenty-one years later, I've published over one thousand stories, which have been read by hundreds of thousands of people. I'm proud to have created a platform for showcasing creativity, with talent as the only criterion for entry.

Fiction on the Web doesn't cost much money, but it costs a lot of time. There are typically a dozen submissions a week. Getting a story into web-publishable format can be a mind-numbing process. In addition, I spend time responding to author emails, promoting the site, and keeping my beloved Patreon crowd engaged – not to mention doing an unrelated full-time job, raising two daughters, servicing my twin obsessions with board games and films, and . . . you know . . . occasionally *writing*.

So, thank you to all of you who have supported the site over the years, by reading and commenting on the stories. Long may it last.

Printed in Great Britain
by Amazon

Coming Soon

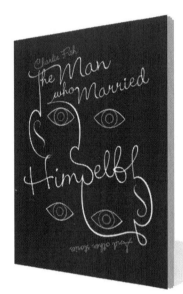

The Man Who Married Himself and Other Stories by Charlie Fish will make you laugh, cry, tremble with fear, but above all – *think*. Stories that address life's big questions: How can I be a good person? What is freedom? Is this penny trying to kill me?

This is the definitive collection of the very best Charlie Fish stories from the last twenty years. Visit www.fictionontheweb.co.uk for more information.

Afterword

The internet was smaller when I started. Modems made strung-out beeping noises, pictures loaded line by line, AltaVista was the only search engine that worked. It was exciting. I wanted in.

I'd always been passionate about short stories, so publishing them seemed a natural fit. I taught myself HTML on my dad's 33 MHz i486 PC, and Fiction on the Web was born.

At the time, there were only a few dozen similar websites, most of them genre-specific. We all linked to each other and helped promote the idea that the web was a great place to find fiction.

More than twenty-one years later, I've published over one thousand stories, which have been read by hundreds of thousands of people. I'm proud to have created a platform for showcasing creativity, with talent as the only criterion for entry.

Fiction on the Web doesn't cost much money, but it costs a lot of time. There are typically a dozen submissions a week. Getting a story into web-publishable format can be a mind-numbing process. In addition, I spend time responding to author emails, promoting the site, and keeping my beloved Patreon crowd engaged – not to mention doing an unrelated full-time job, raising two daughters, servicing my twin obsessions with board games and films, and . . . you know . . . occasionally *writing*.

So, thank you to all of you who have supported the site over the years, by reading and commenting on the stories. Long may it last.

Coming Soon

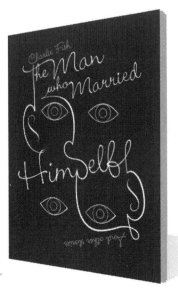

The Man Who Married Himself and Other Stories by Charlie Fish will make you laugh, cry, tremble with fear, but above all – *think*. Stories that address life's big questions: How can I be a good person? What is freedom? Is this penny trying to kill me?

This is the definitive collection of the very best Charlie Fish stories from the last twenty years. Visit www.fictionontheweb.co.uk for more information.

27610810R00309

Printed in Great Britain
by Amazon